MORE THAN RICHES
A LITTLE BADNESS

JOSEPHINE COX

MORE THAN RICHES
A LITTLE BADNESS

BCA

LONDON NEW YORK SYDNEY TORONTO

This omnibus edition published 1995
by BCA
by arrangement with Headline Book Publishing

CN 1445

Printed and bound in Germany
by Graphischer Großbetrieb Pößneck GmbH
A member of the Mohndruck printing group

CONTENTS

MORE THAN RICHES

For darling Anita.

I have shared my joys with all of you who read my books; and there are very many of you now. I have spoken of my sister, Anita, through previous dedications, and on many occasions when I have travelled the country to meet all of you. Now sadly I share a great sorrow with you. I have to tell you that our Anita is gone from us, at the tender age of 36 years.

Those of you who know me, will know how precious my family is to me. Anita was the baby of ten brothers and sisters. In my grief, something happened that tested my faith. Something stranger happened to strengthen it.

On the afternoon when the priest received Anita into God's house, where she remained until the morning, we drove home through a black and rainy day, the sky was dark and ominous when suddenly it split open and a shaft of sunlight pierced the blackness. As we watched, the light spread to the earth, dazzling us.

When I told my sister, Winifred, she said it was a stairway taking Anita to Heaven.

I hope that was true, because only then can some sense be made of such a tragic waste. The post-mortem revealed that there was no medical reason why our Anita died. Maybe there really is another reason we mortals don't understand?

Anita was good and kind and, like everyone who was privileged to know her, I will miss and love her to the day I die.

This book is dedicated to her, because it is the only title that reflects what she was to us.

Goodbye, little sister. God keep you safe until we meet again.

CONTENTS

PART ONE

1948

When We Lie

CHAPTER ONE

Rosie might have been forgiven for thinking this was the worst day of her life. Until she remembered that today was a joy compared with what was to come. The worst was still a month away. After that, all of her chances for happiness would be gone forever.

'Rosie?' The whisper of her name on his lips only made her realise what she had lost.

She didn't answer. Nor did she look at him. In her tortured mind she believed that if she ignored him it might be easier to pretend he wasn't there.

'Rosie!' This time there was a note of urgency in his voice, a rush of anger.

In the ill-lit street, the sound of their footsteps tapping against the pavement made a peculiar melody. Through tearful eyes, she stared at the ground beneath their feet; the hard shiny cobblestones stretched before them like hundreds of newly baked loaves brushed with milk. It had been a glorious June day, and now the evening was sultry, closing about them like the protective arms of a lover.

'What the hell's wrong with you?' His voice was closer now, his head bent to hers. 'You've been like this all day. If there's something on your mind, you'd best speak up now, because I'm sick and tired of this cat and mouse game.' Pressing his hand to her arm, he brought her to a halt. Swinging her round to face him, he demanded angrily, 'I mean it, Rosie. You'd best speak up, because I've had enough of your bloody moods.'

She regarded him with distaste. 'Want to know *all* my thoughts, do you?'

Realising he'd said the wrong thing, he cunningly changed tack. ''Course I don't, but you're so quiet tonight, sweetheart.' His voice was entreating. He didn't want to spoil his chances. 'Is it something I've done?' he asked. 'Something I've said?' Whenever he was close to her, the urge to make love was strong. It was strong now.

'No, it's not your fault,' she assured him. If anything, the fault was hers. He was just a man, and in all truth he had done nothing that she could reproach him for. Yet, in that moment when he tenderly propelled her backwards, leaning with her against the vicarage wall and whispering softly to her, she knew she could never love him in the way she had loved before.

Oh, he was handsome enough. Even though he was small in build, and barely taller than Rosie herself, there was something uniquely attractive about him. He possessed the most beautiful, sinister eyes: one as blue as cornflowers, the other as green as the ocean. His dark brown hair was thick and long to his ears, and he walked with a proud bearing. He could be incredibly charming, able to make a woman feel special and seduce her without her even realising it.

That was how it had begun with Rosie. She'd been swept off her feet, and only now did she realise the enormity of what she had done.

'I want you.'

'Not here, Doug.' It wasn't what she wanted to say. What she really wanted to say was: 'Don't lay a finger on me. Don't *ever* again lay a finger on me.' But she was wise enough to know that rejecting him now would not solve anything. It was too late for that.

'Why not here?' he argued. When she looked up at him like that, she stirred his every sense. In the lamplight, her brown eyes were softly beautiful. 'We won't be seen, I promise you,' he pleaded. 'There's not a soul about.'

Torn by guilt and still deeply disturbed by the letter which had arrived in the morning post, she pushed him off. 'No, Doug!'

'You didn't say that before.'

'No, I didn't, did I?' She ruefully smiled at the memory, hating herself, hating him. That was when it had all started to go wrong.

Mistaking her smile for an expression of affection, he leaned down to stroke her bare leg. 'You're so lovely,' he whispered. He felt confident enough to take her now. Sliding his hand beneath her skirt, he pushed upwards with probing fingers, quickly sliding them between the softer crevice of her thighs. 'You're ready for me now, aren't you?' he murmured breathlessly. He was so excited he could hardly wait. With his other hand he fumbled at his trouser buttons.

With her legs now pushed open, and his moist tongue lightly following the curve of her ear, Rosie couldn't deny that she *was* ready for him. When all was said and done, she was still a woman, warm-blooded, with needs much like his. Turning on him now would be tantamount to destroying herself, and what would that solve? Her mood became defiant. Why shouldn't he make love to her? As she recalled, it had been good before, so why shouldn't it be good now?

She felt herself responding. It was all the encouragement he needed. 'Open up, sweetheart,' he whispered harshly, at the same time pushing up through her knicker leg. It was when she felt him against her inner thigh that she knew she couldn't give herself to him. Not tonight. Not *any* night, if she had her way.

'Take me home,' she snapped. 'Have you no shame, Doug Selby? Are we a pair of curs, to mate in the street? Are we, eh?' A great tide of raging energy coursed through her as she thrust him off. When he stumbled backwards, with his penis jutting out like the sign over the pawn-shop window, a sense of the ridiculous made her want to laugh out loud.

'Christ Almighty! What are you trying to do to me?' he groaned, rubbing one hand over his face and making low guttural sounds as though in the throes of deepest agony. 'You want it as much as me, I know you do,' he pleaded. Reaching out, he touched her on the neck.

The feel of his damp trembling hand had a startling effect on her.

'LEAVE ME ALONE!'

Shocked and limp now, he began yanking his trousers together, anger in his voice. 'What the hell's the matter *now*?'

'I don't want you treating me like a whore, that's all,' she

5

snapped. 'I asked you to take me home, and if you don't want to that's all right by me. I can take myself!' Quickly straightening her skirt, she brushed past him, half running to put as much distance between them as she could. She could hear him yelling, cursing her at the top of his voice. 'To hell with *you* an' all, Doug Selby,' she called back. Tears ran down her face. Tears of shame, and guilt, and frustration. She was trapped, and there was no way out.

Rosie was halfway down the street when he came chasing after her. 'Hey! It isn't me who's at fault here. It's *you*. You've been down in the dumps all day, and now, for no reason at all that I can see, you fly off the handle. What am I supposed to do, eh? Tell me that.'

By the time he'd caught up with her, she had taken off her high-heeled shoes and was sitting on the horse trough outside the railway station. The last train had long gone and the whole place was enveloped in an eerie silence.

When she saw him limping up the road, gasping and wheezing, she couldn't help but laugh. 'Look at you,' she chuckled, 'you're worse than your old grandad.' She felt in a better mood after the exhilarating run. 'I should have thought you'd have been fitter . . . what with carting them coal-bags on your shoulders every day.'

Slumping down beside her, he took time to recover his breath. 'Carting coal-bags might broaden your shoulders,' he pointed out at last, 'but it don't prepare you for a two-mile run.' Dropping forward, he buried his face in his hands. It was a moment before he spoke again, and when he did, it was to say in a harsh voice, 'I want to know what's going on? The truth, mind. Don't take me for a bloody fool.'

'Leave it, Doug. There's nothing to be gained by talking about it.' Lately her life seemed to be fraught with problems.

The look on her face told him enough. 'It's *him*, ain't it?' he demanded sharply. 'I might have known.'

Rosie nodded her head. 'We had an almighty row.'

'Hmph!' He slid his arm round her shoulders. 'About me, was it?'

'Sort of.' She felt him pulling her towards him, and though she desperately needed comfort, couldn't bring herself to lay her head on his shoulders.

6

Fortunately, he didn't sense her resistance to him. ' "Sort of" . . . What does that mean?'

'He found my diary. He knows, Doug.'

'So what?' He gawped at her as though she had said something astonishing. 'I'm glad he knows. He would have found out sooner or later. Anyway, what does it matter?'

Shrugging his arm away, she stood up. 'It may not matter to you, Doug Selby. But it matters to *me*.'

'Don't be silly.' Reaching up, he pleaded, 'Come on, sit here. You and me were made for each other, gal. There was a time when I might have dumped you and chased something else in skirts, but, well, you've kind of got to me. I don't want any other woman, not now . . . *especially* not now.'

'Happen you'd be better off chasing "something else in skirts",' she retorted. But inside, she was more afraid than ever. Things were bad enough now, without her giving him that sort of encouragement.

'Aw, you know I wouldn't do that.' Not right now he wouldn't anyway. Maybe later, when he'd got her out of his system and boredom began to creep in. 'Come on, sweetheart. Sit aside o' me. I promise I won't try it on. We'll just have a cuddle.' He grinned stupidly. 'And happen a little feel, eh?'

She heard the childish sulkiness in his voice and despised him all the more. Ignoring his crude suggestion, she told him, 'I've got to go and face him.'

'What do you mean?'

She hung her head, all manner of emotions coursing through her. 'It was awful, Doug. Dad went mad. I tried to calm him down, but he wouldn't listen, so I just ran out.'

'He had no right looking through your diary! Who the hell does he think he is?'

'He says he knew there was something going on, and he meant to get to the bottom of it.'

'So he read your diary? Christ! He's got a bloody cheek!'

'Well, it's done now, and there are things to be mended between us.'

'Did you put it *all* in your diary . . . *everything*?'

'Everything, yes.' In the half-light her face reddened at the thought of what her father had read.

'Bloody hell! What did you do that for?' He recalled the night they had made love for the first time, and it shook him to think she had written all *that* down.

'Because that's what diaries are for.' Sometimes, like now, she wondered what she had ever seen in Doug Selby.

'Aw, to hell with him!' He suddenly grinned. Come to think of it, he was proud of himself for that night. Happen her old man might see what kind of a man Doug Selby was after all! 'He's never liked me, you know that, don't you?' He was shouting now, growing angry. 'I say to hell with the old sod. Serves him right if he's suffering. It'll teach him not to stick his nose where it's not wanted.'

Suppressing the urge to punch him hard in the face, Rosie straightened her shoulders and turned from him. 'You can't blame him, Doug, it must have come as a shock. It's my own fault. I should have told him earlier.' In her heart she realised she should have found the courage to tell them *both* earlier, because there was still another to be told, and his heart would be broken just as hers was. 'He'll be waiting for me. I'd better go.'

'Do you want me with you?' He held his breath, waiting for her answer and hoping she would say no. There were some things that made him see red, and others that made him a coward.

'No.' She sighed noisily. 'It's best if I face this on my own.'

'Okay.' He got to his feet and draped an arm round her shoulders. When she plucked it off, he stiffened. 'Look! I'll come with you if you want me to,' he offered churlishly.

'I said no. I can manage on my own.'

'Fair enough.' Gripping her by the shoulders, he inclined his head to kiss her. When she resisted, he kissed her anyway. 'Right then. Being as you've no need of my services, I'll take myself off home.'

'You do that.'

'Don't take no nonsense from that old bugger,' he warned in a superior voice. She didn't comment, so he flicked her chin with the tip of his finger. 'We wouldn't have been seen, you know . . . back there.' His loins were still throbbing. He wanted her badly. But he consoled himself with the thought that soon he would have her any time he felt like it. 'Like I said . . . tell him to go to hell,' he suggested grandly.

'*You* go to hell!'

'You don't mean that?'

'Oh . . . go home, Doug!'

A sudden thought made him wary. 'I'd best not call round for you tomorrow, eh?'

'You're a bloody coward, Doug Selby.'

'Sensible, that's all,' he corrected. 'It would only make things worse if I turned up on the doorstep. Whether we like it or not, your dad's never taken to me.'

'I wonder why?' She couldn't keep the sarcasm from her voice.

He shrugged her shoulders. 'It don't bother me.'

'Goodnight, Doug.' She swung away, leaving him standing there.

'I'll see you at the market tomorrow, eh? Midday?' She was already at the bottom of the street. He called a little louder, 'Don't let the bugger get the better of you, sweetheart. If you need me, you know where I live.'

As he strode away in the opposite direction, he mumbled to himself, 'You'll not get me within a mile of her old man . . . not if I can help it. What! If he laid hands on me, the bugger would string me up and no messing!'

The thought quickened his feet. First he was walking, then he was stepping it out, then his boots echoed frantically against the cobbles as he took to his heels and ran.

As she approached the terraced house on Pendle Street, Rosie saw that the downstairs lights were still on. Normally, her father would have retired to his bed long before this hour. 'So you're waiting for me, are you?' she said into the warm night air. 'Mean to have it out, eh?' The thought of a violent confrontation with her father made her slow her footsteps. For one awkward minute, she wasn't certain whether to take Doug up on his offer . . . 'If you need me, you know where I live.'

Suddenly she found herself chuckling. 'A fat lot of good Doug would be,' she muttered. 'Like as not, he'd be halfway down the street even before Dad could open his mouth.' It had taken her some time, but at long last Rosie was seeing a different side to Doug. In the long run, though, she believed it couldn't really change anything.

She didn't need to use her key. The front door had been left on the latch. Inside the dimly lit passage, she took off her long white cardigan and hung it over the hook behind the door. Glancing in the hallway mirror, she patted her long brown hair, pushing it back with her hands so that it didn't tumble over her shoulders in that wanton way Doug liked. She fastened the top button of her pretty blue blouse, and straightened her skirt, blushing with colour as she remembered Doug's rough handling of her earlier.

'Who's that?' She was visibly startled as the man's harsh voice reached her from the back parlour. 'Is that you, Rosie?'

'Yes.' She was surprised at the calmness of her own voice, especially when her stomach was churning.

'Get in here!'

One last look in the mirror. 'Stand up to him, gal,' she told herself. 'You're twenty years old . . . a grown woman. Don't let him bully you.' Determination welled up in her as she went down the hallway towards the back parlour.

'Where the hell are you? I said: GET IN HERE!'

His raised voice echoed down the passageway. All her courage vanished, and the nearer to the parlour she got, the more she wished she'd taken Doug up on his offer; however reluctantly it was given. A little moral support was better than none at all, she reasoned now.

Her father made a formidable sight indeed. A retired miner, he was a big man with a mass of iron grey hair, and pale deep-set eyes that seemed to see right through a body. 'Where've you been 'til this time?' he demanded as she appeared at the door.

He was seated in the high-backed rocking chair by the range. He didn't look round at her, nor did he make any effort to rise from the chair. Instead, he kept it rocking back and forth, back and forth, his deep-set eyes directed towards the empty fire-grate, and his long thick fingers drumming, playing out a feverish rhythm on the curved wooden arms.

'I thought it best to stay away for a while,' Rosie explained quietly, 'I thought it might give us both time to cool down.' She stepped tentatively into the room.

10

'Stay where you are. I don't want you any nearer.' His eyes remained focused on the empty fire-grate, and the chair continued to rock.

'What do you mean, Dad? You don't want me in the parlour?'

'I don't want you in the *house*.' The sound of the rockers against the carpet made a strange swishing noise.

'I came home to talk with you. To explain.'

'There's nothing to explain. I've sired a bad 'un, that's all.'

'I'm not a bad un', Dad!'

'If your mother was alive, she wouldn't walk down the street for the shame of it.'

'I'm to be wed. There will be no shame.'

'One bad 'un wed to another.'

'You shouldn't have read my diary. *That* was shameful.'

'I read the letter too.'

Rosie was furious. 'You had no right!' she said angrily, clenching her fists and wishing she was a man. 'How dare you read my private things?'

'You didn't even have the courage to tell *him*,' he accused. The rockers went faster, and the eyes never flinched. 'I always regretted never having a son, but I never thought I'd raise a bloody coward.'

It was a moment before Rosie answered. Then: 'All right, I won't deny I've been a coward, but I had my reasons.'

'Aye. *Two*! Doug Selby and his bastard.'

'The child won't be a bastard. That's why I'm getting wed.'

'I hope the other one kills him. Then you won't be getting wed, and everybody'll know you for what you are.'

'If, as you say, you've read the letter, you'll know Adam is not a murderous man. He's home on leave tomorrow. I'll tell him then.'

'Get out!'

'What?'

'I want nothing to do with you. I don't want you ever to show your face round these parts again. You'll find your things all packed . . . in the front room.'

'You're not thinking straight, Dad. Let's both get a good night's sleep, and talk about it all in the morning. I love you. I can't just leave you.'

'I don't want your kind under my roof. I'll have no part of

11

you from now on. Get out, I said. NOW!' The rockers were suddenly still. He turned. The deep-set eyes regarded her as though she was so much dirt under his shoe.

'Dad . . .' Her ears were ringing from his harsh words, yet she knew him well enough to realise that he meant every word.

He wasn't listening. The rockers were shifting back and forth, the swishing sound all that could be heard. His eyes were turned towards the empty grate, and his big shoulders were set like stone. The time for talking was long over.

'I'll ask Peggy if I can stay there for the time being,' she offered. He didn't move a muscle. 'All right, Dad,' she murmured, 'if this is what you really want.' No reply. She was devastated.

Going into the front parlour, she collected the portmanteau. It wasn't heavy. Four years ago her parents had been involved in a train accident. Her mother was killed, and her father partially crippled, enough to keep him out of full-time work. Her own job at the post office kept the wolf from the door, but it was never enough to buy fancy clothes and the like. Such things didn't bother her. Rosie was a simple soul, with simple needs.

The front parlour had always been reserved for special visitors. Rosie smiled at the irony of her father placing her portmanteau in here. On the oak sideboard stood a photograph of her mother; a small woman much like Rosie herself, with brown hair and browner eyes. 'Well, Mam,' she told the smiling face, 'you'll be sorry it's come to this. We could have talked it through, but he won't listen. You know what he can be like. Still, happen when he's got over the shock, he'll see reason. But *I'm* not making the first move!' She shook her head and set her mouth in a grim line. 'It's him that's thrown me out, so it's up to him to mend the breach.'

She stood there a while, tempted to take the photograph with her. But she knew her father derived great comfort from it, and so departed without it.

As she quietly opened the front door, her father's voice boomed out, 'LEAVE THE KEY!' For the sake of her mam's memory, she almost returned to reason once more with him. But she knew him too well. In the mood he was in, it was best to do as he asked.

Taking her long white cardigan from a hook on the other door, she felt in the pocket. Withdrawing the front door key, she laid it on the hallway table, then slid the cardigan over her shoulders. Taking up the portmanteau once more, she went out of the house.

The evening air had grown chilly. She shivered. It was a good walk to her friend Peggy's house. But there would be a welcome there, she knew.

CHAPTER TWO

'Oh, Rosie! Why didn't you tell me?' At twenty-two, Peggy Lewis was almost two years older than Rosie, yet she seemed younger somehow. A scrap of a woman, with fair cropped hair, big round blue eyes and a nose that was so large it overshadowed her mouth, she looked to be in a constant state of astonishment. She was neither intelligent nor dim, beautiful nor ugly, and if you dressed her in the finest silk that money could buy, she would still look like a bundle of straw tied up in the middle. But her young heart was big and generous, and filled with love for Rosie.

'I didn't tell you because I was ashamed.'

'Ashamed?' Peggy tutted. 'And what are best friends supposed to be for?' she wanted to know. 'Since when have we ever kept secrets from each other?'

'It wasn't just that,' Rosie assured her. 'This was something I had to sort out for myself. Even if I *had* told you, there was nothing you could have done ... except worry yourself sick.' She smiled fondly. 'And you *would* have worried yourself sick, wouldn't you? Admit it?'

Peggy twisted her mouth to one side, nervously biting her top lip, just as she always did when she was lost for words. 'I suppose so,' she reluctantly confessed.

'There you are then. So I'm glad I didn't tell you. I'm sorry I'm telling you now.'

'What? You don't trust me? You think I'll spread it all over Blackburn?'

'Don't be silly. If I thought *that*, I wouldn't have come here tonight. It's a secret between you and me, and my father, of course ... and Doug. But they won't tell. Dad's eaten with shame,

15

and Doug's promised me he won't let on to *anybody*. He knows I'll hate him if he tells.' She half smiled. 'No doubt he'd like to brag to the world, but I believe he'll keep his promise to me.'

Peggy shrugged her shoulders. Not for the first time, she was tempted to challenge Rosie's trust in that young man but, for the sake of friendship, she decided against it. 'You really ought to try and get some sleep,' she remarked instead.

'I can't.' Rosie glanced at the clock over the mantelpiece. 'Every time I close my eyes, I think about everything that's happened. My Dad . . . Doug . . . Adam . . . all the plans that have been spoiled. And not only *my* plans, Peggy. Dad's right. What I've done is awful, and I deserve to be thrown out.'

'Hmph! Anybody'd think you had caused the problem all by yourself. What about that rascal, Doug, eh? You've already agreed to wed him, more's the pity, so I reckon that's punishment enough.' Rolling her huge eyes upwards, she declared grimly, 'Your dad was wrong to do what he did. Cor! If anybody looked through *my* diary, I'd be hopping mad!'

Rosie was puzzled. 'I didn't know *you* kept a diary?'

'I don't. All I'm saying is, *if* I did.'

Rosie had to smile, and soon the two of them were giggling. 'You're a twerp, Peggy Lewis,' Rosie told her. 'But I don't know what I'd do without you.'

'Throw yourself in the canal, like as not.' Placing her thin hands on the parlour table, she stood up. 'It's four o'clock of a morning, and the pair of us will be fit for nothing come daylight, but now that you've woken me . . . tiptoeing down every creaky stair you could find . . . we might as well raid the pantry.'

'Your mam was angry. I shouldn't have put myself on you like that. After all, she's a widow, and there's four other children besides you in this little house. It was a bloody cheek of me to turn up like that . . . suitcase and all.'

'Take no notice. Our mam's bark is worse than her bite.' She chuckled. 'You'll feel better when I tell you she followed me upstairs to ask how much we should charge you to stop here.'

Rosie laughed. 'And what did *you* say?'

'I told her you'd pay two shilling a week, and teach her to embroider. She's always wanted to embroider . . . drives me mad, she does.'

Rosie was astounded. 'You *must* be mad! *I* can't embroider.'

'There you are then. You can teach each other.' Chuckling, she asked, 'Jam butties and cocoa . . . how does that sound?'

Shaking her head in disbelief, Rosie thought it best to ignore Peggy's little games. 'Sounds great, but won't your mam be angry if we raid the pantry?'

'Not if we don't tell her. I'll stir the jampot afterwards, so it looks full, and you'd have to be Sherlock Holmes to miss a slice off half a loaf. As for the cocoa, I bought it myself, so there'll be nowt said.' As she went into the scullery, she reminded Rosie, 'Anyway, the war's been over nearly four years. There ain't rationing like there used to be, thank God.'

Rosie could hear her bustling about in the scullery. She envied Peggy her peace of mind. 'Will you come with me tomorrow?' she called.

Peggy returned with a tray of jam butties and two steaming mugs of cocoa. 'No, I bloody well won't!' she retorted. 'There's things to be said between you and Adam that ain't for nobody else's ears.' Placing one mug and a small plate before Rosie, she added softly, 'You're made of good stuff, and you're not to worry. It'll be all right, you'll see.'

Unable to stomach the jam butty, Rosie sipped at the warming cocoa. 'I didn't mean for you to come with me into the station,' she explained. 'I thought you might sit with me in the tea rooms, just until the train arrives. Then you could go.'

'That's very big of you,' Peggy teased.

'You'll come then?'

''Course I will. Now, drink your cocoa and we'll try and get a couple of hours sleep.'

There was little to be said for the next few minutes. Peggy was too busy polishing off the jam butties, and Rosie too steeped in thoughts of the coming ordeal.

At four-thirty, the two pals traipsed upstairs and into their respective beds. Peggy soon fell asleep, but Rosie lay awake for what seemed an age. In the soft lamplight, she read the crumpled letter time and again:

My darling Rosie,

I know it's been some time since I wrote, but, like I told

you in my last letter, I had some growing up to do before settling down. I know you understand I had to get things straight in my mind, and how I needed to be out of the Army, before asking you to wed me.

I'm sorry. I haven't been fair to you, and all these months of waiting to hear from me must have been sheer hell. But you knew I would write, and you knew I would never stop loving you. I've always promised we'd be wed one day. Well, sweetheart, the day's arrived! I would have written earlier, but I wanted to surprise you.

I'm on my way home, and I can't wait to hold you in my arms. I've carried your picture next to my heart everywhere I've been. Now I mean to carry you over the threshold of our home, as my wife . . . Mr and Mrs Adam Roach! Sounds great, don't it?

I've managed to put some money by, more than enough for a down payment on one of them little houses in Rosamund Street. See! I didn't forget where you said you wanted to live when we were man and wife. There won't be too much left over for a grand wedding, but we can wait a bit if you like.

Doug's dad always said he'd give me a job when I'm demobbed, and carting coal is respectable enough, I reckon, though I don't intend to do that forever because I've got big plans for you and me.

I plan to arrive at Blackburn railway station at nine forty-five on June 14th. I'll have my eyes peeled for you, sweetheart.

See you then.

    All my love,
      Adam xxx

'I'm ashamed to meet you.' Rosie pressed the crumpled letter to her breast. 'I don't even know if I can,' she murmured. But she could. She *must*! She owed him that much at least.

Sickened to the heart, she lay back against the pillow and closed her eyes. All she could see was the letter, every word imprinted on her mind. Her heart felt like a lead weight inside her. She loved him still, and yet she had betrayed him with his best mate. 'He's too good for the likes of you!' she told herself, bitter tears dampening the pillow. After a while, she deliberately closed her mind to it all and drifted into a restless slumber.

In her dreams she was in the eye of a raging storm, floating on a raft that was being carried swiftly out to sea. Suddenly a ship appeared with two men aboard; one was Doug, the other a handsome soldier. Both were reaching down to lift her up, and though she desperately strived to grasp the soldier's hand, it was Doug who caught hold of her. At that moment, the boat overturned and they were all flung into the waves.

The gales blew them every which way, and the waves drove them down. The nightmare worsened. And even when she awoke, it was still so real she found herself thrashing at the air with outstretched arms.

Unable to sleep now, she got out of bed and sat by the window to watch the dawn rise in a beautiful sky. 'In a little while you'll be seeing him,' she murmured. 'And God help you then.'

'Come on, Rosie!' Peggy stood by the door, hands on hips, a look of consternation on her thin face. 'Look at the time. If we don't get a move on, you'll miss the train. And listen!' She cocked an ear towards the stairway. The sounds emanating from above told their own story. 'Our mam's up and about. Any minute now, she'll be coming down them stairs with a line o' kids behind her. Then I shan't get out for *hours*. What with one thing and another, she'll keep me at it all morning.'

It was the incentive Rosie needed. 'Just coming,' she said, taking one last look in the mirror and patting her thick brown hair. In spite of everything, she so much wanted to look good for Adam.

'Bloody Nora!' Peggy hopped from one foot to the other. 'Will you get a move on?' Her anxious eyes followed Rosie's every move, and as always she was struck by her friend's simple beauty. Rosie was wearing her best frock, a pretty cream material overprinted with shadowy pink roses. Its swirling hem was a fashionable calf-length and the tiny waist was drawn in by a plain grey belt. She was wearing black slim-heeled shoes, and carrying an envelope bag of the same colour.

'I'm so nervous,' she told Peggy as they went out of the house. 'God only knows how I'm going to tell him.'

'You'll just have to take a deep breath and out with it,' Peggy declared. 'As far as I can see, there ain't no other way.' She took a sideways glance at her friend. 'You bugger! You didn't sleep after we went back to bed, did you, eh?' She had seen how pale Rosie was, and how the shadows had deepened round her lovely brown eyes.

'I couldn't,' Rosie admitted, 'I kept reading his letter.' It was in her bag now. She must have read it a dozen times, and each time she felt worse.

The tram was just drawing away as they reached the bottom of Viaduct Street. 'RUN!' Peggy yelled, and the two of them took to their heels, shouting and calling to the conductor to wait for them.

'Another minute and you'd 'ave missed it.' The red-faced fellow rolled their tickets out of his machine and gave the change to Rosie. 'Off to the market, are you?'

Before she could get her breath, Peggy chirped in, 'You're not supposed to leave 'til half-past eight, and it's still half a minute to go.' She pointed at her big round watch.

'You're not telling me that thing's right, are you? Where did you get it ... threepence off the market?' He grinned and turned away.

'Cheeky sod! This cost me half a week's wages.'

'Well now that's a real shame, because it's running slow. If I were you I'd ask for my money back.' Before she could retaliate he'd hurried away, whistling at the top of his voice.

The market was already busy, with people jostling each other and pushing forward for the early bargains. But the tea rooms at the station end were almost empty. Rosie was glad of that. 'I've been all kinds of a fool,' she told Peggy as they collected a mug of tea and went to the table nearest the window. 'I could have been walking down the aisle with Adam, setting up home on Rosamund Street, and having his babies. Now look at me ... three months gone and his best friend the father. Happen my dad's right. I *am* a slut.'

'No you're not. You were lonely, and when Doug Selby made a play for you, you fell for it, just like any other girl would have done. In fact, there's plenty who *have*.'

'Which only makes it worse. I should have known better. After all, he's always had a reputation.'

'He's too bloody handsome, that's what. And he can talk his way into anything.'

'Oh, Peggy, I'm so ashamed. You did warn me about him. Why in God's name didn't I listen to you?'

'Because you weren't thinking straight, and who can blame you? Adam hadn't written in a long time, and as far as you were to know, you might never have heard from him again. If you ask me, *he's* as much to blame.' She was suddenly pensive. 'Being lonely is a terrible thing.'

'Are *you* lonely, Peggy?' In that moment Rosie saw a side to her friend that she had never seen before.

'Sometimes,' Peggy admitted. 'It would be nice to have a fella, but they take one look at me and run a bleedin' mile!'

'Fella's can often cause more trouble than they're worth.' And I should know, Rosie thought bitterly.

'Aye, well . . . there ain't too much chance of being lonely in our house, what with screaming brats and my mam going off half cock when things don't suit her.' She laughed. 'Life would be dull without them, though.' She studied Rosie's sad face before asking quietly, 'How do you feel about Doug? I mean *really* feel?'

'Sometimes I hate him.'

'And other times?'

Rosie had asked herself the same question over and over, so she knew the answer by heart. 'I suppose I've grown used to having him around. But I don't love him. Not in *that* way. I never did.'

'Then don't wed him.'

Shocked at the suggestion, Rosie shook her head. 'Oh, Peggy! I don't think you're listening. I'm with child, and my dad's thrown me out. When Adam hears what I have to say, he'll wash his hands of me and the only friend I'll have in the world is you. I've put myself on your poor mam, who already has more than enough to contend with. I've a few savings put by, but that won't last too long, and in a couple of months' time I won't be able to

21

work at all, and I'll be looking for charity.'

'You're only seeing the bad side.'

'What other side is there?'

'You could stay in our house, and let our mam bring the baby up while you go back out to work. I know she wouldn't mind.'

Rosie realised what a good friend she had in Peggy. '*I* would mind though,' she said gently. 'I couldn't put on your mam like that. I wouldn't. And anyway the whole town would know my shame then. I'd be labelled a bad 'un, just like my dad said, and the baby would be branded a bastard.' The thought horrified her. 'No. Bless you for the thought, but I can't do it.'

'There is another way.' Sipping at her tea, Peggy regarded Rosie through crafty blue eyes.

'Oh?' Intrigued, Rosie put down her mug of tea and stared at Peggy with curiosity. The faintest sense of hope stirred inside her. Though it soon fell away at Peggy's words.

'Get *Adam* to wed you.'

'What are you saying.'

'I'm saying you should keep your mouth shut about carrying Doug's child, and go along with Adam's plans. Wed him. Set up house together in Rosamund Street, just like you've always planned. You love Adam, don't you?'

'You know I do. Even though I'm promised to Doug, it's Adam I'll always want.'

'Well then?'

Rosie smiled. 'Don't think it hasn't crossed my mind, because it has, time and again. But it wouldn't work. Adam's a proud man. He wouldn't want me after what I've done. There's no way I could deceive him, and I wouldn't really want to. Besides, can you imagine Doug keeping quiet? No. He would take great pleasure in telling Adam about what went on when his back was turned. He would never let Adam forget that I was carrying his child.'

'It's worth a try. If you really must, you can tell Adam the truth, about Doug and all. *Then* tell him how you're sorry . . . that it just happened, and you still love him.'

'I intend to tell him all that,' Rosie confirmed. 'But I'm also going to tell him that Doug and I are soon to be wed.'

22

'Aren't you even going to *try* and win him back?'

It seemed an age before Rosie answered. How she wished everything was as simple as Peggy would have her believe. 'No. Like I said, it's all too late. I know Adam like the back of my own hand, and I know it would never work.'

'But if he loves you?'

'No. Even then. He's a fine man but he's proud and rightly so. I don't believe there's a man alive who would want to be reminded day after day that his wife and his best friend were lovers while he was away in the forces. Every time he looked at me or the baby, it would break his heart. It would break mine too. Whatever love we started out with, would soon become loathing.'

'Oh, Rosie!' Peggy's voice broke with emotion.

Moved by her friend's tears, Rosie laid her hand over Peggy's, saying softly, 'You mustn't fret, you know. I'm resigned to what has to be done. I know how concerned you are, and I know you're trying to find a way out of it for me. But I've thought it through, and marrying Doug is the only way.' She smiled wryly. 'Like my dad would say, I've made my bed and I'll have to lie on it.' Peering through the window, she turned her eyes towards the clock over the station entrance. It was almost nine-thirty. 'I'd better go,' she said brightly. 'I don't want to keep him waiting on top of everything else.' She stood up. 'Don't wait for me,' she told Peggy. 'I'll see you later, eh?'

Peggy squeezed her hand. 'Don't forget what I said,' she insisted. 'It's worth a try.'

Rosie's answer was an affectionate kiss on the cheek. Then, without a word, she turned away, left the tea rooms, and was soon lost in the milling crowd of shoppers.

'Best of luck, sweetheart. I'll be thinking of you,' Peggy said under her breath. 'Though I'd rather you than me!'

As she made her way across the market place, the train's whistle pierced the air. She paused for a minute, wondering whether she should go back. Rosie's instructions rang in her ears. Don't wait for me, she'd said. 'I expect she'll want to be on her own for a while,' Peggy thought aloud. Soon she was clambering on to the tram that would take her home, and soon after, much to the amusement of the other passengers, she was light-heartedly arguing with the same conductor who had brought them here.

Rosie paced back and forth. As the train approached, people surged forward to meet the disembarking passengers or to board the train themselves. Once or twice she was given the glad eye by certain young men who took a fancy to the slim pretty young woman, though they soon lost interest when she seemed oblivious to their bold attentions.

The train shuddered to a halt. A cloud of vapour from the engine enveloped the carriages, and Rosie stepped forward. Her anxious eyes scanned the crowds as they converged from every direction. There were men in bowler hats, harassed mothers with small crying children, soldiers and airmen on leave, old folk and young, all weary, wilting in the heat of a glorious June day, and all wanting to get home.

As they made their way along the platform, another figure caught Rosie's eye. A tall uniformed figure which intermittently disappeared and reappeared, a ghostly thing, lost in a billowing haze. 'Adam!' Instinctively she ran towards him, her heart in her mouth; a great longing surged through her as she thought of him, of the way it had been between them.

Suddenly he was there, standing only inches away yet not seeing her. He was more handsome than she remembered, upright and strong, with the same proud bearing which had first attracted her to him. She could recall it as though it was only yesterday. It was a Saturday night in February, a little over three years ago. It was Peggy's nineteenth birthday, and she and Rosie had gone to the Palais to celebrate.

Doug and Adam were best pals, and they were there that night; both in Army uniform, jointly celebrating the end of the war and Doug's imminent demob. Adam though, because he had no family ties, had decided to carve out a career in the forces. They were each handsome in their own way; Doug, with his striking, laughing eyes and tumbling brown hair, was the merry one, outgoing and fun to be with; while Adam was quiet, more serious, and incredibly handsome with his commanding height, dark eyes and black hair.

At first Doug made a beeline for Rosie, but was soon disappointed when it seemed that the only man in the room for her was Adam. Disgruntled, Doug then turned his charm on Peggy, sweeping her off her feet and starting a relationship that lasted only weeks before they began to quarrel and he eventually threw her over for the barmaid at The Swan public house. 'Bloody good shuts!' Peggy told Rosie. And the two of them went out on the town to celebrate.

Doug's best friend, though, wanted none other than Rosie. They were so right for each other, so much in love, and so excited about the future. Soon they were a couple, idyllically happy and making plans for a life together. It soon became evident, though, that there was one area where they disagreed. While Rosie begged Adam to get a civilian job, he was adamant that he would stay in the forces. 'I don't feel ready to come out yet, sweetheart,' he explained, and nothing that Rosie could say would persuade him otherwise.

For a while she went along with his wishes, telling herself that the Army had been his family, and he needed it for a while yet. But, from his letters, it soon became clear that he might *never* leave it. Then came the long empty months when he didn't write and she was left lonely and confused. The loneliness gave way to anger, and it was then that she allowed herself to be seduced by Doug. He seemed always to be near, going out of his way to be both charming and attentive. Peggy warned her against him, as did her father. In fact there were times when her father forbade her to leave the house. He became entrenched in his dislike of Doug, and blamed Rosie for the fact that she and Adam had drifted apart. Inevitably they argued, and Rosie was driven the wrong way by her father's dictatorial attitude; especially in view of the fact that the last letter she had received from Adam warned her that she may not hear from him for a while. 'Got things to think about,' he'd written. 'Not sure what to do.'

Secretly delighted, Doug seized his chance. He was quickly there at her side, to comfort and distract her, especially on the night Peggy was taken ill with the 'flu and couldn't go with Rosie to the Palais. She could remember little of that night. Yet she knew she had drunk too much, and recalled going outside to get a breath of air, and Doug kissing her. One thing followed another and on the way home they made love, right in the middle of Blackburn Rovers football grounds.

Later, when she found she was with child, she was frantic, believing he would want nothing to do with her. Astonishingly, when she told him, he proudly declared that they should be wed as soon as it could be decently arranged. Rosie was under no illusions. It took only a short time for her to see him for the shallow and vain man he was. Even so, he was hard-working, and she never doubted for a minute that he truly loved her.

Adam's letter had re-opened all the old wounds. And now here he was in person, breaking her heart all over again. His head was turned away, his dark eyes desperately searching the platform. 'Adam, I'm here,' she said, her soft voice reaching out to him.

When he turned his dark eyes to her, she trembled from limb to limb. There followed a strange silence when it seemed they were the only two people in the whole world. Then he was rushing forward and she was rooted to the spot, summoning up the courage to do what must be done. In a minute he had thrown off his rucksack and was sweeping her into his arms, laughing aloud, calling her name and crushing her so tight to his chest that she could hardly breathe. Setting her on her feet, he gazed down on those beloved features, his own face suffused with pleasure as he breathed, 'I'd almost forgotten how beautiful you are.' He kissed her then, a long hungry kiss that lit the passion inside her.

Tearing herself away, she told him, 'You look well.' She wanted to say so much more; to tell him how she had missed him, and how she still loved him with all her heart. She wanted to rant and rave, and let him know he had ruined both their lives. But how could she accuse him, when it was she who had been the impatient one?

Overjoyed to be back with her, to have finally come to a decision which would secure their future, he didn't realise there was anything wrong. 'Did you tell your dad I was on my way? He won't mind me staying with you both, will he? At least for a while. Oh, Rosie, you can't know how good it is to be home.' He was excited, and full of things to tell her. 'Tell you what,' he suggested, 'I'm starving! Do you fancy a bite to eat?'

This was Rosie's opportunity. 'I was about to suggest that myself,' she told him. 'There's the tea rooms across the way?'

'Fair enough, sweetheart.' He didn't mind where they went as long as they could be alone somewhere they could talk. Swinging his rucksack over one arm, he cradled her to him with the other. And as they walked the short distance to the tea rooms, he couldn't take his eyes off her.

'Sit yourself down,' he told Rosie, throwing his rucksack to the floor. 'What's it to be? Mug of tea and a sandwich?' He pushed his hand into his trouser pocket and began walking towards the counter. The joy at seeing her was still shining in his eyes as he glanced back.

'Tea, that's all,' she said, making herself smile.

Soon they were seated opposite each other, and he was shaking his head in disbelief. 'I can't believe I'm here with you,' he murmured. 'Miss me, did you?'

'You know I did.'

'I'm sorry I took so long to write, sweetheart.'

'You *should* have written before!'

'You're angry?'

'Yes, I'm angry.'

He cast his eyes down, his fingertips toying with the edge of the tablecloth. 'I thought about you every minute. I always meant to come back.' He looked up. Reaching out, he covered her hand with his. 'It was always on the cards that you and me would be wed. You do believe that, don't you?'

Not daring to look into those dark eyes, she kept her gaze averted. 'I don't know *what* to believe,' she answered truthfully.

'You must know I love you?'

'I suppose.'

Only then did he realise there was something not quite right. Yet he didn't immediately say anything. Instead he bit a chunk from his sandwich, then another, meticulously chewing each bite until it was gone. Taking a great gulp of his tea, he put the mug back on the table with deliberation. For a long silent moment he stared at her, his brows furrowed in thought. And all the while she avoided looking into those dark troubled eyes. At length, he asked in a subdued voice, 'We *are* going to be wed, aren't we?'

'No.' Now that the word was out, she felt stronger somehow, yet deeply ashamed.

Sitting bolt upright, he clenched his fists on the table. 'What the hell do you mean . . . no?'

'I mean, when you hear what I have to tell you, you won't *want* to wed me.' Her stricken brown eyes flickered beneath his searching gaze.

He stretched out his hand and took hold of her fingers. 'It can't be all that bad,' he said fondly.

Sliding her hand away, she faced him directly, dying a little with each word as she described how she had begun to believe that he was never coming back, that he didn't want her any more. She told him how she had betrayed him with another man, and how she was carrying that man's child. Her heart broke when he fell back in the chair as though she had felled him with an axe. 'I'm so sorry, Adam,' she murmured. 'When I got your letter, it was already too late. I'm promised to him, and that's an end to it.'

His eyes were hard as they focused on her. '*Who is he*?' His voice was curiously low, yet forceful.

She was tempted to give him another name, or not to tell him at all. But then she realised that it was only a matter of time before he found out. Once he was settled in her father's house, probably the first person he would want to see was his best friend Doug. He had to know. And it was best he should know now. 'It's . . . Doug.' There! It was said. And now she felt more ashamed than ever.

He stared at her in disbelief. '*Doug!*'

Peggy's words came back to her then, and she knew she had to try. SHE HAD TO TRY! Peggy had said it was worth it, and she was right. The thought of losing Adam and spending the rest of her days with a man she didn't love, was suddenly more than Rosie could bear. 'I don't love him,' she said desperately, 'it's always been you, Adam. It's still you. If only you could forgive me, we could still be wed. Oh, if only you could forgive me it would be all right, I know it would.' She could feel the tears streaming down her face, hot and moist against her skin. She wiped the back of her hand over her mouth, brushing the wetness away, trying so hard to choke back the emotion. But she couldn't.

28

For months now she had bottled it all up, and now he was here, he had held her and kissed her, and her heart was breaking.

Without a word he stood up and slung the rucksack over his shoulder. One last glance from those questioning black eyes, then he was gone. As he strode from the room, she called out his name. He didn't look back. She watched him hurry across the boulevard and re-enter the station. She hoped and prayed, right up to the moment he disappeared from sight and for some time afterwards. But he didn't look back. And in her heart she couldn't blame him.

It was growing dark when Rosie returned to her friend's house. She knew at once that there was something very wrong. Peggy was waiting for her. 'You'd best sit down,' she said gently, leading Rosie into the parlour.

Peggy's face was ashen. The children were all abed and the little house was too quiet. Peggy's mam was seated by the window. She didn't speak, but her pained eyes spoke volumes.

'What is it?' Rosie was afraid. 'What's wrong?'

Peggy looked helplessly at her mam, who quickly nodded encouragement. 'The police were here. We came to the station looking for you, but you'd already gone.'

Rosie was puzzled. 'What do the police want *me* for?' When Peggy was slow in answering, it was as though a light had been switched on in her mind, and it filled her with horror. She was shaking her head, trying to push the truth away. 'It's Adam, isn't it?' she asked fearfully. Running through her confused mind was the possibility of a train crash, or even worse.

'No, it's not Adam.' Peggy held her and then Rosie knew. 'It's your dad. I'm sorry, he's gone. There was nothing anyone could do.' She didn't say how they had found him in the bath, with the razor still embedded in his wrist and the walls splattered with his own blood. Rosie would suffer that later. For now, she needed a friend. 'Shh now,' she said. 'Wait a while, then we'll go and see them, eh?' Rosie felt numb. For a moment she couldn't take it all in. Memories of her lost love filled her sore heart, she could still feel Adam's kiss burning on her lips; she remembered the awful pain in his eyes when she told him the truth. And now her father! It was too much, all too much. She started to shake, but still she couldn't grasp it all. Nothing seemed real to her. Beneath her breath Peggy murmured, 'They say it never rains but it pours.'

And she feared that, for Rosie, the storm clouds had only just begun to gather.

CHAPTER THREE

'Are you getting up or what?' Doug's angry voice carried up the stairs. 'I'm ready for off, and my sandwiches still aren't done!'

Before Rosie could explain that she hadn't got up because she was crippled with pain, another voice intervened: his mother's. 'Leave the lazy cow where she is, son. I got your snap tin ready long before *she* came on the scene, and I can do it now.' There followed a series of loud deliberate noises when, after a few seconds, Martha Selby could be heard stamping down the stairs. 'I warned you she'd be no good, but you wouldn't listen. Oh, no! Happen you'll bloody well listen *now*!'

Inching her legs out of bed, Rosie touched the cold linoleum with the tips of her toes. The pain shot through her like a knife. 'It's started,' she gasped, running both hands over the swollen mound beneath her nightgown. The sweat was pouring from her now, and she could hardly breathe. 'DOUG!' It took all of her strength even to call his name.

Suddenly the door burst open and there he was. 'What bloody game are you playing, eh?' he demanded, striding into the room. 'Since when does my mam have to get herself out of bed at five o'clock on a winter's morning to do what *you* should be doing, eh? EH?' He poked at her with the tips of his fingers, oblivious to the fact that she was in a state of great distress.

Rosie had been sitting with her head bowed, but now she raised her eyes. In the glow from the lamp, she saw his red angry face staring down on her, and the only thought in her mind was to be rid of him. 'Get out,' she said, and he was visibly stunned.

'WHAT!' He looked at her in disbelief before raising his hand to strike her.

If he expected her to flinch, he should have known better. Defiant brown eyes stared back at him. Anger smothered the pain. 'Go on. Hit me then,' she taunted. 'What are you waiting for?'

For a minute it seemed as though he would bring his fist crashing down on her. But then he realised she was not afraid and he laughed out loud. 'Well, I'm buggered!' Sitting beside her, he slid an arm round her shoulders. All anger was gone, and in its place came a mood that was even more repugnant to her. 'You're a fiery bugger and no mistake.' One hand snaked under her nightie while with the other he fumbled at his trouser buttons. Grabbing her hand, he placed it over his exposed member. 'Feel that,' he coaxed. 'Stiff as a broom handle ... aching for you, it is.' When she snatched her hand away, he nuzzled at her neck with the tip of his nose. 'I miss it, you know,' he moaned, frowning pathetically. 'I could have got it elsewhere, but I haven't. Not yet.'

'You'd best go or you'll be late for work.'

'We've time, if you want to.'

'Sod off!'

'Well, that's no way to talk to your old man, is it?'

A vicious pain rippled through her, taking her breath away. 'Please, Doug. Leave me be.'

'What the hell's the matter with you?' He stared harder at her, only then realising that she was deep in labour. Bent double in pain and sweating so much that her nightgown was welded to her back, she didn't have the strength to push him away. 'Christ Almighty!' Running to the door, he began yelling, 'MAM! MAM! SHE'S STARTED!' He didn't come back to the bed. Instead, he stood by the door, yelling for his mam and watching Rosie apprehensively.

Martha Selby came rushing into the room, breathless and red-faced from coming up the stairs two at a time. She was a big woman, grey-haired and scruffy; the dark stain of snuff beneath her nostrils resembled a 'tache. 'Off to work, son,' she told him, planting a kiss on the side of his face. 'Your snap tin's all ready downstairs.'

'She's started!'

'Nothing for you to worry about, son. She ain't the first woman to fetch a bairn into the world, and she won't be the last.' With the flat of her hand, she pushed him out of the door. 'Go on. I'll see to it.'

He didn't need telling twice. He was gone even before she'd finished speaking.

'Now then, young madam.' Regarding Rosie with curious eyes, Martha came across the room. 'I'll not stand for no tantrums,' she said in a hard voice. 'Giving birth ain't easy, but if you start yelling and screaming, I'm buggered if I won't tie you down. Do you understand what I'm saying?'

'I want the doctor.'

'No need for a doctor.' With her hands on her hips, she demanded, 'I asked whether you understood?'

Rosie didn't answer. Racked with pain, she merely nodded. She was in no fit state to fight. The fact was, she was alone in this room with a woman who loathed the very sight of her, and she was at her mercy.

'Good. It seems we understand each other. Now, get off the bed while I roll back the sheets. Them's my best ones and I don't want 'em soiled.' She waited while Rosie struggled to raise herself up against the bed-head, clinging to the brass rail and bearing the throes of labour without even a whimper. 'Lie down flat.' Martha Selby had removed all but the mattress cover. The bedding, even the pillow, was neatly stacked on to a nearby chair.

The bed struck cold as Rosie lay down. Her head fell back, making the pain more intensive. 'Can't I have my head raised?' she asked.

'If your head's flat, you can't see what's going on, and if you can't see what's going on, then you'll not be tempted to shout and holler. Now, let's see.' Rosie felt her legs being drawn up and stretched wide open. 'The little sod's on its way right enough. I'll away down and get things ready.' In that moment Rosie was gripped with a particularly vicious pain, which made her cry out. Her reward was a sharp slap in the face. 'I said there'll be none o' that. I won't stand for no hysterics, do you hear me?' Rosie turned away. 'I SAID, DO YOU HEAR ME?' Rosie gave a nod. 'Right. Do as you're told. Else I'll leave you to get on with it yourself, and then it'll be God help you!' With that she hurried from the room.

Rosie thought she was never coming back, but after an age the older woman reappeared. When she came through the door, Rosie was pushing against the force of the child inside her. 'Don't push, you bugger! You'll harm the child!' Dropping the bowl of hot water on to the dresser, she thrust her hands between Rosie's legs. 'Its head's nearly out,' she cried. 'It won't be long now.'

In spite of everything, Rosie was glad of this sour-natured woman. She was afraid, and lonely, and wondering how bad the pain would get before she had to yell and scream. It got bad, then worse, and still she kept her silence. Above all else, she didn't want to be left alone, and she was under no illusion where Martha Selby was concerned. The woman was hard as nails, with a vicious streak that made her more enemies than friends. If she had threatened to leave Rosie to it, then that was exactly what she would do. Even if it meant both mother and child losing their lives.

It was two agonising hours before the baby came into the world, during which time Rosie worked harder than she had ever worked before. Even then she could do no right for Martha Selby, who yelled and screamed herself as though it was *she* who was giving birth, and not Rosie. 'It's another lad!' she finally cried jubilantly, holding the child aloft. 'Just as well, 'cause I ain't got no time for split-arses.'

She took an unnaturally long time in bathing the newborn. Then she cooed and fussed and worried about what name to call it, and when Rosie asked to hold the child, tutted and moaned and thrust it into her arms with the warning, 'With your mam dead and gone, you'd best not forget I'm his only grandma.'

Wisely, Rosie made no comment, but that evening when Doug climbed the stairs to see her, she gave *him* a warning. 'You've got a month to find us a place of our own.'

'You must be mad!' He hadn't even looked at the child in his cradle, nor had he taken Rosie into his arms. 'Where the hell am I supposed to find a place, just like that? You know very well there aren't many houses for rent now, what with landlords cashing in on this new trend for *owning* property. Every house round here for miles has been sold off. There ain't a place to be rented nowhere.'

'That's rubbish and you know it. You haven't looked hard enough.'

Rosie had spoken the truth and it irked him. Punching the door with a clenched fist, he demanded, 'Bloody hell, woman! We've a roof over us head. What more do you want? My mam's been good to us, and Dad's twice upped my wages for helping him on the coal-wagon. We're living here in comfort, and it's only costing us half what we'd have to pay anywhere else, even if we *could* find a suitable place.' He swung round to face her. 'And if you've got an eye on Rosamund Street, you can bloody well forget it, because I'm not paying fifteen shillings a week for no house, in Rosamund Street or not.'

'I'm not talking about Rosamund Street.'

'Oh? And why's that, eh? There was a time not long back when Rosamund Street was all you could think about.'

'That was *then*.' A great sadness washed over her. Rosamund Street was still close to her heart. But having a house there had been a very special dream. It belonged to her and Adam, and no one else. Well, that dream might be over, but it was all she had left of him, and she didn't want it spoiled. 'I don't care *where* we live, as long as it isn't in this house.'

'Well, that's bloody right, that is!' Striding across the room, he shook his fist at her. 'My mam's had you pegged all along. You're an ungrateful little bugger. You're not asked to do any housework, are you?'

'No.'

'Washing, ironing . . . none of that?'

'No.'

'Well then?'

She looked at him with a dignity that made him feel inferior. 'You just don't understand, do you?' she asked in a quiet voice. 'Does it never occur to you that I *want* to do my own washing and ironing? That I long to clean the carpets and polish the furniture? But I'm not allowed to, because your mam doesn't want me touching her precious things.'

'She doesn't want to put on you, that's all.'

'You're either blind or you don't care. Your mam only tolerates me because she doesn't want to lose you or her grandson. That's

35

the reason she enticed you to live here in the first place, and it's the reason she keeps us here.'

'And what's so wrong with that, eh? She's lonely. What with my dad working all hours God sends on that bloody coal-wagon of his, it's only natural she wants company.'

'Did you know she's busy choosing a name for *our* son?'

'And you object?'

'Of course I object!'

He seemed genuinely shocked by that, but made no comment. Later she would live to regret denying his mother that simple pleasure!

'I mean it, Doug. If you want me and the boy, you'll have to find us somewhere else to live.'

'And if I don't?'

'I'll take him and find lodgings.' The minute the words were out of her mouth, she realised how empty they were.

He hadn't expected a bold statement like that. Such a thing wasn't done round these parts where if a man couldn't control his family, he was not a man. Doug had no intention of being made to look a fool in front of his neighbours. Besides, he still had an uncontrollable lust for this defiant wife of his. 'Try that one and I'll break every bone in your body!'

She didn't answer. What she threatened had no real substance. How could it? Besides, she would never accept charity, so what would she live on?

Troubled by her silence, he came to her. Sitting on the edge of the bed, he said in a softer voice, 'Don't let's fight.' Running his fingers through her thick brown hair, he mistook her shudder of repugnance for delight at his touch. 'I want you so much,' he murmured. 'Yet somehow, I always feel you're never really mine.' It was a deep-down feeling that was increasingly hard to live with. 'I do love you, you know . . . you and the boy.' For the first time his eyes turned towards the cradle. 'Mam says he's just like me when I were a lad.'

For the briefest moment there was a curious tenderness in his voice, and Rosie thought she might have been a little hard on him these past weeks. 'I'm sorry, Doug. I know she's your mother, and happen she means well, but we don't hit it off. She's never liked me, you know that.'

He smiled. 'She can be a cantankerous bugger when she sets her mind to it, I'll give you that.'

'You'll find us a place then?'

He nodded. 'Aye, I expect so.' Having agreed to give her something, he expected something else in return. Kissing her on the mouth, he whispered, 'I don't suppose . . .'

'No. Not yet.'

'For Christ's sake! WHEN?'

'I don't know.'

'Tomorrow?'

'What kind of man are you, Doug Selby? Have you forgotten, I've only just given birth?'

'No, I've not bloody well forgotten. But I don't intend to wait forever, I can tell you that. I've waited long enough, and come the end of next week, I'll be after my rights, just like any self-respecting man.' Putting his hands one either side of her face he squeezed hard, until her dark eyes looked like round brown pools and she was unable to cry out. Then he kissed her so viciously on her puckered mouth that it bruised her. 'I *will* have my rights!' he said with an ugly smile. 'So think on *that* while I'm out searching for a house, eh?'

He went out of the room laughing. When the door was slammed shut behind him. Rosie stroked her sore face and cursed the day she ever set eyes on him. Then she leaned over the cradle and took the newborn into her arms. 'If it wasn't for you,' she murmured, softly crying, 'I wouldn't stay in this house another minute.' But she was trapped. And saw it as just punishment for her sins.

The days sped by. Doug swore he was looking in every direction for a house of their own; Martha Selby couldn't keep her hands off her new grandson; and Rosie spent as much time outside as she possibly could.

In the cold December mornings, she walked all the way to Corporation Park and sat beneath the willow trees by the lake. Here, she would breast feed her son in the wintry sunshine and watch the ducks at play until mid-afternoon, when she would walk all the way back to Artillery Street, where Martha Selby was invariably standing by the door, hands on hips. 'Where the

37

hell have you been all day?' she'd demand. 'Have you no sense
at all, woman? Don't you know it's too cold for my grandson to
be out?' At which point she would snatch the boy from his pram
and hurry inside, always with the same snide comment: 'She's a
bad mammy, ain't she, eh? Lord knows what your dad'll have to
say when he gets home.' And she always made certain that Doug
was riled up two minutes after he walked through the door. 'She's
been wandering the streets 'til all hours again, our Doug. Have
you ever heard the like? Taking a lad of his age out on such a
chilly day. He's feverish, feel his forehead! I shouldn't be at all
surprised if the lad doesn't go down with pneumonia,' she would
crow. 'She's your wife, so it's up to you. If you ask me, you ought
to take a firmer hand with her.'

Today was Friday. Rosie had spent many hours in the park,
and now she turned the pram away from the lake and towards
the main entrance. 'We'll go and see Peggy, shall we?' she
asked the sleeping child. 'We've time enough.' A glance at the
clock over the arches told her it was almost four-thirty. Normally,
she would have made straight for Artillery Street, because she
always made a point of being home before Doug. Today, though,
she wasn't concerned, because she knew he wouldn't be home
until at least six-thirty. After work on Friday, Doug usually spent
an hour with his drinking pals. Rosie was glad of that, because
to tell the truth, the less she saw of him the better.

It was twenty minutes past five when she got to Castle Street.
As she came in at one end, Peggy got off her tram at the other.
The sight of her dear friend cheered her heart. 'PEGGY!' she
shouted, pushing forward at a quicker pace, yet going carefully
over the cobbles so as not to shake the baby.

Peggy's face lit up. 'You're a sight for sore eyes!' she cried,
coming at a run down the street. Her nose was red from the cold,
but her eyes were bright at seeing Rosie. The two of them were
soon hugging and laughing, and in no time at all they were hauling
the pram up the steps and into the house.

Manoeuvring the cumbersome article down the narrow passage
was no easy task, especially when Peggy's mam and four boister-
ous children decided to lend a helping hand. But they managed,
and once the pram was lodged safely against the parlour wall,

the children all disappeared into the back yard, and Peggy's mam took herself into the scullery where, except for the time she reappeared with a mug of tea each for the two young women, she remained throughout Rosie's visit.

'Bless her old heart, she's probably listening through the door-curtain,' Peggy whispered, her blue eyes bright with mischief. 'And what she don't overhear, she'll try and worm out of me later on.'

Rosie laughed. 'She's a good sort is your mam. And anyway, I've got nothing to say that she can't hear.'

'Hmph!' Peggy sat back in her chair. 'I don't expect Martha Selby's making life any easier, is she?'

Rosie told her everything then; how Doug's mother was inter-fering, trying to take charge of the boy; how Doug still hadn't found them a place of their own, and how she suspected he wasn't even looking; and, worse, how he was intent on claiming his rights this very weekend. 'Honest to God, Peggy, I can't stand the thought of it.'

'I don't know what to say,' she admitted. 'Ain't you got no feeling for him at all?'

'Well, of course I have. But I don't *love* him . . . not like a wife should.'

'Well then, to my mind, if you've got even the *slightest* feeling for him, it shouldn't be too bad.' Leaning forward, she confided, 'It has to be better than having no fella at all.'

'You're right. It's not the end of the world. I expect I'm just nervous after the baby and everything.' Rosie cast her mind back over the past year. 'Anyway, far worse things have happened.'

'As for Martha Selby, I'm surprised you ain't given her a right mouthful. Knowing you, I'm surprised you ain't put the old bag in her place by now.'

'It's not that easy. She's a cunning sort, and I have to be careful not to give her more opportunity to cause trouble between me and Doug. No, Peggy. If I'm to get a place of my own, it's best if I play her at her own game. I've been thinking long and hard, and I reckon I'll find a way. It's just a matter of time, that's all.'

The conversation took another turn when Peggy explained how she had been put on the stationery counter at Woolworths. 'We miss you, gal,' she said, 'the others are always asking after you.' Without waiting for a reply she gabbled on, curious about the christening and wondering if she was going to be a godparent. Rosie assured her she would be, and that the christening would likely be when the lad was three months old. She also explained how she'd wanted to call the boy after her own dad, but Doug was having none of it. 'Every time I come up with a name, he finds something wrong with it. As for his mam, she's intent on picking the lad's name herself.'

'You won't let her, will you?'

'Over my dead body!'

'So, what *will* you call him?'

'Doug and I have argued the point for a whole week now.' Rosie chuckled. 'We'll have to see, won't we?' She looked at the child in his pram. 'He's a grand little thing,' she said lovingly. 'It's not his fault if Martha's hellbent on using him as an excuse to cause trouble.'

'Martha won't get her own way, and Doug will want his son to have a good manly name, so I don't reckon you need worry.' Rosie tended to agree, so they talked of more general matters, like Peggy's new fashionable thick-heeled shoes, and Rosie's astonishingly slim figure after the baby and all.

They were just two old friends catching up on gossip and enjoying the experience. After a while the baby started whimpering. 'I'd best be off,' Rosie apologised. 'The lad needs feeding, and anyway I don't want Doug getting home before me, especially if he's had a drink or two and his mam's fighting fit. That would really put the cat amongst the pigeons.'

Peggy's mam emerged then. 'I couldn't help overhearing,' she confessed with a cheeky little grin. 'All men are the same. If you want a peaceful life, you have to let them be boss. As for his mam, you do right to think of playing her at her own game.' She said something then that really caught Rosie's attention. 'In spite of what your fella says, he can't have looked far for a house 'cause there's one here . . . at the bottom of our street.'

Not realising the full impact her words had on Rosie, she then went on: 'Martha Selby always did like having her own way . . . got a nasty streak in her nature, she has. And she was never popular, even at school. She used to argue and fight with every-body. But I will say one thing in her favour... she was never brazen like some of the lasses. What! She used to redden like a ripe tomato if a boy so much as looked at her.' She laughed out loud. 'Not that many of them ever did, because then, like now, Martha Selby was not what you'd call a pretty thing.'

Having said her piece, Peggy's mam returned to the scullery from where she instructed her daughter to: 'Set the table, lass. Tea's ready.' Hearing their mam, the four children came rushing in from the yard. 'Hey! Get in here and wash your hands, you lot.' She lined them up against the sink. 'Look at the state of you!' she remarked. Their noses were running from the cold and their little hands was chapped by the cold. 'What am I going to do with you, eh?' she chuckled. Then, amid wails of protest, she made them wash their hands and face. And: 'Don't forget behind your ears, you little buggers!'

Rosie went off down the street, still chuckling. 'God forbid that I ever have a little army like that,' she muttered with some apprehension. It wasn't that she didn't like children. It was the idea of Doug fathering them she didn't fancy. The cold air sharp-ened with the onset of evening, prompting her to dig out the headscarf from the pram and wrap it securely about her wind-blown hair. 'By! That's got chilly now, sweetheart,' she told the sleeping infant.

The nearer she got to Artillery Street, the more she thought about what Peggy's mam had said: 'Your fella can't have looked far for a house 'cause there's one empty at the bottom of our street.' That was more than enough to get Rosie's hackles up. But what she had later revealed was even more interesting to Rosie, and it had given her the germ of an idea. 'Well, well, Martha!' she said, smiling to herself. 'I just might have found a way to turn the tables on you once and for all.

'Where the hell have you been?' Doug was waiting for her as she turned the corner into Artillery Street. 'It's going on six o'clock!' He was stiff with anger as he came towards her. 'Our mam's been bloody frantic.'

Astonished to see him home, Rosie did her best not to appear alarmed. 'I can't think why,' she answered, her firm voice belying the angry knot in her stomach. 'I'm quite capable of looking after our son.' Turning round at the foot of the steps, she proceeded to pull the pram up backwards until Doug pushed her out of the way to lift the whole thing from the ground. Carting coal gave him the muscles of an ox.

'I asked where you'd been?' he insisted, taking the pram at a fierce pace into the parlour.

'I went up the park, then I went to see Peggy. It's been ages since I saw her. Anyway, I didn't think you'd be home yet.'

'Up the park?' He glared at her. 'Who in their right mind goes up the park when they can stay in a warm cosy parlour?'

The row raged all the while she fed the child. It continued while Martha Selby went about setting the table, and it went on even while Mr and Mrs Selby sat down to eat their meal. Doug was in too much of a fury to eat, and though she had been looking forward to her meal, Rosie had quickly lost her appetite.

When Doug's parents had finished their dinner, Martha slyly remained within earshot while Mr Selby did his usual vanishing trick and retired to the front parlour. Quiet and plain-faced, he was a big man with a broad back and a shrewd business brain. The complete opposite to his despicable wife, he was painfully timid, and whenever occasion allowed, escaped from the traumas of wedded life to read his beloved racing paper in the privacy of the front parlour.

'When I get home of an evening, I want you here, do you understand?' Doug ranted on. Still dressed in his work clothes, he was standing, legs astride, with his back to the fire, his fists clenched by his sides and the leather collar that protected his shoulders from the rough coal-sacks hanging loosely about his neck. The round staring eyes and fine film of coaldust over his face and nose gave him a comical appearance.

'You tell her, son!' encouraged his mam who was seated at the table now, pretending to sip a cold cup of tea. 'Then get your wash and have your dinner while it's hot.'

'SHUT UP, MAM!' He could handle *one* woman, but his mam was one too many.

'Don't speak to me like that.' In a minute she was across the

42

room and confronting him. 'I'm only saying she deserves to be told, that's all.'

'Yes, and it's me that'll do the telling. I've had more than enough of your bloody interference!'

'Well, sod you . . . and sod her . . . and the pair of you can get out if that's how you feel!'

'Aye, and we will. Don't you worry. Soon as ever we find a place, we'll be off.'

Rosie was amazed, wondering whether she was hearing things. The idea of Doug and his mam going at each other like that was unthinkable. Wisely, she remained very still, sinking deeper into the chair and hoping they would forget she was there. But it was too much to hope for.

After the heated exchange, there was a moment of shocked silence when mother and son realised how the row had escalated. 'You mustn't talk about leaving this house, son,' Martha cooed, brushing away imaginary tears. 'As long as me and your dad's alive, this will always be your home.'

He was sullen for a while, but then he answered, 'I'm sorry, Mam. You've been good to us, and I don't mean to be ungrateful. It's just that I've had a hard day.' He didn't mention that he'd lost a deal of his wages on a foolish bet.

Suddenly his mother pointed at Rosie. 'It's all *her* bloody fault!' she cried, glaring at her daughter-in-law who went across the room to gather the child into her arms. 'See how cunning she is . . . setting us at each other's throats like that?'

'Leave it, Mam.' His cold eyes studied Rosie's slim attractive figure as she bent over the pram. He hadn't forgotten. Tonight, he would hold her in his arms and make love to her. The thought made him shiver inside.

His mother opened her mouth to complain, but he silenced her with the promise, 'It won't happen again, Mam.' Smiling, he kissed her lightly on the cheek. 'Now then, can a man have a minute alone with his wife?'

Sensing his intention to paw her again, Rosie gently laid the child in his pram and began clearing away the used dishes from the table, until she felt a vicious poke in the arm from Martha. 'Get away from my table! I don't need your bloody help.'

Rosie was incensed. 'And if you *did*, you wouldn't ask, would you? Why don't you tell him the truth, Martha? You don't want me in this house, do you?'

'No, I don't. To tell you the truth, I think our Doug could have done a lot better for himself.'

Rosie laughed at that. 'It wouldn't have mattered *who* he brought home, you wouldn't have liked them, because you want to keep your precious son all to yourself. Well, you're welcome to him.' Suddenly the child began screaming. 'But you'll not get your hands on this little chap,' she warned, grabbing the child to her and rocking him back and forth. 'Much as you'd like to!'

'I wouldn't be too sure of that, my girl. Anybody can see you're not a fit mother . . . keeping a lad of that age out 'til all hours. Poor little sod, he should have been in his cot an hour since.'

'Leave it, I said, Mam.' Doug stepped between them. 'Can't you find something to do upstairs?' His meaning was clear.

One glance at her son's grim face cautioned Martha not to show too much of her loathing for his wife. There were other, more deceitful ways to oust her. 'All right, son,' she agreed sweetly. With that, she went out of the door and into the passage. Here, she went noisily up the stairs, stopping halfway and stamping her feet a few times on the step before creeping down to sit with her ear pressed to the crack in the parlour wall. From here, she could hear everything.

'Don't take too much notice of our mam,' Doug pleaded. 'She don't mean half of what she says.' He was worried that the ugly scene would mar his first night of love in a long time.

Rosie wasn't easily placated. 'She means every word, and you know it. I'm just a lodger here, and she can't wait to be rid of me.' The child was quiet now, but still fretful. Rosie lowered her voice. 'That doesn't worry me, because *I* can't wait to get out either.'

'I wish you wouldn't talk like that.'

Regarding him with hard brown eyes, she accused, 'You say you've looked everywhere for a good house to rent?'

At once he was on his guard. 'That's right.'

'You're a liar!'

'Who the hell are you to call me a liar?'

'Peggy's mam told me there's a house on the corner of Castle Street. Did you enquire about *that*?'

He looked away. 'I don't need other folks to tell me where there's property!'

'And I don't need you lying to me!'

Spinning round, he grabbed her by the arm. 'I've said I'll find us a house, and I will. But not on Castle Street.' Outside on the step, his mother grinned widely.

'And why not? It's a good house, and the rents are reasonable.' She wouldn't be put off. Not this time. 'Or is it because I'd be too close to Peggy, eh? Has it come to me not being allowed a friend. HAS IT?'

'Don't talk bloody daft.' Stroking her arm, he lowered his voice. 'I've arranged to meet somebody down at the pub. We'll talk about it later, eh?'

'We'd better.'

He stiffened. 'Hey! Watch your tongue. I've said we'll talk about it, and we will.' Tonight, he'd do anything to pacify her. But talking was one thing. Moving to Castle Street or anywhere else was another! 'All this bloody arguing's got me down. Tell my mam I'll have supper when I get back.' Another minute and he was gone from the room.

Turning at the front door, he caught sight of his mother hunched on the stairs. For a minute she looked alarmed, but when he went away chuckling, Martha believed she'd won the day.

Returning to the parlour, she told Rosie smugly, 'You'll never get him to leave his mam. Doug knows where he's best off.'

'Oh?' Taking the child into her arms, Rosie settled herself into the chair by the fire. It was time for the baby's feed. Undoing her top button, she slid out a plump firm breast. The child latched on to the nipple and began to suck. 'Don't underestimate me, Mrs Selby,' she said boldly. 'Doug and I will be leaving this house before the month's out.'

Martha Selby had been clearing the table, but now she paused to look down on Rosie's lovely face. Her gaze fell to the exposed breast. It was the first time Rosie had fed the child in full view of her. 'Cover yourself up!' she snapped, her face reddening with rage. 'Have you no dignity?' Seeing Rosie giving birth was one thing but now, suddenly reminded of Rosie's beauty, she became incensed.

Delighted, Rosie undid another button and eased the breast further out. Normally, she would never have been so shameless, but baring her breast to Martha was all part of her little plan. 'I have as much dignity as the next woman,' she declared. 'It's just that I don't seem to have as much titty.' With great deliberation, she stroked her breast towards the nipple, encouraging the milk to flow. 'We're not all blessed with big breasts, are we, Martha?' she insinuated, momentarily glancing at the bulky outline beneath Martha's pinafore. 'My milk must be strong though, because he's always satisfied.' Looking away so she wouldn't be seen to be smiling, she asked innocently, 'Was Doug always content with *your* milk?'

'I don't remember.' Martha deliberately clattered about as she put the dishes one on top of the other. 'Anyway, I don't think it's the sort of thing I should discuss with the likes of you,' she snarled. 'Save your cheap talk for your friend Peggy.' All the same, she couldn't help but glance at Rosie once more. 'Disgraceful!' she muttered, shaking her head. 'Exposing yourself like that.'

Aware that she was being watched, Rosie squeezed the nipple between finger and thumb until the milky fluid flowed over, oozing out of the baby's mouth and running down its chin. 'Doug *loves* my breasts,' she remarked with feeling. Looking up, she smiled into Martha's eyes. 'You need never worry that he's not all man,' she said meaningfully. 'Because I can tell you that he *is*.'

Martha's eyes widened in horror. 'You little slut!' she screamed, 'I rue the day he ever brought you home.' Grabbing the dishes, she almost ran into the scullery. Rosie was bursting to laugh out loud, but she dared not. Thrilled that her plan was taking effect, she finished feeding the baby in silence.

A short time later, when she went into the scullery to put the kettle on for his wash, Martha fled into the parlour. When Rosie mixed hot and cold water in the biggest saucepan and set it on the rug, Martha set about polishing the sideboard like her life depended on it. After the child was stripped and laid on a towel, Rosie leaned over him, her blouse still loosely open and showing her slight cleavage. Normally, at her grandson's bathtime, Martha would stand behind Rosie, barking out instructions and generally making a great nuisance of herself. But this time she busied herself, rushing back and forth, before disappearing into the scullery where she noisily washed the crockery in the sink.

Rosie was immensely proud of herself because this was the very first time she had been allowed to bathe her own son without a barrage of criticism from her mother-in-law. And it was deeply satisfying. 'I've got your measure now, Martha, you bugger,' she muttered as she carried the child upstairs to its cot. Recalling the look of embarrassment on her mother-in-law's red face when she saw the bare breast and flowing milk, then the horror when Rosie had hinted at how ardent a lover Doug was, she collapsed on the bed in fits of laughter. 'At last I know how to get the better of you!' she chuckled. 'And you'd best watch out, because this is only the beginning!'

It was almost midnight when Doug got home. Coming into the bedroom, he was pleasantly surprised to find Rosie ready and eager for him. For hours she'd waited for him to enter the front door, and when he did, she quickly flung open the big window, then stripped off her nightgown and got back on the bed.

In the soft glow of the bedside lamp, Rosie looked more beautiful than he had ever seen her. Stark naked, she was stretched out on top of the eiderdown, her thick brown hair fanned out on the pillow and her long legs slightly open. 'I've been waiting for you, sweetheart,' she murmured. Her dark brown eyes smiled invitingly.

'You little bitch!' he chuckled, quickly stripping off and lying over her. He had brought the cold in with him and it made her shiver. 'I'll soon warm you up,' he promised. 'You want it as much as me, and you never said.' He would have taken her then, but she wriggled away, confusing him.

'Don't be in a such a hurry,' she chided. 'Play with me . . . like you used to.' Easing him on to his back, she wrapped her small hands round his huge member, gently stroking it and whispering in his ear, 'You don't want it to be over too quickly, do you?'

'Are you after driving me mad!' he gasped. He was deeply flustered, unable to believe his luck. 'You're a wonder and no mistake,' he said, roving his hands over her nakedness. 'I really thought I'd have to fight you for what's mine tonight.'

Gently biting his lip with her teeth, she laughed softly. 'Whatever made you think that?' she asked innocently, stroking her thumb over the tip of his bursting penis.

'For God's sake, woman!' he cried, arching his back and pulling away. 'You'll have me finished before I'm even started.' She laughed out loud then, and he, anticipating the joys ahead, laughed too.

Next door, Martha lay stiff in her bed, trying not to listen, but whatever the weather, she liked to feel the breeze coming into the bedroom, and just as Rosie had intended every lewd sound carried through the open window. Slithering out of bed so as not to waken her husband, she tiptoed to the window and closed it. But still the wanton sounds filtered through the paper-thin walls. She tried putting her hands over her ears, and buried herself under the clothes, almost suffocating. And still she could hear every groan, every moan and cry. And while she detested every sound, her husband revelled in them; lying beside her and pretending to be asleep, but all the while regretting the loss of his youth, and wishing he had chosen a more warm-blooded woman.

She tossed and turned and tried to block out the sounds by pressing her hands to her ears. It was no use. Martha could hear every movement, the rusty bed springs creating telltale images and causing chaos in her mind; the ecstatic cries and frantic moans suggested they were now in the deeper throes of lovemaking. She felt her blood rising and her face growing redder and redder.

In spite of it all, Martha might have remained in control until it was all over. But when the by now highly aroused Mr Selby rolled over and touched her beneath her nightgown, she screamed aloud and leapt out of bed.

Too far gone to hear anything else but his own beating heart, Doug didn't hear his mother's scream. Rosie heard though, and deliberately drew Doug deeper into her, arching her back, widening her legs and moaning so loud that he was driven to greater heights.

When she flung the door open to peer in, the sight of Doug's bare rear thrashing in and out between those slim white thighs was more than Martha could stand. 'I WANT YOU OUT OF MY HOUSE!' she yelled from the doorway. Her round eyes were bulbous and she jabbed frantically at the air, as though fending off something awful.

The intrusion triggered Doug's orgasm, and he collapsed on to Rosie with a great sigh. It was all too much for Martha who fled downstairs and into the scullery where she twice dropped the tea-caddy in her haste to make herself a hot drink to soothe her frayed nerves, after which she sat hunched beside the fire-range until dawn came. When Doug came sheepishly into the parlour, she rounded on him. 'Get shut of her! I don't want her under my roof another night!'

Fulfilled and immensely satisfied, Doug called her bluff. 'Rosie is my wife. If she goes, *I* go.' At the top of the stairs, Rosie kept her fingers crossed.

'Then you can *both* bugger off' The idea of enduring another night like that was unthinkable. 'I want the pair of you out today.' Later, she would deal with her husband, and make him sorry he'd thought to have his wicked way with her!

Rosie took the child out of its cot. 'We've done it,' she whispered, brushing her hand against his little pink face. 'It cost more than I wanted, sweetheart, but I reckon it's not too big a sacrifice if it means we'll have a home of our own.'

The winter sun was unusually warm, and the work was laborious. Doug tipped the coal through the cellar chute, then, wiping the sweat from his face, he returned to the wagon. Throwing the empty sack over the others, he turned to the big man waiting there. 'What do *you* think, Dad?' he asked. It wasn't often he asked his dad's advice because it was usually his mam who had the most to say. This time, though, he felt the need to consult another man, and his dad was nearest.

Mr Selby hitched the full sack on to his broad shoulders. He seemed astonished that anybody should ask him anything. 'Do you *really* want to know what I think?'

'I wouldn't ask if I didn't.'

'Well, I'll tell you.' He leaned his considerable weight against the side of the wagon, arms bent up above his head and the corner of the coal sack securely caught between thick strong fingers. 'I've never said this afore but I'll say it now . . . I made the worst mistake of my life when I wed your mam. It's too late for me. But you've got a good lass in that wife o' yourn, and if you let her go, then you're a bigger bloody fool than I took you for!'

Doug had never heard his father talk in such a forthright way. In fact, he couldn't recall him ever stringing that many words together. Anger and astonishment welled up in him. 'If your marriage ain't as it should be, happen you should look at *yourself* for the reason,' he snapped. 'It can't all be our mam's fault.'

'I thought it were *you* asking *me* for advice?'

Frustrated that his comments had fallen on deaf ears, Doug stared his father out. 'And I'll thank you not to call me a fool,' he said sullenly.

'Then don't act like one.'

'If that's all you've got to say, I wish I'd never asked you.'

The big man shrugged his shoulders, hitched up the sack of coal, and turned away. He'd said his piece. Now Doug could either listen to him or be ruled by his mam.

All day Martha marched about the house doing her chores, and never a word to say to anyone. In the evening Doug came home with two pieces of news. The first was cause for celebration. The second a bitter blow to Rosie, and cruelly curtailed any joy she might have felt. 'I've got us a house,' he told her. 'It's the one you wanted, on Castle Street.'

'Oh, Doug, that's wonderful!' she cried jubilantly. 'When can we move in?'

Swinging the key before her, he said, 'I persuaded Dad to let me take the rest of the afternoon off. Get yourself ready, woman. We're off to old Tom's on Ainsworth Street.'

Rosie couldn't disguise her disappointment. Old Tom kept a second hand shop, selling all manner of paraphernalia. 'Oh, can't we afford *new* furniture?'

'No, we can't. Old Tom'll have some good strong pieces there. That'll do us. Now, are you coming or not?'

Rosie didn't need asking twice. In no time at all, she'd brushed her rich brown hair until it shone, changed into a clean jumper and skirt, put her tweed overcoat on, and got the child tucked up in its pram. 'Ready,' she said, all smiles and lighter of heart. Perhaps life wouldn't be so bad with Doug after all, she thought hopefully.

His next words not only wiped the smile from her face, but made her realise how wrong she was to assume he might be a better man. 'By the way, I've been in to register the lad,' he casually told her as they went down the street. Martha watched from the window, cursing Rosie and wondering how she could split the two of them up.

'So you've been to the registrar? That's good,' Rosie acknowledged with a bright smile. 'I was going to suggest that we do it on the way to old Tom's.' Recalling how Peggy was certain that Doug would choose 'a manly name', she asked eagerly, 'What name have you given him?'

He gazed down on her upturned face, and for one brief moment she saw the spite in his odd-coloured eyes. 'Oh, you'll like it ... I've called him *Adam*,' he said with a grin. 'After your old lover ... my best mate. What's more, I reckon I'll invite him to be godfather. What do you think of that?'

Rosie was shocked. 'I think you're a bastard!'

He feigned astonishment at her reaction. 'My, my! And I thought you'd be pleased. After all, you did love the fella once, didn't you, eh? In fact, if I hadn't come along, you might even have wed him.' He knew Adam Roach was a better man than he could ever be. He suspected also that Rosie still hankered after him. Naming their son Adam was a way of reminding them both that he hadn't forgotten. And he wouldn't forgive. 'We don't want you to forget a fine man like that, do we, eh?' he sniped.

Rosie continued walking in silence, keeping her distance and despairing of her life with him. Until now she hadn't realised how insanely jealous he was. To name his son after Adam was a malicious act. It told her two things; firstly, that Doug wanted to hurt her for having been Adam's love, constantly to remind her that Adam had no claim on her now, and that she and the child belonged to *him*. Furthermore, it revealed how afraid and insecure he was; although she had been careful never to mention Adam in Doug's presence, he had somehow guessed that she was still in love with his best friend.

What Doug hadn't realised in his fever to hurt her, was that he himself would be hurt. Every time he spoke his son's name, it would be like a knife through his heart.

Anger seeped through her. If he'd intended breaking her spirit, he would be very disappointed. 'On second thoughts, I think that was a lovely idea, Doug,' she lied with the sweetest smile, gazing at the child and wishing it could have been Adam's. 'Yes, *Adam*. I think it suits him.'

It was hard to pretend delight when her heart was heavy. But she must never let him know how vulnerable she was. Tomorrow, when he was out of the way, she would go to the registrar. There was time enough and hopefully there would be no problem in rectifying the mistake. For now, though, she would keep up the pretence and show her hand later, when the smile would be wiped off Doug's face.

Rosie kept her secret well. All the way to old Tom's and right up to the day of the christening.

CHAPTER FOUR

Rosie had lived on Castle Street for three months now. The little two-bedroom back to back was her pride and joy. In a row of other like dwellings, it was conspicuous by its whiter stoned front step and new brass door-knocker. Though the window frames were rotten, and there were gaps in the roof where the tiles had fallen away, and though it was cold even in summer and bone-damp in winter, it was her beloved sanctuary, her consolation for having to suffer a man she could never love.

Complaining the whole time, Doug had been persuaded to paint all the walls; cream in the front parlour, blue in the back parlour, and pale green in the scullery. Rosie had lovingly scrubbed the floorboards and helped to lay the pretty floral-patterned lino. The windows were polished until they shone, and at last the green tapestry curtains were hung.

Two days before Christmas, old Tom had delivered the furniture on his wagon: a sturdy iron-framed double bed; a walnut wardrobe and matching set of drawers for the main bedroom; an oak sideboard; a square table and four ladder-back chairs for the back parlour; and a gas cooker that furiously spat out every time it was lit. Rosie went down Blackburn market and bought a number of scatter rugs for ten shillings, and a big flowered pot on a stand with a wilting aspidistra which revived only after a great deal of tender loving care. The furniture, curtains and bric-a-brac cost a grand total of four pounds eight shillings, and though Rosie considered that to be reasonable, Doug complained it was: 'Bloody daylight robbery!'

Rosie had risen early on this Saturday morning. Last night Doug had made love to her, and as always she had pretended to enjoy it. Afterwards she couldn't sleep. She lay in her bed, listening to the rhythm of his snores and staring out of the window at the sky beyond. As the hours ticked away, the need for sleep fell from her. In the half-light of that room, alone with her most secret thoughts, she felt strangely at peace, yet somehow unfulfilled and empty inside.

After a while she gave herself up to the beauty of a new day being born. There was something especially wonderful about watching the dawn break over the land; something so immense and miraculous it made everything else insignificant in comparison.

Doug was away to his work early. 'Jack Farnham's retiring and Dad's bought the best part of his round. Canny bugger never said a word to me neither,' he said, winking at her with the air of a man who was pleased with himself. 'There still ain't enough work to take on another man, so it means we'll have to work twice as hard ourselves. I'm not complaining though because Dad reckon's it'll put a few bob extra in my wage-packet.'

'A few bob?' Rosie had been feeding little Adam, but looked up at Doug's words. 'That's not much for twice the work.'

The smile slid from his face. 'Whatever I get, you needn't worry *your* head about it, my sweet, because I'll be giving you a small increase as well ... happen enough to put a decent breakfast in front of a working man, eh?' he complained. 'I've said nothing until now because I know money's been tight, but you don't come up to Mam's standards. I'll be expecting an improvement. So, think on.'

Rosie met his sly gaze with accusing brown eyes. 'That depends on how much extra I get in *my* wage packet,' she said boldly.

'Watch your tongue,' he warned. 'Don't get clever with me.' When she merely smiled and turned her attention to the infant, he slung his work-bag over his shoulder and stormed out.

'And good shuts to you!' Rosie whispered, smiling at the child and hugging him close when he touched his tiny finger against her lips. 'I would have said he was very well looked after, wouldn't you?' she asked. 'He's never sent off to work without a full belly, and when he comes home of a night there's always a hot meal waiting for him.' Nuzzling her face against the child's pink cheek, she grumbled, 'But I can't be expected to lay a king's table with a peasant's purse.'

In no time at all, the table was cleared and the clean crockery put away; the housework was finished, and little Adam was sound asleep in his pram. The washing was done and blowing on the line outside in the yard, and Rosie was ready for her trip into Blackburn town centre. All that remained was for Peggy to show herself, and the two of them would be off.

Studying herself in the mirror over the mantelpiece, Rosie stroked at the dark shadows beneath her eyes. 'A good night's sleep wouldn't do you no harm!' she chided. 'And your hair wants cutting.' Her brown tresses were shoulder-length, falling into deep shining waves and giving her the appearance of a little girl. But she looked tired. Excitement at having her very own home wouldn't let her sleep, and lack of spare cash wouldn't allow her a visit to the hairdresser. 'Still, you don't look too bad,' she said, winking at her own image and thinking how vain she was. Suddenly she realised she had no real reason to look nice. 'What does it matter?' she asked herself. 'Who's to care *what* I look like?' The thought of Adam flickered through her mind, but she immediately shut it out.

'Where *is* she?' Glancing at the clock, Rosie realised that Peggy was already overdue. She promised to be here at nine-thirty, and already it was a quarter to ten. 'Don't let me down, Peggy gal,' Rosie muttered as she went along the passage to the front door. 'I'll go stark staring mad if I have to keep my own company for another minute!'

It seemed a lifetime since she and Peggy had enjoyed any real time together. When they first came to live in Castle Street, Peggy came round almost every day. But Doug appeared to resent her intrusion and went out of his way to make her feel uncomfortable. Now the two friends got together only when he was out of the house.

Out on the step, Rosie shivered in the keen March wind. Hopefully, she cast her gaze up the street towards Peggy's house, but there was still no sign of her.

'Morning, luv.' Mrs Best from next-door was off to the shops. A big woman with a man-size face, she kept in touch with everything that happened on Castle Street. If you wanted to know anything, you only had to ask Mrs Best. 'Settling in all right, are you?' she enquired as she went by.

'Yes thank you.' Rosie hoped she wouldn't stop to chat, because once Mrs Best launched into conversation, there was no stopping her. Today, though, she appeared to be in a hurry.

'That's good,' she called. 'If you need anything, you've only to ask.' Hitching her basket further up her arm, and bestowing a huge smile on her new neighbour, she quickened her step and was soon gone.

Rosie smiled, her brown eyes growing wistful as she gazed after the woman. At the top of the street a group of children sat on a wall, swinging their legs and laughing aloud as the joker in the pack began doing something to entertain them. Rosie had only lived here for a very short time, but it felt so right. Castle Street was a place where good simple folk lived out their lives in full view of their neighbours. Ragged-arsed children played on the cobbles, and mangy dogs roamed the gutters in search of any tit-bit that might have been dropped. Old women sat on their rickety chairs outside the front door, watching life unfurl around them and dreaming of their own long lost youth. Old men leaned on the walls and sucked their pipes, chatting earnestly to a beloved neighbour and fervently putting the world to rights. Many households relied on wages earned at the mills, quarries and factories. Folks wandered in and out of other homes as though they were one big happy family, and there was a grand sense of belonging. A sense of comradeship. And now, Rosie felt part of it too.

Fifteen more minutes and still there was no sign of Peggy. 'That's it!' Returning indoors, Rosie tucked her brown jumper into the top of her long straight skirt, then put on her smart black coat and matching beret. 'If she isn't coming to us, then we must have arranged to go to *her*!' she told the sleeping child. Softly singing, she pushed the pram up the passage and down the front steps where, locking the pram-brakes, she returned to close the front door. The sound of running feet made her turn round. It was Peggy.

'Sorry I'm late,' she said breathlessly, 'I overslept.' Her hair was standing on end and her coat was haphazardly flung about her shoulders. Running her hands over her hair to flatten it, she shrugged the coat on, buttoned it up, and grinned at Rosie who hadn't the heart to chastise her. Then taking charge of little Adam, who had woken up crying, she pushed the pram along at a furious rate, chattering incessantly about nothing in particular and making baby noises all the way down the street. Rosie couldn't get a word in. But she didn't mind. Peggy was here and they were on their way out. For the moment, that was all that mattered.

The market was busy. Pushing their way through the shoppers, they made straight for the tea rooms; the very same place they had sat on the day Rosie went to meet Adam off the train. She recalled it now, and her spirits fell. In her mind's eye she could see his face, that strong handsome face, and the wonderful smile that fell away at her news.

'Would you believe it?' Peggy plonked herself on the opposite chair. 'I'm buggered if I ain't talking to myself!' She gave Rosie a gentle kick under the table. 'Hey! I might as well not be here at all.'

Rosie was startled out of her reverie. Looking up, she gave a small laugh. 'I'm sorry, Peg,' she apologised, 'I was miles away.'

'I could see that.' She eyed Rosie with concern. 'Do you want to talk about it?'

Before Rosie could answer, the waitress arrived. She was a young surly-looking creature with sharp painted nails and long tendrils of black hair floating about her neck. 'Yurs? What can I get yer?' Rosie ordered tea and Peggy asked for a strong black cup of coffee. Without a word the waitress turned away, frantically scribbling on her pad.

'Miserable sod!' Peggy stared after her.

'Happen she's got sore feet?' Rosie suggested.

'A sore bloody head more like.' Tearing her gaze from the waitress, she turned her attention to the baby. 'Who's a little beauty then?' she cooed, tweaking his fat cheek and groaning when he began to cry. 'Bugger me. *Everybody*'s miserable today,' she remarked, frantically rocking the pram. In a moment he was fast asleep. 'Never could handle kids. They always cry at me,' she confessed with a chuckle. 'Must be my ugly mug.'

'Peggy?'

'Yes?'

Rosie was about to confide in her when the waitress returned. 'One tea . . . one strong black coffee,' she said sourly, sliding the cups along the table. 'You shouldn't really bring carriages in here. The boss don't like it.' She stared disapprovingly at the pram.

'Well now, that's a bloody shame, ain't it?' retorted Peggy. ''Cause the carriage goes where we go.'

The young woman was astonished. She gawped at Peggy, then at Rosie, then shrugged her shoulders and muttered something under her breath as she walked away. After that she kept her distance, though she occasionally glanced at Peggy sourly.

'You were saying?'

Rosie sipped at her tea, wincing when it burnt her lip. Replacing her cup on the saucer, she mused for a while, acutely aware that Peggy was waiting for an answer. Presently, she summoned the courage to tell, her, 'I'm pregnant again.'

'Bloody Nora!' Peggy sighed heavily. 'But you didn't want no more, did you?'

Rosie shook her head. 'I don't mind having babies,' she admitted, looking fondly at her son. 'It's the *making* I don't much care for.'

'What? You mean . . . having it with Doug?'

Rosie smiled. Peggy had never been known for her tact. 'That's exactly what I mean,' she said. 'I know I shouldn't feel that way, but every time we . . . you know . . . I can't help but wish things were different.' It was so good to have Peggy to talk to. With her Rosie didn't have to pretend. 'I still cringe every time he touches me.'

Peggy sighed. 'I ain't much help, but . . . well, I don't see what else you can do. Have you tried denying him his rights?'

Rosie laughed. 'It's easy to see you've never been wed. I've tried it once or twice, but it's difficult to justify it for too long. And anyway, it's easier to keep him happy than it is to live with the rows and long faces. The lesser of two evils, if you know what I mean.'

'Hmph!' Peggy pulled a face. 'There's you fighting it off, and there's me can't get any at all.' When she saw that her attempt to lighten the situation had little effect on Rosie who was genuinely troubled, she frowned. 'I ain't much use to you, am I, gal?'

'More use than you think. To be honest, Peggy, I don't know what I'd do without you. Just talking helps.'

'I suppose I'm a good listener if nothing else.'

The two of them lapsed into silence, Rosie's mind on the past and Peggy thinking about the future. 'When's the baby due?' she wanted to know.

'September.' Rosie had to smile then. 'It's the price I paid to get him away from his mam.'

'Not a bad swap, eh?'

'I don't regret it. Oh, I bitterly regret *other* things. But not this baby.'

'What's playing on your mind then?'

Rosie shrugged her shoulders. 'Same as before, I expect. I'm Doug's wife, and I'm having his second child. I've made mistakes and I'm not likely ever to forget that. But if I'm to live any sort of peaceful life, I'll have to accept my lot.'

'Ain't you happy at all?'

'Oh, yes.' She caressed her son's small hand. 'There's him, and there's the little one on the way. And I've got my own front door key. Isn't that what most women want?

'But not you, eh?' Peggy reached out to cover Rosie's hand with her own. 'You still love him, don't you? Adam, I mean?'

Rosie forced herself to smile. 'Least said, soonest mended,' she said brightly. 'Now then . . . will you be godmother to this one?' she patted her stomach.

''Course I will! I'll be proud to be godmother. But it means I'll have to buy another new outfit,' she moaned, feigning weariness. 'Have you noticed how there's so much more choice now that clothes-rationing is finished? Anyway, you wouldn't want me to wear the same outfit for the christening next week, and then again for the *new* baby's christening, would you?' she asked cheekily. 'Godmothers have to set a good example.'

Her son's christening had caused more rows between Doug and Rosie than she cared to mention. 'I'm sorry, Peggy,' she said now, 'but Doug's cancelled next week's christening.'

'Cancelled!' Peggy was obviously disappointed. 'Why?'

'I wish I knew. He just told me he'd been to the church and stopped it. He wouldn't say why. And he hasn't decided on a new date.'

'You mean he just went out and put a stop to it, without talking it over with you first?' Peggy was appalled.

'You wouldn't be so shocked at that if you knew him better. Doug Selby doesn't believe in consulting *anyone*, least of all his wife.' She smiled wryly. 'But then, there's always his mother. It wouldn't surprise me if she'd had a hand in it.'

'I thought they weren't talking?'

'So far as I know they're not. But if I've learned one thing since being wed to him, it's that he can be very deceitful.'

'But why would he cancel the christening? And how do you feel about it?'

'I was furious!' Rosie recalled the night he came home to tell her. It was midnight. He was drunk, and angry, and something else that she couldn't quite put her finger on. He seemed secretive, gloating somehow. 'We had a vicious row. I told him exactly what I thought about him doing that behind my back. I even threatened to go and see the vicar myself. But he went mad.' Instinctively she put her hand to the side of her face. It still hurt. 'He's not the easiest man in the world to talk to.'

'You mean he hit you?' Peggy had seen the way Rosie subconsciously touched her face. 'The bastard!'

'Like I said . . . least said, soonest mended. The christening's off, that's all I know. When I tackled him about a new date, he mumbled something about having the two babies baptised together. I think there's more behind it than that, but he wouldn't give me an explanation.'

'Well, I suppose, if the truth be told, having the two baptised together isn't a bad idea. It would cut the expense anyway.' She laughed. 'Bugger him! There goes my excuse to buy another outfit!'

'You're right. It would make sense, I suppose.' Rosie agreed. 'But he could have avoided a row and talked to me about it first. I would have gone along with that.'

'Have you asked him? About me being godmother, I mean?'

'No. But you're my best friend, and I can't think of anyone else who would love the children more. Besides, I can't see how he could object to that.'

'Well, I'm here when you want me. Like I say, I'd be really proud.'

'Right! Now that's settled, sup up and we'll have a browse round the stalls.' Somehow, everything always seemed much easier after she'd confided in Peggy.

The morning was delightful. The sun shone and, content in her friend's company, Rosie was soon in a better mood. They wandered the market square, stopping at every stall, examining this and that and making the usual comments women do. 'What do you reckon to this?' Peggy asked, holding up a blue shawl with a long silk fringe.

'You'd look like old Ma Riley in that,' Rosie told her. The trader was so determined not to let them get away that it was a good five minutes before they arrived at the flower stall, where Rosie bought a pretty posy of lavender.

'What am I supposed to do with this bleedin' shawl?' Peggy asked, clutching the unwanted garment.

'You shouldn't have let him talk you into it,' Rosie chided good-naturedly. 'Take it back.'

'What! I daren't go back there,' she protested, eyes as big as saucers at the thought. 'The bugger'll have me buying half his stall.'

Rosie shook her head in frustration. 'You should have said no and meant it,' she said.

'Oh, aye? And what about *you*?' Peggy dipped her hand into the pram and drew out a ghastly red cloche hat with a broken feather. 'Why didn't *you* say no?' Rosie had no answer to that. Instead, she smiled, and soon the two of them were laughing like children. Almost like magic, Rosie's troubles vanished.

'Didn't you say it was your mam's birthday in a few weeks?'

'Yes.'

'And don't you think she'd look a treat in that shawl and hat?'

'So she would!' Peggy declared. 'Why didn't I think of that?'

So it was settled; the shawl and hat were reverently placed into the largest bag and laid on the pram where they wouldn't get squashed. Peggy offered to repay Rosie the threepence she'd paid for the hat, but Rosie declined. 'I would have bought her a little something anyway,' she said. And that was an end to it.

At the bric-a-brac stall, Peggy purchased a blue scarf. 'Ain't it a lovely colour?' she grinned, opening wide her blue eyes. 'It'll set off the colour of my peepers.' Rosie agreed, and promptly spent fourpence on a knitted jacket for her son in the same delightful shade of blue.

They sat beside the horse trough and shared a bag of roasted chestnuts. 'Them'll warm the cockles of yer 'eart!' yelled the newspaper man. 'Fetch us one over an' I'll give you a kiss.' Peggy told him to piss off, and he turned away, roaring with laughter.

Afterwards, they wandered down Ainsworth Street and into King Street. From there they returned at a sedate pace to Castle Street. 'It's been a lovely outing,' Rosie declared. 'It's done me a world of good.'

Peggy had intended going back with Rosie for a while, but she was waylaid by her mam. 'For Gawd's sake keep an eye on these little sods while I go down the market, else we'll have nothing for us dinner!' she wailed.

Peggy argued. 'You knew I was going down the market, Mam. Why didn't you tell me what you wanted?'

'I'm capable of doing a bit of shopping!' she snapped, straightening her hat as she rushed down the street. 'And don't you take no nonsense from 'em!' she cried. With that she went at a run to catch the tram, leaving Peggy and Rosie looking at each other in bewilderment.

'If you ask me, your mam looks like a woman at the end of her tether,' Rosie remarked.

'She's a crafty old sod, that's what she is!' Peggy chuckled. 'I fetched her groceries from the corner shop last night, and I know she don't want nothing at all from the market. It's just an excuse to get away from this brood.' By now the children could be heard causing a rumpus in the passageway, 'Look at that!' Peggy cried. 'Our mam's only been gone two minutes and I'm buggered if they ain't fighting already!' As she went up the steps at a run, the children scattered in all directions. 'I'll tan your backsides when I get my hands on you, you see if I don't!'

Rosie thought that this was as good a time as any to make her way home. 'I'll see you later,' she called, going slowly past the door and peering into the passage. There was no sign of anyone, but the excited screeches emanating from the front parlour told her there was a game of hide and seek going on. 'No wonder your mam's run off,' she called. 'I might do the same if I had that lot to contend with.' Then she went down the street, chuckling to herself all the way.

The following Friday evening, two things happened to rock Rosie's world a little more.

It was almost ten o'clock and Doug wasn't yet home. 'Down the pub again, I expect!' Rosie muttered as she laid the child in his cot. 'He'll be coming in drunk as a lord and wanting his rights.' The thought made her cringe. 'You sleep now,' she murmured, tucking the blanket over tiny limbs. 'You must have had me up and down these stairs a dozen times since I first put you to bed.' The infant was fretful, and she was bone tired. But he seemed sleepy now, and ready to give in. 'Shh now . . . mammy isn't far away.' She stroked his face and her heart melted. His skin felt like velvet beneath her fingertips.

On tiptoe, she went downstairs where she boiled some water and made herself a cup of tea. Holding the cup between her hands, she went to the window and stared out at the yard beyond. 'It's been a long day,' she murmured. In the twilight she could just make out the cumbersome shapes of the blankets hanging heavy on the line. That morning she had gone through the house like a whirlwind; changing the bed from top to bottom and spending two hours on her knees by the tin bath, scrubbing and rubbing, rinsing and dipping those blankets, until they were as clean as the day they were bought. After the arduous task of dragging them out to the yard in the tin bath, and hanging them on the line, still dripping wet, she had then set about polishing the floor. After that she'd cleaned the windows and cleared out every cupboard where the tiniest speck of dust might be lurking.

In between, the child kept her on her feet, and later, when he was sleeping and she fell exhausted into the nearest chair, she felt the tiniest fluttering in her stomach. It could have been an attack of indigestion, or it might have been the new life flickering inside her. But it raised a touchy issue, and she grew determined to have it out with Doug when he got home. This business of the christening had been playing on her mind for too long.

The tea revived her, and she decided to do a little darning. Taking her work-basket from the sideboard, she sat in the big armchair by the fire; she hadn't lit a fire today and now the room was beginning to feel cold. Wrapping her cardigan about her shoulders, she opened her basket and took out the little knitted coat. A pretty lemon thing with silk ribbons, she had bought it from an old woman who came round the houses selling bric-a-brac. One of the cuffs had come unravelled. It was a small repair, but somehow Rosie hadn't found the time to mend it, until now.

In the lamplight, hunched over her work and concentrating on the tiny stitches, Rosie let her thoughts wander. 'Is this it for the rest of my life?' she asked herself. 'One baby after another and waiting for him to come home night after night . . . never knowing what he's thinking, and forever dependent on him?' It was a depressing prospect. The more she thought of it, the more her dreams turned to her first love.

It was gone midnight. The little parlour was quiet with only the sound of the ticking clock disturbing the silence. Rosie's work had slid to the floor and she had fallen into a restless slumber. Even the sound of Doug's footsteps coming down the passage didn't wake her. In her dreams she was troubled. In life her troubles seemed tenfold.

When Adam's hand touched her face, she pressed her own fingers over his. When his warm mouth covered hers, she sighed with happiness and clung to him. It was only when he softly laughed that her joy was shattered. 'Want me, do you, you brazen little bitch?'

'DOUG!' She stared at him with shocked eyes. 'You frightened me.' Instinctively she pulled away.

'Frightened you, did I?' The stench of booze on his breath made her reel. 'Funny. You seemed to be enjoying it.' The smile froze on his face. 'Or were you dreaming of somebody else, eh? Is that it?' His face grew hard.

He was so near the truth she could hardly breathe. 'Don't be ridiculous.'

He merely smiled, a cold calculating smile. 'Ready for bed, are you?' His hand reached out to touch her breast.

'I have some darning to do. I'll be up later.' She stooped to retrieve her work-basket from the rug.

'That can wait 'til tomorrow,' he snapped, knocking it out of her hands. The contents spilled over the floor which seemed to please him. 'Didn't you hear me? I said I was ready for bed.'

Whether it was tasting freedom in her dreams, or whether it was something about the possessive manner in which he gripped her wrist, Rosie didn't know. But something deep inside her made her want to strike out at him. '*You* may be ready for your bed,' she said with surprising calm, 'but *I'm* not. I've told you . . . I'll be up when I've finished my work.' She was astonished at herself.

He too was shocked. 'You what!' he screamed. 'I'll not have no wife of mine trying to get the better of me.' Raising the back of his hand, he fetched it down hard against the side of her face. 'You'll get to bed when I tell you!'

For what seemed an age she stared at him, her small figure stiff and unyielding and her brown eyes swimming with tears. But she wouldn't cry. She told herself she must not give him the satisfaction of seeing her cry. Even when he raised his hand again, she didn't flinch. Instead, in a steady voice that belied the churning inside her, she challenged, 'Hit me again, and you may just live to regret it.'

Amused, he laughed in her face. 'Oh? Threatening me now, is it?'

But he didn't hit her again. And Rosie would never know how her words might have affected him because a knock on the front door startled them both. Slewing round, he almost lost his balance. 'Who the hell's that at this time of night?' His wide eyes and reluctance to answer the door gave Rosie the impression that he was afraid. She wondered whether he had got on the wrong side of some of the seedy characters who frequented the same pubs.

'Hadn't you better go and see who it is?' she asked with

disgust. 'After all, you're supposed to be the man of the house, aren't you?'

Her jibe cut deep. 'I'll deal with you later,' he promised. Then he straightened his jacket and went down the passage on unsteady footsteps. 'Who is it?' His anxious voice carried back to the parlour.

It satisfied Rosie to see that he was a coward. 'I hope it's somebody come to knock sawdust out of you,' she muttered, hastily gathering her work from the floor.

Muffled voices filtered down the passage. Crossing to the sideboard, where she replaced the work-basket, Rosie cocked an ear. What she heard was Doug's voice, raised in surprise at first then talking low and earnestly, and a woman's voice, replying in soft affectionate tones. The voice was familiar. 'No!' Rosie couldn't believe it. But it was true, because almost immediately Martha Selby appeared at the door.

'Look who's come to see us.' Doug was grinning from ear to ear as he ushered his mother into the parlour.

Martha said nothing. Instead she remained upright and formidable as always, her grim face expressionless as she told Rosie, 'I know what you're up to. I've known for a long time, and like a fool I let you get away with it. But I'm telling you here and now, it won't work because I refuse to be parted from my son any longer.'

Rosie was not intimidated. 'I'm not sure what you're talking about,' she lied. She knew very well that Martha was alluding to the brazen manner in which she had 'persuaded' Doug away from his mother's clutches. 'It was never my intention to part you from your son.'

'Don't take me for a fool!'

'All I ever wanted was a home of my own. There's nothing wrong with that, is there?'

The big woman looked around the room. Everything was in order; the ornaments stood proud and sparkling on the mantelpiece, and the floor was clean enough to eat off. She resented that. 'You had a good home in my house.'

'And we have a good home here ... in our *own* house.' She had seen the resentment in Martha's eyes. She had seen the loneliness too. In a different way, it echoed her own. 'It was nothing personal, Martha,' she said kindly. 'You're a woman. You know how special it is, to have your own things about you . . . to have your own front door key.' She waited for a response, but there was none. She looked to Doug for support, but the booze had fuddled his senses and he was slumped against the sideboard with a foolish grin on his face.

Rosie felt very uncomfortable. Her instincts told her she had made an enemy for life in this woman. 'It's very late, Martha. What exactly did you come for?'

She turned away, ignoring Rosie and giving her answer to Doug, who clumsily stood to attention. 'Your father's been ill ever since he got home. I'm to tell you that he won't be in tomorrow. He's paying a call on the doctor. There's nothing for you to worry about, but he's anxious that the wagon's in good hands. Are you able to take care of everything? That's what he wants to know, son. I told him you were. I asked him, "what sort of idiot do you take our lad for?" But he carried on so much I thought I'd better come round and see you. Your dad says if you can't manage on your own, you're to get that lad from Taggett Street.'

Doug laughed. 'What! He's more bloody useless than a boot without laces. I can manage better on my own. You tell Dad that.'

'I already told him, son.'

His face crinkled into a smile. 'Aw, Mam! I'm glad you've come to see us. I didn't like it when we weren't talking.' He glanced at Rosie, but addressed his mother. 'Take no notice of her. She don't mean nothing.'

Martha wasn't convinced. Returning her attention to Rosie, she asked frostily, 'How's my little grandson?'

It was Doug who answered, 'He's abed. You can go and see him if you like, Mam.' He looked at her like a little boy trying to please. 'Up the stairs, first on the left.'

Without a word, but maliciously smiling at Rosie through narrowed eyes, Martha turned and departed, going slowly up the stairs on leaden feet and striking the fear of God into Rosie's heart. She'd never thought to see Martha Selby in this house, leave alone going up the stairs and into the bairn's room. As if

Doug wasn't enough to contend with, she now had his mother on her back again. God forbid!

'You make her welcome, do you understand?' Doug glared at her. 'She's my mam, and there's been enough bad feeling.' That said, he slumped into the nearest chair, laying his head against the wall and closing his eyes. 'I don't feel well,' he moaned.

'Are you saying *I* caused the trouble?'

He didn't move a muscle, but his voice was menacing. 'I'm just saying, don't get above yourself, if you know what I mean.' Rosie knew all right. He was still smarting because, far from cowering when he'd hit her just now, she had dared to challenge him.

When Martha came back down the stairs she was bristling. 'He's too thin by far,' she told Rosie. 'And there aren't enough blankets over him.' Before Rosie could answer, she told Doug, 'I expect you to do something about that.' At once sitting up, he assured her that he would.

'And what about the christening? Isn't it time you got that organised?' She looked from one to the other. 'If it's too much trouble, you'd better let *me* do it.'

Rosie was quick to point out that the date had been set for next week, and she would have let Martha know but, 'Your son cancelled it.' Just as Rosie anticipated, Martha rounded on Doug, and he took it like the coward he was.

After his mother had gone, he blamed Rosie. 'Why did you have to go and tell her that?'

'I wasn't aware it was a secret.' A thought occurred to her. 'Come to think of it, why didn't you tell her we were having another child?' He didn't answer. Unperturbed, Rosie pursued the other matter. 'And why didn't you tell her *why* you cancelled the christening?'

'I'm not answerable to her.'

Rosie was stunned. 'You used to tell your mam everything.'

'Not everything.'

'You do mean for our son to be christened, don't you?'

'Don't be bloody stupid, woman. Of course I do!'

'Then why don't you tell *me* what's behind your thinking?'

'You mean you don't know?' He grinned, crossing his legs and lying back in the chair. His odd-coloured eyes appraised her while he took his time in explaining, and when he spoke it was with a deal of cunning. 'I've written to a mutual friend, and I'm waiting for a reply.'

Something in his manner made Rosie's heart turn cold. 'What do you mean?'

'We can't have a christening without a godfather, can we? And we want the very best for our precious son, don't we?' He was enjoying the feeling of power he held over her at that moment. 'I'm sure you'd agree that the best is Adam.' The horror on her face spurred him on. 'Yes, that's right, sweetheart . . . my best friend, and yours, Adam Roach. Soldier and gentleman. Surely you can't have forgotten him? You couldn't forget a man you once promised to wed? No, of course not.' Stumbling close, he leered at her. 'I've no doubt you didn't resist when *he* wanted to make love, eh?'

Rosie was repelled. 'Are you saying you've actually written to him? I knew you mentioned it some time ago, but I thought you were just being vindictive.' She realised she should have known better.

'I've written to the regiment. No doubt he'll get the letter in good time, and when he does, I expect he'll be overjoyed. After all, if I hadn't taken you from him, you'd be wed to him now, and it might be him asking *me* to be godfather to your son.'

'You'll never let it go, will you?'

Taken aback by the hatred in her eyes, he wanted to tear out her heart. 'I'll let it go when you stop wanting him,' he hissed. Then he covered his head with his hands and bawled like a child.

Sickened, Rosie left him there. That night she slept in the chair beside her son's cot. Dear Lord, don't let Adam come anywhere near us, she pleaded. Because if you do, I can't answer for the consequences.

Doug was right. She would never stop wanting the better man. Adam Roach would always be the man for her. But Doug was the man she had settled for, and that was the ugly truth. Her whole empty future lay before her. There was no hope now. And it was *that* which was so unbearable.

'What am I supposed to do with this?' The plump and homely

Mrs Jason was exasperated as she showed her husband a letter which had arrived that very morning. 'Should I send it back and say he's no longer living here, or should I try and find him? I wouldn't really know where to start though, because he didn't leave a forwarding address. All he told me was that he intended going up in the world, and that one day he meant to have his own coal-merchant's.'

'Sounds like you're talking about Adam Roach?' he remarked. 'I don't know about going up in the world. Not when he couldn't even get a job round these parts.'

'That's because there's very little work to be had in the Midlands right now. If you ask me, it's time the government put its thinking cap on. There are too many young men out of work, more's the pity.' Placing the offending article in front of him, she began to pour out the tea. 'That letter looks important, don't you think?' Sitting bolt upright in the chair, she took up a plate in one hand and a ladle in the other. Scooping out a huge helping from the large oval dish, she dropped it on to the plate. 'Steak and kidney pie. Your favourite,' she announced proudly as the aroma permeated the room. Indicating the various dishes positioned centrally on the table, she told him, 'There's peas and carrots, oh, and both lodgers are out, so there's only me and you for dinner, Ted. So eat hearty. It's a sin to waste good food.'

He was delighted. 'No lodgers, eh? It'll make a nice change to sit at my own table without strange faces watching every mouthful I take,' he grumbled. 'I never did like you taking in lodgers.'

'There, there, dear,' she coaxed. 'When your rheumatism stopped you working, it seemed a good idea to have lodgers. You must admit, they've never been a problem.' She stroked her greying hair and gazed dreamily at the unopened letter lying beside his plate. 'We've had some very nice people staying under this roof,' she said. 'You can't deny that.'

'Hmph!' he snorted. Snatching up the letter, he stared at it through angry eyes. 'I suppose you're talking about *this* fellow again, eh?'

'Adam Roach was a nice young man, and I'm sorry he's gone.'

'Are you now?' He turned the letter over in his hand. 'Well, *I'm* not! You women are all the same . . . all it takes is a good-looking fella and you can't think straight no more.'

'Don't be ridiculous, Ted. I'm old enough to be his mother.' In fact, the reason she had taken to Adam was because she had given away a son many years ago. With his dark hair and black eyes, Adam reminded her of the child.

Ted also had memories. But where *she* kept them alive, he tried desperately to bury them. 'I know, love. I'm sorry. But you can't keep torturing yourself. When you gave that infant away all those years ago, it was because I'd let you down. If I'd offered to wed you then, instead of running off like a coward, we could have kept the boy.' He bent his head and covered his pale eyes with large, surprisingly smooth hands. 'He's gone,' he murmured, 'and he's never coming back.' The look he gave her was filled with pain. 'The sooner you realise that, the better.'

She didn't answer. Instead she looked away and the gesture appeared to infuriate him. 'Let's see what we've got here,' he snapped, staring at the official stamp on the envelope. 'This is from the armed forces. I thought he was demobbed?' He remarked curiously. 'Didn't you say his papers came through to this address soon after he came here?'

'They did. And he *was* demobbed.'

'Oh, aye? A deserter more like!' Ripping open the envelope, he was surprised to find another, smaller envelope inside. Reading the accompanying letter he said aloud, 'It's a forwarded letter.' Tearing open the smaller envelope he read silently, explaining, 'It's from a mate of his . . . Doug Selby . . . wants him to be godfather to his son.' The letter was like salt being rubbed into a wound. 'I'll tell you what to do with this!' he cried. Tearing the two letters into tiny fragments, he dropped them into his saucer and lit them with a match from his waistcoat pocket. '*That's* what you do!' He watched the paper blacken and curl. 'He's gone from this house, and with the help of the Lord we'll never clap eyes on him again.' With that he went out of the room on slow tortuous footsteps. As he went upstairs his crippled legs pained him more than he could ever remember. Once inside the bedroom, he sat in the chair by the window and stared out across the rooftops.

A few moments later his wife found him hunched over and

71

sobbing pitifully. 'I'm sorry,' she said, holding him close.

'No,' he murmured, 'it's me that should be sorry. Sorry for what I've done to you. Sorry for being the failure I am.' He turned to look at her with pitiful eyes. 'But I'm *not* sorry for destroying that letter. That young man who stayed here . . . Adam Roach . . . he wasn't your son, Doreen. I know it and you know it. And you've got to stop imagining that our lad will just turn up on the doorstep one day, because he won't. Do you hear what I'm saying, love? HE WON'T!' He could feel the warmth of her tears on his face and bitterly regretted all the heartache he had caused her. 'We've got each other,' he said. 'And we should thank the good Lord for that.'

CHAPTER FIVE

Adam had worked on the sidings for almost three weeks now. Shovelling coal was a thankless task, hard and back-breaking, but it was good honest work, and in these times of unemployment, he was grateful just to be earning a living. His shoulders were broadened and honed by his labours, and his skin was tanned by the May sunshine that had spilled from a clear blue sky every day since he'd come to work at the yard.

'Put your bloody shovel down, man!' The fat fellow had come up behind him. 'Are you working right through your break or what?' Settling himself on an upturned box which groaned beneath his considerable weight, he swung the bag from his shoulder and took out a snap can. Inside the can was a pile of sandwiches, a great chunk of meat pie, and a container of cold tea to swill it down with. 'By! Me stomach thinks me throat's cut,' he chuckled. 'If it does nothing else, this work builds a man's appetite, and that's a fact.'

Adam leaned on his shovel. Stripped to the waist, he was a fine figure of a man. 'I had no idea it was that time,' he admitted, wiping the grimy sweat from his brow.

'Well, it *is*!' the other man affirmed. 'So knock off, for Chrissake. If the boss sees you working through your break, he'll make it a regular thing.' He frowned, casting a glance towards the shed where the foreman was watching. 'I don't know ... you young 'uns seem to have too much energy for your own good.'

Propping his shovel against the heap of coal, Adam flicked the top layers of dust from his trousers. 'Not so much of the "young 'uns" if you don't mind,' he chuckled. 'I'll be twenty-seven next birthday, and that's only spitting range from being thirty.' He

73

stretched his arms above his head and flexed every muscle in his strong lithe body. Then he went with long strides to the wagon, collected his lunch-box, and returned to sit beside his colleague. 'There aren't many wagons in today,' he observed ruefully. 'I reckon things are slackening off.' He bit into his apple and cast a wary eye along the row of wagons still waiting to be loaded. There were three. Normally there would have been six or seven.

'You're right,' the other man agreed. Blowing the coal-dust from his sandwich and sinking his large white teeth into it, he gazed doefully at the line of wagons. 'Heard summat interesting in the pub last night,' he said confidentially.

'Oh, aye?'

'There's talk that Ben Saxon's in trouble.' He shook his large head, gulped down a mouthful of tea and wiped his mouth with the back of his hand. 'If *he* goes under, there'll be even less wagons, then we'll have to watch out for us jobs. If the merchants are having a hard time of it, they'll not be wanting the coal, and that means *we* won't be needed neither.'

'Surely it won't come to that?'

'I'm telling you! You've only to look at them there wagons.' Pointing to the three vehicles, he went on, 'And not one of 'em belonging to Saxon. It's a crying shame because he's a good man, with a good reputation. It goes without saying that if a man of his calibre can't keep his head above water, there's hard times ahead for us all.' He leaned forward as though imparting a secret. 'Truth is, I've heard he might have to sell up.'

'What? Lock, stock and barrel?'

The other man nodded, his face serious beneath the sooty mask. 'All ten wagons . . . the yard . . . house and everything.' He shook head wisely. 'Ben Saxon's father started that business years ago. If it's sold now, it'll be a household name gone forever. What! Saxon's coal-merchant's was delivering round these parts when I were a snotty-nosed kid.'

Adam was thinking ahead. Though he was sorry for the old fellow, he was excited by a certain idea. 'How much do you reckon he'll get for it . . . if he *does* sell up, I mean?'

The fat fellow shrugged. 'Who can tell? That big old house is run down, the wagons are past their best, and as for the yard, well, there's been good yards standing empty round here since afore the war, so folk ain't likely to be queuing for it.' His white teeth tore off another chunk of the sandwich. 'In these bad times, I shouldn't think the whole lot will fetch more than a couple of thousand pounds.'

'You're forgetting the rounds, goodwill and all that. What price there?' Though two thousand pounds might as well be *ten* thousand, and every penny of it out of his reach, the germ of an idea was growing in his mind, giving him an urge to satisfy his curiosity.

Following Adam's train of thought, the fat fellow laughed aloud. 'Looking to start your own round, eh?' he teased.

'Happen.'

'You must be mad! I *said* you young 'uns had too much energy for your own good!'

'It was just a thought.'

'Have you got a pile of banknotes hidden away?'

'A few.'

'Not anything like enough, I'll bet,' he chuckled.

'No,' Adam confessed. 'Nowhere near. But I've saved most of my wages and I had a fair bit saved before I came here.' For one precious moment he remembered Rosie, and his heart was full. 'Saved it for a wedding that never happened,' he murmured, the memories flooding back to pain him.

His workmate was lost for words. He had seen how Adam's mood had changed. 'A wedding, eh?' he prompted, thinking he might be further enlightened. When Adam kept his own counsel, he quipped good-naturedly, 'I ain't never seen a wedding yet that would cost anything like the money you'd need to set up a coal-round.'

'Start small, grow big,' Adam said.

'It ain't as easy as that. Have you been in business afore?'

'No. But there's always a first time. Every successful business-man has to start somewhere.'

'And how do you reckon you could build up a round from scratch?'

'I'm not sure yet, but if I made my mind up, I'd give it a damn good try.'

'Capable of fighting off men who've already got a foot in

the door, are you? Men who'll stop at nothing to keep their own patch?'

'I'd not be much of a man if I let myself be frightened off.' What had begun as an impossible dream, was now fixed determination. 'Yes. Given the chance, I reckon I could make it work all right,' Adam declared boldly.

The fat fellow shook with laughter. 'Talk about a dog pissing agin the wind!' he roared. When Adam remained grim-faced, he studied him with new respect. 'Tell you what,' he promised in a serious voice, 'the day you make boss, I'll be the first to take me hat off to you.'

The two men lapsed into thoughtful mood. The fat fellow regretted the passing of his youth and all that fire in his loins, and Adam couldn't let go of the idea that he should be looking to start out on his own.

'Happen there's no truth in what you heard?' he suggested. 'About Ben Saxon selling up. You know how rumours run away with themselves.'

'Oh, there's truth in it all right. No rumour starts without cause. Ben Saxon's ready to sell. That's the beginning and end of it.'

'It's a pity all the same,' Adam said honestly.

'Well, the old fella's had a good run for his money . . . been in the business nigh on forty years, has old Ben. I expect he's too long in the tooth now, and what with the young 'uns coming up and snatching the work from under his nose well, it's dog eat dog, and old Ben ain't got no teeth left to fight 'em off.'

'I would have thought there'd be room enough for healthy competition. There'll always be a demand for fuel.' Adam roved his eye over the mountainous heaps of coal. Brought from the pits in railway wagons, the coal had first been graded, then tipped into various bays. The highest grade was black and shiny, large jagged chunks that burned slowly and gave out a strong degree of heat; the lowest grade was little more than grey scrapings that congealed in the fire-grate, and turned to ashes quicker than most. The coal was taken to the merchants, who bagged it and took it round the streets to the householders. It was a dirty messy business, but a necessity of life. 'I'm not arguing that times aren't hard,' he admitted, 'because they are. But when they've to tighten their belts, folk will always put heat and food first,' he observed shrewdly.

'Aye. That's true enough. But coal's expensive, and Liverpool folk are canny. When needs must, they'll burn anything rather than fork out precious money for a bag of coal. Some of 'em will take the doors off the hinges, or rip up the floorboards. And who's to blame them, eh? When all's said and done, the landlord ain't to know, is he? And anyway, there's allus plenty of flotsam and timber lying about the docks. Burns well does that ... especially if it's coated with tar.'

From the window of the shed, the foreman cast a regretful eye over the two men. 'Which one though?' he asked the gangly bespectacled fellow seated behind the desk. 'Now that it's between these two, which of 'em do we let go?'

'Last in, first out,' replied the other man without raising his eyes from his paperwork. 'That's the proper way.'

'Not always the best though. The fat fellow must be knocking on forty.'

'I've known Ted Laing a good many year, and I've always found him to be worth two men.' The boss looked up then, his thin flat face expressionless. 'Has he slacked off or caused any trouble?'

'No. But Adam Roach works like a horse, and he's years younger. That must count for something?'

'In my experience young men become ambitious, and sooner or later they'll be looking to move on. Ted Laing has a family. He can't afford to move anywhere.' His small eyes drilled into the other man's face. 'We've four men working these sidings. With work dropping off, we can manage with three. Get rid of Roach.'

The foreman shrugged his shoulders. 'You're the boss.'

'And don't forget that. You can tell Roach that once work picks up ... and it always has ... he's welcome to his job back.' That said, he returned his attention to the paperwork, leaving the foreman wondering how he might tell Adam that he was to pick up his cards and be on his way.

Three days later, on Friday afternoon, the men queued for their wages. As always, Adam was the last to finish work. By the time he came to the window, the other men were sauntering off, counting the notes in their wage packets and putting aside the price of a jar of ale before they delivered the money to their wives.

'Cheer up, mate,' Adam told the grim-faced foreman, 'it's a Friday. You've a whole weekend before you.'

'I'm sorry.' The foreman regarded him with serious eyes, 'I've been told to let you go.'

'What do you mean, "let me go"?' He knew exactly what that meant, but was reluctant to believe it.

The foreman handed him a fat wage-packet. 'You'll find your week-in-hand, together with a good bonus in there. You've earned it. But the boss says we've to cut down on manpower, and you're it.' He threw out his arms. 'If it had been up to me, I'd have kept you on. I'm sorry, mate.'

Adam was momentarily lost for words. Presently he told the other man, 'As long as it wasn't my work that was unsatisfactory.'

'Good God, no!' The foreman's relief was obvious. He'd seen some men turn nasty when they were handed their cards. And this particular fellow could no doubt flatten him with one blow if he took a mind. 'You're one of the best workers we've had here,' he explained. 'What's more, the boss says when trade picks up, you can gladly have your job back.'

'*If* I want it.' Adam had other things on his mind; like a coal-round of his very own. 'First time in my life I've ever been given my cards. But who knows? It might be a blessing in disguise.'

The foreman was intrigued, smiling with him. 'Oh? Got something up your sleeve, have you?' he queried.

Adam touched his nose with the tip of his finger. 'Who knows?' he hinted. 'I just might come back as a customer.' With that he stuffed the wage packet in his pocket and went away whistling. At the gate he turned back and surveyed the blackened heaps. 'See you,' he called to the foreman, who had followed his progress across the yard.

'Aye. Best of luck, mate,' he returned. Then he went inside to tell the boss, 'In my opinion you've let the best man go.'

'You're not paid to have opinions,' snarled the thin-faced

misery, rising from his seat. Going to the coat stand, he grabbed the black bowler hat and rammed it on his head. 'I suppose I can leave you to lock up, can I?' he said sarcastically. Without waiting for an answer, he went outside and cranked his little black car until it spluttered into life. Clambering inside, he fussed and fidgeted, before being carried away in a series of jerks and spurts as the vehicle negotiated the many hollows and mounds that littered the unmade road. They got as far as the gate before the car coughed and died, reviving only when its ungrateful owner got out and gave it another cranking, swearing and moaning the whole time.

'Serves you right!' The foreman kept out of sight in case he should be called on to exert himself. 'It'd do you good to catch a tram . . . or even *walk* home like the men who sweat for you.' He was still rankled about having to give a good man his cards. Still and all, he felt in his bones that: 'We ain't seen the last of Adam Roach. Not by a long chalk.'

CHAPTER SIX

Dell Place was a miserable little dead end near the Liverpool docks. The houses were terraced and the landlords, greedy to cash in on the shortage of living accommodation in this area, had divided the houses into rooms and the rooms into cubicles, where often a whole family would reside in poverty.

Here, the stench of fish from the docks permeated the air, and the many sounds kept a body from sleeping: drunken sailors released from months at sea and let loose to fill their bellies with booze; street women making love against the walls with men hungry after being deprived for too long. Vicious dogs roamed the neighbourhood, and men fought each other with knives and fists. There were robbers and scoundrels and people who would steal the shirt from your back. But, amid all this, the ordinary law-abiding folk eked out a living where they could; good God-fearing neighbours who helped each other when times were hard.

Adam lived at number two, in a dingy room at the top of two flights of stairs. From his window he could see the cobbled streets below, and if he raised his eyes he could make out ships anchored in the docks, their tall masts and chimneys creating a unique skyline. In this neighbourhood life went on twenty-four hours a day, a throbbing pulsing ebb that flowed from the docks and swamped everything around. He didn't mind it here. He would mind it even less if he lived on Albert Street. That was where Ben Saxon lived.

'Happen he'll sell the furniture with the house,' Adam mused aloud. He stared round the room, a tiny place with a single iron bed up in one corner, a sink in the other, a small table and two chairs, a crotchety old settee with the stuffing hanging out, and a faded rug covering the floorboards in the centre of the room. 'Anything would be an improvement on this lot!'

Since coming in from work, he had sat by the table with a mug of strong tea, his wages spilled out before him, and his heart filled with regret. 'What made you do it, Rosie?' he murmured, gazing at the one picture he had of her.

Held with great tenderness, the picture lay in his palm. So many times he had meant to throw it away, but couldn't bring himself to do it; not even when he reminded himself that she now belonged to someone else. 'I love you so much, sweetheart ... always will. We could have been so happy, you and me.' Big brown eyes smiled back at him, and it was more than he could bear.

Going to the wash-basin, he began to shave. With the lather thick and rich on his face, he studied himself in the discoloured mirror. 'Don't kid yourself, Roach,' he chided softly. 'Rosie made her choice, and it wasn't you. So you might as well get on with your life. There's no future in being head over heels in love with a woman when she prefers your best mate.'

But he *was* head over heels in love, and for too long all his thoughts, all his plans, had revolved around Rosie. He couldn't altogether blame her. He hadn't written, so what was she to think? Even then she might have come to him, but his pride got in the way. He deeply regretted that. Some time ago he had even gone back to Blackburn, only to learn that Rosie and Doug were wed. It had taken him a long time to come to terms with that. Yet every day was like a new penance, and in spite of everything, it was hard to see a future without her.

He shaved, stripped and washed all over. In no time at all he was ready for out. In his blue cord trousers and open-necked dark shirt, he was incredibly handsome. His thick black hair shone like new coal, and his dark eyes sparkled with the confidence of a man with a plan. A plan to set him on a new path.

He gathered up his money. With the back week and the bonus it amounted to forty-one pounds. Together with the rest of his money, which was in the bank – representing the major part of his wages while he was in the forces, and the main bulk of his earnings since – the grand total came to two hundred and twenty pounds. 'It might have been enough to pay for a wedding and a down payment on a house in Rosamund Street.' He hadn't forgotten how Rosie had always wanted a house on Rosamund Street. 'But I can't see it putting me in with the big boys.' His strong features broke into a smile. 'Still, it's a nice little pile all the same. With a bit of luck, it might be enough to get me started.'

After taking out eight shillings for the rent and five for a night out, he carefully replaced his wages behind the loose brick in the chimney-breast. First thing Monday morning, with the exception of a few shillings to feed himself, the money would go into the bank with the rest of his savings.

Winding his way round a warring couple and pausing to play hopscotch with a group of giggling children, Adam came out of Dell Place and into Fish Street. From there he went along Merseyside and down towards Albert Street. He had an idea in mind, and wouldn't enjoy a pint until he'd put the idea to a certain Mr Saxon. The nearer he came to Albert Street, the better he felt and the merrier he whistled. 'Steady as you go, Roach,' he warned himself as he approached the house. 'You're still not certain the old fella means to sell up. What's more, you're a stranger to him and may not be welcome.'

Albert Street was a long winding row of narrow terraced houses. Like every other street of its kind, it had a life of its own. From one house could be heard the voices of a man and his woman having a raging argument; four doors away, a middle-aged mother sat on a chair, her withered breast hanging over a stark white blouse and a tiny infant sucking contentedly at the nipple. Some way off two dogs were fighting over a bone, while nearby a group of children played five-stones on the cobbles.

Ben Saxon's house straddled the corner. It was a big old Victorian building with a multitude of windows and a wonderful carving over the porch. But it was past its prime; the window-frames were rotting and the whole place appeared to be sagging in the middle. Through the wooden gates at the side, Adam could see the yard with its many bays, still half-filled with coal. At the far end, an old grey gelding peered out from his stables, sad-eyed and lonely.

Having come along the length of Albert Street and now

standing before Ben Saxon's house, Adam thought of all kinds of reasons why he should turn tail and head for the pub. 'Happen it *is* all a rumour,' he told himself. 'Happen he'll run me up the road with a shovel . . . and so he should, you cheeky bugger!' His courage almost deserted him when a white head appeared at the window, narrowed eyes regarding him with hostility. But, no. He had come this far, and he might as well see it through.

Adam had his arm raised ready to knock on the door when it was flung open and a little wizened figure thrust itself at him. 'What do you want here?' it demanded, small dark eyes staring him up and down.

Being on the bottom step, with the little man peering down on him, Adam felt at a disadvantage. More than that, he was aware that a group of youths had gathered at the sight of a stranger down their street. One of them was standing nearby with one foot on the kerb. 'Anything wrong, old man?' he asked, addressing Ben Saxon.

The old fellow shook his fist. 'Bugger off,' he snapped.

The young man laughed. 'Threatening me, are you, Grandad?' He leered at the others who sensed a rumpus brewing. 'Hear that, did you?' the scruffy youth asked. 'The miserable old sod don't like me taking an interest.'

The other youths grinned and began to close ranks. 'I'd call that real ungrateful,' said a large red-faced lad. 'Especially when there's a *stranger* standing on his step. I mean . . . how are we to know he ain't here to cause trouble?' He stared at Adam whose expression hardened when the lout asked, 'What have you to say to that, Mister?'

Turning to face him, Adam smiled. 'What would you *like* me to say?' Bracing himself, he remained ready and confident.

The lout laughed aloud. 'See what I mean? This bugger's a troublemaker if ever I saw one!' he told the others. Glaring at the old man, he warned, 'You should know better than to hobnobbing with troublemakers. Round here, we like to keep ourselves to ourselves.' Returning his attention to Adam, he suggested slyly, 'I reckon you'd best be on your way.'

'I'll be on my way when I've finished my business here, and not before.'

Loud hoots greeted his words. 'Oh, and what "business" would that be then?'

'Not *yours*.'

'My, my! Looks like we'll have to teach you a lesson, big fella.' The youth stepped forward, his eyes round and staring as he dipped into his pocket and drew out a chain. Wrapping it round his knuckles, he told the others, 'This one's mine!'

Whipping off his jacket, Adam tied it round his arm. He didn't speak. But there was a look in his dark eyes that momentarily halted the youth, who glanced back to make certain the others were not far away. The only one to move was the old man who quickly shuffled back into the house, muttering and swearing beneath his breath.

'Come on then, big fella!' goaded the youth, giggling nervously when Adam stood his ground, shoulders broad and straight, and grim determination shaping his features. 'I'm gonna have to give you a hiding.' He tightened the chain round his wrist and turned to laugh at his friends.

None of them saw the old man return, and when the broom-head caught the youth in the nape of the neck, sending him sprawling across the pavement, everyone was stunned with shock.

Adam glanced up to see the old man jabbing at the air with his brush and warning the open-mouthed youths to: 'Bugger off, the lot of you! I ain't so old that I've forgotten how to look after myself!'

Suddenly, the one who had first accosted Adam started chuckling. 'You silly arse, Bernard,' he cried, pointing at the lad on the ground. 'Ain't I always told you to watch out for your back!' Soon they were all laughing aloud and the tension was eased.

Even the big lad sprawled on the ground could see the funny side of it. 'I ain't never gonna live this down,' he giggled; in truth he was immensely relieved that he didn't have to test the stranger after all. 'Floored by an old fella with a broom-head!' Gripping the back of his neck, he winced. Which only made the others laugh all the more.

Scrambling to his feet, he glanced first at the old man and then at Adam. 'You're lucky I'm in a good mood,' he bragged. Then he threw his arm round the other lad, and the pack of them went away down the street, their laughter lingering even after they had turned the corner.

'They're all right,' the old man said, 'They're Liverpudlians ... high-spirited that's all.' Propping the broom against the wall, he invited, 'You'd best come in and state your business.'

As they went down the passageway, he turned his head to glance at his visitor. 'What name do you go by?'

'Adam.'

'Adam what?'

'Roach ... Adam Roach.' They turned into the parlour. The stench of damp made Adam wrinkle his nose. He lost no time in putting on his jacket. Outside the May sunshine warmed the air, but in here the cold had bitten right through his shirt.

The inside of the house was surprisingly tidy. There was little furniture in the parlour; only a chest of drawers, two horsehair armchairs by the fireplace – one a rocker and one a tall-backed uncomfortable-looking article, and a square oak table surrounded by four high-backed chairs.

'Sit yourself down. I'll make us a brew.'

Adam did as he was bid. The old fellow ambled into the adjoining scullery, and soon returned with two mugs of steaming tea, one of which he placed on the table in front of Adam. 'I can't recall the name Roach, and I know most of the families about here.' Seating himself, he regarded Adam with some curiosity. 'But then, you don't *sound* as though you're from these parts?'

'I've no family. I went into the forces when I was seventeen, and I'm recently demobbed.' He felt as though he was being interrogated, but the quicker he satisfied the old man's curiosity, he thought, the sooner they could get down to business. 'And you're right, I'm not from these parts. I was born and bred in Blackburn.'

'Hmm. Blackburn, eh? Town of pubs, church spires and cotton mill chimneys. I should have thought you'd have been able to find work there?' He blew on the hot liquid and carefully sipped while waiting for a reply.

When Adam remained silent, he said knowingly, 'Ah! Don't want to talk about it, eh? No doubt there's a woman involved.'

He scanned Adam's handsome face, that coal black tumbling hair and those dark brooding eyes. And he was convinced that some woman somewhere had caused him grief.

'I'm sorry about that little argument out there.' Deliberately drawing the conversation away from himself, Adam recalled the confrontation on the steps. 'They won't give you any trouble when I'm gone, will they?'

Ignoring Adam's question, the old man remarked, 'You could have wiped the floor with the lot of 'em. I'd put money on it. Matter of fact, happen I should have let you get on with it. It's been a long time since I enjoyed a bloody good set-to.'

Adam laughed. 'And what makes you think I could have wiped the floor with them? That red-faced bloke was built like a Churchill tank.' He took a great gulp of his tea. It warmed him through.

'You've worked on the sidings, that's why.'

'How do you know that?'

'I've only to look at you.' He eyed Adam's physique with pride. 'I've been a coal-merchant all my life . . . and my faither afore me. Working on the sidings . . . shovelling the stuff from morning 'til night . . . that sorts the men from the boys, I can tell you.'

'I *did* work on the sidings.'

'Oh?'

'Been given my cards.'

'Can't say I'm surprised. There isn't much money about. Every day it gets harder to earn a living.' He glanced at the picture on the wall. 'That's Arnold Saxon, my father.' Waiting for Adam to turn and look, he went on, 'In all the years we've been coal-merchants, I can't recall a time as bad as this.' He gazed at the picture for a while, lost in the past and despairing of the future.

Glancing round that spartan room, Adam thought it strange there appeared to be no picture of Ben Saxon's mother. He wasn't to know Ben's father burned every reminder of her after she ran off with a tailor from Manchester. The old man was remembering though, and his eyes welled with tears. After a while, he remarked, 'I suppose you know I'm selling up?'

'That's what I heard.'

'And that's why you're here?'

Adam felt uncomfortable. 'I feel a bit like a jackal after blood,' he apologised, 'but you know the way it is . . . if you don't get in quick, you might live to regret it.'

'Go on.'

'I had a mind to set up on my own.'

'What? As a coal-merchant?' The old man's eyes widened in disbelief. 'I've only just told you what hard times we're living through. Besides, shovelling on the sidings is a lot different from being a coal-merchant.'

'I know that.'

'Oh?'

'Before I went into the forces, I worked for a coal-merchant in Blackburn. The hours were long and the work was back-breaking, but it taught me a lot. I reckon I could put all that to good use.'

'What were the name of this 'ere coal-merchant?'

'Selby. He was a good man . . . quiet and hard-working.'

Ben Saxon shook his head. 'Selby, eh? Never heard of him.'

'He had just the one wagon . . . he worked it with me and his son, Doug. Doug and I went to school together . . . grew up like brothers we did.' While he talked he remembered.

Like brothers we were, and while I was still in the forces, he was busy stealing the girl I loved. In his mind's eye, he could see old man Selby, and with that image came the image of Doug and Rosie, and the pain was deep as ever.

'So! You know a bit about coal-merchanting. But you've little chance of making it work here. Go home and think about it, that's my advice to you.'

Adam was undeterred. 'I've got no job, and little prospect of one. As you say, times are hard and there's not much about. What have I got to lose?'

'How much money have you?'

'A little over two hundred pounds.'

The old man roared with laughter. 'You're wasting your time,' he said at length. 'When this lot goes under the hammer, I'm looking for upwards of *three thousand*! Can you raise that sort of money?'

Adam gave no reply. Instead, he sipped at his tea and thought long and hard.

'You can't, can you?' The old man grew angry. 'You're a dreamer, just like the bloody rest.'

Adam looked up. 'The rest?'

'Aye! You didn't think you were the only one that's knocked on that door with an idea to buy me out afore I got to auction?'

"Course not,' Adam lied, 'but I'm not looking to buy you out altogether,' he explained hopefully. 'I never thought I'd have anywhere near enough money to do that.'

'What is it you're after then? Out with it.'

'A wagon. One sound wagon to get me started . . . two dozen sacks of best coal, and a good round. That's all.'

'You've got a nerve, I'll give you that.'

'So we can talk business?'

'No, we bloody *can't*!' The old man leaned back in his chair and looked at Adam through new eyes. 'I've had some cheeky buggers here, but you take the biscuit,' he declared without malice. 'You come to my house with two hundred pounds in your pocket and expect to get started up in business? Have you any idea how much blood and sweat went into building them rounds? Have you the slightest inkling of how much a good wagon costs new?' Before Adam could, answer, he went on, 'Well, I'll tell you! The best part of four hundred quid, that's what. And I've kept my wagons good. They'll fetch a handsome price or my name's not Saxon.'

'You just finished telling me how times are bad,' Adam reminded him. 'The wagons may not fetch as much as you hope.'

The old man studied him for a while before he spoke again. 'Finish your tea and get out.' Standing up, he leaned forward, fists resting on the table. 'You're full of fresh ideas and brimming with energy . . . eager to get started on someone else's back. Well, it won't be *mine*.' He saw himself in Adam, and it only reminded him how old and frail he had become. Once he too had been young and virile, filled with energy and raring to go. Where had it all gone? What happened to his youth? What price the dreams of wife and family? He envied Adam, and it showed. 'Go on! Be off with you.' He snatched the mug of tea from Adam's hands, spilling a dark trail across the tablecloth. 'Your business here is finished.'

'I'm sorry you feel that way,' Adam said, rising. 'But we don't

have to part like enemies.' Extending his hand he waited in vain
for the other man to shake it. 'All right, if that's the way you want
it,' he conceded, dropping his hand to his side and turning away.

The old man followed him to the door. 'You've got a bloody
cheek coming here! I should have known better than to let
you in. You're all the same. Something for nothing, that's what
you're after.'

Before the door was closed on him, Adam apologised. 'You
can't blame a man for trying. But you have my word, I didn't
come here to get something for nothing. I might not have enough
to buy one of your good wagons, but I'll get started somehow,
even if I have to build up a round from scratch. You say your
father did it, so why not me? As for my two hundred pounds,
I agree it isn't all that much, but it's hard-earned and better
than nothing.'

'As good as nothing!'

'Thank you for your time, Mr Saxon.' With a friendly smile he
bade Ben Saxon good day and went down the street, somewhat
disappointed but not dejected. He meant what he said. Somehow,
he'd make his savings work for him, and he *would* find a way to
get started.

Ben Saxon remained at the door, his unhappy eyes following
Adam's upright figure. 'Good luck to you,' he said sullenly. Until
now he hadn't fully realised what the coming events would mean
to him ... no more work, no planning of schedules or passing
the time of day with old customers. Nothing to look forward to
but a narrow terraced house alongside the docks. It was hard
being an old man with nothing else to give when once he had
meant something round these parts.

Suddenly it didn't bear thinking about. Unwittingly, Adam had
made him see what lay ahead, and it crushed his old spirit.
Returning to the back room, he sat on the chair which Adam
had vacated only minutes before. 'Ben Saxon, you're an old fool!'
he said. 'All right! Happen you *couldn't* afford to sell him a
wagon and round for two hundred pounds ... but you didn't
have to pour scorn on his ambitions. Instead, you could have
given him a deal of advice.' Thumping a gnarled fist on the table,
he chided himself; 'You're a selfish, jealous old bugger! It isn't

his fault if the custom's not there. It isn't *his* fault you're having to sell up. And if you were half a decent man, you'd have set him on the right path.'

He paced the floor and thought awhile. And for the first time in months, the glimmer of a smile crossed his aged face. 'So he reckons he can get started on a lousy two hundred pounds, does he? You can't help but admire him, and that's a fact.' Reaching up to take his pipe from the mantelpiece, he chuckled. 'If you can pull it off, you'll be a better man than I gave you credit for, Adam Roach. But we'll see.' Settling in the fireside chair, he rocked it back and forth, seemingly content. 'We'll see!'

CHAPTER SEVEN

As soon as he opened the door to his room, Adam knew the money was gone. The mattress was turned over and everything was in disarray. The few articles from the mantelpiece were littered across the floor and the brick from the chimney breast was flung in the hearth. 'Jesus Christ!' He rushed across the room and thrust his hand into the void where the brick had been. It was empty. All his precious bank-notes gone.

At first he was filled with rage. Then he wanted revenge. Then, after realising that he had no hope of ever finding out who had stolen the money, he sank into a chair, head forward in his hands and his dark eyes staring at the carpet. In his shocked mind he began to work out how the loss had reduced his chances of buying a wagon. 'You're right, Saxon,' he said, laughing cynically, 'I'm just a dreamer, no different than the rest.'

He remained immobile for what seemed an age, despondent and frustrated, angry with himself for having been so stupid as to leave his precious wages where they must easily have been found. 'I should have kept them in my pocket,' he muttered. 'They'd have been safer there!' He wondered how he could possibly start a business on what little money he had left. And the more he thought on it, the more ludicrous it began to seem.

After a while, he collected the few coins scattered on the rug, kicked his way through the debris and went out into the growing darkness. 'Might as well enjoy what's left!' he decided grimly, making his way to the nearest pub. In that moment it seemed all his plans were shattered. 'Whatever bastard took that money, I hope he realises it was hard earned and meant for better things!'

When he came into the pub, his dark handsome looks turned

heads. One particular young woman seated at a nearby table could hardly keep her eyes off him. Connie Wilson was lonely, and far from home. Tall, slim and blessed with china doll looks, she had a warm heart and generous nature. Sipping slowly at her drink, she watched as Adam gave his order. As though quenching a fire within him, he gulped down the first drink and promptly ordered another.

Taking her own drink, she crossed the room and climbed on to the stool beside him. Close to, he was even more handsome than she'd first thought. With one hand thrust deep into his pocket and his long legs straddling the rail at the foot of the bar, he sat on the edge of his stool, dark eyes staring into his drink and a deeply thoughtful expression on his face. He was totally oblivious to her attentions.

'Need some company?' Her soft voice infiltrated his thoughts. When he turned to look at her, she smiled warmly. Shifting nearer, she murmured, 'I'm a good listener.' She made no attempt to touch him. Instinct warned her he was not the sort of man you got too friendly with too quickly. 'We could go somewhere?' she suggested tentatively.

His dark eyes appraised her. How different she was from his Rosie, he thought. 'Thanks all the same,' he answered with a devastating smile, 'but I don't think so.'

'Okay. Suit yourself.' Returning to her table, she watched him for a while. Not once did he turn to look at her. Obviously not interested, she told herself. Pity. He looks a decent sort.

She switched her attention to the two men seated at a table in the far end of the room; one was a thin white-faced creature with bulbous eyes, but the other brown-haired fellow was reasonably attractive, dressed in a pin-stripe suit and smoking a fat cigar. 'Could try your luck there, Connie girl,' she muttered to herself.

When she sauntered up, the two men were deep in conversation. 'Got time for a chat with me?' she asked the man in the pin-stripe suit. When he merely glanced up and looked away again, she seated herself on the chair beside him. 'If you can tear yourself away from your business here, I don't think you'll regret it,' she said, crossing her legs and shifting her skirt in a suggestive manner.

The man didn't speak. Instead, without warning, he clenched his fist and viciously lashed out, catching her on the side of the face and sending her crashing into a group of chairs. While she lay, shocked and bleeding on the floor, he merely grinned and spat over her before calmly resuming his conversation.

He had only spoken two words when he was lifted right out of his chair and knocked to the ground. Stroking his knuckles, Adam stood over him as he lay crumpled on the floor. 'I think you forgot your manners,' he remarked casually.

Dazed, the man stared up at Adam, then, without another word, he scrambled to his feet and staggered towards the door. Alarmed, the thin man followed, and by the time Adam had helped Connie back to her chair, the two were long gone.

'You'll have to watch they don't wait for you outside,' she warned.

'I shouldn't think there's any danger of that,' he assured her. 'Their kind take great pleasure in knocking women about . . . but they've no stomach when it comes to trading fists with other men.' Examining the tear on her chin, he thought it wasn't too bad considering. But she was shocked and bruised.

'What's your address? I'd best see you home before you get into any more trouble.'

'No address. Sorry.'

'What do you mean? You've got a home, haven't you?'

'Nope.' The bruise on her face was beginning to swell. Beneath those wonderful dark eyes, she grew embarrassed. 'It's not your problem, and I'm sorry you were caught up in mine.' She made an effort to stand but almost fell over. 'Don't worry. I can look after myself.'

'Hmph! Looks like it.' Cupping her elbow with his hand, he helped her across the room. Outside, he told her, 'Wait there. I'll get us a taxi.' Stepping off the kerb, he peered up and down the street. It was only minutes before he'd hailed a cab and they were on their way to Dell Place.

As he helped her up the stairs to his room, she wondered what a man like this was doing in such a rundown place. 'How long have you lived here?' she wanted to know.

'Too long. And I know what you're thinking.' Recalling how

the thief had turned the place upside down, he half smiled. 'When you see inside, you might wish I'd left you in the street.'

When the door was opened to reveal the mess the thief had made, she was open-mouthed. 'God Almighty! It's a bloody pig-sty!'

Depositing her in the nearest chair, he confessed, 'I should have cleaned the place up. Truth is, I was burgled, and I was so bloody mad, I couldn't think straight.'

'So you thought you'd go out and get drunk?'

'Something like that.' Going to the sink, he swilled a corner of the towel with water from the tap. 'The bastard took two weeks' hard-earned wages and a handsome bonus. On top of that I've lost my job.' He dabbed so hard at her face that she cried out.

'Hey! It weren't *me* that robbed you.'

Shamefaced, he apologised. Dabbing more gently at her face with the cloth, he explained, 'It's just that the money was for starting up my own business.'

'I'm sorry.'

'So am I.' Lifting her fair hair, he examined the side of her temple. 'You're lucky he didn't split your skull open.'

'Serves me right. I thought it would be easy. I was wrong.'

'You mean you haven't ... done it ... before?'

'Solicited, you mean?' She smiled and he was astonished at her beauty. 'No, I've never done it before. I only arrived in Liverpool this morning ... it's taken me years to summon the courage to leave my old man ... *another* coward who likes to knock women about.' She stood up then. 'I've taken enough of your time and you've got your own troubles. I'll be on my way.'

'Oh, and where will you go?' He had taken a liking to her.

'I'll find somewhere.'

'You could stay here.'

Feigning shock, she teased, 'And here was I thinking you couldn't get me out of the door fast enough, when all the time you can't wait to get me in bed!'

'I should *throw* you out the door,' he said with a grin, 'but you're welcome to stay, at least for tonight. Tomorrow you'll feel better able to find yourself a place.' Pointing to the settee, he explained, 'As for getting you into bed, that's where I'll be sleeping.'

Without a word she got out of her chair and began clearing the mess up. 'You don't have to do that,' he protested. Going to the sink, he washed her blood from the corner of the towel and hung it over the rail. Then he flung his coat off, hung it on the hook behind the door and set about tidying up with her. 'I'd like to get my hands on the bastard who did this,' he muttered.

Replacing a drawer, she paused to look at him. 'Judging by the leathering you gave the man in the bar, I reckon the burglar can count his lucky stars you *didn't* get your hands on him.'

He smiled wryly, but remained silent all the while they were clearing up. Later, when the room was ship-shape, Adam insisted she sat down while he made her a cup of tea. 'Nothing stronger, I'm afraid,' he apologised. 'As a rule I'm not a drinking man . . . one with my mates on a Friday night and that suits me fine.' Handing her a mug of tea, he stretched himself out in the chair beside her, wondering how he would ever get started in business now, with no job and a good chunk of his money gone.

Connie had been secretly watching him. It occurred to her that such a man ought to have a woman sharing his life. 'Do you have a family?'

'No.'

'Parents? Wife? You must have *somebody*!'

'No.'

'But that's terrible!'

'There are worse things.' His smile was cynical.

'I can't think of any.'

'Oh, I can.'

'Such as?'

'Never knowing where you are. Being brought up in a succession of children's homes. Going into the forces and being afraid to come out in case you're lost again. Coming home early to be told your sweetheart is expecting your best friend's child and they're to be wed. Working yourself to the bone with the dream of someday being your own boss. And then having your hard-earned wages pinched by some lazy bugger who's probably never done a hard day's work in his life, and never intends to!'

Sensing the frustration in him, she simply said, 'I see what you mean.'

There followed an uncomfortable silence until she asked,

'What will you do now? I mean, what with all your money stolen and no job. Fresh air won't pay the rent.'

Collecting her cup he went to the sink where he swilled the crockery under the tap. 'I'm not broke,' he answered, at once wondering why he should confide in a complete stranger. 'I have money put by . . . money I've been saving for a business venture.'

'What kind of business venture?' She came to stand beside him. Taking up the kitchen cloth, she wiped the cups and placed them on the drainer.

'I had visions of being a coal-merchant.' Seeing the surprise in her face, he added with a chuckle, 'Oh, it's not glamorous, and happen it won't make me a millionaire, but it's all I know, apart from Army life. And it's good honest work. What's more, there *is* money in it, if you think on a big enough scale.'

'And you meant to do that?'

'The *thinking*'s already done. I meant to have a fleet of my own coal-wagons.' He chuckled. 'They'd all be sign-written in big bold letters: ADAM ROACH, COAL-MERCHANT. In time I would have bought out every small merchant for miles around.'

'And now?'

The smile fell from his face and was replaced with a resolute expression. 'I haven't altogether given up. Not yet.'

She half smiled. 'Somehow I can't see you as a loser.'

Laughing, he pinched his finger and thumb together. 'I'm that close,' he admitted. But, after talking it through, he knew he could never give up his ambitions. 'You're right,' he said finally, recalling what she had told him in the bar.

'Oh?'

'You are a good listener.'

She gazed up at him, her face suddenly serious. 'I'm a good lover too,' she whispered boldly.

To Connie he was just a man, though not quite like any other she had met, and she needed a man. Men were like a magnet to her, but there could be no in between; they were either friends or lovers. She didn't want a full relationship, and the thought of being committed to one man frightened her like nothing else. Now that she had won her freedom, she meant to keep it. All the same, in this instance she was sorely tempted. 'What I said in the bar,' she reminded him softly. 'The offer's still open.'

For a long moment he continued to gaze at her. There was no denying he was attracted to her and God alone knew how much he needed someone. but not *anyone*, he reminded himself. His heart was too full of Rosie. Just as he had not altogether given up on his ambitions, neither had he given up on her; though for the life of him he couldn't see a happy ending to it all. 'It's nothing personal, Connie, but the answer's still the same. No thanks.'

She didn't answer. Instead, she nodded her head wisely and returned to the settee where she spread herself out. Taking a box of matches and a pack of cigarettes from her pocket, she lit one up and all the while her pretty blue eyes followed his every move. When he went to the window, she saw how he stared out, as though expecting someone to walk up the street towards him. 'Want a cigarette?' she asked, holding out the pack of Woodbines. He shook his head but didn't look round. 'Okay. Suit yourself,' she said, thrusting them back into her pocket.

Adam was shocked to see how the night had closed in. He and Connie had talked for so long that the time had flown by without his realising. 'It's late,' he said abruptly. Striding into the bedroom area, he could be heard moving about until a few minutes later he returned, carrying crumpled sheets. 'I'm allowed only one set of clean sheets a week,' he explained. 'I've stripped the bed.' Indicating the laundry in his arms, he went on, 'These will do me. You'll find clean ones at the foot of the bed.'

'Won't you need a blanket?' She was on her feet now, stubbing out the cigarette in the ashtray.

'I'll be fine. Don't worry.'

'We could cuddle up together? Or we could talk, if you'd rather. I'm not ready to go to bed yet.'

'Goodnight, Connie,' he said firmly. To tell the truth he wouldn't have minded sitting up a while and talking. She was easy company, and he hadn't talked to a woman in that way for so long. But he felt he had disclosed enough of his life to her. Somehow she had managed to get under his skin. That troubled him.

'Okay,' she said, peeking through the curtains. 'It's just that where I come from, one good turn deserves another, and if it hadn't been for you, I'd probably be dossing out there on the streets.'

He turned to smile on her and she felt cheated. He was so handsome. 'I'll bear that in mind,' he promised.

'Well, you know where I am if you want me.' When he didn't answer, she closed the curtains and undressed. The act of sliding off her clothes felt sensuous. Sighing, she roved her hands over her warm firm breasts. 'You're sure you won't share the bed with me?' she asked hopefully. 'I promise not to pinch all the blankets.' When he laughed, she was encouraged to open the curtains and look out, making certain that one of her breasts was exposed. He was stripped to the waist, his broad chest tanned and muscular. His beauty took her breath away. 'We could keep each other warm,' she said invitingly.

'Goodnight, Connie,' he told her determinedly, quietly chuckling when she sighed longingly and closed the curtains.

Taking off his trousers, he lay on the settee and covered himself with the sheets. Connie was right, he thought, shivering, it did get chilly of a night. All the same it wasn't long before he was deep in sleep. The booze still lay heavy on him. Since ploughing all his wages into the bank, he wasn't used to upending the number of pints he'd sunk tonight.

He dreamed of Rosie, but she was always out of reach. Yet tonight in his deepest dreams, he felt her touch him. She was warm and soft, and his passions were roused. Half-asleep, he got off the settee and into the bed. 'I thought you'd never find your way in here,' Connie told him. Seeing him now in all his glory, she knew the wait had been worth it.

Hungry for the love of a woman, he played with her awhile, enjoying the velvet texture of her flesh and exploring her until she gasped with pleasure. When, thrilled and impatient, she cried out for him, he pushed himself into her. Their mating was fiery, almost angry. When it was over they fell away from each other, exhausted and immensely satisfied.

In the morning, he could hardly look at her. 'It won't happen again,' he said grimly. The muscles in his face were like chiselled stone.

She too realised it had been a mistake. Not because she hadn't enjoyed it, because she had. Making love with Adam was some-thing beautiful. But she knew he was not making love to *her*. Even in the throes of ecstasy, she sensed that he was somewhere else. His mind was on the sweetheart he had lost to his best friend. 'I'm sorry,' she told him now, 'I'll get out.'

He stopped her then. 'The fault was mine.' He was at the sink shaving. When he turned, the blade nicked his chin and a trickle of blood ran down his chest, but he appeared not to notice. 'You don't have to go.'

She smiled. 'Oh, I see. I'm welcome in your room, but not in your bed?'

Returning her smile, he agreed. 'That's about the size of it, but you *can* stay until you find somewhere else. I don't want to be responsible for you walking the streets.'

'But we can't be lovers?'

'Not wise.'

'Because you still love your sweetheart?'

He looked away, and for a moment she thought she had gone too far. But then he said softly, 'You're a very perceptive woman, Connie Wilson.'

'Friends then?'

'I think so, yes ... friends.' Giving her a quizzical look, he asked, 'Have you given any thought to what I said before? About giving up the idea of soliciting?'

'Yeah. I've thought about it. But to be honest, I can't see myself washing up dishes in some hotel kitchen, and believe me, there isn't much else.'

'Perhaps you haven't tried hard enough?'

'Look. I won't try and run your life, if you don't try and run mine.'

Laying the razor on the edge of the sink, he splashed his face with cold tapwater and towelled it dry. 'Two conditions then. You don't bring your "clients" back here, and I'll expect you to pay a full share of the rent.'

Laughing, she stretched out her arms. 'A deal!' With that she waited her turn at the sink. A few minutes later, she threw on her jacket and went jauntily out of the room. 'See you later,' she called. And he couldn't help but wonder whether he'd made a rod for his own back.

During the following week, while Adam trudged miles looking for work, Connie proved her worth. She kept to their agreement, and though she soon became popular with the many men she canvassed, she never brought them home. When Adam returned, footsore and weary, she would have a meal waiting for him, and a big smile that lightened his heart. 'You don't have to cook for me,' he told her, but she insisted, and so it became a regular pattern. They dined together, and laughed together; they discussed their fears and hopes, and soon became firm friends. She paid her way and even bought odd items of furniture for the flat.

One Friday night she proudly showed him the new floral curtains that decorated the windows. 'What do you think?' she asked, beaming from ear to ear.

'You know what I think,' he remarked, 'I object to you spending your money on this place.'

'But it's our home, and I want it to look nice.'

'Aw, Connie! If it belonged to us it would be a different matter. But it doesn't, so as far as I'm concerned, it's as good as money down the drain.' An unpleasant thought crossed his mind. Glancing furtively at the door, he warned her, 'For God's sake don't let the landlord see how you're tarting this place up, or he'll want extra rent.'

She laughed at him. 'Don't you worry about him,' she said winking knowingly. 'He and I have an understanding.'

Groaning, Adam told her that was the worst thing she could have done. 'Never on your own doorstep, isn't that what they say?'

'Oh, it's all right. I've got him eating out of my hand. In fact, I'm tempted to ask for a reduction in the rent.'

'No! The rent is *my* department. Look, Connie, are you sure you know what you're doing?'

'Of course I'm sure. You don't think I'd do anything to cause you trouble, do you?' She began to explain her relationship with the landlord, saying how he was "a good soul at heart".

Groaning, he pleaded, 'That's enough, Connie. I don't want to know any more. Our landlord isn't the angel you make him out to be, and if you'd been around this neighbourhood longer, you'd realise he's a bad lot. To be honest, I think you're making a grave mistake getting involved with him, but it's your life, and I've never pretended to be your keeper.'

'Quite right,' she answered cheekily, 'I'm done with having keepers. And my life *is* my own.' Her mood had changed. 'I'll get your meal,' she said sharply, beginning to make her way to the oven. 'And don't tell me I shouldn't cook for you because I like to!' she snapped. 'So you'd better bloody well enjoy it!'

Taking a steaming meat pie from the oven, she placed it on top. The gravy ran down the sides as she sliced a huge chunk off and placed it on a large white plate; to this she added a helping of cabbage and a scoop of roasted potatoes from the tin. That done, she enacted the same procedure for herself, with a smaller slice of pie and fewer vegetables. 'I'm a good cook if nothing else,' she declared, carefully setting the plates on the table. 'It's your favourite.' That was something she had soon discovered. She also knew he had a large birthmark on his thigh, and he was ticklish just under his right rib. 'Aw, look, I'm sorry,' she said. 'We're good mates. I don't want to have bad feelings between us.'

'Neither do I,' he confessed. 'And, like I say, you do what you like. It's no business of mine . . . unless it threatens the very roof over our heads.'

'Surely you don't think that?'

'I don't know *what* to think. All I know is, you're playing a dangerous game.'

Smiling, she told him, 'Ain't that what makes life interesting?'

He couldn't help but return her smile. She was like a child. 'I worry about you,' he confessed.

'Well, don't! I can take care of myself.' During the meal she admitted, 'Perhaps you're right and I shouldn't have struck up a relationship with the landlord. But, honest to God, he's not as bad as people make him out to be.'

Adam had warned her to be careful. Beyond that he wouldn't go.

Later, he scanned the local newspaper, looking for work. As usual, there was nothing worthwhile. But something else caught his eye. 'It's tomorrow!' he cried excitedly. 'They're auctioning Saxon's goods . . . wagons, coal stocks . . . the whole shebang!'

Connie was mending a pair of her sheerest stockings, and almost ruined them when he leaped out of the chair. 'A coal-merchant!' she said with immense patience. 'I might have known.' But he wouldn't be put off. His dream was alight again, and he couldn't wait for the morrow.

Suddenly he recalled what Ben Saxon had said, about his not having enough money – and that was *before* he was robbed. 'I don't know what the hell I'm getting excited about,' he told Connie. 'There'll be men there with money in their pockets to make my little bankroll look sick.'

'Do you reckon there'll be much interest then?'

'Enough. When times are hard, you can always rely on two things that folk will spend on. Food and heat. Always a priority.'

'Come to think of it, you might be right.'

'I *know* I am!'

'You've forgotten a *third* priority.'

'What's that?' He was intrigued.

'Love. A man will spend his last shilling for a cuddle and a grope in the dark. Business has been going well, Adam, so if you're short, I can lend you some money.' She wasn't surprised when he graciously declined. 'Suit yourself. But the offer's there if you want it.' He didn't. If she had learned anything else about Adam, it was that he had high principles. That was another of the reasons why she admired him.

Adam arrived at the yard early, but already there were men milling all over the place; eager-eyed merchants looking to increase their own fleet of wagons, and maybe buy up a month's stock of prime coal at half the price. Many of the would-be buyers were strangers to Adam, but he recognised two of the town's most prominent coal-merchants, and his spirits fell. His chance of buying a wagon seemed more remote than ever.

He bought a catalogue for a shilling and found a pencil in his jacket pocket. Might as well take a note of how much it all goes for, he told himself. Soon the auctioneers were set up and every-one gathered round. The air was filled with a sense of excitement, and the first item was put up for offer.

'A fine wagon,' a bald-headed man announced, 'bought last year and only done three hundred miles. The tyres are good as new, and you all know its worth. Right then ... who'll start me at five hundred guineas?' The atmosphere was electric. Silence reigned, and he grew impatient. 'Come on now! Let's get under-way. Five hundred to start?' Again, nobody moved. Everyone was playing the game. Sighing, he scratched his shiny pate. 'All right ... *four* hundred, and I must be mad!'

Straightaway someone's catalogue was raised. Adam recog-nised the man as being Arnie Burton, one of the big merchants. If he was up against people of that calibre, he might as well go home. But he didn't. He stayed, and later had reason to be thankful.

The wagon went for three hundred and twenty guineas. Adam wrote the figure against the item in the catalogue. The sale con-tinued; first the wagons, then the coal.

Dejected, Adam would have walked away then, but he was held, mesmerised by the auction, curious as to what price the coal would fetch, and who might buy it. All around him the serious-faced men made their various moves, indicating to the auctioneer that they were prepared to pay a little more. Suddenly the bidding was less hectic and folk began drifting away to pay for their bargains. Now there only remained the ones who had come for the coal. The auctioneer tapped the hammer once, twice, and a new voice came into the proceedings. Adam's attention was caught. The voice was strangely familiar.

Turning round, he stretched his neck, dark quizzical eyes scan-ning the faces. Astonishment crossed his face when he saw the big man himself. Ned Selby! At first Adam was shocked, but then he reminded himself that Blackburn wasn't all that far away, and after all, why shouldn't Doug's dad bid for that prime coal, along with any other merchant? In fact, judging by the strangers here today, it was plain that a number of them had travelled in from further afield than Liverpool.

Adam's first instinct was to push his way through the crowd and make his presence known to Ned. But a deeper instinct made him look about, searching the faces for another, wondering whether Doug had come here with his dad. He didn't care to see Doug. It was still too soon. Doug was a married man now . . . married to Rosie. Adam could not easily forgive that.

When he was sure Doug was nowhere to be seen, Adam made his way to the big man's side. He owed a lot to Ned Selby. It would do his heart good to talk with him now.

The big man was just as surprised to see Adam. 'Good God above!' he exclaimed. 'I never thought to see *you* here.' Having secured some coal, he was about to make his way into the house where he would pay for it. Now he led the way towards the temporary bar. 'You'll take a drink with me?' he asked. 'I want to know how you've been doing.'

Adam insisted on buying two pints, and when they were seated at the table it was he who spoke first. His question came as no surprise to the big man. 'How is she . . . Rosie?'

'She's fine.' Sipping his ale, Ned Selby took stock of the younger man, and he knew without a shadow of doubt that Adam still ached for his first sweetheart. 'You know she and Doug got wed?' When Adam nodded, he went on, 'Aye. They've a son too . . . and another bairn on the way.' He felt it necessary to tell Adam how Rosie was both a wife and mother now. She was part of a family, and though his son didn't deserve her, Rosie was his wife. Sadly, Ned felt it his duty to remind Adam of that.

'I knew they were to be wed, and that she was with child.' Adam bowed his head. 'I didn't know there was another on the way.' Somehow she seemed further from him than ever. Yet, deep inside, he still couldn't accept that he would never again hold her in his arms.

'Doug wanted you to be godfather to his son, did you know that?'

'I had no idea.'

'Oh, aye. He tried to track you down. When he couldn't find you, he was bitterly disappointed. So much so that he still hasn't had the boy christened.' No sooner were the words out of his mouth than he regretted them. He anticipated Adam's reaction.

'Not christened!' Adam knew Rosie, and he realised with a shock that she would desperately want her son christened. 'What does Rosie think to that?'

106

'I'm afraid it's caused friction between her and Doug.' There was no point in lying. 'And Doug's mam makes it worse by constantly interfering.' Afraid that Adam would say or do something he might regret, Ned hastily added, 'No matter. It's all a storm in a teacup. Doug and Rosie have a good life together, and it'll take more than a little upset to come between them.'

Adam reflected on Ned's words, and felt instinctively that something was horribly wrong between Doug and Rosie. *He wouldn't rest until he'd seen her.* 'If the lad can't get christened unless I turn up to be godfather, then I'd best buy myself a new suit, eh?' He sounded light-hearted, but in fact his heart was heavy. He knew Doug of old, and also knew that he had a sullen and nasty side to his nature.

'You mean you're willing to do it?' Ned had hoped Adam would want no part of it, although it broke his old heart to know his grandson was still not baptised. 'Aren't you too busy?' He glanced around the yard. 'I mean, you must have a business going if you're on the lookout to buy coal and wagons?'

Adam had to laugh at that. 'Chance would be a fine thing,' he said.

'You mean you *haven't* got a business?' He wouldn't have been surprised to learn that Adam was a high-flyer, because, like Doug, Adam was always a hard worker. He also had the ambition and brains to make it on his own.

'Haven't even got a *job* at the minute.' Before Ned Selby could comment, Adam went on, 'I do have aspirations, though, and a decent sum of money put by. So it's only a matter of time before I get something going.' He didn't want to seem like a charity case. Certainly not in front of Doug's father.

Ned nodded his head thoughtfully. 'You don't have to explain anything to *me*, son. Times are hard right now for all of us, but I've no doubt you'll pull yourself up by the bootstraps and make something of yourself. You were always the one with the drive to be a rich man. Like you say, it's only a matter of time.'

Adam was ashamed. 'It's not as easy as I imagined. Just when you think you've got it made, something happens to knock you down.' His jaw set hard. 'All the same, I'm not finished yet.'

'I'm sure you're not.'

107

The two men talked a while longer. Ned explained he was here for the day only, having travelled over on the train, he was now in a rush to catch the next one home. 'I'd best go and pay for that coal before they think I've changed my mind,' he said, glancing at his pocket-watch. 'It's a good buy, and every little helps. Lord knows it's a bit of a struggle at the minute.'

As he walked towards the house, Adam accompanied him. When the coal was paid for, they shook hands and parted; but not before Adam had written down his address, and Ned had put the paper safely in his pocket. 'Tell Doug I'll be honoured to be godfather,' he said. And meant it. Though it would be hard being godfather to Rosie's son when he would prefer to be its natural daddy.

Reflecting on their conversation, he remained on the step of the Saxon's house. There was a sadness about him as he watched Ned Selby's familiar figure walk away. 'So Rosie has a son, and another bairn on the way?' he mused aloud. Somehow he couldn't really believe it. Or didn't want to!

He was so engrossed in his thoughts that he was visibly startled when a voice sounded in his ear. 'You turned up, then? I wondered if you might.' Ben Saxon had not forgotten the young man who had come to see him.

Stepping aside to let another man pass, Adam reluctantly confessed, 'I couldn't stay away.'

'Like them, you mean?' The yard wasn't so busy now, and the auction was almost over. One or two bargain hunters could still be seen pawing over Saxon's possessions. 'I should have stayed away myself,' he mumbled. His eyes were bright with tears. He was an old man, and old men had the right to show their emotions. 'Down there in that yard is everything that made life worthwhile. And now it's all gone.'

'I'm sorry.' Adam was in the right frame of mind to understand how Ben felt.

'Oh? Sorry are you? Sorry for me, or sorry because you didn't get *your* pound of o' flesh?'

'I'm no vulture. All I want is the right to start up on my own, just as you did years ago. Is that too much to ask?' There was an anger in him then.

Ben peered at him with interest. He had spoken harshly and now regretted it. 'I don't reckon it is,' he agreed. 'To tell you the truth, I'm in no position to criticise because it was easier for me. You see, I took over this business from my father so it was all there . . . the wagons and rounds, and all the contacts. Oh, he'd told me tales of how he got started, and by all accounts, that was hard.'

He saw the straight-cut line of Adam's strong jaw and the way he returned his gaze, with clear honest eyes. There was something about his lithe physique and broad shoulders that struck a chord with Ben. 'I'm buggered if you don't put me in mind of my father,' he chuckled. Suddenly he felt a whole lot better for having met this determined young man. Slowly, the tiniest germ of an idea was growing in his mind.

'Come with me. You might be interested to see something.' Without waiting for an answer, he went down the steps into the yard. Bemused, Adam followed him to the big barn at the far end. It was locked. Reaching behind a loose plank, Ben fumbled about until he found the big rusty key. 'I always keep it locked,' he explained. 'Especially today, with all these nosy louts poking about!'

Turning the key in the lock, he swung the door open just wide enough for the two of them to squeeze through. When a man in a flat cap and boiler suit approached, Ben told him, 'Bugger off, mate. This is private property!' With a sour look and a muttered curse, the man turned his attention to a nearby pile of railway sleepers.

Adam stood in the gloom, wondering what this was all about, when the lamp was lit and his astonished eyes beheld a wagon. One of the earliest types, it was propped up on wooden boxes, without wheels or engine. There were no seats in the cab, and two of the boards were missing from the flat carrier at the back, but the paintwork was polished and the chrome gleamed; as he drew nearer he could see his face in it. 'It's beautiful!' he breathed, running his hand over the smooth paintwork.

'It was the very first wagon my father bought.' Laughing, Ben explained how it had been a rogue right from the start. 'We took her out four times, and each time she let us down. One time she lost a wheel and we tipped the entire load of coal in the middle of Albert Street. Before we could rebag it, there were women everywhere. In minutes they'd scooped the bloody lot up and disappeared back inside their houses! Another time we were going up Arnham Hill when the brakes failed. We started rolling backwards and I thought we were goners. Luckily, she veered into a lamp-post and we escaped with a few cuts and bruises. Mind you, the Council charged us for a new lamp-post.' The memory made him laugh. He hadn't laughed in a long time, and it felt good. Slapping Adam on the back, he said in a low voice, 'She's yours if you want it . . . what's left of it.'

Adam couldn't believe his ears. 'You mean it's for sale?'

'I mean what I said. She's yours if you want it.'

'What . . . you mean for *nothing*?'

'That's exactly what I mean.'

Never having been given anything for nothing, Adam was suspicious. 'I don't understand. When I came to you the other day, offering you good money for a wagon, you all but threw me out.'

'That was then.'

'And now?'

'Now, I can see how we can help each other.'

Understanding dawned. 'Ah! I knew there had to be a catch. Before I accept, I think you'd best tell me what you have in mind.'

'Nothing sinister, believe me. All I want is for you to promise me you'll look after this old wagon the same as I've looked after it.' His eyes clouded over. 'When you're old, all you have left are your memories. This wagon is a special part of my life, and I couldn't bear to put it in the sale. Since I won't be keeping this house on, I've been wondering what to do with this 'ere wagon. You seem like an honest fellow. If you tell me you'll look after it, I'll believe you.' Going to the wagon, he took a while to climb on to the cab; his old bones were not what they used to be. Sitting on the wheel arch, he asked, 'Well? Will you give her a good home?'

Adam could only nod, and wonder if he was dreaming. He could hear Ben talking, but he was too stunned to listen. 'Of course you'll have to find an engine for it . . . and a set of wheels, but you reckon you've a bit of money put by, so you should be able to manage that. Once you've got her ship-shape again, you'll have to concentrate on getting a round. You've worked in the coalyards so you know the business there. Getting folks in the street to buy your coal is a different kettle of fish. You'll find it hard, but you're young and eager. All the advice I can give is: don't undercut the opposition by too much or you'll go broke ... and treat your customers fair so they'll always come back to you.' He was standing by Adam's side now. 'Do you hear what I'm saying?'

He dragged his gaze from the wagon. 'How in God's name can I thank you?'

Ben laughed aloud. 'You haven't heard a bloody word I've said!' he spluttered. But it didn't matter. There wasn't much time left now, but there would be time enough to go through it all again.

In that moment, all that mattered was what he saw in Adam's face. It told him that here was a man he could trust. Here was a man who deserved a chance, and who would willingly work his fingers to the bone for it. Today had been a heartache. But now at least he could rest assured that something good had come of it all. And he could go to his maker with a clear conscience.

The month that followed was a busy and exciting one during which Adam worked long arduous hours restoring the cherished wagon. The cost of the spare parts took most of his hard-earned cash, but because he carried out almost all the labour himself, he made a great saving. The only time he called in expert help was when the engine was ready for fitting.

In the week that followed the auction, Ben and Adam talked for hours. Ben explained what made a good coal-merchant, and Adam listened intently. They were good friends, growing closer by the day. But, much to Adam's dismay, all that ended when he started work on the wagon.

Ben took an interest, but only from a distance. Adam thought it strange that he never came to the barn until the end of the day, when he knew Adam would be preparing to leave. At seven o'clock sharp he would stand by the door, hands in his pockets

111

and a faraway look in his eye. He never spoke. One minute he was there, and the next time Adam looked round, he was gone. The first time this happened, he had gone to the house and tapped on the door. 'Ben, was there something you wanted?' he called.

Ben didn't answer then, nor did he answer when, on arriving the next morning, Adam saw him coming out of the barn. He called out, but Ben appeared not to have heard. Without a backward glance he scurried into the house and only came out for that peculiar vigil just as Adam was finishing work. It was plain that he didn't want to talk with Adam, and so Adam accepted his need for privacy.

Something even stranger happened on the day when Adam climbed into the cab and drove the wagon into the yard. He was thrilled and excited, and most of all he wanted to share this moment with Ben. When he saw the older man watching from an upstairs window, he scrambled out of the cab and shouted up to him. 'Ben! Come and see,' he invited eagerly. 'She's purring like a kitten.'

Ben's answering smile was proud. There was a fleeting moment when he gazed on the wagon. Then he was gone. Adam waited, expecting him to show at any time. But the door remained firmly closed, and Adam grew impatient. This was Ben's moment as well as his, and he so much wanted him to drive down the street in this wagon which had been retired since the old Mr Saxon had passed on.

Determined, Adam went to the house and knocked on the door. There was no answer, so he boldly pushed open the door and called out Ben's name. All that greeted him was a chilling silence. Anxious, yet not knowing why, he climbed the stairs. 'Ben! Are you there?' he called. Still no answer. With his heart beating fast he inched open the bedroom doors one after the other. Ben's room was at the front of the house. He had gone to bed. His face was still and white, and there was a wonderful expression of peace in his features.

The doctor said he had suffered a heart attack. Adam believed his suffering was over, and that Ben Saxon had waited until the wagon was working once more. Now he could go to his father

112

with a sense of pride instead of shame. 'I made you a promise,' Adam told him at the funeral. 'Rest in peace, Ben, I won't go back on my word.'

Two days after Ben was laid to rest, Adam received a letter from Doug telling him that his son was to be christened on 2 July, and saying that both he and Rosie would be delighted if Adam could be there as godfather.

Against his better instincts, but longing to see Rosie again, Adam lost no time in writing back graciously accepting the kind offer. Connie told him it was a mistake, but Adam wasn't listening. This time, his heart was ruling his head.

CHAPTER EIGHT

Rosie shivered as she got out of bed. Though it was June and the sun was already shining outside, the air inside the house struck cold. Like all the other dwellings along this street, it was damp and old, and never properly warmed up until the sun had been high in the heavens for at least two hours.

Creeping about so as not to disturb Doug, Rosie threw her robe on and reached into the cot. 'Come on, sweetheart,' she told the sleeping child. 'You'd best come with your mammy because if you start crying for your breakfast and get him out of his bed, we'll not hear the end of it, will we, eh?' Doug had a nasty temper if he was woken before ten o'clock on his Saturday off.

Wrapping the infant in his shawl, she pressed him close and went out of the door. These days, with Rosie nearly seven months pregnant and with a child in arms, it was increasingly difficult to negotiate the narrow stairs so she took her time, inching her way along and being especially careful where the steps curved dangerously halfway down. Behind her she could hear Doug loudly snoring, 'Sounds like a train in full steam,' she chuckled.

Downstairs, she wedged the child between cushions in the corner of the settee. 'You'll be fine while I treat myself to a cup of tea, won't you, darling?' she cooed. But the infant had other ideas. In answer to her question, he opened his big eyes and began sucking on his fist. 'Hungry are you?' she asked, settling herself on the settee beside him. She had hoped he might allow her a few quiet minutes when she could gather her thoughts, but babies were unpredictable as she well knew. 'All right, I'll see to you first,' she conceded. 'Then I'll make myself a cup of tea before getting your daddy's breakfast ready.'

Undoing the front of her nightie, she lifted the child to her breast, laughing when he instantly clamped his mouth round her nipple and began frantically sucking. 'Where are your manners?' she teased. 'Going at your poor mammy like a sink plunger!' But she was never happier than when the child was feeding. Somehow she felt closer to him. While he fed, she allowed her mind to wander, and as always it wandered to the time before Doug, to the time when she and Adam had been together.

The infant was soon fed, washed and changed into his day clothes. Rosie glanced at the clock. It was already half-past eight. There was the dusting to be done, the mats to be taken out and beaten, and a pile of washing a mile high sitting in the dolly-tub. 'No good looking at it,' she said aloud, 'the work won't do itself.'

It was quarter to ten when she came in from the yard where she had been hanging out the washing. 'That's it for now,' she told herself in the parlour mirror. 'You look like something the cat dragged in. Best wash and dress. You know His Majesty moans if you're still in your nightie by the time he gets up.' Going to the stairs cupboard she dragged the ironing basket out and found a clean blue blouse, a straight grey skirt and clean underwear. Taking the garments into the scullery, she heated the iron and ran it over them. In no time at all she was washed, dressed, and feeling good. By the time she had finished washing herself, the water in the bowl had gone cold, and she soon discovered that there was nothing more revitalising than a rush of cold water on your skin.

The aroma of sizzling sausages and frying eggs began to fill the little house. Going into the parlour, she laid the table and checked that the baby was all right. He was fast asleep. 'You're a little beauty,' she told him, tenderly stroking his face. These past few weeks he had changed. His eyes were colouring to a soft hazel hue, and his hair was deepening to a rich brown colour like his mammy's. 'It's been weeks since he mentioned about you being christened,' she said. 'But if he thinks I've forgotten, he's very much mistaken. I intend having another go at him this morning. I mean to get you christened, and I'll fight him tooth and nail until he gives in!'

Returning to the scullery, she glanced at the calendar on the wall.

'June the twenty-fourth,' she said aloud. 'Half the year nearly gone and the bugger's *still* playing games!' She was angry, frustrated, and determined that, one way or another, the christening would take place before the year was out.

She was turning the eggs when suddenly she froze. 'Good God!' A smile spread over her face as she perused the calendar. 'Look at that, gal,' she chuckled. 'June the twenty-fourth 1949. It's my birthday, and I'm twenty-one!' Going into the parlour she leaned over her son to whisper in his ear, 'Shame on you! Fancy sleeping on your mammy's *twenty-first birthday*!'

She had completely forgotten that this was a special day and, for just a brief moment, there was joy in her heart. But it was soon curtailed when Doug appeared at the parlour door, dishevelled and irritable. 'Ain't my breakfast ready yet, woman?'

His irritation transferred itself to her. She wasn't surprised to realise that he too had forgotten her birthday. 'I've only got one pair of hands!' she snapped. 'Your breakfast will be on the table in a minute.' With that she went smartly into the scullery while he seated himself at the table.

Rosie picked at her toast. After all the work she had done in the past two hours, she was famished. Now, though, her appetite had vanished at the sight of his sullen face. Her instinct told her not to broach the subject of the christening just yet. There would be time enough later, after he'd been to the betting shop, when he might come home in a better frame of mind.

'I don't need to ask what *you'll* be up to today,' he grumbled. 'I expect you'll be gadding about with that bloody Peggy.' Viciously stabbing at his food with the prongs of his fork, he rammed it into his mouth, all the while staring at her with those odd-coloured eyes.

'We'll be going to the market together, yes,' she said defiantly.

Jabbing the fork at her, he said, 'I don't like you going about with that one.'

'She's my best friend. My *only* friend, as it happens.'

'That's beside the point. You're a married woman, and she's not. To my mind that spells trouble.'

'Oh? And are you forbidding me to see her?' There was a note of warning in her voice that cautioned him. 'And who says it spells trouble? Your mother, I suppose?'

117

'Watch your bloody tongue when you speak about my mother. She's been a better friend to you than ever your precious Peggy could be . . . let you move in when we had nowhere to go, didn't she? Gives you advice on the lad here, doesn't she?' He jabbed his fork again, this time towards the sleeping child. 'And all you've ever done is throw it all back in her face.'

Wisely ignoring his attempt to draw her into an argument concerning his mother, she asked in a calm voice, 'So, does all this mean you're forbidding me to see Peggy?'

He looked at her then, at her strong brown eyes and the determined set of her pretty jaw, and he knew he was on dangerous ground. 'I didn't say that,' he snarled. Picking up his mug of tea, he swilled the hot liquid down his throat. 'Just think on,' he warned slamming the mug down. 'There's folk watching you, that's all I'm saying.' Pushing his chair away, he left the table and went into the scullery where he quickly washed. Coming back to the parlour, he took his jacket from the nail behind the door. 'I'm off out,' he said, slinging his jacket over his shoulder. As he did so, a white envelope fell out of his pocket. Before Rosie could see what it was, he scraped it up and thrust it out of sight.

'What time will you be back?'

'When I think fit.' Flinging open the parlour door, he went down the passage and out of the house, leaving the front door open and a chill whipping down the passage and into the parlour.

Hurrying up the passage, Rosie closed the door. 'HEATHEN!' she called after him.

Suddenly a smile lit her face. 'Why, Rosie darling,' she mimicked his voice perfectly, 'isn't it your twenty-first birthday today?' Pursing her lips she feigned a kiss. 'Now then, sweetheart, where would you like to go? We can get the old battleaxe to babysit if you like? How about an evening at the Palais? Or we could go to that nice little restaurant on the corner of Dewhurst Street. I'll buy you a nice big box of chocolates afterwards . . . or a bunch of flowers. Or would you prefer a pretty silk scarf? No? What then? Oh! I know. Of course, why didn't I think of it before . . . a diamond ring! That's what I'll get you, sweetheart . . . a beautiful diamond ring. And a new dress! After all, you deserve the very best.'

She smiled and she cooed and she pranced up and down the passageway, fancying herself in this and that, holding out her work-work fingers to admire the diamond ring. 'My! See how it glints and sparkles!' she exclaimed with big surprised eyes. Sweeping into the parlour, she fell into the nearest chair and laughed until she cried.

The stain of tears was still under her soft brown eyes when the knock came on the door. 'Who the devil's that?' she muttered, going up the passage and hoping it wasn't Doug come back.

It wasn't Doug, nor was it the devil. It was Peggy. 'Took your time opening the door, didn't you?' she remarked, following Rosie into the parlour. 'Anybody would think I were the rent-man.' The two often laughed at how Peggy's mam had occasion to hide from the rentman some years back, and one of her indignant brood told the visitor through the letterbox, 'If you're the rentman, our mam says she ain't here!' To which he promptly yelled back, 'You tell your mam who "ain't here" that I've been called some things in my time, but never a rentman. You tell her I'm from the Widows' and Orphans' Charity, and I've brought her a free sack of firewood. But if she "ain't here" I'd best take it to some other deserving case.'

Before he'd even finished speaking, Peggy's mam flung open the door. 'Get inside, you!' She clipped the foolish boy's ear and sent him scurrying to the back room. 'And as for you,' she addressed the young man, 'you'll not find a more deserving cause than me in the whole of Blackburn, so kindly drop the sack of firewood on the step and bugger off!' Instructing the driver to offload one sack of firewood from the wagon, he doffed his flat cap and bade her good morning, and was still laughing as he climbed back into the cab. The incident had been a source of amusement ever since. After that, whenever she found the need to hide from the rentman, Peggy's mam bundled the children behind the settee with her.

Remembering the occasion, Rosie chuckled. 'I'm sorry if I kept you waiting,' she apologised. 'I thought it might be Doug coming back for something, that's all.' Realising Peggy was intently study-ing her face, she said hastily, 'I'll make us a brew, eh?'

Peggy shook her head. 'No, thank you all the same. I've just had my breakfast. But you *can* tell me why you've been crying.'

Seating herself opposite her observant friend, Rosie feigned surprise. 'What makes you think I've been crying?'

'Oh, nothing much . . . just the time it took you to open the door, and your eyes, all red and swollen.' Peggy would not be put off. 'Then there's your frantic hurry to get into the scullery and make a brew, when you know very well I always make *you* one since you've got big with child.'

'You're too clever for your own good, my girl,' Rosie said light-heartedly. She knew there was no use trying to hide anything from Peggy. 'Anyway, I might be "big with child", but I'm not an invalid.'

'Come on. Out with it.'

Rosie sighed wearily. 'It's nothing. Honest.'

'Liar!'

'I had a set to with Doug, that's all.'

'Oh? What about?'

'This and that . . . his mother mostly.' Rosie thought it might sound childish to say she was peeved because he'd forgotten her birthday.

'Has the old cow been interfering again?'

'She thinks our friendship is bound to cause trouble, what with me being married and you being single.'

'I've a bloody good mind to go and have it out with her!'

'Not a good idea.' All the same, the thought of Doug's mam and Peggy going at it hammer and tongs on the street tickled Rosie's imagination.

'Well then, tell her to piss off and mind her own business!'

'Oh, don't you worry. Soon as ever I get the chance, that's exactly what I'll do.'

'Good for you!' Getting out of the chair, Peggy asked coyly, 'Aren't you going to ask me why I'm not at work this morning.'

Going along with her, Rosie put the question. 'All right then. Why aren't you at work this morning?'

'Because our mam's thinking of decorating the parlour and she wants the furniture moved. I told her we could do it tomorrow, but she said not on the Sabbath. Anyway, you know what our mam's like. Once she's made up her mind there's no changing it.

I was due a Saturday off, so I thought I might as well get the agony over with. As it is, there's not much hope of that trip to the market this afternoon. I'm sorry.'

'Do you need any help? Though I won't be any good at shifting the heavier stuff.'

'You're a mind-reader.'

It took fifteen minutes for the two of them to clear away and wash the breakfast things. After which Rosie put the child in its pram and the three of them made their way to Peggy's home.

Peggy's mam was waiting, and so were the children, all standing round the table which was laid with a white cloth, a mountain of home-made goodies, and a round cake in the centre, with icing that spelled out her name. Rosie was completely taken by surprise.

'Well? Ain't you got nothing to say?' Peggy laughed. 'Surely you didn't think I'd forget me best mate's twenty-first?' Taking the child from Rosie's arms, she sat him in the deep armchair and grabbed Rosie in a great big hug. 'Happy Birthday, sunshine,' she said, and the tears ran down Rosie's face.

'I don't know what to say,' she whispered through her tears. 'I was sure nobody would remember.'

'Well, you were wrong, weren't you?' Peggy chided. And without further ado, she fetched a box of matches for Rosie to light the candles on her cake. 'You ain't getting any younger, gal,' she teased. 'There's all twenty-one there, so you'd best take a deep breath and blow them all out together.'

Most of them went out in one blow, but it took two more little tries to extinguish them all; at which point a loud cheer went up and the party began. Twenty-one balloons, blown up the night before by Peggy and the children, were set loose across the room, with the young ones scrambling to pop them before they stuck to the ceiling. The children squealed and laughed and filled their bellies with jelly, cakes, cheese butties, and finally a large wedge of birthday cake, which Rosie vowed was, 'The most delicious I've ever tasted.'

'I've allus been known for my cakes,' Peggy's mam boasted, and Peggy laughingly told her not to get a big head. Rosie gave the kindly woman a heartfelt kiss, and she blushed a warm shade of pink. 'Why's our mam gone all red?' piped up a little voice, and Peggy's mam playfully clipped him round the ear.

By midday, the food was gone and so were the children. 'Gone out to terrorise the neighbourhood,' Peggy joked. The three women set to and tidied up, but when Rosie offered to help wash the dishes, Peggy's mam told her, 'You're a good lass, Rosie Selby, and you've been a good friend to my lass. I'm ashamed to say there have been times when I've been a sour-faced old sod, and I'm sorry about that. I didn't need no asking twice when our Peggy said she was planning a party and needed my help. I've been glad to do it, and now I'll be glad to wash up.'

'Come on, gal,' Peggy said. 'You look worn out. Put your feet up, and I'll do your hair for you . . . a special birthday treat, you might say.'

Rosie *was* tired and couldn't deny it. Her feet ached, her face was flushed and the unborn child inside her felt like a ton weight. Easing herself into the standchair by the table, she watched as Peggy went to the sideboard and took out a shoe-box. 'What are you up to?' she asked suspiciously when Peggy put the box on the table; she was visibly startled when her mam charged in from the scullery, crying, 'It's bad luck to put a shoebox on the table!'

'You mean *shoes*!' Peggy corrected.

'You keep shoes in that box, don't you?' her mam argued. 'So do as you're told and get it off the table.'

Placing the box on a nearby chair, Peggy took out a bowl and another small box. Inside the box was a sachet of dark liquid, a wad of cotton wool, and a small comb. 'I'm going to turn you into a raving redhead,' she told Rosie.

Rosie was horrified. 'You're not, you know!'

'Well, happen I'll just bring out the pretty highlights in your hair then?'

'What's wrong with my hair as it is?' In spite of her fears, Rosie was intrigued.

'There's nothing at all wrong with it,' Peggy assured her. 'It's very pretty. But I can make it glint like gold if you'll let me.' She laid the things out on the table. 'I got it at discount. We've just started this new line in cosmetics, you see, and like I said, it's a special birthday present for you.' She saw how hesitant Rosie was. 'Go on, gal,' she entreated, 'I promise you'll look great.'

Rosie thought of how she never did anything exciting, and how every day ran one into the other without anything to distinguish them. Lately she had been feeling like an old woman, instead of someone only twenty-one. She remembered how Doug had forgotten her birthday and she thought how good it would be to shock him. 'Do what you like,' she told Peggy. 'If I go bald, happen Doug won't want me in bed.'

Peggy's mam could be heard laughing in the kitchen. 'You're a pair o' buggers!' she said, and she was right.

It was ten o'clock at night when Doug came home. He wasn't drunk, but he was in a foul mood. 'What money have you got in your purse?' he asked, glaring at her from the doorway.

'A few shillings,' she answered. 'Enough to see us through 'til payday.'

'Give it here.'

'What for?'

'Never mind what for. I said . . . give it here.' Striding into the room he stretched out his hand and waited for her to empty her purse into it. 'I ain't got time to argue.'

Rosie didn't argue either. She knew it wouldn't make the slightest difference if she did. Besides, she wanted to humour him so she could ask about the date for the christening. With this in mind, she gave him half of what she had. It was enough to placate him. When he turned sharply and went out of the house again, she ran into the front room and peeped through the window. There were two other men waiting on the doorstep. They hurried away once Doug had paid his dues. Rosie suspected they were gambling partners. 'You're a fool, Doug Selby,' she whispered, hurrying back to the parlour. 'One of these days you'll get in over your head.'

When he came back he was smiling. 'I could drink the sea dry,' he said, throwing himself into the armchair. 'Put the kettle on, sweetheart,' he coaxed.

Rosie hated him when he turned on the charm like that. She was about to say she was tired and off to bed, when she stopped herself. Until he set the date for the christening, she would have to humour him. Without a word she went into the scullery, returning with his tea a few minutes later. 'Have you been to see the vicar?' she asked, giving the hot mug into his outstretched hands.

For a moment he stared at her. 'There's something different about you,' he commented, sitting up in his chair.

Knowing how he would react when he saw the red highlights in her brown hair, Rosie had deliberately kept in the shadows. 'What do you mean?' she asked innocently.

He shook his head. 'I'm not sure . . . something.' He stared a moment longer, but he had drunk a pint or two and his vision wasn't perfect at the minute. Puzzled, he sank back in the chair, sipping at his tea and infuriating her.

Just as she opened her mouth to remind him of her question, he astonished her by saying with a smug little smile, 'Not only have I been to see the vicar, but I've set the date for Sunday next.'

Rosie was thrilled. 'Oh, Doug! You can't know what a weight you've lifted off my mind.' If only he hadn't put her through so much, she might have embraced him. But he was too cunning, too arrogant. And her memory was too vivid.

Besides, she thought with amusement, she'd better stay in the shadows. If he was to see the carrot-coloured streaks in her hair, there would be an unholy row. She could handle that all right, but the little one had been fretful with his teething, and she didn't want him woken again. 'I began to think we'd be getting the two children baptised together,' she remarked coolly. 'What made you change your mind?'

'I got what I wanted, that's why.'

'In what way?'

He stared at her again, trying to distinguish what was different about her. 'What have you been up to?' he asked, getting out of the chair and starting towards her. It was then that his eyes caught sight of Peggy's birthday card, which Rosie had stood proudly on the mantelpiece. 'What the hell's this?' Snatching it up, he ran his eyes over it. A look of surprise came over his features, and for a moment it seemed as though he was about to make a comment but he replaced it without saying a word. Instead, he came to where she sat and proceeded to look her up and down. 'It's your bloody hair!' he gasped. 'You've had it dyed ginger.'

Summoning every ounce of courage, Rosie bestowed her loveliest smile on him. 'Don't you like it then?' she asked coyly. She didn't like it either, but she wasn't about to admit that.

He ran his fingers over the top of her head, ruffling the thick strands of hair before viciously grabbing a fistful and demanding: 'Do *you* like it?'

'Yes,' she lied, 'I do.' Standing up to face him, she waited for the outburst but was unprepared for what happened next.

'Your hair's pretty enough the way the good Lord made it, but yes, I think it suits you,' he replied, astounding her.

Before she could answer, he took out the envelope from his pocket and thrust it into her hand. 'After all, I do want you to look your best for the christening. We wouldn't want *him* to think the goods had become soiled, would we, eh?'

'What game are you playing, Doug?' She had known him long enough to realise that he was up to something.

'No game, sweetheart. It's just that things have turned out exactly how I wanted them to.' With that he went up the stairs, chuckling all the way.

Opening the envelope, she read the letter from Adam. It was short and polite, not at all like that of a friend. But it confirmed that Adam had graciously accepted the invitation to be godfather to Doug and Rosie's son. 'Oh, Adam, I thought you of all people might see through him,' Rosie sighed. 'He's using you, just like he uses me.' Now she saw what Doug had meant when he said things had turned out exactly like he wanted them to.

Pacing the room with the letter clutched in her hand, Rosie was tempted to sit down and write to Adam, warning him how Doug had intended to name his son after him only to antagonise her – though he was in for a real surprise when they got to the church. All the same, she wanted Adam to know that he had been asked to be godfather for the very same reason . . . to punish the two of them for having dared to love each other.

But then she realised she would only be hurting herself more by persuading Adam to stay away, because then Doug would never allow their son to be christened. 'And in spite of everything,

I do so much want to see you, Adam,' she murmured, putting the letter against her face. She was both excited and afraid. Excited at the prospect of being in the same room as Adam again, and afraid because, though he was forever out of her reach, she would never stop loving him.

Carefully, she laid the letter on the sideboard where Doug would find it. 'A week,' she whispered, going up the stairs to bed. 'Only one week, and then he'll be here, in this house.' She shivered with delight. When she entered the bedroom and saw Doug waiting for her, the delight turned to dread.

Monday morning brought a wonderful surprise, but not before Doug had alarmed her with the news, 'Dad's losing work hand over fist. There are more folk out of work, and consequently they're counting their pennies. Last month we only sold a hundred and fifty bags of coal, when we normally sell upwards of four hundred.'

As always, Rosie was optimistic. 'Happen it's just a bad month. After all, it is June, and there are only a few people who light a fire in summer . . . old folk and them with small bairns.'

Scraping back his chair, he got up from the breakfast table. 'Don't talk daft, woman!' he snapped, glaring at her as though she was a total imbecile. 'The summer's always been a good time for selling coal. Folks have allus stocked up their cellars while it's cheap, and you bloody well know that.'

Rosie made no comment. Instead, she concentrated on clearing away the breakfast things. Only when she heard him slamming down the passage and out of the front door did she straighten herself from the task, and that was to roll her eyes to the ceiling and say, 'Dear Lord, you made a miserable soul when you made that one!'

The postman was late, but Rosie wasn't worried. He never brought anything exciting, just bills and circulars. When she heard the familiar plop of letters on the carpet, she went down the passage to collect them, absent-mindedly sifting through them as she returned to the parlour. 'Same as usual,' she muttered; there was a gas bill, a reminder about the instalment on the new gramophone, and a leaflet from the chimney-sweep, saying how

126

he could 'Sweep a chimney so clean you could hang your Sunday best coat in it'.

Rosie was still chuckling at that when she came into the parlour. But as her smiling brown eyes saw the writing on the last envelope, her heart almost stopped. The letter was addressed to her, and she had seen enough of his letters to know without a doubt that this one was from Adam.

Seating herself at the table, she opened the envelope and took out the contents. What she saw made her gasp. It was the most beautiful birthday card; in the cream-coloured background, little robins and kittens could be seen nuzzling up to each other, and there were clusters of exquisite red roses in all four corners. Inside there was a simple message that tore at her heart and filled her eyes with tears. It read:

> To Rosie,
> Did you think I would forget your birthday?

It was signed 'Adam'. There was no other message, nothing about the christening or Doug. At first she was puzzled, but then she understood. Adam had effectively shut out everyone but the two of them, and because of that, she would cherish the card all the more.

Her first instinct was to hide it. In fact, she even went so far as to turn back the lace-cover on the sideboard, 'No!' she declared. 'I *won't* hide it. Why should I? It can't hurt Doug to know there are people who think enough of me to remember my birthday.' Having decided to display it, she put it on the mantelpiece alongside Peggy's. 'There you are, Rosie gal,' she said, hands on hips as she stared at the two pretty cards. 'Don't ever say nobody loves you.' She daren't wonder whether Adam might love her still. It would only be wishful thinking, and anyway, even if it were true, all it could ever bring was heartache.

All day long, Rosie went about her work with a song in her heart. That song was cruelly ended when Doug walked in and saw the card there. 'Who's that from?' he wanted to know, striding across the room and snatching it up. He opened the inside and read the message. 'Bastard!' he roared. 'What gives him the sodding right?' Taking the card between his fingers, he began tearing it apart.

Seeing that precious card torn in front of her eyes was like a red rag to a bull. Darting forward, Rosie grabbed at it. There was a fury inside her, an insane rage that had built up over many months and now was let loose like a burst dam. 'He's got *every* right!' she cried, her nails scoring his arm as she struggled to take the card from him. 'Just because I married you instead of him, doesn't mean he can't still be a friend.'

Holding her at arm's length, he peered at her through red, dirt-rimmed eyes. 'Why, you little whore! You want him, don't you?' His voice was low, unsure. Then, when her gaze fell from him, he shook her, his voice rising in a fury. 'Admit it, or I swear I'll take your bloody head off at the shoulders!'

'Oh, aren't you the big man?' she demanded, her brown eyes mocking him. 'If you think there's something going on between me and Adam, why don't you ask *him*? After all, he'll be here on Sunday.'

'You little cow!' With one backward swipe of his hand he sent her crashing against the table. 'If I ever thought you and he . . .' Stretching himself to his full height, he glared down on her. 'So help me, I'll swing for the pair of you!' He made a low guttural sound in the base of his throat, then he was gone: unwashed, unfed, back on to the streets and into the pub, where he could drown his terrible thoughts in a jug of ale.

Covered in the fine coal-dust that had fallen from his clothes, Rosie remained bent across the table, using it to hold her steady. '*You're* the bastard!' she said softly. Any affection she had felt for him had grown cold long since. To tell the truth, she wouldn't care if she never saw him again.

Long after she had washed and changed and all the work was done, she was so churned up inside, she could hardly keep a limb still. Only when the child cooed on her lap and smiled up at her did she begin to melt, and love again. 'I've still got you, ain't I?' she said, holding the child closer. She glanced up at the crumpled card on the table. 'What shall I do with it?' she mused aloud. 'I ought to put it right back on the mantelpiece!' Shaking her head, she gave an odd little smile. 'Better not, eh?' She had been darkly angry, then indignant, and now she was filled with a terrible fear.

Fear for Adam, fear that once the two of them came face to face again, so many feelings would be unleashed. 'It would be better if you stayed away, Adam,' she whispered. 'For all our sakes.'

Later, when the child was asleep in its pram, she took the card, held it close for the briefest moment when she could feel him near. Then, with a firm and final gesture, she threw it in the midden. 'Sorry, Adam,' she said with a wry little laugh. 'The time for pretty things is long gone.'

During the following two days, Rosie remained inside the house, venturing out only to collect the milk from the doorstep; even then she made sure no one saw her. 'Don't want the world and its neighbour to know he's been belting me,' she said, glancing in the mirror at the dark bruise that coloured her eye and cheek bone. 'Best keep myself to myself for a while.'

She reckoned without Peggy's determination though. Twice she had been round to see her friend, and each time she had been sent away by Doug. 'She's not well,' he told her. 'She's taken to her bed.'

Now, when the knock came on the door, Rosie wasn't certain whether to answer it or stay quiet until whoever it was had gone away. She decided to remain quiet, holding her breath and hoping the child wouldn't wake and start crying.

The sound of the letter box being opened almost turned her heart over. 'Rosie!' Peggy's voice sailed down the passage. 'I know you're in there. Open this bloody door or I'll scream blue murder up and down the street.'

Half laughing, half crying, Rosie ran down the passage and flung open the door. 'It's *you*!' she said, ushering her friend in and closing the door before any nosy neighbour might look in.

''Course it's me!' Peggy replied, making her way before Rosie. 'Who the sodding hell did you think it was?' Once inside the parlour she turned to examine Rosie's face. 'I thought so!' Her voice hardened with anger. 'I had an idea you two had been fighting. By! He's a worse coward than I imagined.' Going into the scullery, she put the kettle on. Peering at Rosie through the doorway, she insisted, 'Any man who'd do that to a woman ain't worth spit!'

When she came back into the parlour, carrying two mugs of

piping hot tea, she asked, 'Tell me to mind my own business if you like, but they do say a trouble shared is a trouble halved.' Giving one of the mugs to Rosie, Peggy waited for her to sit down on the chair opposite. Through the scullery window she had seen the sheets and bedding hanging out on the line; the flagstoned floor had been scrubbed until it shone; the mats had been beaten and relaid in the parlour; even the fire-grate was blackleaded, and one glance told her that the child was washed and now fast asleep in its pram. 'Good Lord, you must have been up at the crack of dawn,' she remarked.

'Four o'clock,' Rosie informed her. 'I couldn't sleep. I haven't slept properly these past two days.' After all that had happened, she had been at sixes and sevens. 'Doug wrote asking Adam to be godfather, and he's accepted.'

Peggy's face said it all. 'So *that's* what you've been fighting about?'

'Sort of.'

'What's that supposed to mean?'

'Why aren't you at work?'

'You may well ask. I've been round here twice and that bloody husband of yours has sent me away each time. I began to think the only way I'd find out what was going on was to take an hour off work, so here I am.'

'Oh, Peggy! You'll get the sack.'

She chuckled at that. 'Give over. Didn't you know they've got their eye on me as the next manager?' The smile fell from her face. 'You don't want to tell me then?'

'He saw the birthday card you gave me.' She decided she might as well tell it all. 'Then he saw the one Adam sent.'

Peggy looked surprised. '*Adam* sent you a birthday card?'

'It was innocent enough . . . a simple card, with a simple message.'

'But your old man didn't see it that way, eh?'

Rosie had to laugh. 'He went berserk.'

'That were his lousy conscience, I expect. I don't suppose you had a card from *him*, did you, eh?' When Rosie shook her head, Peggy asked, 'How did he come to see Adam's card?'

'I displayed it next to yours on the mantelpiece.'

Punching the air with her fist, Peggy said, 'Good for you, gal!'

'Now I've got this to show for it.' Rosie pointed to the bruise on her face.

'But you stood up to him, that's all that matters.'

'I sometimes wonder whether it's worth it though.' She smiled a sad smile. 'Oh, Peggy, you should have seen Adam's card. It was so pretty, with roses and everything.'

'I suppose he tore it up, did he?'

'No. It were me who tore it up.' Seeing the look on Peggy's face, she explained, 'I had to, don't you see? I made my mistake way back, and now there's no point spending my days dreaming and wishing. What's done is done, and that's an end to it.'

'Are you sure?' Peggy saw how desperately unhappy Rosie was, and couldn't help but wonder if there was a way out of it.

'Oh, Peggy! Of course I'm sure. What's to be gained by clinging to the past? Adam must have a life of his own now . . . I'm wed to Doug.' She pointed to the pram. 'There's the lad to consider, and I'm nearly seven months with another. Ask yourself, what chance could there be for a woman like me on my own?' When Peggy seemed lost for words, she went on in a softer tone, 'If Adam were to knock on that door right now and ask me to come away with him . . . which I'm sure would never happen . . . I would still have to think twice. Doug Selby is a vindictive and possessive man. You can depend on one thing. He would fight for the children and leave no stone unturned to make my life a misery.' She made an odd little sound that might have been a sob. 'You can depend on something else too. His mother would be right behind him, spurring him on with her hatred.'

'I suppose you're right, gal,' Peggy was loth to admit it, but she could see the awful truth in Rosie's words. 'But I swear if he hits you again . . .'

Rosie interrupted. 'Don't worry,' she promised in a serious voice, 'this is the last time he raises a bruise on me.'

'By! You sound as though you might kill the bugger.'

'Don't think it hasn't crossed my mind.'

A strange silence fell over the little parlour while each young woman considered the implications of what had been said. 'I'm surprised Adam agreed to be godfather,' Peggy commented finally.

'So am I.'

'Are you glad?'

'It means my son can be baptised at last.'

'Oh? And you're not pleased because you'll see Adam again?' Peggy teased with a knowing little smile.

Rosie returned her smile. 'All right then, yes,' she admitted. 'But one look at me and he'll thank his lucky stars he went when he did.'

'Whatever do you mean?' Peggy looked at her. Though Rosie's face was bruised, she was still the loveliest creature on two legs. 'The bruise will be cleared up in time.'

'Maybe. But I wasn't just talking about that.' Stretching her arms out, she invited Peggy to take a closer look. 'I'm big as a barge, my hair needs cutting, and there are bags under my eyes where the baby's kept me awake night after night.' It was a hot and humid July afternoon, and she felt completely drained of energy.

'You're too hard on yourself, gal!' Peggy reprimanded. 'Anyway, you've forgotten about my considerable talents. I haven't been put on the cosmetics counter for no reason, you know.'

'You're not dyeing my hair again!'

'Why not? The dye washed out, didn't it?'

'Yes, and so did handfuls of my hair.'

'All right then, we'll forget that.'

'And anything else you've got in mind,' Rosie said good-naturedly, 'I'm past being a guinea-pig.'

The child woke then. 'It was early when I fed him, so I expect he's bawling for his titty.' In a minute Rosie had collected him and was preparing to feed him.

Lately, Peggy's career had overtaken her desire for husband and children. But now she watched how tenderly Rosie held the boy, and how lovingly she let him suck the milk from her. There was something uniquely special about the relationship that deeply moved her. Oh, she had seen her own mother feed the young ones, but with Rosie it always seemed different. Peggy wondered if it was because her friend was younger than her, yet here Rosie was with an infant son and another bairn due soon. There was no denying that she was not only beautiful in appearance but that she had a warm and giving soul. 'You're so lovely, Rosie,' Peggy told her, 'Adam will rue the day he let you go.'

She smiled. 'I don't think so.'

'That's the trouble with you, my girl!' Peggy's hackles were up. 'You've too low an opinion of yourself. You'll see! I'll have you looking like a million dollars on Sunday.'

Rosie laughed. 'That'll take some doing,' she said, cuddling the boy on her lap. 'I'm a wreck.'

As Peggy cast a gaze over her friend, she experienced a fleeting pang of envy. With her rich brown hair, sparkling hazel eyes and those classic features, Rosie was very special. And even though she had been through the mill with Doug and his hateful mother, her strength of mind had carried her above it all with a dignity that was impressive. 'Trust me,' she said now. 'When Adam claps eyes on you, he'll want you all over again.'

'I'm not sure that would be a good thing.'

'If it makes that bloody husband of yours value you more, then it *will* be a good thing.' Peggy chuckled. 'In fact, I wouldn't be surprised if on Sunday we don't see the cat among the pigeons.'

'I've been thinking that myself.'

'And are you worried?'

Rosie's eyes sparkled with mischief. 'I was. But now I'm really looking forward to it.'

The two friends laughed and talked, and the hours ticked away. When Peggy was gone, Rosie thought about the christening, and how she had told her friend she was looking forward to it. Now, though, in her solitude, she wondered what Sunday would really bring, and a feeling of mounting trepidation rose within her.

CHAPTER NINE

Connie was in tears. Yet again she had been battered by her husband, and now here she was looking to Adam for comfort. As he sat her in the chair, Adam warned, 'If you go back to him, you deserve everything you get.'

Through her tears Connie smiled up at him. 'Thanks for not saying, "I told you so".' It was obvious from her red eyes that she had cried all night. Wincing from the pain in her shoulder, she bit her bottom lip. 'I think he's broken it.'

Tenderly roving his fingers along the line of her shoulder, he was satisfied when she showed how she could raise her arm and bend it at the elbow. 'No. It's not broken . . . badly sprained though.' His mouth drew into a thin angry line. 'How did it happen?'

As always, Connie defended her lover. 'It was my fault,' she insisted. 'I shouldn't have put my shoulder against the door.'

'Ah!' He realised now. 'So, he's thrown you out again?'

Grinning, she admitted sheepishly, 'Looks like it.'

'For Christ's sake, Connie! Why can't you see him for what he is? The fellow's no use to you.' Anger was welling up inside him, forcing him to pace the floor. 'Everyone knows what a womaniser he is. What! There must have been umpteen young women in and out of these premises over the years, and he's used them all . . . he lets them have a room, and for that he takes their rent money *and* expects to bed them.'

'He didn't take any of them into his own house though, did he?'

'Not that I know. But a man like that always has his own devious reasons for doing what he does.' Adam hated raising this particular issue, but felt he had to make Connie see what she

135

was letting herself in for. 'I hope you haven't forgotten how he brought men to the house and expected you to sleep with them?'

'I wish I hadn't told you that.'

'Yes, well, so do I! Because in spite of everything I say, you still think the sun shines out of his arse!'

'I know all the arguments, Adam, so you might as well save your breath.' Very carefully, she flexed her arm muscles. 'I think you're right, it isn't broken.' She sighed with relief.

'But it might have been. That bastard deserves a bloody good thrashing!' Grabbing his coat from the chair-back, he flung it on. 'Matter of fact, I'm in the mood to see to it.' In two strides he was at the door.

Scrambling to her feet, Connie stopped him. 'He's not there.'

'You would say that.'

'No. Honest to God, he's cleared off. Business, he said. But to tell the truth, I reckon he's trying to shake me off altogether.'

Realising she was telling the truth, he took off his coat. 'You'd be better off if he never came back.'

'No, I wouldn't.' Looking pleased with herself, she said, 'I'm pregnant.'

Adam groaned and shook his head in despair. 'And I don't suppose he wants to know?'

'That's why he's took to his heels and buggered off.' She chuckled. 'But he won't get away that easily, because now I've got him where I want him. He can't ignore me, can he, eh?' For the first time her voice wavered and she seemed unsure of herself. 'Can he, Adam? Not even he could desert a woman who's carrying a child.' Tears welled up in her eyes. Now, when Adam opened his arms to her, she clung to him. 'I know I've been a fool,' she confessed, 'but I love him.'

Holding her tight, he reassured her, 'I know. And if he had any eyes in his head, he would see that. Happen he will. Happen he'll change his ways.' He laughed wryly. 'Even a snake can shed his skin.'

'I shouldn't bring my troubles to you, Adam.'

'Isn't that what friends are for?'

Moving away, she asked, 'Can I stay here tonight? I'm not short of money, and I could go to a hotel, but I don't want to be on my own.'

'Of course you can, but only for the one night. I'll be checking out myself tomorrow.'

Her eyes lit up. 'Does that mean you've got Ben Saxon's house . . . the one with the yard and everything?'

'It does.' A look of immense satisfaction came over his handsome features, but it faded when he thought of Ben. 'They say one man's misfortune is another man's opportunity, but I can't help feeling sad for Ben.'

'From what you told me about him, I reckon he would have been pleased to know you had come into good times. I mean, he was the one who gave you the chance of a wagon, and he took a liking to you straight away.'

'God knows why!'

'Because you're a good man, that's why. And Ben Saxon saw that.'

'It's early days yet,' Adam reminded her. 'I've only just really got going, and the rent on Ben's place will be crippling at first. Besides, the house is in bad repair and I won't be able to renovate it for some time yet.' But even though he had a daunting task ahead of him, Adam couldn't suppress his excitement. 'Oh, Connie! At long last I'm seeing it all happen . . . first the wagon, and then the best round in Liverpool, and now the house and yard! Sometimes I still have to pinch myself to make sure I'm not dreaming.'

'You're not the kind of man to waste time dreaming,' she said. 'Whatever you've achieved it's no more than you deserve, because you've worked bloody hard for it.'

'Aye! And I'll go on working hard until every fireplace in Liverpool burns the coal I fetch to the door.' Every day brought a new opportunity, and ambition burned so fiercely in him that he worked with a frenzy. A frenzy that was meant to shut Rosie from his thoughts. It didn't though. And he was a fool to think it ever would.

'I'll find somewhere tomorrow,' she promised. 'It's just that I don't want to be on my own tonight.'

He smiled. 'Reminds me of that first night I brought you here.'

'One of the better things in my life.'

'Where's your suitcase?'

'Outside the door.' He went to get it, and on his return she asked impishly, 'I don't suppose . . .?'

Anticipating her question, he shook his head from side to side, his dark eyes smiling. 'No. I'll sleep on the couch as always.'

'Pig!'

Teasing, he asked, 'Anyway, I thought you were head over heels in love with the landlord?'

'That don't mean to say I can't snuggle up to someone else when he's not around.'

'Bed and breakfast, that's all I'm providing. Do you still want to stay?'

'Okay.'

He laughed aloud. 'I never know what to think of you.'

'I wouldn't mind going out for a drink later . . . cheer me up, it would.'

'I've no objection to that.' Taking her case to the bedroom, he reminded her sternly, 'Then it's you to your bed, and me to mine.'

'All right. I'm grateful for small mercies.' Being in Adam's company always cheered her up. 'In return, I'll help you move out tomorrow.'

'Nothing to move, except myself.' He saw how downcast she looked. 'I tell you what, though. You know I'm travelling to Blackburn tomorrow afternoon?'

'Oh, yes, I'd forgotten. You're going to a christening. After my bad behaviour am I still allowed to go along?'

'You don't deserve to, but I'm sure Rosie and Doug wouldn't mind.'

She was thrilled. 'If you're sure?'

'I know you'll be miserable if I leave you behind,' he said. And so it was settled.

That night, while Adam slept on the settee, Connie came through the room to get a glass of water. On her way back, she glanced at his tousled hair and sleeping face. Women like me don't fall for decent blokes like you, she thought. It's a pity, but we always end up with someone as bad as ourselves. As she clambered back into bed, she stared at the door and whispered in a sad voice, 'I know he's a bastard, but I'd give anything to keep him.' She was momentarily filled with shame. 'Goodnight, Adam. And thanks for being a friend.'

CHAPTER TEN

The family had gathered in Rosie's tiny parlour. Ned Selby looked stiff and uncomfortable in a light grey suit with a striped shirt that was done up so tight round his neck he looked choked. 'I'll have to go home and change into something looser,' he complained to his wife. His neck was red raw where he had constantly run his fingers beneath the shirt collar.

'You'll do no such thing!' While she spoke, Martha glared at him through narrowed eyes. 'I'm not having you in church looking like a rag-bag.' She was dressed in a sober green two-piece that stretched over her ample figure like a net over a bag of peas; every awful curve and wrinkle was exposed for all to see.

Rosie looked unusually lovely in a flowing dark dress that wonderfully camouflaged the round bulge beneath. Her brown shining hair was left loose to her shoulders, and there was a wonderful radiance about her.

For two days now she and Peggy had worked hard getting the little house ready for visitors, finally this very morning laying out the table with all the food which had been made by their own hands, apart from the scones which Peggy's mam had eagerly contributed. Only two hours ago, Rosie was bone-tired and it showed. Now, after bathing and resting awhile, and with the event in sight, she appeared to be more relaxed; though in truth her heart was beating tenfold at the thought of seeing Adam again.

Doug was running back and forth to the door, impatient for Adam to arrive. 'Where the hell is he?' he raged. 'If he don't soon turn up, you can forget the whole bloody thing!' His remarks were aimed at Rosie.

With a calmness that surprised everyone, she walked across

the room to confront him. 'Whether Adam arrives or not, our son *will* be baptised,' she assured him in a quiet voice. 'No more delays, Doug. I won't stand for it.'

He laughed aloud, pointing a finger at her as he addressed the other three. 'Will you listen to that, eh? The little woman's getting too big for her boots, don't you think?'

Ned Selby stared hard at his son, and felt ashamed. Martha, however, stepped forward to tell Rosie, 'It's the *man* who decides these things, my girl, and don't you forget it!'

'And don't *you* forget, we're not in your parlour now, Mrs Selby.' Rosie had long ago ceased to be afraid of this woman, though she was always wary of the influence Martha held over Doug.

Looking smart in a navy-blue two-piece and white frilly blouse, Peggy had remained near the pram, occasionally glancing out of the window and watching for the arrival of Adam Roach. Now, she was relieved to see a black vehicle draw up by the kerbside. 'He's here!' she cried, and when Doug rushed out, everyone else turned their eyes towards the door. A strange atmosphere settled over the tiny parlour. Ned Selby mentally recalled his meeting with Adam and wondered whether he had made headway with his ambitious plans; Martha's thoughts were more vindictive because she remembered how Rosie and Adam had once been sweethearts. Peggy too remembered and was quietly anxious, while Rosie herself was lost in a multitude of emotions, trembling with excitement one minute and filled with dread the next. What would he look like? Would he think she was still attractive? Would he be put off by her swollen stomach and puffy ankles? And what about Doug? She had no doubt he had insisted on having Adam here out of sheer jealousy, and knew he harboured a deal of loathing towards both her and his former friend; her for choosing Adam before him, and Adam for being more handsome, more intelligent, and in Ned Selby's words, 'A decent bloke'.

All manner of thoughts raced through her mind as she heard Doug go to greet Adam. Even the sound of Adam's voice touched her deep inside. 'Here he is!' Doug came through the door first, a look of triumph on his face and his odd-coloured eyes lost in a broad smile. 'The man himself,' he said, stepping aside to let

Adam enter. And all the while Doug kept his sharp gaze on Rosie. She felt his animosity and, not for the first time, was afraid of the awful consequences this day might bring.

Adam came into the room, and at once the little parlour was full of his presence. He was everything Rosie remembered: tall and incredibly handsome, his dark eyes smiling, and his thick mop of black hair spilling over ears and forehead as though it had a life of its own. As he paused, his gaze seeking her out, his broad shoulders seemed to fill the doorway and the parlour was cast into shadow. 'Good to see you, Rosie,' he said, and the sound of his voice turned her heart over.

'I'm glad you're here,' she replied truthfully. She knew Doug's eyes were on her, but couldn't tear her gaze from Adam. For the two of them, time seemed to stand still. It was almost as though they had gone back to that fateful day when he went into the forces. Nothing had happened between . . . no long periods when he didn't write and she was devastated, no Doug, no deceit, no wedding. There was just Adam and her, and a love so powerful it almost breathed.

It was Peggy who wisely broke the spell. 'You ain't changed much,' she remarked. 'But then, I don't suppose any of us has.'

'You certainly haven't,' he said. 'You're still as bright as ever.' He kissed her on the cheek, and would have done the same for Martha if she hadn't glowered at him and stepped away.

'There's no time for all that,' she said sullenly when he shook hands with Ned. Turning to Doug, she suggested, 'We'd best go, son, or we'll be late.'

'Wait, there's someone I want you all to meet.' Adam looked behind him and ushered in Connie who was pretty as a picture in a bright pink outfit and black high-heeled shoes. 'This is Connie,' he explained. Addressing Doug he said, 'I hope you don't mind, only I didn't want to leave her behind.'

Doug's face lit up. 'Mind? Whyever should I mind?' He stared her up and down and was pleased with what he saw. Then he turned to Rosie. 'Come along, sweetheart. Like Mam says, we don't want to be late now, do we?'

In the church, Rosie's son was quiet as a lamb. Instead it was

143

Doug who exploded when the priest declared the little chap's name to be 'Danny'.

'You're wrong,' Doug interrupted, and was embarrassed when all eyes turned to him.

'Oh?' asked the priest, looking puzzled, 'What shall I christen him then?'

Rosie spoke out. 'Danny,' she said calmly. 'His name is to be Danny. That's the name he's registered by, and that's the name he'll be christened.' Fortunately, the registrar was an old man with an understanding nature. Changing the child's name had not been the arduous task she had feared. She smiled at Doug and his eyes bored through her. Some time back she had called on this very priest and she gambled that Doug wouldn't cause a scene here in church in front of everyone. Thankfully, she had been right.

The ceremony continued, and throughout it Rosie could feel Doug's hostility towards her. But she didn't care. Her son had been given the name she had chosen, and if she had to pay the price later, then so be it. For now, the moment was hers, and she was revelling in it.

The child slept when the priest poured water over his head, and snoozed through the heartfelt rendering of 'The Old Rugged Cross'. He slept on while Adam cuddled him, and was still deep in dreams when they arrived back at the house. 'I've never known an infant so good,' Connie remarked, and everyone had to agree.

'I'm proud you asked me to be godfather,' Adam told Doug, who had stopped off at a mate's to collect a crate of ale and was now busy working his way through it.

'Who else would I ask but my best mate?' Doug said sulkily. The more he drank, the surlier he became.

Aware that Doug was deliberately being offensive, Adam guessed the reason and made a great effort to stay away from Rosie. Leaving Connie chatting to Doug, he spent a few minutes making small talk with Martha, who seemed hell-bent on making him feel unwelcome. He was relieved to talk with Ned, who discussed various current affairs, including the recently retired world heavyweight, Joe Lewis, and the lifting by the Soviets of the Berlin blockade. The talk soon came round to home, and industry, and inevitably came the question, 'Are you making your fortune then, Adam?'

'Not yet, but I'm heading in the right direction.' Occasionally he would glance at Rosie, and everything he had achieved so far meant nothing to him. 'I've got one wagon and just recently took on the lease of a yard and premises ... the very same premises where we met at the sale.' Ned Selby seemed impressed so he went on, 'Ben Saxon did me a favour I'll never forget.' He explained how it had all come about, and added, 'It was the kick-start I needed. There'll be no holding me now!'

Especially not now, he mused bitterly, sneaking a glance at the heavily pregnant Rosie and thinking how lovely she was. In fact, he said the very same thing to her when Doug fell asleep on the settee and the two of them were able to sneak a moment together. 'I don't think I've ever seen you look more beautiful,' he said, smiling into her brown eyes.

'Away with you,' she said softly, feeling suddenly shy beneath the intensity of his gaze. 'I'm seven months pregnant and looking like the side of a house.'

'Not from where I'm standing.'

'Thank you for that.'

'Rosie?'

'Yes?'

'Tell me, are you happy? *Really* happy?'

She couldn't bring herself to answer. Instead she looked to where Connie and Martha were talking. 'Your girlfriend ... she's very pretty.' She was grateful that Connie had innocently drawn Martha's attention from her, because ever since Adam had crossed the room to talk with her, Rosie had been acutely aware of her mother-in-law's eyes boring into them.

'Rosie, you didn't answer my question.' Adam was insistent. 'Are you happy?'

'Of course. You can see for yourself.' It was more than she dared do to let him think otherwise. Besides, her pride wouldn't allow him to believe she was less than happy. Not when he obviously had a woman of his own who he 'didn't want to leave behind'.

'You've changed.'

'Oh?'

'You're quieter, more subdued . . . as if the spirit has gone out of you.'

'What nonsense!' She forced herself to laugh. 'How like a man. Here I am, with a bairn in arms and seven months carrying, and I'm expected to leap about like a two year old.' It wasn't his fault but she felt angry, sad even. Perhaps because he was right. She had changed.

'I didn't mean that, and you know it.' He glanced at Doug who had woken up and after talking briefly to his father was now glowering at them from the other side of the room. '*He* hasn't changed at all. He's still fond of the ale, and his temper hasn't improved.' When she didn't answer, he voiced the suspicion that had played on his mind ever since he had arrived here. 'I don't have to ask why he wanted me as godfather?'

'Are you sorry?'

'If he expected me to be that, then he's the one who should be sorry.' He gazed down on her lovely face, and sensed the sadness there. 'Doug should thank his lucky stars that he has a woman like you for his wife,' he murmured. 'Walking out on you was something I can never forgive myself for.' Leaning towards her, he lowered his voice. It was now heavy with emotion. 'If there should come a day when you need me, I'll be there. Always remember that.'

'Thank you, but I honestly don't see how I'll ever have need of you,' she lied. 'Doug has his faults, I know, but he takes good care of us.' Her gaze went first to the sleeping child, and then to her husband. He was beginning to drink heavily and she feared he might cause trouble. 'It seems such a long time since we were all footloose and fancy free,' she mused aloud, 'but that's all water under the bridge.' She wondered how she could sound so matter-of-fact when inside she was crying out for him. 'The past is gone, and it's only the future that counts. We all have our own roads to travel.' In her own way she was trying to tell him that even if she should ever need his help, she could never ask for it.

Her words were like a slap in the face to Adam. 'I'm sorry,' he said, 'I didn't mean anything. It's just that, well, I hope we can remain friends, you and I? But of course you're right. It's no

146

good dwelling on the past. Nothing ever comes of that.' So they talked about the child and how bonny he was. They talked about how Adam was working his way up in the world, and how Ben was a good man who had advised him well. They had a little laugh about how Martha was still an old warhorse, and Rosie told him what a good friend Peggy was. They chatted about everything in general and nothing in particular, and not once after Rosie's timely warning did they talk about themselves. In her heart, though, Rosie cherished these precious moments together, and he was tortured by her nearness.

It was Doug's slurred and bad-tempered voice that broke the spell between them. 'What the bloody hell's this then?' he asked, flinging his arm round Rosie's shoulders and almost knocking her over. 'A secret meeting, is it? Or can anybody join?'

Adam's face broke into a wide smile. 'I was just telling Rosie how well she looked . . . considering.'

'Oh, aye?' Pushing Rosie aside, he thrust his face forward, glaring up at Adam with bloodshot eyes. 'And what's that supposed to mean, eh? Considering?'

Adam knew Doug of old. He had seen him the worse for drink before and, though he could have shaken him by the scruff of the neck, simply smiled and told him, 'Considering the wonderful do she's put on here, the food and everything. It's a credit to her. It can't have been easy.'

Doug laughed. 'Rubbish! This sort of thing is what women are best at.' Turning his attention to Rosie he asked, 'Enjoyed every minute of it, didn't you, sweetheart?'

'If you say so.' Her brown eyes deepened with anger. She didn't like being made to look a fool, especially in front of Adam.

Sensing her animosity, he tightened his grip on her shoulders, making her wince. 'Oh, I *do* say so!' he murmured, kissing her on the mouth and laughing aloud when she pulled away. 'No need to be shy in front of old friends,' he argued.

To make his point he would have kissed her again, but lost his balance. It was Adam who saved Rosie from being squashed against the sideboard. 'Don't you think you've had enough of that?' he asked grimly, pointing to the jar of ale in Doug's fist; most of the frothy brown liquid had splashed over Rosie, but she chose not to make a fuss in front of everyone. Instead she quietly dabbed at the stain with her hankie, realising with dismay that her one best skirt was possibly ruined.

'Stop that!' Doug knocked her hand away. 'Bugger the skirt,' he yelled, 'I'll buy you a new one. Or would you rather *he* bought you one, eh? Then happen he'd have a right to take it off when he felt like it!' With every word he jabbed at her arm until it was red raw.

Something snapped in Rosie then. Whether it was the sight of Martha's smug and satisfied face gawping at them from across the room, or whether it was Adam's grim features that told her he was about to wipe the floor with Doug, or even her own humiliation at being shown up in front of everyone, she would never know. But in a minute she was facing Doug, telling him in a calm and dignified voice, 'Please keep your hands to yourself and lower your voice. Have you forgotten this is our son's christening, and that we have guests here?' Forcing a nervous smile while he stared at her open-mouthed, she went on, 'If you can't behave in a civilised manner, I think it might be a good idea for you to go upstairs and sleep it off.' Nothing in her manner betrayed the fact that she was inwardly seething.

But Doug's fury was written on his face for all to see. 'You little bitch!' Grabbing her by the arms he shook her hard. 'Who the hell are you to talk to me like that, eh? I ought to take the skin off your back!'

'Not if I have anything to say.' Adam had seen enough. Stepping forward, he gripped the neck of Doug's shirt. 'I reckon Rosie's right. I'll even give you a hand up the stairs if you like.' There was a threat in his voice and Doug turned a sick shade of grey.

'Take your bloody mitts off me!' Squirming and kicking, he still couldn't shake himself free from Adam's vice-like grip. 'And get out of my house, you bugger, afore I have you thrown out.' He looked to his father, but Ned was thoroughly enjoying seeing his son being taken down a peg or two. Martha had taken a few steps forward to intervene, but was forced to a standstill when her husband caught hold of her arm. It seemed she was more shocked by his action than by the heated argument between Adam and Doug.

Out of the ensuing awkward silence, it was Rosie who spoke.
'I think you'd better go,' she told Adam. 'And it might be wisest
if you never came back.' He couldn't have known what an
immense effort it took for her to say that. 'I'm sorry,' she whispered. Those last two words were only for the two of them, and
he knew that.

'I understand,' he told her, 'and I wouldn't want to outstay
my welcome.' For a seemingly endless minute his grip on Doug
remained fierce, before he released him with such force that the
smaller man staggered backwards. 'I wish I could turn the clock
back, but I can't. Rosie's your woman now, though God knows
you don't deserve her.' His warning was unmistakeable. 'You'd
best look after her, Selby.'

Doug didn't answer but watched him go, calling Rosie back
when she would have gone with him. 'He can find his own way
out!' he snarled. When Martha rushed to his side to comfort him,
Doug pushed her away. Peggy winked at Rosie who, in spite of
her husband's warning, hurried after Adam and Connie; at the
same time acknowledging Peggy's wink with a knowing smile.

As she came to the door, Rosie's smile froze on her face when
she saw Connie with Adam at the car. Connie was on tiptoe with
her arms round Adam's neck. She was kissing him.

Quickly, before they saw her, Rosie returned to the parlour,
the image of what she had just seen burned on her mind. Yet she
chided herself for feeling hurt. She had no right. Adam was his
own man, and she had only just finished telling him in her own
way that they must not dwell on the past. Yet, she did hurt, and
she envied Connie with all her heart.

'Are you all right?' Peggy met her at the door.

'I'm fine, thanks, Peggy.'

''Course she's all right!' Martha had found her voice and was
fighting fit. 'Why shouldn't she be? If anybody should be upset,
it's our Doug here. That bloody Adam Roach has a thing or two
to answer for!'

'Shut up, Mam!' Swaying on his feet, Doug came across the
room to stare at Rosie. She had never seen him so enraged.

'I *won't* shut up,' Martha cried, coming between him and Rosie.
'I'm your mother, and I don't take kindly to folk like Adam
treating a son of mine like that.' She pushed at Doug's chest with

the flat of her hands. 'You ought to have leathered him. Why didn't you leather him?'

'GET OUT!' He saw her words as an accusation that he was either a coward or a lesser man than Adam. On top of everything else it was more than he could bear. With one great sweep of his arm he lifted her clean off her feet and sent her flying against the heavy oak table. There was a grinding thud, one awful minute when she stared at him with wide open eyes, then she fell to the floor with her back strangely twisted and her arms trapped beneath her own weight.

'God Almighty!' Ned fell to his knees beside her, cradling his wife and afraid to move her. 'She's hurt bad.' Looking up at Doug with accusing eyes, he ordered, 'Get out of my sight, you!' When he spoke to Peggy it was to ask, 'Get the ambulance, lass . . . quick as you can.'

As Peggy fled from the house, Rosie urged her to run as fast as she could. With a surge of compassion she stared down on Martha's unconscious form, and, rightly or wrongly, blamed herself for all that had happened here.

Rosie wasn't to know that Martha's back was broken, and that she would never walk again. In her worst nightmare she could not realise how the events of this day would make her already unhappy life even more unbearable. For the moment all she could think was that Martha had been hurt, and needed help.

Ned and Doug went with Martha to the Infirmary. Before they left, Doug made Rosie a promise. 'I'll teach you to interfere with my plans!' he told her, and she knew he was referring to her having secretly changed the child's name. He then blamed her for his mother's injury. Ned, however, was quick to reassure her.

'It was an accident,' he said softly. 'I don't want you getting yourself in a state.' Glancing at her swollen stomach, he said, 'You've got enough to worry about. Anyway, Martha's a tough old bird. She'll be all right.'

Peggy offered to stay, but Rosie would have none of it.

'You look awful,' Peggy argued. 'Are you sure you're all right?' She wasn't exaggerating when she said Rosie looked awful. Her face was drawn and pale, and she looked desperately tired. Feeling the need to be left alone with her troubled thoughts, however,

Rosie assured her she was fine, and Peggy reluctantly went home to tell her mam what had happened, and to explain how she wouldn't have Rosie's life 'for all the tea in China'.

No sooner had Peggy gone than Rosie felt the first pangs of early labour. Two hours later the pains were intensifying and she could hardly breathe.

In the early hours, doubled up in agony and alone except for little Danny, Rosie made her slow tortuous way down the street. When Peggy opened the door she found her friend crumpled in a heap on the step.

When those brown eyes looked up at her, Peggy's heart turned over. 'Help me, Peggy,' she pleaded. 'I don't want to lose my baby.'

Yet she knew. In her heart Rosie felt the child's life ebbing away inside her. It seemed like a penance, a shocking punishment for secretly wanting Adam's love.

In that moment she prayed she would never set eyes on him again.

CHAPTER ELEVEN

'The end of another week, thank God.' Kindly-faced, with the shoulders of a bull elephant and hands the size of shovels, the man's eyes were stark white in his sooty face, and when he walked across the office little pockets of coal-dust fell from his clothes, leaving a dark trail across the floor. 'Have you ever known such a stifling day?' he groaned. 'Hottest July I can ever remember.' Wiping his brow, he left a smear of white skin exposed beneath.

Adam was busy putting the wages together, his head bowed and his lips silently counting. Undaunted, the fellow continued, 'It's a miracle the way you've picked up more work when other merchants are losing hand over fist.'

'That's because I have a good eye for an opportunity,' Adam teased. It was Friday night, and like his men he felt lighter of heart with a good week's work behind him.

Taking up the envelope, the fellow laughed. 'Hopefully the missus won't miss the price of a pint out o' me wages.' He said something then that struck Adam to the quick. 'What would you know about being wed, eh? You've been too bloody clever to get yourself lumbered with a wife and family.' He meant it as a compliment, not realising how he had touched on Adam's deepest longing.

Tipping the money into his large palm, the fellow counted his wages. 'But you do pay yer men well, I'll not deny that.' Standing up and stretching his back with a groan, he wet his lips with the tip of a pink tongue. 'I reckon a pint of ale would do me nicely. By! I can taste it slithering down me throat . . . dry as a bone I am. Matter o' fact, being as I've done a deal of overtime this

153

week, I reckon I might treat meself to a *couple* o' pints.'

Adam met the other man's gaze, his dark eyes brooding now. 'Off you go then, before the ale gets warm.'

'I can wait, if you want to join me?'

'You'll wait a long time. There's four wagons to clock in yet, and a mountain of work to be done before I can lock up.' He waved a hand over the pile of papers and documents strewn across his desk. 'I'll be honest, Tom. There are times when I wish I was back on the rounds with the rest of you lads. In fact, now that the business is thriving and I can afford it, I've been thinking about getting somebody in to take all this paperwork off my hands. I'd much rather be shifting coal any day of the week.' He stretched himself in the chair and thought of Rosie. When a man's back was heavy with his work, his heart was somehow quieter.

'Don't be daft, man!' At fifty years of age, Tom Lockwood was the oldest man there. He felt it his duty to look after the others, and to this end he spoke his mind now. 'You could get a clerk to do the paperwork, but who could you trust to go after the contracts, eh? Who would grade the coal and haggle about price? What about the buying and selling of wagons? You said yourself we need to keep a good fleet. Get somebody to do the paperwork, aye! No doubt you can offload the financial side of it too. But there ain't nobody who can run this business like you, and it's you we rely on to keep our wages coming in. No. There's more to running a business than doing paperwork and making up the wages. This is your own business. You've worked bloody hard to get where you are in a tough world. And, as far as I'm concerned, there ain't nobody who can look after your own interests better than yourself.'

Adam had to laugh. 'Sounds like I should set *you* on?'

Tom pursed his mouth and winked an eye while he considered that. 'No,' he said at length, vigorously shaking his head. 'You've got the best man doing the job now. Like the rest of 'em, I know what's needed, but there ain't a man here who could do what you've done, and that's the God's honest truth. There's them that lead, and there's them that's content to follow. Besides, think on what you've achieved here. Hand it over for somebody else to take care of, and you could end up with nothing.'

Adam leaned back in his chair. He knew that what had been said made sense. All the same, in spite of everything he had gained, he felt as though he had lost a great deal more. 'Sometimes I don't feel as though I've achieved *anything.*'

'Away with you! To take on a rundown outfit and build it up to a flourishing concern, and all in less than two years. Well, I'd say *that* were some achievement.'

'I was in the right place at the right time, that's all.'

The other man shook his head. 'There's more to it than that. You're a grafter like the rest of us, but you've got brains too. That's what makes the difference between us. And you ain't afraid to take a chance when you see it.' He chuckled. 'To tell you the truth, none of us ever thought you'd do as well as you have . . . but you've proved us wrong, and I'm glad of that.'

'So am I.' Holding out his hand, Adam suggested, 'You'd best let me have this week's work-sheet . . . unless you don't want any wages next week?' In that minute two other men walked in, eager to collect their wages and make for home or the ale-house.

Producing the work-sheet from his overall pocket, Tom leaned forward. Lowering his voice he said, 'I hope you don't mind me speaking my mind?' When Adam assured him that he didn't mind in the least, he visibly relaxed. 'Right then. I'll be off for that pint.'

Once outside, Tom strode off in the direction of The Liverpool Arms. It wasn't long before one of the other men caught up with him. 'Heard you say you were going for a pint,' he confessed, 'I've a thirst of my own. Mind if I walk along with you?'

The two men talked over what had been said in the office, and they were agreed that they would never find a better boss than Adam Roach. 'Still an' all, it's a crying shame,' the second man said, 'a young fella like that . . . living on his own in Ben Saxon's big old house. He ought to have a pretty wife to come home to, and a dozen kids running round his arse.'

'It wouldn't do no harm if he were to tell that brassy blonde where to get off. Old friend or not, she fetches more trouble to his door than any dozen kids. What! It's a wonder there ain't been bloody murder between that landlord fella and our man. If you ask me, there's trouble brewing, and I wouldn't like to make a bet on which one of 'em will come off worse.' From the look on his face when he glanced at the other man, it was plain he was thinking of Adam.

Thankful that the last man had gone, Adam finished his paperwork and locked up for the night. It had been an especially busy week. For months now he had battled to secure the lucrative contract to supply all the coal for the local Infirmary. The competition was fierce, and all the sealed tenders had been submitted last Tuesday. Adam had learned only yesterday that he was the successful candidate, and even now could hardly believe it. He was in no doubt that he had made many enemies over that particular contract, and because of the extra work was forced to consider increasing his manpower and consequently reappraising his whole operation. He was into big business now, and such were the implications that he still had not told the men.

The office was situated in the ground floor of the old house. When Ben Saxon was alive, the room had been a junk-hole, cluttered from top to bottom with rubbish. Since Adam had taken over the house some two years back, the room had been transformed; there was a desk and two filing cabinets, and the walls were painted a quiet green.

The window of this particular room still overlooked the street, but Adam had commissioned builders to knock through a door leading straight to the yard. It had proved to be a real asset because now there was easy access in and out of the office and the men could come straight in on pay-day instead of going all the way round to enter the house from the scullery door.

In fact, the entire house had been subject to a great deal of change. The large room at the back was now a comfortable place where Adam could relax at the end of a long day. The freshly painted walls reflected the light, and were now hung with pictures; landscapes mostly, though there was also a seascape whose quiet mood and sun-kissed waves never failed to soothe his troubled heart. The big black fire-range had been restored to its original beauty, and the new light oak furniture was both attractive and serviceable. Where the floors had been covered in tattered old carpet, the boards were now exposed. Adam had spent many back-breaking hours sanding and polishing the boards, until now the beautiful grain in the wood made a splendid sight.

When Adam took over the tenancy on this house, every room was neglected and dingy. Now, they were bright and easy to live in. The kitchen had been remodelled the most with Adam ripping out everything that could move and refitting it with a new sink, a shiny gas-cooker, and a large pine dresser that was six feet wide and reached almost to the ceiling. Right along the wall nearest the sink, he had fitted a deep shelf that served as both table and a working surface.

The bedrooms were all painted in soft colours and, like the downstairs living-room, every floorboard was exposed and polished, with soft scatter-rugs spread to give a homely feel. The main bedroom, which overlooked the street, had a huge four-poster bed which he had acquired from the rag-man after a long and enjoyable haggle. Built of dark oak and draped with a patchwork eiderdown which Connie had bought in a curio shop, it was a wonderful, comfortable thing. Together with the dark oak dresser and wardrobe and two armchairs which he'd rescued from the tatter's wagon for a pound and recovered with his own hands, the room reflected his own strong personality. It was undoubtedly a man's room. Yet, every time he entered it, Adam saw how it lacked a woman's touch, and couldn't help but think about Rosie, and wonder what other touches she would bring to the whole house.

Now he wandered from room to room, feeling incredibly lonely, and wondering, not for the first time, where his life was leading. He felt empty, unfulfilled and immensely sad. Suddenly he could feel her in his arms, soft and warm, loving him as he loved her. 'You bloody fool, Roach!' he snapped angrily. 'When will you learn, she's done with you for good?' The truth seemed finally to overwhelm him, and suddenly all the trappings of success meant nothing.

The mantelpiece clock struck eight-thirty. After a long soak in the bath-tub, and afterwards an enjoyable meal of crusty bread and cheese, Adam was seated in the living-room. The *Evening Telegraph* was set out before him on the table. He kept a close eye on local adverts, for you never knew when a bargain might crop up, or who was undercutting who in the coal war.

The sound of a knock on the door startled him. He wasn't expecting anyone, but his thoughts flew straight to Connie. 'Surely to God she's not been fighting with him again, has she?' he asked himself as he went quickly to the front door. When he opened it, he was astonished to see not Connie but Ned Selby. 'Good Lord! You're the last person I expected to see,' gasped Adam.

'I'm sorry to disturb you.' Doug's father looked haggard, and his shoulders were stooped as though he was carrying a heavy load. In these two years since Adam had last seen him, he had aged more than ten. 'I've been meaning to come and see you for weeks now,' he explained as Adam led him into the living-room. 'Only it's taken some courage, and lately I don't have too much of that, I'm afraid.' A look of embarrassment crossed his downcast features. 'I shouldn't have come so late. I can always come back tomorrow.'

'You'll do no such thing!' Adam told him. 'I'm delighted to see you, Ned, and now that you're here, I won't let you go that easily.' He ushered him into the most comfortable armchair. 'What'll it be . . . a jug of ale down at the pub, or a mug of tea?' His smile was designed to relax the older man, and it did.

'I don't feel like going to no pub, lad.' Even though Adam was now a mature man of thirty, Ned still saw him as the boy who'd grown up with his own son. 'If it's all the same to you, I'd rather stop here. What I have to say isn't for any other ears.'

'Fair enough.' Adam was both intrigued and bothered by Ned's comment. 'A mug of tea then, eh?'

Ned shook his head. 'Not for me,' he declined. 'Like I said, it's taken a lot of courage to come here, and if I don't speak my mind now, that courage will be gone.'

At once Adam sat down, his dark-eyed gaze settling on the older man's face. 'Go on, Ned,' he encouraged kindly, 'I'm listening.'

Ned couldn't speak for a minute. He wiped his hands over his face, then sighed and looked up through workworn fingers. His eyes were those of an old, old man, and when he spoke the words

158

were barely audible. 'I've come to the end of the road, lad,' he murmured, and his voice broke with emotion.

Adam was loth to reply. He felt instinctively that to do so would be an intrusion. The eyes that stared at him now were tear-filled in the folds of that aged face, reflecting the tortured soul inside. When it seemed as though Ned was lost for words, he said softly, 'You're safe enough speaking your mind here. Whatever you have to say won't go no further, I can promise you that.'

Taking his hands from his face and leaning back in the chair, Ned sighed deeply, his gaze never leaving Adam's concerned face. 'I don't know how to start,' he confessed. 'So much has happened that you don't know about.'

'Is it Rosie? Is she in some kind of trouble?' Sitting bolt upright now, Adam was ready to leap from the chair.

'No. I didn't come to talk about Rosie . . . at least not directly.' When Adam relaxed into the chair, Ned went on, 'It's not one thing in particular. I wish to God it was, because then I might be able to cope.'

'Whatever it is, Ned, I'm sure you're man enough to deal with it. And if I'm able to help in any way, you know I will.' This man had been like a father to him.

'I know. And I'm ashamed that I didn't reply to your letters.'

'I thought you must have your reasons.'

'Oh, it was all to do with our Doug and misplaced loyalty, I suppose. And, to be honest, I'm a bloody coward. In spite of what you might think, I've *allus* been a coward at heart. But I've kept them all, though, and I've read them time and again.' He smiled for the first time since entering Adam's house. 'I'm proud of you, lad. You've done well for yourself.' He glanced around the room. 'Your own business, and a grand place like this to come home to. By, you have! You've done well.'

'It was you who taught me everything I know. The master and the boy.' Memories came flooding back as Adam looked at Ned with affection. 'I owe you a lot.'

'Aye, maybe, lad. But now the master's gone down in the world while the boy has gone up. And rightly so, because I couldn't see what was happening under my own nose.' No sooner were the words out then Ned clamped his lips together for fear he might let slip more than he'd intended. *The last thing he wanted was for Adam to suspect how Doug had been robbing his own father blind.*

'You're not making too much sense, Ned. What exactly do you mean about not seeing what was happening under your own nose?'

Thinking swiftly, Ned sought to allay any suspicion. 'What I mean is, I should have seen it coming . . . the market failing the way it did . . . customers going elsewhere to save a penny or two.' He slammed one gnarled fist into his palm. 'Damn and bugger it, Adam! I should have seen it. But I didn't, and now I'm in a spot o' bother.' He laughed, a low ugly sound. 'In fact, I'm about to lose it all.'

Adam sat up. 'Not if I have my way! How much, Ned? How much to keep you on top?'

Ned smiled again, and this time it was filled with warmth and regret. Oh, if only his own son was made of the same stalwart goodness. 'Bless you for that,' he said, 'but I've not come here looking for a loan.'

'What then?'

'I want you to buy me out.'

Adam couldn't believe his ears. 'Give over, Ned! You've *years* before you need to think of retiring.'

'Oh, I don't mean to retire, lad.' Now that the subject had been broached, he was more at ease. 'Whatever would I do with myself, eh? No, what I'm asking is this . . . buy me out at market value, then let me carry on as though it were my own business? That way, I'd have the capital to get myself out of debt, and the only people who'd know that the business was yours and not mine, would be the solicitor and the two of us. Then, when the time *does* come for me to retire, it'll be yours to do with as you like.'

Adam didn't care for the proposition. 'You built that business up with your own sweat and blood, and believe me, Ned, I know now just what that entails. Besides, it was always there as your security for when you grew old. If I buy you out, where will that security be then, eh?'

'Look at me, son,' Ned entreated. 'I *am* old.' Following Adam's thoughts and afraid that he would turn him down, he went on,

'If I don't sell to you, I'll sell to somebody else, and they'll not give me a fair price the way things are. There are jackals out there, lad, and if they smell blood, they'll move in for the kill. As it is, I've still got two good rounds . . . not as lucrative as they once were, I'll admit, but they're good rounds all the same. If I could get a fair price, an outright sale should fetch enough to get me out of trouble, and happen leave a little to put by for a rainy day.'

'You really mean to sell, don't you? Whether it's to me or to somebody else?'

'That's right. I've already made discreet enquiries . . . sounding out one or two possible buyers. Honest to God, son, you wouldn't believe the measly offers I've had. Daylight robbery, that's what it is.'

'And you'd want to stay on, you say?'

'I'll run it well for you, you know that. Besides, to tell the truth, I need the wages.'

'What about Doug?' Always, his thoughts came back to Rosie.

'He doesn't work for me any more.' Quickly now, before Adam could voice the questions forming in his mind, Ned added, 'We went through a real lean time last year. I told him to keep his eyes open for a more secure job. He found it with Leyland's.'

'I see.' Adam pictured Doug leaving his own father floundering, and hated him for it.

'No, you *don't* see!' Ned had been worried that Adam's instincts would tell him a story. Afraid it might be the right one, he said, 'It were *my* decision that Doug should go, not his.' That at least was the truth, though he was careful not to reveal that he had sacked Doug after a bitter argument. 'There are other things too,' he went on. 'Things that have taken their toll on both me and the business. Martha had a bad fall . . . her back was broken and she's paralysed from the waist down. She's confined to her bed, and there are times when I have to neglect my work to look after her.'

Adam was shocked. 'I'm sorry to hear that.' He had always been in awe of Martha, and knew what a taskmaster she could be. All the same, it was a terrible thing. 'Is there anything at all that I can do?'

'There's nothing anyone can do. The thing is, she's become harder, more difficult to handle. Earlier on, I paid for a nurse to look after her . . . most of the money I earned went on medical expenses and the like. But I didn't mind that, because it meant I could work all day same as usual, and at night I tended her best I could. That went on for about a year, until she became hostile to the nurse, and every blessed other that came after.' He smiled, but there was sadness in his face. 'At least I knew she was feeling better, because she was getting more like her old self.'

'So you had to stay with her all day?'

'I couldn't very well leave her on her own, though I'd be a liar if I didn't say she wore me to a frazzle. Like the little trooper she is, our Rosie offered to go round each day, but Martha went mad at the idea.' When he saw the surprise on Adam's face, he quickly explained, 'There's always been resentment there. Martha's never really forgiven Rosie for taking Doug away. Anyway, the fact of the matter is this . . . she wouldn't let nobody but me take care of her. Consequently, the business was badly neglected at a time when I should have been concentrating all my efforts on keeping it afloat.'

'Let me lend you the money you want, Ned. Take as much time as you like in paying it back. I would never press you, you know that.'

Ned was adamant. 'You should know I'm not a man to borrow,' he said firmly. 'I've made up my mind. The business has to go. There's nobody else who'll buy it at the right price, and pay me a wage to stay on. If you're not interested, I'll be on my way. If I've caused you any embarrassment, I'm truly sorry.' He made to rise from the chair, but sat down when Adam began to speak.

'What price had you in mind?'

'I'm open to offers.'

For the next half hour they talked earnestly, and a deal was done. Adam would pay Ned a generous lump sum for the goodwill and all equipment, and in return, for an exceptionally handsome wage, Ned would stay on to run it as he had always done. The transaction was to remain a secret between the two of them; with the exception of the solicitor named by Ned.

'I wouldn't be in this dire position if I'd had the guts to stand up to Martha when she insisted I look after her. But all that will change now, and you can be sure I'll look after your interests. First thing on the morrow, I intend to find a nurse to stay at the house while I'm out at work.' Ned smiled wryly. 'I'm certain that if Martha is made to realise how much money we owe, she'll come to her senses right enough. Of course I shan't tell her how, thanks to you, we're now able to rid ourselves of debt. I'm not denying she's been ill, and my heart goes out to her for the predicament she's in. For a woman like Martha, paralysis must be the worst punishment of all. But she's made of hard stuff, and to be honest I reckon it's time she was made to realise the world doesn't revolve round her all the time.'

'It's a sorry situation, and I don't envy you, Ned.'

'I've been too bloody soft! What's happened has made me see that.' His face hardened. 'Like I say, things will change from now on.'

'I hope it all works out for you.' Adam could never remember the big man being so furious. But then he recalled everything Ned had told him, and it seemed that, though Martha had suffered a sad and terrible affliction, Ned had gone out of his way to protect her from undue hardship or discomfort. Like the man he was, he had shouldered all the responsibility and allowed himself to be dominated. It seemed that Martha's unfortunate accident had not only ruined her life, but everything Ned cherished along with it. And, seeing him now, Adam could only imagine the state of affairs that existed between him and his wife.

'Don't forget what I said . . . if there comes a time when you want to buy back the business, you've only to ask.'

Ned stood up then, his hand outstretched. 'I'll never be able to thank you enough,' he said, taking Adam's hand in a firm grip. 'As for buying the business back, it's all too late for that. No, I'll be satisfied just to earn a wage and let someone else do the worrying.'

'Ned?'

The big fellow smiled. 'I might be an old fool in some ways, but I know what's been on your mind ever since I stepped through that door. You want to know about Rosie?'

'How is she . . . really?'

'She's well. They all are.' He was careful not to mention how Rosie had lost the child she was carrying.

Adam eyed him curiously. 'I've written many times and sent presents for my godson, but as yet I've had only one reply, and that was a very polite letter from Rosie. Doug has never written.' He thought on that for a minute. 'I've been tempted to go and see them, but wondered if I'd be welcome after what happened at the christening?'

Knowing in his heart that Adam was the right man for Rosie, Ned wondered whether he should tell him everything ... how Rosie was suffering too. Time and again Ned had threatened Doug himself after discovering he had beaten Rosie for no good reason. And though she could give as good as she got, the constant rows and unhappiness were beginning to tell on her. Yet, for all that, he had to deter Adam from ever visiting. 'I'm afraid what happened on that day has turned Doug against you. And you're right, I don't think he would welcome another visit from you, more's the pity.'

'That's what I thought.' Adam had long suspected that, but to hear Ned say it now was upsetting.

'Still, you never know,' Ned remarked in a brighter voice. 'He's bearing a grudge now, but happen there'll come a day when he'll value the friendship you once had.' Like any father would, he lived in hope that Doug would come to his senses and that he and Rosie would resolve their differences. Even though he could not in all honesty see that happening, he still couldn't put the final nail in the coffin by telling Adam what was really going on. Ned was in no doubt that if he knew of Rosie's miserable life, Adam would move Heaven and earth to get her back. He couldn't risk that. He had to cling to the smallest hope. 'Rosie and Doug have never been happier,' he lied, and felt the shameful flush creep up his neck. 'I'd best be off,' he said, wanting to get away. 'Thanks to you I've got a new lease of life, and there's a lot to be done.'

They shook hands on the doorstep. Adam went back inside and Ned went on his way to the railway station.

'Well, look who's here!' Connie's voice came at him out of the darkness. 'It's me, Connie!' she laughed, holding on to the lamppost for support. 'You remember ... Adam brought me to your grandson's christening.' Swaying and laughing, she was obviously the worst for drink.

Ned recognised her at once. 'Of course.' He recalled how Connie and he had talked, and he had thought her a delightful creature. 'How could I forget?' In the halo of light she looked like a child. 'I've been to see Adam,' he explained. 'A matter of business.'

'Business, eh? Well, you couldn't find nobody better than my lovely Adam. He's becoming a wealthy man now, did he tell you that? I love him to bits, but it ain't for his money, oh no! Between you and me, I don't know what I'd ever do without him. What! I'd have been in the gutter before now. But he's always watched out for me. And no matter what some people think, he always will.' Stepping towards him, she rubbed her hand up and down his shirt collar. 'He's a good man. One of the best.' Holding out her hand, she said, 'Look . . . a wedding ring. You're talking to a married woman now. Bet he didn't tell you that, did he, eh?' In the lamplight the ring flashed like so many stars.

'No, he never mentioned it.' Ned felt elated and dismayed at the same time; dismayed because he had been so bent on talking about himself and his troubles that he hadn't even asked Adam about his own life. And yet he felt elated because now it was clear that Adam had finally put his love for Rosie aside and taken a wife. The news couldn't have been better. 'Congratulations,' said Ned, putting out his hands to steady her. 'You're right. Adam is a good man.'

She giggled at that. 'And you should know. Adam tells me you were like a father to him.' Lurching sideways, she would have fallen had he not caught her.

'I think I'd best get you to your door,' he offered, gently propelling her up the street towards Adam's house. 'Been out celebrating, have you?' He couldn't help but wonder whether she and Adam had rowed. Sadly, he thought, it seemed to be the way with married folk these days.

'I've been enjoying a women's night out,' she said with a twinkle in her eye. 'And I've had a little too much to drink. Oh, but don't you worry about me,' she chuckled, 'Adam will put me to bed as usual.' Realising he was holding her upright, she told him haughtily, 'It's very kind of you to help me, but I *can* manage, thank you.' Shaking herself free, she toddled off.

He watched her go up the steps, and waited for the door to open. He saw her fall into Adam's arms and went on his way with a smile on his face. 'Looks like you've got your hands full with that wife of yours, lad,' he said. With Adam agreeing to help him, and now, seeing how Adam had taken himself a wife, Ned felt as though a lead weight had been lifted from him. All in all, his visit here had been more worthwhile than he could ever have hoped.

'What in God's name have you been up to now?' Adam was exasperated. 'You shouldn't be wandering the streets at this time of night . . . and drunk into the bargain!' He almost had to carry her into the living-room.

'Now now, don't scold me.'

'I ought to tan your backside.' He tumbled her into a chair. 'Go on then. What's it about this time?'

'He's a pig!'

'I told you that before you married him.'

'I know, and I should have listened.' She giggled again. 'Oh, but I do love him.' She sat up at the sound of someone knocking on the front door. 'If that's him, tell him you haven't seen me.'

'I'm not lying for you again, Connie.'

'Don't tell him I'm here!' she pleaded. 'Please, Adam.'

Tutting, he shook his head. 'I should feel sorry for him. I don't know who's the worst, you or him.'

'It's *him*!' she retaliated, 'And I'm teaching him a lesson, that's all. It'll do him bloody good to worry about me.'

He had to smile. 'I know the feeling,' he chuckled, going to the door. 'It's the last time though, Connie.'

'Okay.' Her pretty blue eyes grew wide.

'Stay quiet then.'

'Okay.' Her eyes grew wider still. 'I know what to do.'

He knew from experience there was no use trying to reason with her, so he hurried down the passage to open the front door. 'Oh, it's you!' He hoped he sounded suitably surprised.

His previous landlord was a greasy little man with a pencil thin moustache and a weaselly smile. 'Is Connie with you?' he wanted to know. From the doorstep he peered down the passage. 'When we have an argument, she always comes to you.' He sounded peeved.

'Not this time.' Adam had no intention of letting him in. He had never liked the fellow. 'I haven't seen her for a fortnight.' Under his breath, he asked the good Lord to forgive him.

'I don't know where to look next. One minute she was putting April to bed, and the next she'd disappeared.'

Adam was alarmed. 'If Connie's gone missing and you're here, who's with the little girl, now?'

'Oh, don't concern yourself. We've got a friend staying, and *she's* keeping an eye on April.' Connie's daughter was now a delightful toddler. On the many occasions when Connie had fled to Adam for comfort, he and the infant had become fast friends.

'You should know Connie by now. I dare say she'll come back when she's good and ready.'

'If she comes here, you'll tell her to come straight home, won't you?'

'Depends.'

'On what?'

'On whether you've been hitting her again.'

The little man grinned. 'These days it's more likely to be *her* hitting *me!*'

'I hope you're not looking for sympathy?'

Bestowing a sour expression on him, the man turned away to go at a fast and furious pace down the street.

From behind him Adam could hear Connie shouting, 'Good shuts to the old bugger! It'll serve him right to think I've done a bunk!'

Coming into the living-room, he wasn't surprised to see her lounging in the chair with her bare legs hanging over the side. She looked as though she'd been in the wars; her yellow hair was unkempt, the top two buttons of her low-cut blouse were undone, and her tight skirt had ridden up her thighs. 'He'll be sorry,' she muttered, and for the first time that night a note of bitterness crept into her voice.

Patiently, he looked at her pretty face, which was made up like a clown's. 'All right, what have you been up to?'

'Teaching the bugger a lesson, that's what.'

'You heard what he said?'

'About you sending me home? Ah, but you wouldn't turn an old friend away, would you, eh?'

He chuckled. 'I must have been a fool to tell you where I'd moved to.'

'At least I don't have to sleep on the settee these days.'

'I should make you sleep out in the yard.'

'But you won't.'

'Fool that I am.' He rolled his eyes and sighed. But something about her cheeky manner ensured that he could never stay angry with her for long.

'Same bedroom?'

'You know where it is,' he answered wearily. After saying goodnight, he went to his own room while she made herself a hot toddy. Some time later, his bedroom door opened and Connie peeped in. 'Want some company, big boy?' she whispered.

'Goodnight, Connie!' The tone of his voice brooked no argument.

'Goodnight then.' He heard her singing as she went along the landing. Then the slam of her bedroom door. And he knew that, like so many times before, when he woke, she would be gone.

The house grew quiet and the night became darker. Soon the darkness lifted with the promise of a new day, and still he couldn't sleep.

Ned had set him off thinking about the past, and Rosie. Though he carried her lovely image deep in his heart, it had been an age since last he saw her. But now he felt so close to her that he could hardly breathe.

CHAPTER TWELVE

Peggy's mam was goggle-eyed. 'Oh, you should have seen it!' she gabbled excitedly. 'There we were, all crammed into the grocer's front parlour . . .' She glanced at Peggy and Rosie to make certain they were still listening, then, with a proud little smile she went on, 'Of course he invited only his very best customers, and Lord knows I spend enough money to have *bought* him that blessed television set, so it's only right that I should watch the Coronation on it. Mind you, it were stifling hot in that little room. Twenty-two of us there were . . . packed in like sardines.'

'Well, you wanted to see it, our mam, and now you have, so stop moaning.' Peggy winked at Rosie and as always, Rosie enjoyed their light-hearted banter.

'Too right I wanted to see it!' Peggy's mam exploded. 'And so did you two buggers, but you couldn't, 'cause you ain't customers.' Recalling the physical discomfort of being pressed between Mrs Armitage and that big woman from Leyton Street, she blew out her cheeks and flapped the top of her blouse. 'Good job an' all if you ask me, 'cause two more bodies in that parlour and we'd have all fainted right out.'

'You shouldn't have been too uncomfortable, our mam,' Peggy argued. 'It were a miserable day . . . cold and raining.'

'Oh, aye! And wouldn't you know it would be the coldest wettest June *outside*, but inside that parlour it were like a bloody hothouse.' She smiled then and said dreamily, 'Oh, but you should have seen it. I'm telling you, it were a sight to last me a lifetime. Did you know there were two million people waiting outside in the rain?' Without waiting for an answer, she went on: 'It were wonderful! Our Elizabeth looked so tiny and fragile, a princess

169

made Queen . . . Oh, and the pageantry! June the second 1953 . . . a red letter day I'll never forget.'

'No, and I don't suppose you'll ever let *us* forget it either.' Getting up from the table, Peggy took out the cups and washed them at the scullery sink. 'Anyway, I thought you and the kids were going to the flicks?' she called out. 'They've been waiting out there for ages.'

'My God! I forgot about them.' In a minute she was gone, leaving the instruction: 'Mind this place is tidy when I get back, or I'll want to know the reason why!'

'Honest to God, she gets worse as she gets older.' Peggy laughed as she flopped into an armchair. 'Come and sit here,' she told Rosie, who was still seated at the table where the three women had enjoyed a light tea, along with the exciting report on the new Queen's Coronation.

'I'll help wash up the tea things while little Danny's still fast asleep,' Rosie offered. Her brown eyes glanced to where her young son lay fast asleep on the settee. Now four years old, he was making a fine young lad. His mop of thick hair was the same dark brown colour as Doug's, but his eyes were warm and brown like Rosie's. She had always been thankful for that because one set of odd-coloured eyes staring at her was more than enough.

'Hey!' Peggy's commanding voice stopped her in her tracks. 'I didn't ask you over so you could wash up the tea things. Come and sit down. It ain't often these days we can have a natter, and it'll not be long before our mam's back. It's the first time she's taken the kids to an early evening matinee, and it means she'll have to let them stay up late.' Laughing aloud she promised, 'I wouldn't mind betting she'll be back within the hour on some excuse or another.'

Rosie was glad to sit and talk. In her heart she was deeply unsettled. Yet, even when she was seated in her armchair, she couldn't bring herself to talk about certain matters. Instead she said, 'I would have loved to have seen the Coronation on television.'

'You heard it on the radio, didn't you?'

'Well, yes. But it's not the same, is it?' She didn't reveal how Doug had thrown the radio across the room, and now it was broken beyond repair.

'I suppose not.' During the brief silence that followed, Rosie seemed a million miles away, unaware that Peggy was regarding her with concern. It was only when Peggy spoke, asking whether she had something on her mind, that Rosie looked up with surprise. 'What do you mean?' She had been thinking of Adam, and of what Ned had told her some time back. The news that Adam was married had raised all manner of emotions in her, and even now, after all this time, she couldn't stop thinking about him.

'I know you.' Peggy half guessed the truth. 'Whatever's on your mind, the best thing is to talk about it. A trouble shared is a trouble halved, they say.'

'Do you think he's completely forgotten about me?' Her brown eyes were soulful.

'Ah! Adam, you mean?'

'You knew I was thinking of him, didn't you?'

'I've known you for too long, gal. And no, even though he's married and should have, I don't expect for one minute he's forgotten you. After all, *you're* wed, and you ain't forgot him, have you, eh? You love him just as much as you've ever done. And what good will it do, tell me that, for God's sake?' She thought about Rosie's hard life and that miserable husband of hers, and wished with all her heart that it could have been different. But it wasn't, and now perhaps it never would be. Shaking her head in frustration, she pleaded softly, 'Oh, Rosie, will you *never* stop tormenting yourself?'

'When Ned told me he'd married that young woman who came to the christening, well, I don't mind admitting, I was surprised. Oh, it's not that I didn't think she was nice, because she was. But somehow she just didn't seem to be the type I imagined he'd settle down with.'

'I thought the same, and yes, she did seem nice enough in her own way . . . chatty and friendly. But, like you, I never saw Adam as going for the brassy hair and deep cleavage type.'

'Happen we're being unkind?'

'Happen.'

'I *hope* he's content. It would be nice to think he had a family of his own . . . children . . . a son maybe.' She smiled, but it was an unhappy expression.

'It's just as well he got wed because now you know he's out of reach.' Peggy believed the only way to be kind was to be cruel.

'You know he's done well for himself?' There was pride in Rosie's voice.

'I should know, gal. You've told me a million times.' Like Doug and Martha, they believed what Ned had told them about bumping into Adam at another sale two years back. They weren't to know he had sold his business to Adam.

Deliberately thrusting Adam from her mind, Rosie was genuinely delighted to report, 'Ned goes from strength to strength. Lately, he's a different man. It's as though somehow he's shed a deal of worry. Certainly his business is picking up, and what's more, he's just taken delivery of a new wagon.' Rosie had a great deal of affection for her father-in-law, and had never blamed him for sacking Doug. The only regret she had was that Doug could not be the man his father was.

Thankful that Rosie had wisely changed the subject, Peggy answered, 'I've always liked Ned Selby, and I'm glad he's doing better these days. Do you think he'll take Doug on again?'

Rosie's eyes darkened with anger. 'Why should he? Doug's unreliable, lazy, and half the time he's drunk. I'm not surprised Ned's turned his back on him. Besides, he's got his hands full with Martha.' Every day she grew more and more vindictive, making that poor man's life an absolute misery. And though she did feel sorry that Martha must be suffering too, Rosie couldn't help but wonder at Ned's immense patience.

'What? You mean she's playing up again? I thought she'd got to like this new nurse.'

'You know her. She can't like anyone for more than five minutes at a time. Yesterday when I went round to see if I could be of help in any way, Martha was throwing a terrible tantrum. Ned was sitting at the kitchen table with his hands over his ears, and the nurse was close to tears.' She sighed. 'If you ask me it's only a matter of time before that one follows the others out of the house. Soon Ned won't be able to get anybody to look after her.'

'By! She's a wicked old sod. If I was Ned, I'd bugger off and leave her to it!'

Rosie shook her head. 'Never. Ned's a good man. He'd have

to be at his wit's end to do a thing like that.'

'Oh, aye? And how long will it be before he is at his wit's end? The man isn't a saint, when all's said and done.'

Noises from the front hallway made Rosie look round. 'Sounds like your mam's back,' she said with a chuckle.

Peggy listened too. 'Well, I'm buggered!' she exclaimed. 'So she is. What did I say, eh? I knew it. She must have ants in her pants because she can't sit still for two minutes at a time.'

After a lot of shouting and pushing and cries of, 'I wanted to see the end of the picture!' the little tribe came bundling into the parlour. 'These two wouldn't keep quiet,' Peggy's mam moaned. 'Three times the usherette threatened to throw us out.' She cuffed the three eldest round the ears. 'Get washed and off to your beds.'

'We wanted to watch the end,' they argued in unison. But when she glared at them, they soon scooted into the scullery.

'An' this little sod wet himself!' she explained, pushing the young one before her.

'I ain't!' he wailed, tears in his eyes as he appealed to Peggy. '*I* wanted to watch the end an' all.'

'Why didn't you wait for the end, our mam?' Peggy wanted to know. 'There's nothing worse than seeing a picture nearly all the way through, and not knowing what the end is.'

All she got for an answer was the suggestion that she: 'Mind your own bloody business!' It was obvious that taking all the children to the pictures had turned out to be more of an 'adventure' than Peggy's mam could cope with. She looked harassed and weary. 'I'd best make you a brew,' Peggy offered.

'That's nice, dear,' sighed her mam. Then she fell into the nearest chair as though her legs had given out.

When little Danny woke with a start and began screaming at the top of his lungs, Rosie thought it was a good time to leave. She said goodbye to Peggy's mam, who smiled wanly from the depths of the chair. 'See you later,' she called out to Peggy who was in the scullery overseeing the younger ones. But Peggy was being bombarded with complaints and didn't hear.

Outside, Rosie sighed and glanced at her son, who was now contentedly walking along beside her, his hand securely tucked into hers as they made their way home. 'It's a madhouse,' she said, ruffling his brown hair. 'But it's a happier house than ours, and that's a fact.'

That night, Doug came home late. He was in a foul mood. 'Old Leyland's going senile,' he complained. 'He says I came back to work drunk after the break. He's a bloody liar. I was sober as a judge.' His face twitched as he spoke. It was obvious to Rosie that he *had* been drinking and that he badly needed a drink now. 'What money have you got?' he asked, pushing his tea aside. The meat pie had been light and fluffy, oozing with gravy and crispy at the edges when Rosie baked it earlier. Now, after being kept warm for two hours, it was dry and shrivelled.

'None for booze, I can tell you that.' Taking up the poker she jabbed at the coals with it. All day she had felt a chill, and now she feared she was coming down with 'flu.

In two strides he was across the room. Snatching the poker out of her hand, he flung it into the grate. 'What the hell have you got a fire lit for?' he snapped. 'It's the middle of summer for Christ's sake. We ain't got money to waste!'

'No, and if you get sacked from Leyland's, for being drunk at work, we won't have money to feed us neither.' Her eyes were hard and bright as buttons.

Incensed when she dared to defy him – and that was too often lately – he insisted, 'You've got money all right. I know you keep a few shilling tucked away.' When she said nothing but continued to challenge him with those forthright brown eyes, he reached out to touch her mouth. 'You're a handsome-looking woman, Rosie,' he murmured. 'To be honest, I don't know which I want most . . . a pint of ale at the pub, or an hour on the floor with you.'

She hated it when he talked like that, as though she was little better than a jar in his fist. 'There's two shilling under the clock.' In that moment, giving him the few coins she had put by was the lesser of two evils. 'Take it, and to Hell with you!'

For a long unbearable moment he stared at her with avaricious eyes and she felt herself cringing. Taking her by the shoulders he leaned forward to cover her mouth with his. 'Later,' he promised, reluctantly pushing away. He laughed in her face before taking the money from the clock and making a hasty exit. 'Right! I'm off for a pint or two okay?' he said brightly. She didn't answer. She was astonished that he should expect her to.

After he had gone, she went upstairs to check her son. Sound asleep and contented, he had obviously not stirred since she took him up some two hours before. 'You're such a little innocent,' she murmured. 'But you're growing so fast, and I'm afraid he might pass his bad ways on to you.' When Danny was a baby, the fear wasn't so great. But now that he was a little man in his own right, talking and listening and looking up to his dad with the loving eyes of a son, she was desperately afraid. 'I won't let him ruin you,' she vowed.

But that night, when Doug stumbled into the bedroom, blind drunk and hardly able to stand, she wondered whether in the end he would ruin them all.

Over the next few days, Rosie kept out of Doug's way as much as possible. When they went to bed she pretended to be asleep, and when he woke in the morning she was already downstairs preparing his sandwiches for work. Two out of three nights he managed to arrive home sober, and though he badgered her for money, she was determined that he would not have the money which she had hidden in the rent book.

The days came and went and each was the same as the one before. As though in defiance of her mundane existence, Rosie sang at her work, keeping the little house clean, taking advantage of the fine weather to dip the blankets and scrub the mats. Every grubby garment in the house was washed, ironed and neatly stacked into the laundry cupboard at the top of the stairs, and the windows were cleaned until they sparkled. Even grumpy Ada from the bottom house had to admit, 'By! Them windows look a right treat, lass. Happen you should come and do mine?' If Ada had been badly or old, or if her legs were swelled up with varicose veins, Rosie might well have offered, but the woman wasn't much older than Rosie herself. She was also known to be bone idle so Rosie just smiled and thanked her, and quickly retreated into the house.

On Thursday night Doug went out on money borrowed from 'an old mate'. Peggy popped round and told Rosie she just had to get out of the house. 'I've had a bad day at work and the kids are making that much noise I'm tempted to suffocate the little sods,' she groaned. They talked until nearly midnight and Doug still wasn't home. 'Happen he's found another woman and run off with her?' Peggy suggested.

'I should be so lucky!' Rosie laughed.

Realising how the time had run away with them, and that her mam would have put the children to bed by now, Peggy rose to leave. 'Keep sane, kid,' she told Rosie, and Rosie promised she would.

After letting Peggy out, she locked the door and went to bed. A quick peep into the smaller bedroom told her that little Danny was still sleeping. *She* couldn't sleep though. Her mind was too alive. She thought on what Peggy had said just now, about Doug running off with some woman. 'There's no other woman would have you!' she muttered, her gaze following the antics of a spider on the ceiling while she reflected on her own life.

After a while she slid down between the sheets and closed her eyes. She felt strangely afraid, as though waiting for something to happen. It was an odd and eerie feeling, so strong that she had to get out of bed and go downstairs again. 'You must be losing your mind, Rosie gal,' she chuckled. Making herself a cup of cocoa, she curled up in the big armchair, thoughtfully sipping at the hot drink and warming her hands on the mug at the same time. 'It's freezing in here!' she moaned, taking Doug's overcoat from the back of the door to fling over her legs. Once the night had settled, the cold chilly air from outside seeped in and the temperature dropped.

She finished the cocoa and put the cup in the hearth. She felt tired, yet not tired enough for sleep. She dozed and woke, and thought awhile. The clock ticked the minutes away, chiming the hours between, and soon the night was almost gone and the sky infused with the colours of morning. And still Doug wasn't home. 'Why should I care if you choose to stay out all night?' she asked aloud. 'God only knows, I should be pleased to see the back of you.'

All the same she couldn't help but worry. When all was said and done he was her husband and, even though she was eaten up with regret for having committed herself to him, she was essentially a woman who took her marriage vows very seriously. This was the first time he hadn't come home, and she began to wonder whether he really did have a woman who served him better. That made her smile. If there was a woman out there who wanted him, she only had to ask.

Having sat in the chair for so long, she began to ache all over. The mantel clock struck four, and above the chimes came the sound of a child crying. Hurrying up the stairs, she found the boy on his feet and rubbing his eyes. 'Shh, sweetheart. It's all right.' He felt cold to the touch as she helped him back to his bed. Tenderly she settled him beneath the blankets. 'Mammy's here,' she coaxed, Lying down beside him, she folded him in her arms and there she fell asleep.

It was the rattle of the milk cart that woke her. Sitting up with a start, she was momentarily confused. With sleepy brown eyes she glanced round the room and finally her gaze fell on the lad sleeping beside her. Realisation dawned and she got carefully from the bed.

It was only a few steps along the landing, but even before she had opened the bedroom door, she sensed that Doug was still not home. When he was here there was a brooding atmosphere in this house she loved. Whenever he was out, it was as though the sun shone in every room.

Dropping on to the bed, she drew her hands over her face as though to wipe away the sleep that was still on her. 'Where in God's name is he?' she murmured. Going to the window she looked out. Apart from the milk cart that was already turning the bottom of the street, there wasn't a soul to be seen. A quick glance at the bedside clock told her it was still only five. Soon the street would be filled with the sound of people wending their way to work, but for now the men were still snoozing, although the women were no doubt busy in their kitchens, packing sandwiches and making flasks of tea.

Wide awake now, Rosie went downstairs and boiled a kettle full of water. That done she tipped most of it into the bowl, tempered it with a rush of cold water from the tap, and stripped off her nightgown; a thorough strip-wash, and then to work. She cleaned out the ashes from the fire-grate, washed the hearth and brought the tiles to a high polish, then she pushed the sweeper over the carpet and dusted the furniture. By that time it was nearing six-thirty.

Just as she was straightening her back from her labours, a small voice called out from the parlour doorway, 'I'm hungry.' The little fellow looked tousled and tired as he came into the room.

'You're as bad as your mam,' Rosie softly chided when he put his small hand in hers. 'I reckon we both look the worse for wear.'

Fastening his pyjama top, she sat him up at the table. 'What do you fancy, little man?' she asked, tickling him under the chin with the tip of her finger.

'Chuckie egg,' he said, his drooping eyes growing round with anticipation. 'And soldiers.'

'Well now, that's just what your mammy fancies too,' Rosie told him. 'But we don't have our breakfast before we've washed, do we?' He shook his head. 'Right then. I've had my wash, so now it's your turn.' Lifting him from the chair, she took him by the hand and together they went into the kitchen. Using the remaining water in the kettle she soon had him washed, dried and dressed in clean grey trousers and pale blue jumper. 'There!' Running the comb through his bouncy brown locks, she regarded him with pride. 'You're a handsome fellow, I'll not deny it,' she told him. But he wasn't listening. Instead, he was reaching into the cupboard where Rosie kept his toy box. 'Play trains,' he said proudly. Falling to his knees, he tipped the entire contents on to the carpet.

'All right,' Rosie said. 'But only until I've got breakfast. Because then we're going out. I want to catch Grandad Selby before he goes to work.' She would need to be quick, as these days he always left home sharp at eight o'clock. 'Happen *he* might know where your daddy got to last night . . . and where he is now!' she muttered beneath her breath.

The breakfast was soon got ready, and though Rosie's appetite vanished once the soft-boiled egg was in front of her, little Danny eagerly devoured his, together with Rosie's toasted soldiers as well as his own.

'Come on then. Let's be off.' She wiped his face with the flannel and soon the two of them were ready for the chilly morning air, the boy looking smart in his short grey jacket and cap, and Rosie wearing her best tweed coat and the new red scarf which Peggy had bought her last Christmas. 'If we hurry, we'll just catch the early tram,' she said, gripping Danny's hand and running him down the street.

The tram was about to leave, but the driver saw them and waited. When the conductor swung the boy on to the platform, Danny thought it was all a wonderful game and, much to the annoyance of a fat woman with a snappy pooch, insisted on pulling faces at it all the way to the next stop where he and Rosie disembarked.

Ned Selby's house was only a short walk from the tram stop at the bottom of Artillery Street. As they approached, Rosie saw the wagon parked on the common opposite. It was Ned's. 'Good. Your grandad hasn't left yet,' she said, hurrying the rest of the way. Excited at the prospect of seeing his grandad, the boy ran ahead.

By the time Rosie got to the house, Ned had already answered the door. 'By! I thought you were gonna knock the blessed thing down,' he chuckled, stooping to swing the child into his arms. Smiling at Rosie, he added, 'It's a mercy he didn't wake Martha or I'd have got the length of her tongue and no mistake!' It was obvious she had been difficult again.

As he led the way into the back parlour, Rosie sensed there was something very wrong. Usually proud of his appearance, Ned was wearing a grubby shirt which was haphazardly rolled up at the sleeves and hung open to the waist. He was unshaven and red-eyed, looking much like Doug when he'd been on one of his drinking binges. 'Is everything all right?' she asked, taking off her coat and eyeing him with concern.

He didn't answer straightaway, obviously aware that the boy was paying attention to all that was being said. 'Let's get your coat off, young 'un,' he said, undoing the buttons on little Danny's jacket. 'Then, if you're quiet, you can play with your grandad's lead soldiers.' No sooner were the words out of his mouth than the boy was off. He knew the soldiers were kept in a tin box beneath the sideboard, and would play contentedly for hours if let be.

'What's brought you and the young 'un here so early?'

Conscious that he must look a sight, Ned hastily rolled down his sleeves and did up the top buttons of his shirt. His self-conscious action only heightened his unkempt appearance.

Standing by the table, Rosie leaned forward, her hands supporting her weight, and her dark eyes worried as she remarked pointedly, 'Ned! You didn't answer my question.'

'What was that?'

'I asked if anything was wrong?' When he hesitated to answer, she came round the table and looked fondly up at him. 'There is something, Ned. I could tell the minute I walked in. For a start you're not shaved or dressed properly, and normally you'd be ready to leave for work.'

'I'm not going to work today, lass.'

'That's not like you, Ned.' A thought struck her then. 'It's Doug, isn't it?' If so, it wouldn't be the first time he had caused trouble in this household. Many was the time he had taken his mother's side, even when he knew his father to be in the right.

Ned was surprised she should ask such a question. 'You must know I haven't clapped eyes on Doug for weeks. He's never forgiven me for sacking him, and only visits when I'm out. Even then he manages to upset his mother so she's difficult to handle for days after.' He raised his eyes to Heaven. 'Though, God knows, it wasn't him this time.'

Rosie had her answer as far as Doug was concerned. He hadn't been here last night, and he wasn't here now. But Ned was upset, and for the minute her concern over Doug took a back seat. 'Is Martha being difficult? Is that why you're not going to work?'

He sighed and closed his eyes. 'You could say that. She's been impossible these past few days. Last night when I got home the nurse met me at the door. Her face was bleeding where Martha had thrown a cup at her. So now she's gone and she's not coming back.' He dropped his head and stared at the floor. 'I've failed her, but as God's my judge, I can't think where I'm going wrong.'

'Oh, Ned!' This new nurse had been with Martha for even less time than the last one. 'You've done more than any man could be expected to do, and still she won't help herself. Why can't she see what she's doing to you?'

Seeming not to have heard, he went on, 'I can't blame the

nurse. Poor thing, she were only a young lass, and Martha's enough to try the patience of a saint. Honest to God, I don't know what to do next.' He sounded desperate. 'Sometimes, I'm tempted to take off and leave her to her own devices, then she'd be put in a place where they'd know how to deal with her.' His eyes were moist with threatened tears as he looked up for reassurance. 'I know it sounds heartless, lass, but what am I to do, eh? Tell me that.'

'You say she's in a sulk?' To tell the truth, Rosie was tempted to go up there and give her a piece of her mind. But she knew from past experience that it would go in one ear and straight out the other.

'She's sleeping now, and she bloody well ought to be 'cause she's kept me awake all night with her bawling and shouting. When the lad knocked on the door just now, I half expected it to be the neighbours come to complain.'

'They're good folk, Ned. I'm sure they understand.'

'Mebbe, but I'd like to bet they'll not put up with it for much longer.' He glanced up at the ceiling. 'She can be a wicked bugger when she sets her mind to it. I've told her I can't afford to lose my work . . . that we have to have someone in to take care of her, but she won't listen.'

Sad to see him like this, she made up her mind. 'Don't worry, Ned. I'll stay with her.' Though she had always disliked Martha, Rosie had never been afraid of her. 'You get yourself off to work.'

He was astonished. 'I can't let you do that. What! She'd take a deal of pleasure in making your life a misery.'

Rosie smiled craftily. 'She's been trying to do that for years, but so far I've survived. She won't get the better of me, I can promise you that.'

His eyes lit up and a smile crept over his tired old face. 'Are you sure, lass?'

'I'm sure. Now be off before I change my mind.'

He gazed at her and for a minute he was too choked to speak. But then he grabbed her by the shoulders. 'You're a good lass,' he muttered. 'And though I say it as shouldn't, our Doug doesn't deserve you.'

She laughed wryly. 'I'm always telling him that.'

He rushed around, getting a wash and telling Rosie how he'd already got everything prepared for Martha's breakfast. 'She normally wakes with the appetite of a bull elephant,' he said. In a surprisingly few minutes he was ready for off. 'I'll try and be done early so you can get home,' he promised. 'I don't want you getting in trouble 'cause Doug's tea's not ready when he gets in.'

Rosie had had no intention of telling him about Doug, but somehow it slipped out. 'That's *if* he comes home.'

'Are you saying he's taken to staying out?'

'Something like that.' When she realised it was only another worry for Ned, she quickly assured him, 'I'm not too worried so you mustn't be. No doubt he'll turn up with his tail between his legs and a fine excuse to tell.'

Ned paused, ready to take off his coat again. 'But it's not like him to stay out, is it? It hasn't happened before, has it?'

'Many times,' she lied. 'Now get off to work. I saw a gang of big lads hanging round your wagon. If you don't hurry, they'll be off up the street in it.' That did the trick. There was nothing more precious to Ned than his lovely coal-wagon. In a minute he was out of the door and away. When Rosie went into the front parlour and looked out of the window, it was to see him driving past the house, looking far more contented than when she'd arrived. 'Now for the old battle-axe!' she said through gritted teeth. 'Like mother like son, and that's a fact.'

'I want Ned. Where's Ned?' Martha was shocked to open her eyes and see Rosie standing there with her breakfast tray. 'Get out of my house. Bugger off, damn you!' She was a terrible sight to see. Her eyes were sticking out like hatpins and her hair was a spiky mess because she had flatly refused to let the nurse comb it. Stretching her neck, she yelled at the top of her voice, 'NED! NED, GET HER AWAY FROM ME!'

'You can shout 'til the cows come home.' Rosie calmly placed the tray on the bedside table. 'But he won't hear you because he's gone to work.' With her hands on her hips she stared at the other woman, a quiet test of strength going on between them.

'You're a bloody liar!'

'No, I'm not.' Rosie smiled sweetly. 'It's your own fault. After what you did, the nurse won't show her face again. Ned's gone to work, so I've come to look after you for the day.'

Martha's eyes were bulbous and her face turned a deep shade of red. 'You'll get out of my house now, or I swear to God I'll raise holy hell.'

'Hmh! Sounds like you've already been doing that. If you hadn't attacked the nurse, she would still be here now. As it is, Ned's running out of capable people to take care of you.'

'None of your business what goes on in this house.'

Rosie's face was grim. 'I'm very fond of Ned and I don't like to see you hurting him the way you do . . .' Martha was about to interrupt, but Rosie shouted her down. 'No, you're going to listen to me. It's about time somebody told you what a tiresome and selfish creature you are. All right, so you've had a tragic accident and I'm truly sorry that it happened to you. But there's nothing I can do to change that, and neither can Ned. Though no man could have done more to make you comfortable.'

'NED, YOU BASTARD . . . I KNOW YOU'RE HIDING DOWN THERE.' Martha had her hands over her ears and a murderous look on her face.

'He's gone to work, I tell you.' In a softer voice, she appealed to Martha's better instincts. 'Don't you realise how worried he is, Martha? If he doesn't go to work, he can't pay the rent and you'll be evicted.'

'Don't talk bloody stupid! Ned will provide for me. He always has.' There was just the faintest note of concern in her voice.

'He's always provided for you because he's always worked. Take away his work, and the money dries up. You know what I'm saying is the truth. Ned might have had a bit of money put by for a rainy day, but the rainy day's come and it won't go away. Think about it, Martha. Where do you suppose the money came from for the nurses you keep frightening off? And what about the special aids he's got for you?' Pointing to the strap above the bed, she explained, 'This useful contraption for instance . . . the special bath, and the wheelchair . . . it all cost money. You know yourself the coal industry has been going through a bad patch and it's dog eat dog. But, as you say, Ned's always provided, and he will go on providing – if you treat him like the human being he is, and not something to be whipped and tortured, as though what happened to you was his fault.'

'It *was* his fault! And yours too. I blame the lot of you.' Turning away, she grabbed the pillow and pressed it to her ears, at the same time yelling and screaming for Ned to come and: 'GET THIS BITCH OUT OF MY HOUSE, DAMN AND BUGGER YOU!'

Rosie sighed and shook her head. She could only imagine what Ned had been going through and her heart went out to him. As always, Martha had no intention of listening to reason. 'All right, Martha. I've had my say, and I'll leave you alone now. After you've had your breakfast, I'll give you a wash.'

'You come anywhere near me and I'll wring your bloody neck!' She glared at Rosie and her eyes were dark with loathing. 'I might have lost the use of my legs, but the Devil compensates. The strength has all gone to my arms. I mean what I say, so you'd best stay away from me.'

Rosie shook her head, considering what to do. The mood she was in, Martha might work herself up to a fit. Then Rosie would never forgive herself. 'I see. There's no getting through to you, is there? All right then. I won't come upstairs again, unless you want me to. But you have to eat, and you'll need to go to the toilet.'

'I'll eat nothing, and Ned can take me to the toilet.'

'You'll be waiting a long time, Martha, because he won't be home until this afternoon.'

'Piss off.'

Undeterred, Rosie lifted the tea cosy from the teapot and pushed the tray closer so it was within easy reach. 'If you need me, tap on the floor with your stick.' Ned had given Martha a cane and with it she had driven him almost beyond endurance, banging on the floor to summon him up the stairs so he could suffer tirades of abuse. When Rosie told him he was too quick in responding, he said he was afraid to keep her waiting in case she was really in trouble. But she never was.

With as much dignity as she could muster, Rosie departed from the room, to the tune of Martha swearing and threatening. 'You'll be sorry, Ned Selby,' she told the bedroom door. 'I don't know what game you're playing, but you'll be sorry!'

Closing the door, Rosie leaned against the wall outside, her eyes closed and her face raised to the ceiling. 'God give me strength,' she murmured. And, as the day wore on, she certainly needed it.

'What's the matter with Gran'ma?' Frightened by all the noise, Danny was waiting at the foot of the stairs.

'It's all right, sweetheart.' Rosie ushered him into the front room. 'She's in a bad mood, that's all.'

'She's *always* in a bad mood.' There had been a time when Martha doted on her grandson, but these days she was only interested in her son, Doug. Even though he had crippled her, he was the light in her life, and he could do no wrong.

'I'll tell you what, sweetheart.' Rosie sat on the rug beside the upturned cardboard box. 'I reckon Grandad would be thrilled if you could give all these soldiers a really good clean.' Plucking one up between finger and thumb, she said, 'If I give you a rag and some polish, do you think you could have them all ready for inspection?' Her smile was bright, but she was subdued after the scene with Martha. She was also riddled with guilt. The woman was disabled after all. So had she gone too far . . . or been too cruel in her frankness? Should she have merely humoured her? But then the answer came back . . . a resounding no! Martha had punished Ned for too long, and it was time she was told a few home truths.

'Can I wash their faces too?'

Deep in her own thoughts, Rosie's attention had wandered. 'What? Oh, yes, 'course you can,' she laughed, giving him a cuddle. 'I think that's a marvellous idea.'

For the next few hours Rosie busied herself about the house, and her son washed and polished the lead soldiers. In between making a meat dumpling and scraping the potatoes ready for Ned's evening meal, Rosie willed her mother-in-law to knock on the ceiling. But the silence was unnerving. Compelled to go up and check that everything was all right, she climbed halfway up the stairs but restrained herself from entering the room, especially when she could hear Martha still chuntering madly to herself. 'I'm here if you want me,' she called in a soft voice.

'You've only to knock on the floor.'

The chunnering stopped and Martha's voice fell quiet. 'All right, I'll play your little game,' Rosie told her, going down the stairs. If that was the way Martha wanted it, there was little she could do. And anyway, it wouldn't be too long before Ned was home. With a bit of luck, he might have managed to find someone who was prepared to look after the cantankerous old bugger.

What with the baking and clearing up after, and the games between with little Danny, Rosie was surprised at how quickly the morning sped by. But the next two hours crept along, and still Martha remained sullen and un-cooperative.

At five minutes to four Ned returned. 'Finished early,' he told her with a bright smile. 'By! That does me good to get out of the house.' His smile faded as he remembered what lay waiting for him upstairs. 'How is she?'

'Same as usual. She hasn't thrown anything at me, but that's because I was ordered out of her room and threatened with certain death if I returned.' Rosie had to chuckle but her sympathy was with him. 'I'm sorry, Ned. I did try but she's been calling for you.'

His whole countenance changed. Where there had been a light in his eyes when he came in, there was now only despair. 'It can't go on like this,' he murmured, sinking into the fireside chair. 'You'd think there'd be somebody who could help, but it seems when you're in this situation, you're expected to cope best you can. Oh, the authorities do their bit, but it never seems to be enough. By rights she should be in a hospital of sorts.'

Before Rosie could answer, another voice intervened. 'You'll put her away over my dead body!' Doug strode into the room. 'What the hell's going on here, eh?' he demanded. 'It seems I've arrived just in time. By the sound of things you're all set to put my mam in a home.' He stared from one to the other, condemning them with his expression.

'Oh? So you've decided to show your face then?' Rosie was astonished that he wasn't rolling drunk.

'I'll deal with you later,' he snapped. 'Right now I'm having words with my dad here.' Addressing Ned, he went on, 'Well? I

186

reckon you've got some explaining to do.'

At once Ned was on his feet, eyes blazing. 'Don't question what you don't understand!' He hadn't forgotten how this man, his own son, had robbed him blind when every penny was needed for Martha. 'You of all people should know I do my level best by your mother,' he said, controlling his anger. 'As for an explanation, I'd say I don't owe you *anything*.' The look on his face conveyed his meaning, and Doug was momentarily conscience-stricken. 'Now, if you don't mind, I think your mother needs me.'

When Ned had gone, Rosie was compelled to ask, 'What did your father mean . . . "you of all people"?' Something in Ned's manner told her there was something very wrong between these two, something she had not seen before.

'I think you might be forgetting your place, woman.' Doug sauntered over to the fireplace and stood with his back to it, his odd-coloured eyes regarding her with contempt. 'You'd do well to keep your mouth shut.'

'Forgetting my place, eh?' Rosie mimicked. 'And where exactly do you think my "place" is?'

'You should be at home. I'll want my tea on the table when I've finished here.'

'Oh? And what about you? Shouldn't *you* be at home?' Stepping closer she remarked in a low voice, 'I don't suppose you'll tell me where you were last night?'

'What's been going on here?' Deliberately evasive, he answered a question with a question. It wouldn't do to let her know how he'd been subbing from work, and had spent an entire week's wages. On top of that, he'd been late there today after spending the night with a whore. The boss had given him a final warning, and now he was in the right frame of mind to cause a heap of trouble here. 'If he thinks he's putting my mam in a home, he's got another think coming.' He would have gone on, but Martha's call cut across his words. 'You get home!' he told Rosie. 'There's things to sort out here.'

As he went from the room she shouted after him, 'It's not for *you* to sort out.' When he ignored her and ran up the stairs, she sensed trouble brewing and wanted the boy out of the way. Taking his coat, she went to the front room and quickly dressed him for outdoors. 'Come on, Danny, let's be off, eh?'

'Why's Daddy shouting?'

What she said was, 'He was just calling up to his mam.' What she *thought* was: because he's a bloody bully.

'Can I put Grandad's soldiers away?'

Having always taught him to tidy up behind himself, Rosie could hardly argue now. ''Course you can, but hurry up, there's a good fella.'

There was an unholy row building in Martha's bedroom. First she could be heard yelling, then came the murmur of Ned's controlled voice, then the sound of Doug's above it all. 'Don't listen to him, Mam. I caught them talking about it . . . THE BUGGERS WANT TO PUT YOU IN A HOME!'

One minute Rosie was tempted to intervene, and the next minute she couldn't get away from that house quickly enough. Dropping to her knees she helped the boy put away the soldiers, and soon the two of them were outside and going down the street at a run. 'If we hurry, we'll just catch the five o'clock tram,' Rosie said breathlessly.

The boy giggled and she was relieved that he thought it was all a game.

On the tram he fell asleep, and she lapsed into thought. She imagined the row still to be raging, and wondered whether she had done a cowardly thing in running away. But then she had the boy to think about and it was unhealthy for him to witness the scene that she believed was now taking place in that sad house. Moreover, even if she *had* stayed, she knew from experience it would have made no difference. Martha would still shout, and Ned would still try to reason with her. Doug would still come between them like he had always done, and in the end the outcome would be the same. *And she dared not think too much about that!*

She cared for neither Doug or his mother, but she felt deeply concerned for Ned. When she had first arrived that morning, it was plain to Rosie that here was a man in the depths of despair. She hoped he would stand his ground against his wife and son. She believed he would. 'Ned's made of strong stuff,' she told herself in a whisper. 'He'll manage.'

But he was only flesh and blood, a man who, after giving his all and being scorned for it, had come to the end of his tether. Even while Rosie thought of him, he was losing ground between these two selfish creatures who cared only for themselves. 'Doug heard wrong,' he argued, red in the face from trying to explain. 'As God's my judge, I wasn't planning to put you away. All I said to Rosie was that you really ought to be in a hospital where they could look after you properly.'

Martha would have none of it. 'You're a liar!' she told him, 'Do you think I'd believe you before my own son?'

Ned sighed. 'No, Martha,' he admitted, 'I don't believe that for one minute.' He glanced sideways at Doug, who was standing at the head of his mother's bed, one arm draped round her shoulders and a look of cunning on his face. 'You've always believed him before me, so why should it be any different now?' He was beaten and knew it. It showed on his face, and in the stoop of his broad shoulders. 'I think Doug should go now. It's better if you and I talk this thing through, Martha. There's only the two of us can find a solution.'

She stiffened. Clinging to Doug's hand, she declared in a resounding voice, 'He's not going anywhere.'

Ned stared from one to the other. His heart was weary, and he had no more stomach for these awful set-tos. But he was still master of his own domain and felt the need to remind them of that. 'This is *my* house, and I don't want him here. In fact, it wouldn't bother me if I never saw him again after what he's done.' He saw Doug's face and knew the taunt had hit home. 'I reckon it might be a good idea if he goes before I say too much I might regret.' He was alluding to the money which Doug had robbed from him.

Martha caught the look that passed between them, and her curiosity was aroused. Looking first at Doug she saw that he had turned a shade paler, and she was instinctively suspicious. All the same she refused to accept that he could have done anything really wrong, so when she addressed Ned, it was angrily. 'Stop bloody well insinuating, you old fool! If you've summat to say to our Doug, get on with it.'

Tired of always being the one in the wrong, Ned answered,

'When will you come to see that you've a liar for a son? I'm telling you the truth, Martha. I wasn't planning to put you away, like he says. Your precious son is out to cause trouble, and he doesn't care if you get hurt in the process.'

'Why would he want to cause trouble?'

'Because he's never forgiven me for sacking him.' There! It was said. That would give her something to think about.

Martha couldn't believe her ears. 'What! You sacked your own son?' If she could have got from the bed, she would have thrown herself at him. 'You've gone bloody mad!'

'I was mad to trust him in the first place.'

'What are you getting at? Why did you sack him? I want to know.'

Doug was frantic. 'Whatever he tells you, Mam, don't believe him. He had it in for me because I turned up late once or twice. Honest to God, I didn't do nothing to deserve the sack!'

'You can believe him if you like, Martha, but it's time you knew what kind of man your son is.' Now that it was all coming out, Ned had no intention of keeping anything back. If he could get her to see the truth, it might be just the shock she needed to make her mend her ways. 'While I've been breaking my back to earn the money needed to keep you comfortable, *he's* been robbing me behind my back . . . collecting money and short-changing me. Money that should have gone on you, but went instead on booze and women.'

'Lying bastard!' Doug launched himself through the air, sending Ned backwards when his fist crunched against his jaw.

Horrified to see them fighting like two wild dogs, Martha screamed for them to: 'STOP IT!' But it was too late for that. There was too much anger, too many years of suppressed emotion.

Doug fought with the brute strength that comes from a kind of madness, and Ned, though fit and able, was no longer a young man. When Martha saw her husband falter, she whipped Doug into such a frenzy that he soon overpowered the older man.

When it was over, Doug kicked at the figure lying on the floor. 'Get up,' he snarled. 'You ain't half the big man now, are you?'

Ned gave no answer. Instead he got to his feet and stood up

as straight as his painful bones would let him. Staring at Doug through bruised eyes, he said in a wonderfully calm voice, 'No. It seems *you're* the big man now.' He wasn't angry any more, nor was he filled with a lust for revenge. Instead, he was strangely elated, as though he had been released from his burden.

Doug burst out laughing, giggling insanely as he snatched a glance at his mother's smiling face. 'I gave him a bloody good beating, didn't I, Mam?' He was like a child hoping for a reward.

It was Ned who answered. 'I'm only sorry I didn't give *you* a similar beating when you were younger. Happen then you might have turned out to be a son I could have been proud of.'

'That's enough,' Martha ordered. 'I want you to take him back. It's only right that father and son should work together. And if he did help himself to a bit of money, it doesn't really matter. There'll come a day when he'll inherit the business anyway.' She smiled encouragingly at Doug and he smiled back, but their smiles fell away when Ned spoke in his new dignified voice.

'He can't inherit what isn't mine.' Delighted by their astonishment he went on, 'I sold the business some while back, soon after I discovered there was money missing. What with all the expenses and business being quiet, I had no choice. So you see, there's nothing to inherit.'

Doug stared at him with disbelief, and Martha was trembling. 'Who did you sell it to? she hissed.

There was a world of regret in Ned's voice, but strangely enough he was smiling as he went to the door. 'Adam Roach,' he said, and heard them gasp aloud. Before they could recover, he made a further statement. 'I won't be coming back again,' he told them. Nothing else. Just that. And their shocked silence was immensely satisfying to him.

CHAPTER THIRTEEN

'God Almighty! Why didn't you put a stop to it?' Peggy was horrified to learn that Doug had moved his mother in with him and Rosie.

'What could I do, Peggy?' As they hurried across the road towards the park, Rosie held hard to the boy beside her. Daniel was a sturdy little fellow, with a ready smile but a quiet disposition. 'Hurry up, sweetheart,' she urged, always wary of crossing the road with him, though there was not much traffic because it was Sunday and most people were either in their beds or talking to the Lord in church. 'My hands are tied and they both know it,' she told Peggy now.

'Is there nothing at all you can do, gal?' Coming to the bench just inside the park, Peggy fell heavily on to a seat, her blue eyes watching Rosie's every move as she took off the boy's jacket and folded it over her arm. The July sun was beating down and his face was growing redder by the minute. When he asked if he could play in the sand, Rosie let him go, but warned him not to stray. After he'd toddled off to make sandcastles, Peggy resumed her questioning. 'Have you talked to Doug about it . . . having his old woman there, I mean?'

''Course I have.' Day and night, whenever he was sober enough to listen, she had gone over the same arguments that Peggy was raising now. 'I've told him time and time again that it's impossible for the four of us to live under the same roof.'

'And?'

'He doesn't want to know. He just says I'm selfish, and that I should be glad it's not *me* lying in bed and having to rely on other folks.' Rosie had come to the end of her tether, but she couldn't help wondering about what Doug had said. 'The trouble is, he does manage to make me feel guilty because it's true, isn't it? Evil as she is, Martha must feel every bit as bad as me. After all, she can't really want to live with me, hating me like she does.'

Peggy sat bolt upright, her blue eyes blazing. 'What! She's probably enjoying every minute of it . . . knowing how unhappy she's making you. You're just too kind-hearted, that's the problem, and the pair of 'em are taking advantage.'

Rosie knew it. She also knew that the situation was an impossible one, and that there was no easy solution. Leaning back on the hard bench, she let her eyes rove over the colourful flower-beds. At home there was an atmosphere you could cut with a knife, while here in this lovely place there was a sense of peace and her heart felt at ease. 'I've thought and thought about what to do, but I can't see a way out and that's the truth.' Her sad brown eyes gazed at Peggy, and not for the first time she envied her friend's independence.

'You could leave.' Peggy voiced the same possibility that had lately crossed Rosie's mind. 'If you like, I'll help you to find a place of your own?'

She answered with a sigh, 'I've already been looking at rooms to let, and I can tell you, it's a thankless task. These past weeks I've lived on the tram, going in every direction. Last week it was Darwen, the week before that it was Accrington, and the day before yesterday I walked the streets of Bolton.'

Peggy sat forward, an expression of surprise on her face. 'You little sod! You never told me that.'

Rosie winked cheekily. 'Makes a change for me to be one step ahead of you.'

'So when are you moving out?'

'I'm not.'

'*Why* not?'

'It's the same old story, Peggy . . . no money to speak of, and a young child. I'd be struggling worse than I am now, and on top of that Doug's already threatened that if I should try "taking my hook" as he puts it, he'd have Danny away from me.'

'Happen he'd *try*! Knowing you, though, you'd fight him tooth and nail.'

'Oh, I'd do that all right, but it's a risk I'm not prepared to take.' Rosie's whole life revolved round her son. 'Besides, I've thought the whole thing through, and I've decided I'm staying put. Not because of his threats to take the boy, and not because of his mam's wickedness.'

'I think you're mad. If it was me, I'd be off in a minute.'

'No, you wouldn't, Peggy,' Rosie answered softly. 'Not if you think about it. At first I felt exactly the same. I was afraid and unhappy about the situation. I still am. But why *should* I leave? That little house is my home. I've loved it since the first day I walked through the door.' Rosie's brown eyes shone defiantly. 'No, Peggy. I'm on to Martha's nasty little plan. She thinks she can get me out, but she'll be sadly disappointed because I'm staying!'

Peggy's smile said it all. 'I should have known. If Martha wants a fight, she's met her match in you, I reckon.' In a softer voice, she went on, 'Be careful though, gal. She's a wicked old biddy and she'd stop at nothing to see you out on the street.'

'Happen she's forgotten I'm a fighter.' When she'd got up that morning, Rosie had felt as though she was carrying the world on her shoulders. But now, in Peggy's company, relaxing in this lovely old park, she felt stronger of heart. 'So you reckon I'm right to stay put then?'

Peggy nodded. 'If it were me, I'd have cut and run the minute she came through that bloody door, gal. But I ain't made o' the same strong stuff as you, and yes, thinking about it, I reckon you're right to stay. If you cleared off, the artful old sod would have won the day.' She laughed out loud then. 'Who knows? When she sees the other side of you, happen she'll bugger off herself.'

'Do you know what *would* be nice?' Without waiting for an answer, Rosie went on, 'If we really *could* live together. I mean, without all the rows and her dreadful temper. After all, she is my son's grandmother.'

'I thought you said she doesn't have much to do with him now?'

'Not since the accident.' Rosie had always wondered about that. 'Do you know, Peggy, she's so deranged I sometimes think she suspects the boy to be Adam's.' The words came out without her meaning them to, and now she blushed to the roots of her hair. 'I know it's impossible, but why else would she turn on her only grandson?' she finished lamely.

Peggy was quick to notice Rosie's frustration, and equally quick to put her at her ease again. 'She's turned on the lad because she's an old cow, that's why. And for no other reason.' Following Rosie's gaze to where Danny was playing, she suggested, 'It's such a glorious day, why don't we walk back by way of Blakewater?'

Rosie didn't need asking twice. Having mentioned what had been in her heart these past weeks, she now wished the earth would open and swallow her up. Time and again, she had been tempted to contact Adam, but each time she cursed herself for such weakness. There was nothing to be gained from contacting him, and besides, there were other reasons why she hated herself for even having entertained the idea. She had cut him out of her life, and rightly so. The Adam she had known was not the same as the one who had snatched an old man's living from under him. Ever since Doug had told her how Adam had schemed to price his father out of the market, she had felt like a traitor. It was obvious he wasn't the same man she had known.

But then, so much had happened. So many years had passed. He had changed, and so had she. Unwilling at first to accept Doug's version of the story, she had spoken to some of Ned's old cronies. But they had only borne out what Doug told her: how Adam Roach had bought him out, and it had broken his heart. The story was that Adam wanted Ned out altogether, but the older man had made it a term of the contract that he stay as an employee. Even now Rosie found it hard to believe that Adam could have done such a callous thing. Yet it was true, and like poor old Ned, she had to accept it. But in spite of all that, and even more to her shame, she still held a deal of affection for Adam. Strangely enough, Peggy touched on that very issue now.

'It would have made it so much easier.'

'What do you mean?'

'If the boy had been Adam's son.'

'He's not, and you know that.'

'I know. All the same, it's a pity, because then Doug couldn't really threaten to take him from you.'

'As long as I live and breathe, Doug will *never* take Danny from me.' The dark and forbidding look in Rosie's eyes momentarily subdued her companion.

'Have you forgiven him?' Peggy's thoughts were running along the same lines as Rosie's.

'Who?'

'You know who. *Adam*, that's who. Have you forgiven him for taking away Doug's inheritance?'

'Doug lost the right to that a long time ago. Ned's business was his own . . . built up over many years. I don't believe he had any intention of leaving it to Doug. Oh, it might have been different years ago when Doug was a boy. But, thanks to Martha, whatever respect there once was between father and son long ago turned to indifference.' There was bitterness in Rosie's voice. 'I've never heard Doug say one kind word about his father.'

'It shocked me, I can tell you, when I heard about Adam Roach buying Ned out. I never believed he would part with his beloved wagon and trade. You know, gal, I reckon there's more to all this than meets the eye. Ned wouldn't have sold easily, I'm certain.'

'I don't suppose we'll ever know what actually happened to make Ned sell. Apparently he was in financial trouble, and I'm not surprised at that. Happen he had no choice but to sell, and happen it was forced on him, I don't know. But I do know this much. Ned taught Adam everything he knows, and all the thanks he got was to become Adam's next takeover. It's common knowledge how Adam Roach is fast becoming one of the county's biggest coal-merchants.'

'I suppose we should be proud of him. When all's said and done, you don't achieve that unless you work damned hard.'

'Or *cheat* damned hard.'

'Aren't you being a bit hard on Adam?'

Rosie's lovely face set. 'I don't think so. There's something else. According to Doug, his dad borrowed money from Adam in the lean times, and Adam used that to drive him under.'

'Doug doesn't always tell the true story.'

'I know that. But the fact of the matter is this . . . Ned lost his business, and now he's gone. Adam Roach has painted his own

197

name on the wagon, added another two routes and expanded Ned's old ones. *That* tells me the truth. He isn't the man I knew and loved. As far as I'm concerned, Adam has beaten a good man in Ned, and I'll never forgive him.'

'Have you heard from Ned?'

'Just that brief letter soon after he left, telling me he was all right and asking me to take care of his grandson.' She recalled how there had been no mention of either Doug or his mam, and that night Doug had gone out on one of his worst drinking binges yet. 'We knew Ned was having a job to make ends meet. It stood to reason, with Martha needing a nurse and everything. But I didn't know how troubled he must have been, and I never imagined he would turn to Adam.' She had tried so hard not to believe it, but she knew now that Adam really had taken advantage of the situation. 'Ned lost everything he'd worked for. I can't forgive Adam for that.'

'Come on, gal.' Peggy rose from the bench and stretched her limbs. Afterwards she surprised Rosie by saying softly, 'One way or another, we're *all* carrying a cross of sorts.' When Rosie tried to draw her on the remark, she would have none of it. But it left Rosie unsettled, wondering whether she had misjudged Peggy's cavalier attitude. Happen she was not so happy to be footloose and fancy free after all?

While Rosie was gathering the boy's coat, Peggy made her way to the sand-pit. 'Come on, young 'un,' she said in a brighter voice. 'We're off home now.'

It was nearing midday when they passed St Peter's church. The congregation spilled out of the great doors, keeping Rosie and Peggy to one side of the pavement. When the path was clear again, they went away at a slower pace. 'I keep promising myself to go to Mass,' Rosie murmured, ashamed. 'Next Sunday, I will.' And, come what may, she would, because lately she had a desperate need for the Lord's guidance.

'You know, I'm not sure we should believe everything we hear, gal,' Peggy remarked. 'Why don't you contact Adam? Get his version of the truth?'

'I *know* the truth, Peggy.' Rosie had asked many questions after Ned's disappearance. 'There's a pattern to it all. Adam

Roach is eaten up with ambition. He buys out the smaller merchants to eliminate competition. It's common knowledge. You've said so yourself.' Soon after Ned went, she had been tempted to get in touch with Adam. But commonsense prevailed, and now she was glad she had resisted the temptation. 'I never want to set eyes on him again!' she said firmly.

'Are you saying you don't have any affection for him at all?' Peggy sensed Rosie's despair, and could only imagine what her friend was suffering.

'I suppose if I'm honest I do still love the Adam I remember,' Rosie reluctantly admitted. 'No woman can easily forget her first love. But I loathe what he's become. Doug has his failings and they're many, but he's weak more than wicked.'

'You and Doug . . . how are things between you now?'

'The same. He hates me when he's sober, and wants me when he's drunk.' A wry little smile appeared at the corners of her mouth. 'Fortunately for me, when he's drunk he falls asleep before he can get his pants off.'

Peggy laughed out loud. 'Poor sod!' she cried. 'What happens then?'

'I throw a blanket over him and he sleeps where he drops,' Rosie answered merrily.

'It must be rotten when *he* wants it to stand up, and all *it* wants to do is lie down.' Peggy's laughter was infectious, and the two of them were still laughing when they turned into Castle Street.

The laughter was short-lived. At Peggy's house they parted company and Rosie made her way along the street with a heavier heart. The thought of Martha sitting up there in the bedroom, waiting to spoil what little pleasure Rosie and her son had got from the morning's outing, was more than enough to take the smile from her face. Little Danny said it all now when he whispered, 'I don't have to go and see Gran'ma, do I?'

'Not if you don't want to, sweetheart,' she answered, giving him a hug. Fumbling in her purse she took out the key and unlocked the door. 'If you like, you can play in the back yard while I get some food on the table. No doubt your daddy will be home soon, starving hungry as usual.' She smiled, but there was no smile in return.

As soon as they were inside, the boy lost no time in making his way to the back yard. 'Wish I could do the same,' Rosie muttered, watching him through the window. No sooner had she spoken than Martha's voice called down, 'Rosie, you bugger! Is that you?'

Going to the foot of the stairs, she called back, 'Can you wait a minute? I'm just about to get the food ready.'

'No, I bloody well can't. Get up here now.'

Rosie shook her head. Every day she hoped Martha's mean mood would improve, and every day it seemed to get worse. 'On my way,' she replied, reluctantly climbing the stairs. As she went, she mimicked Martha's voice, muttering beneath her breath, 'Where've you been all this time? You're a heartless bugger, Rosie Selby, leaving a poor defenceless woman to fend for herself. One o' these days you'll come back and find me lyin' here dead! But I expect that's what you want, ain't it, eh? Clap your bloody hands if I should pop off, wouldn't you, eh?'

At the top of the stairs, Rosie took a deep breath. 'Do your worst, you old sod!' she said, glaring at Martha's bedroom door and imagining the hostile face behind it. Going the remaining few steps along the landing, she pushed open the door. Straightway Martha's voice took up where Rosie's had left off, repeating word for word what she had said while climbing the stairs. And all the while, Rosie stood by the door, waiting for the tirade to end. But when it did, it was on a note of such malice that it made Rosie shiver. 'You've been with a fella, ain't you?' Martha sniggered. 'Look at you, you dirty little bitch, breathless and red-faced, still panting from what you've been up to.'

Tempted to cross the room and ram the pillow down that wicked throat, Rosie forced herself to remain calm. 'If I'm red-faced and panting it's because no sooner am I back from a long walk in the warm sun, than you're yelling for me to run straight up the stairs. You don't even give a body time to get her breath!'

'Been for a walk, eh? More like you've been rolling in the grass with a fella. What! You've only to look at your face to know you're guilty as hell. And I'll tell you this – our Doug will know the minute he gets home, because I'll make it my business to tell him.'

'Well, now you've got all that off your chest, Martha, what can

I do for you?' Rosie's voice was deliberately kind and soft, and there was even a smile on her face.

'I've shit the bed!'

The smile fell from Rosie's face. 'I don't believe you.'

'What? Same as I don't believe *you*?' She chuckled and clapped her hands at the horrified expression on Rosie's face. 'Don't smell too sweet, do it, eh?' she pointed out with glee.

'If you *have* messed the bed, you've done it on purpose.' Rosie made no move. Instead she remained by the door, letting her disapproval be known.

'So say you.' The ugliness of Martha's soul showed in her countenance. Her eyes had grown smaller from years of being narrowed with hatred. Her brow was furrowed in a permanent deep frown, and her greying hair stood up round her large head, as though she'd been caught in a high wind. There was shocking satisfaction in her smile. 'You'd best clean me up, hadn't you? Miss High and bloody Mighty.'

Rosie stood her ground. 'You've never messed yourself before.' She had always admired Martha for her ability to do most things in spite of her disability. 'How come you can manage to use the pan yourself whenever Doug's home, but when I'm out, you find it impossible? You *did* do it on purpose, and I've a good mind to let you swill in it.'

Martha was pleased. 'Be very careful, lady,' she warned gruffly. 'My Doug would be upset to hear you threatening me like that.'

'Happen "your Doug" should clean you up then.'

Rosie turned as though to leave, but swung round when Martha screamed out, 'Don't you dare turn your back on me!'

Rosie was suitably wide-eyed and innocent. 'I'm so sorry, Martha, was there something else?' she asked in a dignified voice.

'All right, you bitch! I *did* do it on purpose, but I ain't sorry.'

'Well, you should be. Your grandson hardly ever moves out of this house, and today was the first time he's been to the park in weeks. I don't often leave you, but when I do I always make sure you've everything to make you comfortable. And I always ask Ma Rushden next-door to keep an eye on you. You know perfectly well you've only to knock on the wall and she'll be here in a minute.'

'Sod Ma Rushden!' Martha began thumping her fists against

the covers. 'You'd best clean me up or I'll yell blue murder!'

Seeing that she was fighting a losing battle, Rosie conceded. 'All right. Give me a minute to boil the kettle, and I'll be straight back.'

'And fetch the boy.'

Rosie glared at her. 'We'll see.'

'I need to see him now! Or shall I tell Doug that on top of everything else, you're trying to keep my own grandson from me.'

'You know that's not true, Martha. I've never refused to let you see him.' Not that she wouldn't *like* to because the boy was obviously frightened of his grandmother. 'It's just that I'd rather you were in a better mood, that's all.'

'You bloody well fetch him, do you hear?'

'All right, I'll fetch him. But not until after you're washed.' Martha's smile widened and Rosie hurried from the room.

Downstairs, Rosie was shocked, when she glanced at the clock over the firebreast. It was almost two o'clock. 'God Almighty! He'll be in any minute, and no food on the table.' Before she went out that morning, she had cleaned the fish, prepared the vegetables and set the table, so all that remained was for her to place the fish in the oven and put a light beneath the pans. She did that now, then checked that her son was all right, and finally boiled a kettle full of water and got the bowl ready for Martha. And, above it all, she could hear her mother-in-law shouting for her to: 'Get up here, damn and bugger you!' To which Rosie replied under her breath, 'Your language doesn't change, Martha. It's still colourful as ever.'

A short time later, after the vegetables were nicely simmering and the aroma of baking fish was gently issuing from the oven, Rosie tested the water in the bowl, making sure it was neither too hot nor too cold. She dropped a flannel and soap into it, draped a large towel over her arm, and went back upstairs, being careful not to slop the water over her own legs.

'About time too,' Martha complained. She complained when Rosie turned back the covers and she complained when her clothes were stripped away. She swore that the water was: 'Hot enough to scald the skin from me back,' and she grumbled the whole time she was being washed, dried and dusted with powder.

Finally the task was done, and Rosie prepared to leave. 'Your dinner won't be long,' she said. Her every bone ached. Martha was no easy handful, and had gone out of her way to make the job more difficult.

'You can fetch the young 'un now.' Sitting up in bed, Martha finally looked presentable, with her freshly laundered nightgown and pretty pink bed-jacket, and her hair combed to a semblance of order. 'I'm waiting, so get a move on.'

Rosie's answer was a forlorn shake of the head. She had hoped Martha would change her mind about wanting to see the boy. Instead she was adamant, and Rosie was obliged to comply. But she would watch her! Like a hawk, she would watch Martha's every move.

'I don't want to go up.' Danny tugged at Rosie's skirt and pleaded with big frightened eyes. 'She's been shouting again. She'll shout at *me*.' Martha's room overlooked the yard where he had been playing, and her voice had carried to its every corner.

Rosie's heart went out to him, but she knew it would be wrong to encourage the bad feeling that was beginning to develop between her son and Martha. 'Your grandma's not well, sweetheart,' she explained. 'She didn't mean to shout.'

He blinked away the tears, dropped his head to his chest and cast his gaze to the floor. 'If I go, will you come too?'

''Course I will.' She took hold of his hand. Slowly, the two of them went up the stairs, he in front and Rosie behind, and it was hard to tell whose heart was sorrier for that short journey.

Martha's smile was terrifying. 'Come to see your gran'ma, eh?' she asked, grinning through yellowing teeth. 'Come on then, right up to the bed.' She beckoned him closer and, on hesitant footsteps, Danny went to her. Anxious as ever, Rosie stayed close behind.

At first, it seemed as though the boy would turn tail and run. But then Martha became surprisingly charming, asking him about the park and the sandpit where he played. 'And did you build any castles?' she asked, affectionately ruffling his hair. Her warm smile was totally disarming. Slowly but surely the child warmed to her, and Rosie began to think she had judged Martha a little too harshly after all.

Danny told her about this and that, and Martha kept on with her questions. When they discussed his grandad's soldiers, and Martha asked whether he would like to keep them, Danny nodded excitedly. Chuckling, she produced the soldiers from the bedside cupboard, and he was enthralled. He even laughed a little and seemed to forget his past unease with her. Watching from nearby, Rosie was delighted that they were getting on so well. It was all she had ever wanted. If Martha was bound to remain in this house, and it seemed as though she was, then it would certainly be wonderful if they could all live peacefully together. For whatever reasons, her son had already lost his grandfather. It would be some compensation if he should gain a grandmother who came genuinely to care for him. After all, she did once love him dearly. Surely that feeling was still alive deep down in Martha's heart?

When Doug's voice called from downstairs, Rosie had few qualms about leaving the two of them together. 'I'll be back in a minute,' she promised, and they hardly glanced up as she departed. However, Martha did bestow a smile on her, and Rosie hoped that at long last everything might be coming right between them.

Doug wasn't drunk, but he was merry. 'I've been at a mate's house,' he explained. 'Had a game of cards, and look at this!' He produced a wad of notes from his pockets and grabbed her into his arms. 'Your old fella's a canny bugger when it comes to cards.' His open smile took her back to when she first fell for his charms. Even now, after all that had happened between them, he could still raise a smile from her.

'It's nice to see you're not drunk on your winnings,' she said simply. 'Happen you can fork out for some new clothes for your son.' When he pushed a couple of notes into her hand, she could hardly believe it. 'What are you after?' she asked light-heartedly. When he was like this, she could forgive him at least some of his behaviour.

He tickled her under the chin and clicked his tongue at her. 'You're a real beauty, do you know that, Rosie Selby?' His lascivious gaze travelled over her classic features, the small heart-shaped face and the straight proud nose, her rich brown hair that looked the colour of ripe chestnuts against her pale skin, and those pretty brown eyes with their long lashes and perfectly shaped eyebrows above. Pushing closer, he put his arm round her, his eyes boring into hers. 'Where's the boy?' he asked in a voice hoarse with passion.'

'Upstairs with your mam.'

'We've time then?' His fingertips crept over her throat, then down to the neck of her blouse. Sliding his hand in, he stroked the small taut breast, expertly rolling the hard nipple between finger and thumb. Bending his head, he opened his mouth over hers, at the same time gruffly whispering, 'I've wanted you all day.' Pushing her backwards against the sideboard, he began undoing his trousers. 'We've time,' he kept saying. 'We've time.' In a minute his member was thrust out, large and erect in his hand.

'What the devil's the matter with you?' Rosie was mortified in case the boy should see. 'Have you no sense of decency?'

'Aw, come on, we'll be over and done before they know it.' He was frantic by now, and in no mood to be refused.

Before Rosie could push him off, he was all over her. But then he was startled by the sound of Danny's voice calling out for his mammy. 'Ignore the little brat,' he gasped, his whole body forcing her down.

When Rosie heard the boy running down the stairs and loudly sobbing, she gathered every ounce of her strength to push Doug's weight off her. 'You're like an animal,' she accused. 'If you ask me, you wouldn't even *care* if the boy saw us at it.'

His face was flushed with anger. 'To Hell with him,' he snapped. 'To Hell with *both* of 'em!'

Astonished to hear him cursing his mother, Rosie pushed him aside and ran to meet the child. He was deeply distressed. When she opened her arms to him, he collapsed into them. 'Gran'ma hurt me,' he cried, lifting his face to show the red weal that went from one side of his forehead to the other.

He was still crying bitterly when Rosie brought him into the living-room. 'You'd best have a word with her,' she told the disgruntled Doug. 'Because if you don't, I will. And I can promise you, I won't be so particular in what I have to say!'

Incensed at being cheated out of his lovemaking, the anger

was still on Doug when he stormed towards the door. 'Is there no peace for a man in his own house?' he demanded. When he ran up the stairs two at a time, Rosie took the child into the kitchen and set about washing the wound on his forehead. Thankfully the skin was unbroken, but he had been badly frightened. Little by little, Rosie discovered what had taken place up there in Martha's room. First she had quizzed Danny about whether his mammy had met a man in the park. Then, when they were playing cowboys and Indians, she took a knife to his head and threatened to 'scalp' him if he didn't tell her 'the truth'. Rosie was made to wonder whether the old lady had finally lost her mind.

Upstairs, Doug vented his frustration on his mother. 'This is *my* house, and don't you forget it,' he told her. 'No wonder Dad buggered off. But I'm not as soft as the old man, and I'll not stand for your peevish little games so you'd best be warned. If you can't behave under my roof, you can bloody well find somewhere else to make mischief.'

At first, Martha turned on the tears fantasising to herself that Rosie's old meat knife had been under her pillow for protection. But when she realised her cunning wiles were getting her nowhere, she flew at him in a rage, 'It shouldn't be *me* you're yelling at,' she snarled. 'It's that wife o'yourn. *She's* the one who needs throwing out, the little baggage.'

All the while she was speaking she dabbed at her eyes with a hankie, making small sad noises in the back of her throat. 'I may have been a bad 'un to your dad, but I never cheated him, not once all the years we were wed.' Through her fingers she spied Doug's face, satisfied when it turned a pale shade of grey. 'It's *her* you should be turning on, not your poor old mam.'

He was bending over the bed, one hand on the brass headrail and the other clenched into a fist not far from her face. But now he straightened his back and stared down at her, his odd-coloured eyes like round glittering marbles. 'You'd best tell me what you're getting at,' he instructed in a strangely quiet voice.

Leaving him to brood on the suspicions she had planted in his mind, Martha sighed and groaned and muttered her discontent. She plumped up her pillows, then tidied the neck of her nightgown, and now, much to his frustration, was patting at her dishevelled hair.

When he made a small grunting noise and bent over her again, she looked up and saw she had punished him long enough. 'Don't you think you'd better ask *her*?' she suggested. All trace of her distress was now gone and in its place was a bristling authority. After being belittled by Rosie, it felt wonderful to relive the power she'd had over her husband, now over her son. 'You can ask her, but I doubt if she'll tell you the truth.'

'I'm asking *you*!' His face was twisted with rage.

'All I'm saying is, you should keep your eyes open. It wouldn't be the first time a woman strayed when she thought her husband wasn't looking.'

'You're a bloody liar!'

'You think so, do you?'

'If she was carrying on with another bloke, I'd know, I can promise you that.'

'Then there's no need to worry, is there?' The damage was done. The seed was planted and she could leave it to grow. 'Go away and let me sleep,' she grumbled. 'I'm tired. First *she* upsets me, then the brat, and now you.' She flung herself to the far side of the bed and began softly crying. 'I've always done my best by you, and now none of you want me. Shame on you!' She buried her face in the pillow and waited for him to go. Once the door was closed, she raised her head and chuckled to herself. 'Talk down to your betters, will you Miss High and Mighty? Well, now you'll see who comes off worse, won't you, eh? Happen you'll remember in future ... make trouble for Martha Selby and you'll get more than you've bargained for.'

Rosie was curious as to what had gone on between mother and son. But when Doug came downstairs, he had nothing to say. He remained quiet throughout the meal, and afterwards sat sullen and moody in the fireside chair. Occasionally he would glance at her as though on the verge of saying something, but then he would look away, eyes downcast and his fingers playing on the arm of his chair.

'Your mam's fast and hard asleep,' she told him, returning to the living-room with Martha's tray. 'I thought to wake her, but then I decided to let her sleep a while longer. I'll steam the meal up later. It won't spoil.' What she had really wanted to do when she stood over Martha just now was to tackle her over what she had done to the boy. But she reasoned that, if Doug had dealt with it, she ought to let it rest, although Hell would fuse with Heaven before she ever again left her son alone with Martha.

'I'm tired, Mammy.' Danny was heavy-eyed and still upset from his ordeal at Martha's hands. He had barely touched his meal, and was now clambering down from the table.

'All right, sweetheart.' Rosie led him into the kitchen. Normally he would have been given a thorough strip-wash before being allowed up to his bed. But on this occasion, Rosie gave his hands and face a quick lick-over with a damp cloth, before returning him to the living-room.

'Say goodnight to your daddy,' she said, and was astonished when Doug opened his arms to hug the child. As a rule it was a quick 'Goodnight, son', and the boy was sent straight off to his bed.

Tonight, however, Doug held on to the boy for a full minute before thrusting him away. He hadn't spoken one word since his confrontation with Martha, and Rosie was deeply perturbed by his strange mood. She felt guilty without knowing why.

Upstairs, she helped Danny to change into his pyjamas. She reassured him when he looked fearfully at the door and remarked in a small voice, 'I don't like Gran'ma any more.'

'If you want me, I won't be far away, you know that,' Rosie told him.

He didn't want to let her leave. 'Sing to me, Mammy,' he begged, and she did.

The nursery rhyme was an old favourite of hers. The words calmed her fears and lifted her spirit, and soon her soft lilting voice was lulling Danny to slumber. 'Go to sleep my baby, close your big brown eyes . . . Angels watch above you, peeping at you from the skies.' Even before she had finished the verse, he was sound asleep, a look of contentment on his face and his arms stretched out above his head. 'Sleep well, little one,' she whispered, tucking the blanket over him. She kissed him gently on the forehead and tiptoed from the room, softly closing the door behind her. Outside she paused a moment, listening. All was quiet. A smile wreathed her face as she murmured, 'If I never have anything else in this life, I'll always thank the good Lord for you.' More and more, her son had come to mean the world to her.

Before going down again, she took a look in Martha's room. Her heart turned over when her mother-in-law sat bolt upright in bed and grinned at her. 'Got the brat to sleep, have you?' Her voice was low and grating, her eyes glittered with malice, and Rosie's dislike of her intensified.

She had promised herself she would leave it to Doug to deal with Martha. But, at that moment, it was obvious to her that he had made little or no impact on his mother. There was something very wrong about Martha. Something sinister. 'I ought to see you through that front door for what you did to my son . . .' Rosie started.

'Don't threaten me,' Martha interrupted. 'You can't do anything to harm me, and you know it. This is my son's house, and I'll answer to *him*, not you.' She smiled, sending shivers down Rosie's spine. 'You can leave now,' she said.

Rosie was convinced. '*You're completely mad*,' she murmured.

'I don't want no dinner either. How do I know you ain't trying to poison me?'

'We're not all painted with the same brush,' Rosie said sharply. 'But if you don't want your meal, that's fine by me. I'll leave it steaming until you do.' She knew from old that Martha would soon be demanding her food. 'But before I go, I want you to know that if you ever hurt my son again, you'll answer to me.'

'Is that so?'

'You can depend on it,' Rosie insisted angrily. When Martha merely smiled, she thought it best to leave. If she stayed she might be tempted to do something she would regret.

'Must you go out?' Doug was putting on his coat when Rosie came into the living-room. 'I really wouldn't mind some company tonight.' Martha's oddness had unnerved her. But then she recalled how Doug himself had been in a strange mood since talking to her. Between the two of them, Rosie was made to feel insecure.

He stared at her for a minute, his mouth set in a grim line. He shrugged and fastened his coat, and as he was leaving, asked cynically, 'Are you sure it's *my* company you're after?' Before she could question his remark, he was gone, slamming out of the house and leaving her in a quandary.

She went about her work with a vengeance. When everything was done, she got out her sewing basket and replaced all the loose buttons on her best frock. She stitched the tear in little Danny's play trousers, and darned the sleeves of Doug's jumpers. When that was done, she turned on the radio and tried to get interested in the mystery story. It was already halfway through. Unsettled, she turned it off and went to the bottom of the stairs where she listened a while. Silence. Not a sound came from upstairs. 'You ought to sleep, you old bugger!' she murmured. 'But it's a wonder your conscience will let you.'

In the kitchen Martha's meal was slowly steaming but the water in the pan was almost gone. Filling the jug from the tap, Rosie poured the contents into the pan until it was nearly full. After taking a look at the food, she set the plate on top once more; the meal was nicely kept and would remain so until Martha started shouting for it. 'I ought to chuck it in the bin!' Rosie grumbled.

For the next two hours she looked for things to do, and the more she thought about what Doug had said, the more she was ready to have it out with him. She felt angry, confused by his parting remark, yet convinced Martha was behind it all.

It was midnight when he came home. Rosie was in bed fast asleep. She had tried to stay awake, but it had been a long and arduous day and the minute after her head touched the pillow she was in a deep, if restless, slumber.

It was a sense of horror that woke her. At first when she opened her eyes, she couldn't see him. The room was steeped in darkness, the only relief being the slit of moonlight that cut through the narrow opening between the curtains. With a gasp she sat up, clutching the bedclothes to her breast. 'Who's there? Doug, is that you?' Fear was betrayed in her voice.

His reply was low and angry, his voice slurred with drink. 'Expecting somebody else, were you?' Narrowing her eyes, she could just make him out, slumped against the dresser, his face like a pale mask in the gloom.

In a minute she was out of the bed and reaching for the light-switch. A ripple of fear went through her when his fingers quickly locked over her wrist. 'I'm sorry if I've disappointed you,' he hissed, tightening his grip on her arm. 'But then, I'm only your husband when all's said an' done.'

Anger bubbled up in her. Wrenching herself away, she demanded, 'It's your mother, isn't it? Something she said to you before you went out has got you all riled up.' Snapping on the light, she stared into his face, her brown eyes alive with anger. 'For God's sake, Doug, can't you see what she's trying to do?'

The sudden influx of light made him blink. Impatient, he switched off the light. 'It's got nothing to do with her,' he lied. 'But I'll tell you this . . . if I find out you're seeing another man, I'll kill the pair of you.'

Rosie should not have been surprised, but she was. 'So, she *has* told you I've got another man? Are there no depths to her wickedness?' Martha's spitefulness had always been foreign to Rosie's more generous nature. 'I take her in, run up and down the stairs at her beck and call, wash her, feed her, wait on her hand and foot, and *still* she's bent on making trouble between us.' Something inside her snapped. 'If you're fool enough to believe the lies she tells you about me, then happen I should take the boy and clear off.'

'It's lies then?'

'Of *course* it's bloody lies!' Stiffening with rage, she swung away. Throwing herself on to the bed, she sat upright and grim-faced, her troubled eyes staring out of the chink between the curtains. The sky was dark as black velvet. Out there was another world, one she had never really explored. 'I can't take much more of her,' she confessed. 'I do what I can, but it's never enough. Happen it really would be better if I found somewhere of my own?' At this minute in time, it seemed so simple. 'Besides, after what happened with Danny today, I'm afraid. She hates him, you know that, don't you?'

'Don't talk daft! He's her grandson. Why would she hate him?' There was something in his voice that told Rosie he also had been deeply shocked by what had taken place here today.

'I don't *know* why. But she's turned on him, and you can't deny it.'

'You swear on Danny's life . . . you're not seeing another man?'

'I'll do no such thing!' Rosie rose from the bed and crossed the room. 'You can believe what *she* tells you, or you can believe *me*. I am NOT seeing another man.' She actually laughed out loud. 'God Almighty! Don't you think I've learned my lesson with *you*? One man is more than enough.'

He let out a great heaving sigh. 'I know I'm not the best husband in the world, Rosie, but I do love you.'

Hating the dark, she again flicked on the light and was astonished to see him crying. Huge teardrops rolled down his face. With his hands thrust deep into his trouser pockets and his head inclined to one side, he looked a pathetic sight. Yet her heart remained hardened against him. He was ready to believe anything of her. She could not easily forgive him for that.

'She's been a good mother to me, but lately she's changed. Or I've only just begun to see her as she really is,' he confessed. 'She's a wicked old biddy, and I'll have to take a firmer hand with her,' he promised. 'Only please don't leave me. I'd be nothing without you.'

Rosie was torn in so many directions. There was no longer any love in her heart for this man. The only real thing that tied them together was the fact that he was the father of her child. In many ways he was too much like his mother. There were times when she loathed the very touch of him, and there were times when he was more of a child than Danny. She looked at him now, and felt ashamed. She also felt more trapped than ever. Why couldn't she have seen all of this years ago? Before it was all too late? But she hadn't, and there was only herself to blame. She could never love him again, never as long as she lived. Hers was a life without love. Only her son touched her heart, yet he was only half hers. She felt instinctively that if she left, Martha would side with Doug, and between them they would move Heaven and earth to take the boy from her. No. She had made her own decision in life and, rightly or wrongly, would have to live it through; for the boy's sake if not her own.

'I'll never let another man come between us.' There was murder in his words, and it startled her.

She gave no answer. His remark needed none.

When he laid her on the bed, she made no resistance. She didn't want him, but neither did she want the upheaval of turning him away. Quietly, she submitted. The sooner it was over with, the better, she thought bitterly.

The smell of booze on his breath was nauseating, though he was not so intoxicated as not to have his way with her. 'Take your nightgown off,' he said. Before she had time to refuse, he was pulling it up round her waist. She could feel his hard member against the warmth of her skin and, for one regretful minute, she was roused. Sensing it, he coarsely laughed as he began probing into her. He had been interrupted before, and his appetite was all the more ravenous because of it.

This time he was deep in the throes of ecstasy when the cries of his son cut through his passion. He would have ignored the cries and carried on to fulfilment, but Rosie wriggled away and ran from the room, leaving him bitterly frustrated and in a dark rage at having been deprived yet again.

When Rosie opened her son's bedroom door, what she saw would live with her for the rest of her days. The light from the hallway flooded in. Martha was lying on the floor, twisted and wild-eyed. The child was caught up in her arms and she was holding a knife to his throat. His brown eyes were huge with fear, and his little hands were pulling on his grandmother's arms in a futile attempt to loosen her deadly grip. Tiny droplets of blood trickled over his fingers, and Rosie's heart turned somersaults.

'Let him go, Martha. *Please* . . . let him go.' Her voice was astonishingly calm, belying the terror she felt inside.

'Didn't hear me, did you?' Martha's laugh was terrible to hear. 'Didn't hear me crawling along on my belly, did you, eh?' she asked again. 'Oh, but I heard you . . . and him. I heard you going at each other in there.' The smile slid from her face. 'I told him about you, but you talked him round, didn't you, eh? You managed to convince him you ain't got another fella, when you and I know you bloody well have!'

'Please, Martha . . . let Danny go now.' Rosie had a mind to dart forward, take her unawares, but instinct warned her not to.

As though reading her thoughts, Martha warned in a sinister

213

voice, 'Be very careful, dearie. He means nothing to me.' Her gaze went beyond Rosie to the doorway. Doug had come upon the scene and was momentarily struck dumb, his odd-coloured eyes going from his mam to the boy and then to Rosie.

At the sight of Doug, Martha's face broke into a wide smile. 'Send her away, son,' she pleaded. 'We don't need her. We don't need *either* of them.' Digging the blade into the boy's tender skin, she chuckled when he began sobbing again.

Hastily dressed in pyjamas, and slightly swaying from the effects of booze, Doug ventured further into the room. 'That's enough, Mam. Let him be,' he instructed. His voice was quick and angry. 'Whatever you think of Rosie, it has nothing whatsoever to do with the boy.'

Martha met his gaze with bold eyes. 'That's where you're wrong, son,' she declared knowingly. ''Cause this boy is right at the heart of it all.'

'Do as I ask you, Mam. Let Danny go.'

'You don't believe anything I say, do you? You and me, son, we were fooled all along. I believed the child to be my grandson, and you imagined him to be your own flesh and blood. Well, he ain't! He don't belong to neither of us, 'cause it were another man as fathered him.'

'You'd best stop, Mam. You're letting your tongue run away with you, and I don't want to hear no more of your mischief-making.' He took a step into the room but paused when she jerked the knife up against the boy's chin.

Behind Doug, Rosie was frantic, warning him in a hoarse whisper, 'For God's sake, be careful!'

He glanced round as though listening more intently to what she had to say, and even later, when she recalled the awful thing that happened, Rosie could never pinpoint the exact second when Doug bounded forward and launched himself at Martha. She heard an ear-splitting scream, and the dull thud as the two of them fell backwards together.

She saw Martha's surprised face, the wide open eyes and lolling mouth. Suddenly there was blood everywhere. It spurted up on the bedspread and spilled over the carpet, and the sound of Doug's cries rose above her own. She saw and heard all that, yet she could not say how it happened exactly. In that same split second, she darted forward and grabbed her son from beneath Martha's crumpled body. He was bleeding badly and limp as a rag doll in her arms. But he was breathing. Thank God, he was still breathing!

'She's dead!' Doug's voice was like a dull rhythm in her head. 'Mam's dead!' He kept repeating it. 'She's dead. Mam's dead!'

Beneath his weight, the knife had somehow embedded itself in Martha's neck. Now the handle was in his fist, and Martha was staring at him through flat glazed eyes. He began screaming. He was still screaming when Rosie summoned help from next-door, and was quietly sobbing when the police took him away. Like a child, he wanted his mam. They had to tear him from her, and as they walked him across the bedroom he turned his head to look on that familiar face, now shockingly quiet. In repose it seemed too normal, too devoid of expression.

He was still looking at her as they took him out of the door. Never once did he glance towards Rosie or the boy. He didn't show any interest when the ambulance-man gently took Danny from his wife's arms. Nor did he care.

All the way down the stairs he could be heard crying, 'I've killed her!' Over and over, 'I've killed my own mam. *May God have mercy on my soul.*'

CHAPTER FOURTEEN

It was the last day of July 1953, and the first time since Doug had been taken into custody that Rosie was able to visit him. Since that dreadful day, she had been torn between her love for her son – who was still not fully recovered from his ordeal – and her loyalty as a wife.

Last Friday the postman had brought the visiting voucher which she was to present at the gate on arrival at Strangeways Prison in Manchester. The voucher was for Tuesday. That was tomorrow, and already Rosie's stomach was turning somersaults at the thought of seeing Doug again. She was ashamed to admit it, but since he had been locked up, she hadn't missed him for one minute; though there were times when the house seemed strangely silent and empty with only her and Danny here. In fact, Rosie loved it with just the two of them.

After a restless night, she awoke feeling troubled. Leaving Danny sleeping, she hurried downstairs to find a letter on the mat by the front door. As soon as she picked it up, she recognised the handwriting. It was from Ned. Switching on the passage light, she read it where she stood. Ned was never known for his letter-writing, and she was surprised to find that it was long and soul-searching:

Dear Rosie,

You must think me all kinds of a coward for not coming to Martha's funeral. The truth is, I believe she would not have wanted me there. But you must know that.

Like I said in my earlier letter, I was deeply shocked by what happened. When I read the newspaper reports of what

217

Doug had done, my first thoughts were for you. But even then, I could not bring myself to come back. I couldn't explain it in my first letter, and I can't explain it now; except maybe I really am the worst coward.

There is no love in me for Doug, but I do miss you and my grandson. One day, when I miss you both enough, you'll find me on your doorstep.

Forgive me, Rosie. Please don't tell Doug you've heard from me. We've been like strangers for too long now. I know he would only reject anything I have to say.

Please accept this five-pound note. Give Danny a big hug for me. Tell him my work keeps me away, but I will not forget him.

Keep well.

Yours affectionately,

Ned

'Shame on you!' Neatly folding the letter, Rosie replaced it in the envelope, and this she put in the pocket of her dressing-gown. Switching out the passage light, she made her way to the living-room. Once there, she took out the letter and opened the sideboard drawer. 'I won't hug your grandson for you, Ned,' she said bitterly. 'When he needed you, you weren't here. We've both done our crying for you, and now I'd rather he forgot you ever existed.'

Opening the drawer, she was about to put the letter inside when the other envelopes caught her eye. There were four of them, an earlier letter from Ned, and three from Adam. She didn't need to read them for she knew every word; especially the ones from Adam. After Doug was arrested, Adam had offered his help. She didn't answer that one so he wrote again, this time threatening to come and see her. She replied then, a cursory note to say that she wanted nothing more to do with him. She told him how she believed she was partly to blame for what had happened, and asked him never to write again, or try and contact her in any way. Taking out the last letter, she read it once more:

Dearest Rosie,

   I was sad to receive your note, but not wanting to add to your distress, of course I'll do as you ask though it goes against my natural instincts.

You must know I still love you.

If you want me, I'll be here. You have my address.
    Yours always,
      Adam

Incensed that any man could write such a letter when he was married to another woman, she had thrust it in the drawer with the others, and there it had remained. Now, before she could ever be tempted to read it again, she tore it into little shreds, before throwing it in the bin along with all the others. But it was engrained on her mind. I love you. 'Damn you, Adam Roach!' Because she loved him too, and she always would.

Busying herself in readiness for the day ahead, Rosie quickly put the letter out of her mind. The idea that soon she would be sitting in the same room as Doug was more than enough to occupy her every thought.

Peggy was on her annual fortnight's holiday, and had agreed to stay in Rosie's house with Danny. 'With school out, that lot indoors would drive him crazy,' she laughed. She laughed a lot lately, and Rosie knew it was for *her* benefit. Like Rosie, Peggy had been stunned by the whole ordeal, and neither of them had yet talked about what the future might hold for her and her son. It was a subject that dogged Rosie day and night, and she could see nothing ahead but trouble and heartache.

'You look real smart,' Peggy told her on this Tuesday morning. In her brown two-piece and white blouse with the frill at the neck, Rosie did look smart. She had on her best black patent shoes and wore a deep-brimmed cream hat that suited her shoulder-length brown hair. But her eyes were shadowed with tiredness, and her face was pale and gaunt. She had lost a deal of weight and her jacket looked too big across her frail shoulders. There was a haunted expression about her that persisted even when she smiled, and when she spoke it seemed as though her mind was elsewhere.

'You're not listening, are you?' Rising from her chair, Peggy crossed the room to where Rosie was looking in the sideboard mirror and fiddling with the neck of her blouse. Putting her two hands on Rosie's shoulders, Peggy gently turned her round until they were facing each other. 'You don't really want to go, do you?' she asked softly.

Suddenly Rosie was opening the drawer and her hand was on the letter. 'This was lying on the mat when I came down,' she explained, handing it to Peggy. 'It's from Ned.'

She read the letter. She had also read the first one so the contents didn't surprise her. 'Don't blame him,' she said. 'Nobody knows what he went through with Martha.'

'He should be here, Peggy, and you know it.' Rosie didn't find it so easy to forgive. 'Whatever happened between Ned and his wife and son is no fault of Danny's. To a child, everything is black and white. How can he understand why his entire family have been taken from him? How in God's name can I ever hope to explain such a thing?' She choked on the words. 'Ned should have been here. Now we don't need him.'

'I know how you must feel, Rosie,' Peggy entreated. 'But you can't really know what he's thinking right now. What happened has affected all of you . . . not just Danny.'

'It's Danny who's suffering the most because he doesn't understand. If Ned had been here, we could have helped each other.' Rosie was not convinced that he should be cleared of all blame. 'What kind of man can stay away when his wife is murdered and his son is imprisoned? What kind of a man is it who won't come to his grandson when he needs him?' She shook her head. 'No, Peggy. Until Ned has the guts to face me, I can't altogether forgive him.'

Momentarily silenced by Rosie's outburst, Peggy was lost for words. Presently she said, 'I don't think I've ever heard you speak so harshly. Don't shut Ned out, Rosie. Everyone has their own way of dealing with tragedy.'

There had been a terrible anger in Rosie until that moment when she looked into Peggy's dear face. Suddenly the anger softened and tears welled up to choke her. 'Oh, Peggy, I don't know what to think. Sometimes I believe it was all *my* fault, and I can't bear it.' Her lovely brown eyes were hauntingly sad. 'If it hadn't been for me taunting Martha, maybe none of this would have happened.' The tears had been held back, but now they spilled over and, throwing herself into Peggy's arms, Rosie sobbed like a child, words tumbling over one another. 'Oh, Peggy, I wish to God I could turn the clock back.'

Peggy let her cry. Rosie had comforted her so many times, and now it was *her* turn. She held on to that dear soul, horrified by how thin Rosie had become, and wondering where it would all end.

Ashamed, Rosie drew away. 'I'm sorry,' she murmured, 'I shouldn't heap my troubles on you.' She felt better for crying, but there was a great hard lump in her heart still, and nothing she could do would break it down. Suddenly weary, she sank into the fireside chair. 'I don't know how I can face him,' she murmured. 'I won't know what to say.'

'You can't think *he* blames you?' Collecting Rosie's hat from the floor where it had fallen, Peggy came and sat opposite. 'You mustn't think that.'

Rosie opened her mouth to speak, but her throat was tight and her heart too full. Eventually she whispered, 'He killed his own mother, Peggy, and it was me who called out for him.'

'Well o' course you called out for him!' she retaliated. 'So would any other woman. Martha was holding a knife against your son's throat. What else could you do?'

'Happen I could have talked her out of it?'

Peggy shook her head. 'Didn't you try that? Before Doug came into the room, didn't you try and talk her out of it?' She was desperately concerned for Rosie. Day by day she had seen her going downhill until now she hardly ate and it was obvious from the dark circles beneath her eyes that she was not sleeping either.

'I did try! Honest to God, I did try.' In her heart, though, she was convinced that there must have been something more she could have done . . . been a better person perhaps? . . . kinder to Martha? . . . kept a lock on little Danny's door? She hadn't even realised that Martha was becoming a much more dangerous

221

enemy. Now she was cold in the churchyard, and Doug was locked up for her murder.

The funeral had been a strange affair, with curious crowds lining the way, but only herself and Peggy at the church. Even the service had been short and to the point. When Martha was laid into the ground, the earth was quickly shovelled over and she was lost to sight as though she had never been.

'Look, Rosie, I know we mustn't speak ill of the dead, but the woman was completely mad,' Peggy remarked now. 'Folks round here heard her screaming and yelling at the top of her voice at all hours of the day and night. Like I said, it were a tragedy waiting to happen. And if you didn't realise it, that's because you've a kind heart and see only the good in people.'

Rosie gave a wry little laugh. 'You're wrong, Peggy. I saw the evil in her all right. But I mistook it for wicked mischief.' Clasping her hands together, she stood up, driven by the awful memories. 'When she hurt Danny that first time . . . made a mark on his forehead, I should have known. I should have been more on my guard.' She breathed in, a long slow breath, and then let it out on a great sigh. She pushed Martha from her thoughts. 'I'd better be going or I'll be late, and like as not they won't let me in.'

Realising that Rosie had deliberately changed the subject, Peggy also stood up, to remark in a lighter voice, 'As long as they let you *out*, gal, that's all as matters.'

The typical remark made Rosie smile. Reaching out she took Peggy in her arms and the two of them hugged each other tightly. 'You're a good friend,' Rosie acknowledged. 'I don't know what I'd do without you.'

'You'd go to ruin, I expect,' Peggy said in a mock serious voice. They laughed then, and the tension was broken.

Surreptitiously brushing away a tear, Rosie went to the mirror and put on her hat. Then she patted the creases from her skirt and picked up her bag from the chair. Peggy watched her every move. 'Thanks for looking after Danny,' Rosie said simply. 'I checked him just before you came in, and he was sound asleep. Let him be. He's had little enough rest lately.' Not a night passed without her being woken by his cries. The nightmares never seemed to end.

Peggy walked her to the door. 'I know somebody else who hasn't had much sleep either,' she chided. 'And I've come to a decision.'

'What?'

'There'll be time enough to talk about that when you get back. Now be off with you!' Giving Rosie a little push, she nudged her out of the front door. 'And don't worry about the lad, I won't disturb him. I'll be too busy doing your ironing.'

Before Rosie could protest, the door was closed and Peggy was inside, leaving Rosie standing on the pavement, a little smile lifting the corners of her mouth. Gazing at the house, she shook her head and fondly imagined Peggy inside. 'God bless you,' she murmured. Then, before she might change her mind, set off at a brisk towards the tram-stop.

Having missed the ten o'clock tram, she had a fifteen-minute wait for the next one. The minutes seemed like hours, and she grew more and more nervous. It was bad enough going to prison in the first place, without being late. The queue began to swell, and many of the women knew her by sight. Normally they would have passed the time of day, but this morning they turned to talk to each other, ignoring her as if she wasn't there. They all blame me for what happened, Rosie thought bitterly. Suddenly the sun went in and the skies darkened over. It turned chilly and she wished she had put on her mackintosh.

'They don't mean any harm, luv.' Mrs Norman from two doors down had never liked Martha Selby, and was quick to state her support for Rosie. 'Folks is funny,' she added with a smile. 'They're embarrassed, d'you see? They don't rightly know how to behave in matters such as these. Some are quick to point the finger, others reckon it's none o' their business, and them like me want to help but don't know how.' Her round face beamed a smile that lit up Rosie's sorry heart.

'I know,' she declared gratefully. 'On the whole, people have been kind.' She was thinking about the grocer who had sent a basket filled with food; the postman who expressed his sympathy at what had taken place; neighbours who had carried out the old tradition of going round the houses for a small contribution which was then given to the bereaved. When Mr Pope knocked on her door a week back, Rosie had been tempted to refuse the gift. But to do so would have been an insult, so she had thanked him kindly and spent the whole two pounds on a wreath for Martha. Though she knew there would come a time when that money might be sorely needed, Rosie couldn't bear the thought of spending it on anything else. The large floral tribute was the only one on Martha's coffin, and had made a lonely sight.

'And how's your little lad, me dear?' The entire episode had been reported in the newspapers, down to the smallest detail, together with a description of how the boy had been used.

'Mending well,' Rosie told her. There was no need to say any different.

'Aye, that's the way.' The older woman nodded and beamed, and turning to the queue, declared in a loud voice, 'It's a pity folks don't realise at times like these, it's just a bit o' kindness that's needed!' She was particularly alluding to a fat brassy-faced lady in a blue hat and carrying an umbrella. 'Isn't that right, Dora Lockley?' Widow Lockley had a vicious tongue and the declaration was more of a warning than retribution, because, with regard to the Martha Selby affair, she had so far managed to keep her opinions to herself.

Silence ensued, during which Rosie didn't know which way to turn. But then the woman in question came and stood before her. 'I know I'm an old gossip,' she apologised, red-faced, 'but I swear I've never said one bad word against you. In fact, I can only imagine what you went through with that dreadful woman. Believe me, Mrs Selby, you do have my sympathy.'

'Bless you for that,' Rosie said. And at once there was a chorus of cheering and laughter, and light-hearted shouts for Dora Lockley: ''Ere, you old bugger, get yerself back to the end of the queue!' The tram arrived. Rosie sat in the first seat and, as they each passed her, the passengers tapped her affectionately on the shoulder. 'Keep your chin up, lass,' they said. And Rosie arrived at her destination with a lighter heart.

The forbidding sight of Strangeways Prison wasn't enough to dishearten her. Neither was the long wait and the curious stares of the wardens, nor the miserable room into which she was eventually shown; though she did feel highly apprehensive while seated at one side of a table, with a prison warden behind her and a vacant seat for Doug opposite.

Rosie believed she had prepared herself for anything. But when Doug came through the door, she gasped aloud. He was a shadow of his former self. In his drab prison garb and with his hair cut within an inch of his head, he was almost a stranger. Yet there was something horribly familiar about him, a kind of intimacy that shook her to the core. For one unnerving moment, when Rosie looked into these wild odd-coloured eyes, it was Martha who stared back at her. And it was Martha's voice that addressed her in clipped tones. 'You're late!' Grabbing the back of the chair, Doug drew it out and sat down. 'Couldn't face the thought of seeing me, eh?' he demanded sharply.

'I missed the tram.' It seemed such a lame thing to say, but it was the truth. 'I'm sorry.' She half smiled, but it died on her lips when he sat before her, his peculiar eyes boring into her face.

'I suppose when it came right down to it, you couldn't stay away. Curiosity got the better of you, did it? Wanted to see the kind of place you'd put me in, did you?' When she hesitated, he raised his voice. 'ANSWER ME, BITCH!'

At once the officer stepped forward. 'All right, officer,' Doug acknowledged humbly. The officer stepped back, and Doug returned his gaze to Rosie. It wasn't humble now. It was hard and penetrating. 'I've had time to think in here.' Though he spoke in a quieter tone, his voice was sharp and cutting. 'Oh, yes, I've had plenty of time to think.' His hands were clenched together on the table, and while he spoke he rubbed the palms one against the other. They made an odd rasping sound, like two dry pieces of wood.

'I've done some thinking too,' she told him softly. There was an air of dignity about her that momentarily silenced him. Her eyes regarded his ashen face. 'There's been a great deal on my mind of late.'

'Hmh! Not about me, that's for sure.'

'Yes. About you, and Martha, and how desperately sorry I am for what happened.'

'Sorry!' he sneered. 'Won't bring her back, will it, eh? Won't

225

save me from the gallows either.' He watched her reel back at his words and was glad to have shocked her.

'Surely to God it won't come to that? I mean, they can't hang you for defending your own son.' The idea that he could be hanged had never seriously entered her head. 'She would have killed him, Doug. I *know* she would have killed him.'

'Happen I should have let her.' His lips curled wolfishly. There was so much loathing in his eyes that Rosie could almost feel it.

'Why would you even think such a terrible thing?'

'Because he ain't mine, that's why.' His fingers shot out and gripped her hand. 'That's what she said, weren't it, eh? The little bastard ain't mine.' His fingers closed tighter until she winced with pain.

'You *know* he's yours.' Shocked and enraged, Rosie wondered how in God's name Doug could think otherwise.

'Mine, eh! And how would I know that? You were always yearning for Adam. Even after we were wed, you still wanted him. Oh, don't deny it. Every time I looked at you, I could see it. I could feel it whenever I took you, and as far as I know you *still* want him! How can I be sure you and that bugger didn't copulate behind my back, eh? Come to think of it, the boy don't even look like me.' All these things had been churning over in his mind since he'd been put away. Now it was all he could think of. Eating, waking and sleeping, his mother's vicious accusation burned in him until he was almost crazy. 'If you ask me, it were all a set-up!' His finger-nails dug so hard into Rosie's skin that they drew blood. 'You deliberately antagonised my mother. That night, you could have handled her, but you called out for me. Why? I'll tell you why! Because it were all part of your plan. You wanted me locked up, so you and Adam Roach could have it all your own way.' Kicking away his chair, he dragged her up by the hair. 'My mam knew what you were up to, and you *wanted* her dead, didn't you, eh? You wanted me out of the way and her dead! That's right, ain't it?' In his madness he had lost all reason.

The pain was so bad, Rosie couldn't even scream. It was as though her scalp was being torn off. Suddenly the officer was grappling with Doug, and she was caught in the middle. A whistle sounded, and the door was flung open. It took four burly men to

226

tear him from her, and when he was led away, she was left bleeding and deeply shocked. 'It's all right, luv.' The officer gently showed her to an office. From a distance she could hear Doug yelling: 'He can have you . . . you *and* the little bastard! But I'll find you. I swear to God, if I get out of here, I'll hunt you down wherever you are!'

'Not the nicest fella that ever walked, is he?' The officer stayed with her while she received first aid. Handfuls of hair came out with the bathing, and there were deep scratches all over her forehead. 'You can press charges, you know.'

She shook her head. 'I don't want that.' Even now, Rosie was reluctant to make things worse for Doug. But, as far as she was concerned, they were even. If she had ever blamed herself for what happened to Martha, her guilt had now turned to contempt. How could he have believed his mother's vindictive lies about Danny being Adam's son? God! If that had been true, she would have gone with Adam right from the first. Marrying Doug was the biggest sacrifice she had ever made. And the reason was because she was carrying *his* child. When Danny was conceived, Adam was serving in the forces. Doug knew that. And still he was taking Martha's word against hers. If only she'd been given the chance, Rosie would have argued this with him.

The kindly officer escorted her to the front gates. As he let her through, he eyed her up and down. 'You don't deserve a man like that,' he declared. 'But when he's allowed visitors again, you'll be safe. I can promise you that.'

Glancing beyond him to the barred windows and the open yard, she replied simply, 'I won't be visiting again.'

His lined face softened slightly. 'I understand,' he said, closing the gates.

The sound of the huge bolts being thrust home sent a shiver down Rosie's spine. For a long poignant moment she remained perfectly still. In her mind's eye she recalled the awful scene in that tiny room. When Doug accused her of bearing Adam's son there was such loathing in his voice it had made her blood run cold. When he'd dragged her up by the hair, there was murder in his eyes.

There in the street, with the smell of the prison still on her,

Rosie made a heartfelt vow. 'Doug Selby, even if you were to be set free tomorrow, it's all over between us. As long as I live, I can never forgive you for renouncing Danny.' Danny *was* Doug's son. Now, he was an outcast without a father. 'But he'll have *me*,' she murmured, making her way to the tram-stop. 'With the help of the Lord, I can be mother and father to him.'

Peggy knew as soon as she opened the door that there was something wrong. She saw the way Rosie's hair was pulled over her forehead, saw the determined expression on that lovely face, and sensed there had been trouble of a kind. But the only comment she made was to assure Rosie, 'Danny's been as good as gold. He ate all his breakfast and now he's playing in the yard.'

'Thanks, Peggy.'

'I'll put the kettle on, shall I?' Peggy suggested. When Rosie gave no answer, but instead closed her eyes, Peggy went to her. 'Was it such a dreadful ordeal?' she asked kindly.

Turning, Rosie smiled, but it was a sad little smile. 'I shan't be going to see him again.' Coming away from the door, she sat herself at the table. 'Doug and I have nothing more to say to each other.'

Astonished, Peggy followed and sat in the chair opposite. The tea could wait. This couldn't. 'I can't say I'm sorry,' she confessed. Leaning forward on the table, she put her chin in her hands. 'I knew there was something the minute I saw you. What happened in that place?'

Rosie described everything. About how Doug believed Danny was not his, and how he'd viciously attacked her and had to be dragged away screaming. 'There's no future for us, not now,' she explained decisively. 'For Danny's sake more than mine, I've turned a blind eye to many things. Now that he's rejected his son, there's no need for me to go on pretending.' Though her heart was breaking for Danny, the fact that she would never live with Doug again was a great relief.

'You could go to Adam?'

'I could no more go to him than I could love Doug! You know how I feel about Adam taking Ned's business. Besides, one way or another, Adam is at the bottom of everything that's gone wrong in my life.' She could hear herself saying these things, but she was not entirely convinced. She might hate herself for loving him, but she couldn't stop that same love from growing more intense over the years. Adam was her first love. He was her *only* love. Now, though, it was all too late. 'Please, Peggy. Don't ever speak of him again.'

'If that's what you want?'

'Haven't I said?'

'Okay. But there's something *I* want to say, and the sooner I get it off my chest, the better.'

For the first time since she came through the door, Rosie smiled, a one-sided, knowing little smile. 'Go on then,' she suggested. 'You've been itching to tell me something since this morning, so you'd best let it out before you burst.'

'I want to come and live with you. I've been thinking about it for ages, gal. You and me, in this little house with Danny. It'll be really cosy. I can pay you a proper board, so you won't be too strapped for cash. I'll help with the cooking and washing, and I'll even mind Danny if you want to go out once in a while of an evening . . .'

'Whoah!' Rosie laughed. 'What brought all this on?'

'Well, it makes sense, don't it?'

Rosie shook her head. 'Thank you, sweetheart, but no,' she said. 'I know why you want to do this, and I'm deeply grateful.'

Looking Rosie in the face, Peggy blushed, 'I never could hide the truth from you, could I?'

'Not that I can remember.' She met Peggy's contrite gaze and her heart was warmed. 'Like I said, Peggy, no one could have a better friend. But your place is with your mam, and you know it. Danny and me, we'll manage well enough.'

'I'm really worried about you, Rosie, especially now, when you say you and Doug are finished for good an' all. You're on your own, and it's a cruel place out there for a woman on her own.' There was genuine concern in her voice. 'It's going to be real hard.'

'I know.' In fact, Rosie was acutely aware of her desperate situation. A short time ago she was a married woman with a regular, if small income. Now, suddenly, she was on her own, with a child to care for and no man in her life. What with her meagre savings all gone, and the authorities dragging their feet to help out, the time had come to make serious decisions. The last thing she wanted was to receive her friend's charity. Such a thing didn't bear thinking about! 'I intend getting a job,' she announced proudly.

'What about Danny? He can't start school until next year, can he?'

'I've thought about that.' Rosie hesitated, not certain how Peggy would react. 'And I'm going to ask your mam if she'll mind him. I know he'll be well taken care of, and I'll pay her good money.'

Peggy was thrilled. 'She'll like that. She keeps on about how we'll all be leaving home afore too long and nobody will want her then.' She laughed aloud. 'Honestly, the way she carries on at times, anybody would think she were headed for the rubbish tip.'

'So, you really don't think she'd mind me asking?' Rosie was visibly relieved. 'Only I wasn't sure.'

'What! She'll bite your hand off!'

'I'll ask her first thing in the morning.' Rosie felt as though she was once again in charge of her own destiny. 'Then all I need to do is find a job.' That would be the hardest thing because well-paid jobs without Saturday work were still hard to come by.

Sitting back in her chair, Peggy quietly regarded her. 'Are you any good at figures?' she asked.

'All right, I suppose.' Rosie was curious. 'I managed to feed and clothe us all on what little I got from Doug. And I was never more than two weeks behind with the rent.' She sat up, frowning. 'Why?'

At first Peggy was coy. Rosie didn't realise how lovely-looking she was. Once she was let out, men would fall over themselves to court her. Someone like Rosie could bring trouble on her own head without even realising it. 'There's a job going in the offices,' she said reluctantly. As soon as the words were out, she regretted them. It would be ironic if Robert, the office manager, took a liking to Rosie.

Rosie's brown eyes danced. 'Oh, Peggy, do you honestly think I stand a chance?' The idea of making her own way in the world was both daunting and exciting. 'Won't they want someone with experience? After all, it's been a long time since I went out to work. And anyway, I've *never* worked in an office.'

'You're right. They may not want you. But then again, the job's been vacant for a couple of weeks and, as I understand it, they haven't found anyone suitable yet. I even considered going after it myself, but I'm hopeless at figures and wouldn't know one end of a ledger from the other.' She giggled. 'Give me twenty-four hours and I'd have the whole place in chaos. The orders would be all wrong, and I'd be bound to get the sack.' She looked at Rosie and saw a different kind of trouble ahead, but knew that nothing she could say would stop her friend now. 'It's up to you,' she said. 'If your mind's made up, give it a try. What have you got to lose?'

While Peggy was talking, Rosie was thinking and now could hardly contain her excitement. 'I've got nothing at all to lose,' she said, suddenly pacing the floor and thinking aloud. 'I do have a bit of experience because a couple of times I prepared Ned's ledgers for the accountant. It was easy. All I did was copy some invoices into the book, and tot up the total at the end. But in a big store like Woolworths, there must be mountains of paperwork.' Her courage began to waver. 'Oh, Peggy! I'm so afraid something will go wrong . . . either I won't land a job, or your mam won't agree to have Danny.'

'She'll have him all right.'

'If I don't see her right now, I won't sleep tonight.' For the first time in years, Rosie was beginning to think of herself. It was a good feeling. 'If she says yes, that will be the biggest obstacle overcome, because I wouldn't dream of leaving Danny with anyone else.'

'By God! You don't let the grass grow under your feet, I'll give you that.'

'Will you mind Danny for a few minutes?' Rosie didn't want to take him with her. 'I know he wouldn't object to staying with your mam because he likes her a lot. But I won't mention it to him until it's all settled.'

'Go on then.' No sooner had she said it, than Rosie was out of the door and away down the street. 'Me and my big mouth!'

Peggy chuckled. 'If Robert takes a fancy to her, I've only myself to blame.'

Peggy's mam was delighted. ''Course I'll have the lad,' she agreed. 'And if you're still at your job when he starts school, I'll take him and fetch him home. It won't be no trouble, luv.' Her face beamed from ear to ear. 'By! And here were I thinking me useful days were nearly over.' A shadow crossed her face when Rosie reminded her that she hadn't yet got a job.

'Oh, but I will!' she promised. 'I'll have work before the week's out, you see if I don't.' Suddenly the whole world was opening up and nothing would stop her now.

Peggy wasn't surprised to learn her mam had agreed to have Danny. 'I told you she'd bite your hand off.' Strangely subdued, she made her excuses and left soon after. Rosie noticed the change in her mood, but put it down to tiredness. After all, Danny could be a handful when he put his mind to it.

After Peggy had gone, Rosie couldn't settle. The idea of being responsible for her own life again, made her nervous. At the same time she was looking forward to it immensely. Strange how unforeseen circumstances can change a woman's life overnight, she thought. When Doug was here, the idea of going out to work and leaving Danny with someone else was unnecessary and unthinkable. Then, when Martha came to live with them, Rosie became a prisoner. Now, because of a series of tragedies – Ned losing his business and deserting his wife, Martha's death and Doug's imprisonment – she was set free. Everything was changed forever.

Thinking of all that had happened, Rosie's joy faded. Going to the back window, she watched her son at play. He was a fine boy, and yes, Doug had been right because, except for the colouring of his hair, Danny bore little resemblance to his father.

When emotion threatened to overwhelm her, Rosie launched into a fever of cleaning. She cleaned the cooker and washed the curtains. She scrubbed the kitchen floor, then, when Danny came in tired and hungry, set about making the evening meal.

When at last she sat down with him, weariness washed over her like a tide, seeming to take the last vestige of her energy. Watching the boy tuck into his fish-dabs and scallops, she envied him his appetite. For days now she had been unable to eat. She couldn't recall the last time she had slept soundly, and though she knew the damage she was doing to herself, had seemed powerless to reverse the downward spiral. Now, though, when she began toying with the food on her plate, she was surprised and delighted to find that she was really hungry. She took one mouthful of fish, then another, and before she knew it, had finished the meal, leaving her plate as clean as Danny's.

Rubbing his eyes, he climbed down from the table. 'I think it's time you were in your bed,' Rosie told him. And he didn't argue.

When he was washed and in his pyjamas, she took him by the hand and led him upstairs. Normally he would talk all the way, but tonight he was unusually quiet. 'Where's my little chatterbox then?' she asked, tucking him into bed. She felt his forehead. There was no fever. 'It's all that fresh air made you tired, I expect,' she surmised. 'Peggy told me you played out all the time I was gone.' Reaching out, she took his favourite teddy from the bedside cabinet and laid it beside him.

In a move that took her by surprise, he grabbed her hand. His big eyes looked up, moist with tears, as he asked in a whisper, 'When's Daddy coming home?'

For one awful minute she was uncertain how to answer. Danny had asked the same question many times since Doug had been put away, and each time her heart was torn in two. 'Not yet, sweetheart,' she told him. He had suffered enough since that night, and she had to protect him from the truth for as long as possible.

'Is he with Gran'ma?' A tremor of fear touched his voice, and he visibly shivered. 'Has Gran'ma taken him away?'

'Don't you remember, I told you how Gran'ma went to Heaven?' The boy nodded so she went on, 'And no, he isn't with your gran'ma. He's just gone away for a while.'

'Is he coming home?' That same question, over and over.

And always the same answer: 'I don't know for sure.' But now she *did* know for sure, because 'home' was her and Danny, and Doug had forfeited the right to both. As far as the house itself was concerned, if the day ever came when Doug walked in through the front door, she and Danny would pass him on the way out. But Danny was too young to be caught in the middle of the bad feeling between them. 'I'm sure Daddy will come home as soon as he can.' She hated herself for misleading him, but what else could she do? If she told him the truth, the nightmares would start all over again, and he might never mend. Later, when there was no option, there would be time enough for the truth. Right now Danny desperately needed reasssurance.

'Is he a long way away?'

'Not too far, sweetheart.'

'Does he still love me?'

Rosie's heart almost stopped. 'I thought you already knew that?'

He considered her reply before raising his arms and wrapping them round her neck. Placing a sloppy kiss on her mouth, he said sleepily, 'Night, God bless.' He fell back into the pillow and closed his eyes.

'Night. God bless, sweetheart.' It was a long time before Rosie could tear herself away. She sat on the edge of the bed, gazing down at that small sleeping face and silently offering a prayer. 'You ain't given me much in life, Lord,' she whispered, 'but this little fella makes up for it all.'

After a while she returned to the living-room. From the door, she let her gaze roam round the room, from the few stalwart items of furniture to the threadbare carpet and yellowing net curtains. She recalled the very first time she had set foot in this house. After living with Doug's folks, it was like a dream come true; her very own place, a sanctuary from Martha and her vile ways. Now, Martha had tainted this place too, and it would never be the same again. 'You're still here,' she said aloud. 'You and him. You'll always be here.' Their presence was like a tangible thing, pressing down on her. But she wouldn't let it! In her heart Rosie had a new dream. A dream that didn't include Doug. It was just her and Danny, living in a different place, a place where they would be safe from the past, a place where nobody knew them. A safe and quiet place where they could start afresh. Not much to ask, but for now it was an impossible dream.

Rosie actually laughed aloud. 'Stop fooling yourself, gal,' she chided. 'First things first. Get yourself a job. Come next year

Danny will be starting school, and wanting all kinds o' things. Meanwhile, there's two mouths to feed, the rent to be paid, and decent clothes for your backs.' Tomorrow, she would put on her best bib and tucker and present herself at the Woolworths offices.

Coming into the room, she began clearing the table, all the while wondering what to wear. She had a nice two-piece, two pretty frocks, one best blouse and two well-worn skirts. She also had a very smart jacket hanging upstairs in the wardrobe. Yes, she might wear that. 'Best try it on before you decide,' she told herself. 'You've lost that much weight, it might resemble a blanket on a scarecrow.'

Her thoughts flew in another direction. Wonder what he's like this Robert Fellows? Until now, she had felt confident. Suddenly, with the office manager to confront, she was apprehensive. 'Don't get above yourself, my gal,' she warned. 'Happen he'll take one look at you, and show you the door.'

With that sobering thought, she washed the dinner things, locked up and went to bed. But she couldn't sleep. Instead, she conjured up all manner of appearances for Robert Fellows. She regretted not asking Peggy about him. Was he tall, short, thin or fat? Dark-haired or fair? Did he have a kindly manner, or was he sharp-tongued? But, whatever he was, she was determined to make a good impression. 'You can be sure of this, Mr Robert Fellows,' she muttered, 'if there's a job going, and I can do it, you'll find I'm not easily put off.' With that she drifted off to sleep. But it wasn't Robert Fellows she dreamed of. It was Doug. And beside him stood Adam, and it was like looking through a mirror at everything that had ever happened in her life. Soon, Doug's image faded and she was left alone with Adam. In her dreams, she let herself love him. When he took her in his arms the tears of joy ran down her face, and all her fears were gone.

When she awoke in the light of a new day, the tears lay stale against the coldness of her skin. There was a pain in her heart that wouldn't go away, and even when she threw back the curtains to let the sunshine flood in, it didn't lighten her spirit. Instead, she recalled how she had felt in Adam's strong warm arms, and was filled with the deepest regret. At that moment, she felt she was the loneliest creature in the world. 'Come on, Rosie gal!' she told herself. 'Feeling sorry for yourself won't pay the rent.'

Going to the wardrobe, she sifted through the meagre items until her hand came to the jacket. Drawing it out on the hanger, she took it to the mirror and held it against herself. It was a fitted style, slate grey in colour, with a dark velvet collar and velvet pocket flaps. 'That'll do,' she decided. 'It looks smart enough, and I reckon it will still fit a treat.' If not, she could always move the big bone buttons to make it fit better.

At nine o'clock on the dot Rosie went down the street hand in hand with Danny. He was excited about staying with Peggy's mam and chatted non-stop all the way there. 'My! You look very posh.' Peggy's mam regarded her with a critical eye. 'If you don't get the job, I'll eat me best Sunday hat!' she exclaimed. Rosie looked very elegant in her straight navy skirt and grey velvet-trimmed jacket. The hardest thing to decide was which blouse to wear beneath, but eventually she'd settled for the white one with the frilly collar; though the frill hid most of the velvet collar, it lent a touch of efficiency to her appearance, which she thought might appeal.

'Why, thank you,' Rosie said, flushing with pleasure. 'You don't think I've overdone the make-up?' Normally she wouldn't wear such a strong shade of lipstick, but Peggy assured her it suited her.

'You look grand, lass.' Peggy's mam beamed her approval.

'And the shoes?' Rosie raised her foot to show the black patent shoes. 'You don't think the heel is too high?' They were a heady three inches and already they were killing her.

'I reckon you look a real treat,' Peggy's mam told her firmly. 'Now be off about your business.' She smiled at the boy who was still clinging on to Rosie's hand. 'Me and Danny have got things to do.' Stooping to whisper, she told him, 'I thought we might go into town and have a sticky bun in that little cafe near the railway station. What do you say to that, eh?'

'Can I, Mam?' Looking up at Rosie, Danny's eyes were shining at the prospect.

''Course you can, sweetheart.' She took him in her arms and they clung together for the briefest minute, before he was running up the steps. 'You be good now,' Rosie warned.

It was Peggy's mam who answered. 'He'll come to no harm,' she said. 'Now be off with you.'

Going down the street, Rosie recalled where Peggy's mam was taking the boy, and her heart was heavy. It was the very same cafe where she had told Adam she was marrying his best mate.

The memory stayed with her on the tram, and it was with her when she stopped off the tram outside Woolworths. 'It's now or never, gal,' she told herself. 'So put your best foot forward.' She did, and it hurt. In fact, she would be surprised if the wretched shoes hadn't crippled her by the time she got home!

Taking a deep breath, she went into the main store. Peggy was the first to see her, and came rushing forward. 'Shouldn't leave me counter,' she said, furtively glancing round, 'but I saw you come in and wanted to wish you luck.'

'Where's the office?' Rosie felt completely out of place, and already her confidence was vanishing.

The woman came out of nowhere. 'Back to your counter, Miss Lewis,' she said in a frosty voice. And, with a little grimace at Rosie, Peggy hurried away. 'Is there some problem, madam?' Tall and sharp-featured, with her fair hair rolled into a sausage shape, the young woman was immaculately dressed in a black two-piece, with just a touch of white at the throat and a silver bar across her breast-pocket. The bar was etched with the words 'Miss B. Emmanuel, Floor Manager'. The woman looked Rosie up and down as though she was tasting something nasty. 'Perhaps I can help?' Her smile was stiff and her hands were constantly agitating against her skirt. She made Rosie feel nervous.

'I've come about the vacancy in the office.' When the woman closely scrutinised her, Rosie was tempted to turn tail and run.

'I wasn't aware they were interviewing anyone today.' Holding out her hand, she asked, 'May I see the letter?'

'I haven't got a letter,' Rosie explained, shifting from one foot to the other and wondering why she had been so vain as to wear such uncomfortable shoes. 'I heard there was a vacancy, and called in on the off-chance.'

The woman's face lit up and her smile broadened. 'Oh, I see!' she exclaimed. 'In that case, you've made a wasted journey, Miss . . . ?'

'It's *Mrs.*' More's the pity, Rosie thought. 'Are you sure I couldn't have a word with someone? Perhaps the office manager, Mr Fellows, might see me?'

She knew at once she had said the wrong thing because the smile slid from Miss Emmanuel's face and in its place came a look of horror. 'Good Heavens! Mr Fellows is far too busy to waste time on someone who just walks in off the streets. No, I'm sorry. You must write in with all your particulars, and, if you're lucky, you may be called for interview. Good day, Mrs . . .?' She paused, her mouth open, waiting for Rosie to provide the necessary information.

She bristled. She had taken an instant dislike to this arrogant woman. 'The name is Mrs Selby, and I would appreciate it if you could go and ask the gentleman himself. After all, it would be *his* time I'm wasting, not yours.'

The woman was adamant. 'We follow a procedure here, Mrs Selby.' Her voice was controlled, but her attitude was hostile. 'And I can assure you, there would be no point whatsoever in my going to Mr Fellows because his answer would be exactly the same.' Her handsome grey eyes were enhanced by thick mascara and a heavy pencilled line. Now, when they opened wide and stared at her, Rosie was put in mind of a panda. They opened even wider when a man's voice intervened.

'I heard my name mentioned, Miss Emmanuel?'

Both Rosie and the woman were startled. But it was the woman who became flustered at the sound of Robert Fellow's voice. 'Oh, Mr Fellows!' She swung round and almost fell over. 'It's this young woman.' Casting a cursory glance at Rosie, she went on, 'I *have* tried to explain that we can't just interview anyone who walks in off the street. I have also suggested she should follow regular procedure. But I'm afraid Mrs Selby is being rather rude and aggressive.' She sulked a little and her crimson lipstick stuck to the corners of her mouth. Rosie tried not to look, because it was one of those things that would irritate her all day.

Robert Fellows had a nice face. Not as handsome as Adam's, Rosie thought, but pleasant to look on. He was much the same build as Adam too, with strong broad shoulders and an easy manner that put her at ease. His eyes were softly brown, not dark like Adam's, and when he smiled, like now, she smiled with him. 'I think I can spare a moment for a little chat,' he told Miss Emmanuel in a charming voice. 'After all; we've already interviewed several people for the post, and as yet we've not been able to find one suitable candidate,'

'But we do have a proper procedure, Mr Fellows,' she protested haughtily. 'And I don't think we should make any exception.' She was aware that certain members of staff, including Peggy Lewis, were watching, willing her to lose the argument. 'It would set a bad example, if you see what I mean?' What she really meant was that she might lose face if he went against her advice.

Stepping between her and Rosie, he smiled. 'Oh, I think we can be forgiven in this instance.' Turning to Rosie, he said, 'All the same, I do hope you're not wasting my time?'

'So do I.' Rosie calculated him to be about thirty years old, yet he had a boyish charm that made her want to giggle. Strange, she thought, how she was constantly comparing him to Adam.

'To the office then.' He set off towards the bottom of the store and she followed, finding it difficult to keep up with his long strides, especially when the shoes on her feet were gripping her toes like a vice.

They passed Peggy's cosmetics counter. She gave Rosie the thumbs up sign. For her trouble, Peggy got a severe glare from Miss Emmanuel who was fuming by the front doors and blocking the shoppers' access. Then past haberdashery and on to the confectionery counter. At the point where the fabric racks met houseware, Robert Fellows took a left turn. For a frantic moment he was lost to Rosie's sight, but then she caught a glimpse of him hurrying up the stairs. Breathless, she ran after him. When she got to the top, she paused for breath. 'You ain't as fit as you thought, Rosie gal,' she chuckled. When she raised her head, Robert Fellows was looking at her, and she blushed to the roots of her hair.

A long, meandering room with large windows all round, the office was surprisingly welcoming. There were three desks with members of staff sitting at them. One man was aged and grey, the other fat and balding. At the third was seated a kindly-looking woman aged about fifty. She put Rosie in mind of Peggy's mam. Each desk has a large black telephone, and they all started ringing at once. 'We're a team,' Robert Fellows explained. Seating himself in a big leather chair behind his desk, he gestured for Rosie to occupy the upright chair immediately in front. 'Some people object to working in one big office, you know. They prefer to be shut away in a little room on their own. How do you feel about that?' His question was abrupt, taking her by surprise.

'I like the idea of working as a team,' she answered truthfully. 'And I would imagine it to be more efficient.'

His eyes gleamed. 'My sentiments exactly, Mrs . . .?'

'Selby.' She wished it could have been any other name, because no sooner was the word out of her mouth than the three clerks swung round to stare at her, three pairs of eyes all looking her up and down as though she was a curiosity. Robert Fellows appeared not have noticed so she went on, 'I'd best tell you straight off, I don't know the workings of a big office. The only ledger I've ever tended was my father-in-law's, and that was just to tot up the coal invoices.' That information appeared to have confirmed the three clerks' suspicions because they turned to stare at her again, although the woman did give her an encouraging smile.

Robert Fellows quietly regarded her. He liked what he saw. She was smart and presentable. She was not coarse or loud, like many of the applicants he had seen. And from what he could gather downstairs, she had stood her ground with the formidable Betty Emmanuel. As far as he was concerned, that alone spoke volumes for her character. On top of all that, she was exceptionally lovely; a little thin perhaps, but that was by the way. 'Write your name and address for me,' he suggested, pushing a fountain pen and a sheet of paper towards her.

As she wrote, he watched her closely, noting the rich brown hair that tumbled to one side of her face when she inclined her head, the long thick lashes and that perfectly formed face. It was one he would never tire of looking at.

'I'm sorry.' Pushing the paper back across the desk, she apologised, 'My handwriting isn't all that wonderful.' The truth was, she hadn't had much practice, and all the while she was writing she had been aware of his gaze on her. It had made her tremble

240

a little. Consequently, the writing was unsteady.

He studied it. 'You have a fine hand,' he told her truthfully. 'You say you know how to keep ledgers?'

'Well, it was only my father-in-law's, and just the one. I entered invoices and totted them all up at the end.'

'One . . . ten, it's all the same.' He smiled encouragingly. 'Are you good at sums?'

'Good enough, I think.' In fact arithmetic had always been her strong point.

'And the telephone?' When she frowned, he added, 'You'd be amazed at how many people are frightened to use a telephone.'

'I don't have occasion to use a telephone all that much. I don't have one at home.'

'What? You mean your husband hasn't had one installed?'

Rosie felt all eyes on her again, and thought the time had come to put her cards on the table. 'My husband is in prison.' Since the others knew, there was no point in pretending otherwise.

In fact, he had already sensed the atmosphere when she mentioned her name, and knew of the case. He doubted whether there was one person in the whole of Lancashire who hadn't read about Doug Selby and the tragedy that had led to his mother's death. He hadn't mentioned it because he wanted the truth to come from her. 'I know,' he said. And once again his smile put her at ease.

Rosie stood up then. Now that the truth was out, there was no point in continuing. She cursed herself for even thinking she could get a job. No one in their right mind would employ a woman with her background. She had intended lying, but the clerks had known instantly. While she carried the name Selby, she also carried its stigma. 'I'm sorry,' she apologised, preparing to leave. 'It seems I have wasted your time after all.'

'What are you like at making tea?'

'Nobody makes it better.'

'When can you start?'

'Tomorrow, if you like.'

'See Meg Benton.' He gestured to the kindly-faced lady, who readily beckoned. 'Give her your details, and I'll expect you to report for duty at nine o'clock in the morning.' With that, he pushed the chair back and strode out of the office, leaving Rosie too stunned to take it all in.

'You're one of us now, dear,' Meg told her.

Rosie couldn't believe her ears.

CHAPTER FIFTEEN

Rosie had been employed at Woolworths for five weeks. With Danny being well taken care of, and not seeming to miss her too much, she was happy in her work, and learning more by the day. Soon after she started, Robert Fellows went away on a course and one of the clerks fell ill, so it was left to the others to carry the extra workload. Rosie didn't mind; in fact, she liked to be kept busy, because it made the day go quicker before she went home to Danny. Now though, all the office staff were present, and Rosie had learned a great deal about the running of the place.

'Open that window, there's a dear.' Meg Benton loosened the collar of her blouse. 'I've never known it so hot in here.' She peered at Rosie from over her tiny rimless spectacles; teetering on the bony precipice of her nose, it seemed that any minute they would slip over the narrow edge, but they never did. 'Thank you, dear,' she said, when Rosie threw open the window and resumed her seat.

'Would you like me to fetch you a cup of tea from the canteen?' Rosie too was feeling uncomfortably warm. The August sun blazed in through the window, warming everything in its path; including the clerks bent to their work. 'It's almost lunch-time anyway.' She had arranged to meet Peggy in the canteen and, as always, was looking forward to their daily chat.

'That would be nice, dear.' Like the other two, Meg always ate her sandwiches at her desk. During this time there would be a smattering of small talk and gossip; the most recent discussion being the hanging of John Christie, found guilty of 'the most horrifying murders'. Beside this was the recent Commons debate on whether to suspend all death penalties for five years. Meg

Benton agreed. Horace Sykes declared: 'Hang them all', and Mr Mortimer had little opinion either way. As for Rosie, she still wasn't altogether convinced that innocent people would not be hanged.

'If you're going to the canteen, you might fetch me a glass of water?' That was old Mr Mortimer. He had worked in this office for many years now, and, as Meg Benton whispered to Rosie on her first day here, he was 'almost part of the furniture'. With his grey hair and starched white collar, he resembled a vicar. Old-fashioned and blessed with a sharp mind, he kept himself to himself, usually only making his presence known by loudly blowing his enormous nose.

Addressing Horace Sykes, Rosie asked, 'Can I get you something while I'm down there?' He was a sullen little man, balding on top but with a wild tuft of ginger hair sticking out over each ear. In fact, old Mr Mortimer had more hair than Horace.

Without looking up, he merely grunted. Rosie took that to mean no. 'I'll just finish this,' she said, feeding the invoice figures into the adding machine. 'If I leave it halfway done, I'll forget where I've got to.' Quickly now, she wrote down the sum total and ticked off the spent invoices.

'Oh, I'm sure you wouldn't do that, dear.' Meg Benton regarded Rosie through her tiny specs. 'You know, it really is remarkable how quickly you've picked up the routine here. If you continue to make progress the way you have these last few weeks, I shouldn't be at all surprised if you were next in line for a wage rise.' Broadly smiling at one and all, though neither men noticed, she pointed out, 'Mr Fellows always rewards the good workers, you know, and before long, you'll be quite indispensable.'

Mr Mortimer blew his nose. 'Nobody's indispensable!' he muttered, glaring at Meg Benton.

Horace Sykes had his say too. 'I really don't see how you can call Mrs Selby a good worker. What with Mr Fellows away on a course I'm amazed she could ask for tomorrow off. Selfish, I call it. It will only make more work for the rest of us.' Since Rosie had made it known that she would not be reporting for work tomorrow, it had been a bone of contention with him.

Meg wagged a finger at him. 'Now then, Horace Sykes! You know very well why Rosie can't come in tomorrow.' In fact, the whole of Blackburn knew that Doug Selby was being brought to court to answer the charge of murder. Smiling encouragingly, she turned to Rosie. 'Besides, I'm quite certain our newest recruit will bring all her accounts and figures up to date before she leaves today.' Regardless of what she might say, she didn't like the idea of having her own workload increased either.

'My desk will be cleared, I promise,' Rosie assured them. 'Even if I have to work through most of my lunch-break.' As she spoke, the big clock over the door chimed twelve. 'I'll come straight back with your drinks,' she said, rushing from the office.

Outside, she paused, leaning against the wall, with her gaze turned towards the ceiling and her mind in chaos. 'Bugger you, Horace Sykes!' she muttered. 'You make it sound like I'm going on a picnic.'

She was still fuming when she joined the queue for the drinks, 'One glass of water and a cup of milky tea, please,' she said. Within minutes the burly woman had put them on a tray, taken her money, and was already asking for the next order before Rosie turned away. 'Hmph! *She's* in a bad mood!' remarked Liz Rothman from houseware. 'I expect her old man refused her again last night!' Rosie left her giggling with her friends. If she didn't get a move on, she wouldn't even have time to eat her meat and potato pie.

Though the window was open and allowing a breeze through, the office was stifling after the coolness of the canteen. Mr Mortimer thanked her kindly for the water, taking it quickly from the tray and swilling it down his throat at an alarming rate. The glass had a magnifying effect on his nose and from where Rosie was standing, it appeared to fill the tumbler.

'If you like, I'll bring you another glass when I come back.' Collecting her lunch-box from the top drawer of her desk, Rosie waited for his answer. When none came, she said aloud, in a voice very much like Mr Mortimer's. 'Why, no thank you, Rosie, but it's very kind of you to ask.' He didn't even look up, but as she hurried away he blew his nose and said in an odd squeaky voice, 'All the same, nice of you to offer.' He ain't such a bad

245

old geezer, she told herself as she went down the stairs two at a time.

Peggy was seated by the table nearest the door. 'I've got your mug o' tea,' she said. Shifting along the bench, she made room for Rosie. 'How's it going then, gal?'

Rosie took a refreshing gulp from her tea. 'By! That's good,' she said. Running her fingers through her hair, she pushed it from her face. 'Apart from it being like a steam bath up there, it's going all right,' she answered. Undoing her lunch-box she took out a paper bag. Curling the top back, she inched the pie forward until only half was showing. 'I can't stop long,' she declared between bites, 'I've got a stack of work to do. Horace and Old Mortimer are already making sly remarks about me having tomorrow off.' She was quiet then, recalling how nasty Horace had been.

'You ain't taking notice o' them two, are you?' Peggy tapped her consolingly on the hand. 'Come on, cheer up. Tomorrow will be here and gone before you know it.'

'I wish the others would see it that way.' She sighed. 'Honestly, Peggy . . . why do some folk get so much pleasure out of being miserable?' Miss Emmanuel walked by just then, giving them each a fiery glance. 'Her and Horace should swap notes,' Rosie said with a giggle. 'They'd have a great time being miserable together.' She didn't feel like laughing, but it was either laugh or cry, and she had done enough crying to last a lifetime.

'Bugger her, and bugger Horace!' Peggy exclaimed. 'It ain't *them* who's got to face the judge tomorrow.' Lowering her voice, she added softly, 'I've said I'll come with you if you like?'

Rosie shook her head. 'No. Can you imagine if you were to ask for time off an' all? Likely we'd both lose our jobs.'

'You love your job, don't you?' She had seen a remarkable change in Rosie during these last weeks. Her brown eyes shone like chestnuts and there was a certain sparkle about her that made people stare when she walked by.

'I feel useful again, if that's what you mean.' But it was much more than that, and Rosie knew it. For the first time in years she had a real purpose, getting up in the morning with somewhere to go and knowing that come Friday she would have a wage,

enough to pay the bills and even the occasional shilling or two
to put by. She alone was responsible for herself and Danny, and
she liked that. For too long, she'd felt as though she had shrivelled
and died, and now something inside her was beginning to blossom. It was a good feeling. 'The best thing of all is that Danny
really loves staying with your mam.'

Peggy laughed. 'The feeling is mutual, I can assure you. What!
It's Danny this and Danny that. But he's a smashing kid. You've
done a good job with him, Rosie, gal.' In a more serious voice,
she asked, 'Do you reckon his grandad will turn up tomorrow?'

'Who knows? He might, but to tell the truth, Peggy, I've given
up on him.' Her troubled brown eyes belied her flippancy. 'All
the same, it would be nice if he did, for Doug's sake at least.'

'Happen Doug doesn't want him there?'

'Happen not.'

'Do *you* want him there?'

'I'm not bothered either way,' she lied.

'And Adam?'

Rosie was shocked. Peggy couldn't have known how, in that
very moment, she had been thinking of Adam. 'Anybody can
turn up. As far as I can tell, it's open to the general public.'

'I didn't ask that,' Peggy insisted. 'I asked whether you wanted
Adam there.'

Rosie thought long and hard. Did she want him there? Yes!
Did she love him? Yes! Was she ready to admit it? No! He was
married, and so was she. Taking a deep breath she answered
truthfully, 'It would be better for everyone if he stayed away.'
She took another gulp of her tea, then absent-mindedly twiddled
her hair between her finger and thumb. Now she was looking
at Peggy with fire in her eyes. 'Why do men always take us
for fools?'

Peggy laughed. 'Robert Fellows could take me for a fool any-
time.' She pursed her lips in a kissing gesture and made clicking
sounds with her tongue. 'Nice bit of all right, he is.'

The mood was lightened, and the minutes ticked away agree-
ably. 'I'd best get back. See you later.' Before Peggy could answer,
Rosie had replaced her empty cup on the rack and was soon
gone from sight. 'Like a flaming will-o-the-wisp!' Peggy chuckled.

Rosie's half-eaten pie was lying on the plate. 'Waste not, want not,' said Peggy, tucking in.

At half-past five, Rosie had finished the bought ledger. 'Good girl,' Meg Benton said as she put on her coat and left. Half an hour later, Mr Mortimer departed, grumbling at how 'some people have no consideration for others'. When Rosie asked him what he meant, he blew his nose twice and made a hasty exit.

'Ah, good!' exclaimed Horace Sykes as he passed Rosie's desk on the way out. 'I see you've started entering the stock orders for tomorrow.' He peered at the pile of sheets before her and, smiling to himself, went on his way. 'I hope your wife's burnt your tea!' Rosie mumbled after him.

When Peggy tapped on the door soon after six o'clock, Rosie was only halfway through. 'You'll have to go without me, Peggy,' she apologised. 'I've got to finish this or my name will be mud round here tomorrow.' She didn't want to give either of the men an excuse to complain about her. 'I did warn your mam I might be late, but she said not to worry... that she'd give Danny his tea.'

''Course she will,' Peggy confirmed. 'Do you want me to wait for you?'

'No, thanks. You get off home. Tell Danny I'll be as quick as I can.'

'All right, but I think you should have left it for them to do. *I* would have!' Making ghostly noises, she went down the stairs. 'Mind the bogey man don't get you!' she called out, and her echoing voice sent shivers down Rosie's spine. Soon everyone but the night watchman would be gone, and most of the place would be in darkness. Frantic, she sent her pen across the pages at a faster pace. 'If anybody puts a hand on me, they'll be sorry!' she warned Mr Mortimer's creaky old desk. And for the next half hour, even the smallest sound had her peering into every corner.

The office clock loudly ticked away the minutes; tick-tock, tick-tock, the rhythmic sound reverberating from the walls. It was half-past six, then quarter to seven, and still she seemed to be making little impact on the stock sheets.

At five minutes past seven, she turned over the last page and gave a sigh of relief. 'If I hurry, I might just catch the seven-fifteen tram!' When a man's voice answered, she almost leaped out of her chair.

It was Robert, and she had been too engrossed in her work to hear him come in. 'No need to rush for the tram,' he said, smiling as he came towards her. 'I'd consider it a pleasure to take you home.' In fact, he had just taken delivery of a new Vauxhall Velox, and would welcome the opportunity to show it off.

'Mr Fellows!' Rosie gasped with relief. 'You gave me a fright.'

'Well now, I certainly wouldn't want to do that.' Seating himself on the edge of her desk, he asked with genuine concern, 'What are you doing still here at this time of night?'

'As I won't be in tomorrow, I wanted to get the stock-sheets done.' She thought he looked incredibly handsome. She had only ever seen him in his office suit, with a sober tie done up at the neck and his fair hair slicked back. This evening, though, he was dressed in brown cord trousers and a grey cotton roll-top jumper. His thick fair hair was tumbling loose about his ears, and he had a sense of devil-may-care about him. For some reason, his closeness was making her nervous. 'I'm finished now, so I'll be on my way. Thank you for the offer of a lift, but the tram-stop is only a few minutes' walk. It drops me off right outside my street, you see.' Fumbling for her bag, she leaned forward. It was then she smelled the drink on him. She hadn't noticed it before, but now she could see he'd had one over the eight. 'Goodnight, Mr Fellows,' she said, quickly turning away.

'Please.' Putting his hand on her arm, he said softly, 'Let me take you home. Besides, I've been waiting for the chance to get to know you better.' Drawing her to him, he smiled into her eyes. 'You're very lovely. As soon as I saw you, I knew you would brighten up this dreary office.'

Rosie was affronted by this remark. 'Oh? And is that why you gave me the job?' she asked angrily. She made an effort to release herself from his grip, but his fingers were like iron bands round her arms.

'At first, maybe. But in those first few days when you showed yourself to be remarkably able, I realised I'd found the best of both worlds . . . a good-looker who could actually *work*!' When he realised she was not favourably impressed with his flippant remarks, he apologised in a sincere voice. 'Please, Rosie, don't be offended. I do mean it as a compliment.'

'I'm sure you do.' She struggled against him. 'But I really don't wish to discuss it. Right now I have a son waiting for me, and I mean to catch the seven-fifteen tram.'

With one mighty twist of her arms, she managed to free herself. Leaving her cardigan draped over the back of the chair, she grabbed her bag and made for the door. But he was right behind her. Before she could open the door, he stretched out his arms and pressed her to the wall. 'So you won't let me take you home?' he murmured brushing his face against her neck. 'If that's the way you want it, fine. But surely you won't deny me one little kiss?' Swinging her round, he brought his mouth down on hers. The kiss was long and passionate, with Rosie struggling beneath him and his arms wound tightly about her.

Just once he loosed his hold on her, and that was when the kiss was over. 'I think I love . . .'

Rosie didn't give him time to finish his sentence. Taking the opportunity, she lashed out with her foot and caught him on the shins. When he reeled back, she was out of the door and down the stairs. Even before he recovered from the vicious kick, she was running down the street. The tram was just drawing out. Quickening her steps, she reached it before it got up full speed. With one mighty leap she fell on to the platform and straight into the conductor's arms. 'A threepenny ticket, please,' she gasped breathlessly, then fell into the nearest seat and closed her eyes.

When she opened them again, she peeped out of the window to see how far the tram had got. 'This isn't the way to Castle Street,' she told the conductor.

'I should hope not!' he replied, his eyes twinkling. 'This tram goes to Whalley End.'

It was ten minutes to the next stop, quarter of an hour before the right tram came along, and gone eight by the time Rosie knocked on Peggy's door. Danny came running down the passage to meet her, and Peggy announced, 'About time too. We thought you'd decided to stay the night.' Rosie was tempted to explain there and then, but decided against it. Instead, she made her apologies all round and went home with Danny. Once there, she sat him on her knee, and he told her about everything he'd done that day.

Normally, Rosie was all attention when Danny described his little escapades. Tonight, though, she found it hard to concentrate, because something else was cluttering up her mind. It was Robert Fellows, and that long passionate kiss. It was the realisation that he was a very handsome man. It was the way his eyes made love to her. And, much to Rosie's astonishment, she was recalling it all with a great deal of pleasure. 'Watch yourself, Rosie, gal!' she muttered beneath her breath. 'He's probably had more fools like you than you've had threepenny tram rides.'

The court was assembled. The public galleries were full to bursting. 'Answer the questions truthfully, and explain it exactly the way it happened,' the lawyer told Rosie. She was fine until Doug was brought into the court flanked by two burly officers. Their eyes met and he was still staring at her when she looked away. If she had entertained any hope that he regretted all those terrible things he had said to her, she saw her mistake then. Hatred for her shone out of his eyes and smothered her.

Court was quickly in session. The jurors' heads followed the prosecutor like spectators at a tennis match, first this way then that. The pathologist gave his evidence. 'Killed by a single stab wound to the neck,' he said. When the clear plastic bag containing the knife was held up for the jury to see, there was an audible gasp from the galleries. Rosie hung her head. In her mind she was reliving every detail of that night, and she felt sick to her stomach.

The day wore on. Rosie was called to the stand, and in as clear a voice as she could, gave her version of what took place on that awful night. 'Martha had a knife to my son's throat,' she said, her voice falling to a whisper as she looked on the long sharp blade.

'Is this the knife in question?' she was asked. The bag was thrust under her nose. She was allowed to handle it, but the touch of the bag made her flesh creep.

'As far as I can tell,' she answered, quickly returning it. The knife had a white bone handle which was secured to the blade by the means of round flat rivets. It had been Rosie's meat knife, which had gone missing some time back. It made her shiver to think how many times she had used it for mundane tasks in the kitchen. She wondered again how Martha had laid hands on it. Perhaps it had been in an upstairs drawer all along.

'Describe the incident in question, exactly as you remember it,' she was urged. And a great hush fell over the court.

Rosie took her time. Doug's life was at stake and she did not want to get anything wrong. She explained how she and Doug were in bed when they heard the scream. She went on to describe how she was the first to enter her son's room, and was horrified to see that Martha had him and was threatening to kill him. 'She looked completely mad. Danny was crying,' Rosie recalled. And the memory was overwhelming.

'Please speak up.' The voice was not unsympathetic.

Clearing her throat, Rosie went on, 'I knew if I made even the smallest move, she would kill him.'

'Please tell the court what happened then?'

'Doug . . . my husband, he came into the room and tried to reason with her. But she wouldn't listen. She . . .' It was on the tip of her tongue to say how Martha claimed that Danny was not Doug's but Adam's. The mere thought of revealing such a thing made her hot with shame because, even though there wasn't a vestige of truth in it, she had often wished that it was so.

'Yes? You were about to say?'

'She was insane.'

'That was what you assumed?'

'Yes, sir.'

'Can you think of any reason why your mother-in-law should want to attack your son?'

'She had always been very fond of him.' Rosie silently prayed he would not press the point.

'Had you yourself rowed with her on that day?'

'Martha was not the easiest woman in the world to get on with.'

'I asked . . . did you row with her on that day?' Pausing on his way to the jurors' bench, he swung round and stared at her from beneath long bushy brows.

'Not a row exactly.'

'What then?'

'Martha liked to make things difficult for everyone she came

252

in contact with.' Glancing at the day nurses who had already given evidence as to Martha's unpredictable character, she wondered why they had to keep asking the same questions. It was almost as though *she* was on trial.

'Apart from the deceased . . . and your son, whose evidence has already been read out, the only other witnesses to what actually happened were yourself and your husband?'

'Yes, sir.' My God! She *was* on trial! Suddenly she was even more aware of the many accusing eyes all focused on her. In that split second her gaze fell on Doug's face. His smile was sinister, and she wondered whether he wouldn't mind being hanged, as long as she was hanged with him. There was a moment of silence when she felt as though the whole world had her in its sights.

There were more questions. 'Was there bad feeling between the accused and the deceased?' 'What exactly happened in that moment before the accused lunged forward?' 'Describe it to the court.' 'What happened immediately afterwards?' The interrogation was relentless. Then, just when Rosie had reached screaming point, the examination was over and she breathed a sigh of relief. 'Thank you. You may now step down.' Her legs felt like jelly as she made her way back to her seat.

After Doug's evidence was heard, and was seen to be compatible with her own, the jury retired to consider their verdict.

When an hour passed, and then another, many people left the court to gather in small chattering groups in the outer hall. Rosie remained in her seat. Almost alone and feeling totally exhausted, she stared up at the huge domed ceiling; carved with crowns and eagles, it was a spectacular feat, and even in her dilemma she couldn't help but admire it. In these awe-inspiring surroundings, she felt like an insignificant little speck. What would it matter if they *did* take her away and hang her? At once she thought of Danny, and was horrified by her own thoughts. 'God forgive you, Rosie,' she whispered, and her voice came back like an echo.

Unbeknown to her, when she had suffered all manner of fears in that confined witness box, Adam had lived the moments with her. From the back of the courtroom, he had willed her to be brave and not be afraid. He had listened to her version of what happened and had seen how distraught she was at the memory.

253

And he had loved her with all his heart. Yet, when the jury was sent out, he made no attempt to let Rosie know he was there. He was so afraid she would turn him away. He needed to think, to decide whether he should approach her. He vividly recalled her reply to his letter, when she had made it clear he was not welcome in her life. It was true that she was married and he accepted that. Even so, if she would only have him, he would spend the rest of his life taking care of her and Danny. As the years passed, he found it increasingly harder to accept that Rosie was not his, and neither was Danny. What made it worse was that they *might* have been his, if only he hadn't been so blinded by jealousy on that day she told him the truth about her and Doug.

Now, after all that had happened, the last thing he wanted was to alienate Rosie even more, and so, with this in mind, he went away to think. His heart told him to go to her. But his instincts warned him otherwise. After all, Doug had made no secret of his loathing for Adam, and he was still Rosie's husband. As far as Adam could tell, she must be suffering agonies for him. If either of them saw him there, it was bound to make matters worse. The best thing you can do is stay out of sight, he decided, cursing himself for having made the journey here. But his love for Rosie would not let him stay away.

As the crowd surged out, he went with them. In the grimy little cafe across the road, he ordered a strong black coffee. After paying, he took the coffee and himself to the farthest corner where he sat alone and friendless, his heart and mind with Rosie. And his thoughts in chaos as he wondered whether or not to return home without making his presence known to her.

It was mid-afternoon when the jury returned, and all this time Rosie had not moved from her seat, except to pace up and down when her legs grew stiff and sore. Deeply agitated, she wondered how Doug was bearing up. Her mind went from him to Danny, and then she was filled with fear for all their futures.

Suddenly the crowds were pouring back and the court was in session again. The jurors filed into their seats and, when requested by the judge, the foreman stood up to give the verdict. As he read it out, Rosie's heart almost stopped. Doug had been cleared of murder, but convicted of manslaughter. The judge's voice rang out in sentencing him. Doug stood in the dock, pale and nervous, his hands gripping the rail as though he desperately needed that support.

Rosie leaned forward as the sentence was given. 'Five years' imprisonment.' The words echoed over and over in her mind. Doug was to be put away for five years.

It was finished. She felt empty, shocked, but relieved that Doug had been cleared of murder. As he was being led away, he called her name. She looked up to see him struggling with his captors. His head was turned towards her, his face twisted into a grotesque mask. 'Five years, then I'll be back,' he yelled, that same sinister smile on his face. 'Mind you wait, my lovely!'

Long after he had gone from her sight, Rosie could see that devilish smile. She could hear his words, and knew they were a warning. Doug blamed her for what had happened, and would make her pay. *That* was the veiled warning he meant to convey. And, because of it, he had committed her to the same sentence he himself had received, just as surely as if the judge had put them away side by side.

From his place at the back of the court, Adam also heard Doug's message. But, unlike Rosie, he had not seen the wickedness on Doug's face. He wasn't aware of the awful rift between these two. Nor was he aware that Martha, and now Doug, had come to believe that he and not Doug, had fathered the boy. Adam knew nothing of all this. So, when the court was almost emptied, he remained, waiting for Rosie to pass by, and marking the moment when he could talk to her. She needed a friend. He could be that much at least, he thought.

Rosie took a moment to recover from the ordeal, though she would remember every minute for as long as she lived. Now, collecting her bag and fastening the buttons on her jacket, she turned – and almost fell into the arms of Robert Fellows. 'I've come to take you home,' he said. He studied her lovely face, and was touched by the sadness there. 'I behaved like a fool last night,' he murmured regretfully. 'Can you forgive me?'

'You have no business here, Mr Fellows,' she said sharply. Seeing him was quite a shock. 'As for last night, it was plain to me that you'd been drinking. I've seen that kind of behaviour

255

before and it's never very pleasant.' She had seen it all too often, she thought bitterly. 'Now, if you'll excuse me, I have to go . . . that is, if you think I should be allowed to live a life outside office hours?' Her voice was deliberately sarcastic. The truth was, she felt he had a bloody cheek coming here. Not only had it angered her, she felt mortified with shame.

'I deserve that,' he admitted. 'But I promise you, Rosie, it won't happen again.' He looked like a small boy caught out in mischief. 'Won't you give me a chance to make amends? After what's happened here, won't you at least let me see you safely home?'

Rosie was about to give him a piece of her mind when something happened that took her completely aback. The moment she raised her eyes, she saw Adam coming down the steps towards her. He was smiling. Then he was saying, 'Can we talk, Rosie?' And her heart was leaping out of control. With Robert Fellows on one side, and Adam on the other, she felt trapped. Which way should she turn? For the briefest moment she was tempted to go with Adam. But then she remembered. If only he hadn't turned from her years ago, they might have been together now. Yet it was she who had gone astray, and not him; she must not forget that. Still, hadn't he conned Ned out of his business? Wasn't he also married? And wasn't she? On top of all that, her husband had just been jailed for five years, and here Adam was, asking if they could talk. What in God's name was he thinking of? Surely he must know his presence was like a red rag to a bull!

Her steady gaze belied the turmoil inside her as she told him in a cool calm voice, 'I really don't think we have anything to talk about.'

Acutely aware of the other man standing nearby, Adam murmured his reply. 'I wouldn't agree, Rosie. But if that's the way you feel?' His broad shoulders stiffened and his dark haunted eyes set her alight.

'I do.' Her voice was crisp and hostile. 'Besides, I have a business matter to attend to.' She bestowed a smile on the bemused Robert Fellows. 'I think we should leave now.' He nodded and gestured her to lead on.

All the way up the aisle she could feel Adam's eyes on her. When she thought about it later, she didn't know how she stopped herself from running back to fling herself into his arms. Leaving him there was the most painful experience of her life.

'Handsome bloke.' Robert Fellows was faintly jealous. 'Married, I hope?'

Rosie turned the question. 'Are *you?*'

'What?'

'Married.'

Momentarily astonished, he stared at her then grinned, showing a good set of teeth. Except for one which jutted out at an odd angle to touch his lower lip – though it took nothing away from his good looks. 'You know very well I'm not married.'

'Makes no difference to me whether you are or you're not.' Come to think of it, she didn't even know what she was doing giving him the time of day.

'That bloke ... he seemed to care a great deal for you.' His gaze dwelt on her face. 'Who was he?'

'No one you know,' she said curtly.

'In other words, mind my own business?' He smiled, amused but curious. Back there he had sensed hidden emotions.

'If you say so.'

Afraid that Adam might be watching, Rosie allowed herself to be shepherded into the big black car. Soon they were driving away from the court and towards the narrower streets of Blackburn town. 'Castle Street, isn't it?' He gave her a sideways grin. 'You'll have to direct me.'

Too engrossed in her own thoughts, she made no answer. But when they neared the area, she indicated which way he should turn. Outside the house, she quickly disembarked, having spoken no more than two words the entire time. 'Are you all right?' he asked, walking with her to the front door. 'I can stay a few minutes if you like?' He *wanted* to stay. He wanted to take her to bed, but he knew he had to be very careful or he would lose her altogether.

'Thank you for the lift,' she said, deliberately putting herself between the door and him. She wasn't ungrateful. In fact, she had taken a liking to him.

'See you tomorrow then?' His brow furrowed. 'Only if you feel able, of course?'

'I'll be in tomorrow, Mr Fellows. You can rely on it.' There was

257

no point in sitting at home moping. For the time being, work was her salvation.

He nodded and smiled. Then he climbed into his grand car and drove away. She didn't watch him go. She didn't turn around when he had to slam on his brakes because he was staring at her and didn't see the lorry almost on top of him. Instead she quickly unlocked the front door and hurried inside where she fell against the wall and sobbed her heart out. 'You fool, Rosie!' she sobbed. 'Adam was there, and you let him go!' So much had happened that day, and all of it bad. All of it, that was, except for seeing Adam. In her mind's eye she recalled the desperate longing in his beautiful dark eyes. It was the same as her own. And it was wrong. That was what she must keep telling herself. The love she felt for Adam was wrong. And, however much it hurt, she must harden herself against it.

'I've got to know, Adam, how did he seem when they led him away? And what about Rosie . . . did she look well? Was she taking it all right? And what about the boy? Did you get news of him?' Ned Selby had been a haunted man when he first came to Adam some weeks back. He was still troubled, and it showed in his haggard face as he leaned over Adam's desk, pleading for news of his family.

'Sit down, Ned.' He waited until the older man was seated, then stared at him, shaking his head in frustration. 'For God's sake, man, you look dreadful,' he chided. Ned was unshaven, his hair was now streaked iron grey, and his face that of a man at war with himself. 'Where the hell have you been? By all accounts you never turned up for work yesterday, and here it is, eight o'clock, and I'm just about to finish for the day.'

'I'm sorry. I couldn't face work. I wandered about . . . just walked and walked. It were late when I got to bed, and late when I woke up. I've come straight here.' His large work-worn fists plucked at the baggy material of his trousers. 'I ain't been drinking. You know I don't touch the stuff.' His bloodshot eyes closed, he groaned and asked again. 'What happened? I need to know.'

'I don't expect you've had anything to eat?'

'*Couldn't* eat.'

Closing the ledger before him, Adam got out of his chair. 'Come on. I dare say Mrs Jessup has left more than enough for one.' He intervened when he saw how Ned was preparing to speak again. 'We can talk later. You look as if you're ready to drop. Come on.' He rounded the desk and heaved the big man out of his chair. Ned felt lifeless and heavy in his grip. 'Let's get you washed and shaved, then I'll tell you all you want to know while we eat. A deal?' He looked Ned in the eyes, his warm smile encouraging the other man.

'All right . . . a deal.' Ned actually returned the smile. It was a rare occurrence these days.

While he used the upstairs bathroom, Adam waited in the living-room. Mrs Jessup had left a note on the mantelpiece. 'Lit the fire in case there's a nip in the air. The dining table's set, and your meal's all ready on the table. Though why I couldn't have got you a roast of sorts, I do not know!' Adam chuckled. She was a real old tartar, but worth her weight in gold was Mrs Jessup.

Ned came down looking a changed man. He had combed his hair and shaved the grey stubble from his chin, his shirt-collar was done up, and as he came into the room, he told Adam 'You're right, son. I thought I weren't hungry, but now I'm bloody famished!' He rubbed his great fists together and stood awkwardly at the door.

Instantly putting him at his ease, Adam strode across the room and grabbed him by the shoulders. 'Here's another one who's famished,' he laughed. 'So we'd best go and see what the wonderful Mrs Jessup has to offer.' He led the way into the kitchen, and there, spread out on the table, was a feast; there were numerous dishes, all covered with pretty little cloths hung with beads; one contained a huge slice of salmon, another was full to the brim with tiny potatoes cooked and cooled in their skins, there were peas and carrots, and plump green beans, and right at the back on a long-stemmed earthenware dish stood a thick round apple pie and beside it a jug of pouring cream. 'By! It's enough to feed an army,' Ned declared, his eyes popping out of his head and his stomach playing an audible tune.

'Mrs Jessup has turned out to be a real gem,' Adam readily

259

admitted. 'She comes in every day from nine to five and I never have to worry about clean shirts, unmade beds or dirty dishes in the sink. Her only fault is trying to fill me with meat puddings and piping hot stews in the height of summer.'

Ned laughed at that. 'She wouldn't be looking for a husband, would she?' he teased. Then he remembered Martha, and the smile fell from his face.

Adam was quick to notice how Ned's mood had changed. 'You take these two dishes,' he pointed to the peas and green beans, 'and I'll take the rest.'

In the dining-room, the table was set for Adam. It took only a minute to lay another place opposite. When Ned was seated, Adam brought the jug of ice-cold water from the fridge. Placing another tumbler on the table, he said, 'If water isn't to your taste, there's beer ... or I could make you some strong black coffee?'

Ned waved away his suggestion. 'Water's fine, son. Anything else would only spoil Mrs Jessup's beautiful food.'

Aware that Ned was hungry, not just for food but for news of the trial, Adam told him. 'The verdict was manslaughter. Doug was sentenced to five years.' He spread the napkin across his knee and sat, still and upright, looking at Ned and feeling great sympathy for this man who sadly appeared to have lost his way in life.

Sighing, Ned closed his eyes, slowly shook his head and spread his hands over his face. For what seemed an age he remained like that, with his head drooped on his chest and his thick fingers hiding his eyes. Then he raised his face and his hands fell away to his knees. 'For what he did, five years ain't so bad.' He smiled faintly. 'And how did he take it?'

'He appeared to take it very well. Certainly he seemed in high spirits when they led him away.' He was remembering how Doug had called out Rosie's name, and how he had asked her to: 'Wait for me, my lovely.' The words were imprinted on his brain. 'He and Rosie appear to have been happy together, Ned,' he said now. 'Being separated this way will be hard for them both.'

For a moment Ned was tempted to tell Adam everything, to reveal how there was very little love between Doug and Rosie, and that for some long time she had led a bitter life with him. But, even now, he felt it was not for him to expose these things. He reasoned that if Rosie wanted Adam to know, she would tell him. 'And how was Rosie?' If he was mortally ashamed, it was because he had abandoned her and the boy, not because he had any lingering feelings for either Martha or Doug. They were two of a kind, and had made their own beds.

'Rosie's made of strong stuff,' Adam replied softly. Almost to himself, he added, 'I don't think I've ever seen her looking more beautiful.'

'Did you speak to her?'

Adam frowned as he recalled the man who had left with Rosie. 'I spoke to her only briefly. But she was fine, don't worry.'

'And the boy . . . my grandson. Did you get to see him?'

'No, I'm sorry.'

'Still, I know he's all right. Rosie would never let any harm come to Danny.' He swallowed hard. 'Was it all as they said in the papers? Martha threatened to kill the boy? She really did that?' At times he'd wondered whether there was any end to that woman's wickedness. But it was ended now, wasn't it? And who could have imagined it would take Doug to put an end to it? Yet, in spite of that, he couldn't feel any compassion for his son, no forgiveness or affection, no sympathy or sense of family feeling. Instead, he felt only the repugnance that Doug had felt for him.

'Everything was exactly as the papers reported it,' Adam confirmed. 'It's done now, Ned, and there's nothing you can do to turn the tide.' He had never seen the big man so devastated, and it touched him deeply. 'Why don't you eat?' he asked. 'Happen later, in a few days or weeks when the dust settles, you can visit Doug . . . go and see Rosie and Danny. Heal the rift, Ned. You can do that.' He would have given anything to enjoy that same freedom. But, for reasons known only to herself, Rosie had shut him out.

Seeming to consider what Adam had said, Ned heaped the vegetables on to his plate and cut himself a slice of that succulent salmon. He took a bite and moaned with satisfaction, then put down his fork and told Adam in a thoughtful voice, 'It's too late for that. What I did was unforgivable, and I can't ever go back.'

Adam didn't argue. A man had to come to terms with his own failings; just as he himself was trying to do.

At half-past nine, after the meal was ended and the two men had relaxed awhile in the big armchairs, Ned stretched his legs and stood up. 'I'd best be off,' he said, looking down on Adam. 'Or I'll be shut out of me lodgings.'

'You could always stay here, Ned. You know that.' Adam stood before him, and his words were sincere.

'Naw.' Ned shook his head. 'It wouldn't work, and you know it.'

'Happen you're right,' Adam conceded. 'But while I've a roof over my head, so have you. Remember that.'

'I will,' Ned promised. 'But you've done enough, son. No man could do more for a friend. You've given me a job, so I can hold my head up among my own kind, and you pay me more than I deserve . . . especially when I left you in the lurch after you were good enough to buy me out. If it hadn't been for you, I'd have slid deeper in debt and happen be in prison myself now.' When he'd turned up some weeks back, ill from sleeping rough and full of remorse at having left Martha, Adam had taken him under his wing and made him whole again.

'I thought we'd agreed never to talk about that matter again. Besides, there was nothing lost. It's now a flourishing business and, like I've told you, Ned, you can be part of it any time you want. To my mind, you're still the best coal-merchant there ever was. It isn't your fault you came on hard times.'

Ned put his great hand on Adam's shoulder. 'Happen not,' he said gratefully. 'But I've done my share of worrying about contracts and coal-rounds, and how to balance the books. Shovelling coal and doing odd-jobs suits me just fine. Besides, there are far sharper men than me out there now, son, and you know it.' He grinned. 'Look at yourself,' he pointed out. 'Young and ambitious enough to make it all come right. What's more, the buggers don't come much sharper than you, and that's a fact.'

'I've had some lucky breaks, that's all.'

'And you've made the most of 'em, son. That's what sorts the men from the boys.' He reached out to shake Adam by the hand.

'Goodnight, son, and thanks again. I'm a different man from the one you saw a few hours back. And you needn't worry, I'll be in the yard sharp on seven tomorrow morning.' He looked embarrassed. 'I don't know what got into me yesterday. I'm not sorry I stayed away from the trial. It's just that, well, everything got on top of me, and I couldn't think straight.'

'Enough said, eh? Get off home to your bed.' Ned was special to him, a lovely man Adam was always delighted to help.

He watched Ned amble down the street, and was glad to have been there for him. As Ned rounded the corner and Adam turned to go back inside, his attention was caught by two more figures hurrying towards the house; one was a man, the other a small girl. She was crying bitterly. The man was dragging her along, viciously tugging at her arm when she resisted. Adam recognised them at once. They were Connie's husband and daughter April. 'What the devil do you think you're doing?' he demanded, running down the street towards them. By this time the girl was in a dreadful state and the man was red-faced with fury. 'What kind of man are you?' Adam snapped, straddling his legs and blocking the path so there was no way past. 'You'll break her arm, pulling her along like that.' It was all he could do not to lash out with his fist. But the child was upset enough, and he thought the best thing now was to contain the situation.

'She's gone.' The little fellow spoke in a sob, snatching at his face with the tips of his fingers as though some insect was plaguing him. Adam recalled how Connie laughed when she told him: 'Sometimes I upset him just to watch how he grabs at his face until it's red raw.'

'She's gone, I tell you!'

'Who's gone? *Connie*?' The child had stopped crying and was staring up at Adam with red eyes. He wanted to snatch her up, but he hadn't the right.

'Who else?' the other man snapped. Suddenly he produced a note from his pocket. 'Read this, you bastard!' he snarled, thrusting the note into Adam's hand. When the child whimpered, he tugged at her again. But he stopped when Adam glared a warning at him.

In the lamplight, Adam read the note. It was short and cruel:

I've stuck it as long as I can. Don't look for me this time, because I'm never coming back.

I've taken only what's mine, apart from the girl. But you don't need to be lumbered with her, because she was never yours. She belongs to Adam.

Goodbye and good riddance,
Connie

Adam was shocked to the roots. 'Good God above!' He put out a hand and leaned his whole weight against the wall. Could it be true? In his frantic mind he tried to calculate when it was he had made love to Connie. The child had passed her third birthday some months back, so when was it he and Connie made love? When? For God's sake, he couldn't even think straight. No! The girl couldn't be his. But could she? Happen it wasn't altogether out of the question.

Before Adam could answer, the other man thrust the child at him. 'Take the brat! And to Hell with the lot of you! I must have been mad to get mixed up with the slut in the first place.' With that he swung away and almost ran down the street, leaving the sobbing child clinging to Adam's trouser leg, and looking up at him with big sad eyes that tore him in two.

'Well now. It looks like you'll be staying with your Uncle Adam for a while.' The child smiled through her tears when he told her, 'I've got apple pie and cream. Want some, do you?'

Blinking away the tears, she nodded eagerly.

'But you needn't think you're getting it *all*, gutsy.' She giggled at that, and he hoisted her on to his shoulders. As they went down the street, he muttered through his teeth, 'You bugger, Connie. You've really dropped me in it this time!' What the authorities would say about it all, he really didn't know. 'And whatever will Mrs Jessup have to say when she finds out?' That made him laugh. And the sound of her Uncle Adam laughing aloud was such a tonic that the child began laughing too.

'Laugh today, tears tomorrow!' Adam muttered. He couldn't get it out of his mind that Connie had said he was the girl's father. What he felt was hard to describe. But it was a mingling of sheer frustration, dark anger at Connie for having done such a cowardly thing as this, and a sense of bewildered pride that such a beautiful and lovely-natured girl as April might really belong to him.

CHAPTER SIXTEEN

'You surely can't be so heartless as to turn me away on Christmas Day?' Robert Fellows stood at Rosie's front door, a great bunch of flowers in one hand, and under his arm a pile of boxes all wrapped in pretty festive paper. 'Ask me in, and I promise you won't be sorry,' he pleaded in his most charming manner.

It was obvious he had made an extra effort on Rosie's behalf. He looked attractive in a long dark overcoat and white scarf. His shoes were highly polished as usual, and his hair carefully smoothed down from a side parting, making him look older. Snow was just beginning to fall. It settled on his shoulders like a sprinkling of flour, and the breeze which had chilled the air all morning gathered momentum. He visibly shivered, asking through numbed lips, 'Or would you rather I froze to death on your doorstep?'

'Whatever are you doing here?' she asked incredulously, her brown eyes widening with astonishment. 'It's Christmas Day, for goodness' sake. Have you no home to go to?' When the knock came on the door, Rosie was just taking the mince pies out of the oven. After that, she and Danny would be ready to take the presents along to Peggy's house; there was a new scarf for Peggy's mam, a pair of pearl-drop ear-rings for Peggy, and a selection of inexpensive games and trinkets for the younger ones.

Convinced the visitor must be Peggy, she was taken aback when she opened the door to Robert Fellows.

'No home, no woman, and no one to share the festivities with,' he replied. He looked like a lost soul, and Rosie couldn't help but smile.

'In that case, you'd better come in.' Stepping aside, she waited for him to pass her, then shut the door on the weather and shuddered. 'Brr! You've brought the cold in with you. Give me your coat. I don't want snow all over my new front room carpet.' It wasn't entirely new; in fact it was showroom soiled, but she had got it for two-thirds of its value. Best quality, with a dark red background and big cream roses all over, it gave the room a cosy feeling. Next, Rosie wanted two new fireside chairs and perhaps a dining table . . . a round oak one, and four tall-backed chairs with pretty seat cushions. But money was still short and her savings didn't mount up as fast as she would have liked, so a new table and chairs would have to wait. Meanwhile, she enjoyed window shopping in the big stores in Manchester and Blackburn. On top of that she comforted herself with the knowledge that she was keeping up with the rent and when it was cold outside, there was always a cheery fire in the grate, Danny had a new coat, and the larder was full to bursting. Life was ticking along without too much upset, and that was enough to be thankful for.

These days, since Martha and Doug were gone from it, the house had taken on a new lease of life. Thinking of her husband made her blood run cold. Two days ago she had received a letter from him. It was the letter of a madman.

'You really don't mind my calling round like this, then?' Robert's voice shook her out of her reverie.

'You're here now,' she said absently, her thoughts lingering on Doug and the letter. As for Robert Fellows, she *did* resent his arriving unannounced, even if it was only because this was hers and Danny's day. Coming up to Christmas, the store was busier than usual and everyone, including Rosie, had been called on to work extra hours. Though she loved the job and knew that Danny was content with Peggy's mam, Rosie had been eager for Christmas Day when she and her son could make up for lost time. For that very reason, she had even turned down Peggy's invitation for her and Danny to spend all Christmas Day at their house. Now, Robert Fellows' arrival was an intrusion, and though Rosie hated herself for thinking of it in that way, she still didn't know whether to be angry or pleased that he was here.

He seemed to know what she was thinking. 'I wouldn't have intruded like this, Rosie,' he claimed. 'Only, it is Christmas, and there I was, all alone in that miserable flat, and I couldn't stop thinking of you.'

She didn't answer straightaway. Instead, she shook the snowflakes from his coat and hung it on a peg, and placed the scarf over it. Now she was regarding him with friendly brown eyes that sent a thrill through him. 'I suppose it must be lonely all on your own. And after all, it *is* Christmas . . . goodwill to men and all that.' Even when he smiled, or perhaps *only* when he smiled, there was something about him that disturbed her. Yet, at the same time, she was grateful for the friendship that had developed between them these last few weeks. Certainly he had helped her get over the trauma of the trial, and how could she deny that his interest in her as a woman was very flattering?

He seemed peeved. 'I hope it isn't only because it's Christmas that you've asked me in?' he said softly. 'I'd much rather it was because you want me with you?'

'Look, Robert, I really am sorry to sound inhospitable.' It was strange how these days his first name sprang easily to her lips. In the office it was always 'Mr Fellows', but outside working hours they had seen more and more of each other. So much, in fact, that Rosie believed it was time for her to keep her distance. 'It was just that I didn't expect you to turn up here today,' she told him. 'Still, now you're here, you're very welcome.' A genuine smile appeared despite herself. 'Go on through. I know Danny will be pleased to see you.'

Regarding her with flat hard eyes, he said softly, '*Danny* might be pleased to see me, but you're not, are you, Rosie?' It was more of a statement than a question.

'If you must know, Robert, I'm thinking of the neighbours. I'm also thinking how I've been seeing a lot of you lately, and I think we're getting too involved . . . taking Danny to the Saturday afternoon matinee . . . walking arm in arm through Corporation Park . . . eating hot chestnuts from the barrow in the boulevard. The three of us acting like a family, when we're no such thing. It's wrong, that's all I'm saying. And it's not fair on Danny.'

'How can it be unfair on Danny?' he demanded. 'We take him everywhere we go, except for that one time when I finally managed to have you to myself. And don't say you didn't enjoy it, because I know you did ... a day in London, dinner and dancing at the most expensive night club.' His meaningful smile spoke volumes. 'It was only spoiled when you refused to come back home with me.'

'I'm not denying I enjoyed it,' Rosie assured him. In fact, it was one of the most memorable events of her entire life. 'It's just that I can't afford to make mistakes. Whether I like it or not, I do have a husband. I also have a son I dearly love, and people's tongues can be wicked.'

'What are you saying, Rosie?' He reached out, the tips of his fingers stroking her face. Her skin felt soft as velvet beneath his touch. Her obvious reluctance to accept the growing affection between them only made him more determined to have her. 'Have I offended you? Are you saying you don't ever want to see me again?'

Rosie sighed. The last thing she wanted was to hurt him. In fact she had a very soft spot for Robert. 'All I'm saying is this ... if the circumstances were different, I'd be delighted to go on seeing you. I like you, you must know that.' But she didn't *love* him. She loved Adam and always would. 'But we can't forget I'm a married woman. Even more important, I have Danny to consider. Tongues are already wagging. It's got out that we're seeing each other, and now here you are, turning up at the door, laden with presents. You've been seen, you can rely on that. And your visit here will be common knowledge all over Blackburn before the week is out.' Anger rose in her, and her brown eyes darkened. 'I'm not blaming you, but that's the way it is.'

'Do you want me to go?' Whatever her answer, he had no intention of leaving.

'I didn't say that.' All the same, she would have felt better if he'd stayed away. Some neighbours would understand, and others would make a meal of it. Malicious gossip could lead to all kinds of trouble.

'Say you're pleased to see me then?'

'All right. I'm pleased to see you.' Oddly enough, she was regretting having been too honest just now. Robert had been good company. He'd taken her out when she was at a low ebb, and restored her faith in herself as a woman. It wouldn't do any harm to make him feel welcome today. Besides, what woman wouldn't enjoy a good-looking man wanting to spend some time with her? Just as long it stayed within certain limits.

She ushered him through to the living-room. 'Of course I'm glad you're here. What's more, if you have nothing else to do, you're welcome to stay all day.' God! What was she saying? When would she learn not to let her tongue run away with her like that?

He stared about the room. It was warm and cosy, and the small Christmas tree for which Rosie had paid half-a-crown at the market stood bright and sparkling in the corner. He wrinkled his nose. 'Something smells delicious.'

'It's a turkey I bought for me and Danny. I left it cooking all night on a low light, and at six o'clock it was done to a turn.' The air was warmed by all manner of aromas; the newly baked mince pies, the simmering brandy pudding, and the bacon rolls lying crispy and hot atop the turkey. 'I hate leaving everything 'til the last minute,' Rosie explained. It had been hard work to get everything done, but it had been a labour of love.

'You're a real little homemaker,' he declared, seeing the blazing fire in the grate.

Excited, Danny leaped up from the rug where he'd been sitting cross-legged with his new jigsaw. 'It's *you*!' he cried, flinging himself into Robert's arms. In a minute he was being swung into the air as Robert sat him on his shoulders, nearly knocking the ceiling light down in the process. 'Your mam says I can stay all day if I like,' he told the excited boy. 'What do you think, Danny, shall I accept?'

'Yes, yes!' the boy cried, and the argument was won.

'In a little while, Danny and I have to play Father Christmas to the Lewis family,' Rosie explained, 'so you'll either have to amuse yourself here while we're gone, or you can come with us. Which is it to be?'

'I'll come with you, of course.' He thought it might be a good time to let the neighbours know he had staked a claim on Rosie.

Peggy was delighted when she saw Rosie at the door, but her smile fell away when she saw who was with her. 'You know Robert Fellows?' Rosie said as they all entered the hallway. Danny ran ahead, but Rosie stayed with Robert. She sensed

Peggy's hostility and felt the need to protect him.

'Rosie kindly invited me to share Christmas Day with her,' he said in his most endearing manner. 'I hope you don't mind my coming along?'

Peggy merely nodded, her face stiff. Turning her back on him, she led the way to the living-room. Behind her, Robert glanced at Rosie, and she returned a reassuring smile. Unbeknown to him, Rosie had already suffered a warning from Peggy where he was concerned. 'He'll bring you nothing but trouble, gal!' she'd said. But Rosie paid little mind. Instead, because she suspected Peggy's warning was not without a touch of envy, she explained how there was nothing serious between her and Robert. In fact, they were more good friends than lovers.

Peggy's mam was up to her elbows in baking. 'It's like feeding a bloody army!' she chuckled. 'I've been at it since yesterday morning and there's still the chicken to gut and stuff.'

'Away with you, our mam,' Peggy chided. 'You know very well you love it.' Turning to Rosie, she added, 'Honest, she's like a great kid at Christmas. I've told her I'll do the chicken and veg, but do you think she'll let me, eh?'

''Cause you've done your share, that's why,' her mam argued. 'If it weren't for your wages, happen we'd be having sparrer instead of a fat juicy chicken. So you look after your friends and leave me to do woman's work.' With that, she pushed the rolling pin over the pastry and began singing.

'There'll be no talking to her for hours yet,' Peggy laughed. 'What with her singing and that lot creating bedlam in the front room, I don't know whether I'm on my head or my feet.' It sounded like all hell was let loose in the front room. 'They opened their presents at four o'clock this morning,' Peggy groaned. 'You should see it in there. Honest to God, Rosie, it'll take a week to clean up the mess.'

She handed over her parcels. 'The more the merrier,' she said. 'But you can always hide them 'til next year.'

'What! That would be more than my life's worth.' Taking the presents, Peggy put them under the tree, all except her own. When she opened it and saw the pretty pearl-drop ear-rings there, she hugged Rosie hard. 'They're lovely,' she said. In fact, they were the very ear-rings she had admired in Slater's shop window when she and Rosie had taken a walk during one lunch break. 'You never forget a thing, do you, you bugger!' she said, eyes shining with affection.

Rosie's presents were from the whole Lewis family; a bottle of perfume and a pair of sheer stockings. She was horrified at what they must have cost. 'Oh, Peggy! How lovely. But I dread to think how much they were. I'd have been delighted with just *one*.'

'I know that!' Peggy exclaimed. 'And what they cost don't matter.' She shook her head and grinned. 'Anyway, it's me own fault for having a friend with expensive tastes, ain't it, eh?' Suddenly her mood was serious. Gazing fondly at Rosie, she said softly, 'You're the best friend in the whole world, Rosie gal, and after all you've been through, I wanted to get you something really special.'

Rosie was speechless. Her brown eyes softened with tears as she looked on Peggy's dear face. Choking back her emotion, she flung her arms rond her friend and hugged her hard. 'I love you, you bugger,' she whispered. When Peggy suggested they should get a drink from her mam's secret hoard of gin, tears turned to laughter.

Robert gave a slight embarrassed cough, and Rosie was mortally ashamed. 'We're neglecting our guest,' she told Peggy.

'He ain't *my* guest,' Peggy said stiffly. But when Rosie gave her a pleading glance, she relented. In a warm voice which hid her true feelings, she told him, 'But you're welcome to a drop o' the old stuff, if you don't mind drinking out of a cup. You see, we don't drink in this house as a rule, and we only ever had two glasses. Our kid broke them when he was searching for his presents, so I'm afraid it's cups for now.'

Sensing her hostility, he decided that if he wasn't going to alienate Rosie, he had better play along. 'Thank you, a cup will be just fine.' His smile was devastating.

When the bottle of gin appeared, so did Peggy's mam. 'You little sod, our Peggy!' she exploded. 'I thought I'd hid that good and proper.'

'Do you want a drop or not?' Peggy asked her, slyly winking at Rosie.

Before you could say Jack Robinson she'd scurried into the kitchen and fetched out a mug. 'And don't be mingy with the measure!' she warned, holding it out. When Peggy was too cautious with her pouring, her mam tipped the bottle in her own favour. 'That should warm the cockles of me old heart,' she chuckled, returning to the kitchen with her good measure of gin. In no time at all she was singing louder than ever. 'Canny as a barrow-load o' monkeys, is our mam,' Peggy said. And Rosie was glad to have them for her friends.

Half an hour later, Peggy showed her visitors out. 'Don't forget we're going to the sales in the morning, kid,' she reminded Rosie. 'There are only one or two shops open on Boxing Day, so we'd best be away by eight if we're going to snap up the goodies.' Then she shot a last speculative glance at Robert and closed the door.

'I don't think she cares much for me,' he said as they walked back to Rosie's little house. What Peggy Lewis thought didn't worry him the slightest, but he didn't want that silly little cow setting Rosie against him.

'It isn't you personally,' Rosie explained. 'It's what I was saying before. The neighbours have started to gossip, and Peggy's worried it might backfire on me and Danny.'

'I can see she's a good friend.' There was a bad taste in his mouth when he uttered these words. All the same, he knew them to be true.

'The best.'

'I care for you too, Rosie, and I wouldn't do anything to harm you or Danny. You must know that?'

Rosie didn't want to be drawn deep into conversation just now. So she was immensely grateful when Danny commandeered Robert to 'Play with my new jigsaw', leaving her to bustle about preparing the lunch.

Everywhere she moved his eyes followed, unsettling her, making her wish she hadn't opened the door to him. Yet, for all that, she found a certain comfort in the idea that, on this special day, Danny had a father figure in the house. The two of them made a heartwarming sight, sitting on the rug together, finishing the jigsaw, with Robert looking like any loving father with his son.

In one quiet moment Rosie paused by the kitchen door, observing them together. The jigsaw depicted a giant and a boy, and Robert was telling Danny the story of David and Goliath. She wondered whether she had been too hard on Robert. She couldn't know that even at that moment he was play-acting, aware that she was watching, and hoping to get to her through her son.

'Up to the table, you two.' Lunch was ready. Decorated with parsley and wearing white frills, the turkey was laid on a large flowered plate in the centre of the table. Round the rim of the plate the bacon rolls made a colourful contrast. There were numerous deep dishes, one with crispy baked potatoes, another containing small round Brussels sprouts, and a third filled to the brim with fluffy mashed potatoes. Alongside stood a small shallower dish holding six tiny Yorkshire puddings, and nearby a pretty floral-patterned jug filled with rich brown gravy. The delicious aroma permeated the air. 'I'm starving!' Danny exclaimed. Robert said it was no wonder when they were faced with such a wonderful spread. And Rosie took all the compliments like any woman would, with a knowing smile and a large pinch of salt.

During the meal, she relaxed her rule of no talking at the table, and the excitement of Christmas spilled over. Danny laughed and giggled, he chatted and threw his arms in the air when relating to Rosie the tale Robert had told him of David and Goliath. Robert was his usual good company. When, after picking at his food as he always did, Danny declared he didn't want any more, Robert persuaded him he should eat up all his greens and grow as big as the giant. Danny's eyes grew wide at the thought, and Rosie couldn't help but laugh.

When the meal was over and the table cleared, she realised that she had thoroughly enjoyed herself. In fact, she felt more relaxed than she had for a very long time. 'You don't have to do this,' she told Robert when he picked up a tea-towel and began drying dishes.

'And you didn't have to invite me in,' he said fondly.

As the day wore on, Rosie came to believe that she had done the right thing. Certainly Danny loved Robert, and he appeared to feel the same affection for the boy. She was torn two ways.

When the time came to shut Robert out of their lives completely, it was bound to be a real jolt for Danny. Conversely, how could she deny him the relationship that was already growing between these two?

The afternoon went quickly, and soon it was evening. Everyone was still too full up to want any tea, so while Danny insisted that Robert should finish the jigsaw with him, Rosie listened to a Sherlock Holmes mystery on the radio. Now and then she glanced at the two on the rug, and a warm feeling came over her. A little wry smile covered her face as she wondered whether it was the gin she'd downed at Peggy's house.

'I'm tired, Mammy.' At half-past nine, Danny rubbed his bleary eyes and fell into her lap.

'I should think so!' Rosie declared. 'It's way past your bedtime, young man.' Taking him into the kitchen, she undressed him and washed him all over. Normally she would have had a fire burning in the tiny grate, but what with all the baking and the oven remaining hot for some time yet, it wasn't needed.

'Can I help?' Robert got up from his chair when he saw Rosie carrying the sleeping child.

'He just keeled over,' she replied, her smile soft and loving as she gazed on the boy. 'But he does weigh a ton, so yes, I'd be grateful if you could carry him up for me.' Carefully, she delivered her son into his arms, and the three of them went out of the room and on up the stairs.

As she led the way, Rosie wished it had been like this with Doug. Even more so, she wished she had not lost Adam. Suddenly she brought herself up sharp. Who was she fooling? She *had* lost Adam. And even by the longest stretch of imagination it had *never* been like this with Doug.

To her surprise, she found herself wondering whether it would be so bad if she was to continue seeing Robert. Defiance grew in her. After all, she had no intention of ever living with Doug again. And if the neighbours gossiped, so what? It wasn't them who had to live her life. It was her. She was responsible for her own actions, and she was responsible for Danny. She had asked nothing from nobody, and while she had a strong back and two strong hands, she never would.

But when she looked at Danny, lying there in his bed, all her doubts came back. It did matter what the neighbours said, because gossip had a way of reaching the school playground and there was no one more wicked than children if they had a mind to bully. With Danny starting school after the holidays, she didn't want anything to go wrong. Then again it was common knowledge how his grandma had been stabbed to death, and that his daddy was in prison for it. So he already had his cross to bear.

'Penny for them.' Robert had laid the child in his bed before turning to see Rosie deep in thought.

She gave no answer, merely smiled, took him by the hand and led him out of the room. Once outside she closed the door and whispered, 'Thank you.'

He was pleasantly surprised. 'For what?'

'For making this Christmas Day so special for Danny.'

'And have I made it special for you?' His voice was soft, sensuously persuasive.

She thought a moment and then answered truthfully, 'Yes, I think so.' He was looking at her in that certain way again, and it made her tremble inside. In the half-light, his eyes seemed darker. The very nearness of him was intoxicating.

'I love you, Rosie.' Reaching out he put his hands around her face and kissed her on the mouth.

'No!' Her voice was strong, but inside she was weakening. It was so long since she had been with a man in that way, and like any woman she was hungry for love. The feel of his mouth over hers had awakened something in her, something she couldn't deny any longer. More than that it brought back tender memories of Adam, and with the memories came a kind of rage. The rage became passion, and passion blinded her to reason.

'Don't push me away, Rosie.' He kissed her again, and this time she responded. Encouraged, he murmured sweet endearments, tickling the inside of her ear with the tip of his tongue to set her pulses racing.

The need in her was as great as his own. 'Not here,' she said, glancing worriedly at Danny's door. Curling her fingers into his, she led him down the landing to her own bedroom. The room had been hers and Doug's. Now it was newly decorated, with a brand new bed and two pretty rugs that were soft underfoot. It was as though Doug had never been there. But none of that mattered now. He was out of her life and she was her own mistress.

Inside the room, she half drew the curtains, some deep instinct in her making her ashamed. Slowly, she undressed. He watched her; first the straight blue skirt that showed off the shapeliness of her ankles, then the cream blouse with its deep revers and pearly buttons. Then her full-length slip with the lacy hem. Now the see-through brassiere and flimsy knickers.

While she took them off one by one, he watched lasciviously, apreciating the slim and lovely form that was being temptingly revealed to him. At last she stood there in all her naked glory, and he gasped aloud. He had never seen such beauty. He knew he never would again.

Quickly now, all reserve gone, he threw off his clothes and took her in his arms. The small taut breasts touched the hardness of his chest, making his skin stand up in goose-pimples. 'You're magnificent,' he breathed. She didn't answer. She wanted him, and was not ashamed. He swept her into his arms and carried her to the bed. There he laid her down. All tenderness was gone now. Like a wild animal he cried aloud, gathering her to him and driving deep inside her. Hard and penetrating, he took her to himself in a frenzy, frantic she would escape him. And she returned his passion with the same ferocity.

Afterwards they lay, side by side, bathed in sweat and clinging to each other. 'I knew you would be wonderful,' he murmured. In bed, in the throes of lovemaking, she'd been as wild as he.

Rosie climbed out of bed. She dressed with haste, a sense of guilt overwhelming. Before he could realise her intention, she went from the room and made her way downstairs. The guilt went with her, the awful shame of what she had done.

He followed. When he came into the living-room, she was sitting in the fireside chair, her shoulders hunched forward and her troubled brown eyes staring into the dying embers of the fire. 'I want you to go now,' she said. Her voice was firm. It startled him.

Sensing her mood, he thought it best not to provoke her. Some women were like the spider, so filled with malevolence after mating that they devoured their mate. 'If that's what you want, Rosie.' She didn't answer. He felt uncomfortable. Glancing at the clock, he saw that it was gone ten. 'It might be just as well,' he conceded. 'But I will see you tomorrow, won't I?'

'Maybe.' It wasn't him she hated. It was herself.

He came to her then. 'Rosie, we made love just now. Doesn't that mean anything to you?' He actually believed it had given him a claim on her for all time.

The desperation in his voice made her look up. 'Of course it did,' she told him kindly. 'But it's been a long tiring day, and it's getting late.'

'But we *will* see each other again?'

'Why not?' She wasn't certain, but she could think about that later.

'Tomorrow?'

'No.'

'When then?'

'After I'm back at work.' She needed to spend the rest of the holiday with Danny. Just the two of them. Somehow, she felt as though she'd betrayed him.

'Whatever you say, Rosie. Just as long as I haven't done anything to turn you against me.' As far as he was concerned, the fun was only just beginning and if it was to be ended, it would be him and not her who did the ending.

'No. You've done nothing,' she promised him. Standing up, she kissed him lightly on the cheek. 'I'll see you out.'

They didn't exchange words at the door. He whispered goodnight, and she nodded. Then she closed the door and shot the bolt. A few moments later, she had a strip-wash after which she kissed Danny goodnight and went to her room, where she sat before the mirror brushing her thick brown tresses. 'You've done it now, Rosie gal,' she told herself in the mirror. 'The bugger won't leave you alone now.' She smiled, her mouth wide and beautiful in the mirror. 'Maybe that won't be so bad,' she murmured. 'Happen when you've got Doug out of your life forever, there'll be a better future with Robert Fellows. Danny won't mind, that's for sure.' Before she could stop herself she was saying what was on her mind. 'And what about Adam? What would he think of your behaviour tonight?' Instantly her mood changed, and the pain was unbearable.

When she climbed into bed, she was still thinking of Adam. And when she slept, she dreamed of him.

'ROSIE!' Peggy's voice sailed up from the street. 'You lazy little sod, get up and let me in.'

Half-asleep, Rosie hoisted herself up on to her elbows. It was a minute before she realised it was daylight. One glance at the bedside clock told her it was already eight o'clock. 'Gawd! Half the day's gone!' With one bound she was out of bed. As she reached the window, a stone clattered against it and Peggy's voice yelled, 'ARE YOU BLOODY DEAD IN THERE?'

Raising the sash window, Rosie leaned out. 'It wouldn't matter if we were, gal,' she shouted back. 'Because you're enough to *wake* the dead. And stop throwing stones! If you break this window, it'll cost you.'

Peggy laughed. 'Oh? And who's got up in a crotchety mood this morning, eh?' Kicking the door with the tip of her shoe, she moaned, 'Get a move on, gal. It's bloody freezing out here.' The milkman hurried by, his arms laden with bottles.

'I'll warm you up if you like,' he promised.

'Huh!' she retorted. 'It'll take more of a man than you, Ben Slater. Anyway, you've been handling them bottles and your hands must be like ice, so you can bugger off.' He went on his way chuckling to himself.

Rosie inched open the door. 'Get in here, you,' she ordered. 'Before the whole street's up.' As Peggy rushed in, the cold came with her and Rosie's teeth started chattering.

'The whole street *is* up, gal.' Marching into the living-room, Peggy went straight to the window and threw back the curtains. The daylight flooded in. 'It's a bloody good job we managed to get this holiday off, 'cause I don't reckon you'd have made it to work today anyroad.' She regarded Rosie with suspicious eyes. 'It ain't like you to oversleep, gal,' she teased. 'Ain't you well?'

'I'm fine.' Rosie went into the kitchen and filled the kettle. While she was lighting the gas ring, Peggy came in. She didn't say anything, but stood there, her eyes following Rosie's every move.

Rosie put the kettle on the ring and scooped up a bundle of kindling wood from the pile in the corner. Taking it into the living-room, she proceeded to light the fire. She knew Peggy was waiting for an explanation, and was unsure how to start. Little by little the events of last night were coming to mind, and were very disturbing to her.

'You slept with him, didn't you, gal?' Peggy knew Rosie like the back of her hand. 'You *did*, didn't you?' Coming into the living-room, she sat in the fireside chair. Rosie was still on her knees, blowing into the grate, trying to fan the flames through the kindling wood.

When it got hold, she leaned back on her haunches and looked up at her friend. 'Can't hide anything from you, can I?'

Peggy stared at her. 'You bloody little fool!'

Rosie shrugged her shoulders. 'Happen I am.' Clambering up, she rubbed her knees. 'I'll just go up and see if Danny's all right.' With that, she hurried from the room, leaving Peggy exasperated.

When Rosie returned, her friend was just pouring the tea. 'Is he awake?' she asked. She was quieter now, more understanding.

Rosie shook her head. 'He's still fast and hard asleep.' Now that she had her dressing-gown on, she was more comfortable, but still shivered when her bottom touched the cold wood of the dining chair. 'I'm sorry,' she said when Peggy sat down beside her. 'I know I promised I'd be ready by eight, but we can still make the ten o'clock tram if you like.'

'Don't fret, gal,' Peggy answered. She slurped her tea and stared at the tablecloth. 'Last night ... do you want to talk about it?'

Rosie peeped at her from the corner of her eyes. She did want to talk, yet she didn't. In the end she decided to stall. 'I had a letter from Doug the other day.'

'Oh?'

'I think he's gone off his head.'

'If you ask me, he was *always* off his head.' Her mind was still on Robert Fellows, and she was just the tiniest bit jealous.

Rosie got the letter from the drawer. 'I'm afraid for Danny,' she whispered, handing it to her. 'Read it, and you'll see what I mean.'

Sensing the fear in Rosie, Peggy unfolded the letter and read:

My darling wife,

I expect you're wondering why I haven't written to you, especially when you've so often taken the trouble to write to me?

I've been thinking of you a lot lately, and it's time, my love. Time to lay down some rules and regulations. You see, I have to abide by them, and it's only right that you should do the same.

How is the boy? Are you looking after him? I want you to keep him well for me. I wouldn't like it if you let him forget me. It was a shock to discover that he wasn't mine, but soon as ever I get out of here, I plan to deal with that little matter.

I'll be home sooner than you think, my love. Meantime, don't do anything that might anger me. I think you know by now that I'm not a very forgiving man.

I'm being made to pay the price for what I did. I think you should be punished too, you and the boy.

I know you must be lonely for me, but it won't be too long now.

Your loving husband,
Doug

Peggy dropped the letter on to her knee. 'I see what you mean,' she said, looking up at Rosie with shocked eyes. 'It ain't what he says . . . it's what he *don't* say that's so frightening.'

'Do you get the feeling that he means to hurt Danny?' Rosie spoke in a whisper in case the boy should come creeping down the stairs.

Instead of answering, Peggy put her own question. 'I didn't know you'd written to him several times?'

'I haven't,' Rosie confessed. 'I wrote to him just the once, soon after he was locked away. He never answered, so I didn't write again.'

'After he threatened you in court like that, you shouldn't have written at all.'

'I thought I should. He was under stress that day, and though I know it's over between us, I couldn't altogether abandon him.'

282

Rosie was frantic. 'This letter . . . tell me what you really think?' Taking the letter from Peggy, she absent-mindedly folded it, over and over, until it was small enough to hide in the palm of her hand. The very sight of it sent shivers down her spine.

'You're not to worry about it,' Peggy entreated. 'It's plain he doesn't know what he's talking about. I mean, fancy thinking Danny ain't his!' She shook her head in disbelief.

'It was Martha who put the idea into his head, and where his mother was concerned, Doug could never think for himself.' Every word she spoke brought back the horror of that night. 'He means to hurt Danny, I just know it.'

Peggy forced a smile. 'Give over, gal. How can he hurt anybody when he's locked away in jail?'

Now for the suspicion that had haunted Rosie since she'd received the letter. 'I'm sure he plans to escape.'

Peggy was adamant. 'Never!' She came to Rosie and put her arm round her. 'You're letting him get to you, kid, and that's exactly what he wants. Doug is a bad lot but he's a coward. Mark my words, gal, while he's in there, he'll toe the line. He'll do his time, and when he comes out, you and Danny need have no fear of him.'

'I wish I could believe that.' Rosie had tried hard to put the letter out of her mind, but it was always there, festering away in her mind. Suddenly she leaped up and threw it into the flames. It curled in the heat and then was gone, eaten up, like Doug was eaten up with jealousy and madness.

'That's the best place for it,' Peggy told her. She had returned to her chair and now was looking up at Rosie. 'Get on with your life, gal,' she said. 'Doug had his chance. Now it's yours.'

'What if I took up with Robert Fellows?'

'I reckon you'd be jumping out of the frying pan and into the fire.'

'Why?'

'Because, in a different way, he's as bad as Doug.' She was on her feet now, showing her anger. 'Robert Fellows has played around with everybody. He'll use you just like he used them. Once he's got what he wants, he'll be gone, looking round for another plaything.'

The only young woman he hadn't played around with, was Peggy herself. She bitterly resented that.

'He doesn't seem that kind of man to me.'

'Well, you can take my word for it. You'd do well to steer clear.' She didn't wait for Rosie's response. Instead she asked quietly, 'What happened here last night?'

'We had a wonderful day, the three of us. Last night after Danny was asleep in bed, we just . . . sort of fell into each other's arms.' The memory brought mingled pleasure and regret. She recalled the wild and wanton way she had behaved last night. That wasn't love. It was a raging desire for sex, and now she questioned herself as to why it had happened. It seemed like another person had been in his arms, not her. Just thinking about it sent a pink flush over her face.

'I've got to be going.' Peggy suddenly made for the door. 'I expect I'll see you later, gal.'

Rosie ran down the passage after her. 'Wait a minute, Peggy, I thought you wanted to go into town?'

'Changed me mind.' The door slammed and woke Danny up. After that, Rosie had little time to think about Peggy's abrupt departure.

An hour later, when breakfast was over and the two of them were getting ready for the ten o'clock tram, Rosie was fastening Danny's coat up. She couldn't think why Peggy had behaved in such a strange manner. It was when she began going over what they'd discussed that it suddenly dawned on her. When she'd first started at Woolworths, Peggy had mentioned that she liked Robert Fellows. But Rosie had taken that to be a bit of fun, something and nothing that she'd taken little notice of. 'Gawd! I must be blind,' she chided herself. 'Hurry up, sweetheart,' she told Danny, who had run back into the living-room for his lead soldier. 'I want to call on Auntie Peggy.' If she didn't put things right now, she would never forgive herself.

As Rosie closed her front door, Peggy came out into the street. For one uncomfortable minute the two of them stared at each other. Then Peggy laughed. And Danny laughed. And Rosie shook her head, a smile on her face and a lilt to her heart as Peggy came towards her. 'What must you think of me?' she asked.

'I've already told you,' Peggy replied, 'I reckon you're a bloody fool.'

Rosie laughed then. 'So do I. What's more, I'm not even sure he's worth it.'

'But you can have a bloody good time finding out, eh?'

'Friends then?'

'What else?'

'A long walk into town if we don't catch that tram.' With that, they went at a smart pace along the street and down towards the tram stop. Danny skipped all the way, and Rosie felt that everything would come right, as long as Peggy was beside her.

CHAPTER SEVENTEEN

Ned was all done up in his Sunday best. He knocked on the door and stood back, his shoulders against the wind. In no time the door was opened and Adam was heartened to see him there. 'By! Here it is February, and there's still no sign o' this shocking weather easing up,' Ned complained. As Adam opened the door to admit him, he took off his hat and shook the snowflakes on to the front doorstep.

'It's good of you to come round on a weekend.' Adam quickly let him in. As they went across the spacious hallway, Ned was surprised to see that he was being led towards the library. Still, he said nothing. However close he and Adam were, and however much Adam would have argued, he was still only a guest in this house. All the same, usually when he paid a visit, he was always made welcome in the grand living-room. There must be a reason for Adam receiving him in the library, he thought, but it wasn't for him to question why.

The reason was soon made clear. 'Sit yourself down, Ned,' Adam invited. Taking the other man's coat, he flung it over the back of a chair, oblivious to the little pool that was formed on the carpet as the heat of the room melted the snowflakes. He poured Ned a stiff whisky. 'That'll get the blood moving again,' he chuckled. Raising his own glass, he took a great swig.

Ned was shocked to see him drinking like that. As a rule, Adam rarely drank anything stronger than a pint of best or a glass of red wine with his meat on a Sunday.

'Mrs Jessup's in the other room with April.' Adam smiled and it was a smile filled with love. 'The little beggar won't sleep, and she's running rings round that poor woman. Still, since the dear old soul was widowed and came to live here, she's been a real godsend.' He strode to the window and stared out. 'Anyway, I don't want April hearing what I have to say, so I thought it best if we talked in here.'

'What's on your mind, son?' Still suffering the effects of the bitter wind outside, Ned sipped eagerly at his drink, shivering when it fired his veins.

Silence greeted him. He looked up to see Adam staring out of the window, his head bent and his dark eyes pained, and knew straightaway what was on his mind: the same thing that had been on his mind these past weeks; the same thing that drove him half-crazy when another day passed and still she wasn't home. 'You'll have to face it, Adam,' he quietly pointed out, 'Connie's not coming back.'

Deep in thought, Adam appeared not to have heard the older man's statement. Now, he swung round to face him. 'For God's sake, Ned, how could Connie just walk out and leave her child?' Slamming his fist on the window frame, he strode to the desk and sat down heavily in the chair. Picking up a pencil, he turned it over and over against the desk top, 'If she wants to end the marriage that's fine. It was always rotten anyway, and it's got nothing to do with me or anyone else. But the girl's a little innocent.' April was a warm and delightful little creature and he couldn't understand how Connie could have left her.

'It's no use. You'll have to go to the authorities,' Ned told him. 'Happen they'll find Connie.'

'Oh, aye! And happen they'll put April in some bloody awful institution.' The very idea was loathsome to him.

'Look, Adam. You've done all any man could be asked to do for a friend. But Connie's clearly gone forever, and you can't hold on to that child indefinitely . . .' He paused, making his next words convey a particular meaning. 'Unless, of course, she really *is* yours?'

Adam leaned back in his chair. 'I don't know, Ned, he answered truthfully. 'I can't say she is, and I can't say she isn't. All I know is this . . . until Connie tells me otherwise, I've got to behave as though she is . . . and that means taking care of her when there's no one else.'

'And how long is that?'

'As long as it takes.'

'It's been almost six months since she's been gone, and there's been no word whatsoever. Why don't you have another go at her old man?'

'Because he's about as bloody useful as an empty paper bag! I've lost count of the times I've tried to reason with him.' Adam had come close to thumping Connie's husband in the mouth on more than one occasion. But violence never solved anything, and it certainly wouldn't do the child any good. 'He swears April is mine, and so does Connie . . . the letter's in the cupboard there, you've seen it yourself. Anyway, it doesn't matter now whether she's mine or whether she isn't. The lass is with me, and she's staying put. And even if Connie's old man was to go down on bended knee, neither Hell nor high water would make me hand her back to that bloody little creep. Not when he's thrown her out and turned his back on her, like she was so much muck out of the midden.'

'Well, he's not likely to want her back, is he?' Ned snorted. 'Or he wouldn't have disowned her in the first place.'

'To tell you the truth, Ned, I don't know who's worse, him or Connie. I just thank the good Lord the child is too young to know what's happening.'

'Does she still ask questions . . . about her mam and dad, I mean?'

'Not any more. I don't have to tell you how distressed she was at first. But, thanks to Mrs Jessup, she's happy as Larry now.'

'Is there no news from that private detective?'

Adam sighed. 'No, not yet. But he's only been on her trail for a fortnight. There's time enough yet.' Groaning, he leaned forward to push his long fingers through his mop of hair, his whole expression one of misery. 'Dear God above! How can any mother leave her own flesh and blood like that?' He had come to love the child as his own, and now wanted only to keep her. Looking up with tortured eyes, he said in a gruff voice, 'The trouble is, Ned, even if Connie does come back, I won't want her to take April away.'

'I told you to watch out for that.' Time and again, Ned had

warned Adam he was getting too close to the child, and that it would only end in heartache; not just for Adam but for April too. 'When the time comes for you to give her up, will you cope?'

Adam gave a wry little smile. 'I don't intend giving her up,' he confessed.

'What in Heaven's name are you talking about?' Ned was horrified. 'If Connie turned up tomorrow and demanded the child back, there wouldn't be a single thing you could do about it.'

'There is just one. I'm not searching for Connie so she can take April away. When I find her, I mean to ask her to marry me.'

Ned couldn't find words to speak. Instead he stared in disbelief. Presently he warned, 'You'd only be making real trouble for yourself, son. Connie's already brought you enough grief. And besides, she's already married, or have you conveniently forgotten?'

Adam shook his head. 'No, I haven't forgotten. But for the legalities, that marriage is already over. It's April we have to think of now.'

'You don't love Connie, do you?'

'Not in that sense.' How could he love her? How could he love anyone when he only had thoughts for Rosie? But she had thrown him aside, just like he had thrown her aside all those years ago, just like Connie had thrown her daughter aside now. Thinking of Rosie made him sad. But then a little glow came into his heart. The child was the best thing that had happened to him since Rosie. Though she may not be his own, April loved him as though she was. She had even begun to call him Daddy. And why not? Certainly she had no one else but him. And he had no one else but her. Nothing in the world would be allowed to spoil the loveliness that had grown between them.

'Adam, think what you're saying. If you don't love Connie in that way, then how can you even think of marrying her?'

'If it means keeping April, I'm prepared to do almost anything.' He got out of the chair and came round the desk. Perching on the edge of it, he regarded Ned with honest eyes. 'You're the only one I can talk to, Ned. I need to know what you think. Sometimes it takes a different point of view to spot the pitfalls. What do you think? I mean, *really* think?'

Ned thought long and hard. He knew Adam had come to adore the child, and he knew that he was not prepared to give her up without a struggle. A fight for custody would harm everyone involved, particularly the child. Connie had claimed the girl was Adam's. She could have lied just to spite her husband. Equally, she could lie again, in court, on oath. Connie was the kind of woman who would break all the rules to get what she wanted. And even now, nobody knew what it was she really wanted! Moreover, a court case like that would cost Adam a small fortune. At the end of it all, he still might not have the child. 'As you've asked me, I'll tell you exactly what I think . . .' he said now.

'So, to my mind, he concluded, 'marrying Connie to keep the child might be the lesser of two evils.'

Adam sighed with relief. 'Everything you've just said only echoes my thoughts. I've agonised for weeks on this, Ned. At first, I wanted Connie to come home and take charge of her daughter. But gradually I began to think it could be the very worst thing that could happen to April. I've always known that Connie didn't care one way or the other about the girl; she saw her as a nuisance, someone who got in the way of what she wanted to do with her life. She even blamed April for ruining her marriage. Now she's just up and left, leaving a note claiming I'm the father. God Almighty, Ned! He might have done the child harm. He was certainly in a rage when he turned up here with her, and that's a fact.'

'So your mind's made up?'

'It is. And I'm not likely to change it.'

'Then there's nothing else to be said. But what if you don't find her?'

'I'll give it a few weeks, then I'll have to talk to a solicitor.' His face stiffened. 'But I won't let them take April away. I'm a wealthy man now. I can give her the best education that money can buy, and I'll see to it she never wants for anything. I've got the letter, signed by Connie, saying I'm the father.' His dark eyes glittered with defiance. 'Let anyone try and deny that, and they'll wish they'd never been born!'

Some time later, when Ned left, Adam returned to the living-room. Mrs Jessup was just coming back from the child's bedroom. 'She's wide awake,' she said with a patient smile, 'and she'll not sleep 'til you've been up and told her a story.' Shaking her head she began mumbling about how, 'Auntie Jessup ain't good enough to tell her a story! Auntie Jessup don't do it properly . . . not like Daddy does!' She wagged her finger at him and chortled, then shuffled off to the dining-room where she would lay the table ready for breakfast. After that, she would wash and make her way to her own room at the back of the house. There she would fall on her knees and say her prayers before gratefully falling into her bed. 'That little rascal would wear an elephant out!' she called after Adam as he went up the stairs two at a time.

He opened the door cautiously, in case April had gone to sleep. But no. As soon as he poked his head round the door, she was squealing with delight: 'Daddy! Daddy! April wants a story.'

'You should be hard and fast asleep, my girl,' Adam lovingly chided. No sooner was he seated on the edge of the bed than two thin little arms wound round his neck and his face was wet where she'd planted a sloppy kiss. 'Daddy tell April a story?' Her whole face lit up with joy on seeing him. It was the tiniest heart-shaped face, with a small upturned nose and the prettiest mouth; her fair hair curled about her neck and ears, and her huge brown eyes put him in mind of Rosie.

Suddenly the sadness had returned, and his mood was changed; though he was careful not to let the child sense it. 'Shall I tell you about someone I once knew?' he asked softly. 'A lovely creature by the name of Rosie.'

'Rosie.' The child mimicked the way he spoke her name and it was beautiful to his ears. He began. First he told her about the prince who used to be a soldier. 'The prince had fallen in love with a beautiful princess,' he went on. 'All his life he'd loved her, but while he was making up his mind to go home to her, someone else came and took the princess away.'

'Did the prince cry, Daddy?'

Not wanting to convey his own sadness to the child, he changed the story, gave it a happier ending. And soon the brown eyes closed and she was sound asleep. But as he turned away, there were tears in his own eyes. 'You were all kinds of fool, Roach,' he told himself. 'If you'd only been half the man you are now, you might never have lost her.'

He sat in the library until the small hours. The clock struck midnight, then it was two o'clock, and now the daylight was beginning to peep over the horizon. Tired and weary, but with the tiniest hope in his heart, he took up the pen and began to write:

Dearest Rosie,
Won't you see me? There are so many things I need to say to you. So many times I've started out with the intention of coming to you. But then I've realised you would only turn me away.
With Doug imprisoned, I wonder how you're coping? Is there any way I can help? All you have to do is ask, you know that.
The man who escorted you from the courtrooms, he was a stranger to me. Is he Doug's solicitor? Was he a friend? Does he have your interests at heart?
Oh, Rosie. How can I say it without it sounding wrong? I love you. As long as I live, I will always regret losing you . . .

He stared at the partly written letter, and his heart was broken. 'You bloody fool! What makes you think she'll even open it?' Torn in so many directions, he knew he could never send that letter. Now, when he voiced his thoughts aloud, he realised he had no claim on Rosie, and never would. What right have you to say such things to her, with Doug in prison and Rosie trying to make her way without him? She loves him . . . not you! You lost the right to Rosie years ago, and now it's too late. He crumpled the letter in his fist. Then, like all the letters before, when he'd poured out his heart and seen the futility of it all, he flung it in the bin. Besides, you have to think about April now, and Connie. And how, if your plans work out, you'll soon be a married man yourself.

Later, when he lay in bed, in the quiet, he couldn't shut Rosie out of his thoughts. When he slept she was there; when he woke, and all day as he worked, she was with him, breathing every

293

breath he took, like a tangible presence that wouldn't leave him. And though he was prepared to move Heaven and Earth for that dear rejected child he adored, nothing in life could compensate for having lost Rosie. And just as surely, he believed, nothing would ever bring her back to him. As he surveyed the years ahead, with or without Connie, all he could see was a great empty void that not even the child could fill. And he was desolate.

PART TWO
1955
When We Love

CHAPTER EIGHTEEN

'Let me look at you, sweetheart.' Rosie gazed down on her son, and her pride was so strong it was like a physical lump in her breast. 'My! You look so grown up,' she said, her smile enveloping him, 'It's hard to believe you've been at school for a whole year.'

During this past year he had taken on the appearance of a real little gentleman. Dressed in short grey trousers with knee-length socks, a smart dark blazer and a little cap adorned with the school badge, he was different somehow. Already she could see the man in him, and the realisation brought its own kind of regret. Somehow, Rosie couldn't help but feel that in her son's transition from bairn to boy she had lost something very precious to her, something that was gone forever and could never be recaptured.

'Oh, Mam!' Danny had acquired a habit of biting his bottom lip when he was worried. He did that now as he glanced at the mantelpiece clock and it told him they had only five minutes to get to the tram-stop. 'Miss Jackson will only shout if I'm late again,' he groaned.

Rosie feigned a look of horror, 'And we mustn't let *that* happen, must we, eh?' In fact, Miss Jackson was a kindly soul who had brought Danny's learning on in leaps and bounds, and Rosie viewed her with great respect, 'Get your overcoat on,' she told him, 'it's still snowing outside.' The snow had come with the beginning of January, bursting from the skies with a vengeance. The next day it fell steadily, and now, two days later, had lessened to a slight trickle. But the wind had grown in strength, and Rosie was wakened that morning when the windows began rattling in their frames.

Danny put on his coat. 'I don't want my scarf on,' he grumbled. 'It tickles my neck.'

'Sorry, love, but your mam wants you to wear it.' Rosie wrapped the scarf round his coat collar and tied it securely at the front. 'It's freezing out there.'

'Are *you* wearing a scarf?' He fidgeted, tugging at the scarf and grimacing.

'I'm not going out there without one, that's for sure.' Taking her long brown coat from the back of the door where she'd hung it the night before, she threw it on and quickly buttoned it up. Fishing a soft blue headsquare from the pocket, she wrapped it round her head, tying the knot tightly and tucking the ends beneath her coat collar. Next came woollen gloves. Now she felt ready to brave the elements.

Collecting a smaller pair of mittens from the sideboard drawer, she handed them to Danny. 'Here you are, young man. 'You'll need these.'

She watched him pull the mittens over his fat little hands. Satisfied, she collected her handbag from the chair, glanced round to make sure everything was ship-shape, and, propelling the boy before her, went along the passage and out into a cold wild day. 'We'd have done better to stay in bed,' she said through chattering teeth. Danny would have gladly gone off snowballing, but she dragged him back. 'There's no time for that,' she reminded him. 'We've a tram to catch.'

Peggy's voice sailed along the street. 'Hey, you bugger! Wait for me.'

Rosie was astonished. Not wanting to stand in the howling wind, she slowed her pace until Peggy caught up. 'I thought it was your day off?'

'It was. Until your fancy man asked me to come in.' Bending her head against the wind, she shivered and moaned, 'If I'd realised how bloody cold it were, I'd have stayed where I was . . . nicely tucked up in a warm bed.'

'Robert Fellows isn't my fancy man,' Rosie reproved. 'Anyway, I didn't know he'd asked you to come in.'

'Well, you would have if only you hadn't buggered off at half-past three of an afternoon, when the rest of us were still working,'

Peggy complained indignantly. 'You don't expect to know what's going on if you ain't there, do you now?'

'Aw, give over, Peggy.' Rosie said light-heartedly, 'I *start* an hour earlier, so I'm entitled to leave an hour earlier.' Lately, Peggy seemed to go out of her way to antagonise.

'Oh, I'm sorry, gal,' Peggy apologised. 'Take no notice of me. I reckon I've just got out the wrong side of the bed. Besides, if I had a lad to take care of, I expect I'd rearrange my hours an' all.' Glancing sideways at Rosie, she explained, 'There ain't no real mystery about why I'm trudging in this morning when I should be abed. All of a sudden we're one short at work, so I were asked to substitute.'

'One short. How come?'

'You know that silly little sod from stationery . . . Meg Withering, as big as a bloody ship an' ready to drop any minute?'

''Course she's not!' Rosie argued. 'She's only five months gone . . . still got two weeks before she finishes at work.'

'Aye, well, that's what she wanted everybody to think, so she could earn a few more wages. Crafty sod.' Shivering aloud, Peggy pulled her coat collar up. 'The bugger's *eight* months gone, and if your fancy man hadn't rushed her to the Infirmary in his car, happen she'd have given birth there and then, on the floor behind her counter, in full view of everybody.'

'Why didn't you tell me this last night?' Clutching Danny's hand, Rosie quickened her steps. Peggy had made them lose a few minutes and if they missed the tram they'd have to stand in the freezing cold waiting for the next one.

'I was about to. In fact, I were halfway down the street when it struck me that *he* would probably turn up any minute. I reckoned three would be a crowd, that's all.' There was just the slightest hint of envy in her voice.

Rosie still wasn't certain whether Peggy had forgiven her for spending more and more time with Robert. 'That's nonsense, and you know it,' she said sharply. 'You're always welcome in my house, whether there's anyone else there or not. And anyway, he didn't turn up, so I knew nothing about Meg Withering and her little drama.' She chuckled. 'Was it panic stations?'

Peggy giggled. 'You *could* say that. Meg were just serving this big fat fella when she grabbed at her stomach and screamed out that the baby were coming. Honest to God, you should have seen his face! He went bright red, then he went a dirty grey colour and looked like he were about to throw up. Then he turned and ran. Well, he waddled at a fast pace anyway ... his huge arse knocking all the displays over as he went. Cor! You should have been there, talk about a mess! Still, it ain't surprising when he were as far round as the bloody gas works, and his belly hung over his shoes.' She laughed aloud, then clamped her lips shut when the cold made her catch her breath. 'Bleedin' weather!' she said through stiff lips. 'I should'a stayed in me bed.'

She lapsed into a sullen silence, but Rosie chuckled all the way to the tram-stop. There was little said until the tram pulled up outside the school where Rosie saw Danny safely off. As he went through the gates with all the other children, she called out, 'I'll see you this afternoon. Wait inside the classroom now.' He waved and nodded, and in a minute was lost in the playground amongst the other children. The teacher blew the whistle and the children quickly formed straggly lines outside the door. The tram trundled away and Danny was lost to sight. 'It doesn't seem possible he's been at school for a whole year,' Rosie said, shaking her head and thinking it seemed like only yesterday that he was a newborn in her arms.

'A year, eh?' Peggy nodded her head, blue eyes surveying Rosie with curiosity. 'That's how long you've been seeing your fancy man.' When Rosie seemed preoccupied with her own thoughts, she went on, 'I expect you'll be announcing your engagement soon, eh? Then it'll be off with the jailbird, on with the new, wedding bells and happy ever after.'

Turning in her seat, Rosie looked her in the eye, 'What's bothering you, Peggy?'

She blinked with embarrassment. 'What d'yer mean?'

'You still don't like me going out with Robert, do you.'

'It ain't up to me.'

Rosie sensed the undercurrents and didn't like what was happening. 'Look, Peggy, you and me have always been able to talk things through. Why can't you say what's really on your mind?' When Peggy remained sullen, she murmured, 'Please. You've

300

always been like a sister to me. Don't let anybody spoil that. Not Robert, not anyone.'

Peggy looked into those troubled brown eyes and felt ashamed. 'I'm sorry, gal,' she said sincerely, 'I don't want to mar any happiness you might have found, because God only knows you deserve it. But, well, to be honest, I just don't trust the bugger.'

'It's got nothing to do with you wanting him then?' Rosie knew if she was to protect her close friendship with Peggy, it was cards on the table time. This wasn't the first occasion they'd discussed Robert Fellows, but Rosie always felt that they had only ever skirted the real issue.

Taking a deep breath, Peggy sighed. 'All right. Happen I do still fancy him,' she admitted. 'But he ain't got the time of day for me. He never has had. So even if you were to finish with him tomorrow, it wouldn't make no difference as far as I'm concerned.'

Rosie looked away. 'I honestly don't know what to do,' she said softly, looking out of the window and watching the thickening snowflakes splash against the pavement. 'I hate it being this way between you and me.'

'Do you love him?'

'I like him a lot.' She met Peggy's gaze honestly. 'I haven't really thought too much about it.' Rosie had grown closer to Robert without even realising it. 'But he's good and kind, and Danny has really taken to him.'

'I know all that. But you're not answering my question. What I said was, do you love him?'

Rosie smiled, but it was a sad smile. 'Happen I could learn to love him, but no, I don't feel that way now.'

'Still Adam, eh?'

This time Rosie smiled widely, but said nothing.

Peggy was relentless. 'Would you wed Robert Fellows if he asked you?'

'I'm married, Peggy. Don't forget that.'

Something in Rosie's voice made Peggy regard her more closely. 'My God! He's already asked you, ain't he?'

Rosie turned away, her attention caught by a group of youths throwing snowballs at the tram. The day was grey and bleak, just

301

like her heart. 'He asked me a week ago, when we went to the pictures,' she admitted softly, thinking it was a good job the tram was nearly empty. These days more people went on the buses. Soon the trams would all be gone, and that would be a terrible shame, she thought sadly.

'Well, you little sod!' Peggy cried in a hoarse whisper. 'And you never even said.'

'There was no point.' The reason she hadn't said anything was because she didn't really know how Peggy would react. The last thing she wanted was to hurt her friend's feelings, and anyway things were already delicate between her and Peggy. The thought of losing what she and Peggy had was a source of great pain to Rosie.

'And what did you tell him?' Peggy's voice betrayed her disappointment.

'I told him I already had a husband.'

'And what did he say?'

Rosie was reluctant to answer, because if she did she would have to tell the truth. 'Divorce him then,' Robert had said. 'I'm prepared to wait for as long as it takes.'

Peggy had guessed. 'Don't tell me. He wants you to get a divorce from Doug?'

'Something like that.'

'And will you?' Her voice was low and cynical. 'After all, it's over between you and Doug, ain't it? I mean, he's threatened to hurt you, and you ain't got no feeling left for him anyway. So you might as well put an end to it, ain't that right?'

Wisely, Rosie turned the tables. 'What would *you* do, Peggy? I mean, if you were in my shoes.'

Peggy was taken aback for a second, then she laughed. 'You know bloody well what I would do,' she confessed. 'I'd drop Doug like a hot cake, then I'd set myself up with Robert and look forward to a cushy life. *That*'s what I'd do. But then you ain't me, are you? You've got values and a high-minded sense of right and wrong. I mean, look how you took care of that bloody old battle-axe Martha Selby, even after she made your life a misery. Me? I'd have laced her fried eggs with poison and danced on her bloody grave!'

302

'No, you wouldn't.'

'Hmh! You've got a better opinion of me than I have of meself, gal.' She sniffed. There was an awkward silence between them, before Peggy cuttingly remarked, 'So? I expect you'll be dumping Doug for Robert, eh?'

Before Rosie could answer the tram pulled in to the kerb. In a minute the two of them were tumbling off and rushing through the cold towards Woolworths main doors. The warmth inside the building did little to melt Peggy's hostility. 'Well?' she asked as they wended their way between the counters, Peggy to the cloakroom and Rosie to the bottom of the stairs which would take her up to the offices. 'Do you mean to wed him?' Her blue eyes were cold as the day.

'I don't know,' Rosie answered truthfully. She had seriously toyed with the idea, but it was a complex issue, and always at the back of her mind was the fear that everything could go wrong.

'You'll be sorry if you do.' Peggy whipped her coat off. Normally she would leave Rosie with a smile on her face, but not today. Today she was unhappy. 'Like I said, I don't trust the bastard.'

'What do you mean, Peggy? *Why* don't you trust him?' Strangely enough, there were times when Rosie herself had her doubts, though she couldn't say why.

'Just a feeling, that's all. Happen it's 'cause I'm just a jealous bugger who wants him for herself, eh?' With that she swung open the doors to the cloakroom and left Rosie feeling dejected. For a minute she was tempted to follow, but then decided against it. This was neither the time nor the place for a heart to heart with Peggy. Tonight, though, after work, it would be a different matter.

Rosie was the first to arrive in the office. She hadn't been at her desk for more than five minutes when Robert came in. Striding across the office, he went straight to her and kissed her on the mouth. 'How about a meal and a show tonight?' he asked. 'Afterwards, maybe we could go back to your house.'

He sat on the edge of her desk, looking splendid in his well-tailored suit and with his fair hair neatly parted. His wide smile as always was a sight to see and his eyes sparkled. Rosie couldn't help but think about Peggy's words just now. 'I don't trust the bastard,' she had said. Now Rosie felt uneasy. 'Not tonight,' she replied.

'You still haven't given me an answer to my other question.' His smile was gone and in its place was a look of expectation. 'You promised to put me out of my misery in a week. Time's up, my lovely.' Leaning forward, he breathed in her ear, 'When can we be married?'

'There's so much to think about. It won't be easy. There's Doug and everything.' Rosie was shocked to hear herself using him as an excuse.

'You're not leading me on, are you?' Robert was smiling again. 'I wouldn't do that,' Rosie answered truthfully.

'Good. Because I wouldn't like it if you did.' He took her in his arms, and she couldn't help feeling it was good to be wanted.

The outer door swung to and in came Meg Benton, puffing and panting from the long walk up the stairs. 'By! It's cold out there,' she complained. Having taken off her coat in the cloak-room, she was still wrapped up like an eskimo, with a high-necked blouse beneath a thick woolly jumper haphazardly tucked into the waist of her long tweed skirt. She was wearing ankle boots and blowing into her frozen fingers. 'I'm getting too old to come out in this kind of weather.' Seating herself at her desk, she put on her tiny rimless spectacles and stared at Robert Fellows, who was still perched on the edge of Rosie's desk. 'Good morning, Mr Fellows,' she said in a loud bold voice. Judging by the look on her face, she obviously disapproved of the boss fraternising with the workers.

'Good morning to you, Mrs Benton,' he returned, at once clambering from the desk and straightening his tie.

The two men came in together. Mr Mortimer's eyes were watering from the cold and he coughed all the way to his desk. Horace Sykes took a minute to rub the warmth back into his balding head, then glanced at Rosie, shifted his gaze to Robert and remarked rather loudly to Mr Mortimer, 'Some of us are born to work, and some of us would rather play!' With that, he went to the filing cabinet and slammed the drawers about.

Putting his two hands on Rosie's desk, Robert Fellows leaned towards her. 'I'll pop round to your house this evening,' he told her softly. 'I promise you, my lovely, I won't take no for an answer.' He winked and hurried away, and she was left in a turmoil.

'You want to be careful,' Meg Benton warned quietly. 'Men like that can get you in trouble.'

Rosie smiled and bent her head to her work. Strange, she thought, because Meg's warning was the second of its kind today. She was beginning to wonder whether others knew more about Robert than she did.

As always when Rosie buried herself in her work, the morning was gone before she knew it. The telephone started ringing at nine o'clock, and it was still intermittently ringing at five minutes to twelve, when she thankfully made her way down to the canteen.

Halfway down the stairs she looked out of the window. The snow had stopped falling, and the watery sun was already breaking through. 'Thank God for that!' she exclaimed, running down the stairs. She was in a hurry to see Peggy. They had parted on bad terms, and it had worried Rosie all morning.

The canteen was always busy at this time of day, and there was already a long queue for the tea counter. Searching it for Peggy and realising she was nowhere to be seen, Rosie tapped one of Peggy's work colleagues on the shoulder – a big girl with huge bosoms, and peroxide hair piled high on her head. 'Have you seen Peggy?' Rosie asked. The girl shook her head. But from further along the queue came the reply, 'She's up with Mr Fellows. Been up there over an hour now she has. And I'm bloody well fed up, because I'm having to cover her counter as well as my own. Where the bleedin' hell is she? you ask. And that's what I'd like to know an' all!'

Rosie was astonished. What on earth was Peggy doing with Robert for over an hour? Surely to God she wasn't in trouble? How could he reprimand her for anything when she had turned out 'specially today to cover for an absent colleague? On top of that Peggy was a loyal and conscientious worker.

As she neared Robert's office, Rosie forced herself to be calm. It wasn't unusual for one of the floor staff to be called into the office; often it was merely a matter of quality assessment, or something to do with holiday periods, and sometimes it was the member of staff who called the interview. But an hour! Rosie felt instinctively there was something very wrong here.

At the same moment as she reached the top of the stairs, Robert came out of his office. 'Rosie!' He came towards her, eyes glowing with pleasure. 'Were you coming to see me? Have you decided to make an honest man of me then?' He would have kissed her but she drew away.

Glancing through the open office door, Rosie was surprised to see that except for his secretary, who was preparing to leave for her lunch, the room was empty. 'Where's Peggy?' she asked, turning to Robert with a puzzled expression.

He smiled, then gently ran his fingers down her face. Now he was drawing her towards the office. 'She's gone.'

'Gone?' Rosie was vaguely aware of the secretary passing them on her way out. 'Gone where? Isn't she well? Is she in some kind of trouble?' She and Robert were facing each other and he appeared to be concerned by her distress.

'No, my lovely,' he said. 'She is not in trouble, and as far as I know she's quite well. Or at least she was when she left me.'

'If she isn't in trouble and she's not ill, where is she?' Rosie was growing impatient, sure in her mind that whatever was wrong with Peggy, it must have something to do with the conversation they'd had that morning. Certainly Peggy had not been in her usual bright mood when they parted. In fact, now that she thought more deeply on it, Peggy hadn't been happy for some time. A sense of guilt spiralled up in Rosie. Maybe she should have been more tactful about her relationship with Robert? Happen it would have been better if she had tried to find another job? Whatever the reason for Peggy's problems, Rosie somehow felt it was all her fault.

'Sit down, Rosie.' Robert Fellows stood over her while she sank into the chair then sat on the desk before her, his legs stretched out and his face concerned. 'There's nothing at all wrong with your friend,' he assured her. 'Peggy came to see me about a certain professional matter.' He sighed. 'All right, my lovely, in the circumstances I'm sure she wouldn't mind my confiding in you. Peggy Lewis is a bright young woman who wants to better herself. Apparently she's been toying with the idea of applying for a training post in London.' He saw the light dawning in Rosie's eyes and quickly prompted, 'You know the one . . . a year's intensive training in one of our bigger stores, with a view to management?'

Rosie nodded. 'I pinned the details on the notice board myself,' she recalled. 'And you say Peggy's applied for it? Funny, she never mentioned it.' Something occurred to her then. 'You're not telling me she's gone straightaway? I mean, how could she?'

'She *wanted* to leave right away. I rang head office, told them she was the perfect candidate, and of course there was no objection. So, yes, she's probably on her way home to pack. After that no doubt she'll be travelling to London before the evening. As I say, it's all been arranged, right down to her accommodation.' He grinned handsomely. 'If it's handled right, these things can be done very quickly.'

Rosie was stunned. 'Was it you? Did you encourage her?' Suspicions were forming in her mind. He appeared too smug about the whole thing, too full of his own importance. Too pleased at the outcome.

'Shame on you, Rosie!' His eyes grew round with horror. 'What are you saying?' He came to her and placed his hands either side of her face. Expecting her to raise her face to his, he was shocked when she tugged away. Standing to confront him, she said angrily, 'There's something about you that seems too good to be true. I couldn't see it before because I was too blind and too hungry for affection. But now I'm beginning to wonder. Peggy's warned me about you all along. You can't deny it would be better for you if she was a long way away from here, far enough away so she can't come between us.'

Taken aback, he confessed, 'No, I won't deny that. It's also no secret she's made eyes at me in the past and I've made it clear I'm not interested. She's never forgiven me for that, and you know it.' His voice softened. 'You can't hold me to blame for whatever decisions she makes. And, as God's my judge, all I care about is you and me, and our future together.'

'I wish I could believe that.' Rosie wasn't altogether convinced.

Groaning, he declared, 'Believe me, Rosie, I had nothing what-soever to do with it. I was just as surprised as you are. Peggy asked to see me, and I honestly didn't have a clue what it was all about until she requested to be transferred to London at the earliest opportunity. I did what she asked, and that was all there was to it, I swear.' He sounded desolate.

'I'd best get back to my work.'

'Oh, look, Rosie, have you had your lunch? We could go out somewhere. What do you say?'

'I'm not hungry. Besides, there's a lot to do before I collect Danny.' And a lot to do before she knew what was behind Peggy's disappearance, she thought worriedly.

'All right, my lovely. Have it your way.' Putting his arms round her, he drew her from the chair. 'I do love you, you know.' His mouth was close to her face, and he stole a kiss. Though he regretted it when Rosie shrank away. 'It's clear you're not in the mood for company,' he said, releasing her. 'But I will see you tonight, won't I? You haven't forgotten I'm still waiting for an answer?'

She looked at him then, at his forlorn face and bright eager eyes, and her heart melted a little. Perhaps she was being unjustly hard on him? After all, it wasn't his fault if Peggy had decided to up and off. What was more, she must have sneaked out through the tradesman's entrance or Rosie would have seen her leaving. 'I haven't forgotten,' she said softly. 'Make it around eight o'clock. I know Danny will want to see you before he goes to bed.' She laughed, and he thought she was never more lovely. 'You'll be taken through every lesson he's had today,' she warned.

'I'll look forward to that,' he promised. And she believed him. She wasn't to know that on the stroke of three that afternoon, something would happen to betray to her the kind of man he really was.

Meg Benton bustled out of the office with a fistful of papers. Two minutes later she bustled back in again. 'Honestly!' Slamming the papers down on her desk, she groaned, 'It's no wonder the work never gets done around here. I've got a whole pile of queries which I want Mr Fellows to check, and there's no sign of him.'

Mr Mortimer coughed and said, 'That's because he's in consultation with the floor manager downstairs.' Smiling irritatingly, he reminded her, 'It's almost three o'clock, my dear. Have you forgotten they meet every week at this time?'

'Bloody management!' muttered Horace Sykes, scratching his near-bald head. 'I wouldn't give a shilling for any of 'em.'

'What about his secretary then?' demanded Meg Benton. 'She's nowhere to be seen either.' She glanced at Rosie, but looked away when the girl appeared too busy to hear.

'You know what they say?' interrupted Mr Mortimer sulkily. 'While the cat's away, the mice will play.'

Resuming her seat, Meg Benton put the papers aside. When the telephone began ringing, she warned, 'If that's a call that should be going through to *his* office, I'll scream down the line!' It was. And she didn't. Instead, she spoke in a very refined and polite manner that made the other three chuckle. Though when she put the phone down, she had plenty to say.

For the next ten minutes, the phone constantly rang, and each time the call was for Mr Fellows. 'That's it!' Flushed with anger, Meg Benton pushed her chair back and stood up. 'I haven't even had time to pick up a pen, and my work is mounting by the minute.' Striding to the door, she declared, 'I intend to find that secretary and give her a piece of my mind.' With that she was soon gone and the others, including Rosie, couldn't help but laugh.

Rosie was eager to be done and get home. She hoped Peggy hadn't yet gone because there was a great deal she had to say to her. Feverishly she tore into the last pile of stock-sheets, moaning beneath her breath when the jangling ring of the phone interrupted her line of thought. 'Good afternoon. May I help you?' Pressing the phone to her ear, she tried to write with her other hand. It was impossible so she paid attention to the voice at the other end. It was a woman's voice, soft and pleasant. 'I'd like to speak to Mr Fellows, please?' she said.

'I'm sorry, but Mr Fellows is in a meeting right now.'

'Oh!' There was a pause. Then, 'Who am I talking to?'

'This is Rosie Selby. Would you like to leave a message for him? I'll make certain he gets it the minute he returns to his office.'

'Could you please put me through to his secretary?'

Rosie sighed. 'I'm sorry, but she's out of the office right now.

She should be back any minute. Perhaps if you called again later?'

There was a sigh followed by a request that shocked Rosie to the core. 'I have to go out in a minute so I'd better leave a message. Would you please tell him his wife phoned? Has he managed to acquire a house for us yet? Ask him to ring me this evening, would you? Oh, and tell him his daughter Sadie sends her love. Thank you so much.'

'Good Lord, you've gone a pale shade of grey!' Mr Mortimer peeped at Rosie from beneath his reading glasses. 'An irate customer, was it?'

Even Horace Sykes was made to look up, mouth open to deliver some scathing comment. The fact that Rosie was sitting bolt upright, phone in hand and all the colour drained from her face, struck him dumb. Without a word he bent his head and resumed his work.

Just then Meg returned. 'Would you believe she was downstairs chatting to the floor supervisor?' Falling heavily into her chair, she explained, 'Apparently, Mr Fellows has put his foot in it by allowing someone to leave at short notice, at a time when we're desperate for floor staff.' When nobody commented, she grunted, scraped forward her papers, and began scribbling. 'Anyway, she's back at her desk now, so we shouldn't be bothered with any more of her calls, thank goodness!'

Rosie's mind was preoccupied by the woman's words . . . 'Tell him his wife phoned . . . His daughter Sadie sends her love.' She couldn't think straight. It was impossible to settle her thoughts enough to continue with her work. When she glanced up at the clock, she was greatly relieved to see that it was almost three-thirty. 'I'll be away now,' she said, collecting her belongings together.

'What? There's still a few minutes to go yet.' Horace Sykes had found his tongue, and it was as sharp as ever.

'You get off, my dear,' Meg Benton said. 'If the truth be told, you do more work than the three of us put together.' Glaring at the little man, she silently dared him to say another word.

When Rosie was out of the door, however, a little argument ensued. It took only a few chosen words to silence the two men, and for the remainder of the afternoon the atmosphere was so thick it could have been cut with a knife.

All the way home, Rosie tried to reason with herself. Was it a mistake? Had the woman somehow got the wrong number? Did she really say 'Mr Fellows', and did she mean Robert? 'You're a fool, Rosie gal, she muttered as she looked out of the tram window. 'Peggy was right about him, and you've fallen for the worst trick of all.'

Aware that she was talking aloud she glanced nervously about. With the exception of an old man who was buried in his racing paper, the tram was empty. Just as well, she thought, or they'll have me locked away for being out of my mind. She chuckled to herself. She *was* out of her mind, or she'd have seen him for what he was months ago!

The bad feelings began to subside, and in their place came a calm and rational mood. He didn't know she had spoken to his wife. So, as far as he was concerned, nothing had changed, and he was coming round to see her tonight. Want an answer to your 'proposal', do you? she thought bitterly. Stepping off the tram and on to the pavement, she went straight to the school gates. As she scoured the yard for a sight of her son, she forced all thoughts of Robert Fellows out of her mind.

The children were pouring out of the school doorway. Danny saw her and ran forward. 'Mam, look what I've done today!' Wide-eyed and excited, he raised a huge square of paper for her to see. It was a colourful drawing of nothing she could identify. 'Why! That's lovely!' she exclaimed, her face wreathed in a smile. Taking the paper between her hands she turned it this way then that, and still she couldn't understand what the coloured blobs were meant to signify.

'It's *you!*' he told her, eyes shining.

'Well, of course it is,' she returned, giving him a hug, 'I knew that all along.'

There wasn't another tram for fifteen minutes, but the bus was waiting as they ran up the street. 'I'm hungry,' Danny moaned, clambering into the seat beside her. When Rosie produced a digestive biscuit wrapped in foil from her handbag, he sat back

311

in the seat and contentedly nibbled at its edges all the way home. When they got off the bus at the end of Castle Street, he popped the last bit in his mouth and grinned up at her. 'I love you,' he said.

'Only because I gave you a biscuit,' she teased. Then she grabbed his hand tightly and hurried him away. The wind was as keen as ever, and the thought of a cosy fire grew more and more welcome the nearer they got to home.

Rosie's first stop was Peggy's house. 'I need to talk with her,' she told Peggy's mam, who quickly ushered her and the boy in out of the cold. She would have taken them into the parlour, but Rosie graciously refused. Her instinct told her that Peggy was not here.

'I'm sorry, luv, but she's gone ... been gone this past hour.' The older woman chuckled. 'By! That were a turn up for the books, eh? Our Peggy's gone on a training course to London. The next thing you know she'll be after the manager's job.' Her eyes grew round as two silver shillings. 'She's done her old mam proud, that she has.'

Rosie was disappointed to have missed her. 'Did she say where she'll be staying?'

'Nope!' She shook her head, frowning hard. 'But I expect I'll know soon enough. She's promised that soon as ever she's settled, she'll write, and if our Peggy says she'll write, then she will.' Suddenly she was going into the parlour at a run. 'I nearly forgot. She's left a note for you.'

She disappeared into the far room. For the next few seconds Danny hid behind Rosie's skirt when Peggy's Mam could be heard shouting and bawling at one of the children, 'Clean up this bloody mess, unless you want yer arse belted!'

It wasn't long before she came rushing out again. Handing a long white envelope to Rosie, she explained, 'Peggy said I was to give you this the minute you came round.' She peered at Rosie through curious eyes. 'You two fallen out, have yer?'

'We had a few words,' Rosie admitted. Waving the letter in the air, she added hopefully, 'Happen this will put it right.'

'Aye, happen. But I wouldn't count on it, lass. I'll not ask

312

what's come atween yer, but I know this much . . . our Peggy can be a stubborn little sod when she's put out.' She shook her head and saw Rosie to the pavement. 'Get away in, luv. It's enough to freeze the balls off a pawnshop sign.' Without further ado she slammed the door shut and, even as Rosie and her son walked away, the dear soul could be heard threatening blue murder at one of her hapless brood.

Rosie would have opened the letter straight away, but Danny was shivering and hungry, and so was she. 'Come on, sweetheart,' she told him, reluctantly placing the letter in a drawer. 'You lay the table while I light the fire.'

As always Rosie had already laid the paper and kindling wood before she went to work that morning, so the fire was quickly alight. Danny slowly but happily set about laying the table although he had the knives and forks round the wrong way, and brought out pudding dishes for dinner plates. But Rosie was grateful, and told him so. Besides, it took only a minute for him to rectify his mistakes.

Soon the living-room was warm as toast, and not long after the smell of meat pie and vegetables cooking in the kitchen permeated the air. 'I'm hungry!' Danny wailed, again sniffing the air.

'Do you know, so am I!' Rosie was surprised that she could even think about food after the shocks of the day. But she was even more surprised to discover she was oddly relieved that Robert was already married. This way she was off the hook. She even chuckled as she went about her work. Wait until she told Peggy! No doubt her reaction would be: 'Told you so'. But Rosie wouldn't mind a bit. In fact, she felt she deserved it.

Within an hour of arriving home, the meal was set before them, and they ate heartily. 'What else did you do at school?' Rosie asked with interest.

'I spilled paint all over Bobby Dixon,' he announced proudly. Seeing the horror on Rosie's face, he giggled. 'We all painted his picture, and Susie Lock got jealous and knocked my paint tray over, and it went all across my drawing.' He pulled a face. 'I don't like her any more.'

'Oh, Danny, I'm sure it was an accident.'

313

'No, it weren't. She did it because I wouldn't kiss her in the playground.' Picking up a piece of pastry he pushed it into his mouth and would have gone on muttering, but Rosie told him to finish his dinner and they could talk afterwards. Unable to speak, he nodded his head and forked another piece of pie into his mouth. When his cheeks bulged out and his eyes began to pop, Rosie warned him not to take such big bites or he might choke. He heeded her warning, and the meal was finished in silence.

Insisting he should help, Danny carried his own plate to the kitchen where Rosie was already running the hot water into the bowl ready for washing up. 'After everthing's put away, you can tell me what else you did at school,' she invited.

'Will you read me a story?'

'If you like.'

'Will you read me Auntie Peggy's note?'

'I don't think so, sweetheart,' she said solemnly.

'Why did you and Auntie Peggy fall out?'

'Who said we have?'

'Her mam.'

She nodded. 'Oh, so you heard that, did you?' Dropping the dishcloth into the water, she wiped her hands and put them on his shoulders. 'You know how you fell out with Susie Lock at school today?'

'I hate her!'

Rosie smiled. 'Do you *really* hate her? Do you think she *meant* to spill that paint over your drawing?'

He shrugged his shoulders. 'I 'spect not.'

'So she's forgiven, eh?'

'I 'spect so.'

'Why?'

He looked astonished that she should even ask such a thing. ''Cause she's my friend!'

'That's right, Danny. And Peggy's *my* best friend. We did have a falling out, but I hope it won't spoil our friendship either.' She went to the sideboard. With trembling fingers, she took out the envelope and opened it. The note inside was short and to the point:

314

Dear Rosie,

You may think I had no right to say the things I said. And you may think I never stood a chance with Robert Fellows. All I know is he had started noticing me. Then you came along, and I had no chance at all.

By the time you read this I'll be on my way to London. No doubt you already know all about it, seeing how close you are to *him*.

Don't try and contact me, because I've got a lot of thinking to do.

  Peggy.

'Oh, Peggy!' Rosie was desolate. It was so ironic, especially when Robert was already married and had no right to promise either of them anything.

'Is she still friends, Mam?' Danny came in, covered in suds and the front of his jumper soaking wet. 'Has she gone away for ever and ever?'

'We'll see.' Rosie's bright voice belied her true feelings. Taking off his jumper and draping it over the chair in front of the fire, she told him softly, 'Good friends don't ever say goodbye, do they?' She hoped not. Oh, she really hoped not.

At half-past eight, Danny was ready for bed. Rosie read him a story about a little boy who went on a great adventure, and before she reached the last page he was fast asleep. 'Goodnight, son,' she murmured, tucking the blanket about his shoulders.

She then dimmed the light and went on tiptoe into the bathroom. Here she bathed and put on her dressing-gown. She too was ready for an early night, and it was obvious Robert had changed his mind about calling. 'More's the pity,' she said, glancing out of the window and down the street. 'I was looking forward to passing on your wife's message!'

Downstairs, she tucked herself into the big old armchair and settled down to read the book which she had bought a few days before. It was a romance, and somehow it only reminded her of Adam and what she herself had lost. Disillusioned, she dropped it in the drawer and re-read Peggy's letter. 'All I can do is wait for you to come to me,' she said. After that, she sat in the chair, raised her legs beneath her chin, criss-crossed her arms round them and stared forlornly into the fire, watching the flames leaping and dancing, and wondering how poor folk ever managed to keep warm on a night such as this.

With the warmth fanning her face into a rosy pink glow, making her deliciously sleepy, and her far-off thoughts carrying her first to Peggy then to Adam, she didn't hear the knock at the door. When it sounded again, this time with more determination, she sat up, startled. A glance at the clock told her that it was almost ten-fifteen. 'Good God above, whoever's that at this time of night?' Springing from her chair, she drew her dressing-gown closer about her and went along the passage to the front door. 'Who's there?' If Peggy had been home, she would have assumed it was her. Certainly it was too late for Robert Fellows to come calling.

'It's me . . . Robert.' At once she recognised his voice. 'I'm sorry it's so late,' he apologised in lower tones. 'Let me in, my lovely. It's freezing out here.'

The tiniest smile crept over her face as she opened the door, but when he looked at her the smile was radiant. 'Robert! It doesn't matter whether it's late or not,' she cooed coyly, 'I'm just so pleased to see you.' He would have taken her in his arms but she quickly closed the door and went before him down the passage. 'I was just thinking about you,' she lied, coming into the room and watching him take off his coat. 'I've got the answer you've been waiting for.' Now she let him take her in his arms and kiss her. She returned his kiss passionately and was secretly delighted when she felt him harden against her.

'You've decided to marry me?' he declared eagerly, gazing down on her with the look of a cat who's got the cream.

'How could any woman resist?' she purred, and he kissed her again.

'Why don't we celebrate . . . let me spend the night?' His hands were probing beneath her dressing-gown, exciting and repulsing her all at once.

'Why not?' she murmured. 'Especially now that we're to be wed.' She opened her gown and he was shocked by her beauty; the taut pert breasts and the long shapely legs, the tiny waist and that dark enticing area between her thighs. Groaning, he gathered her to him. 'I've been thinking about you all day,' he whispered in her ear. 'Wanting you until I'd go half-crazy.' Quickly, he began to undress. He didn't see her smiling to herself.

When the two of them were naked, she held him off a moment longer. 'I'm so looking forward to being your wife,' she said softly. 'Mrs Fellows . . . it has a nice ring to it, don't you think?'

'Must you drive me mad?' He was kissing her hair, her eyes and ears, murmuring words of endearment, while she was pushing at his chest with the flat of her hands, and rolling her lovely brown eyes with childish excitement. 'I think I'll have my dress hand-made . . . you can afford that, can't you, Robert?' When he groaned and nodded, she went on, still resisting when he would have pushed her to the floor. 'And where shall we live? I'd like a big house in the country. Can you afford that too, Robert?' He nodded again, this time succeeding in laying her beneath him. He was about to push into her when she said in a low trembling voice, 'Of course, your wife won't like it. I mean . . . hasn't she been waiting for you to find a house for her . . . and your daughter Sadie?' Her eyes darkened with anger as they looked up, meeting his horrified gaze calmly.

His face was stark white in the firelight. 'How did you find out?' His voice was harsh and broken as he shivered with fright.

Lowering her gaze, Rosie saw that his member, which had been large and erect, was now shrivelled. It gave her a curious sense of satisfaction. 'I'm sorry if I spoiled your enjoyment,' she said cuttingly, getting up to replace her gown, 'I think you'd better go.' Fastening the belt around her waist, she gazed down at him with contempt.

'Bitch!'

'Don't come to my house ever again,' she warned.

He quickly dressed. When he was ready to leave he boldly suggested, 'Tomorrow, when we've both calmed down, perhaps we can talk this through? I could take you to lunch. I know a nice little place on the Preston New Road . . .'

While he was talking, Rosie was thinking ahead. It was obvious he'd had a great shock. It was also obvious that he would still pursue her for his own ends. Men like him never gave up their quarry. 'I won't be in tomorrow,' she said. 'Nor any other day. In fact, you can send me my cards and money owing.'

'You'll regret this, I promise you.'

'I'm already regretting it.' With that she opened the front door and pointed to the cold black night. 'Like I said ... don't ever come round here again.'

As he brushed past her, he murmured, 'You're a fool, Rosie!'

'No,' she corrected him, 'I've *been* a fool. Not any more though.' That said, she physically pushed him out of the door and closed it against him.

While Rosie returned to her cosy parlour, Robert climbed into his car, his face like thunder and his heart as black as night. 'You'll be sorry, Rosie.' He smiled, his white teeth shining in the moonlight. 'You *will* be sorry!' He started the engine, and was still smiling wickedly as he turned out of the street.

Rosie had made a bad enemy. The consequences of this night would turn her world upside down.

CHAPTER NINETEEN

Adam had interviewed at least twelve suitable men since Monday. It was now six o'clock on Friday evening and he was facing the final candidate. The man seated before him was in his early-thirties, broad of back and experienced in the coal-business. 'You'll have no cause to complain about me,' he promised now. 'Like I said, Mr Roach, I can lift a full sack of coal better than any man. I use a shovel like it were part of my own arm, and I'm trustworthy as they come.'

'Do you have a family?' Almost the minute this man had walked through the door, Adam had taken to him. Over the years he had learned to trust his instincts. He trusted them now, believing Roger Leyton to be the kind of fellow he was looking for. Built like a bull elephant, he was also likeable and intelligent.

A flicker of doubt crossed the man's face. 'I have a woman,' he said. 'Hopefully, the family will come later.'

'I see.' Adam had sensed the man's change of mood, and realised there was something painful there. Never one to pry where he wasn't wanted, he stood up to shake the man's hand. 'I'm glad you responded to the advert,' he said.

The man looked disappointed. 'Will I hear from you?'

Adam walked him to the door. As the man passed to leave, he told him, 'Report to me at six o'clock four weeks from Monday. The job's yours if you want it.'

Relief appeared on the man's face. 'How can I thank you?'

'By proving I've done the right thing in taking you on.'

'I'll do that right enough, don't you worry,' he said. Then he crossed the yard at a run and went down the street whistling a merry tune.

Ned looked up as Adam approached. 'By the look of it, you've given him the job.'

'He were the best man for it, that's why.' Slapping Ned on the back, Adam invited him inside. The yard was empty now. As usual, Ned was the last to leave.

Dropping his shovel into the bay, he shook the coal-dust from his clothes and followed Adam through to the office. 'Now then, happen you'll tell me what you're up to?' he suggested, pointing his thumb to the outer yard. 'There's no vacancy out there, yet you've taken on four new men to start in a month's time. There's summat up, ain't there, you artful bugger?'

While Ned talked, Adam brewed a strong pot of coffee. He poured the dark liquid into the mugs, adding milk and sugar as he pondered on Ned's words. 'You're right,' he began. 'There *is* summat up, as you put it.' Handing Ned one of the mugs, he took his own and sat on the edge of the desk. 'I'm not telling you anything you don't already know when I remind you how a man by the name of Len Sutcliffe has carved quite a business for himself. To tell you the truth, Ned, if I hadn't nipped in there when I did, he'd have snapped up many of the big contracts.'

'Len Sutcliffe?' Ned's expression hardened. 'By! He spreads his wings, don't he, eh? That bugger has a habit o' moving in on the lame, and sucking at their blood, and I should know. Thanks to you, though, he got his nose pushed well out of joint, I'm happy to say.'

Adam took a long warming gulp of his coffee, his dark eyes regarding Ned over the brim of his mug. Presently, he put the mug on the table before saying, 'Well now, you might be happy to know that he's got his own comeuppance, because I've just bought him out, lock, stock and barrel.' He grinned widely, cocking his head at Ned, and taking delight in the look that came over the other man's face.

Ned was on his feet in an instant. 'You sly bugger, and you never said a word!' he cried jubilantly. Wrapping his two huge hands over Adam's, he shook it up and down. 'By! But you're a canny businessman, Adam Roach, that you are!'

'There's still a lot to sort out. And I'm keeping the name Sutcliffe's,' Adam informed him. 'At least until I've got it running on the straight and narrow. It's a well-respected name, and there are still those who are fiercely protective of Sutcliffe himself. There are debts to settle and bridges to cross before I'll risk putting my own name on the trucks and letter-heads.'

Ned was back in his seat now, his brow furrowed as he listened to Adam's plans. 'I think you're right,' he agreed. 'Sutcliffe is a powerful name in coal-merchanting, and there are still those who haven't forgiven you for snatching my contracts from under his nose.' Leaning forward, he asked in a low voice, 'But what of Sutcliffe himself? You must know he's the kind of man who wouldn't hesitate to spread the poison about. It wouldn't matter a jot to him that you'd saved his bacon. He's a spiteful nasty bugger when all's said and done.'

'You've no need to worry on that score,' Adam told him confidentially. 'I'm one step ahead of him there. It's all written into the contract of sale. One false move from him, one malicious word in the wrong quarter, and it'll cost him every penny he's got.' Adam levelled his gaze at the other man. There was something more important he had to say. 'As far as I understand, Sutcliffe intends to move right away. However, we do have another problem, and I'm hoping you can help me there, Ned.' Since the deal was done, Adam had agonised over a particular quandary. To his mind, there was only one man besides himself who could turn Sutcliffe's business around. That man was Ned. But, for various reasons, Adam was reluctant to broach the subject. But broach it he must, so taking a deep breath, he declared confidently, 'I want you to run the Sutcliffe contracts.'

Ned was shocked silent. He stared at Adam with quizzical eyes, then dropped his gaze to the floor. 'I can't do it,' he said.

Adam couldn't hide his disappointment. 'I understand,' he replied. 'I had to ask though, but I don't want you to fret on it.'

Ned shook his head. 'I'd *like* to help you out, son,' he said sorrowfully, 'because God knows you've done enough for me. But it's memories, you see? I honestly don't think I could go back.'

'Then it's enough said, and I'm sorry I asked you. It was wrong of me to put you in that position.' Secretly, Adam still hoped Ned would reconsider. He felt it would be good for him to face the things that haunted him still, and he could only do that if he went back to where it had all taken place. Besides, with Doug in prison, it would be comforting for Rosie to have Ned close at hand.

Still, he respected and loved the older man, and right now, he half regretted ever raising the subject. 'Tell you what,' he said, his mind racing ahead with an idea. 'why don't you and I meet in the pub later, have a pint or two, and you can give me the benefit of your experience? After all, I've a mountain of decisions to make in the next month.'

Ned shook his head. 'I've already decided to have a night in,' he apologised. 'But I'm here now, so if you've any other ideas to bounce off me, I'm in no hurry.'

Adam laid out his plans then for how he meant to build up Sutcliffe's round and eventually merge it with his own. He told Ned he intended to send four of his most trusted and able men to get it off the ground. 'I've yet to approach them about it, but none of them has a family, and as far as I can tell, they'd have no objection to a spell away. The four new recruits will come here in their place.'

'And who will you send to manage?' In spite of himself, Ned was curious. Not realising that Adam had counted on that, he fell headfirst into the trap.

'If you didn't want it, I thought maybe Jack Rutherford. He's been with me from the start, and he knows the business inside out. He's good with figures, and seems to get on with everybody.'

'That's just it, son.' Ned shook his head.

'You're saying you've got reservations about him?'

'Like you say, he's a good man. But I work with him on the ground, and I reckon he falls short of what makes a good manager.'

'Oh?' In fact, Adam already knew what Ned was getting at. Though Jack was an excellent man in many ways, he was not managerial material. Suggesting him for the job was Adam's way of drawing Ned out. 'I reckon he'd be ideal.'

Ned shook his head again. 'You're wrong, son,' he insisted, standing up to make the point. 'He's *too* pally. A manager has to raise himself above that, while at the same time being access- ible to the workers. It's all a matter of balance . . . discipline with respect.' He groaned. 'I'm sure I don't have to tell *you* that?'

'I'm sorry, Ned, I don't agree,' Adam fibbed. 'As far as I'm concerned, Jack's the only other man for the job. I intend to put it to him at the first opportunity.' Walking to the door, he thanked Ned. 'I hear what you say, but this time we'll have to agree to differ,' he remarked craftily. He then repeated his invitation for Ned to join him in the pub later.

'No. Like I said, I'm in for an early night.' Ned's voice was sharp and he didn't look up when he spoke.

Adam saw that as a good sign. 'Goodnight then. See you Monday,' he said. When Ned had gone, he closed the office and went through to the living-room where April was waiting for him.

'Daddy kiss,' she said, wrapping her arms round his neck when he picked her up.

'There's a man waiting to see you,' Mrs Jessup told him as she lifted the child from his arms. 'I've put him in the library.'

The man was the private detective hired by Adam to trace Connie. 'I've found her,' he said, 'but it's not good news, I'm afraid.'

'You mean she won't co-operate?' Adam was at the end of his patience where Connie was concerned.

'I mean she *can't* co-operate.' He explained, 'She's in a bad way. According to the doctors, it's only a matter of days, hours even.'

Adam was frantic. 'Why in God's name didn't you phone me?'

'Because I thought it more appropriate to bring that kind of news personally. Besides, there's no time wasted. I only just found out myself, and I've come straight here.'

'Which hospital?' Reaching for the telephone, Adam began dialling. 'How long has she been there? Dear God! What happened?'

'She's in the Liverpool General . . . been there about three days, according to the pub landlord.' He could have told Adam that Connie had been earning a living as a prostitute, but in the circumstances he thought better of it. 'Run over she was, that's all I could find out.'

Just as suddenly as Adam had snatched the phone up, he slammed it down again. 'No answer!' He groaned. 'Look, get yourself off to this address.' Feverishly scribbling into a notepad,

323

he read out the name and address of Connie's husband. 'Give him this note.' Handing the scrap of paper to the little man, he ordered, 'Be as quick as you can.'

Even before the other man was out of the door, Adam had informed Mrs Jessup that he didn't know when he would be back. In another minute he was in his car and heading towards Liverpool General. Being Friday night, the workers were pouring out of the factories and many of the roads out of town were busy with traffic. The journey seemed neverending, and he knew he would not forget it for as long as he lived. He had sent for Connie's husband, but he wasn't too hopeful that the man would have either the decency or the inclination to come. There was too much hatred there, too much water had flowed under the bridge.

He prayed all the way there, and when he was taken to see the doctor in charge, felt physically sick when told, 'I'm sorry, Mr Roach, but there is nothing else we can do.' As he walked towards the side ward, the doctor's words rang in his mind . . . Nothing else we can do . . . nothing else we can do. Try as he might, he couldn't believe that Connie was on her deathbed. Connie, that wild vibrant creature who could always laugh in the face of adversity; Connie, unfettered and free, madly infuriating, the waif who could never cope with responsibility; alive and laughing, forever young and devil-may-care. 'Dying?' The word fell from his lips. 'No!' His protest was lost in the clatter all about him. Nurses going about their daily work, doctors rushing back and forth, the lady down the corridor pushing a tea-trolley and humming a merry melody. And Adam, striding towards the room where Connie was, afraid and angry all at the same time. It wasn't true. It couldn't be!

Everything the doctor had said played over and over in his mind. According to their information, Connie had been drunk and dazed when she wandered into the road. 'There are several witnesses who all say that she didn't even look where she was going . . . could hardly stand up, said one.' The doctor went on to explain how, when the lorry hit her, Connie's internal organs were crushed beyond repair, 'I'm so sorry,' he finished. And the sorrow showed in his face.

Coming into the side ward, Adam was taken aback by the sight that met his eyes. A frail bruised figure lay buried beneath swathes of bandages. 'Gently does it,' warned the nurse, 'We've given her the strongest painkillers, but I'm afraid she's still in great discomfort.'

While the nurses discreetly withdrew, Adam came closer. There were tears in his eyes as he gazed down on what had been the prettiest face, now swollen almost beyond recognition. 'Oh, Connie . . . CONNIE!' Raising his face to the ceiling, he swallowed the choking tears. Inside he was all churned up. All this time he had been trying to find her, to lay all manner of guilt and shame at her door. Well, now it was *he* who felt guilty. *He* who was ashamed.

Desolate, he sat in the chair beside her, and held her hand. Somehow the warmth of his touch alerted her, and she opened sad eyes to look at him. 'Adam.' The voice was soft and loving, the very same, it had not changed. 'I knew you'd come to me.' Squeezing his fingers with surprising strength, she gave the merest glimmer of a smile. It cut him in two.

Returning her smile, he wanted to speak but the words wouldn't come. His eyes burned with threatened tears. But he knew he must not show them. It was when she said, 'I don't mind if you cry,' that they trickled down his face. 'What am I going to do with you, eh?' he asked softly.

'Hold me,' she said. And he did, ever so gently.

Taking her in his arms was like gathering a fragment of the past to himself. Like the past she felt brittle and delicate, yet she clung to him ferociously, flesh and blood, memories and regrets, touching his heart and breaking it.

For what seemed a lifetime he held her there, his free hand tenderly stroking her hair and his face close to hers. Suddenly she shivered in his arms and softly laughed. 'Some women always find the rotters, don't they?'

'Don't think about that now,' he begged.

Closing her eyes, she smiled. In the smallest whisper she pleaded, 'Look after her for me.' Then, before he could answer, she gave a shuddering sigh. When he looked into her quiet contented face, he knew Connie's suffering was ended for all time. 'I'll look after her,' he promised. And it was a promise from the heart.

'She left this for you.' The nurse gave him a note which Connie had dictated. In it she gave Adam all legal rights over her daughter April. 'Who else could be her father but you?' she wrote ambiguously. It was plain that she was taking the truth with her to the grave. But, whatever the truth, Connie had secured the child's future. It was her legacy to Adam, a great big thank you for all he had been to her. More than that, she knew the girl would be safe with this gentle giant, the kindest, strongest man she had ever known. She would rest now. And he would never forget her.

During the following week, Adam took it on himself to arrange the finest funeral for her. His own work took second place, and everything he had planned was postponed. 'It can wait,' he told Ned. 'Some things are more important than work.' The hardest thing was how to tell April about her mother.

'The truth, son,' Ned advised. 'You must tell the truth.' And that was what he did. Two days after Connie died, Adam broke the news to the child, telling her that her mother had been a warm and lovely creature who had placed her only child in his care before going to stay in Heaven. But the child was too young to understand the full impact of what he was saying. She thought on his words, and looked at him with worried eyes, then she threw her arms round his neck and asked in a tearful voice, 'You're still my daddy, aren't you?'

His answer was to hold her close and reassure her, 'I'll always be your daddy.' A moment later she was laughing, and it was as though he had said nothing of Connie to her. But that was the best way, he decided. In the future, he would only talk about Connie if the girl asked. In his heart he was content, and so was she.

It was a bright cold day when Connie was laid to her rest. The mourners numbered two: Ned and Adam. Connie's husband never came to the hospital. Nor did he turn up for the funeral. And, as far as Adam was concerned, it was just as well. In his heart he knew Connie would not have wanted him there.

Afterwards, when it was all over, Ned told Adam he had made up his mind. 'Whenever you're ready,' he agreed. 'I feel a need to be near Rosie and the young 'un.' Something about the events of the past week had raised a great longing in him.

Adam was both delighted and sad. 'It would help us both to lose ourselves in our work,' he said. But now he regretted ever asking Ned to take on the new acquisition. For the moment he had a temporary manager running the new contracts, so he would have Ned with him for at least another month. All the same, the thought of losing his friend brought on a great feeling of loneliness. More than that, the idea that Ned would be so near to Rosie, and he so far away, was almost unbearable.

CHAPTER TWENTY

The clerk smiled frostily. 'I'm sorry, Mrs Selby. You left work of your own accord. I'm afraid it will be weeks before we can help you.'

'But I've got a child to take care of. What are we supposed to live on in the meantime?' Rosie was desperate. It had taken a great deal of courage for her to call on the Welfare, and now here she was, being told by a scrap of a girl that she couldn't be helped. It was humiliating. 'It's not as though I haven't *tried* to find work,' she exclaimed. 'I've applied for that many jobs my fingers are worn ragged, and I must have trudged miles these past weeks.' For some reason she couldn't fathom, no one was prepared to take her on.

The clerk picked up her pen. 'I really am sorry,' she said, writing furiously on a piece of paper which she then passed to Rosie. 'I've made an appointment for a month's time. We can review the situation then.' She was already turning her gaze to the next candidate when Rosie crumpled the paper into her pocket and walked away.

'Thanks for nothing,' she muttered defiantly. But there were tears in her eyes as she emerged into the unusually warm sunshine of a February day.

Dejected, she thrust her hands into the pockets of her overcoat and made her way to the railway station. Here, she went to the cafe where she had parted from Adam. These days, it was the only place she could find sanctuary. There were memories here, both good and bad. Here in this cosy welcoming place she confessed her betrayal to her first and only real love. Here she had talked with him, longed for him to forgive her, and lost him because of her own foolishness. In this place she and Peggy had spent many a busy hour, gossiping and making silly plans for the future. 'What's the future now?' she asked herself. 'With Adam gone . . . Peggy gone, and now my work, the only thing that made me feel useful. What is there for me to look forward to?'

With the realisation that she was fast falling into debt and could see no way out of it, her spirits fell like a lead weight inside her. Taking off her coat, she hung it over the back of the chair. Thoughts of Danny flooded her heart, bringing a smile to her face. Suddenly the day seemed so much brighter. 'We'll manage,' she promised herself. 'Somehow we'll manage.'

'Mornin', luv. What can I get yer?' Mrs Brown was the owner of these premises, and never a day went by when she didn't have a broad smile on her face.

'A cup of tea and . . .' Rosie pressed her face to the glass cabinet. Inside was the most delicious display of fresh cakes and buns '. . . one of your Eccles cakes,' Rosie decided, and when she smiled at the round rosy face before her, her own smile was dazzling.

'Still ain't got a job then?' Mrs Brown always showed an interest in her regular customers.

Rosie shook her head. ''Fraid not,' she replied. 'But it isn't for want of trying.' In fact, today was the only day she hadn't done her usual rounds . . . all the big stores, the smaller shops, and even the factories hereabouts. 'It seems nobody's setting on.'

'Hmph! It's their loss I'd say.' Mrs Brown carefully placed Rosie's order on to the tray and slid it across the counter. 'There y'are, luv. That'll be one and ninepence.' While she got Rosie's change from half a crown, she chatted on. 'I can't understand it,' she said thoughtfully. 'You know you told me last week you'd been to that big store on the corner and they turned you down?'

'Taylor's store, you mean?' Rosie recalled it very well. In fact she had seen the advert on Monday, applied the very next day, sending her references and everything, and on Thursday she was called for interview. However, when she got there she was told there had been a mistake and that the post had already been filled. It puzzled her then, and it had puzzled her ever since.

330

'You went for an interview, didn't you . . . on the Thursday if I recall correctly?'

'That's right. I was told there had been a mix-up and that the job had already been given.'

Mrs Brown leaned close, as though about to impart a confidence. 'Then how come Judy Craig from Harper Street got set on, for the very same job you applied for . . . on the *Friday*?'

Rosie was astounded. 'Are you sure?'

'Sure as eggs is eggs!' She put the change into Rosie's outstretched hand and left her to think about it.

For a full hour Rosie sat at the table, her gaze following the passersby outside the window. Her thoughts however followed Mrs Brown's remarks. It seemed inconceivable to Rosie that the office manager of a large store should deliberately lie to her. Yet what else was she to think? Certainly there were any number of possibilities as to what had happened. Maybe the girl who was promised the job had failed to turn up, and they merely called the next person on the list? On top of that, maybe this Judy Craig was better qualified than she? Either way, Rosie told herself, it was no use crying over spilt milk. Maybe she'd be luckier the next time?

Yet the more she thought on it, the more she felt there was something not quite right. Why had she been turned down for so many jobs? Work of a kind that was exactly what she had been doing for Robert Fellows, and doing very well? Why was it that the employers always seemed keen until she sent in her references? And of course she was obliged to offer her previous employer as reference.

Slowly but surely, the merest glimmer of suspicion crept into her mind. The idea was so shocking that she startled the couple at the next table when she cried out, 'Surely to God, it *can't* be!'

Mrs Brown however, was not startled. She knew the reason why Rosie had given up her job, and though she suspected there was a smear campaign being mounted against her, was not one to get drawn in. Now though, hearing Rosie's exclamation, she was satisfied that she'd got the message across without actually having to spell it out.

Rosie glanced up to see the kindly soul looking at her, and her doubts vanished. Rising from her chair, she put on her coat and took the tray back to the counter. 'You knew, didn't you?' she said softly.

Mrs Brown still wouldn't be drawn. 'Mum's the word,' she replied, pressing a chubby finger to her lips. Then she took the tray and attended to the next customer.

Robert Fellows was not surprised to see Rosie. In fact he was delighted. Dismissing his secretary, he closed the door. Turning to Rosie, he said charmingly, 'I wondered how long it would be before you paid me a visit.'

Looking at him now, she was amazed that she could ever have been fooled by him. 'You've blackened my name, haven't you?' There was no use beating about the bush. She had never been surer of herself, so the best thing was to come right out and say it. 'You're giving me bad references, and don't deny it!'

'My, my! Are you telling me you can't get a job?'

He sat on the edge of his desk in that arrogant fashion she had foolishly mistaken for elegance. In that moment Rosie had to fight down an urge to knock him sideways. 'I'm warning you here and now, I intend to report you to a higher authority. If it was known what you're doing, you'd be shown the door pretty damn quick.' Inside, she was boiling with rage. Outside, she kept a cool head. It shook him just a little.

'I hope you can prove everything you're saying, my dear?' he was the cool one now. 'Wait just a minute.' He strode out of the office and returned a moment later with the entire office staff.

Lining them up, he explained in a bold voice, 'Mrs Selby has made a very serious allegation against me.' He gave a small laugh, effectively ridiculing her. 'Now then, if any of you are aware, or indeed suspect, that I am returning bad references on her behalf, or casting the slightest doubt on her ability, I want you to speak up.' The charm was gone as he glared from one to the other. Finally fixing his gaze on Rosie, he snapped, 'Apparently this vindictive young woman intends to complain to the highest authority. If that be the case, then each of you will be called on either to substantiate her story ... or uphold my own blameless character.' With his hands behind his back, he walked down the

332

line, smiling at each one in turn. 'Mrs Benton, what have you to say?'

Meg Benton's face grew scarlet and she could not bring herself to look at Rosie. 'I would rather not be involved, if you don't mind,' she muttered. When he stared at her, she quickly added, 'Not for one minute could I say you would do such a thing.' With every word her face grew hotter, until she was visibly uncomfortable.

Mr Mortimer shuffled his feet. 'I would have to agree with Mrs Benton,' he offered. Then he had a coughing fit and Mrs Benton had to fetch him a glass of water.

Horace Sykes grunted and complained that, 'If you'll excuse me, sir, I have better things to do with my time than to stand here and listen to spiteful accusations. As far as I can see, a respected member of this establishment is being wrongly accused, and I would have no hesitation in saying so, if called upon!' Having said his piece, he curled his bottom lip over his top one, and stood smartly to attention.

The secretary swore she had seen every reference sent out on Rosie's behalf. 'As far as I'm concerned, they gave an excellent report of your work here,' she lied brazenly.

Robert Fellows was pleased. He knew every one of his staff and how to play on their weaknesses. When all was said and done, nobody wanted to lose their livelihood. 'Thank you. That will be all,' he said, sending them all out.

'You should be ashamed.' Rosie knew she was on to a losing battle. 'Somehow you've got them all to lie for you.'

He laughed aloud. 'You really are the limit!' he told her. 'First you accuse *me*, and now you're accusing the entire office staff.' Perching himself on the edge of the desk, he wagged a finger at her. 'I think I warned you that you'd be sorry,' he murmured.

Rosie was incensed. Realising she could do nothing without involving those people outside, she decided to settle her account another way. 'I could tell your wife how you proposed to me,' she said sternly. 'But that would hurt her, and to be honest, I don't know if I could bring myself to do it.'

Relieved, Robert chuckled and her temper broke. 'You bastard!' With one great swing of her arm, she caught him sideways.

333

He lost his balance and fell to the floor. 'I don't need your references anyway,' she said, looking down at him. 'I'm only sorry I couldn't see what a pathetic trickster you were. But they do say sometimes you can't see the wood for the trees.'

Shocked, he made no attempt to get up. Instead he asked in a small voice, 'You didn't mean it did you? About telling the wife?'

She gave him a withering look. 'I haven't decided yet,' she declared, then straightened her shoulders and walked sedately to the door. 'Goodbye, Mr Fellows. Oh, and by the way, don't kid yourself that you're good in bed . . . more passable I'd say.'

With that scathing remark she swept out. It was only when she got to the street door that she began chuckling. She felt elated, wonderfully satisfied. Robert Fellows would never know whether she meant to contact his wife or not, and that was the way she wanted it left. 'Let the bugger suffer!' she told Mrs Brown later. 'It's what he deserves.'

For the rest of that week, Rosie lowered her sights, going round the coal-yards and into the marketplace, searching high and low for any kind of work. Unfortunately, though Robert Fellows' influence hadn't reached this far, there was no work. 'If you were a fella with arms like Popeye, I'd set yer on straightaway,' the fishmonger said. 'Them crates have to be packed, lifted, weighed and loaded on to yon lorry. It needs a man. Sorry, luv.' The message was the same wherever she went. 'Not strong enough' . . . 'Need a bloke with a broad back' . . . 'You can make the tea but these fellas swear like bloody troopers and, besides, I can't pay above four pounds a day.'

It was Friday night. Weary but not beaten, Rosie had just put Danny to bed and was sitting by the fire wondering what to do when a knock came on the door. It was Peggy's mam. 'Saw you come home earlier,' she said. 'You looked fair worn out, so I thought I'd come and keep you company for a while. What's more, I've some news that might cheer you up.'

Rosie went into the kitchen and made them each a brew of tea. 'I need cheering up,' she confirmed. 'Look at them.' Pointing to a pair of battered shoes, she explained, 'They were hardly worn when I left Woolworths, and now I can feel the pavement through the soles.'

'By!' The older woman slowly moved her head from side to side, loudly tutting and looking sorrowful as she gazed at the shoes. 'You poor little sod, I'd no idea.'

'Oh, don't worry,' Rosie told her. 'I ain't given up yet.' It was funny, she thought, how she had reverted to saying 'ain't' when all the time she was working, she would say 'isn't'. Laying a comforting hand on the older woman's arm, she urged, 'What's this news you've got that might cheer me up then?'

'I had a letter from our Peggy . . .'

Before she could finish, Rosie's brown eyes were shining with excitement. 'Did she mention me? Is she getting on all right? Coming home for a weekend, is she? Oh, I'll be that glad to see her.' One of her greatest regrets was the rift that had developed between her and Peggy.

'No, lass, I'm sorry.' Unable to look Rosie in the eye, she lowered her gaze to the crumpled letter clutched in her hand. 'She never mentioned you at all.'

Rosie looked away. 'That's a real shame,' she said with heartfelt disappointment. 'Still, we mustn't blame her, eh? Happen she's too busy to think about me.' What she said was one thing. What she thought was another. Now, when she glanced up at the other woman, her smile was painted back on. But it didn't fool Peggy's mam.

Her eyes sparkled with anger. 'She wants a bloody good shaking if you ask me. An' I've told her that! Every time I write, I'm full of what you've been doing . . . how you've packed up your job, and now you can't seem to find another. I've told her how things is getting really difficult for you, and that you miss her.' She tutted loudly again. 'And still she makes no mention! By! I shall give her a piece of my mind when I write back, an' that's a fact.'

'No. Please don't do that.' Rosie didn't want to be the cause of bad blood between Peggy and her mam. 'If our friendship is worth anything, she'll mend it in her own good time.' Hesitating, Rosie added softly, 'Or not at all.' The very thought of never again having Peggy for her friend was overwhelmingly sad. So she chose not to dwell on it. 'How's she doing anyway?'

'Well, that's what I came to tell you,' came the proud answer. 'She's going through the course with flying colours. According to

335

this 'ere letter, the bosses are really pleased with her.'

Rosie nodded approvingly. 'That's the way,' she said, 'I'm glad it's turning out right for her.'

Stuffing the letter into her pinnie pocket, the older woman regarded Rosie with admiring eyes. 'You're a grand little thing,' she said. 'And I'm a silly old bugger.'

'Whatever do you mean?'

'Well! I mean fancy me boasting about how well our Peggy's doing, when here's you with two mouths to feed . . . out of work, let down by the Welfare, and not knowing where the next shilling's coming from. By! I must have me brains in me arse.'

That remark was so characteristic of Peggy that Rosie laughed out loud. 'You're a tonic, that's what you are,' she chuckled. And Peggy's mam giggled like a schoolgirl.

'Children abed, are they?' Rosie asked brightly.

'Aye. I've put 'em abed early, 'cause bed's the warmest place. Especially when that silly bloody coalman ain't brought me weekly ration. Honest to God, Rosie gal, I've a mind to change to Sutcliffe's.'

'I should think twice about *that*!' Rosie urged. 'From what I've heard, folks are leaving him in droves. What with late deliveries and high prices, it's a wonder Sutcliffe's are still in business at all.'

'According to her from the draper's, there's a new manager, and things is a lot better now. Happen I'll give him a try.' Stretching out her hands to warm them, she was mesmerised by the leaping flames and the hazy glowing coals beneath. 'That's some good coal, lass. Where'd you get it? Not from *my* coalman, I'll be bound.'

Rosie smiled wryly as she explained, 'I can't afford a full sack at a time, and the coalman won't deliver less, so I get it by the shovelful from the corner shop.'

'Cost you more in the long run, though. Surely the coalman will let you have a full sack if you pay half one week and half the next?'

'I've already tried that, but he won't do it. Not since I've lost my job, he won't.' Rosie laughed. 'Miserable old bugger! Happen I should teach him a lesson . . . get myself a truck and set up against him.'

'Aye, an' I'll bet you could show him a thing or two.' Peggy's mam saw it for the light-hearted suggestion it was. 'I mean, you had a good teacher in Ned Selby, ain't that a fact?' Unaware that Rosie had lapsed deep into thought, she yawned and stretched her fat little figure, then said, 'Right. I'd best be off, else Lord knows what that lot'll be getting up to.'

'Wait a minute,' Rosie told her. Quickly now, she tipped a small pile of coal out of the scuttle and into a cardboard box. 'Take this with you,' she offered, pushing the box into the other woman's arms. 'There's nothing worse of a morning than getting up to a cold house.'

Dumbstruck by such kindness, Peggy's mam could only stare. When she caught her breath, she gasped, 'God love and bless yer.' Tucking the box under her arm, she made her way to the front door, where she promised to return the favour the following week.

Rosie threw the bolt home and went back to the living-room. Here she stood before the fireplace, her eyes searching her own features in the mirror. Something Peggy's mam said had set her thinking.

It wasn't quite thought through yet but the germ of an idea was planted in her mind, and now it was slowly beginning to blossom. Suddenly, Rosie's face broke into a smile. 'That's it, Rosie gal!' she cried, thumping her fist against the mantelpiece. 'Buy the coal from the sidings and build up a little round of your own, why don't you?'

Staggered by the measure of her ambitions, she fell into the chair and for a long time gazed into the red raw heat of the fire. Excited and daunted all at the same time, she made herself be calm. 'Think it through,' she murmured. 'There must be dozens of folk like you ... folk who can't afford a full bag of coal, and who have to cart the smaller bags on their back from the corner shops. On top of that they're made to pay the earth for it.' Now the idea was really beginning to take shape. 'The regular merchants won't split a bag in two. Nor are they too willing to take half payment one week, and the rest the next.' She was on her feet now, eyes glowing as bright as the coals and her heart going ten to the dozen. 'Do it, Rosie!' she whispered harshly.

'Get together every penny you can, and give it a go. You've got nothing to lose.' She chuckled. 'Well, happen the few pounds I put by for a rainy day. But the rainy day is here now. The Welfare won't help, so the money will be gone soon enough. Why not put it where it might reap rewards?'

Thrilled, she even did a little jig on the spot. After that she went to the sideboard and took out an old tea-caddy. Taking off the lid, she tipped it upside down on the table. A small bundle of notes fell out, together with some loose coins. 'How much have you got then, Rosie, gal?' she asked herself. A quick count produced twelve pounds and eighteen shillings. 'Will it be enough to carry us over?' she wondered. Only time would tell.

Carefully, she replaced the tin and went upstairs. Danny was fast and hard asleep. 'We're going into business, sunshine,' she told the sleeping form. 'What do you think to that, eh? Rosie and son . . . coal-merchants.' She smiled a soft and secret smile. 'Sounds good, don't it, eh?' she murmured. At the door she turned. 'You and me, we're off to see the man at the sidings tomorrow.' It was something to look forward to. At long last she had a real reason for rising from her bed. It was a good feeling.

Excited by her new enterprise, Rosie hardly slept a wink. Consequently, when she sat opposite Danny at the breakfast table the next morning, her head was thumping like an old steam engine and she had no appetite. 'If you don't want your cornflakes, I don't want mine either,' Danny declared. And because she wanted him to set out with a full belly that morning, she forced every mouthful down her throat.

First stop was the rag and bone man, 'A pram, you say?' he repeated, rubbing the stubble on his face. 'There's a couple down the yard, I reckon, but one's got a wheel missing, and the other ain't got no bottom to it. You can have the pair on 'em for half a crown.' He blew his nose through his fingers and regarded her with amusement. 'It's Doug Selby's missus, ain't it?' he asked meaningfully. 'Well now, I thought your old man were in prison? Been naughty, have you, eh?' He winked at her and she was nauseated.

'What I want the pram for is none of your concern,' she said, putting him smartly in his place. 'I'll give you one and six for the both.'

'There must be summat wrong with your ears. I said half a crown.'

'If you know so much about me, you must also know there's no money coming into my house.' Meeting his leer with defiance, she said, 'Two shillings. That's my best offer. Take it or leave it.'

Spitting on his hand, he held it out. 'Let's shake on it.'

'I don't think so,' she replied, grimacing.

Roaring with laughter, he took her money and pointed the way to the corner where the prams were stacked. There was a black tatty one, and a navy blue thing with a great hole in the bottom. 'We can't get no coal in there,' Danny said, getting down on his knees and peeping up at her through the pram bottom. 'And that one's only got three wheels.'

'Then we'll take a wheel off the one with no bottom, and put it on the other,' Rosie declared. She lifted the prams one at a time and examined them. The one with only three wheels had a sound base, strong enough for her purpose, at least until she could buy a hand cart. But she was thinking ahead of herself. 'One step at a time, Rosie gal,' she cautioned.

'Can you change the wheel, Mam?' Mimicking her actions, Danny was pretending to examine the articles.

'It's not a big job.' She tousled his hair. 'But we'll need a spanner.'

No sooner had she said it than he was running down the yard. A minute later he came back with the man in tow. 'The hire of a spanner will cost you sixpence,' he told her, handing it down.

'Fair enough,' she said, 'I'll give you sixpence, and you can give me a shilling.'

'How do you make that out?'

'Because I paid for two prams and I'm only taking the one.'

He coughed and stared and coughed again. 'All right,' he grumbled. 'Take the bloody spanner and we'll call it quits.'

'And I'll need that hand-shovel.' She pointed to a small black scoop lying on top of a scrap heap.

'Take the bloody thing!' he snarled. He stalked off, leaving Rosie very pleased with herself. 'This spanner will come in handy,' she told Danny. And he was never more proud of her.

The foreman at the sidings was astonished. 'What! You're telling me you mean to take that monstrosity round the streets and sell coal from it?' He walked round and round the pram, grinning from ear to ear. 'I'd rather you than me,' he declared.

'Nobody's asking you to do it,' Rosie reminded him. 'All I want from you is a load of coal, enough to fill the pram to the very top.'

'You've got some balls, I'll give you that.' He was standing before her, hands in his pockets and a look of admiration on his face as he glanced from her to the pram and back again.

'I don't know whether to take that as an insult or a compliment,' Rosie returned. Impatient to be gone, she enquired, 'How much will it cost me . . . to fill the pram right up to the brim?'

'All depends what grade coal you're after.'

'I want the best.' Just in case he had it in mind to cheat her, Rosie reminded him, 'And don't forget I knew Ned Selby for a while, so I do know muck from gold.'

He laughed at that. 'I'm sure you do,' he confessed, 'I'm sure you do.'

Satisfied that Rosie and the boy were following, he strode to the far end of the yard. 'You'll not get better than that,' he pointed out, indicating the pile of shiny black nuggets piled high in the bay. He watched her go over and take a piece in her hand. He saw her expression fall, and knew she wasn't fooled. 'Is there a problem?' He winked at Danny, who gave him a withering look.

'I said I wanted the "best",' she retaliated angrily. 'This is too scaly. It'll spit and fizz and be gone in minutes.'

'Well now, you *do* know your coal, don't you?' he said with renewed interest. 'I'm impressed, lady.'

'I don't want you impressed. I want my pram filled. How much will it cost me?'

'Let's see now.' He scrutinised the pram, weighing up the contents in his mind. 'Three shilling . . . happen a bit more.'

Rosie stared at him in disbelief. 'Try again.'

He knew he'd met his match, 'All right, pay what you can afford. Wheel the thing over here. I'm a busy man with a yard to run, so the quicker we get it done the better.' He had enjoyed his fun. Now it was a nuisance. 'We don't normally trade this way, with folk just coming in off the streets,' he advised her. 'What's more the merchants wouldn't like it.' He again winked at Danny, who surprised and amused him by winking back.

He stood at the door to his office as Rosie and the boy trundled off with the coal-laden pram. 'Good luck to you,' he muttered under his breath. 'You're a trier, I'll give you that. I'm buggered if you don't deserve to do all right.'

As he went back into the warmth of his office, he wondered whether he'd see her again. In fact, so successful did she become that Rosie was destined to return to his yard again and again.

First stop was Albert Street. Mrs Lewis couldn't believe her eyes. 'You're a godsend,' she declared; a wizened little thing with poor eyesight, she was virtually housebound. 'Our Katie in Bolton, well now, *she* has a lovely coal-merchant by the name of Anstee. It's a pity the ones round here aren't like him. The one I've got is such a surly devil. He'll not split a bag, you see, and he won't give credit. Being on a small income, I find it very hard to pay the price of a full bag all at once.'

'You can have as much or as little as you like from me,' Rosie explained. 'And I'm not against giving credit if needed.' Realising she had to earn this week to pay for her next load, she warned, 'I'm only just starting up, so I can't carry debt beyond a week.'

'Oh, I can pay for what I have,' came the answer. 'I don't burn much more than a couple of shovelfuls a week . . . have to ration myself, do you see?' Peering into the pram, she asked, 'Good stuff, is it? Long-burning?' Rosie reassured her and so her next question was, 'How much a shovelful . . . heaped up, mind?'

Rosie had already calculated she would need to charge two shillings a shovelful if she was to make a profit. 'Can't really do it for less,' she apologised. After all, she had to find food and pay the rent the same as anyone else.

Mrs Lewis was delighted. 'If I were you, I'd call on Mr Runcorn at number four. He and the coalman had one blister of a row last week. Since then he's been without coal.'

Mr Runcorn had three shovelfuls. The next-door neighbour had two. And by the time Rosie got to the end of the street she was sold out. 'I can't believe it!' she laughed, hugging Danny, the two of them covered in coal-dust. 'We've sold out! Do you know what that means?'

'Are we rich?' Danny's big eyes shone like candles out of his smutty face.

Rosie was choked. She looked into that small dirty face, and her heart was full to bursting. 'What say we sit right here on the kerbside and count our earnings, eh?'

And that was just what they did. Spreading the shiny coins over Danny's grubby little palms, Rosie reckoned they had got their money back, plus a small profit. Taking the shillings which she had paid for the coal, she dropped it into her purse. 'See that, son?' she said, pointing to the remaining coins. 'That's our reward for working hard.'

His reply was to lift her own small hand and touch the blisters there. 'Your hands are bleeding, Mam,' he murmured, 'I don't like that.'

She looked at him as though seeing him for the first time, and her love for that little man almost broke her heart. Wrapping her arms around him, she tugged him into an embrace. 'If we want to be rewarded in life, we *must* work hard,' she whispered. 'We haven't made a fortune today, but it's a start. That's all we need. The rest is up to us.' As she held him close, Rosie was unaware that the tears were running down her face to create tiny rivulets through the coal-dust. 'There's no shame, in hard work, son. Always remember that.'

'Yes, Mam.'

'Hungry?'

'Yes, Mam.'

Rosie smiled. 'Do you reckon we've earned a treat from the fish and chip shop?'

Danny leaped high in the air. 'I want a great big fish with a tail that hangs right out of the newspapers!'

'So do I!' she announced. And it was quick march to the fish and chip shop. 'Good Lord above! Have you been up the chimney?' asked fat Mrs Heeney as they went in.

'We've been working hard,' Danny told her proudly. 'And we've earned our reward.' At that everyone laughed, and he got an extra big fish, with an extra long tail.

'That'll put hairs on your chest,' said the man at the end of the queue. Danny told him he didn't want hairs on his chest. When he and Rosie left, the laughter followed them all the way down the street.

'Do you know what, Mam?' Danny asked, stuffing a coal-smeared chip into his mouth.

'No, but you can tell me.'

'If we had *two* prams, we'd have been twice as rich.'

The very same idea had crossed Rosie's mind. 'Or if we had a hand cart, son. Now, *that* would take three times as much coal as this old pram. What's more we only went down *one* street. There are hundreds of others yet.'

'Thousands!' He dropped a chip on the pavement and would have picked it up if Rosie hadn't stopped him.

By the time they got home, both she and her son were bone-tired. Their clothes were stripped off and put into soak. Danny was bathed and put to bed; no sooner had his head touched the pillow than he was fast asleep. A few moments later, Rosie too bathed then fell thankfully in between the clean white sheets.

But she couldn't sleep. 'Today is just the beginning,' she told herself. 'Before the month's out, I mean to have a hand cart, and a sign written on it with the name ROSIE AND SON.' The idea grew and grew, until she realised that nothing less would do. 'Carting coal is what I know best,' she whispered into the darkened room.

She wondered what Adam would think of her enterprise, and smiled. Then she thought of Doug, and the smile slid away. 'Oh, Adam, if only we could turn the clock back,' she sighed. But the years had ticked away. There was no going back. Only forward. That was her path now, and she must travel it; however daunting it might be.

Doug watched the warden out of the corner of his shifty eye. He was nervous, anxious that all would not work to plan. But he wasn't reckless. Oh no! He had waited for this moment a long time. He could wait just another few minutes, long enough to make certain that everything was in place.

The big man with the rough face moved nearer. It was

unbearably hot in the kitchens. The sweat ran down his face, glistening on his chin stubble and meandering along his neck in slow-moving, jerky rivulets. 'Now, Doug?' he grinned childishly, displaying an uneven row of yellow teeth. His great fists gripped the handles of the cauldron; it was a huge iron thing, blackened by use and weighing upwards of twenty pounds. 'Look!' He inclined his head towards the warden. There was another man with him now, distracting his attention, 'Taylor's there. I'll do it now.' He grew excited, edging towards Doug, the sweat pouring down his face as he begged, 'Please, Doug. Let me do it now!'

Glancing up, Doug satisfied himself that the warden's attention was taken by the third man, a slim figure, a 'trustee' lately in Doug's pay. 'I knew we could count on Taylor,' he muttered. He grinned as the big man moved in.

In that moment, Doug Selby showed the madness that had overwhelmed him. Suddenly, his broad grin became an expression of fear as the big man raised the cauldron. A moment's hesitation, then: 'For Christ's sake, get on with it!' Out of his mind with hatred and the thought of revenge, he could see nothing beyond that. Nothing else mattered.

When the cauldron came smashing down to slice off his toes, his cry of agony echoed across the kitchens and beyond, bouncing off the prison walls. Then he slithered to the floor, and all Hell was let loose. 'He needs surgery of a kind we can't do here,' the doctor said. 'He'll have to be taken to an outside hospital.'

Drifting between sense and unconsciousness, he heard every word. It was exactly what he'd wanted to hear. Everything was going to plan. They gave him an injection to put him to sleep, and out of his misery. But he couldn't rest. For the umpteenth time he dreamed of his mother, of the hatred she had always felt for Rosie. He remembered how she had wanted to kill the boy. It wakened a thirst in him. She was right. She had *always* been right. And he had not seen it until it was almost too late. Oh, but it wasn't too late yet. Not yet. Not until Rosie and the boy had been punished.

Only then could he rest. When he had carried out his mother's wishes, like the good son he was.

CHAPTER TWENTY-ONE

On Friday 2 March, Rosie collected Danny from school. All the way home he chatted about how he had: 'Got two stars for helping to put the ink-pots away.' He related how he and Bob Marcus had made friends again, after having several tiffs over the last few days, and Rosie told him how pleased she was at his good news.

She, however, had some good news of her own, and found it really hard to keep the secret. When they got off the bus, she almost ran him all the way home. 'How much coal did you sell today, Mam?' he asked, puffing and panting as they went at a fast pace up the street.

'More than yesterday,' she answered, with a twinkle in her brown eyes. 'And a lot more than the day before.' She too was puffing and panting. After having been at work all day, and now with a surprisingly warm sun beating down on her back, she suddenly felt exhausted. At the same time she was exhilarated by what had taken place only two hours earlier.

As they neared the house, Rosie slowed the pace. Glancing down, she watched the boy's expression turn from astonishment to curiosity. 'Look, Mam!' he cried. 'Somebody's left a hand-cart outside our house.' Breaking free from her, he ran towards it. The cart was quite small, not much longer than a pram in fact. But it was deep and cavernous, with sturdy wooden sides and huge spoked wheels. Painted white, with blue along the carved rim, it was a thing of joy. The shaft was not too long, but, being sturdy and wide, was big enough to house a small horse or donkey. But the most exciting thing of all was the name emblazoned on the side in large gold lettering . . . 'ROSIE AND SON' it read 'COAL MERCHANTS'.

'It's ours, sweetheart,' Rosie murmured, watching her son's eyes widen with disbelief as he carefully read the letters out loud.

'*Ours*?' Swinging round, he stared at her, his whole face open with surprise. 'Where'd you get it, Mam?'

'Well, you know the wheel on the pram was beginning to wobble?' He nodded so she went on, 'I took it down to the rag'a'bone man, to see if I could buy some other wheels.' She pointed to the handcart. 'I saw this and fell in love with it.'

'Did it cost *all* the money we've earned?'

'Not quite. It's made a great hole in it, but we're still in profit, and we're getting more customers every day. *And* I got half back on the pram what I'd paid for it.' She chuckled. 'That's not bad, especially when we've had the best out of it.'

'Can I play with the cart?' His chubby hand roved lovingly over the wheels which were taller even than he was.

'It's not a plaything.'

'Can I polish it then?'

'I don't see why not.' She had already washed and polished the cart, especially where the lettering showed. But she didn't want to dampen his enthusiasm, so told him it was a wonderful idea. 'Tea first though,' she declared. 'Then into your old togs.' Before she finished speaking, he was waiting at the door. When she turned the key in the lock he was gone, along the passage, up the stairs two steps at a time, and down a minute later, changed out of his school-clothes and into his play-things. 'Ready, Mam!' he called as he ran into the living-room where she was waiting at table for him; the fish pie had been left gently baking while she went to the school, and now it was done to a turn.

'Wash your hands,' she told him, glancing at the dust he had gathered from the cart wheels.

Several times through the meal Rosie had to caution him. 'You'll choke yourself eating as quickly as that, my boy!' Danny sighed and took his time. But it was plain he couldn't wait to get out and into that cart. 'Go on then,' Rosie agreed. 'There's a tin of polish in the kitchen drawer, and a box of polishing rags under the sink.' Before she could draw breath he was out of the front door, with the articles held firmly in his arms. When she looked out of the front room window a minute later, he was proudly showing the cart to Peggy's younger brother and sister. 'That's me there,' he said, pointing to the word 'Son'. 'And that's my mam . . . "Rosie".'

The big lad shoved him playfully. 'We know that, you little squirt. Here, let me polish the wheels.' At first Danny resisted when the lad picked up a polishing cloth. But then the lad's pretty sister smiled at him, and he went all silly. 'Do *you* want a polishing rag?' he asked shyly. She shook her head and hurried away. 'Take no notice of her,' the lad said. 'She's a pain in the arse.'

An hour later, Danny came back in. He was covered in polishing wax and smelled like a perfume counter. 'Can *I* pull the cart tomorrow, Mam?' he asked, standing at the door with the polish in one hand and a clutch of rags in the other.

'I don't think so, sweetheart.' Taking the rags and polish from him, she drew him into the kitchen where she proceeded to take off his shirt. She had already run a bowl of hot soapy water for his wash.

'Why not? I nearly come up to your shoulder, don't I?'

'I'm afraid you'll need to grow just a bit more,' she explained. 'The cart is different from the pram, sweetheart. You see, it was much easier with the pram, because you *pushed* it along. But the cart has to be *pulled*, and besides, it will be carrying nearly three times as much coal.'

'I want to help though,' he insisted, a frown darkening his face.

'And you will, I promise. Anyway, I don't know if I could manage without you,' she said, humouring him.

'When I'm at school, you'll have to,' he solemnly reminded her.

'Well, then, I won't put so much coal in the cart, eh?' she fibbed. That seemed to satisfy him. 'Now then, get yourself washed and into your pyjamas, and we'll spend an hour on your jigsaw before bedtime.

They were halfway through the jigsaw when Danny suggested

they should bring the cart into the house. 'In case somebody pinches it.'

'Now, who on earth would want to pinch our cart?' The idea was unthinkable.

'If I can't pull the cart, can I sit on it then? When it's not too heavy,' he quickly added.

''Course you can,' Rosie assured him.

'I love you, Mam,' he said, planting a sloppy kiss on her face. 'And I love our new cart.' A look of seriousness came over him. 'Are we rich yet?' he asked.

'Not yet,' she said, laughing. 'But we're doing all right.'

'When will we have enough money to buy a horse?'

'When we've sold a good few cartloads of coal, I should think.' With that they finished the jigsaw, each of them preoccupied with their own thoughts and growing more bone tired by the minute.

At half-past eight, Danny went to his bed. Rosie went to hers an hour later. 'It's up with the lark for us tomorrow,' she muttered, climbing into bed. But she wasn't daunted by the thought. In fact, she was happier than she had been in many years.

It was the dark hours when Rosie woke with a start. The circle of light travelled over the bedroom, sweeping from wall to wall and over the ceiling. At first she couldn't make out what the light was. Then she realised. It was a torch. Someone outside was shining a torch into the bedroom.

Scrambling out of bed, she turned on the overhead light and rushed across the room to open the window. Down below in the street, she could just make out the dark shapes of two men standing in front of the steps. There was another figure at the door, and a fourth one standing beside a car. It was a police car, and the men were uniformed. 'Sorry to wake you, Mrs Selby,' said the officer nearest the door. 'But we need to talk with you.'

Trembling in the cold air, Rosie put on her dressing-gown and went down to open the door. Afraid even to wonder why they were here, she merely stepped aside to let them in. The one who had first spoken to her removed his helmet and stepped inside; his colleague, a tall fellow with a round friendly face, accompanied him. The other two remained posted outside.

Once they were inside the living-room, the round-faced officer addressed Rosie in quiet, considerate tones. 'Mrs Selby, isn't it? Husband by the name of Douglas Selby?'

'That's right.' Rosie trembled as she clutched her dressing-gown about her. Try as she might, she couldn't stop herself from shivering though the room was still quite warm, and the fire had not altogether died down in the grate. 'What's happened?' she asked nervously, looking from one to the other. Her stomach was churning over. She felt physically sick.

'Sit down, luv.' The round-faced officer gestured for her to sit in the armchair. 'It's not what you think.'

As Rosie sank into the chair, she wondered how he could possibly know what she was thinking. All sorts of terrible possibilities assailed her mind. Was it Ned . . . had something happened to him? *Or Adam*? Oh, dear God above! She couldn't bear to think on it. Suddenly, her instincts came into play, and every muscle in her body seemed to relax. 'It's Doug, isn't it?' Yes. She was sure now. But why were they here? Had he got into a fight and been killed? Her thoughts flew to Danny. He would suffer too. Not now, but later, when the truth came out about his daddy, he was bound to suffer.

'Yes, Mrs Selby. It is. I'm afraid your husband has escaped.' Unaware that she wasn't listening beyond those words, he went on to explain how, following an accident some weeks back, when Doug lost most of the toes on his right foot, he had been confined to hospital. 'Of course there were men posted outside, and he was regularly checked. But somehow he fooled the night duty constable, and managed to get out of the hospital unseen.'

Rosie had not heard a single word, other than that Doug was on the run. Would he try and get right away from this area? Or would he head for home? The idea that he should come here terrified her.

'Mrs Selby?' Seeing how the colour had drained from Rosie's face, the constable sat in the chair beside her, his quiet voice betraying his concern. 'Are you all right?'

Rosie mentally shook herself. 'I'm sorry, I didn't hear what you were saying?'

Patiently, he repeated everything he had told her. 'We found a trail of blood along the corridors,' he revealed. 'Your husband is obviously in urgent need of medical attention. According to the doctor, he's lost a great deal of blood, and can only get steadily weaker.'

'What do you want from me?'

'If he turns up here, or if you hear from him, we want to know. Will you do that?'

'Yes.'

'You haven't had news of him already, have you? I mean . . . he hasn't been in touch?'

'No.'

'Do you mind if we look around?'

'I don't know. My son's asleep upstairs. I don't want him frightened.'

'It's all right.' His face beamed. 'We may look like big hulking lumps, but you'd be surprised how quiet we can be.' He jerked a thumb at his colleague who went softly out of the room and up the stairs. A few minutes later he returned, went into the front room, and finally came back to report, 'Nothing, Sarge.'

'Right.' The senior officer nodded at Rosie. 'We'll leave you in peace then. Thank you for your time.' He turned to go, but looked round to instruct her. 'Lock the doors behind us, and be careful when you go about your business.'

'What do you mean?' Fear clutched at Rosie's heart.

'I don't want to worry you unduly. But, well, he did make a threat in court, didn't he?'

Rosie hadn't forgotten. 'Thank you, officer,' she said, following him to the door. 'If I hear anything . . . anything at all, I'll let you know. And don't worry, I'll be careful.' And she would. Normally she left the kitchen door unlocked of an evening. But from now on, when she and Danny were in the house alone, all the doors would be locked and bolted.

Rosie didn't go back to her bed. She wouldn't have been able to sleep anyway. So she made herself a cup of tea and piled a few more coals on the fire. 'You'll have to get past me to get to him,' she muttered. If it came to it, she would gladly lay her life on the line for that innocent little boy upstairs.

When the dawn broke through, Rosie was curled up in the chair fast asleep. Tiredness had overtaken her. But when the sun came filtering into the room she opened her eyes. The events of the night came back to her, bringing a new and strange kind of fear.

Her waking instinct was to run upstairs to see if Danny was all right. He was stirring as she came into the room. 'All right, sweetheart?' Sitting on the edge of his bed, she stroked the tumble of hair from his forehead.

'I dreamed about our cart, Mam,' he yawned, rubbing the sleep from his eyes. 'Can we fill it right to the brim?'

'You see if we don't!' Rosie was thankful that his dreams had been much happier than her own.

Fed, washed and dressed for carting coal in worn old clothes that had seen better days, Rosie and her son emerged to a new morning. The mantelpiece clock struck seven as they went out the front door. Peggy's mam was just collecting her milk bottles from the step. 'Morning, dear,' she called. With thin straggly skeins of hair wrapped round numerous flat tin curlers, and her feet clad in enormous red slippers, she made a frightening sight. 'Saw your new cart last night. It'll do you a good turn, will that.'

Taking Danny with her, Rosie went to the other woman. 'Any news from Peggy?'

'Only the usual . . . telling me how she's going on.' She looked downcast. 'I'm sorry, lass, but there's no word for you.'

'Oh, it's not your fault,' Rosie comforted. 'Besides, that's not the only reason I came to see you.'

'Oh?'

'I wonder if you'd do something for me?'

'You've only to ask, you know that.'

'Did you hear anything untoward last night? In the early hours to be exact?'

She shook her head, sending a tin curler clattering to the ground. Bending to retrieve it, she grunted, 'Can't say I did. But then, I've always slept like a log.' Hugging the milk bottles she asked, 'Why? Was there a disturbance?'

Rosie was glad she didn't need to go into any detail. 'I just thought I heard something,' she said. 'It's made me a bit nervous, leaving the house empty all day an' all. Could you maybe keep an eye on things?'

'Goes without saying, dear.'

Rosie put on her brightest smile. 'Right then, I'd better make tracks or the best coal will be all gone.' She hurried Danny away, sat him on the cart with his little legs dangling over the side, and trundled off down the street, dragging the cart behind her.

Peggy's mam watched until Rosie and son had turned the corner. Shaking her head, she muttered harshly, 'By! It's coming to summat when a lovely young woman like that has to fit 'atween the shafts of a cart, like a bloody donkey!' With that, she thanked her lucky stars, and went indoors to write Peggy a stinging letter.

If Peggy's mam had stayed on the doorstep a few minutes longer, she would have seen a crouched bedraggled figure sneak out of a doorway some short distance down the street. She would have seen him go, in a slow painful gait, after Rosie and the boy. And never in a million years would she have believed that Rosie's pursuer was none other than her own husband, now an escaped convict. His injuries had become badly re-infected and his blood was carrying the poison to his heart. He was dying. And he meant to take Rosie and the boy with him.

A short time after Rosie left Castle Street at one end, the dark saloon drew in from the other. Ned was in the passenger seat. Adam was driving. 'I'm not sure about this, Ned,' he protested. 'I'd much rather have gone straight to the hotel. You could have come back on your own once we'd made all our other calls.'

'That's an empty argument, and you know it,' Ned chastised. 'Castle Street is on our way in to town. It makes more sense to see her now. You said yourself we've enough appointments to keep us going 'til dark, and what with everything else, and the pair of us having to get back the day after tomorrow, it won't leave that much time for visiting.' Consulting the address on a slip of paper in his hand, he stretched forward to read the number on the door. 'This is it,' he said. 'Pull over.'

Edging the car into the kerbside outside Rosie's front door, Adam was thrilled yet nervous, his knuckles chalk white as he gripped the steering wheel. 'I shouldn't have let you talk me into this,' he groaned.

'Like I said, it makes sense to call in. We're practically passing the front door anyway.'

'I doubt if she's up at this hour of a morning.' Adam looked at his watch. 'Good God, man! It's not yet eight o'clock. *And* it's Saturday. If she's got any sense she'll still be abed.'

'It's no good you using that as an excuse to drive away. Rosie was never one for staying in bed of a morning, and I can't see why she'd change the habit of a lifetime now.' He glanced at Adam and was moved by his plight. There was no doubt that Adam adored Rosie. 'I wish you'd come in,' Ned pleaded.

Adam groaned. 'I can't, Ned. There's bad feeling between us, and if I barge in without being asked, it will only make matters worse. Her last letter made it very clear she wanted no contact with me whatsoever.' The memory of that cold short letter cut through him. 'I have to respect her wishes. You must know that.'

'I'm sorry, son.' Ned still made no move to get out of the car.

'If you're going, you'd best get a move on.' Leaning over, Adam unlocked the door and pushed it open. 'I know you mean well, Ned, but you're only prolonging the agony. You go. I'll wait here.' He thought it strange he could sound so calm when his insides were in turmoil. It was all he could do not to leap from the car and bang on that front door. To see Rosie again, to feel the warmth of her radiant smile, would be the most wonderful thing.

'All right. But I'd like to bet that once she knows you're here, she'll be straight out to see you.' He climbed out of the car and poked his head back in to say, 'Our Rosie was never one for bearing grudges.'

'It's not a matter of bearing grudges and you know it.' Slowly winding the window up, he urged, 'Go on, Ned. And look, it might be best if you don't let her know I'm here.'

'Whatever you say.'

Twice he knocked on the door, but there was no answer. Turning to look at Adam, who was peering from the car window, he stretched out his arms in a gesture of helplessness. 'Seems like there's nobody in,' he said, expression downcast.

Peggy's mam was just putting out the empties. 'It's no good you knocking on that door,' she told him sharply, 'because Mrs Selby ain't there.' Regarding Ned through suspicious eyes, she came a step closer. 'What's your business with her anyway?' She hadn't forgotten how Rosie had asked her to keep an eye on the house.

'I'm her father-in-law ... Ned Selby.' As he came towards her

353

his face was wreathed in a friendly smile. 'It's been a while since I've seen Rosie. We're in the area and, to be honest, I thought it was time I mended a few broken bridges between me and mine.'

'Hmh! Ned Selby, you say?' Retreating up the steps, she eyed him up and down. 'As far as I'm concerned, you could be Jack the bleedin' Ripper, 'cause I ain't never seen you in my life afore.' Oddly enough, though she knew of Ned Selby, and Peggy had mentioned him umpteen times, Peggy's mam had never clapped eyes on him.

Ned was faintly amused. Out of the corner of his eye he could that Adam also appreciated the situation. 'I've never been accused of being Jack the Ripper before,' he told her. 'Honest, luv, I really *am* Ned Selby, and if our Rosie was here, she'd vouch for me right enough.'

'Well, she *ain't* here, is she? What's more, if she *was* here, you wouldn't need vouching for, would you?'

'You're right, I wouldn't.' Reaching into his waistcoat pocket, he withdrew a pen. Fishing out a scrap of paper from his jacket pocket, he asked, 'I don't suppose you'll tell me where I could find her.'

'Nope!'

'But you won't refuse to give her a message?'

'I suppose I could do that all right.'

Pressing the scrap of paper to the wall, he scribbled:

Rosie,
    I'm sorry I missed you today, but I'll call round later tonight. Hope that's all right? I need to explain why I stayed away. I hadn't realised how much I'd miss you both. I'm here for only a couple of days, and there's so much to tell you. Look forward to seeing you and Danny.
    Love,
    Ned

He folded the note and gave it to Peggy's mam. 'It's important,' he said, and there was a strange kind of sadness in his voice. The exchange ended, he climbed back into the car. When he saw her crumple the note into her pinnie pocket, he muttered, 'I hope she remembers to give it to Rosie.' Pushing himself down into the seat, he wondered how his daughter-in-law might welcome him.

Adam gave no answer. He was engrossed in his own thoughts and, as always, Rosie was at the heart of them.

The guv'nor of the sidings had stopped being astonished at Rosie's fever for work. Every morning, six days a week, she would arrive at the yard at seven-thirty on the dot. There was always a smile and a cheery greeting as he came to help her fill her pram. This morning, however, even with her new cart and the prospect of earning more, there was no cheery greeting, and her face was serious as she paid over her money. 'I don't know what time I'll be back,' she said. 'There's enough in the cart to take me twice as far as usual on the first round.'

'If you had a horse to pull it, you could fill the cart right to the top,' he declared, trying to bring a smile to her face.

'Well, seeing as it's *me* that's doing the pulling, I'll settle for what's in it now.' While she and the guv'nor were talking, Danny had wandered away. Suddenly she caught sight of him and her heart froze inside her. 'DANNY, NO!' Her voice sailed across the yard as she took to her heels and headed towards the railway tracks; the coal-filled wagons were silently shunting towards the bays where they would off-shoot their loads. Danny was close to the tracks. Too close for safety.

'Jesus Christ!' The guv'nor saw Danny only seconds after Rosie spotted him, and now she was running like the wind, terror in her eyes as she realised that Danny was unaware of the wagons creeping up on him.

Rosie heard the guv'nor calling out way behind her, fearing that she too was in danger of slipping beneath the wagons. But there was no stopping her now. All she could see was Danny, and he was in terrible danger. 'DANNY, COME AWAY!' Her voice sounded like that of a stranger, and her chest was so tight she could hardly breathe.

Before the big man could catch up, she had grabbed Danny and swung him out of the way. Clutching him to her, she watched the big iron wheels trundle by, and gave up a prayer of thanks. 'Cut a man in two them wheels would.' The guv'nor leaned forward, hands on his knees, gasping for breath. His small eyes were fierce with anger. 'How many times have I told you to keep away from this part of the yard?' he croaked.

'I think he's learned his lesson,' Rosie replied protectively. She could feel the boy trembling in her arms.

Staring at her, the guv'nor snapped, 'I shouldn't really let you in here at all, bugger it!' He had been frightened out of his wits. His fear made him angry, and the fact that he hadn't been able to catch up with a slip of a woman like Rosie irked him down deep. 'It'd be my bloody job on the line if they knew I let you in here.' Having regained his breath enough to stand up, he breathed hard through his nose. The next rebuke came out on a rush of air. 'What have you got to say for yourself, young fella?' he demanded stonily.

'It won't happen again,' Rosie promised. Holding Danny away from her, she looked into his white face. 'Isn't that so?' Her voice was hard, chastising, and he knew she had been terrified. 'You will never come near this part of the yard again, will you?' He shook his head and she was satisfied.

'I don't know.' The guv'nor scratched his head and thought. He had a great sympathy for Rosie. She was a woman with a man's heart, a fighter he couldn't help but admire. Yet, when she looked at him now, it was through the soft, pleading eyes of a mother. He couldn't turn her away. 'All right,' he conceded. 'But he's not to leave your side.' Glaring at the boy, he asked, 'D'you understand?'

Danny nodded. 'I'm sorry.'

The guv'nor studied him awhile. He studied Rosie, and told them both, 'I must be stark staring mad!' Then he ushered them back to the far end of the yard, where the cart was ready for off.

Only when they had gone with Rosie between the shafts and the boy pushing the cart from behind, did he go into his office.

Always too far behind to grab her, and wanting to be sure that the moment was right and she could not escape him, Doug Selby had followed Rosie to the yard. Exhausted and in crippling pain, he dropped behind one of the railway bays. His weakness and the altercation between Rosie and the guv'nor were enough to keep him there, with the intention of recouping his strength. 'So you're coming back, are you?' he sneered, settling deeper into the coal pile. 'Well, you can be sure I'll be waiting, Rosie my lovely.' He laughed softly and it was a chilling sound. 'How could I think of leaving without you?'

He rolled his agonised eyes to the heavens, but it was Hell he was contemplating.

The guv'nor put the kettle on. 'Need a brew to calm my nerves,' he muttered. Taking out a whisky bottle from the filing cabinet, he poured a measure of the golden liquid into a cup. 'And a bit of fire to drive away the cold,' he chuckled.

An hour later, he sat down to sort the mail. It was three days old, and he still hadn't got round to dealing with it. 'Best get this lot out of the way before the postman arrives with another bag full,' he grumbled, slitting open the envelopes one after the other. There were two bills, a catalogue for shovels and equipment, a reminder that the holiday periods had to be entered, and a letter. 'Hello, what's this then?' Normally there were no letters as such, only official documents and trade brochures.

The letter was from Adam Roach, advising the guv'nor that he would be calling in at the sidings Saturday at midday: 'to discuss business'. 'Bloody Hell!' He glanced up at the clock in horror. 'That's *today*.'

The clerk, who up to now had made himself scarce in the back office, poked his head round the door. 'What's that, guv?' A small thin man with a flat face and a great shock of black hair, he resembled a floor mop.

'You should have checked this mail, bugger you. Am I expected to do everything round here?' Like all men in high places, he knew how to delegate the blame.

'I've no idea what you're talking about.'

'I'm talking about this.' He threw the letter down. 'I've a meeting with Adam Roach, you daft sod, and thanks to you, I knew nothing at all about it.'

'I don't see how you can blame me.' Collecting the letter from the floor the clerk read it and replaced it on the desk. 'Especially when I'm not even allowed to open the mail.'

''Course it's your bloody fault! Keeping tabs on things like that is what you're paid for.'

'If he's not due 'til midday, there's plenty of time yet,' came the cheeky reply. 'I don't know why you're panicking.'

'He's one of the biggest coal-merchants in the North . . . he's built up Ned Selby's old round into a huge concern, and now he's looking to expand,' gabbled the guv'nor. 'Happen *that's* why I'm panicking.' Growing thoughtful, he rubbed the flat of his hand over the stubble on his chin. Eyeing the other fellow with a grim face, he murmured, 'The word is, Roach has bought Sutcliffe out. If that's the case, he'll be looking for a supplier. Happen he's coming here to talk terms.' The prospect brought a smile to his face.

'We could do with a few big contracts an' all.'

''Course we could. We've not yet found a market for all the tons we normally supply to Sutcliffe. You know yourself how that contract has been falling away these past months. Why do you think I'm letting such folk as Rosie Selby come in here with a bloody hand cart, eh? Because we need all the help we can get, that's why! What's more, Roach won't just be coming *here*, you can bet on that. There are other suppliers beside me, and with a man like that, you can depend on it he means to see every one of 'em.'

'Then we'd best get this pig-sty cleaned up, eh? First impressions count, or so they say.'

'Not so much of the we. *You* can get on and clean the place up while I attend to the more important part. He won't be looking for a tidy office. He'll be looking at the quality of what we can offer. And that's out there . . . in the yard.' That said, he grabbed a clipboard and pen, and stormed out. He wasn't seen again until gone ten-thirty.

In the time between, he calculated the amount of stock on the ground, and assessed the different grades of coal readily available. 'Anybody'd think it were royalty coming, instead of Adam Roach,' he declared sullenly, striding across the railway tracks to examine the stock on the other side. He muttered and moaned, and checked his watch every few minutes. At half-past ten he reminded himself, 'If the bugger's coming here at midday, that gives me just over an hour to work out my best figures. By! And they'd best be favourable, unless I want him to take his money elsewhere.' With a greater sense of urgency, he pushed the pen behind his ear and went at a smart pace back to the office which was now clean and tidy as a new pin.

Fearing every minute he might be discovered, the bedraggled creature pressed down into the dark coals; covered in a thick film of dust, he was barely detectable. 'Seems it's my lucky day,' he chuckled wickedly. 'Rosie and the boy, and now Roach . . . and all I have to do is be patient.' Taking the crudely made gun from his trouser belt, he stroked it lovingly as a man might stroke a woman. In prison he had made many friends, all of his own devious kind and all from different walks of life. The man who had made the gun was a blacksmith. The one who had smuggled it out was a trustee, working in the prison library. 'Nice to have friends in high places,' he laughed. It was good to laugh out loud, and know that for the moment he could not be heard. Soon though the laughter turned to whimpers of agony. One glance at his leg told him it was beyond redemption. 'Rotten,' he observed without regret. 'Like me.'

Hearing the rumble of trucks, rolling into the yard for their second load of the day, he slunk deeper, lying silent, hoping he would not be exposed to curious eyes. When the trucks went by, he breathed a sigh of relief. Already that morning the loaders had dipped into the bay where he was hiding. Now they were here to load only slack and top quality coal.

An hour later, when the trucks had left and all was quiet again in the yard, Rosie came through the gate. Danny was helping her to push the empty cart. He was also complaining that he was 'starving hungry'.

Rosie had heard it all before. 'You're *always* hungry. You had two helpings of porridge and both my sausages for breakfast,' she reminded him good-naturedly. 'I'm beginning to think you've got hollow legs.' She was not unaware how hard he had worked that morning, and thanked the Lord for such a plucky little chap. 'What about that apple Brenda Watson gave me? Will that keep you going for a while? On the way to Whalley Banks, I'll stop at the bakers on King Street, and you can get us each a meat and potato pie.' She now realised just how hungry she was too.

359

'All right, Mam.' He held out his hand for the apple, then groaned when Rosie produced a small damp towel from beneath the cart instead. 'Oh, Mam, you're always washing me.' He wrinkled his face while she rubbed it with the corner of the towel.

'Just because we sell coal don't mean to say we have to look like chimney-sweeps,' she scolded. She then wiped her own face and hands, and gave him the apple from her pocket, first taking a bite herself. 'That should keep you going,' she said. When he ate it in two great bites, she was afraid he might eat his arm into the bargain. 'Anybody would think you were starving,' she laughed. Pushing against the wagon, she started it moving forward. 'Come on. We'll pay for the next load and be off. We'll have to look sharp because we've still got four streets to do, and I don't want us making our way home in the dark.'

'Mam?'

'What now?' Every bone in her body ached and she could hardly put one foot before the other.

'Are we rich yet?'

Rosie laughed out loud. 'Not yet, but we're getting there.' She jangled the coins in her pocket. 'We've made more money this morning than we normally make in a full day.'

His face lit up. 'Can we do *six* streets before we go home?'

Rosie frowned at him. 'Are you trying to kill your poor mam off?'

Danny was horrified. 'I don't care if we're *never* rich!' he declared, and she hugged him until it hurt.

Rosie was halfway between the office and the gate when *he* saw her. His eyes lit up. 'At last,' he whispered. Edging himself out of the bay, he stalked her as far as the railway tracks. Summoning every ounce of strength left in him, he got in front of her to hide behind the tall shuttering. From here they could not be seen from the office. It was a perfect place for an ambush, he thought. He watched through an open knot in the planks, chuckling to himself as Rosie and the boy came nearer. He could hear them talking and laughing, and the hatred in him grew until he was out of his mind.

Rosie stopped to shake the dust from her skirt. 'It'll be nice to get a bath,' she said.

'When we're rich we can have a bathroom each, can't we, Mam?'

Rosie smiled her approval. 'And gold taps.'

'And big silky towels with swans on?'

'And a deep soft carpet that shows your footprints after you've walked on it.'

'I'd like that, Mam.'

'Oh, I expect by the time we're rich, you'll have a wife and a home of your own. And you can share all these things with her.'

'I won't.'

Rosie stopped the cart and looked at him. 'Oh, and why not?'

''Cause when I grow up, I'm going to marry *you*!'

There was no answer to that. Instead, Rosie started forward again.

She was humorously mulling over what Danny had said when a furtive movement in the bays made her swing round. Like a fiend from Hell he was on her. In his blackened face his eyes were stark white, almost luminous. As the twining coiled round her neck, Rosie's first thought was for her son. In a strangled cry she told him, 'RUN, DANNY! FOR GOD'S SAKE, GET HELP. RUN! RUN!'

'That was a stupid thing to do, my lovely.' Doug's voice reached her through the fear. 'Be careful, this twining can cut through your throat like a wire through cheese.' But Rosie's fear was not for herself, because even while he was speaking another, even greater fear rippled through her. Her eyes were on Danny as he ran away, stumbling and crying. Rosie's prayers went with him. In his haste, Danny fell over again, and Rosie was frozen in horror as Doug tightened his hold on the twining, almost throttling her. He then raised his free arm and took aim, deliberately taking his time as Danny struggled to get himself upright.

In sheer desperation, and without a single thought for her own life, Rosie began violently struggling, desperately trying to knock Doug sideways. But the twining was embedded in her throat, stifling her breath and slowly killing her. Suddenly there was an explosion. Danny was lifted off his feet and hurled forward, lying where he fell, silent and twisted, his small white face turned towards Rosie. In that moment it was as though all the life

361

drained out of her. She felt the heat of her tears as they flowed down her face. She heard Doug's sinister chuckle, but it held no fear for her. Not now. Not any more. All she wanted was to be with Danny.

The two men in the office ran to the window. 'That was a gunshot, I'm telling you!' The clerk pressed his nose to the pane, but he made no move to go outside.

'Gunshot!' the guv'nor scoffed. 'What in blazes would you know about a gunshot?'

'There!' The younger man pointed to the small twisted bundle lying halfway across yard. 'What's that?'

He came to the window, straining to see. 'God Almighty! It's Rosie's lad.' Running across the office, he flung open the door and raced down the steps. The clerk, a self-confessed coward, remained in the safety of the office. Watching from the window, he saw the other man run towards the boy. Before he could reach Danny, another shot rang out, forcing the older man to take cover. 'Come back, you bloody fool!' yelled the clerk.

But there was no way back without crossing the gunman's sights. 'Call the police . . . and an ambulance,' came the reply.

As the clerk grabbed the telephone receiver, Adam's car turned into the yard. The guv'nor saw him and ran round the back, approaching the car from another direction. 'Go back!' he cried, frantically waving his arms. 'GO BACK!'

'What the Hell's the matter with him?' Ned was the first to see him. But Adam was quick to slam on the brakes.

'You'd best get out of here,' the guv'nor told them. 'There's a bloody maniac out there. He's got a gun, and he's already shot the lad . . .' His eyes grew wide with shock as he realised who he was talking to. 'Ned Selby!' He had expected Adam Roach, but not Rosie's father-in-law. There was talk that he'd either gone abroad or died long since.

'Anybody'd think you'd seen a ghost,' Ned exclaimed as he and Adam climbed out of the car.

Adam glanced about the yard. 'What's going on in there, you say?' he asked impatiently. 'Spit it out, man, spit it out.'

He hesitated. Sweat was pouring down his temples as he looked from Adam to Ned and back again. 'It ain't your problem. It'll be taken care of,' he promised. 'Police and ambulance are on their way.' How could he reveal that it was Ned's own grandson who was lying there shot, probably dead? His nerve failed him. 'Get back in your car and turn it round. Get out of here, I'm telling you.'

Adam placed his hand on the man's shoulder. 'Calm down. We might be able to help. Now then ... tell us exactly what happened here?'

It took only a moment for him to spill out the details of how he and his clerk had heard what sounded like a gunshot. They had looked through the window and seen a child lying in the yard.

Sensing there was more to it than that, Adam insisted he should show them. 'And what was a child doing in the yard? You should have had more sense than to allow it.' He knew the rules, and he was angry.

Ned and Adam were taken to a safe spot from where they could see what had taken place. The man pointed to the bundle. He looked at Ned, saying in a small frightened voice, 'I don't know how to tell you this but ... it's your grandson.'

Ned stared at him, a look of sheer horror crossing his features. It was Adam who spoke. 'What are you saying? The child out there is *Danny*?'

When he nodded, Ned would have charged out. It was only Adam's restraining hand that stopped him. 'Easy, Ned. If the boy's alive, we want him to stay that way.' Incredibly calm but thinking fast, he addressed the guv'nor in a solemn voice. 'You say the police and ambulance are on their way?'

'Yes, I've told you.'

'Who's out there?'

'I don't know.' With the flat of his hand he wiped the sweat from his face.

Now the question that Adam was afraid to ask. 'And Rosie? Where is Rosie?'

Again, the man shook his head. 'She and the lad came in for a load this morning, and I saw them leave the yard myself. I didn't see them come back, and I don't know what's happened here. All I know is what *you* know.'

'Came in for a load?' Adam couldn't believe his ears. 'I think you'd better explain,' he said in a hard voice.

The other man gave a sigh of relief when he heard the sound of sirens piercing the air. 'They're here,' he cried, racing to meet them. 'The police are here.'

'I'm going out there.' Adam moved forward. 'I've got to get the boy . . . got to know that Rosie's all right.' Before Ned could stop him, he was already walking out, arms in the air as he went towards Danny. 'I'M GETTING THE BOY,' he called. There was no answer, so he kept walking, nearer and nearer, until now he was standing over the child. 'Alright, son,' he murmured as he took the limp figure into his arms. His heart lurched when the boy's head dropped. There seemed no life at all.

'STAY WHERE YOU ARE.' Doug's voice sailed across the yard. 'I'VE GOT ROSIE. IF YOU WANT HER, YOU'D BEST COME AND GET HER.' He laughed then, and it was the laugh of a maniac.

Adam was astounded to recognise the voice. 'DOUG!' He brought his arms up to give the boy more protection. All manner of emotions went through him. What was Doug doing here? Shouldn't he be in prison? Why had he shot his own son? And why was he holding Rosie in terror? It was obvious he had lost his mind. 'WHY ARE YOU DOING THIS?'

Laughter again. Then: 'YOU SHOULD KNOW, YOU BAS-TARD.' His voice fell away. 'You and her . . . cheating on me behind my back. I'm glad the boy's dead. You're next. Then her.'

'You're so wrong, Doug. Rosie has always been faithful to happened at once.
ambulance here. Let me take the boy, and I swear I'll come back. It isn't Rosie you want. It's me. Don't hurt her, Doug. Rosie has safe, sweetheart.' Her smile was full of pain.

'Danny?' she whisright, I'm taking the boy now.'

'MOVE ONE INCH AND I'LL CUT YOU DOWN.' The shot rang out, hitting the ground before him. When Adam looked up, he was horrified to see Doug standing before him. Rosie was pressed to his side, with a length of twining round her throat, and a look of sheer terror in her brown eyes. Where the twining had cut deep, there was a smudged trail of blood. Weak now, she could hardly stand. She couldn't speak. She couldn't move. But through those lovely stricken eyes she told Adam everything he wanted to know. 'Let her go, Doug,' he pleaded softly. 'She's done you no harm. Neither has the boy. It's me you want. You have to let them go.' It broke his heart to see her like that. Now her eyes were on Danny, and she was softly crying.

'Oh, you'd like that, wouldn't you?' Doug sneered, tightening his hold on Rosie and making her wince. 'You think I'm mad, don't you?' He took a step forward and cried out with pain. Neglect and rough living had turned his leg gangrenous. He knew he had nothing to lose. 'I can't let her go. She has to die.' He aimed his gun at Adam's temple. 'But first she can see you and the bastard lying at my feet. It's only right.' His eyes narrowed as he prepared to pull the trigger.

Not far away, the police were closing in, ready to move. But the situation was fraught with danger, and one wrong move could end in tragedy. Adam saw them creeping forward. 'Think what you're doing, man,' he said sternly, 'Rosie and the boy, you have to let them go.' If it wasn't for them, Adam would have launched himself at Doug and taken his chances.

'Say your prayers,' Doug advised, grinning. 'Are you watching, Rosie?' Tugging on the twining, he made her cry out.

Incensed by her pain, Adam twisted sideways and kicked out with the intention of knocking Doug off balance. He caught Doug on the shin, causing him to double up in pain. Suddenly, out of nowhere, Ned's burly figure crunched against Doug, sending him back with such force that Rosie was thrown sideways. Everything happened at once.

Gently taking the twining from round her throat, Adam cradled Rosie in his arms. 'You're safe now,' he whispered. 'You're safe, sweetheart.' Her smile was full of pain.

'Danny?' she whispered hoarsely. When Adam told her that her son was in good hands, her eyes closed in relief.

Behind them was chaos. Police emerged from every direction. Ned's formidable weight had driven his son to the railway tracks, and now he was holding him down, pressing his back to the iron tracks.

Warnings were being shouted that the wagons were bearing down on top of them. He wasn't listening. Instead, he was cursing

365

his son for being the despicable person he was. 'I can't altogether blame you for what you are,' he said finally, his voice and heart broken. 'Happen if I'd been more of a father to you, none of this would ever have happened.'

Crippled with pain, Doug told him wickedly, 'I never wanted you. It was my mother I loved, not you.'

Ned shook his head in despair. 'And I hated her,' he said simply. 'Like you, she was a wicked creature. Never happier than when she was hurting others.' The memory of all those wasted years with Martha was more than he could bear. Now the evil in her had been perpetuated in her son. Something inside him opened out to swallow him up. *And, at long last, he knew what he must do.*

The police were helpless. They saw Ned pin his son flat with the weight of his own body. As the laden wagons sliced through the two squirming figures, there was an odd murmuring sound, almost like a prayer, and then a shocking, deathly silence.

Adam was devastated and yet, in some strange way, he understood. Then he turned and went to Rosie. That was where his future lay. If only she would have him.

CHAPTER TWENTY-TWO

On 20 July 1955, Rosie sat by the empty fire-grate inside her little house in Castle Street. As she looked around that familiar living-room, with its sturdy well-polished furniture, low ceilings and black-leaded range, she was filled with nostalgia. 'There are both good and bad memories here,' she told Peggy, who was seated opposite. 'I'll miss it.'

'No, you won't,' Peggy declared brightly. 'You've got too much to look forward to.' Lowering her gaze, she flushed with shame. 'I'm sorry if I made you unhappy,' she said softly. 'I didn't mean to.'

'Don't, Peggy, that's all in the past.' Reaching out to touch her hand, Rosie assured her, 'You're here now, and we're friends again. That's all that matters.'

Peggy groaned. 'God! I can't believe what a bitch I was to you. And all because of a swine like Robert Fellows.' She saw Rosie smiling and laughed out loud. 'Got what he deserved though, didn't he?' she chuckled.

'Honestly, Peggy, I think it was rotten of you to tell his wife he was carrying on with every female in the office.'

'Got him transferred though, didn't it? Pity it didn't get old Meg Benton and that measly pair thrown out too. Especially after the way they let you down.'

'All water under the bridge,' Rosie said. 'Best forgotten.'

'What time is he coming for you?'

Rosie glanced at the mantelpiece clock. 'Any minute now.' Her stomach fluttered as she realised the moment was almost here.

'Rosie?'

'Yes?' She knew what was coming, but she didn't know how to answer.

'Do you think you and Adam will get wed?'

'It's too early to say. So much has happened, Peggy. I have to be sure.' Adam had asked her to be his wife weeks ago, and still she hadn't given him an answer.

'Surely it wasn't all his fault? Think about it, Rosie. Take your mind back over the years. He came home, hoping to marry you, and you tell him you're expecting his best friend's child. Wouldn't *you* have walked out? And as for Ned's business, well, hasn't he explained all of that to you . . . about how it was Ned himself who asked him to take the responsibility off his shoulders? We all knew Ned was in debt . . . that Martha was dragging him under. You believe Adam's account, don't you?'

'Of course I do. Deep down, I expect I knew it all along.'

'And he wasn't married to that poor young woman who died?'

'I've told you.'

'He's handsome as ever, don't you think?'

Rosie blushed pink. 'As ever.'

'And Danny loves him, doesn't he?'

'I've never seen him so happy. Those two are so right together. When Danny was in hospital, Adam was always there for him . . . and me,' she added softly. 'Since Danny's been home, the same.'

'You've already admitted you love him.'

'Since the day I met him, I've never stopped loving him. All through the awful years with Doug, I kept on loving Adam. Even when he walked out on me, I couldn't help but love him still. And now, with everything that's happened, I love him more than ever.'

'Then why can't you tell him you'll marry him?' Given half the chance, Peggy would have jumped at the offer. But then she was one kind of creature, and Rosie was another. 'It's time you had some happiness,' she said. 'You and Danny. And Adam too.'

'I know.' Rosie gazed at her dear friend and all her emotions were laid bare. 'It's not Adam,' she murmured. 'It's *me*.'

'What do you mean?'

'It's the guilt *I* feel. The awful things *I've* done.' Sighing, she stood up and walked to the window. The July sun was blazing down. Outside it was warm. In her heart it was cold. 'Doug was cruel, I know. But I was worse.' Peggy would have spoken then, but Rosie put up her hand. 'No, Peggy, hear me out. In the beginning, Adam did what he thought was right, and he deeply regrets it. Doug did what he did because he was tortured by jealousy. But me ... there is no excuse for what I did? Since Doug and I were married, every minute of every day I was with Adam, through every waking hour, in my heart and soul, I was committing adultery. How can I forgive myself for that?' She was crying now, the tears rolling down her face. 'Oh, Peggy, I feel as though I have no right to happiness now. If only I'd been a better wife to him. What happened to Doug and Ned, I feel it's my fault.' The sobs racked her body, and all the pent-up emotions flooded out. 'I'm a bad woman,' she said. 'Adam deserves better.'

Peggy went to her then. Taking her in her arms, she said softly, 'You mustn't punish yourself like that, Rosie. What happened was never your fault. If anyone was to blame for what happened to Ned and his son, it was Martha. The woman was evil through and through. She controlled Doug in a way that you and I could see, and Ned too ... but Doug never realised. He was a victim of her tyranny, just as Ned was. You must see that?' She gently shook Rosie. 'What happened to them was not your fault, and you have a right to happiness. Take it, Rosie. For once in your life, put yourself first. Open your heart and go to him. Spend the rest of your life with the man you've always loved, and don't be ashamed or guilty. There's no need.'

Rosie looked into those sharp blue eyes and laughed through her tears. 'You're a bossy bugger, Peggy Lewis,' she said.

'So you'll do it?'

Taking a hankie from her skirt pocket, Rosie wiped her face and blew her nose. 'We'll see,' she said. Then brightly she declared, 'Oh, Peggy, I'm glad we're friends again. I honestly thought you'd turned your back on me for good.'

'Silly cow that I am!'

These two had cried together, and now they laughed together, and Rosie's heart was full. 'I'll be in touch.'

'You'd better.'

'And you'll take care of everything while I'm gone?'

'I said, didn't I?'

'Do I look all right?'

Taking a moment to study her, Peggy thought Rosie had never looked more beautiful. She was dressed in a soft blue blouse with a sweetheart neckline, and a straight knee-length skirt which showed off her shapely legs. Her rich brown hair, which had grown longer, was tied with a pretty blue ribbon and draped over one shoulder; tiny wispy curls framed her lovely face, and her brown eyes still sparkled with tears. 'When were you ever anything but all right?' Peggy said, with only the tiniest hint of envy.

Collecting her coat, Rosie draped it over her arm. Then she picked up her suitcase and went with Peggy to the door. Danny was sitting on the step, watching the corner of the road. 'He ain't here yet, Mam,' he said mournfully.

'Anybody would think you hadn't seen him for months,' she said. 'It's only been a week since Adam was here.'

'He would have stayed if you hadn't sent him away.'

'We're not the only ones he loves, you know,' Rosie reminded him. 'He has a little girl waiting at the other end, don't forget.'

'Are we staying long with him?'

'We'll see.'

Peggy's voice whispered in her ear. 'I hope you don't come back at all.' When Rosie stared at her, she went on, 'I hope I get a letter from you ... telling me to sell everything, and send you the money. I hope the letter says you're to be married, and I'm to be maid of honour. And I hope the letter isn't long in coming.'

Rosie might have answered, but Danny's whoop of joy deafened them both. Adam's car turned into the street and Danny was limping along the pavement, waving his arms and yelling for Adam to hurry up. 'The little bugger might have been close to death's door a few months back,' Peggy recalled. 'But it ain't hurt his lungs, that's for sure.'

Rosie's face clouded over as she remembered how Danny had been shot through the thigh. He had lost a great deal of blood, and for a time it was touch and go. But then he rallied round, and now even the limp was less pronounced. 'Take care of yourself,' she told Peggy, hugging her close.

Adam ushered Danny into the car before coming to put his arm round Rosie. 'Hello, sweetheart,' he said, sweeping her into his arms and kissing her shamelessly. 'You look good enough to eat.'

'Not in front of the neighbours if you please,' Peggy protested good-naturedly. 'We're not used to such goings on down our street.'

'You're a good friend to Rosie,' Adam said, 'I won't forget that.' He kissed her lightly on the cheek. Taking the case from Rosie, he told her, 'Danny and I will wait for you in the car.'

'You've got a good man there, Rosie gal,' said Peggy. 'Don't let him go a second time.'

Rosie hugged her again. 'Take care of yourself,' she said. In a minute she was hurrying after Adam.

'And don't forget that letter,' Peggy called as the car drew away. 'I'll be watching for it.'

'What letter's that, sweetheart?' Adam asked, steering the car with one hand while with the other he took hold of Rosie's.

'Oh, just something Peggy and I were talking about.' As she glanced at him, she wondered whether she would ever send that letter to Peggy. For now, she felt safe, confent to be with him, and deeply in love as always. But the guilt and the doubts still lingered. She wasn't sure if they would ever leave her.

CHAPTER TWENTY-THREE

'They get on so well, and to think I was worried.' Adam beckoned Rosie to the window. 'Look there,' he said, sliding his arm round her waist. Outside, sitting on the step, Danny and April were laughing together.

Rosie laughed. 'She knows how to flutter her eyelids.'

'She's making a lovely person,' he agreed, 'both in appearance and personality.'

While he lovingly gazed at the children, Rosie lovingly gazed at him. Though they were both seven years older now, and so much had happened during those long years when they had been apart, there was still something uniquely wonderful between them. Physically, Adam had not changed all that much. He was just as strong in physique, and his dark eyes were still filled with the same vibrant passion whenever he looked at her. But now there was something else. Something even more precious. There was complete trust, a warm and glorious contentment she thought could never happen. And, even as she was thinking it, he turned to her, gazing at her through dark love-filled eyes. 'I love you, Rosie,' he murmured.

'And I love you,' she said.

'We could be married next month,' he said, half-afraid. 'You would make a wonderful August bride.'

Rosie was glad when a small voice piped up, 'April wants to be bridesmaid.' It was Danny. He had a protective arm round the little girl. 'And I want to live here forever,' he told Rosie.

Sensing her dilemma, Adam reminded them, 'You two, go and ask Mrs Jessup to wash your hands and face. We're going out. Or have you forgotten I have something to show you?' When they raced off, screeching with excitement, Rosie asked, 'Where are you taking us?'

'You're worse than the children,' he teased, kissing her on the mouth, delighting her when he pressed her close to him. 'Don't you know you should never tell secrets?'

Within minutes the four of them were in the car and heading towards the outskirts of town. 'Where are we going?' asked the children excitedly. And Rosie did the same.

'Wait and see,' they were told.

Half an hour later Adam steered the car into a country lane. At the bottom stood a thatched cottage, with wild brambles and honeysuckle climbing all over the walls. The windows were crisscrossed with leaded lights, and the beautiful gardens seemed to go on for miles. 'It's yours if you want it,' Adam said, turning to Rosie, his eyes alight with hope.

'We want it, don't we?' Danny asked April, and she screamed with delight. Adam opened the door and, after issuing the warning 'Stay where we can see you,' he let them loose.

'So this is your surprise?' Rosie whispered, looking up at him with soft brown eyes.

'Do you like it?'

'I love it,' she said. 'It will make a wonderful home for a growing family.'

'So, you'll stay?'

'You think I'll stay because of the cottage?' She was offended.

'You know better than that.'

She fell into his arms and they kissed long and passionately. 'Are two children enough for you?' she asked.

'Not really.' His eyes twinkled mischievously.

'I've always thought the more the merrier.'

'My own sentiments exactly,' Adam murmured, kissing her again. 'Shall we go and see what the little monsters are up to?'

When they were out of the car, she led him in another direction. 'Now it's my turn to ask where we're going?' he declared curiously.

Linking her arm with his, she explained, 'I saw a post box as we came in just now.' Taking the stamped letter from her pocket, she said, 'I wrote this last night. I intended posting it first thing this morning, but you whisked me off to see your surprise instead.'

'Sounds like it's urgent,' he remarked, squeezing her tight. 'Who's it for?'

'It's for Peggy,' Rosie told him, popping it in the post-box. 'This is a very special letter. She'll be waiting for it, I know.' Then, her brown eyes twinkling, she turned him back towards where the children were playing. 'Now then, about this cottage.'

'You don't like it after all?' His spirits fell to his boots.

'Whatever gave you that idea?' As she urged him on, his hopes soared. 'I think we should go and see if it's big enough for *four* children?'

Now it was Adam's turn to whoop for joy. Lifting her from her feet he carried her through the front door. 'This is our new home,' he told the children.

'Are we rich now, Mam?' Danny asked excitedly.

Rosie's brown eyes brightly twinkled, and there wasn't a single shadow of doubt there. 'What we have, sweetheart,' she told him, 'is much more than riches.'

On the last day of August 1955, Adam and Rosie were married in a simple ceremony at the town register office. Peggy was maid of honour. It was a happy affair, attended by Peggy's family and many of Adam's friends and colleagues. Mrs Jessup was there too. The cottage was being extended to make three extra bedrooms, and she was to move in with them. Rosie chose to go to Weymouth for her honeymoon, and the children went too.

Fifteen years later, on a beautiful day in June 1970, Danny and April made their vows. This time, the ceremony was in the church of All Saints. April looked exquisite in her ivory gown and satin slippers. The two younger children, Susan and Martin, aged eleven and nine, attended the happy couple. The honeymoon was to be in Cyprus.

'It's times like this when you realise your age,' Rosie sighed, walking through the church, her arm linked with Adam's.

Drawing her to a halt, he regarded her through a lover's eyes. She was now turned forty, but ever slim and lovely, and her brown eyes still sparkled in that magic way he had loved from the very first. 'We'll never grow old,' he said. 'We're too much in love.' And they were.

A LITTLE BADNESS

Molly Irvine and her family have known me for many, many years.

Molly knew me as an urchin; she saw me courted and wed, and has followed my writing career with pride and joy.

God bless you, Molly sunshine.

Who couldn't love you!

CONTENTS

PART ONE

1900

Dreams Can . . .

CHAPTER ONE

Rita Blackthorn's heart was barren and hard. In all of her life she had never truly loved. *But she had hated*. She hated now, so deeply she could almost taste it. Beneath the loving gaze of her daughter's soft green eyes, her heart swelled with dark and dangerous emotions. 'Don't stare at me, child!' she snarled through gritted teeth. 'Get up from the floor, damn you.'

Curled up like a kitten, Cathy was a slim homely creature, with a nature as warm as her mother's was cold. She was barely sixteen years old. Since the day she was old enough to realise her mother hated her, she had yearned for one kind word, one affectionate glance. 'I love you, Mother,' she murmured. 'Don't turn me away.' The softly spoken words were uttered from the heart.

Rita made no move. She gave no answer. But Cathy's simple plea burned like fire in her brain. The emotions that swept her then should have been those of joy and belonging. Instead, her loathing clenched like a fist in her breast.

The girl's voice trembled as she dared to ask, 'Have I made you angry, Mother?'

Cold and aloof, the woman gave no answer.

Again the child entreated, 'Why don't you love me?' Beside her mother's chair, Cathy ached to touch those long slim fingers, to curl her fingers about them and to press them against her face. In the whole of her life, she had never experienced any loving response from her mother. Now, it had taken all of her courage to get out of her chair and bring herself this close. Her timid gaze swept the woman's face. As always, it was cold, forbidding. Her mother was so near, so tantalisingly near, yet Cathy dared not reach out.

Rita Blackthorn appeared not to have heard. Her handsome face was set like stone. Painfully aware that Cathy had come to kneel at her feet, she was almost overwhelmed by the desire to kill.

For a moment it seemed as though she might reply. But then she began rocking the chair in a frenzy, her long busy fingers moving skilfully over the embroidery in her lap. It was not a labour of love. The needle wove in and out with vicious rhythmic movements. For a while, the only sounds that could be heard were the muffled sigh of the rockers against the carpet, and the loud ticking of the mantelpiece clock.

Keeping her fingers clear of the rockers, Cathy studied her mother's beautiful face. Even now, she could not see the ugliness beneath.

Certainly, at forty years of age Rita Blackthorn was a vibrant, handsome woman. Having borne only one child, she had a firm, attractive figure and, with her flowing dark hair, magnificent green eyes and arrogant nature, she could have had any man she wanted. But she wanted none, not even her long-suffering husband, who cherished the ground she walked on. One quiet look, one soft word from her, and he was lost.

'Leave me now.' The movement of the chair was brought to an abrupt halt. Reaching down, she dropped her needle and silks into the sewing box. Savagely slamming shut the lid, she hissed, 'Get washed and away to your bed.'

On her feet now, Cathy resented being treated like a child. 'But I promised Margaret I would wait up for her.'

'You had no right to make such promises!' Getting up from the chair Rita said in a low trembling voice, 'Or do I have to fetch the stick?' She glanced at the door where, propped up in the corner, was a long willow stick. As a child, Cathy had been beaten with the stick many times.

'I'm not a child any longer.' The green eyes hardened.

'Don't defy me, girl! You may be sixteen years old, but you're not too old to be beaten.' With a grim expression on her face, Rita made a dash for the stick, but on hearing Cathy's footsteps and then the door closing softly behind her, paused, smiling with satisfaction. When she turned again, Cathy had gone. Softly laughing, she collected the sewing box, put the stocking inside and, with growing irritation, returned the box to the dresser.

Upstairs, Cathy sat at the window, her sad eyes scouring the countryside for a sight of her beloved Margaret. When it became clear that Margaret would be a while yet, she sighed and went about her preparations for bed. She washed at the basin, cleaned her teeth, then put on her nightgown before going to the dressing table to brush her hair. Perched on the edge of the stool, she swept the brush through her long, corn-coloured locks.

Afterwards, she sat on the window-seat, her knees to her chin, and her head resting on them. 'Hurry up, Margaret,' she pleaded aloud. But Margaret was nowhere in sight.

For what seemed an age she gazed forlornly out of the window, her heart missing a beat when she heard her mother climbing the stairs. For one awful minute, the footsteps paused outside her room.

'Don't let her come in,' Cathy whispered, her green eyes turned to the heavens. '*Please don't let her come in!*' She waited for the footsteps to carry her mother away. The silence was ominous.

Suddenly the door handle began to turn. Quickly now, the girl ran across the room on tiptoe and crawled into her bed. Turning on one side, she closed her eyes and pretended to be asleep.

Rita Blackthorn swept in. For a while she remained at the door, her hard gaze on the bed. She half-turned, satisfied that Cathy was sleeping. But then she changed her mind and, on stiff reluctant steps, came to the bed. Here, she leaned forward, staring at the long fine fingers that clutched the pillow, that pretty slim neck with its pink young skin, then the lovely face with its high cheekbones and perfect shape. 'You're too attractive for your own good,' she murmured bitterly. She wanted to tear herself away, but could not. Her envious gaze lingered, travelling the long corn-coloured hair and the thick dark lashes that fringed the closed eyelids. She imagined those striking green eyes beneath, eyes that were almost the mirror image of her own, and it was more than she could bear. 'You asked me if you had been bad,' she whispered. 'You were *always* bad. The badness is in your smile . . . it's in your laughter and your

goodness. Since the day you took root in me, you've been bad.'
Her features hardened. 'I wanted a son, and I got you!' Shivering with loathing, she rasped, 'I'll never forgive you for that.'

Incensed, she turned away. Her parting words cut the girl deep. 'As for "loving" you? *Never!* Not as long as I live.'

When the door was closed and she was alone again, Cathy was filled with sadness that permeated through and through. Confused and hurting, she returned to the window-seat.

Through a blur of tears she searched the countryside for another woman, one who was more of a mother than her own could ever be, a woman with a heart as big and warm as the summer sky, a dear and gentle soul who had loved her brother's child these past years, and was destined to be with her through all the years to come.

Burying her face in her hands, the girl pleaded, 'Please, Margaret . . . please come home.' The tears rolled down her face. Soon there were sobs which racked her body. Only the thought that Margaret would soon be home offered any consolation.

In that moment a sound made her look up. The squirrel had scurried up the tree outside her window and was almost near enough for her to touch. Cathy's face shone with delight. 'Oh, you lovely thing. I knew you'd be back.' Touching the window-pane she giggled when the squirrel sat staring at her, its mouth and nostrils working, almost as though it was trying to tell her something.

Softly now, Cathy slid open the window. 'Come for your tea, have you?' she asked. Taking a nut from a corner of the window-ledge, she held it loosely between finger and thumb. 'It's not very nice, but it's the best I can do.' Scolding the inquisitive creature, she explained, 'It's your own fault, because you haven't been to see me for a long time, and now they're all dried up.'

Creeping forward on the branch, the squirrel plucked at her hand until the nut was firmly grasped between his claws. He turned it over and over, his quick brown eyes examining every detail. At first he seemed not to want it. But then, with a little encouragement from the girl, he put it between his sharp teeth, split open the shell, and began nibbling at the contents.

'There!' she cried softly. 'It's still good.' Enchanted, her face shone with delight which deepened when she caught sight of a small familiar figure coming over the far hill. From the blue dress to the short fair hair glinting in the sunshine, there was no mistaking who it was. Margaret was on her way back.

Margaret Blackthorn paused for breath. It was a long walk to Nan Foster's cottage, and though she could have travelled on the tram from the end of the main road, she preferred to cut across the fields; especially on a day such as this, when the sun had shone gloriously down.

Shading her eyes with the flat of her hand, she squinted up at the sky. 'What a pity Cathy wasn't allowed to come with me,' she murmured, her brown eyes shadowed as she walked quickly on. There was still a way to go, and she knew the girl would be waiting for her. 'A woman like that should never have had a child in the first place!' she declared under her breath.

'They do say as how talking to yourself is the first sign of madness.' The man's voice was warm and kind, but it startled her.

'Good heavens!' Margaret reeled back as he came out of the woods and stood before her. 'Mr Leyton!' Relief flooded her face. 'You gave me a fright.'

'Sorry about that,' he apologised, then, holding up a large empty crate, he explained, 'I'm on me way back from the market, and this is all I have to show for me troubles.' Before she could express her curiosity about the crate, he pointed to the lane where his wagon and horse were waiting. 'That downpour last week opened up the potholes, and the lane's a shocking mess, I can tell you.'

Margaret smiled. 'You don't have to tell me,' she assured him. 'Why do you think I prefer to cross by way of the fields?' As always when she came into contact with Owen Leyton, she was struck by his handsome looks. He was not much taller than herself, but his figure was proud and upright, his muscles hard, and his shoulders broadened by labouring on the land. Owen Leyton caught the eye in a way she could never explain, and his manner was always most charming. With the sun streaming down on him, his brown hair gleamed, and his dark eyes twinkled as he spoke.

'You've still a way to go,' he pointed out. 'Why don't I give you a lift on the wagon?'

Margaret eyed the rickety wagon with suspicion. 'Are you

likely to hit any more potholes?' she asked wryly.

He laughed out loud. 'I'm offended,' he teased. 'You're talking to a man who was *born* on a wagon. What! I drove one almost as soon as I could walk. Me ... hit a pothole? Whatever gave you that idea?'

'Shame on me,' Margaret responded with a grin. 'For ever thinking such a thing.'

'You'll travel with me then?'

Margaret nodded. 'Why not? My legs are aching, and I've the longest mile to go yet.' She began walking alongside him towards the lane. 'I've had a good day ... spent an hour or two browsing in the Blackburn shops, then stopped off at Nan Foster's cottage on the way back.' Her gaze softened as she glanced to the big house in the distance. 'All the same, I'll not be sorry to get back. I expect Cathy's been watching for me all afternoon.'

He nodded as though agreeing with her. 'Aye. She's a lovely lass. An' if you don't mind me saying, Miss, I don't reckon I've ever known a mother and child to be so unalike. Oh, I know the girl has the stamp of her mother ... and that's not a curse because the mother is a good-looking woman.' On seeing Margaret's curious glance, he quickly added, 'But their *natures* are as far apart as heaven from hell.' He kicked at the ground. 'I expect you know how your sister-in-law has a mind to put up the rents on all the tenant farms?'

Margaret should not have been shocked but she was. Trying hard not to show her anger, she merely answered, 'Is that so?'

'Aye.' His face was turned to hers and his eyes burned with a fury that almost matched her own. 'I'll not deny the prospect of finding more rent has caused me a deal of grief, especially as we've had a hard winter and the crops were recently beaten down by the rains.' Sensing he had said enough, he lowered his gaze.

It was on the tip of her tongue to reassure him that her sister-in-law had no legal right to make such threats. But she knew how devoted to Rita her misguided brother was, and how, if it pleased her, he would let her meddle in affairs that were none of her concern. So Margaret merely answered, 'My brother has said nothing of rent rises to me.' She gave a short laugh that lightened his dark expression. 'But then, like all women I don't have a head for business. Much better to leave such matters to the men.'

He eyed her with renewed interest, saying in a pleasant voice, 'Don't pretend you haven't a good head on your shoulders, Miss . . . we all know different.'

'Oh?' She was flattered.

'I'm talking about the way you step in whenever you think your brother is being too harsh. Like last year when it seemed he might levy a milk tax on us. If he'd gone ahead with that idea, I'd have been driven under for sure.' He nodded his head as though agreeing with some inner prompting. 'I've never really said thank you for putting a stop to it, but I'm thanking you now, Miss. There's no mistake about it, you saved my livelihood.'

'And if I said I know nothing about it?' She was astonished. How in God's name had he learned of her brother's plan? It was all exactly as he described and, for the first time since she and her twin brother had inherited the land and cottages, she had felt it morally right to oppose him on a business decision. But, as far as she knew, it had been discussed in private, and had not gone beyond the walls of the big house.

As though reading her mind, he answered cleverly, 'Walls have ears, Miss.'

'You mean the tale was carried out by someone from the house? Are you telling me it was Ruby?'

'Happen . . . and happen not.'

Her smile was friendly, forgiving. She found him wonderfully easy to talk to. 'Meaning?'

'If it *was* the housekeeper, you wouldn't tell your sister-in-law, would you?'

'What do *you* think?'

Grinning, he visibly relaxed. 'Well now, Miss. Taking into account the fact that Ruby Adams has no family but yours, and has served you well these many years, and knowing you have a gentle heart, I don't reckon you would punish her.'

'Ruby is in a position of trust, and she did wrong.' When she saw his expression fall, she quickly assured him, 'I intend to have words with her. But, no, I won't punish her, and neither will I speak to my brother about it.'

'Thank you for that, Miss.' His face hardened. 'If word of

Ruby's little indiscretion ever got to your sister-in-law's ears, she'd take great pleasure in making an example of her.' In his mind's eye he could see his landlord's spoilt wife, handsome, arrogant ... *and immensely desirable.* Thrusting such dangerous images from his thoughts, he exclaimed, 'By! She's a hard one! I had a bull like that once ... magnificent to look at, but get on his wrong side and he'd rip your heart out.' Suddenly he was trembling, whether from fury or desire he wasn't altogether certain. All he knew was that Rita Blackthorn had the power to shake his emotions like nothing he had ever experienced. And he hated himself for it.

Secretly amused by his comparison of Rita to a mad bull, Margaret let the matter lie. 'What's the crate for?' she asked brightly.

Momentarily surprised by her question and realising she wanted to change the subject, he answered gratefully, 'It's empty now, but it weren't an hour back.' Giving no more information than that, he strode along, swinging the heavy wooden crate as though it was no weight at all. 'Where in God's name has he got to?'

'Who?' she asked.

Pausing in his stride and turning his attention to the spinney, he didn't hear her question. 'It's no use him searching now,' he groaned. 'If I know anything at all, they'll be long gone.'

Margaret was intrigued. Standing some way behind, she watched him put down the crate. He then cupped his big hands round his mouth and emitted an ear-splitting whistle. It took her by surprise. Fascinated, she came to his side. Looking with him towards the spinney, she wondered what might suddenly emerge.

When only silence followed, he enacted the same procedure again. This time the whistle was so loud that Margaret was forced to press her hands over her ears, at the same time thinking she might have got home quicker if she hadn't accepted a ride in his wagon.

Suddenly the spinney came alive when two large birds burst from its cover. 'Well, I'm buggered! He found 'em after all.' Falling to his knees, he pulled her with him. 'Keep down, Miss,' he whispered. 'If they catch sight of us they'll be gone like the wind.'

The birds were in a panic. Flying a short distance then falling to the ground again, they flailed the air with their wings and nervously fluttered about.

'Is that what was in your crate?' Margaret recalled him saying he'd been to Blackburn Market.

'That's right,' he confirmed. 'Until we rumbled over the potholes and the blessed thing broke open.'

'Shouldn't you get after them?'

He shook his head. 'No. They're spooked enough. Best to stay put. I've taught him well. He knows what he's doing.' That said, he strained his eyes towards the spinney. 'There!' he whispered. 'D'you see?'

Margaret followed his gaze. Creeping from the spinney on all fours was a young man. Inch by inch he came up on the birds who were pecking at the ground one minute, and in the next squaring up to tear each other's eyes out. 'Careful now. Or it'll be *your* eyes they'll pluck out,' Owen whispered. Margaret remained silent, but watchful.

Suddenly there was a flurry of feathers as the birds went for each other, and in that same minute were grabbed by the young man. Wrenching them apart, he dropped each one into a separate sack before loosely tying the necks and setting towards the onlookers across the field. When he saw Owen, he grinned from ear to ear. 'I'd have bagged them in the spinney if your whistle hadn't scared 'em off.'

His father beamed with pride. 'I might have known he'd track the blighters down,' he laughed. 'Just as well too. They're valuable birds ... champion cockerels, that's what they are. And I don't mind telling you, they cost me a pretty penny.'

Together, Margaret and Owen followed the young man's progress across the field. At eighteen years of age, David was the elder of Owen's two children. The only son, he was the apple of his father's eye; the kind of son a man could boast of. Tall, well-built and incredibly handsome, he was also hard-working and possessed of a warm likeable nature. With his wild dark hair and smiling dark eyes, he had the makings of a heartbreaker.

'He's a fine young man,' Margaret declared as David strode towards them in that easy confident manner he had. 'And a good friend to Cathy.'

Owen snorted through his nose. 'Aye! And how long d'you reckon it'll be before *she* puts a stop to it?' Jerking his thumb towards the big house, he went on in a harsh voice, 'From what I know, your sister-in-law would rather wipe her boots on my son than have the girl speak to him.' He rolled his eyes to heaven. 'By! If she knew how her daughter was teaching David to read and write, there'd be hell to pay!'

'Then we'd best not let her find out,' Margaret said softly. 'What she doesn't know won't hurt her.'

'She'll not hear of it from *me*, that's for sure.' He rubbed his chin with the flat of his hand. 'All the same, I reckon it'll end in trouble.' As he dwelt on the possible consequences of the growing friendship between the two youngsters, a deep frown creased his forehead and he opened his mouth to say something else.

Margaret put up her hand and intervened. 'Do you want me to stop calling?'

''Course not.' The very idea would be like a slap in the face, for Margaret had brought great comfort to his poorly wife. 'What! Maria would never forgive me.'

'Do you want me to stop bringing the girl then?' Margaret was testing him, though she guessed he was made of sterner stuff than to let Rita Blackthorn dictate the pattern of his life.

'Then David would never forgive me.'

'I could always say it was my idea?'

'Then I'd never forgive myself!' Perceiving her little game, he shrugged his shoulders. 'Shame on you, Miss. You know well enough how I want our David to have the learning I never had. Cathy Blackthorn is the best thing that ever happened to him, and as for yourself, Miss, you must know how me and the missus appreciate your help.'

'That's very kind. But we're not talking about me in particular. What we're discussing is whether or not you still want things to carry on as they have these past few months? In other words, Owen Leyton ... are you happy for me to go on visiting your wife? And is Cathy still welcome at your house?' She eyed him with serious brown eyes, the smallest suspicion of a smile appearing at the corners of her mouth. 'I must say, I never thought you were the kind of man to let a woman frighten you.

That's all she is, you know . . . just a woman.'

He was embarrassed then. 'She doesn't frighten me, Miss.' His hackles were up now, and his jawbone working in a fever. 'It's for *him*, isn't it? For David. And to hell with Rita Blackthorn!' His gaze went to the young man who was almost on them, and at once his eyes softened. 'Who am I to say he can't have his chance, eh? He's a good lad, and one day he'll make a better man than his father.'

There was regret in his voice, and something so painful that Margaret was obliged to comment. 'How can you say that?' she asked kindly. 'No son could wish for a better father.'

When he looked into her eyes, she was disturbed by his fleeting expression of guilt. 'You think so?' he murmured, dropping his gaze. 'Mebbe! But I wouldn't be much of a father if I robbed him of his chance to read and write now, would I, eh? David was always a loner, never one for mixing, especially with members of the opposite sex.' He chuckled knowingly. 'But that lovely girl of yours has opened up a whole new world for him. She's not only befriended him, she's taught him a love for words . . . given him the talent to write and read . . . something his father never could do.' He grimaced. 'It's the biggest shame of my life, not being able to read and write. All these years, I've felt only half a man. I don't want that for David. Until the girl came along, he still hadn't mastered the pen and page. Oh, it's not that he hasn't the brains because he has. He just didn't have the *heart*.' He chuckled. 'He hated every minute at school.'

'There's nothing wrong with wanting to be out in the fields instead of being squashed into a row of desks, with only the four walls to look at.' Margaret worried that Owen might see this as a flaw in his son's character. 'David is a bright intelligent young man, with a great love for God's wonderful creation.' She swept out her arms. 'And this is where he belongs, where he feels at home. It isn't surprising that he didn't enjoy his schooling.'

Soon they were all loaded on to the wagon; Margaret seated up front with Owen who had put on his cap and pulled the brim down over his forehead; David in the back, with the crate securely tied to the wagon rim. 'I'll have you home in no time,

Miss,' Owen declared as he gently tapped the whip against the horse's rump.

'I'm later now than if I'd walked,' she said, desperately hanging on as the cart lurched forward. With her free hand she dipped into her basket and drew out a scarf which she wrapped round her neck. Suddenly there was a light wind blowing and the sun was hiding behind a cloud.

'Looks like rain,' Owen remarked. Staring up at the sky, he drove the wagon on. The potholes were thick and fast, and with every turn of the wheels the wagon found them out.

'Miss Blackthorn?' David's voice cut through the air.

Not daring to glance round, Margaret replied, her voice vibrating as she was thrown from side to side, 'Yes? What is it, David?'

'Will Cathy be coming to the farm tomorrow?'

This time it was Owen who spoke. 'Talk sense, lad! It's Sunday tomorrow. Miss Blackthorn never visits on a Sunday.'

There followed an awkward silence. But then Margaret's warm voice answered, 'If the weather is as glorious tomorrow as it's been today, I have a mind to take Cathy on a long walk over the fields. I dare say we could make a detour to the farm.' She turned round then. Happiness shone in his face like a beacon. 'What's so special about tomorrow?' she asked.

His smile fell away. It was something secret between him and Cathy and, as much as he liked Miss Blackthorn, he had promised Cathy that no one would know about it until it was all finished. 'It doesn't matter,' he said quietly. 'It can wait till Monday.'

Margaret sensed his disappointment. 'I'm sure Cathy would be delighted to pay a visit tomorrow,' she said wisely. 'But, as I say, it's a Sunday so there'll be no reading or writing.' When she looked at him again, he was crouched before the crate, tenderly stroking the birds, a little smile on his face.

The short journey to Blackthorn House took only fifteen minutes during which the conversation embraced the Boer War, the assassination of the German Ambassador in Peking, and the opening of London Underground's central line.

'As you know, I was bitterly disappointed not to have joined the fighting force,' Owen lied.

'It wasn't your fault,' Margaret reassured him. She had heard the tale time and again, and knew it inside out.

'I should have been more careful. Two days before leaving, and I had to shoot myself in the knee with a shotgun!'

'It's no good blaming yourself, Dad.' David had remained quiet until now, just listening and enjoying the ride. But now he felt he had to defend his father. 'You have to be thankful you didn't lose your leg.'

Margaret sensed Owen's disgust at himself. 'Sometimes bad things happen and we just have to make the best of them,' she said softly. Her thoughts wandered. She thought of Cathy, and of how Rita had never deserved such a lovely child. She recalled how the girl had always craved her mother's affection but been constantly rejected, and she burned with shame at the way her own brother accepted the situation. In his eyes Rita could do no wrong. Some day, Margaret knew, he would regret the way she had twisted him round her little finger. But for now Frank Blackthorn could not see what was right before his eyes, and there wasn't a thing anyone could do about it.

'You're very easy to talk to,' Owen's voice interrupted her thoughts. 'You're a good woman with a sense of right and wrong.' Under his breath he added warily, 'The wife has always said you're a misfit in the big house.'

Margaret was made to wonder about this, and for some reason she was not too happy about it.

Fearing he had overstepped the mark, Owen quickly urged, 'Take no notice of me, Miss Blackthorn. Sometimes I let my tongue run away with my brains.' He blamed her too. Some people were so easygoing and kind that they made it too easy to be familiar.

Margaret smiled at him. He smiled back. But still he felt uneasy.

Conversation was at an end. Instead, he began softly whistling. Margaret thought about her aching feet and the few purchases she had made at the market. Behind them the young man lay on his back, stared up at the gathering clouds and dreamed of Cathy. So much separated them. So many things decreed that they could never be together as lovers. Yet he was determined: one day in the future, they *would* be lovers. One day in a far-off summer, when he was a man and Cathy was a woman, they would be man and wife. It seemed an impossible dream. Right now, the way things were, it *was* impossible, he knew that. But one day it must happen, or all of his life would count for nothing.

When the wagon drew up to the front door, two pairs of green eyes were watching from the house. Downstairs in the big front parlour, Rita was incensed that a tenant farmer should have the gall to drive his wagon right up to her front door; while upstairs, Cathy was delighted, her fond gaze going from David to Margaret, and back to David. He didn't see her at first. But when he looked up, his heart turned over and the smile on his face told its own tale.

Gathering up the hem of her dress with one hand, Margaret reached out with the other to take hold of Owen's outstretched fingers. 'Don't forget your basket, Miss,' he reminded her as she stepped to the ground. Sweeping the basket from the wagon, he handed it to her, afterwards tipping the neb of his cap and remarking that the clouds had darkened, and, 'It won't be long before the downpour.'

Almost before the words were out of his mouth, Rita's angry voice demanded, 'How dare you bring that filthy contraption to the front of the house?' Before he could answer, she rounded on her sister-in-law. 'As for *you*! I don't know what you're thinking of. I'm ashamed, that's what I am . . . *ashamed!*'

Brushing a cloud of dust from her dress, Margaret smiled sweetly. 'But there's nothing for you to be ashamed of, Rita, dear,' she remarked with feigned surprise. 'It wasn't *you* who rode home on the cart.'

Fuming, Rita turned to Owen Leyton. 'My husband will hear of this,' she warned. 'And when he does, I shouldn't be at all surprised if you and yours weren't thrown out on the streets where you belong!'

Owen stared at her for a moment, before saying in a soft persuasive voice, 'If I've offended you in any way, Ma'am, I'm sorry.' He thought her a splendid figure of a woman. Such was the effect she had on him, he gazed on her from top to toe, mentally ravaging her almost without realising it. He was acutely conscious of the shapely pair of ankles that showed from beneath the hem of her straight-skirted cream dress; the tiny waist and the long dark hair that was caught up on her crown with an expensive mother-of-pearl comb. He was aware of the soft creamy skin that showed at her neck, the exquisite ears and the hard set of her small square chin. He looked into those blazing green eyes and could hardly control his passion. He wanted her. He had wanted her from the first minute he'd seen her.

For a long moment Rita looked up at him, at those dark secretive eyes that seemed to touch her soul, and she couldn't tear her gaze away. She had seen Owen Leyton from a distance on many occasions. She had never been this close to him: never realised how devilishly handsome he was. Something stirred in her. Something deeply disturbing. It warned of shocking things to come; things that would alter the course of all their lives.

He smiled and the spell was broken. Her anger erupted. 'Be off,' she cried. 'And if you know what's good for you, you'll stay well away from this house.'

Without a word, he made a small bow with his head, touched his fingers to the brim of his cap, and swung into the wagon. In a minute he was gone. But his presence remained. And Rita was awed by it.

'Where's your sense of dignity?' she demanded of Margaret. 'You have a reputation to keep up.'

'There's no harm done to our reputation,' Margaret patiently assured her.

'We'll see what Frank has to say about this!' Rita brushed by, storming into the house and slamming shut the door.

'My! My!' Margaret tutted. 'What a sulk.'

After surreptitiously winking at Cathy, whom she had seen watching, Margaret went towards the house. Now a hundred years old, it made a pretty picture with its red-tiled roof, long stone-embrasured windows latticed with lead, and every inch of its brick walls festooned with climbers from which hung many colourful blooms. Her admiring eyes rested on the place that had been home for longer than she cared to remember.

In 1810, Edward Blackthorn, the love child of a country squire and his lowly mistress, came into a handsome legacy. When the house became available, together with some considerable acreage, he fought off all competition and paid a handsome price for it. A farm hand all his life, and possessing a great love for the land, he took on fellow labourers but worked himself into an early grave – and no doubt turned in it when Joshua Blackthorn, his only son and heir, vowed never to turn a shovel or darken his hands with the earth.

When Joshua's wife bore him twins, the boy, Frank, inherited his father's indifference to the land, while the girl, Margaret, shared her grandfather's love for it.

The house was many things to many people. To Rita it was a symbol of her higher status in the community. Her husband Frank was there merely because *she* was there; if she had lived in a pigsty, he would have grovelled in the dirt with her. To the tenant farmers, Blackthorn House was a formidable place, a place from which the 'Squire' presided over them, a place they were forbidden to enter. To Margaret and young Cathy, however, it was home; a place to come back to after a long walk across the fields, a place where they could hide away and tell each other their dearest dreams and wishes, a warm and welcoming sanctuary where they could shut out the hostility that surrounded them, and grow in the strength of each other's love.

As Margaret came into the hall from the front entrance, a small round figure with grey hair bustled in from the back kitchen. Ruby Adams was as much a part of this house as the foundations themselves. Now sixty years old, she had served the Blackthorns for over forty years. Hired by the infamous Joshua Blackthorn, she had cleaned his house, tended his wife, and, on a dark stormy night when the doctor couldn't get through the floods, she had brought the twins, Frank and Margaret, into the world. Less than a year later, deeply affected by her husband's blatant affairs with other women, Annette Blackthorn ran off and was never heard of again.

Afterwards Joshua Blackthorn brought one woman after another into the house. People came and people went. Money was scarce, then it was abundant. There was scandal and chaos; no servant ever stayed for more than a month – and throughout it all, caring for the children, protecting and loving them, Ruby remained ever constant. Even when, twenty years later, Joshua Blackthorn was found drowned in the river, she was there, a sane, familiar figure in a changing world; the same warm, kindly soul she was now.

Though older, and with the habit of speaking her mind to everyone but the arrogant Rita, for whom she had little time, Ruby was indispensable. Cathy and Margaret adored her. Frank had a lingering affection for her. And Rita tolerated her because she was a sort of family heirloom, handed down with their other possessions.

'Whatever have you been doing?' Ruby gently scolded. 'You've sent the mistress into a terrible rage.' While she talked, she collected the basket from Margaret's arm and walked through to the kitchen.

Leaning closer to the round grey-haired figure, Margaret looked into her eyes – pink because she had a liking for 'a drop o' the old stuff... for me poor old bones, you understand?'

'I rode home on Owen Leyton's wagon,' Margaret answered her question.

'You never did!' Ruby's pink eyes twinkled.

'Have you ever ridden on a wagon?' Margaret asked mischievously.

The old woman chuckled. 'If I have, I'm not about to tell you,' she said, blushing to the roots of her grey hair.

Margaret was intrigued. 'Why, Ruby Adams!' she teased. 'Whatever secrets are you keeping?'

'Not telling.' She grinned broadly, showing a row of baby-pink gums. 'And anyway, it were years back... when I were young and beautiful.'

Margaret burst out laughing. 'You were never young and beautiful.' It wasn't meant as an insult, and they knew each other well enough to understand that.

Ruby thought a while, then cocked her head to one side before replying wryly, 'Well... happen not "beautiful". But I wore the frilliest bloomers, and I walked off with the best-looking fella out the lot.' She shook her head and tutted. 'I'll never know why the bugger wed Alice Clegg when he could have had me!'

Margaret hugged her warmly. 'Because he was blind,' she declared.

'Aye. Well, good shuts to him, that's what I say.' With that she informed Margaret that there was a snack ready if she was hungry. Inclining her head towards the drawing room, she whispered, 'Her Highness just informed me that she don't want dinner served.'

'Why's that?'

'Because the master ain't home, and she's in a foul mood.'

'Has Cathy eaten?'

'Not yet. She's been sent to her bed. But I can fetch a tray up for the two of you, if you like?'

'That's a good idea, Ruby. Give me half an hour though. I need to wash the day off me first.' She also needed to have a word with Rita. 'Foul mood' or not, it was unfair of her to take it out on Cathy.

Impatient to see her niece, she went straight upstairs. A gentle tap and the door was flung open. Cathy threw herself straight into Margaret's arms. 'I'm so glad you're back!' she cried. 'I thought you were never coming home.'

'Well, you thought wrong. Not only am I home, but I've brought you a present.' Going into the room, she laid the small parcel on the bed. 'Open it,' she urged, sinking on to the bed beside it, and watching Cathy's excited face as the present was revealed. 'Do you like it?' she asked. But she already knew the answer. Cathy's face said it all.

'Oh, it's beautiful!' With great tenderness, Cathy cradled the brooch in the palms of her hands. An oval-shaped cameo set in silver filigree, it was the same brooch she had sighed over in Harpur's shop window the last time she and Margaret had gone into Blackburn town.

Going to the mirror, she pinned it to the neck of her night-gown. In the light from the window it shimmered and glowed. 'Oh, look!' she cried, glancing at Margaret in the mirror. 'The lady's smiling at me.' And, just for a moment, when she moved and the dying sunlight caught the cameo face, it did seem so.

'That's because she knows what a delightful creature you are.' Margaret came to her then, resting an arm around the girl's shoulders and gazing into the mirror at her. There was a world of love in her eyes.

Pressing one hand into Margaret's, and holding the brooch

against her throat with the other, Cathy told her softly, 'I do love you.'

Sensing the girl's dilemma, Margaret assured her, 'You don't have to tell me if you don't want to.'

The words tumbled out. 'She said she could never love me.' She believed her mother's words would haunt her forever. '*Why?* Why won't she love me? I've done nothing wrong, have I?'

'No, and don't think that.' She sought for a way to explain Rita's coldness towards her own daughter. It was hard. Instead, she gave Cathy a degree of hope. 'We're all different,' she began. 'Women are complex creatures . . . some love their children even while they're carrying them. Others love them from the minute they're born. And there are those who simply don't have the capacity to love . . . they can't open their hearts to *anyone*.'

'*She's* like that, isn't she?' Cathy stiffened in her arms. 'She meant what she said. For all my life, she'll never love me, will she?'

Margaret wanted to say the right thing, something that would help Cathy . . . give her hope, but not too much, because there was no hope of Rita ever loving this precious girl . . . no hope that her heart would soften with the passing of the years. It wasn't Rita she cared about now. It was Cathy. And the only solace she could offer was to say, 'Be patient, sweetheart. Give her time, and she might turn out to be the mother you want.'

'I wish you were my mother.'

'I'm not your mother, Cathy,' Margaret said regretfully. 'But, with the help of the Lord, I'll be here for as long as you need me.' They clung to each other then, and the world was right again.

'Anyway, you're not the only one who got on her wrong side.' Margaret chuckled at the way Rita had laid into her about riding on the wagon.

'Tell me all about it. How did you come to be on the wagon? And David? Did he ask after me? How soon are we visiting again?' The questions came thick and fast, and Margaret answered them as best she could. She outlined the sequence of events, and finished by assuring Cathy, 'I've promised we'll pay a visit tomorrow afternoon.' That brought a smile to her face.

So did the news that Ruby brought. 'I'm to tell you that dinner will be served after all, and you're *both* to be at the table. The master's home and roaring hungry,' she announced wryly. 'What's more, he's brought someone back from London with him . . . though he must be a ghost, 'cause I ain't seen hide nor hair of the fella!'

On the stroke of eight o'clock, Cathy and Margaret came into the dining room; Cathy looking fresh and bright in a pale blue dress, and Margaret feeling just a little bit special after washing and changing into her favourite cream-coloured blouse and long straight skirt; scalloped at the hem, it showed more of her legs than her brother thought proper.

'Be quick! Be quick!' Frank Blackthorn was already seated at the table. A big man with a soft face, sad blue eyes and wild brown hair, he was normally a quiet and reserved soul. Tonight, though, he was greatly excited, and could hardly keep still.

The new maid, Milly, recently taken on because of Ruby's worsening gout, was standing ready to serve soup. As yet there was still no sign of Rita. 'Where on earth is she?' Agitated, Frank got up from his chair and proceeded to walk backwards and forwards, anxiously peering through the door whenever he came to it, and feverishly rubbing his hands together behind his back. 'He's like the rabbit in *Alice in Wonderland*,' Cathy whispered, but fell silent when Margaret shot her a warning glance.

It was ten minutes past eight when Rita arrived. The maid was nervously shifting from one foot to the other; Frank was beside himself with impatience; Margaret was toying with the idea of expressing her curiosity regarding the 'fella' Ruby had mentioned earlier; and Cathy was busy listening to the tune her hungry stomach was playing.

Rita swept in as though she was royalty about to meet her subjects. Bedecked in a crimson dress and matching shoes, and with her dark hair curled about her ears, she looked magnificent. 'My dear, you look wonderful!' As usual, Frank was besotted. Springing forward to lead her to her chair, he fussed over her all the way.

Looking about her as Frank returned to his own seat, she asked, 'Where is he?'

Frank gave a little secretive smile. 'Who, my dear?' He was obviously enjoying himself.

Impatient, Rita banged her fist on the table. 'Your guest, of course ... the man you brought from London!'

'All in good time, my dear,' he replied, beckoning the thankful maid to serve the first course. 'Ruby should be attending to him now. I'm sure he'll join us soon enough.'

In fact, it was sooner than he had intended. They were half-way through the main course when screeches of horror were heard from the hall. Before Frank could get to his feet the doors had burst open and all hell was let loose. The fleeing dark shape flitted through the room, ducking and darting and letting out cries like a banshee. Behind him came Ruby, wearing a dirt-stained pinafore and looking flustered. 'He 'scaped from me!' she wailed above Rita's screams. 'The bugger took off when I were getting the soap!'

'Got you!' Frank lunged at the shape and hoisted it up for all to see. When it wriggled and squealed, Rita screamed the louder, Cathy giggled, and Margaret was astonished when she saw what Frank was holding. 'It's a *lad!*' she exclaimed, though she could hardly see its features beneath the layers of grime.

'A street urchin,' Frank corrected. 'It tried to pick my pocket outside the club in Piccadilly ... would have been carted off and thrown in prison if I hadn't arranged for it to be brought here.' He seemed very proud of himself. In fact, there was much more to the young urchin than he intended revealing.

'You must be mad!' Rita yelled, wrapping her handkerchief over her nose. 'Get it out of here!'

Frank's reply was calm and sincere, and everyone there was silenced by it. 'No, my dear,' he answered. 'The boy stays. He'll be the son we never had.'

Lost for words, Rita stared at her husband as though he had lost his mind. Margaret was shocked to her roots. And Cathy could only watch with disbelief; she had always believed it was her *mother* who bitterly regretted never having a son. Now she realised it was her father also. She looked into his face, that big soft face that was now hard and unyielding. And, for the first time, she really despaired of ever winning her parents' love.

Margaret too saw the possessive look in her brother's eyes. She saw that Rita was reluctantly intrigued by the intruder. She looked at the boy, a surprisingly well-built creature, with dirt-encrusted hair hanging to his shoulders, the whites of his eyes staring out of a blackened face, and like Cathy she wondered what manner of chaos he would bring to Blackthorn House.

In those few moments before Ruby led the urchin away, no one there could ever begin to imagine the sequence of events that even now were being unleashed.

CHAPTER TWO

'Do you think he'll run away?' In spite of her generous nature, Cathy sounded hopeful.

'Who knows?' Margaret replied as they crossed the brook. 'Why? Do you *want* him to?'

Cathy thought for a while, then answered sincerely, 'At first I resented him. But now, I'm not sure how I feel.' She looked up with anxious green eyes. 'Mother said I was wicked. Maybe she's right.'

Stopping at the top of the bank, Margaret pulled her up short. 'Your mother's wrong,' she said softly. 'You're *not* wicked! Don't ever think that, sweetheart.' When Cathy seemed not to be convinced, she went on, 'When your father brought that boy into our lives, he gave us all something to think about. After all, we don't know anything at all about him . . . who he is or where he's come from.'

'Do you want him to stay?'

'Like you, I'm not too sure.'

'What about Mother?'

Margaret's expression darkened. 'I'm sorry, sweetheart, I can't answer for her.' Sensing that the conversation might take a much more serious turn, she took hold of Cathy's hand and headed quickly towards the Leyton smallholding. Above them the sun shone out of a sapphire blue sky, and the sound of birds filled the air. It was a glorious day, and it was Margaret's intention that nothing would spoil it. Cathy was still smarting from her mother's treatment of her, and now there was the urchin to contend with. Not for the first time, she wondered where it would all end. 'Remember, it's Sunday,' she reminded Cathy. 'You're only visiting . . . not working.'

Cathy's thoughts were still at Blackthorn House, with her mother and the boy. 'He seems to be worming his way into Mother's affections,' she recalled. 'When he spilled tea on the tablecloth at breakfast, she didn't even scold him.' Casting her gaze to the ground, she was quiet for a moment, before recalling an incident she would rather forget but could not. 'When *I* dropped my spoon on the floor last week, she slapped me really hard.' Subconsciously caressing the side of her face where Rita had struck her, she gave a small sigh. 'The other night, when she thought I was asleep, I heard her say I was bad ... and that she never wanted me. She only wanted a son.' Looking up at Margaret, she asked forlornly, 'Now they have a son, they won't want me any more, will they?'

They had come to a narrow lane. 'Come and sit here, sweetheart,' Margaret coaxed, pointing to a derelict cart. 'We deserve a breather, I think.' What she really wanted was to put Cathy's tortured mind at rest.

Easing herself up on to the shaft, Cathy sat alongside her aunt. 'As long as I've got you, I don't care,' she lied, but the despair in her voice betrayed the truth.

Taking a deep breath, Margaret smiled into her upturned face. 'You don't have to pretend with me,' she said, shaking her head in disapproval. 'I thought we always told each other the truth?'

Cathy was ashamed. 'I'm sorry.'

'I should think so too.' She put her arm round the girl's slim shoulders and drew her close. 'Now you listen to me, and listen carefully,' she began, and Cathy looked at her intently. 'First of all, you must never make hasty judgments ... sometimes people say things they really don't mean. Like you said just now, about not caring whether they loved you. Oh, I know it's hard, and I'm sorry you heard your mother say those things about wanting a son. But she didn't know you were listening, did she?'

'No.'

'Have you ever heard her say that before ... about wanting a son?'

Cathy thought hard. 'No, I've never heard her say that before,' she confessed.

'Have you ever heard your father say he doesn't want you?'

'No.'

'Well then! As far as I can tell, he loves you very much.'

'He never tells me that.'

'I know, and it's a great pity. But even if he doesn't tell you so, you know he loves you. In your heart, you know. Don't you, eh?'

'I suppose so,' she admitted in a brighter voice.

'Good. By the way, it might be wiser not to mention the boy to anyone. I think we'll let your father do the explaining, shall we?' She was amused by the idea ... it would be a sort of punishment for what she believed to be his foolhardy action. When she spoke again, it was with a serious voice. 'After all, it was all his idea and, to tell you the truth, I'm afraid he may very well come to regret it.'

'I was going to tell David about him, but I won't.'

'Right then! Let's make our way, or it'll be dark before we get back.' She swung off the shaft and, with Cathy beside her, quickened her steps away from the lane.

Disappointed, Cathy glanced towards the cottage at the end of the lane. 'I thought we were calling on Nan Foster?'

'We are. But on the way back,' Margaret explained.

'Do you think he's a bad lot?'

'Who?'

'The urchin.'

'I think we should give him the chance to prove himself one way or the other.'

'He was picking Father's pockets.'

'I know, but from what your father told me, he has no home or family. Perhaps he was driven to it.'

Cathy thought on that for a time. Then, 'He has a nice face, don't you think?'

'Yes, I think he does.'

'Mother thinks he's handsome.' A shadow crossed Cathy's face.

'I suppose she's just pleased he looks more like a human being, now he's been washed and dressed like a little gentleman.'

'She'll probably dote on him.'

Margaret laughed. 'I don't think so. Tomorrow she'll probably throw him out on his ear.' In fact, Margaret too had been surprised when her sister-in-law made no objection to the boy's

remaining at the table throughout breakfast; though she made
no effort to put him at his ease, she glanced his way occasionally
when she thought no one was looking. 'Anyway, I have the
feeling he would much rather be out on the streets, picking
pockets.'

'He ate more than all of us put together.'

Margaret laughed. 'I expect that's because Ruby threatened
him with all manner of horrors if he didn't eat her beautifully
cooked food.'

'Would you say he's good-looking?'

'I suppose he is, yes.'

Like everyone else, she had been astonished at the change in
the urchin. Ruby had scrubbed him until he glowed, then she
cut his hair short and dressed him in the clothes which Frank
had already bought from a shop in Blackburn. The result was
astounding. Gone was the filthy bundle of rags, and in its place
was revealed a young man who, though half-starved and pale,
appeared to be about Cathy's age. With his thick mop of fair
hair and light hazel eyes, he had a certain appeal – though there
was nothing appealing about his manners or his speech. On
being summoned to the breakfast table, he boldly warned his
host, 'Don't think about callin' the rozzers, guv, cause I'll be
long gone by the time they get 'ere!' However, once Frank
assured him he was safe enough, he sat at the table and proceeded to fill himself with every morsel in sight.

'I'm a bit wary of him.' Cathy didn't care much for the way
he stared at her, as though silently assessing her.

'No need to be,' Margaret assured her. 'He's probably more
wary of you.' With that, she quickened her steps; over the hill,
past the spinney, down through the valley, and it wasn't long
before the Leyton smallholding was in sight. A tall red-brick
house with square windows and a litter of farming implements
outside, it was always untidy. But, nestling between the curve
of a tree-lined river and the rising hills behind, it was situated
in one of the loveliest spots around.

Cathy ran on ahead. By the time Margaret got to the back
door, David and Cathy were already deep in conversation. Pausing to look on for a moment, Margaret saw the change in Cathy.
Her eyes were sparkling and her face was alive with joy, as it
always was when she was with David.

'Don't wander off,' Margaret warned. 'And mind what I said . . . no working on the Sabbath!'

'Come in, Miss Blackthorn . . . please.' The voice was weak and thin, like its owner. Maria Leyton was not yet fully recovered from a long and debilitating illness. Frail and painfully thin, with greying hair and tired blue eyes, she looked much older than her forty-one years. 'Our Teresa's about to put the kettle on.' Her smile was warm and genuine. 'You'll take a brew with me, won't you?'

Margaret followed her into the scullery; a cramped but cosy room, it contained a sofa, a straight-backed chair, an empty fire-grate, and a big earthenware sink. Above this was a large window through which sunshine flooded in, falling on the girl who stood there.

Eighteen next birthday, Teresa Leyton was only a year older than Cathy, but she could not have been more different. Thick-set, tall for her age and with staring blue eyes and shoulder-length brown hair, she was possessed of a devious mind and a quick temper. When the two women came into the room, she didn't turn round. Instead, she pumped the handle that much harder, and silently cursed when the water merely trickled out.

'Hello, Teresa,' Margaret said cheerily. 'If you want to go out in the sunshine, I can finish that.' She gestured to the kettle in the girl's hand.

'It's all right,' came the sullen reply, 'Dad said I wasn't to leave until the kettle was boiling on the stove.' With that she rammed the spout of the kettle beneath the tap and stood stiffly while it began to fill.

'Sit yourself down, Miss,' urged Maria Leyton. Embarrassed by her daughter's open hostility to their visitor, the woman made a mental note to scold her later.

When Margaret sat herself in the upright chair, Maria smiled with relief. Easing on to the sofa, she said, 'You've just missed Owen. He's off over the fields . . . after a fat juicy rabbit to fill the pot, y'see.' Chuckling, she pointed to the wood-stove. 'He's lit the stove all ready, so he'll not be long afore he's back, an' I know he'll be glad to see you.'

'It's you I've come to visit,' Margaret assured her. 'How are you feeling, Maria?'

'Oh, up and down. Getting stronger by the day.' She tugged

at the embroidered bed-jacket given to her by Margaret on a previous visit. 'I've been real glad o' this,' she said. 'I can't keep the warmth inside me bones, y'see. But this jacket's been a real godsend.' Her voice fell to a whisper. 'These past months . . . you've been that good to me, Miss. As God's me judge, I don't know what I'd have done without you . . .' Her eyes swam with tears of gratitude.

'I'm a neighbour, Maria,' Margaret murmured, 'I'm sure you would do the very same for me.'

'Oh, I would!'

Another voice intervened then, a hard and spiteful voice. 'No, you wouldn't!' Teresa swung round to address her mother, her blue eyes brilliant with hatred. 'Folks like us can't hardly help ourselves, let alone help others.' Casting a derisory glance at Margaret, she declared in a harsh voice, 'It's easy for the likes of you, Miss Blackthorn, because you don't know what it's like to go without. Up there in your warm house, what would you know, eh?' Tossing her head, she snapped, 'Me dad might be easily fooled by a pretty smile, and me mam might be glad of you with your presents and your do-gooding. But not me! I can see right through your kind, and I don't want you here! Do you understand what I'm saying? You're not wanted here!'

'Teresa!' White-faced and shocked to the core, Maria struggled from the chair. 'Your father would flay the skin off your bones if he could hear what you're saying. Miss Blackthorn has been a real good friend to this family, and well you know it!' Having worked herself up, she fell back on the sofa, coughing and gasping. 'Shame on you,' she spluttered, and as Margaret rushed to the woman's aid, the girl made haste towards the door.

'It's the truth!' she cried from the doorway. 'She might seem to be helping us, but she ain't no better than the rest of 'em who live up at the house!' Staring with contempt at her mother, she sneered, 'She makes me sick . . . coming here in her fine frocks and fetching basketfuls of goodies. And what about the *other* witch who threatens to put us out of house and home?'

Though deeply hurt, Margaret addressed the girl in a cool voice that betrayed nothing of what she was feeling. 'My sister-in-law and I may live under the same roof, but that doesn't make us the same in nature.' She paused a moment, not wanting to say it, but knowing she should. 'Any more than it makes you and your brother of the same nature.' It pleased her that the girl was brought up sharp by the remark. 'As far as being put out of house and home is concerned, all I can promise is that it won't happen if I can help it.'

Choosing to ignore what she knew to be the truth, the girl claimed viciously, 'You come here to spy, don't you, eh? Spying and taking tales back to that sister-in-law of yours. You're all in it together: wanting to make life harder and harder for us, threatening this and that, wanting to take the bread from our mouths, making us live in fear. You and the high and mighty Rita Blackthorn . . . you're all the same. You've got money and we ain't. But it don't make you any better than us!' White-faced with rage, she stormed out, slamming the door behind her.

'God help us, what have I raised?' Maria was in tears. 'You surely don't believe anything she said, do you?' she entreated. 'I'll not deny we've no liking for your sister-in-law. But you must know that me and Owen value you as being somebody special. What! If it hadn't been for you, I don't think I'd ever have made it through the winter.' She clung to Margaret. 'I'm sorry, lass,' she groaned, 'I don't know what came over her to say such dreadful things.'

Margaret too had been taken aback by the assault on her. But she saw that the other woman was making herself ill and was quick to reassure her. 'It's all right, Maria,' she murmured, 'you're not to worry.' She recalled the girl's words and saw a vestige of truth in her accusations. 'To some extent it's right what she said. After all, my sister-in-law *has* threatened to put you out of house and home – for no other reason than that she's a selfish and spiteful woman – and has gone out of her way to make life difficult for you . . . for Nan Foster too! What's more, perhaps it's wrong of me to think I can give my help without being asked for it.'

'Oh, no! You mustn't believe that.' Maria sat up straight, her gaze downcast as she ruminated on what she was about to reveal. 'No mother should have to say this, but . . . well, Teresa is not a very nice person. When I were taken badly, so ill I could hardly move from me bed . . .' She gave a deep sigh and raised her head to look straight into Margaret's clear brown eyes. 'What I'm trying to say is that some folk can't abide illness. They turn away, fearing it might strike them down.'

Margaret had not realised but she saw it all now and it came as a shock. 'Are you saying Teresa turned away?'

'Aye. That's exactly what I'm saying, lass. When I were too ill to put one foot afore the other, Teresa showed her true nature. All the time when Owen thought she were tending me whenever he were out, it were our David who fetched and carried for his poor old mam. It were him who fed and washed me. Teresa kept out of the way, with never a word of comfort in passing and hardly a glance to see how I were faring. It were as though she couldn't care whether I lived or died.'

'No, that can't be right, Maria.' Margaret was loth to believe such a thing.

'Oh, it's right,' she declared sadly. 'Our Teresa has shown her true colours. And now, by saying what she's said to you, she's made me ashamed.' Suddenly she squared her shoulders and announced in a firm voice, 'I shall have to tell her father this time! He'll tan her arse good and proper, that he will!' She blushed to the roots of her hair. 'I'm sorry, Miss! I should never have used such language in front of a lady.'

'Away with you, Maria Leyton. Do you think I've never heard a bad word before?' Margaret's hearty chuckle put the woman at her ease, 'Anyway, you're as much as a lady as I'll ever be.'

'By!' Maria shook her head. 'You're a tonic, that's what you are. God knows how I'll ever repay you for the friend you've been to this family. Aye! Even to our Teresa, though she ain't got the sense to see it.'

'There *is* one little thing you can do, Maria.'

'Name it.'

'Do you really mean to tell Owen about Teresa's outburst?'

'What! Just see if I don't!'

'I'd rather you didn't.'

'Whyever not? That young madam has earned herself a leathering.'

'I'm sure she didn't mean half the things she said. What's more, I wonder about the reason she didn't help you when you were at your worst. She was probably more upset than you realised, afraid she might lose you and unsure how to deal with it all.'

Maria was made to think. 'Aye, happen you're right. Happen I'm being too harsh on her.' Her eyes crinkled into a smile. 'What you're saying is, you don't want to see her get a leathering from her dad?'

'I don't think *you* want to see it either. Isn't that so?' Margaret believed that, in spite of Teresa's behaviour, Maria loved her deeply.

Maria was quiet for a while. She needed to think. Presently she answered, 'I'll not tell her father this time.'

'Thank you, Maria.'

In a more relaxed atmosphere, Margaret poured the tea and they chatted a while longer. They talked of the beautiful weather and of how Maria had sat outdoors yesterday. 'Owen wanted me to see how his new cockerels strutted amongst the hens,' she laughed. They discussed the manner in which the birds had escaped from the wagon, and Maria giggled at Margaret's account of what followed. They spoke proudly of David and his learning, and how quickly he had mastered the arts of reading and writing. 'It's all because of your lovely niece,' Maria said. And Margaret replied by telling her how a teacher was only as good as the scholar. Then they parted affectionately.

Cathy and David were seated on the bank of the river. 'Your aunt's coming for you,' he said, catching sight of Margaret as she made her way towards them. 'I wish you didn't have to go.'

'So do I,' Cathy said wistfully.

They had spent these precious minutes together, laughing and talking, and delighting in each other's company. Suddenly, they were painfully shy. David gazed at her sweet face, at the stunning green eyes and full half-smiling mouth which he had wanted to kiss for ever and dared not. He resisted the urge to stroke the flowing corn-coloured hair and had a desperate need to hold the small hand that rested near to his. All these urges rose up inside him like a tidal wave, threatening to overwhelm him. In a rush he whispered her name. 'Cathy?' The word was a caress. His heart was thumping and his mouth was painfully dry as he wondered how he might begin; how he might tell her that one day he meant to wed her.

She had turned her eyes from him to watch the ducks on the river. But she was always aware of his closeness, his strength and dark good looks, and now, when he murmured her name, she brought her gaze to his face. In that moment, like so many times before, she was confused by her own feelings. 'Yes, David?'

He took a deep breath. It would need all of his courage to say what was in his young heart. He even began, 'There's something I have to . . .' Hesitating, he squared his wide shoulders and gulped hard. 'Something I want to tell you.' He felt hot and cold all at the same time, and the palms of his hands were sweating.

'Yes?' She shifted closer. And his courage was gone.

'It's nothing.' Astonished that he could not bring himself to say what was in his overflowing heart, he felt a rush of anger. 'You'd better go.' Stretching out his long legs, he stood up, addressing Margaret now. 'Hello, Miss Blackthorn. Did Mam tell you she sat out in the sunshine yesterday?' When he spoke of his mother his eyes shone with pride.

Margaret said how pleased she was that Maria was making such good progress, and after a brief and friendly exchange they said their farewells.

As they came to the gate, Margaret asked the girl, 'Did you and David have an argument?'

'No.' Cathy was surprised. 'We had a lovely time.'

'Oh, well, if you're sure.' Margaret wasn't altogether convinced. She had sensed the atmosphere between those two, and it made her curious. 'I had a lovely time too,' she declared. 'David's mother is much stronger today.' She made no mention of Teresa's bitter words. There was nothing to be gained by Cathy knowing how the girl felt.

She was also greatly relieved that Teresa would not be punished. 'It's a pity you and Teresa can't get on,' she remarked casually. 'She doesn't appear to have many friends, does she?' In fact, Margaret couldn't recall any time when she had seen Teresa in the company of others.

'That's because she doesn't *want* friends!' Cathy replied. 'I've tried to be nice to her, but she won't let me. And I know she doesn't like me teaching David to read and write.'

Margaret thought it wisest to make no comment. Instead she turned her mind to the malice in Teresa's attack. All the way to Nan Foster's the incident dominated her thoughts. She thought about the way in which Teresa had neglected her ill mother, and wondered what David must have thought about that. She knew the sorry situation had cut Maria deep, and her heart went out to the unfortunate woman.

Alone with her own troubled thoughts, Maria knew her husband would not be home for hours yet. Bitter and unforgiving, she made him a promise: 'One of these days, Owen Leyton, you'll pay for your womanising.' Disturbed and unhappy, she fell asleep.

Teresa stayed in the barn. From there she had watched the visitors depart. She had seen how her own brother longed for the Blackthorn girl, and was charged with such a loathing that she could hardly breathe. Unable to resolve the turmoil within her, she took to the fields, sometimes running, sometimes walking. It would be many hours before she returned home, and even then it would be with great reluctance.

Standing on the very spot where Cathy had left him, David continued to stare after the disappearing figures. Angry with himself, he kicked at the earth. 'What a fool you are, David Leyton!' he chided himself. 'You lost your opportunity.' He thrust his hands into the pockets of his trousers and stared up at the sky. Suddenly he laughed at the way he had hesitated, amused now at the manner in which he had lost his tongue when he needed it most. 'Not to worry,' he consoled himself. 'There'll be another day.'

The thought brought a smile to his dark eyes and a merry tune to his lips. With a lighter heart, he went into the house to see if he was needed.

At the bottom of the lane where they had previously rested stood the ancient cottage. Now, recovering from the long walk, Cathy and Margaret took a moment to gaze on it. An old thatched place of diminutive proportions, the cottage had once been picturesque and desirable; surrounded by lovingly kept gardens profuse with many coloured blooms whose fragrance mingled with the song of birds. Now the garden was overgrown, and birds were seldom seen there. Once the cottage had housed a family of twelve. Its walls and grounds echoed to the laughter of ten children. But they were long gone and in their place rested one lonely soul by the name of Nan Foster.

As they approached the front door, it was opened to them by a woman of some seventy years; though she stooped slightly from the shoulders and her mouth trembled as she spoke, she still carried a certain grace and beauty. Her hair was now white and her eyes the most wonderful shade of violet, though the once beautiful face was lined with the cruel ravages of time. She wore a long grey dress that had seen better days yet she remained a proud, independent woman. 'I saw you pass by,' she told Margaret in a curiously refined voice, 'and I was afraid you might not find the time to come and see me.' When she smiled, her eyes were lit from within and the lines on her face simply melted away.

'You know we would never miss an opportunity to see you,' Margaret told her.

The old lady led them into the cottage. Though it was a mess outside, it was meticulously neat inside. The curtains were sparkling clean, and the fire-range was polished until it reflected every corner of the living room. The furniture, however, was of poor quality and the rugs were threadbare. A smell of damp permeated the air. 'I wish you'd let me talk to my brother,' Margaret protested. 'This place needs a great deal of work done on it.' Time and again she had argued with the old lady, but Nan would not be budged.

She wasn't now. 'Sit down,' she said, and as always it sounded more like an order than a request. Cathy and Margaret sat on the wooden-framed sofa with their hostess opposite, looking regal and dignified in a high-backed chair with straight legs and curved arms. 'Please don't fuss, dear. I'm happy the way things are.' A shadow darkened her face. 'Besides, it would mean noise and dust, and people trampling all over.' She stared at the glass-fronted display cabinet and was momentarily lost in a world of her own. 'Strangers touching my precious belongings... I couldn't bear that.'

'We wouldn't let that happen,' Cathy promised. 'Aunt Margaret could arrange for all of your belongings to be stored, and while the work was going on, you could come and stay with us at Blackthorn House.'

The old lady looked at her for a moment and there was a strange kind of sadness in her eyes. 'I know you mean well, and I thank you for that, dear,' she said through trembling lips, 'but you're asking too much. We've been through all this before, and the answer is still the same.' She smiled serenely. 'Oh, I know the cottage has seen better days. It's everything you say ... poky and draughty ... riddled with woodworm and warped with age.' She laughed aloud. 'But then, so am I!'

'No, you're not!' Cathy was appalled.

'Oh, but I am. I'm old and withered and past my prime.' Nan laughed and in a more serious voice continued, 'This little cottage has been my home for too long now. I've seen out seven winters in it ... two of them the hardest I can ever recall in my lifetime ... and here I am, still healthy and strong. I have enough for my needs. A larder full of food, logs to make a fire when the wind howls, and all manner of God's tiny creatures coming to call.' Something from the past touched her memory. It was like a knife through her heart. Shaking the melancholy from her, she told Cathy in a brighter voice, 'When I saw you both earlier, I got the sarsaparilla ready. It's on the tray in the scullery. Save an old woman's legs, dear. Pour three glasses, would you?'

Before she'd finished speaking Cathy was on her way to the tiny scullery, leaving the old lady and Margaret together. It was exactly what Nan Foster wanted.

'Please, Margaret, don't think I'm not grateful for your offer,' she said. 'It's just that, well—' She hesitated before going on, 'I've never spoken to you about my past life ... where I come from, that sort of thing. But if you knew the turmoil, the heartache ...'

Margaret stopped her there. 'You don't owe me any explanation. You needn't worry because, as far as I'm concerned, the cottage will stay exactly as you want it, unless you tell me otherwise. Will that do?'

The old lady reached out to touch her hand. 'You're a good soul,' she said softly. 'And, yes, that will do.' She gazed round the room, at the thick oak beams and crooked windows, and was astonished that she had remained here for so long. 'I won't deny I've lived in grander places ... known better times. But now, I'm happy to end my days here.'

'I understand.' In a strange way, Margaret really did understand.

The old lady studied the younger woman and was strangely moved. 'In all this time you've never asked anything of me,' she said. 'You've given of your friendship and wanted nothing in return.'

'What should I want?'

'I can't say. But it seems so unfair that I know a great deal about you, while you know nothing at all about me.'

'I know more than you think,' Margaret teased. 'Let's see.' She turned her eyes to heaven. 'I know you came to this area seven years ago, and in all that time you have rented this cottage from my brother.' She met the old lady's fond gaze with a smile. 'I assume you pay your rent on time, or my sister-in-law would have shouted it from the rooftops. I know we have a good relationship, you and I. Cathy adores you. And, though you keep the cottage beautifully clean and tidy, I can see you hate gardening.' She clapped her hands together. 'You're intelligent, articulate, and so graceful that you make me feel positively clumsy. There! What do you think to that?'

'I think you know more about me than is good for you.'

'What a strange thing to say.'

'You didn't describe me as being lonely.' The old lady skilfully avoided responding to Margaret's comment. 'Here am I, some seventy years old, living on my own, with not even a dog or cat to keep me company. I shy away from people and could count on one hand the number of times I've travelled into Blackburn town. Indeed, in seven years I've hardly set food outside this cottage, except to walk around it on a summer's day. I have almost all my needs delivered in cardboard boxes. As you can see I live well, dress well, and though I have no visible means of support, am not without money. Does that not make you curious, my dear?'

'Material things never make me curious.'

'Ah! That's because you think with your soul.'

'If that means I believe there are more valuable things on this earth than material possessions, then yes, I think you must be right.' Margaret sensed there was much more to this conversation than the old lady would admit. She felt the strangest impulse to leave. In fact, for one awkward minute, she was tempted to call Cathy and draw short their visit. Instead she warned, 'Your past is your own. Like I said, I know all I need to know.'

The old lady was silent for a time. When she spoke, it was almost to herself. 'There are things about me you really should know,' she murmured. 'Precious things ... close to my heart.'

Before Margaret could comment, Cathy was back. Setting the tray down on the table, she handed out the tumblers of dark liquid.

The old lady took a delicate sip from her own glass and settled back in the chair, seemingly content. 'Now then,' she said at length, 'who's going to tell me all the gossip?'

In a furtive whisper, Cathy suggested to Margaret, 'I'm sure it would be all right for Nan to know about the urchin.' Taking up her glass she told them, 'I'm going outside in the sunshine.' What she really wanted was to sit on the back doorstep, think about David and wonder what it was he had almost confided in her.

'What's all this about an urchin?' Nan was intrigued.

After Margaret had finished telling her all about how Frank had caught the boy picking his pockets and had decided to bring him home, telling Rita he would be the son they never had, Nan was horrified. 'Whatever does your sister-in-law say?'

'Strangely enough, she seems to have taken to him. At least that's what Cathy thinks, and I'm inclined to agree. Though of course it's early days yet.'

'It's a very dangerous thing your brother has done.'

'I'm inclined to agree with that too.'

'What possessed him then?'

Margaret shrugged her shoulders. 'Who knows? It's true they've always wanted a son, and though Rita is the dominant partner, he can sometimes rebel in a most unpredictable manner. But, to be honest, Nan, I think he must have had a brainstorm this time.'

Nan seemed to brood then. 'Goodness knows what will come of such a thing,' she muttered presently. 'It changes everything. No! I won't allow it!'

'Sorry, Nan, I didn't quite hear.' Not certain whether the old lady was addressing her or talking to herself, Margaret leaned forward. 'Or was it not meant for my ears?' she asked with a smile.

At once the older woman was on her guard. 'Oh, I'm sorry, my dear,' she apologised. 'I suppose I was thinking out loud.' She laughed nervously. 'At my age you begin to do silly things like that.' Eager to allay any suspicions, she quickly added, 'It was only an echo of your own anxieties though. An urchin off the streets! It's bound to turn everything upside down, wouldn't you say?' She glanced towards the door, not wanting Cathy to hear her next words. 'And what about Cathy? It must have come as quite a shock when her father arrived home with this boy. Is she *really* expected to accept him as her new brother?'

'I've been very concerned about that, Nan.' Margaret had spent a sleepless night worrying over that very issue, and what she had decided was this: 'I honestly don't think my brother has thought this business through. He did it on the spur of the moment, and I think ... *hope* ... he will come to regret it and send the boy packing. Oh, not just for Cathy's sake, you understand? There are other issues at stake here, not least of which is his own well-being.'

'You mean, if the boy turns out to be a bad one?'

'I don't really know *what* I mean,' Margaret admitted. 'It's true the lad is a pickpocket, but does that make him "a bad one"? Why not merely a desperate character? More importantly, who exactly has Frank brought into the household? He intends to raise the boy as a gentleman ... the son he and Rita never had. But who is this lad? Where does he come from? Has he any family? Will they come looking for him?' She ended on a sigh. 'I've made light of it for Cathy's sake, but I don't mind admitting I'm uneasy about the whole incident.'

'Well then, let's hope that's all it is ... an incident. Have you talked out your fears with your brother?'

'I mean to do just that when I get back.'

'I should if I were you, my dear.'

The conversation ended when Cathy returned.

Rising from her chair, the old lady told her, 'I have something very special to show you.' Taking Cathy by the hand, she led her to a small oak sideboard. Here she turned to address Margaret. 'It might be as well if you hear what I have to say,' she pleaded, and there was a strange excitement in her violet eyes.

With Margaret standing to one side of her and Cathy to the other, she opened the drawer. Like every corner of that tiny cottage it was astonishingly neat inside; containing a batch of old yellowing letters, a long slim case whose contents were not visible, and a soft round bag that tied at the top with a pretty blue ribbon. 'I've been wanting to show you this for a very long time,' she told Cathy. 'I thought it could wait a while longer, but I see now it can't.' Fearful they might guess her real reasons, she said with a wry little laugh, 'You see, I'm very old . . . seventy-one this year. If I don't make my wishes plain to you now, I may never again get the chance.'

Margaret had seen a certain look in the old lady's eyes, a look that spoke of regrets and sorrow. It moved her deeply. 'Are you sure you wouldn't rather leave this business for another day. It troubles you, I know.'

The old lady shook her head. 'The only thing that troubles me is my great age. Oh, not that I'm afraid of dying or anything like that. In fact, there are times when I truly believe it would be preferable to living.'

'What then?'

'Oh, how shall I put it? The past? The future? Sins and forgiveness?' Her smile was beautiful. 'One day I might find the courage to confide in you. Until then, there is still so much to be done, and time is running out for me.' She turned to reach into the drawer. Withdrawing the round silken pouch, she placed it on top of the sideboard and opened it. Inside, jewels shimmered and sparkled: a gold ring with a huge emerald stone; a pair of diamond earrings with platinum clasps; a silver latticed bracelet; and, nestling on top, a magnificent wedding ring. 'Mementoes,' the old lady whispered. 'Nearly all gone now.'

'Are you saying you've been *selling* them to stay alive?' It was all clear to Margaret now.

'It's ironic, isn't it? In a different way these beautiful trinkets carried me through my youth. Now they're carrying me through my old age.' Touching the tip of her finger against the wedding ring, she said softly, 'There was a time when this above all else meant everything to me. Now it means nothing. Even the touch of it makes me cringe.' She shivered as though icy water flowed through her veins.

'Cathy?'

'Yes, Nan?'

'I want you to listen very closely to what I'm about to say.' With trembling fingers, the old lady plucked a fold of silk from the back of the pouch. 'Come to the table, child,' she requested, beckoning Margaret as she turned. When they were all three seated round the table, the fold of silk was put between them. 'Of all the things I've sold and all the things I've kept, this is the most beautiful.' Opening the fold of silk, she laid bare its contents. The tiny heart-shaped box was fashioned in gold and platinum and inlaid with vivid rubies. No more than three inches in diameter, it was a work of art.

'Why! It's exquisite!' Margaret was stunned. Never before had she seen such a delicate thing.

'Is it a box?' Cathy wanted to know.

The old lady's answer was to click the lid open and let her have a brief glimpse inside. 'It's a very special one,' she said. 'While I'm alive I can't let it be parted from me. But one day, Cathy dear, it will be yours.'

Reaching up to kiss the old lady's face, Cathy assured her, 'I want you to stay alive forever, Nan. But if the box ever comes into my keeping, I promise I'll take very good care of it for you.'

Margaret had remained silent, but she spoke now. 'The box must be worth a small fortune. Are you sure you want to do this?'

'It's already done, my dear. The wheels have been set in motion.'

They said their goodbyes and, concerned about the darkening sky and the threat of rain, hastened on their way. 'It's getting late,' Cathy remarked. 'Ruby will be wondering where we are.'

The old lady stood at the window until they were no longer in sight. 'This urchin troubles me,' she murmured. Returning to the trinket box, she took from it a small faded portrait. Raising this to the light, she stared at it through a blur of tears.

Two pairs of eyes gazed back at her. Two tiny faces that almost broke her heart. All these years she had carried the crippling guilt with her. Now, though, her heart was more tranquil. Old age had a way of quieting the heart and easing the mind. Yet still she couldn't rest. Not yet. Soon maybe, but not yet.

She took a while to remember how it was all those years ago. She kissed the two small faces. 'All these years I've watched over you,' she said brokenly. 'When I'm gone, you'll be given into the safe keeping of your daughter.' Pressing the portrait to her breast she sat in the rocking chair and rocked gently back and forth, until sleep came over her, lulling her old heart and taking her back over the lonely years.

CHAPTER THREE

'You'll take his land only over my dead body!'

'Calm yourself, Margaret.' Frank was caught between his wife and his sister and, on this occasion, had to admit his sister was in the right. Rising from his comfortable armchair, he crossed to the sideboard. 'I'm sure the three of us can talk this through in a civilised manner, over a glass of sherry.'

'Thank you, but no.' Margaret rarely showed her temper but when she had learned of his plans to recall four acres of land from Owen Leyton she had realised she would have to take a very firm stand. 'I won't allow it, Frank. Time and again I've stood by you while you've made plans without consulting me. I see now that was very foolish.' She glanced meaningfully at Rita who, until now, had remained silent.

'It's only four acres, for heaven's sake.' Sensing that her husband was weakening, Rita felt she must intervene.

'Four acres is almost half the land he rents from us,' Margaret persisted. 'It's difficult enough for him to make a living as it is.'

'How others fare is not our problem.' Rita took the sherry her husband offered and gulped it down. 'Frank and I are decided. We need to recall that land and, make no mistake, we shall have it.' If she had seen the warning expression on Frank's face she might have guarded her tongue.

'I think you're forgetting something, aren't you?' Margaret was only made the more determined by Rita's arrogance.

'Oh? And what might that be?'

'Though it doesn't amount to a fortune, Father left everything equally divided between me and Frank.'

'What are you saying?'

'I'm saying what I should have said long ago. Frank has no

427

right to make decisions without consulting me. It was a mistake to leave the running of Blackthorn Estate to him.' Addressing herself to Frank she said calmly, 'I'm sorry, but if you persist in this, I'll have to fight you.'

'Good grief! Whatever's the matter with you? *Fight me?*' Falling into the chair, he stared at her as though she was out of her mind.

'If you ask me, she's gone completely mad!' Sitting bolt upright in her chair Rita slammed her empty glass on to a side table. 'It's all this mixing with lesser people. It's affecting her reason.'

'I don't know what you mean by "lesser" people,' Margaret declared. 'What makes you think we're any better than they are? We may own this house, two dilapidated cottages and a few acres of second-grade land, but that only means we don't have to tend the earth to make a living. It certainly doesn't mean we can look down on our neighbours!'

'They're not neighbours.' Rita stared defiantly. 'They're tenants . . . *our* tenants. It's right that we hold ourselves above them.' Turning to Frank, she pleaded, 'Your sister is undermining our authority. Look how that insolent fellow drove his filthy wagon right up to our front door. It wasn't bad enough that a member of this family actually travelled home in the contraption, but he had the nerve actually to speak to me . . . to *me*! Filthy, he was! Looked like he hadn't had a wash in weeks.'

Margaret sprang to Owen's defence. 'The man had only just returned from a day at the market . . . on top of which he'd been in the spinny. Owen Leyton is a respectable working man, as clean and proud as any of us.'

Rita was made to recall the incident more closely. The memory of his dark eyes on her was more than she could bear. Since that day she had felt a strange kind of longing, and it frightened her. Clutching at her throat, she rasped, 'You'll have to speak to him, Frank.' Scowling at Margaret, she added vehemently, 'Moreover, you must forbid your sister from visiting these people.'

Frank looked from one to the other and felt out of his depth. 'I'm not really in a position to insist on that,' he said lamely.

'Why not? You're the head of this house. The man who makes all the decisions.'

It was Margaret who answered. 'I think what Frank is trying to explain is that he isn't the elder. *I* am. By twenty minutes.' Her implication was plain as she now addressed him in a softer tone. 'No doubt you're thankful I was born a woman?'

Glancing sheepishly at the plush red carpet, he fingered his waistcoat buttons then toyed with a stray thread on the arm of the chair. Without looking at her, he replied, 'I'm sorry, but I have to agree with my wife. The fact is I have taken on the role of head of the house, and for some long time you have trusted me to do what's right for us all. I really think you're being a little too protective of our tenants. After all, we don't owe them anything, do we? If they were to leave, no doubt there would be a queue of others waiting to take their place.' Suddenly filled with a sense of his own importance and encouraged by Rita's curt nod of the head, he squared his shoulders and announced smugly, 'About recalling the four acres. I think you should give my little plan some further thought.'

'Think what you will, but I won't allow Owen Leyton and his family to be impoverished. That land is his livelihood.'

Rita smiled at her. 'Anyone would think you had a soft spot for him,' she suggested wickedly.

Frank was horrified. 'Now now, Rita. I won't have that.'

Returning his gaze to his sister, he urged, 'Be reasonable. After all, four acres isn't a great area.'

'Is it your intention to sell the land?'

'Of course not. No self-respecting landowner would ever *sell* his land.'

'I think you mean *our* land?'

'Of course.' He seemed to blush. Or it could have been a drop too much sherry that made him suddenly go a bright shade of pink.

'Do you intend to work the land then?'

The suggestion made him laugh. 'Are you trying to kill me off?'

'You're right. A spell of hard work probably would kill you off.' She stood up, preparing to depart. 'I'm well aware of what you mean to do with the land. You and Rita have made no secret of it. First you bring a street urchin into the house. Then you begin grooming him to be the "son you never had". You shamefully neglect your own daughter, denying her the pony

429

she's always craved, yet you plan to buy this urchin an expensive animal the cost of which would keep us all fed for the best part of a year. And now you mean to lay out four acres of farmed land so your new "son" can practise the pursuits of a gentleman.'

Rita eyed her with glee. 'You sound almost envious,' she purred. 'Is that what all this is about? Do you see Jack as taking your place in Frank's affections?'

The idea gave her immense satisfaction. In fact, she had been all for sending the boy back where he came from, but had thought better of it. The more Margaret and the girl were hurt by the boy's presence here, the more she meant to pamper him.

Margaret rounded on her then. 'As far as I'm concerned, you and Frank are free to do as you please with regard to the boy. It's just a great pity you can't lavish a measure of love and attention on your own daughter.'

Frank took offence at that. 'What a wicked thing to say,' he said sullenly.

'Really?' Margaret stared him out. 'I suggest you think about it, Frank.' Addressing her sister-in-law, who was still smiling, she said coldly, 'I suggest you *both* think about it.'

As she walked across the room, Frank asked, 'So you won't reconsider . . . about the four acres?'

'No.'

Rita's voice dripped with malice. 'Is there something between you and Owen Leyton?'

Margaret swung round, her face chalk-white. Inside she was burning with rage. Outside she was astonishingly calm. 'How clever of you!' she answered, and Rita's eyes grew wide with surprise. 'You're right. There *is* something between me and Owen Leyton. But it isn't what you would like to think, Rita dear. What Mr Leyton and I share is a love for the land, that's all. But then, I can't expect someone like you to understand that.'

An awkward silence followed, during which Margaret made her way to the door. If she didn't get out of here as quickly as her feet would take her, she might forget she was a lady and stuff Rita's malicious words down her throat.

'Margaret?' Frank had been stunned by his wife's suggestion

that Margaret was having an affair with Owen Leyton.

'It's no good arguing, Frank. I won't change my mind.'

'I can see that.' He straightened his back and assumed his most authoritative expression. 'No. It's something else that makes me curious.' Clearing his throat, he glanced nervously at his wife before going on, 'There have been some very harsh things said here, and I'm saddened by them.'

'Then I suggest you speak to your good wife.'

Rita sniffed. 'I never take back what I've said.'

'*Please!*' Frank sighed aloud. When his wife merely smiled triumphantly he continued his appeal to Margaret. 'You've taken a dislike to Jack, haven't you?'

'I don't know him well enough to take a dislike to him.' He had hit on a sore point with her. 'However, I do feel the pair of you should be more cautious.'

'In what way?'

'Just now you said you wondered if I had lost my mind. Well, I must admit there have been times over these past weeks when I've wondered that about *you*!' He had asked her, and she meant to tell him. 'This boy . . .'

'Jack!' Frank grew impatient. 'His name is Jack.'

'That's the name *you* christened him,' Margaret retorted, 'because he refused to give you his *real* name! And what else is he keeping from you, I wonder?'

'Explain yourself.'

'I wouldn't have thought it needed any explaining. Who is he, Frank? Where does he come from, and what's he doing here? You know nothing at all about him.'

'I know enough.' In fact he knew a great deal more than he was prepared to divulge, and if the truth ever came out all hell would be let loose.

'What? *What* do you know? That he was picking your pockets? That he lived on the streets . . . earning a living by using his wits? Does he have friends, I wonder? And are they likely to turn up here? And if they do, are you prepared to take them in as well?'

'I can't believe I'm hearing this!' Springing out of his chair, Frank took a step towards her. 'I expected you of all people to understand.' He was pleading now. 'You were always the tender one ... the one who championed the underdog, the one who abhorred everything harsh and unfair in this world. The boy has had a hard life. Surely he deserves to be loved and pampered now?'

It was a moment before Margaret replied. When she did it was with a harshness that shocked them both. 'And what about your own daughter? Don't you think it's time *she* was loved and pampered?'

'But she *is* loved!'

'Then tell her.'

He bowed his head. 'You know I can't speak of such things.'

'Then *show* her!'

'How do you mean?'

'In the same way you show this boy your affection.'

'I wasn't aware I did.' He stared from Margaret to his wife, then back to Margaret again. Suddenly he felt as though he was greatly in the wrong, but didn't know why.

'Oh, but you do, Frank.' Her voice softened. 'You take him to town and buy him clothes. You walk the fields with him, and spend hours talking with him.' She choked on the words. 'And there is a special softness in your voice when you speak to him.' She glanced at Rita who was intrigued and delighted by Margaret's distress. 'You *both* pander to his every need while denying your own child's. Do you really think Cathy doesn't see all this? Do you believe she isn't deeply hurt by it?'

Rita stamped her foot. 'That girl wants for nothing! Her wardrobe is filled with clothes. She has a shelf crammed with books, and each year she's allowed to take a holiday with you. What more does she want?'

Margaret shook her head. 'If you can't see, then I'm just wasting my time.'

Frank hated the way his wife and sister seemed to bring about the worst in each other. Appealing to Margaret's better nature, he explained, 'It's in a man's nature to want a son. Rita and I have been denied that.' He gave his wife a tender glance. 'Now here is a boy without family or home ... an orphan driven to desperation through no fault of his own. He's strong and healthy, with an attractive appearance. He's already proved his determination to break from his unsavoury past, and has it in him to be a good citizen. I intend to give him every opportunity.'

Margaret dwelt on his words for a moment, realising how deeply he felt about the project he had taken on. There was no doubt that he had become strongly attached to the boy. In that light, she questioned her own right to interfere. It was not in her nature to be hard or disagreeable and, for one moment, she might have relented. But then she remembered her own greatest love. 'What about Cathy?'

'I don't understand. We're discussing the boy! A son for Rita and me.' Frank shook his head in frustration. 'For heaven's sake, Margaret, you haven't understood anything I've said.'

'No, Frank.' She gazed at him sadly. 'It's you who haven't understood anything I've said.'

Spreading his hand before his face as though to blot out her presence, he interrupted, 'There's clearly no point in discussing it any further. The boy stays. He has been here almost four weeks now, and never put a foot wrong. In fact, with the exception of the first few days, his good behaviour has only strengthened our belief in him.' He looked at Rita and beamed, not realising how his intimate smile sent a shudder through her.

'I can see the two of you are very proud of yourselves,' Margaret observed dryly. With that she went smartly out of the room.

Rita's voice followed her through the open door. 'You really should be nicer to Jack,' she called arrogantly. 'It won't be long before you're his aunt, because we're already planning adoption. Being our son will also give him certain rights. In fact, I shouldn't be at all surprised if his rights proved to be greater than his little sister's.' Slightly intoxicated by the sherry, she began laughing.

Frank brought her up sharply with a stern warning. 'Careful, my dear! It isn't wise to make enemies.'

It was midnight. Ruby woke in a sweat. 'Who's there?' Sitting up on her elbows, she squinted into the gloom. 'Is somebody there?'

When there was no answer, she clambered from the bed, lit the lamp and threw her dressing gown about her shoulders. 'You old fool!' she chided herself. 'What would anyone want to come in here for? There ain't no jewels nor money, and I don't know any man who'd want to spend the night with an old crow like you.' The idea was so outlandish that she burst out laughing.

Taking up the lamp, she crept up on the door and snatched it open. There was no one in sight and she was puzzled. 'I were sure I heard a noise,' she muttered, glancing up at the ceiling. 'Bleedin' rats I shouldn't wonder.'

The sound of a door closing startled her. 'I'm buggered if there really ain't somebody larking about!' she whispered furtively. Leaning over the banisters, she stared down into the tiny hallway; no one there either. Still not convinced, she went cautiously down the narrow stairs, in and out of the scullery, through the parlour, searching everywhere, and still there was neither sound nor sight of what might have caused her to wake. 'Must'a been them pickled onions I ate at supper,' she chuckled. 'Should'a known I'd suffer for it.'

Before returning to her bed, she gingerly inched open the door which led from her own humble quarters to the big house. All was quiet and in darkness, everyone sleeping, she thought.

Nodding with satisfaction, she closed the door and went back upstairs. Here she crossed the room to stare out of the window at a beautiful moonlit night. 'Even the owls are fast asleep,' she muttered, yawning and stretching her podgy arms. 'Got more sense than folks like you, Ruby, you daft old bugger!' With that she hoisted herself into bed and was soon snoring.

Margaret remained at her window a moment longer. She too had been woken by strange sounds. But, when she could see nothing untoward, she got back between the warm sheets and lay there awake, her mind in turmoil after the day's events. Soon, overcome by weariness, she closed her eyes and slept. But it wasn't a restful sleep. Instead she tossed and turned, and in her worst nightmares feared for young Cathy's future.

Two rooms away, Rita feigned sleep. It wasn't sounds that had woken her, but the urgent needs of her husband. Pushing his naked body against her, he grew with excitement. 'I want you so much,' he murmured in her ear. 'I've wanted you all day.'

'I don't want you.' His breath was warm and nauseating on her face. His weakness made her bold. 'Go back to sleep.'

'How can I?' he wailed. 'You've roused me now.' Stroking

her face with his fingers, he muttered impatiently, 'I'll only sleep after I'm satisfied.'

Inwardly groaning, Rita mentally prepared herself for yet another bout of what she considered to be an undignified and loathsome act. She knew from experience that he would not leave her be until she had succumbed. 'All right,' she snapped, rolling on to her back. 'But be quick!'

While he fumbled at her nightgown, she lay like a corpse, cold and unyielding, her eyes fixed on the ceiling, arms pressed to her sides as though to restrict his embrace. She had no intention of helping him to invade her. In fact, she turned her mind to other matters. 'What will you do about your sister?' she asked coolly. 'Surely you don't mean to let her dictate to you?'

'For God's sake, woman!' Gripping her nightgown with both hands, he thrust it above her waist. 'I don't want to talk about that *now*!'

She knew then he would not assert himself over Margaret. And she despised him. 'Be quick, I tell you.' Even the touch of his skin against hers was nauseating. When he slid his fingers into the crevice of her thighs, it was all she could do not to leap from the bed and flee the room.

But she stayed. Like so many times before she stayed, because it was her duty, and because it was the one thing that gave her power over him, the one thing above all others that made him like clay in her hands.

'Love me,' he moaned. Easing her legs apart, he mounted her.

She made no reply, gave no encouragement. She wanted no more than that it should soon be over. *But then a strange and unpredictable thing happened.* When he probed inside her with the tip of his erect member, she held herself rigid as always, setting her mind against the tedious ordeal to come. She amused herself by wondering how such a big-built man could have such a small penis; reminding herself at the same time that she had no means of comparing it because she had never seen another man in the flesh. But then, without warning, her mind was filled with the image of a man who had looked at her and seen something of her soul.

Owen Leyton rose up in her mind like a physical presence.

Recalling the intimate look that had passed between them, she remembered how handsome he was, those brooding dark eyes and the strong squareness of his chin, the high cheekbones, the brown hair that fell lazily below his ears, and those broad ox-like shoulders.

She wondered about Owen Leyton. He was a big man yet not in the same way as her husband, because one was flabby and the other hardened by hard work. Her husband's hands were soft and white, while the younger man's were coarse and brown. Frank was always meticulously attired in silk cravats and fancy waistcoats while Owen had worn little better than rags.

She had used every argument to discredit him in front of her husband and sister-in-law. Yet her instincts told her that Owen was a better man than her own husband. Rough and ready, one with nature, exactly as Margaret had described him, he intrigued her. Never before had she looked into the eyes of such a man. Normally she would look away, walk on the other side of the road, disown the very idea that they might share the same thought. But this man was different. She had met him in a rage, and he had seen right inside her. It was a frightening thing. Yet it was exhilarating.

The more she thought of him, the more he intrigued her. Even his name sounded right. 'Owen,' she whispered aloud. 'Owen.'

Lost in his own delight, her husband didn't hear the name she called. He heard only the sound, a sigh of contentment that sent shivers down his spine. 'Come on,' he pleaded. 'Show you love me.'

She heard him coaxing but her heart was like stone. When he now pushed rhythmically in and out, licking her lips with his long wet tongue and stroking her private parts with frantic fingers, she wondered how *he* might do it. Would Owen Leyton cover her in the same manner? Was every man the same? Was the act of lovemaking all for the *man's* satisfaction? Did Owen Leyton have a different way? Could he persuade her to give of herself? Actually to enjoy it? She was immensely curious, imagining the younger man unclothed and wondering how they would differ, he and her husband.

One thought loomed in her mind to overshadow all others.

Owen Leyton had fathered a *son*. That one splendid achievement raised him in her esteem. Some small fragment of her
fevered mind wanted it to be Owen Leyton who was using
her body now. Loathing seeped back.

Her husband became frantic, lunging into her again and again,
uncontrollably excited. She knew how it would end, how it
always ended, and this time was no different. With a long shivering groan he gave one almighty thrust and crumpled in a heap
on top of her, his weight crushing her. After a moment he rolled
away and she turned from him with contempt. She had never
hated him more.

Long after her husband was contentedly sleeping, Rita Blackthorn paced the floor, driven by a demon, unable to rid herself
of the feeling that *he* too was pacing the floor, thinking of her
just as she was thinking of him. 'I don't know if I'll see you
again, Owen Leyton,' she whispered. 'It might be wisest to stay
clear of you.'

Outside, the wind blew stronger, cutting through the trees with
a whistling sound. 'Sounds like the banshees have been let loose,
don't it?' The woman looked to be in her late thirties, of slim
build and clothed in a long dark skirt and brown-fringed shawl.
Her face was partly hidden by the shawl which she had drawn
tightly about herself, but her eyes were visible: very beautiful,
large childish eyes of deepest blue. Desperate now, she pleaded,
'You must come back!' She glanced about, crouching fearfully,
as though suspecting someone might be watching. 'If he finds
out, he'll flay me alive!'

Her pleas left the boy unmoved. 'How did you track me
down?'

'It took me an age. But I were determined, that's all.'

'I'm not coming back, so you can forget it. As for *him*, I
couldn't care less.'

'And what about me?'

'I'm not coming back.'

'I swear he'll kill me!'

'Let him kill you then.' Lashing out with a spiteful push, he
sent her staggering backwards.

'How can you do it?' Tears swam up in her beautiful sad

eyes. 'I've never done you no harm.'

'Get away from here.' Being the same height as the woman, he could look her straight in the eyes. Putting his face closer to hers, he whispered a warning. 'If I ever see you round here again, I'll set the dogs on you.' Certain that she would leave without a fuss, he made his way back to the house.

By the time he had stealthily entered his bedroom, the woman had climbed on to the cart and seated herself on the hard wooden bench. With one last look at the house, she dug in her heels, took up the reins and urged the old horse: 'Home, boy. We've a long way to go, God help us.'

The morning arrived in a blaze of sunshine. Raising her eyes to the blue sky outside her window, Ruby moaned, 'Can't see what you've got to smile about. Some of us ain't had no sleep at all.'

She glanced anxiously at the kitchen clock. 'Six of a morning,' she tutted. 'I've been up nigh on an hour already, and since that useless maid cleared off, I still can't seem to get meself on a right footing.' With renewed determination, she went quietly about her duties. There was the range to be lit, a mile of floor to be scrubbed, the breakfast table waiting to be laid, and she had a head that felt the size of four. 'Bugger it!' she said, slamming shut the range door. 'One o' these days I'll take up the life of a gypsy and wander the roads.'

She peeped through the back door; though the sun was rising gloriously, the howling wind was bending the trees and rattling the buckets against the outer wall. 'On second thoughts,' she grimaced, 'I don't reckon I'd be well suited to the outdoors.'

In spite of Ruby's misgivings, breakfast was ready on time. The routine had not changed since she first came into service at Blackthorn House. Eggs, bacon, sausages, kippers and porridge were all served in rose-coloured tureens which were set out on the sideboard. Tea and toast were brought on request, and Ruby was then free to go about her other duties. It was a good system all round. Everyone could have as much or as little of what they fancied, and there was no standing on ceremony. Rita would have dearly liked to be surrounded by servants, but this household didn't have the money for such luxuries.

'Something smells good.' As usual Frank was the first down. Going to the tureens he piled his plate with scrambled eggs and streaky bacon. 'Nothing like a good breakfast,' he declared with a broad smile. After having one appetite satisfied last night, he was now assuaging the other. 'Tea for me, Ruby,' he told her. 'No toast.' When she hurried out, he began softly whistling until he gathered a mound of scrambled egg on to his fork and thrust it into his mouth. After that he wolfed down everything on his plate, drank four cups of tea, and was still seated there, mopping his face with a napkin, when his wife came in. 'Oh, there you are, dear.' Leaping from his place, he ran to pull out her chair. 'Sleep well, did you?' he asked meaningfully, winking and watching her as she reluctantly joined him.

'Say what you want and I'll get it for you. Eggs? Bacon? Maybe a little helping of porridge?'

Rita was not impressed. 'Don't be absurd.'

Ruby emerged with a fresh pot of tea. 'Get me some toast, and be quick about it,' she was told. The order was given with a scowl.

' "Get me some toast" . . . "Get me some toast," ' Ruby mimicked all the way to the kitchen. 'That bugger thinks her arse don't stink.'

'You were a bit harsh on Ruby, weren't you?' Frank complained half-heartedly.

Rita's answer was to glare at him in the hope that he might leave the room.

Much to her annoyance, he inched his chair closer to hers. 'Last night was wonderful,' he murmured. 'There was something . . .' He thought hard. 'Oh, I don't know . . . something different about you.' He reached out and touched her hand, which she instantly withdrew. 'You were kinder . . . softer, somehow.'

His words struck fear into her. Had she allowed her thoughts of Owen Leyton to convey emotion to this odious man who was her husband? If so, she was a fool. 'Have you finished your breakfast?' she asked coldly.

'Yes, and a very good breakfast it was too.' He irritated her by smacking his lips. 'You don't appreciate Ruby, I know, but she really is a treasure.'

'If you've finished your breakfast, I suggest you leave and let others enjoy theirs.'

He sat back as though slapped in the face, but still couldn't believe he was being dismissed. When she ignored him, he sighed and said in a little boy's voice, 'You're being rather cruel this morning.'

'And you are being obnoxious.'

'Did last night mean nothing to you?'

'I refuse to discuss it.'

'Will you stroll with me after breakfast?'

'I would rather not.'

'Will you ride with me later then?' He frowned. 'I have the onerous job of collecting rent from the tenants.'

'If you hate it so much, why don't you employ a rent collector?'

'You know very well why. I don't employ a rent collector for the same reason I haven't filled the house with servants.'

'You're always pleading poverty. It's embarrassing.'

'Not half as embarrassing as it would be if we took them on and couldn't pay their wages.'

'The answer is simple, then.'

'Oh?'

'Raise the rents.'

He bowed his head and thought a while, then stood up, clenched his fist and hit it gently against the table. 'You know very well it isn't always easy.'

Ruby returned with tea and toast. 'There you are, Ma'am,' she said cheerily. All she got for her trouble was a hard look. Sensing the bad atmosphere, she quickly collected Frank's dirty plate and departed. 'Sour buggers!' she muttered, thankful when she came into the sanctuary of her beloved kitchen.

Margaret and Cathy came down together. Cathy ate heartily, but Margaret had little appetite. After nibbling at a spoonful of scrambled egg, she prepared to leave. 'I'll be in the sitting room when you've finished,' she told Cathy. 'I thought we might get started on your schooling early this morning.' She looked at the girl and saw a woman. 'Soon you won't need me as an instructor any more, then how will I fill my hours?' Before anyone could answer, she hurried away.

'I'll always need you,' Cathy murmured. Apart from Ruby, Margaret was all she had.

At the bottom of the stairs, Margaret met Frank and the boy.

'What do you think?' Frank asked, pushing Jack forward for Margaret's inspection. 'A fine-looking fellow in his Monday suit, isn't he?'

It was courtesy rather than curiosity that prompted her to run her gaze over the young man. He was dressed in a blue serge suit, white shirt and black polished shoes. His thick fair hair was combed back, and she had to admit he looked smart. 'He's very presentable,' she agreed. 'Now, if you'll excuse me, I have to get ready for Cathy's lessons.'

Barring her way to the sitting room, Frank stood his ground. He grunted and sighed and finally declared in a foolish voice, 'As you know, I've been grooming Jack in the manners of a gentleman.' He slapped his hand on the boy's shoulder. 'You must agree he's made admirable progress.'

'Without a doubt.' Margaret had no idea what her brother was leading up to, but knew he must have something in mind. 'You've done a good job.' Moving forward, she told him with a hint of impatience, 'I really must get ready for Cathy's lessons.'

He coughed and smiled and grew a little pink in the face. Addressing the boy he said, 'Off you go and get your breakfast. Remember what I told you. Don't leave the breakfast table until you're sent for.' Once the young fellow was out of earshot, he told Margaret, 'Give him time enough before you collect him.'

'What do you mean?' Margaret had hoped she needn't play a part in the boy's upbringing. 'Are you asking me to school him?'

Frank beamed with relief. 'Yes! That's exactly what I'm asking.'

'But I thought you had it in mind to engage a male tutor?'

'Well, yes, and so I will . . . next season. For now, though, I want you to train him in the rudiments of reading and writing.'

'What you really mean is you don't want to be embarrassed by the fact that here is your son . . . fifteen years of age if he's telling the truth . . . who still can't read or write.'

Frank was indignant. 'Hiring a male tutor is a very expensive business. More so if he has to start right at the beginning.'

'Frank Blackthorn, you're a hypocrite.' He was an easy man to see through. 'This isn't a matter of money, you and I both know it.'

'What are you getting at?' The colour drained from his face. Fearing she had somehow discovered the awful truth about the boy, he visibly trembled. 'Come on. Out with it! What are you saying?'

Margaret mistook his anxiety for rage. 'It's no good you getting angry or trying to bully me. I have a mind of my own, you should know that by now.' She waited a moment, half expecting he would yell and shout. When he didn't, she answered, 'What I am saying is this . . . you should be ashamed! You obviously don't want the world to know you're about to adopt a boy who can't read or write.'

Relieved she knew nothing that could threaten him, he hung his head, saying sheepishly, 'Such a thing might cause tittle-tattle in the village, and I would rather avoid that if possible.'

'It isn't the boy's fault he can't read or write.' Margaret was astounded to find herself defending him. 'He obviously comes from the sort of background where it's more profitable to learn the art of pickpocketing than to know how to write his own name. In that respect, he has an excuse for being illiterate.'

'I knew you would understand, and because of the way you feel about my having brought Jack here, I realise I'm asking a lot of you. Especially as I can't pay you, and you already tutor Cathy without a penny reward.'

'I have no need of your money, Frank.' Margaret was insulted. 'Even if you offered me wages for teaching Cathy, I wouldn't accept them. Seeing her grow intellectually is my reward. And, after all, I am a trained teacher, or have you forgotten?'

'No, my dear. In fact that's the very reason I know you'll do a good job with the boy. Moreover, he's family now, and you might as well accept it.' Playing on her professional pride, he urged, 'Please. Take him on for a while. All I ask is that you send him to his new tutor with at least the basic rudiments of education.'

Margaret began to see it as a challenge. 'All right. But I would much rather put aside another time, when I can give him all my attention.' Though she couldn't refuse to teach the boy, Margaret saw him as being a possible distraction to Cathy. 'Your daughter is nearing the end of her schooling, while this fellow is only beginning.'

'I've already told him he's to start lessons this morning. Surely it's more expedient to teach two pupils at the same time?'

Reluctantly, she agreed. 'Very well, Frank. But if I'm to be responsible for his learning, I won't have you interfering.'

'I wouldn't dream of it.' His face broke into a triumphant grin. 'I knew you wouldn't let me down.'

Hating the way she had been manipulated, Margaret told him sharply, 'I'm taking him on a week's trial. If in that time he displeases me in any way, that's an end to it.'

The grin vanished and in its place came a penitent expression. 'Of course.'

'Tell him to report to the sitting room in half an hour.' Pushing by him, she continued on her way, hoping she might never come to regret the decision she had just made.

The morning went swiftly. Cathy was surprised to find herself seated at the same table as Jack, though Margaret had been wise enough to put them at separate ends. While Cathy kept her head down to her advanced studies, Margaret went through the alphabet with the boy. She wrote the letters down and he copied them. She spoke each one out and he repeated after her. By the end of the first lesson, he was scrawling his name. 'J . . . a . . . c . . . k'. As he wrote, he spelled the name out. When it was done, he stared at it for what seemed an age. 'I've written my own name,' he muttered with delight. 'I've written my own name.'

Cathy was also delighted. 'David can write his name now,' she said with pride. 'He can read too.'

'Who's David?' Though he tried hard not to show it, the boy was jealous.

'Work now, talk later,' Margaret intervened. She sensed more than curiosity in Jack's voice, and it only deepened her reservations about him.

At midday the lessons were over. Cathy walked out in the sunshine and Jack followed. From the window, Margaret saw them together, seated on the bench by the apple tree. 'How can I keep them apart?' she murmured.

'You can't!' Rita had come into the room unheard.

Startled, Margaret swung round. 'What do you want here?'

'Only to ask how the boy fared with his lessons.' She was too sweet, too smiling.

'And if I said he was a poor scholar?'

'I would blame the teacher.'

Margaret nodded. 'Of course you would.' Coming from the window she took up the pile of books from the table and leisurely stacked them in the cupboard. Her deliberately methodical movements annoyed Rita beyond endurance.

'How *did* he fare?' She struggled to keep her composure.

'As a matter of fact, he fared very well. He wrote his own name for the first time.' In spite of her coolness, she couldn't stop the pride from creeping into her voice. 'You say you would blame the teacher if the boy stumbled at his lessons,' she prodded. 'So now, you may praise the teacher for a job well done.'

Rita stiffened. 'It's the boy who deserves the credit. He obviously has intelligence.'

'I won't argue with that.'

'Just now . . . when I came in?' Rita seated herself at the table, her green eyes glittering and hostile as they raked the other woman's face. 'You were watching them.'

'And if I was?'

'You don't like the boy, do you?' Her handsome features were wreathed in a devious smile. 'You'd prefer him to be thrown back on to the streets, wouldn't you?'

Margaret knew from old that she was being drawn into a trap. But she could not be less than honest. 'You're wrong,' she confessed. 'I don't dislike the boy.'

'You'd rather he hadn't been brought here though, wouldn't you?'

'I can't deny that.'

'You're afraid he'll steal Cathy's rightful place in this house?'

'Hasn't he already done that?'

'I hope so.' Her smile deepened. 'The girl should know she must take second place.'

For the first time, Margaret could see through the whole charade. 'My God!' She dropped the pile of books on to the table, her face openly astonished as she accused Rita, 'You don't want the boy at all, do you?'

Rita outstared her. 'What a thing to say.' She cursed herself for having almost given the game away. 'Why should I take the boy on if I don't want him?'

'To hurt Cathy. That would be reason enough for you.'

444

Margaret rounded the table and, for one frightening minute, Rita feared she would be attacked. 'You've always treated Cathy with contempt!' There was no stopping her now. 'Why do you think I gave up my career to care for her? You took me on as nanny, but I've been mother and father to that lovely child. I've loved her like she was my own, and now you expect me to stand by and see her totally humiliated.'

'You're hysterical.' Secure in the knowledge that her sister-in-law was too much of a lady to hit out, Rita dared to torment her further. 'Frank and I have a son now, and he must be our first priority. Cathy will be taken care of, I dare say.' She was feeling smug, capable of anything.

'Oh, she'll be taken care of all right, you can be sure of that.' Incensed, Margaret slapped her hand on Rita's shoulder. 'Now get out!'

Standing up, Rita casually brushed down her skirt and adjusted her waistband. Smiling once more, she said with malice, 'You won't be able to keep them apart. They're brother and sister now.' She said something then that made Margaret's heart grow cold. 'Unfortunately, however much Frank and I would want it, the boy is not our flesh and blood. It's to be hoped that Jack and Cathy don't become *too* close. After all, she's fast becoming a very attractive young woman.' She gave a small laugh. 'But I expect you were thinking of that when I saw you at the window just now.' In a harder voice she added, 'You do right to be concerned. But human nature being what it is, I shouldn't try too hard to keep them apart. Your efforts may have just the opposite effect.'

Margaret could see it all now. 'You're a witch!'

'And you are a thorn in my side.' With that Rita swept out.

When Margaret returned to the window, she was dismayed to see Cathy and the boy laughing together, he with his arm resting on her shoulders and Cathy looking up at him with affection. Pushing open the window she called out, 'Cathy!' Jack turned and looked, but Cathy appeared not to have heard. She called again, louder, 'CATHY!'

This time Cathy heard and came running, leaving the boy smiling after her. 'He seems nice enough,' she told Margaret. 'He's been asking about David . . . wants to meet him.'

Margaret knew she had to be very careful. 'I'm not sure we should take a stranger to Mrs Leyton's house, certainly not without asking permission first.'

Cathy chatted on and it soon became obvious to Margaret that the boy was already worming his way into Cathy's affections. She recalled the two of them just now, the way he had draped his arm round Cathy's shoulders and the possessive manner in which he was looking at her. Moreover, it was disturbing the way he had chosen to ignore her call for Cathy to return indoors.

It was almost as though Rita had set a serpent loose in the house, a viper to charm and destroy her trusting daughter. It was all a plan, she could see that now. An evil and vindictive plan, to punish Cathy for not being the son Rita had yearned for. 'She'll ruin you over my dead body,' Margaret promised softly. And vowed to watch over Cathy as never before.

Unnerved and excited by her encounter with Margaret, Rita strode through the streets of Langho, nodding a greeting to others as they passed, and enjoying the admiring glances of plain and uninteresting women. There was a defiant spring in her step as she went along by the post office and down through the rows of terraced cottages, despising the people who resided there and thinking herself above them.

'Mornin', Ma'am.' The old cobbler sat outside his shop, his cap drawn down to protect his eyes from the sun, and a pipe of baccy jutting from his thin-lipped mouth. 'Off for a stroll, I see.' A man of a simple nature, he spoke to everyone in the same friendly manner.

As Rita glared at him with open hostility, he visibly cringed, at the same time making a mental note to keep his mouth firmly shut whenever she crossed his path.

'Snooty cow!' Ada Long from number ten was never one to pick and choose her words. 'Who the bleedin' hell does she think she is, eh?' She held a squealing child in one hand and a stick in the other. When the child struggled to be free, she whacked it hard with the length of the stick. 'Keep still, yer bugger!' she chided. 'Yer to come in for a wash an' that's an end to it.' The other three, all aged under six and daring her to take them in, suddenly realised she was not in a mood to be tampered with. In a matter of minutes they were all walking sedately beside her as she marched them back to the house. 'Yer little sods!' she yelled, clipping the biggest round the ear. 'Next time I shout for you to get inside, happen you'll move yerself a bit quicker.'

After she had ushered the last one into the house, she sneaked an envious glance towards Rita. "Tain't fair the way some folks have it all an' are never satisfied,' she sighed. Then she sighed again and followed Rita out of sight. 'She's a looker, I'll give 'er that,' she muttered grudgingly.

Though not many people cared for her, Rita certainly attracted attention. She wore a long beige-coloured skirt and matching jacket, small low-heeled shoes and a white beret over her flowing dark hair. She felt beautiful. As she came away from the houses, she let her thoughts run free. She thought of Frank and hated him. She recalled the confrontation with her sister-in-law and her face hardened. When she remembered how she had gone along with Frank's outrageous plan to adopt a complete stranger, she felt a tinge of regret. But the regret was soon swamped by an immense surge of satisfaction. Things would turn out exactly as she planned. Moreover, the boy was making a handsome addition to the Blackthorn family. Margaret had confirmed his intelligence. He had shown a healthy appetite to learn and, much to her own surprise, Rita found herself being drawn to him. A son was what she had always wanted. *Someone else's* son had at first seemed daunting. Now, though, she was warming to the idea; especially when Margaret had so set herself against it. And even more so when it was becoming increasingly obvious how Cathy's life might be turned upside down by the arrangement. The whole situation appealed to her wickedness; so much so that revenge blinded her reason. As she climbed over the stile and into the open fields, she actually laughed out loud.

An hour later, her laughter had turned to tears. As she pushed her way through the spinney, she was suddenly startled by the screech of a bird. When she looked up, it was to stare straight into the glassy eyes of two dead rabbits; strung across the fork of a tree, their heads were dangling almost to her shoulder.

Fresh blood from their wounds dripped on to her neck and sent her into a frenzy. In that moment there was the sound of a gun being fired, followed by a man yelling. It was all too much. With a piercing scream, she took to her heels, breathless and panic-stricken as she scrambled towards the edge of the spinney. Flailing branches tore at her clothes as she ran, and jagged thorns rent her skin.

Driven by fear and seeing the open fields so close, she didn't notice how the ground fell away beneath her. By the time she realised, it was too late. With a cry of horror, she plunged sideways, crashing to the bottom of a steep bank where she rolled against a tree trunk and lay bruised and unconscious.

Owen Leyton had been rabbiting in the spinney. Having already bagged two and just shot another, he was celebrating his good fortune when he heard the scream. Slinging both rabbit and shotgun over his shoulder, he ran towards the spinney, just in time to see Rita tumble over.

At first he made no move to lift her. Instead he stood over her, his dark eyes drinking in her beauty. Taking the gun from his shoulder he laid it on the grass next to her; the rabbit was dropped at her feet. Kneeling down beside her, he tenderly raised her in his arms, his gaze softening as he looked into her face. 'You're even more handsome close to,' he murmured. Her long hair fell over his hands and he could feel the trim curves of her body beneath his fingers. Beads of perspiration stood out on his forehead.

Rita couldn't recall how she had come to be lying there, dazed and hurt. Her eyes closed, but she heard his voice, felt his arms round her, and for just one brief, wonderful moment she felt safe. Slowly she moved, wincing as the torn skin twisted. With confused green eyes she looked up at his face.

'It's all right,' he told her softly. 'You slipped down the bank, but you're safe now.' When she seemed confused, he whispered, 'You're very beautiful.'

His smile mesmerised her. When she looked into those dark brooding eyes she knew where she had seen him before. Rage gathered in her. But something else, something far more powerful, took hold of her. 'Leave me be,' she told him weakly. 'I can make my own way home.' She struggled, before falling back exhausted into his arms, her gaze meeting with his.

Fired by her beauty, he could contain himself no longer. Leaning over he kissed her hard on the mouth, astonished when she seemed to enjoy it. 'You want me, don't you?' He smiled, stroking her face with the tips of his fingers. 'I saw it in your eyes the first time I looked at you.'

'You filth!' With a vicious sweep of her hand she caught him hard on the side of the face. 'What makes you think I could want *you*?'

Though his cheek throbbed and his first instinct was to slap her hard, his voice was soft with admiration. 'No use denying it,' he said arrogantly. 'You want me every bit as much as I want you.'

She stared at him long and hard. Then she softly laughed. 'I want no man,' she scoffed. 'Least of all you.'

Sensing a weakness in her, he boldly opened the neck of her blouse. Without a word he bent his mouth to her nipple, gently sucking like a child, sensuously playing his tongue against the hardening mound.

Never before had she experienced such feelings. He was like an animal, wild and frenzied, filled with an urgency that intoxicated her. Shivering with delight, she made a show of pushing him away. 'No,' he murmured in her ear. 'It had to happen, you know that.' And she could not refuse him.

By the time she was delivered safely home, Frank was beside himself with worry. He thanked Owen profusely, and ordered Ruby to take care of her mistress at once.

He saw the unguarded look that passed between Owen and Rita but, not realising its significance, paid no mind to it. Yet one day in the not too distant future, when a price must be paid for pleasure enjoyed, he would live to remember that day with burning regret.

CHAPTER FOUR

'Mind you behave while I'm gone.' About to depart for London, Frank loathed the idea of leaving Rita behind. 'Won't you come with me?' he begged for the umpteenth time. He couldn't understand her reluctance. In the past whenever he'd had call to visit the city she always insisted on accompanying him.

'I'm not pleasant company at the moment,' Rita told him, pressing a handkerchief to her nose. 'I have a cold coming on.' She gave a little cough.

'I've a good mind to stay.' He took her in his arms, offended when she pushed him away.

Alarmed he might change his plans, she reminded him, 'I thought you needed to see your financial adviser?'

'Well, yes, I do. These six-monthly meetings are essential, to keep the house in order so to speak, and I want to know whether or not we can afford to send Jack away to a fine school.' He smiled grandly. 'I'm proud of that boy!'

Ignoring his comment, she gave another little cough. 'I think I'll go back to my bed.'

'I really *should* go to London, my dear. But it will mean me staying overnight. I can postpone it if you want?'

'No.' In a move which both surprised and delighted him, she threaded her arm through his and escorted him to the front door. 'I'll be fine,' she insisted. 'Your precious Ruby will see to that.' She allowed him a brief peck on the cheek. 'You'd better go or you'll miss your train.'

'It's *you* I'll miss.' He fussed over her all the way across the hall and on to the doorstep. The keen October wind took his breath away. 'Get back inside, before you catch your death.' He gently pushed her into the vestibule. Blowing a kiss, he got inside the carriage and hung out of the window, waving frantically until he was out of sight.

Thankful that he was gone at last, Rita put on her coat and hat and prepared to leave. As she opened the front door, Margaret came out of the sitting room. 'Spying on me, are you?' Rita demanded angrily.

'I have better things to do with my time.' Margaret had heard certain rumours which deeply troubled her. 'I was hoping to have a word with you.' Going across the hall, she stood before the other woman, wondering how she should broach the subject, or even whether she had a right to.

'What can we possibly have to talk about?'

'Has my brother gone yet?'

Rita's answer was short and sharp. 'If you've something to say, get on with it. I can't stand here all day.'

Margaret took a deep breath. 'There are rumours . . .'

'Rumours?' Rita's face turned a shade of grey and she seemed visibly to shrink. '*What* rumours?'

'I think you know.' She saw the guilt in Rita's face and was shocked. 'You and Owen Leyton. It's true, isn't it? I couldn't bring myself to believe it, but now I'm not so sure.'

Rita laughed in her face. 'Me and Owen Leyton!' She was a mistress of deception. 'You must be out of your mind.' Straightening to her full height, she set her shoulders and declared haughtily, 'If I were you, I should be very careful what you say.' Before Margaret could answer, she was out of the house and striding down the path.

'Where's she going?' Jack had come out of the sitting room and was staring out of the open doorway. 'Have you two had an argument?' The corners of his mouth curled into a smile. The idea of everyone at each other's throats amused him.

'Go back to your lessons.' Hurrying across the hallway, Margaret closed the door and escorted him to the sitting room.

Cathy, too, was curious. 'Has Father gone?' She knew it was too much to expect him to say goodbye. Why should he change the habit of a lifetime?

'I believe so, sweetheart.'

Jack butted in. 'He's gone to see his financial adviser and won't be home till tomorrow.'

Margaret stared at him with astonishment. 'You seem to be very well informed, young man.' Even she didn't know Frank's plans.

'That's because it has to do with me.' He was very pleased with himself. 'Father says you've taught me well but I have to move up soon, so he has to see this man in London . . . about finances and everything.' Coming to where Cathy sat, he stroked her long fair hair. 'Don't worry about Father,' he said. 'You've got me, haven't you? If you like we can go down to the brook after lessons?'

'We have other plans,' Margaret quickly told him. 'Now, please sit back at your work. I want the essays completed before we break in an hour.' She glanced up at the mantelpiece clock. It was five minutes to one. Nan Foster was expecting them by three. She had arranged a little tea party to celebrate her seventy-first birthday, and was baking a cake especially.

'Am *I* invited?' Jack enquired boldly.

It was the last thing Margaret wanted. 'I think not,' she answered.

Seeing his disappointment, Cathy felt for him. 'I'm sure Nan wouldn't mind.'

Margaret considered for a moment. 'All right.' With Frank away and Rita in one of her moods, it might be wise to keep the boy where she could watch him. 'But I hope Nan doesn't mind.'

These past four months she'd worked hard to keep Cathy and the boy apart. But it was proving to be an impossibility. He always seemed to be there and, while she had every reason to resent his presence in her parents' house, and though Jack was too secretive for Margaret's liking, Cathy sought the good in him.

In view of her acceptance of him, Margaret reluctantly decided to give Jack the benefit of the doubt. But her vow to watch him closely was stronger than ever. There was something very mysterious about the boy, and she couldn't help but feel he was not all he seemed to be. Time and again she had discreetly quizzed him about his background but, apart from telling her what she already knew, he was suspiciously secretive.

Coming to the end of the lane, Rita turned left, towards the community of Langho, and Dickens Street. She hated Dickens Street. It ran like a vein right through the heart of Langho, a long meandering street of back-to-back houses, everything she despised. There was poverty in Dickens Street, with the men earning a pittance from the cotton mills and factories hereabouts, and the women raising hordes of children; ragged snotty-nosed children, who filled the street with their laughter and sat on the kerbstones with their feet dangling in the gutter. The women wore turbans and white-stoned their front doorsteps. In the evening the men stood about on the street corners or went to the Red Lion pub, where they sat and supped their beer and afterwards stumbled home with pickled brains and a hankering to enjoy their wife and make another child.

There was no other route to the doctor's surgery so, while she wended her way along the pavements of Dickens Street, Rita Blackthorn tried not to think too much about the people who lived here. Instead, she quickened her footsteps and was soon crossing the market square towards the big red house that stood on the corner. In a minute she was knocking on the door, impatient to be let in.

'I'm sorry, Mrs Blackthorn, but the surgery is already finished and the doctor is on his way to the hospital. I can make an appointment for him to call on you though?'

'Just tell him I'm here. He'll see me.'

'I've already turned away two people, Ma'am.'

'I am not "people"!' Rita thumped her clenched fists on the wooden counter. 'Do as you're told, girl. Tell him I'm here, and I have no intention of leaving until he's seen me.' That said, she sat herself on the nearest chair and kept her stony glare on the girl.

'Very well, Ma'am. I'll tell him.' The girl had never liked Rita Blackthorn. She liked her even less now. 'But he's in a hurry and I know he won't see anyone else,' she said boldly.

Almost at once the doctor emerged. Unlike his receptionist he had always admired Rita Blackthorn as a woman of beauty and determination. 'Come with me,' he said softly, leading the way into his consulting room.

Rita smiled serenely as she followed him in. As they went into the consulting room she glanced at the girl with a smirk of satisfaction.

454

Some minutes later, the doctor's words wiped the smile from her face. 'I think congratulations are in order.' He beamed. 'You are definitely with child.'

He was surprised by her reaction. She seemed neither pleased nor disappointed. But she was in a great hurry to leave, and he assumed she couldn't wait to relay the news to her husband. 'I'll make another appointment,' he said. 'If I remember rightly, you had complications during your previous pregnancy.' He rubbed his hand against his chin, thinking hard and recalling aloud, 'Threatened miscarriage, wasn't it?' He nodded and made a note in his pad. 'I shall have to keep a closer eye on you this time.'

Outside on the pavement, she couldn't decide which way to go. In the end she walked to the market square and there flagged down a cab. 'Brook Lane,' she said, climbing in and making herself comfortable. As they drove away from the houses and out into the countryside, she thought on the doctor's words. 'If I remember rightly, you had a difficult pregnancy last time.' She thought of Cathy and her mood darkened. 'Pity the brat ever drew first breath.'

Settling back in the soft leather seat, she mused aloud. 'If I'd given birth to a boy, things would have been different.' Rubbing her stomach, she whispered lovingly, 'Owen's child will be a boy, I'm sure of it.'

During the short journey, she convinced herself that she was carrying a son. In strange mood, she was both thrilled and afraid. What if Frank found out? He was a man of mild and gentle manner but where she was concerned, he was madly possessive. Yet even the fear of Frank's finding out was itself exciting to her. 'What do I care if the whole world knows!' she muttered defiantly. 'I've been clever enough to hoard a nest of money, and Frank would have to make a decent settlement on me. Yes, Owen and I will move away . . . we'll make a new life together.' The more she thought on it, the more like reality it became. She was convinced that all she had to do was tell Owen she was carrying his child, and everything would be just as she had planned.

'Do you want me to wait, Ma'am?'

Dropping the fare into the driver's grubby hand, she told him sharply, 'No. Be off with you.' Fastening her coat tighter about her, she hurried away, head down against the wind as she went towards the house where Owen lived with his family.

It was Owen himself who opened the door. 'What the devil are you doing *here*?' Quickly, before his wife might grow curious, he closed the door and spoke with her on the step. 'I told you never to come here.'

'I had to.' Rita wanted to throw her arms round him, but something about his manner made her nervous. 'I've just come from the doc—' Suddenly the door was opened and there stood Owen's wife. She didn't speak, but looked from one to the other with quizzical eyes.

'It's Mrs Blackthorn.' Owen quickly stepped back. 'She's come to discuss a business matter.' He smiled at Rita as though she was little more than a stranger. 'Isn't that so?' he urged, widening his eyes in a warning.

Rita rose to the deceit magnificently. 'You're looking well, Mrs Leyton,' she remarked casually, thinking how much better it would be if the woman was suddenly to drop dead. 'My husband has been rushed away on business and he asked me to speak to Mr Leyton here ... about the fencing alongside the lane.' The excuse just popped into her mind. 'We've had one or two complaints, you see.'

'Complaints?' Maria was puzzled. Turning to her husband she asked, 'Didn't you repair that fencing only last week?'

'That's right, I did. The wind must have brought it down again.' When he saw how she shivered from the cold, drawing her shawl over her bony frame as she stepped deeper into the hall, he put his hands on her shoulders and took her back inside. 'You've no business standing in a draught,' he scolded. Easing her into a big armchair, he wrapped a blanket round her legs. 'You're doing so well, I'll not have you making yourself ill again.' When she looked up, he kissed her on the forehead. 'What would I do without you, eh?' he asked fondly.

'Oh, you'd do all right, I dare say.'

'Don't you believe it.' Lately he had come to know the value of Maria.

Jerking her head towards the door, she said meaningfully, 'I expect *she* feels the cold too. You'll either have to fetch her in and give her a brew, or send her on her way.' Chuckling, she leaned forward to whisper. 'To be honest, I'd sooner you sent her on her way. She's a right uppity bugger... not like Miss Margaret at all.' Screwing her face up, she added, 'On second thoughts, get rid of her.'

'Right then.' He got his jacket from the back of the door. 'I'll send her away, then I'll go and take a look at the fencing. When Teresa comes in, tell her to start the tea for you. I'll not be gone long.'

He laughed when she said she was capable of getting their tea without Teresa's help. 'And eat it too if you're not back,' she joked.

Ushering Rita away from the house, he thrust her angrily into the barn. 'What the hell d'you think you're playing at?' he hissed. 'Do you want her to find out? Is that what you're after?'

Rita was thrown by his manner. She knew he would be angry at her going to the house, but she hadn't expected him to be so hostile. 'I had to see you.'

'We arranged to meet tonight. What's so important it couldn't wait?' Whenever he was near her she swamped his senses. It was like that now. 'Never mind... just don't do it again.' Taking her roughly by the shoulders, he jerked her towards him, raining kisses on her face, neck and every inch of skin that was visible. 'You drive me crazy,' he groaned. He stripped away her hat to let her long hair tumble through his fingers. Now he took off her coat and pawed at her breasts. 'You're poison to me,' he murmured in her ear. 'The pity of it is, I can't get you out of my blood.'

Desperate for him now, the news she had brought him could wait. He still wanted her, that was all she needed to know. 'Take me,' she moaned. And he did, with the same wild lust as before, biting and bruising her, bringing her to a fulfilment she had never found with Frank.

Later, when passion was spent and they sat together in that cold draughty barn, he told her grimly, 'If you ever knock on Maria's door again, I swear I'll kill you.'

She laughed at his threat. 'Anyone would think you loved her.' Though she laughed at the idea, she was mortally afraid it might be true. 'You *don't*, do you?'

Standing up to fasten his trousers, he grew anxious that David would soon be home. If he was to see his father here, with another woman! The idea didn't bear thinking about.

Suddenly Rita was there before him, her fingers gripping his arm. 'Did you hear what I said?'

He looked down to see her green eyes blazing with anger. There was a vindictiveness about her that struck fear into his heart. 'Sorry,' he said. 'I was just thinking.' Glancing towards the big doors, his nervousness increased. 'You'd better go. David could arrive back any minute.' Looking towards the far corner and the empty stable there, he explained, 'He's only as far as the spinney ... setting rabbit snares.'

'I'll go when I'm ready.'

'You'll go when *I* say.' He realised now he'd been a fool ever to have tangled with her. She was trouble he could well do without.

'Do you love her?'

'What are you talking about?'

'*Her*!' She snuggled up to him. 'Your wife. I couldn't stand it if you loved her.'

'I don't know what you want me to say.' He had on his jacket now, and was ready to go. 'Maria has nothing to do with what's between us.' He shrugged her off. 'Leave her out of it.'

'Tell me you don't love her!' She stiffened against him, drawing her head back to look into his face.

His instincts told him to be wary. Gripping her arms, he dug his fingers into the flesh. He wanted to hit her, to let her know that he was already eaten up with regrets. 'Bitch!' Intoxicated by her beauty, he bent his head and kissed her hard. 'Does that answer your question?'

She seemed satisfied. 'It's just as well you don't love her,' she said with a cunning smile, '*because I'm expecting your child*.' She saw the colour ebb from his face, and still she didn't realise the way he felt. 'I know it's a boy ... a son for me at last.'

'God Almighty!' He saw his whole life turning upside down. 'With child? Are you sure?'

She laughed. 'I came straight from the doctor to you.' She was so full of the news she couldn't see how devastated he was. 'What's the matter, Owen? Aren't you thrilled?'

His voice shook with emotion. 'How do you know it isn't

your husband's?' He clung to a glimmer of hope.

'Don't worry, my love.' She actually believed he would have been disappointed if the child was Frank's. 'It can't be his. Since you and I have been together, I've used every excuse to turn him away.' She was lying. In fact she had given in to Frank on two occasions since that day when she and Owen made love. 'In any case, this is a boy.' She took his hand and stroked it over her stomach. 'Frank was never man enough to make a son,' she said bitterly.

Startled by the sound of someone pushing open the big doors, he put his finger to his lips and ushered her out by the back way. 'Make your way home before dark falls,' he warned softly. 'And remember . . . you must never come to this house again.'

Angered because he hadn't offered to see her home, she demanded, 'You *are* thrilled about the baby, aren't you?'

'You know I am,' he lied. 'Now get off home.'

Still she resisted. 'I have a certain amount of money, and Frank will be made to see me all right. You say you don't love Maria, so you see how easy it all is? There's nothing at all to stop us making a life together.'

The big doors were open now, letting the light in. 'For God's sake, Rita!' He pushed her out. 'Don't worry . . . I'll make plans.' The 'plans' he had in mind did not include her, but he mustn't let her know that. 'It'll take time. It must be done right. Meanwhile, this is our little secret. Do you understand what I'm saying?' He was frantic in case she was foolish enough to confront her husband with the information.

She smiled then. 'I won't tell a soul, I swear,' she assured him. The smile fell away and her face darkened. 'You won't let me down though, will you?'

Not for the first time, he saw the bad side of her and knew she would make a dangerous enemy. 'Trust me,' he pleaded. Later, he would have to consider moving away. For now, though, he had no choice but to play along. 'Not a word to anyone or it could ruin everything.'

'I'll do as you say,' she agreed. 'And anyway, who would I tell?'

The silhouette of a young man leading a horse could clearly be seen entering the barn at the other end. 'Dad? Is that you?'

David peered deeper into the barn, coming closer with every step.

'Go! Quickly. Keep to the high ground.' Mortified that his son might see her, Owen thrust Rita out of the barn. 'Wait for me to contact you.'

'Don't make it too long,' she replied softly. Then she was gone.

Almost as soon as she emerged from the rear of the barn, Rita saw a face staring down. It was Jack! Leaning against the trunk of an oak tree, he was smiling at her, a sly knowing grin that made her heart turn cold. Quickly now she ran the other way, across the valley and along by the brook. But she couldn't get his expression out of her mind. 'He knows! He saw us!' The idea that he might tell Frank before she was ready spurred her on. 'Perhaps he didn't see us after all,' she hoped aloud. 'We'll see.'

Unaware that they might have been seen, Owen breathed a sigh of relief. But it wasn't over yet, he reminded himself. Rita Blackthorn was carrying his child! The thought filled him with dread.

'How come you're home so early? Have you set all the traps?' Once he'd made his presence known to his son, Owen forced himself to talk about mundane matters.

'Every one of 'em,' David replied with a grin. 'And I'm home early because I've been invited to a party.'

'A party?'

'Nan Foster saw me making for the spinney and came after me. It's her birthday and she's having a party.' A soft blush spread over his handsome face. 'Cathy will be there,' he said. The touch of her name on his lips was warmer than a summer's day.

Relieved that David had not seen Rita Blackthorn, Owen shook his head and tutted. 'By! A party, eh? Some folk do have grand ideas and that's a fact.'

'That's because Nan Foster is a grand lady.'

'I'll not deny that. Though how she came to be living alone in a dilapidated cottage is a mystery to me.'

His thoughts flew back to another 'lady'. The one who lived up at Blackthorn House. The one he'd been unwise enough to become involved with. Some women knew when an affair was over. Some women could take no for an answer, but not Rita Blackthorn. This time he had made a mistake, but he would put it right. Somehow he would put it right.

As he and David walked back to the house, Maria watched from the window. There was something about her husband ... But she wasn't sure. It was always worse when she wasn't sure.

'Come in! Come in!' Nan Foster had on her best dress, a fancy cream creation, with beads at the neck and hem, and a cameo clasp at the throat. In her white hair she wore a headband of blue. 'I'm so glad you're here.' She looked from Margaret to Cathy and then noticed the boy. Studying him for a moment, she frowned deeply. He was everything Margaret had described, handsome and mature for his fifteen years. His fair hair was superbly cut and his sturdy figure seemed at ease in the expensive clothes his new 'father' had provided.

While she studied him, he appraised her through bold hazel eyes. 'Am I right in thinking you're Jack?' she said in a curious voice. Her greeting was neither friendly nor hostile.

Cathy stood alongside him, her pretty face troubled. 'You don't mind our bringing him, do you, Nan?' she asked worriedly.

The old lady merely smiled and continued to regard the boy, grateful that none of them could read her thoughts. She glanced at Margaret and saw her own reservations echoed in those serious brown eyes, but it was to Cathy she spoke. 'I expect there's room at my table for one more.' This was her birthday treat. She had here the two people she loved most in all the world, and she was determined that nothing should be allowed to spoil it all.

As she led the trio into the tiny sitting room, the old lady softly sang her favourite lullaby. Margaret had heard it so many times before, she felt as though she had known it all her life.

'There! What do you think?' Standing proudly before the small square table, Nan waved her hands in an extravagant gesture. 'Have I done you proud?' The table was covered in a white lace cloth, and the cloth was covered in porcelain dishes filled with fish and meat and fancy titbits to whet the appetite. Set about the edge of the table were four small white plates

461

with dainty blue borders, knife, fork and spoon beside. 'I've only set four places, but it won't take a minute to put out another one.' Nan glanced meaningfully at the boy. A part of her wished he hadn't come here. Yet another, greater part of her was glad. Better to know the enemy than to be taken by surprise, she thought.

'Who else is invited?' Margaret had been led to believe it was just herself and Cathy.

'That nice young David Leyton,' the old lady explained. 'He's always been very good to me ... cutting logs for the fire and fetching the odd rabbit to make a fine stew.' She went out to the scullery and brought another setting. Laying it on the table, she shifted everyone along a place. 'There! Now we can all be comfortable.'

'What do you want me to do?' Cathy asked. 'We're here to help as well, you know.'

'Thank you, dear, but I've been up since the crack of dawn, and everything's ready.' She smiled graciously. 'I've made my first cake in years, and I must say I'm very pleased with myself.' She sighed wistfully and in a softer voice appeared to be addressing herself. 'It's been so long since I really entertained.'

Cathy was about to make a comment, but the knock on the front door interrupted her. 'Shall I answer it?' she asked.

'You'll do no such thing!' Nan chided. 'You can take off your coat and see these two do the same.'

Hurrying to the front door she began softly singing the lullaby. It was a strange plaintive melody that never failed to touch Margaret deeply.

By the time Nan returned, Cathy and Jack were seated comfortably on the settee, and Margaret was putting a chunky log on the fire. 'Thank you, dear,' Nan said. 'It wouldn't do if we were to have our tea in front of a dying fire.' She pushed David forward. 'Here we are,' she said grandly. 'Another handsome fellow.'

David's dark eyes surveyed the little group. They lit up on seeing Cathy, but grew hard at the sight of Jack. The whole village had heard about this new addition to the Blackthorn family, but few people had actually seen him. Frank Blackthorn kept him close. 'Hiding him away' was how some put it.

The two young men regarded each other for what seemed a long awkward time but was in fact only seconds, with David inwardly flinching at the sight of Cathy and Jack sitting so close and Jack staring at David with a half-cunning grin. The atmosphere struck cold and, for some reason she couldn't fathom, Margaret thought the old lady was studying the two with some degree of satisfaction.

'Come and sit here,' Cathy invited as David came deeper into the room. She too had felt the coldness between the two young men, and wasn't quite sure what to make of it. She thought David might be jealous of Jack, but hoped not. After all, he was to be her brother. The growing affection she felt for him was altogether different from the deeper emotions that David raised in her. She had no experience of love between a man and a woman, but often wondered if that was what she felt for David. Certainly he made her feel warm and wanted whenever he was near, and when they were apart she was incredibly lonely.

Nan intervened. 'You can all sit at the table now,' she announced. 'The tea's ready and I can't wait to show off the cake I've made.' As they went to the table, she went to the scullery. 'Sit where you like,' she called. 'It doesn't matter.'

With the chill of the outdoors still on her, Margaret chose to sit closer to the fire. Cathy sat to her right, Jack placed himself beside Cathy, and David, wishing he hadn't come, hating the idea of sitting next to Jack, made his way to the place on Margaret's left side, leaving a seat vacant for Nan between himself and Jack.

It was only a minute before she returned, carrying a wonderful cake, her face wreathed in a glowing smile. 'Made of fruit and brandy, spread with marzipan and iced by my very own hands.' Setting it in the centre of the table, she gazed at it and sighed. 'I can't thank you all enough for coming,' she said warmly. But when she looked at the faces round her table, she deliberately avoided looking at Jack.

Margaret said it seemed a shame to cut the cake, but everyone had a slice and remarked on how good it was. As the time sped by, they chatted and laughed; Jack and David avoided each other, and Cathy exchanged intimate glances with David.

Finally, Nan opened the presents they had brought. A pair of patchwork cushion-covers from Margaret and Cathy, sewn from odd pieces of material which they had carefully saved and sorted especially for Nan's birthday. Jack presented her with an expensive porcelain vase, and there was a large fruit bowl from David, crafted by his own hands from a small beech log. 'They're all lovely. Thank you so much,' Nan cried. She hugged Margaret and Cathy, and smiled at the two young men; though the smile she gave David told him she valued his present above that of Jack. Later she was to tell Margaret, 'The porcelain vase brought by Jack might well have cost a deal of money but what David gave, and you and Cathy also, was precious time and skill, and a measure of love.'

When the tea was finished, Margaret and Cathy offered to help with the dishes. 'You'll do no such thing,' Nan objected. 'You're my guests, and anyway, there'll be plenty of time for that after you've gone. I've got little else to do.'

She did set the young men a task though. 'Jack, would you kindly have a look at the window fastener in the bedroom? It won't hold tightly, and I'm afraid the hinge might be broken.' She suspected he wouldn't have a clue about what to do, but it would keep him busy for a while, giving Cathy and David a chance to talk.

'What can *I* do?' Cathy was eager to help.

'You can go with David and draw two buckets of water from the outside pump. Oh, and while you're at it, David, could you clear the fallen leaves out of the trough, or the water won't be able to drain away.'

'I did offer to fell that tree for you,' he reminded her. 'Being close to the pump, it'll always cause you trouble. And anyway, it's on its last legs.'

'So am I,' Nan chuckled. 'Does that mean I should be done away with too?'

'Sorry.' He grinned. 'I didn't mean it like that.'

'I should hope not!' Nan was grateful for his offer. 'All the same, you're right. Come and see me tomorrow, and we'll discuss a lesser punishment for the tree. It was here when I came and I hope it will be here long after I've gone.' A fleeting sadness shadowed her face. She had a lot to do before that day ever came. 'Perhaps we can just cut back some of the overhanging branches?'

'Whatever you say.' Ever since he was a young boy, the old lady had lived in the cottage. She had put him in mind of an angel, with her gentle smile and snow-white hair. 'Just tell me what you want and it's done,' he promised. Stepping back, he allowed Cathy to go before him.

As they left the house, the two were happy enough to be in each other's company at last. Jack however, glowered at them through the upstairs window, slamming and banging at the window fastener, until Nan was forced to call up the stairs, 'Be careful, young man. I want it mended, not broken altogether!'

She made a fresh brew of tea and sat with Margaret in front of the cheery fire. 'What do you make of him?' she asked, jerking a thumb towards the ceiling.

'I'm amazed by the way he's settled in, and he's so quick at learning there soon won't be very much more I can teach him. Still, I understand Frank intends to have him tutored by better than me.'

'Don't belittle yourself.' Nan knew how talented Margaret was. 'And, anyway, I wasn't referring to how clever the boy is. What I wanted to know was what you thought about him, now you've got to know him better?'

'That's just it, Nan. I *don't* know him better.'

'How do you mean?'

'I've tried to talk about his background with him, but he's very secretive and gives nothing away. All I know is what Frank has told me. He's an orphan, made by circumstances to wander the streets, stealing and doing goodness knows what, until Frank came across him and gave him a better life.'

Nan thought on this a while. 'It's very little to know about someone who shares your house, don't you think ... a stranger who stands to inherit everything your brother owns?'

Margaret smiled wryly. 'Of course I would rather know more about him. In fact ...' she leaned forward and spoke more intimately '... lately I've been toying with the idea of hiring a private investigator to find out what he can. But there is precious little to go on.' She drew back. 'I'm torn in so many ways about the whole business, Nan. I think Frank was foolish to do what he did, yes. But he and Rita have craved a son for so long that they can't see clearly any more.' She had agonised over the situation, and now Nan was echoing all the fears she herself

465

felt ... for Cathy and Frank ... even Rita, because what hurt his wife hurt Frank more.

'David doesn't like him.'

Margaret peered out of the window. The greyness of a late-October day made the little cottage seem like a haven. 'David is a fine young man. Like me, he senses the badness in Jack.'

'Ah! So you do think he's bad then?'

'Maybe "bad" isn't the right word. I don't know.' She tried to rationalise her suspicions. 'All I do know is he makes me feel uncomfortable, as though he's waiting ... keeping secrets.'

'He seems to have an eye for Cathy. That spells trouble.'

Margaret nodded. It was uncanny how the old lady could read her thoughts. So many answers raged through her mind in that moment, but all she said was, 'I wish he hadn't come into our lives.'

Nan leaned back in her chair and began softly humming that lilting lullaby, her thoughts reaching back over the years. It was a long moment before she spoke again. 'Life is a trial,' she said softly. 'Sometimes we have to do things we're ashamed of.' She lowered her gaze to the floor and was silent a moment longer. Presently she declared in a brighter tone, 'But you mustn't be too concerned, because Cathy will be fine.' Her face set and her hands, which were resting in her lap, clenched into fists. 'I would never let anything harm either you or the child,' she said grimly.

Momentarily taken aback by the old lady's manner, Margaret was lost for a reply. Laughter from outside caused her to peer through the window to see David and Cathy flicking water at each other. 'Look at them, Nan,' she urged. 'I know they're very young, and still have a lifetime of experience to be lived, but if ever two people were made for each other, it's those two.' There was something beautiful about their relationship. She had seen it time and again, and it never failed to move her.

'If the hearts are together, age doesn't matter,' the old lady murmured. 'But a bad marriage can ruin your life forever.' All the awful memories came rushing back, overwhelming her. Should she tell Margaret? Could she bring herself to say: 'I am the mother who walked out on you all those years ago?' Margaret would be shocked. It could mean the end of their relationship. She couldn't risk it. For now, at least, she must keep her secret close. One day her daughter would know. They would *all* know. Until then, she had to keep them safe, protect Margaret and Cathy from events that might overtake them.

Cathy sat on the edge of the trough, her collar turned up about her ears and her hands thrust deep into her pockets. She watched David lift the second bucket. 'I don't want to go in yet,' she said. 'I want to stay with you a while longer.' She was always happiest in his company.

'Aren't you cold?' David swung the bucket on to the ground and sat beside her. Pulling her two hands into his, he rubbed them with his own. 'Your hands are like frogs' backs,' he said.

She loved the feel of his hands on hers. She smiled up at him and in his dark eyes could see a reflection of herself. It made her feel closer to him somehow. 'I'm glad you're here,' she said. 'You made Nan's party even more special.'

He looked into that sweet uplifted face with its heart shape and stunning green eyes, and trembled inside. She made him feel like a man, creating emotions in him that left him shaken. 'Do you ever think about the future?' he asked softly.

His hands lay still and warm over hers. Whenever he was near she could think about nothing but him. Yet there were times like now when the intensity of her own emotions confused her. Bending her head she stared into the bottom of the trough, where the spilled water lay blackly. It looked dark and deep and she couldn't see through it. That was how she felt about her future. 'That isn't up to me,' she said in a small voice. Suddenly he had made her sad.

'If it was up to me, I'd carry you away and spend my life making you happy.' He felt her hands trembling in his and loved her more than she could ever know.

'What a lovely thing to say.' Her eyes sparkled with pleasure as she brought her gaze up to his handsome face. 'Would you really want to spend your whole life with me?' The prospect excited her.

'Every minute of every day.' He stroked her face. 'Do you know what I mean?'

Her response thrilled him. 'I feel the same as you.'

467

'Do you like being with *him*?' His expression darkened as he glanced towards the house.

'Do you mean Jack?'

'That isn't his real name, is it?'

'I'm not sure.'

'Who is he, Cathy? I mean . . . where does he come from?'

She studied David's face, wishing she could put his mind at rest. 'You don't like Jack, do you?'

Evading her question, he remarked, 'You're shivering. I think we'd best go in.'

'I'm not ready to go in yet. Besides, you didn't answer my question.'

'I won't lie. The truth is, no, I don't like him.' He put one hand on the handle of a bucket, preparing to lift it. 'Now are you ready to go in?'

She grinned and squeezed his free hand. 'You're not jealous, are you?' she teased.

'A little, I suppose.'

'Oh, David! That's silly. I feel sorry for him. He has no family but us, and sometimes he's very lonely.'

'*He* told you that, did he?' There was resentment in his voice.

'It would be nice if we could all be friends.' All afternoon Cathy had sensed the distrust between these two and it was painful to her. 'Won't you please try?'

'If that's what you really want.' How could he refuse her?

Her answer was to snuggle up to him. 'I love you,' she whispered.

It was on the tip of his tongue to ask in what way did she love him? But the time wasn't right yet, and it was enough for him to know that she cared. He had often argued with himself that they were too young for real love, yet what he felt for Cathy burned in him day and night. There had been a time when he felt as she did, when he could say he loved her and think nothing more of it. But that day was long gone, vanished with his childhood. All he could hope was that the same thing would happen with Cathy; that one day she would wake and realise she could not face life without him. In his heart he knew this moment was not too far away. And he could wait. If it was for Cathy, he could wait for ever. He must be patient, bide his time, and all would be well.

Jack's calling voice interrupted his thoughts. 'Cathy! It's time we were going.' He sauntered up to them. 'Are you ready?' He stared at David. 'You shouldn't have kept her out so long. Can't you see she's freezing?'

'He didn't keep me out,' Cathy corrected him. 'I wasn't ready to go in yet.'

Grabbing up both buckets, David looked Jack straight in the eye. 'Since when have you been Cathy's keeper anyway?' he said angrily. Already he was regretting the promise he'd made. He could never be friends with this sly fellow.

'What's a brother for?' came the arrogant reply.

'Don't argue, you two.' Fearing a confrontation, Cathy stepped between them. 'We'd better get back. I expect Margaret will be wondering where we are.' Turning to David she said, 'The buckets must be heavy, filled to the brim. Jack can carry one.' In fact she was disappointed he hadn't already offered.

Jack seemed taken aback by her remark. The last thing he wanted to do was to carry a bucket filled with freezing cold water. On the other hand, he was determined to make a good impression in front of Cathy. More than that, he intended to make David look like a fool. 'Only be too pleased,' he scoffed. 'After all, we can't let poor David carry them both, now can we?' With a deliberately rough action, he wrenched at the bucket. David was taken unawares, and Cathy cried out as a deluge of cold water drenched her legs and feet.

Secretly delighted, Jack made a show of being outraged that such a thing could have happened. 'You did that on purpose!' he yelled, throwing himself at David and lashing out with his fists.

Taken by surprise, David staggered backwards, dropping the buckets and trying to fend off Jack at the same time. The water spilled out over the ground and soon the two of them were rolling about in the mud.

'Stop it!' Cathy tried to intervene, but they were hell-bent on hurting each other. Going like the wind, she ran into the cottage where Margaret and the old lady were deep in conversation. 'They're fighting!' she cried. 'David and Jack are fighting.'

At first there was no stopping them. Locked together in hatred, they drove into each other with clenched fists. 'You need to be taught a lesson!' Jack cried, at the same time kicking out with his feet and catching David hard in the stomach. 'Living on the streets teaches a fellow how to handle himself,' he gloated when David reeled back in pain. His triumphant cry turned to agony as David lifted him off his feet by the scruff of his neck and slammed him effortlessly into the side of the cottage.

'That's enough!' Rushing over, Margaret pressed her hands into David's chest. It was like holding back a bull elephant. 'I know how you feel,' she whispered. 'But he's not worth it.'

Behind them, Jack had recovered enough to snatch up a large piece of timber, and was silently creeping up on the unsuspecting pair. Raising his arm to strike, he would have brought the timber down on David's head. But just in time Margaret spun round and caught him in the act. 'Shame on you!' she snapped. 'What kind of coward are you?'

David eyed him with contempt. 'The worst kind,' he answered. His dark eyes sought Cathy, who had defied the old lady and come rushing from the cottage. A fond look passed between them before he turned back to Margaret. 'He's a bad 'un,' he warned. 'And if I were you, I'd watch him closely.' Without another word, he strode away, his blood boiling with rage.

Rita was ashamed when Jack returned home with a bloody nose and his clothes caked in mud. 'Why did you let him do that to you?' she demanded.

'If he hadn't run off, I'd have laid him out!'

All the way home, Jack boasted about how he could have beaten David to a pulp. 'If you hadn't stopped me, I'd have taught him a real lesson,' he told Margaret. His bragging made no impact on her, other than making her see him for the despicable character he was.

Cathy remained silent until they reached the back door of the house, where she told the astonished Ruby, 'He picked a fight with David.'

'Good God above!' Ruby declared, stifling her giggles. 'I'm surprised he's still walking upright.'

Now he was washed and changed, and standing before Rita. 'You'd best go to your room and don't come down until breakfast,' she decided. Later that evening she told Margaret, 'If Frank was to find out about this, he'd throw the Leyton family out on their ear.' She was in a dilemma, and too involved with Owen for such a thing to happen.

'Anybody would think you actually cared what happened to them.' Margaret eyed her suspiciously. 'I should have thought it suited you to have them thrown out?'

'So it would.' Regretting her earlier remark, Rita chose her words carefully. 'But in *my* good time, not theirs.' Turning away, she smiled at her little secret. Once she and Owen had carefully laid their plans, he would be leaving the area anyway. What happened to the rest of his family was no concern of hers.

'So you agree that Frank should not be told about the incident?' Margaret had argued for that since arriving home. She never imagined that Rita would be so easily convinced.

'In this instance, yes, I think it would be wisest to say nothing.'

'I see.' She didn't 'see' at all, but was thankful for small mercies. 'I'll speak to all concerned and make sure they understand that.' Not wishing to stay in Rita's company any longer than was necessary, Margaret took her leave. She was relieved that Frank was not to be told. On the other hand, she couldn't help but wonder at Rita's peculiar change of heart.

The following evening, two things happened that gave Margaret even more food for thought. She and Cathy had gone to the Leyton house where Teresa answered the door. 'What do you want?' Surly as usual, she obviously had no intention of letting them in.

'I would like to speak with your mother about the fight between the two young men.' Margaret felt she needed to apologise on behalf of Jack. After all, he was now a Blackthorn in all but blood. She'd suggested he should make his own apologies but, true to form, he had merely laughed at the idea.

'I knew you'd be here.' Teresa glared at her. 'I warned our mam that David would get the blame.' Giving Margaret no time to explain, she went on, 'I was right an' all. Well, you can clear off. We don't want you here. Mam don't want you visiting, and David don't want no more reading lessons from *her*.' Staring at Cathy, she was pleased when her words seemed to wound.

'You're wrong.' Margaret had half expected Maria to be unnerved by the incident and was anxious to put matters right. 'No one's blaming David. In fact, I've come here to apologise.'

'I've just told you. We don't want your sort round here any more.'

'If that's what your mother wants, then of course I'll leave and won't intrude again.' She stared the girl out. 'But I would rather hear it from her.'

With a half-smile, the girl pushed open the door. Keeping a wily gaze on Cathy, she yelled into the house, 'Mam ... it's the Blackthorn woman and the girl. Tell 'em what you told me.'

The voice was shaky, but unmistakably that of Maria Leyton. 'Go away!' she called out. 'Teresa's right. You lot up at the house have too much over us.'

'Satisfied?' Closing the door, Teresa couldn't hide her delight. 'We don't want none of you here.' Casting a dark look in Cathy's direction, she told her, 'Especially you. You've caused our David enough trouble.'

'Is he here?' Cathy was only concerned that she might never see David again.

'No, he's not. And even if he was, he would only tell you what I'm telling you now. He doesn't want nothing more to do with you lot.' When she realised her words were getting through at last, she drove the point home with a softer voice. 'I'm really sorry, but that's what he said, and after what happened, you can't really blame him, can you?'

Dejected, the two of them made their way back to Blackthorn House. 'She's right, you know,' Margaret mused aloud. 'You *can't* really blame them for not wanting us in their home. Maria Leyton has always been a little nervous about us visiting, but she needed help when she was ill, and when you started teaching David to read and write, she was so proud ... she didn't have the heart to put a stop to it.' She gave a little smile. 'I know how fond you are of David,' she said kindly, 'but we have to abide by their wishes.'

'I wish Jack hadn't caused all that trouble.' Cathy's heart felt like a lead weight inside her; especially now, when she truly realised how much David meant to her.

'It seems he has a way of causing trouble.' Margaret had tried but could not feel any affection for Frank's protégé. Not wanting to transmit her true feelings to Cathy, she said brightly, 'Still, I expect your father will soon be packing him off to some fancy school, and we'll see less of him.'

'I wouldn't like to be packed off.' In spite of her mother's indifference and her father's neglect of her, Cathy would never want to be too far from Margaret. And the idea of leaving David behind was unthinkable.

'You're not likely to be packed off, sweetheart,' Margaret assured her. 'It's different with young men though . . . important for them to be well educated in all subjects. Like it or not, women don't command the same importance.'

Cathy's thoughts strayed. 'Do you think David will avoid me now?'

'I honestly don't know.' She sensed the girl's pain, but had no way of easing it. 'David doesn't seem like a young man who would bear a grudge, though of course his mother may have given him an ultimatum.' Taking hold of Cathy's hand, she urged her on with the encouraging words, 'If he wants to remain close to you, I'm sure he'll find a way. You'll just have to wait and see.'

Teresa rubbed her hands at the fire. 'It's bitter cold out there,' she said. 'Our David should have got more logs in before he and Dad went across the fields.' She took another log from the laden basket and thrust it into the flames.

Maria rocked back and forth in her chair, all the while regarding the girl through narrowed eyes. 'The lad filled the basket to bursting,' she replied sharply. 'There's enough to keep us warm till they come home.'

Pleased with herself, Teresa seated herself opposite her mother. 'I sent 'em packing, didn't I?'

'Aye. Yer did that right enough.' She studied the girl closely. Teresa was a handsome young woman, and Maria should have been proud. But there was a terrible hardness about her daughter, a bitterness beyond her years. 'Enjoyed it an' all, didn't yer, eh?'

'I only said what you told me.'

'You had no right to speak for David.'

'And he has no right making eyes at the landlord's brat!' She leaned forward, her blue eyes bold as she demanded, 'You won't tell him, will you?'

'Serve you right if I did. What! He'd skin yer alive if he knew yer'd sent that nice young lass packing.' She liked Cathy. In fact she owed the girl a great deal, because hadn't she taught her

473

son to read and write? Maria sighed heavily, lowering her gaze to stare into the flames. 'Still. Happen it's just as well you've driven a wedge between her and David. He's grown too fond of her by half.' David was a sincere young man, and he would never easily commit his affections. These past months, though, she'd seen her son and Cathy growing closer, and to her regret had ignored the danger signs. 'Don't worry,' she told the anxious girl, 'I'll not tell him. If he doesn't see the Blackthorn lass again, it'll suit me just fine.'

'I can't understand why you ever had them here in the first place.'

'They were good to this family, and don't you ever forget that.'

'Then why did you turn them away?'

Impatient now, Maria snapped, 'Enough questions! There's work to do about the house ... the chickens want feeding and there's room for a few more logs in that basket. Get on with it.'

Sulking, Teresa sprang out of the chair and slammed the back door as she went out.

'Yer surly little bugger!' Maria's voice sailed after her. When only silence greeted her, she fell back into the chair, filled with regrets at having turned friends away from her door. Getting out of the chair, she went to the window. In the far distance two small figures could be seen going in the direction of Blackthorn House. 'It were a bad way to repay you for all your kindness,' she murmured sadly. 'But it's all for the best.' When a chilling breeze found its way in through the old window frames, she drew her shawl tight about her. 'It ain't your fault,' she said. 'It's *his*.' Her expression grew sad. 'Some women have lazy husbands ... others have them as gamble away their money. Me? I've got one that can't keep his hands off other women!'

She returned to her chair and rocked silently for a while, weighing the consequences of things. 'You're a fool, Owen Leyton,' she growled. 'Do you think I haven't known when you've bedded other women? I've known every time, and kept me peace 'cause I knew yer'd allus come back to me once yer'd had yer fun. But this time?' She pondered awhile. 'This time I'm frightened. Yer've picked a rotten apple outta the barrel an' it's sticking to yer fingers. *You're* the reason I've sent two good friends away.' She shook her head forlornly. 'Being Blackthorns is the only crime them two have committed.'

She stared towards the sideboard, at a photograph of her and her husband on their wedding day. 'I turned them away, an' it ain't their fault. It's yours, yer bloody fool! *Your* fault. Yer brewing up more trouble than you can handle, an' if I'm not careful we shall *all* be dragged under!'

She'd been angry, then afraid. Now a little smile brightened her face. 'You've had your fun, an' it don't matter to you who suffers for it. But it won't be me and the young 'uns, I can tell yer that. Not if I have *my* way, it won't.'

'Goodbye, Mr Blackthorn. Have a pleasant journey, sir.' The hotel clerk handed over the receipt, his smile becoming a frown when Frank returned only the smallest coin for his trouble.

The porter led Frank out into the night. It had rained all day, but now the air was calm and the sky speckled with stars. 'Right you are then, guv.' Throwing Frank's portmanteau in beside him, the porter held out his hand, astonished when he received twice the tip given to the clerk. 'Gawd bless yer!' he said, reverently touching his cap as the cab pulled away. 'Though yer might have found an extra sixpence if yer'd dug a bit deeper!'

At King's Cross station Frank checked the timetable, cursing when he realised he had just missed the eight o'clock train for Blackburn. 'You've a fair old wait 'til the next one,' he was told. 'The tea-bar's open though, and they do a tasty bacon sarnie.' The ticket clerk grinned like a Cheshire cat. 'An' I should know, 'cause it's my old woman as makes 'em.'

Tired, and with his head still aching from the meeting with his accountant, Frank picked up his case and trudged along the platform. The clerk was wrong. The tea-bar was closed. 'Hmph! His missus obviously doesn't tell him everything,' he groaned.

Whether it was the prospect of a tasty bacon sarnie or a refreshing cup of tea, Frank couldn't tell, but he was suddenly stricken with the need for refreshment. Realising he had time to kill, he decided to go back to the streets in search of a public house or a café of sorts.

Half a mile from King's Cross station, he found what looked like a respectable public house. Inside it was warm and cosy, and a few minutes after giving his order he was seated at a table. In no time at all he was brought a meat pie and a jug of ale with a deep measure of froth on top. 'That should warm the cockles of yer 'eart,' the waitress laughed. She said exactly the same ten minutes later, when Frank ordered a second helping.

Halfway through his second jug of ale, he was convinced someone was watching him. When he glanced up, his heart stood still. Some short distance away, a couple stood by the bar: the man was a big burly fellow with a shock of red hair and a loud mouth; the woman with him was a pretty little thing, with long brown hair and big sad eyes. She was looking straight at him! He knew her at once. How could he forget?

Flustered, he grabbed his case and fled into the night. The woman followed him. 'I only have to raise my finger and he'll tear you apart,' she threatened.

Instinctively drawing her into the shadows, Frank gave his own warning. 'If he knew the truth, it would be *you* he'd tear apart.'

'What makes you think he doesn't know?'

In spite of her bravado he knew she was lying. 'Because if he did, you wouldn't be here to tell the tale.'

She had no reply to that, except to hang her head in shame.

'So! You haven't told him. I knew you'd have more sense.' It was the first time he had come face to face with the man, and he didn't particularly like what he saw. 'He's an uncouth sort. You deserve better than him,' he remarked kindly.

'Who then?' Her sad eyes mocked him. 'You, maybe? Do I deserve *you*?'

He looked at the ground, absent-mindedly studying the puddles which had gathered in the cracks between flagstones. He couldn't answer. She should have known better than to ask such a thing.

Sensing his embarrassment, she laughed gently. 'After all this time, it hasn't changed, has it? I'll never be good enough for you, will I? Even if I was you'd never leave that wife o' yourn . . . tied to her for life, ain't you?' She looked into his face. She didn't hate him. She didn't even know him all that well, but in spite of everything, she believed he was a good man. 'By! I've never known a man so besotted with his own wife.'

'You knew that all along. I never kept the truth from you.'

'No, you didn't,' she admitted. 'You turned my life upside down. But you never lied to me.'

'If it's money you want . . .?'

'No, it ain't money, Frank.' She raised her eyes to the dark sky and gave a sigh that sent a shiver through him. 'Though God knows he spends it faster than I can earn it.' Inclining her head to one side, she glanced meaningfully towards the public house.

Frank was horrified. 'Are you telling me he's spent all the money I gave you?'

Her sad eyes looked him up and down as though she was seeing him for the first time. 'You've got a short memory, Frank,' she chided. 'You didn't *give* me anything.' The impact of what she'd said struck her as being ironic. 'Well . . . apart from the boy. You gave me him sure enough!' Her blue eyes hardened. 'Then you took him away.' Her voice broke. 'That was cruel, Frank. Oh, it was so cruel.'

'It was all meant to be, can't you see that?'

'No, I can't.' In the cold of the evening, she trembled a little. Recalling something he had told her in one unguarded moment, she thought to use it for her own ends. 'You have a daughter . . . Cathy, isn't it?'

He seemed surprised she should remember that much about him. 'What of it?'

'Have you considered her? If you mean the boy to have your name, won't he be able to take everything that should rightfully be hers?'

'Every man needs a son. What use is a daughter?' Only now did he fully realise the contempt he felt for Cathy.

'Don't punish me for one mistake,' she pleaded. 'It was only one night, Frank . . . just one night. He'd thrown me out, and you were so kind.'

'I was *drunk*! That's what I was.' Disgusted with himself, he spat the words out. 'Rita and I were going through a really bad patch and I felt lonely.' He groaned at the memory. 'God Almighty! If she should ever find out what happened, I'd lose her forever. I couldn't bear that.'

'What if I was to tell her?'

Grabbing her by the wrist, he made her cry out. 'You do that and I'll make sure your man in there knows every detail of that night ... how we made a child ... how you gave birth to a boy he thought was his. What would he say, I wonder, if he knew how you came to me for money soon after the boy was born? We made an agreement, you and I.'

'I should never have promised you the boy.' She was crying now.

'But you *did*! And I paid you a handsome sum twice over. Then you ran out on me. I searched high and low and it was as though you'd vanished from the face of the earth.' He took a deep breath, a sigh of satisfaction. 'No doubt you cursed the fate that made the boy pick my pocket ... his own father's pocket.'

'Yes, I curse that night. And I curse ever having come to the police station. I should have let him take the consequences of his own action. Instead of that, I rushed to help him.' She shook her head and rolled her eyes in anguish. 'You could have knocked me down when I saw the "kindly gentleman" who was reluctant to press charges.'

'I was even more shocked when it was you who turned up to collect the boy. It was very wise of you not to block my generous gesture of offering him a good home. If you'd gone against me, I would have pressed charges and had him locked away for a very long time.' He regarded her with a deal of admiration. 'I must say you behaved very well in front of the officers present . . . never once letting the truth be known.' An unpleasant thought occurred to him. 'When you and the boy were allowed a minute together, you didn't tell him he was my son, did you?'

'I'm not altogether stupid.' She glanced nervously towards the public house. 'All these years that brute in there believed the boy to be his. If he knew I'd slept with another man ... that he'd raised one of the gentry's kids.' She closed her eyes in anguish. 'You don't know him, Frank. He can be murderous.' There were tears in her eyes. 'The boy's run away before when they've rowed, so he's not suspicious.' A shadow washed over her face. 'But he's never stayed away too long, you see.' She appealed to Frank's good nature. 'I want the boy back. He's my only comfort.' His silence made her bold enough to threaten him one more time. 'I'm sure if your wife knew how the boy was got, he'd be shown the door right enough.' She trembled again, but this time it wasn't the cold that got to her, it was fear. Fear of the man she had deceived for so long. 'And if you should tell *him* . . .' Her round blue eyes stared defiantly. 'I suppose I could always take the boy where he'll never find us.'

'*I'll* find you though.' In the darkness his eyes glinted like broken glass. He was a gentle soul but when it came to the threat of losing Rita, he was prepared to do anything . . . even murder. He sensed her horror and forced himself to smile. 'Be sensible, my dear. And besides, what makes you think the boy would come with you?'

She had to be careful because he had no inkling that she had already been to his house, seeking to lure the boy home. His harsh words still haunted her dreams. 'He'd have no choice if he was thrown out.'

'I advise you to forget the whole idea.' His voice was cold as the night. 'The boy is my son . . . all my wife and I have ever craved. I really couldn't allow you to ruin everything.' Digging into his pocket, he withdrew a wallet. 'What will it take for you to forget he ever existed?'

She lashed out with her fist, sending the wallet flying to the pavement. 'I've told you! I don't want your filthy money!'

'What the bleedin' 'ell's going on?' The burly fellow had come in search of his mate. Unsteady from the booze, he studied the situation before squaring himself up to Frank. 'Why was this bastard offering you money?' Giving Frank a hefty push that sent him staggering back against the wall, he demanded, 'There's summat funny going on 'ere. What's your game, matey?' He drew a knife from his pocket and held it to Frank's throat. 'Out with it! Why were you offering my good woman money?'

'Leave him be!' Desperately afraid the truth might come out, she got between them. 'He was mistaken, that's all. The poor sod thought I was a prostitute.'

Far from calming him, her words appeared to enrage him. Swinging round, he caught her by the hair, twisting it over and over in his fist until she screamed for mercy. 'Thought you were a prostitute, eh?' he sneered. 'Why would he think that?' His face was almost touching hers, his bloodshot eyeballs protruding from his head as he shook her like a rag doll. 'A man ain't likely to think a woman's a prostitute unless she gives him good cause. Is that what you did, you bitch? Did you give him good cause?' Raising his fist he brought it crashing down into the woman's face. 'Slag! Answer me! What made this bastard think you were a prostitute?'

'I don't know!' Kicking out with her foot, she tried desperately to throw him off balance. There was a fierce scuffle and the two of them fell to the ground. In the awful silence that followed, the woman stirred beneath the burly fellow, her sad blue eyes turned towards Frank. 'Make a little gentleman of him,' she whispered. Her head lolled to one side, she gave a sad smile and all was silent.

Stunned, Frank remained like a statue, unable to take his gaze from her face. A tiny trickle of blood oozed from her neck and dripped to the pavement. 'God above!' He couldn't believe what his own eyes told him. 'You've killed her!'

The burly fellow lay beside his woman, his head bleeding where it had come into contact with the wall. Barely conscious and groaning in pain, he made a valiant effort to stand up. But his strength gave out and he fell back with a thud.

While Frank made good his escape, a group of men came out of the public house. There was a cry of 'Murder!' and the sound of running footsteps. Frank didn't look back. 'I've done nothing wrong,' he told himself, and by the time he arrived at Blackburn station he was totally convinced it had all been a tragic nightmare.

CHAPTER FIVE

The small headline caught his attention and he froze:

WOMAN STABBED IN LONDON STREET

The account told of a lover's tiff, describing how the woman had been taken to hospital, where she remained in a very serious condition... 'not expected to survive'. The man with her was arrested and charged with the attack. His claim that another man was involved was being investigated but, according to witnesses who arrived on the scene before police, there was no sign of this other man. Another witness who knew the couple said this was not the first time the woman had been subjected to a violent attack by her husband.

'Thank God nobody saw me!' Tearing the newspaper into shreds, Frank stuffed it into his wastepaper basket. 'Cancel all newspapers from today,' he told Ruby at breakfast. 'They're an unnecessary expense.' He smiled at Jack across the table. 'Now that we've found you a suitable tutor, we mustn't waste money. Isn't that so, son?' He frowned, dabbing at his mouth with the napkin and seeming suddenly irritable. 'Though why you don't want to attend a fine school like Harlington, I will never know.'

'I would rather stay here with you and Mother.' Jack was wily. Here he could keep an eye on things and, more importantly, worm his way deeper into the Blackthorns' affections. He wasn't satisfied to share things with Cathy. He wanted it all.

Frank beamed with pride. Looking at Rita, he announced, 'Aren't you pleased, my dear? The boy would rather stay here with us. Why! I might have saved myself the bother of going to London after all.' He grew agitated. 'Rita dear ... you haven't heard a word that's been said. Is anything the matter?'

Fearing he might come and actually put his big paws on her, she made herself smile. 'I heard every word,' she lied.

'And don't you agree, the boy is a treasure?'

'He is.' She bestowed a half smile on Jack. Lately she had lost all interest in him, not caring whether he went or stayed. In fact she cared for nothing but Owen and being with him for all time. Frank's interruption into her thoughts aggravated her. She felt unwell, acutely aware of the child growing inside her. Her nights were sleepless and she had been sick every morning for a week. Her only consolation was knowing that Owen was making plans for them to be together, and that at long last she would have a son of her own.

'The boy is quite the little gentleman now, wouldn't you say?' Frank insisted. 'Not at all like the wild thing that first burst into this dining room.' He laughed at the memory.

Glowering at Cathy, who had remained silent throughout, Rita answered deliberately, 'I believe he could teach the girl a few social graces.'

'How do you mean?' Up until then Frank had hardly noticed Cathy. He noticed her now and, like his wife, stared disapprovingly at her.

'Can't you see?' Pointing to Cathy's full plate, she said angrily, 'Good food . . . all wasted!'

It didn't matter to Frank whether Cathy had eaten her meal or not but he felt duty bound to chastise her. 'Really, young lady! I've only this minute explained to Jack that we should not waste money, and here you are, turning your nose up at Ruby's excellent food.' Leaning over the table he demanded, 'What have you to say for yourself, eh?'

Cathy had very little to say for herself, except, 'Sorry, Father. I'm not hungry.'

'Hmph! Sorry indeed. I should think so too.' He glanced at his wife, who was stony-faced. 'You've managed to offend your mother yet again,' he complained angrily. 'Leave the table this instant.'

As Cathy left the room, Margaret also excused herself. 'I have a great deal to do,' she said. In fact the truth was that these past few days since Jack had been taken out of her care, she had more time to call her own.

Cathy made straight for the kitchen, where Ruby was having a welcome cup of tea while she waited for the family to finish their meal. 'I'm sorry I didn't eat anything,' she told the homely soul. Sitting down at the big pine table she looked very lonely.

Ruby felt cheered at the sight of her. 'Aw, lass, yer don't have to apologise for not eating what I cook,' she gently chided. 'There's plenty folk round here who'll be glad of a few titbits.' Pointing to a large white bowl covered with muslin, she explained. 'There's bacon strips and plump sausages in there ... all left over from yesterday.' Wiping her hands on her pinnie, she poured out another cup of tea. 'There! I'm sure you can manage that,' she said with a grin.

Taking up the cup, Cathy took a big sip. 'Thank you, Ruby.' She looked at the white bowl. 'What will you do with the bacon and sausages?'

'I shan't throw it in the midden, that's for sure,' Ruby declared, shaking her head indignantly and sinking her chin into her neck. 'Not while there's worse off than you and me. No indeed. Them's for the coalman. It's his day today, and he's got six childer who'll polish that lot off afore you can see the whites of their eyes.' She chuckled. 'They shall have a deal more an' all,' she promised.

Margaret had been concerned when she couldn't find Cathy upstairs in her room. 'Here you are,' she said, 'I've been looking everywhere for you.'

'The lass is having a cup o' tea.' Ruby quickly poured another from the big brown teapot. 'Sit yourself down, Miss,' she invited, pushing the teacup and saucer across the table. 'If you'll excuse me, I'd better go and see if they've finished.' With that she bustled away to see what was left for the coalman's brood.

Cathy was so quiet that Margaret was prompted to ask, 'Are you ill?'

'No.'

'What then?'

'I'm frightened.'

'Whatever do you mean?'

Cathy shrugged her shoulders. How could she explain to Margaret when she didn't even understand it herself? Lately, all manner of feelings had plagued her. 'Everything's changing,' she admitted sadly. 'Jack's going to a new tutor. Mother doesn't talk to me at all any more except to rant and rave, and David's turned his back on me.' That was the hardest of all.

Without a word, Margaret took the girl in her arms. For a few precious minutes they stayed like that, shutting out the world. Presently, Margaret told her, 'Some things *have* changed, sweetheart. The world turns and things are bound to change. But some things remain the same. *I* haven't changed, and neither has Ruby. More than that, I really don't believe David has turned his back on you.'

'Why hasn't he been in touch then?' Teresa's words had cut deep. Even now Cathy believed them to have come from David himself. 'Why doesn't he wait by the stile like he used to?'

'I don't know for sure.' Margaret, too, had noticed how David was never at the stile when she and Cathy went on their frequent walks. 'Oh, I'm not saying he isn't angry about what happened with Jack. And I'm not saying he isn't just the teeniest bit jealous. On the other hand, he might be taking time to think about what happened . . . to assess his relationship with this family. Then, of course, we have to remember he may be under pressure from his mother to keep a distance. Or it could be because of work. After all, there's the late potato crop to be got in and taken to market . . . cabbages and brussels to be set. And after that, the land needs to be got ready for the next planting. When you realise there's only David and his father to do the work, it's not too surprising if he can't find the time for anything else.'

Cathy's spirits lightened. 'Do you think he'll get in touch when all the work's done?'

'I shouldn't be at all surprised.'

When Ruby came back, loaded with plates and dishes, Cathy offered to help her. 'My! You've cheered up an' no mistake,' she exclaimed. A few minutes later, she chased the two of them out of her kitchen. 'So I can get on with me duties, you understand,' she declared, blushing pleasantly when Cathy treated her to a big hug.

At twelve noon, after she had finished her lessons, Cathy accompanied Margaret to the drapers. The November day was bitter cold, so the two of them wrapped up well; Cathy in her ankle-length blue coat and matching beret, and Margaret in a brown cape with a hood. 'I don't intend to stay out long today,' she said. The sky was heavy with the threat of snow, and the icy wind cut right through a body's bones.

Teresa was just coming out of the butcher's. She would have gone on without speaking, but Margaret wanted to know, 'How is your mother?'

'She's all right.' As usual, Teresa was scowling. The threadbare coat she wore was no protection against the cold. 'We're *all* well,' she insisted.

'And David?' Margaret asked only for Cathy's sake. 'Is he still angry?'

'No. He ain't angry. But he don't want nothing to do with any of you.' She eyed Cathy with hidden malice. 'In fact, he said if I saw you, I was to say how he was very sorry about what happened. But it were only to be expected, and it's best if he don't have no more truck with you.'

'He really said *that*?' For Cathy's sake, Margaret had hoped there would be something left of the friendship between them. Now, though, it seemed David had chosen to sever all ties.

'I've just told you.' Teresa had seen how Cathy's face clouded over with disappointment, and she was in her element. 'Our mam was sick with worry when David told her he'd been fighting with the lad from Blackthorn House. She were convinced we'd be thrown out. The fact that we only got a warning letter from Mr Blackthorn himself don't make no difference. Next time it could be notice to quit. David should never have let himself get caught up in a fight with a Blackthorn. Not when they own the very roof over our heads! He knows his mistake now, and he has to put his own family first.' She glanced at Cathy. 'You do understand that, don't you?'

In spite of everything, she tried to understand. 'It was as much my fault as David's,' she said. 'But, yes, I do understand, and I'm sorry.' She was more than that. She was devastated.

'Should I go and see him?' she asked Margaret on the way back.

'No, sweetheart. I imagine David must have thought long and hard before coming to his decision, and however much it hurts, I want you to promise you'll abide by it.'

485

'I will,' Cathy murmured. As she looked up she was smiling. But the thought of never seeing David again, never sitting on the bank of the river with him, never laughing together or sharing little secrets, weighed heavy on her young heart.

Teresa chuckled all the way home. She was still chuckling when she passed the big barn. David saw her and came out. 'Have you been to the shops?' he asked. He had been mending the tractor and was covered in grease.

'What's it to you?'

'I just wondered, that's all.' Cathy was never out of his mind.

'What you mean is, did I see any of the Blackthorns?'

'Well, did you?'

'I saw the one who used to visit our mam.' She paused, making him suffer. 'She had the girl with her.'

'*Cathy*!' He could hardly contain himself. 'Did you speak to her?'

'I wasn't going to, but she spoke to me.'

'What did she say?'

'Only that you'd caused a lot of trouble by fighting with that other one. She said you should be ashamed, and hoped you would never speak to her again.' She delivered the torrent of lies without any sense of shame, or even the slightest tremor in her voice. She even feigned sympathy. 'I know I didn't always see eye to eye with you about the Blackthorns coming here,' she said softly, 'but I know how you liked the girl, and I'm really sorry.'

Turning away, he felt a great anger rising in him. 'Happen I should have known better,' he said harshly. If Cathy could throw aside their friendship just like that, maybe he'd been a fool all along. Telling himself that didn't help though. He still loved her. Whatever she did and however much distance she put between them, he would always love her.

CHAPTER SIX

Cathy loved the snow. For six days now it had poured relentlessly from the skies. She and Margaret had built four wonderful snowmen; there was one with a twisted nose and a loose mouth dressed with a twig for a cigar, another merry-faced, round-bellied fellow wearing one of Frank's discarded waistcoats and a pair of furry mittens, a third lumpy character who had fallen all to one side and resembled a drunk. And the latest, created on this Friday morning, and Cathy's favourite: small and chubby, with a toothless grin and bright round eyes made of black coal. It was dressed in one of Ruby's old shawls. On its head it wore a vivid pink home-made turban tied with an extravagant bow; Cathy had stuck various bits of bracken all round the edges of the turban, giving the illusion of a full head of hair beneath. The result was almost lifelike. 'By! You've used me for a model without me knowing,' Ruby chuckled. When she saw the three snowmen and one snowwoman all lined up outside the back door like visitors waiting to be let in, she screeched with feigned horror. 'It's no use you scraggy lot thinking yer can sit at my table, 'cause I'm particular who sits in my chairs. Be off!' Shaking the broom, she ran at them. 'Off with yer!' she yelled. 'Yer not getting in ol' Ruby's kitchen, an' that's a fact.'

She only stopped when Margaret and Cathy laughed out loud at her antics. 'Come away in, you two.' Breathless and full of fun, she gave her orders. 'Get in, I say. It's enough to freeze the nose off a parker out 'ere. I've a fresh brew o' tea made that'll warm yer blood rosy.'

'You two go in,' Margaret said. 'Thanks to Cathy dragging me outside, I still haven't put the school-books away.' She went one way and they went the other. 'Keep the tea hot, Ruby. I'll be along in a minute.'

Inside, sitting round the big friendly table, with her coat hanging over the hook in the kitchen door and the smell of meat pie emanating from the cooking range, Cathy felt warm and cosy. 'Did you ever make snowmen when you were young?' she asked Ruby, who was seated opposite. With her two hands wrapped round the cup Ruby had given her, she slowly sipped at the steaming hot tea, her face growing pinker by the minute.

'Did I make snowmen?' Ruby peered at her from beneath bushy eyebrows. 'Happen I did, and happen I didn't,' she said with a twinkle in her eye. 'It ain't one o' the things I recall most.'

Cathy grew curious. 'I can't imagine you being a girl,' she said truthfully.

'Well, I can promise you, I *were*!' Ruby winked, tossing her head with a little burst of pride. 'I weren't quite as pretty as yerself, mind. But I were slim and tidy, and I expect I did fancy meself just a bit.' She waited for the next question, and when it came it stunned her to silence.

'When you were my age, Ruby . . . did your mother and father love you?' Though she had wisely come to terms with her parents' indifference, it was something Cathy would never understand. Margaret had taught her to accept it, but it didn't make it any easier.

Ruby floundered. 'What a strange thing to say, child.' She knew well enough what Cathy meant, for wasn't it common knowledge in this household how Frank and Rita Blackthorn shamefully neglected their own daughter?

Lost in thought, Cathy spoke softly. 'I suppose they did love you, because parents *are* supposed to love their children, aren't they?' The whisper of a smile lit her features. 'When I had David I didn't mind so much. Now, I only have you and Margaret.'

'Aw, lass. You do miss that young fellow, don't you, eh?' Ruby chose not to comment on the disturbing subject of Cathy's parents. Lord knew they were a strange pair and, after all these years, she didn't understand them any better than Cathy did herself.

'David was special.'

'Ain't yer Aunt Margaret special?'

'Yes, but David was different.' She had often wondered about her feelings for him. 'I love Margaret more than I love my own parents.' She felt ashamed to admit such a thing, but was sure that Ruby would understand. 'With David, it was another kind of love, I think.'

'How do you mean, child?' Like Margaret, Ruby felt it was always best to let a niggling worry out into the open. She sensed that Cathy needed to talk, and so made time to listen. 'Is it because David and you are nearer each other's ages?'

Cathy thought on that. Feeling the need to put the record straight, she answered, 'No, it's more than that.'

'Hmh.' From what Ruby could tell, Cathy was in love. 'You're neither of you children any more, are you? What! When I were your age, I'd been in service for two years, and looking after the master's three young 'uns.' She shook her greying head at the memory. 'By! They were a handful an' no mistake.' Realising she had wandered off the point, she prompted, 'What were so special about David then?'

Cathy smiled and she was never more lovely. 'David seemed to know everything I was thinking,' she said. 'It was strange, Ruby ... but when I was with him, it was like there was no one else in the whole world.' Her voice broke a little and she bent her head to take a sip of her tea. Using the moment to compose herself, she continued, 'Now he doesn't want to talk to me any more.' Suddenly she was conscious of how she had opened her heart. She blushed deeply and her brighter smile would have fooled anyone who didn't know her.

Ruby studied Cathy's pretty face for a while, before saying smartly, 'Shall I tell you what *I* think?'

'I'd like that.' Having known Ruby all her young life, Cathy trusted her implicitly.

'*I* think he's a fool to turn his back on a darling like yerself ... especially when you've spent so much time teaching him to read and write an' all.'

'I really enjoyed doing that, Ruby, and you'd be surprised how quickly he learned.' Pride surged up in her. 'He was a natural scholar.' Being close to David, with their heads almost touching as they pored over the books, was a memory she would keep forever.

'Aye, well ... I reckon he couldn't have been the friend you thought he was. What's more, I believe he'll want you long afore you want him, an' that's a fact.' Taking the empty cups she walked over to the sink. 'Men can be so ungrateful, an' ain't it true that he's a man in the making?'

'Did you mean what you said? About him wanting me before I want him?'

Coming back to the table with a cloth to wipe the spills, Ruby affirmed, 'Well, o' course! It's allus the same, lass. These men go off at the deep end, then soon enough they realise their mistake.' While she spoke she flicked the cloth over the table top before ambling back to the sink. 'The trick is to let 'em get on with it.'

'I thought I might go and see him, but Margaret says I ought not to.'

'What! I should think not, lass.' Turning to look at Cathy through knowing old eyes, she said softly, 'You were a fine friend to David Leyton. Either he values you or he don't. An' if he don't, then you're best off without him.' With that she began peeling the vegetables, thinking of all her regrets. Still, she had known the love of good parents, while this lovely girl had been hurt time and again. She thought of how David had hurt her now, and had to have her say. 'No, lass. If David Leyton don't want yer near, then stay well away. That's my advice if yer want it.'

It was bitter advice. 'I'd better go. Thank you for the tea, Ruby.'

'Aw, yer welcome, lass.' When she smiled her old face crinkled into a thousand lines. 'Think of what I've said now. But don't go telling that Jack I've entertained yer in the kitchen, 'cause I don't want him sitting at me table.' She gave one of her cheeky winks. 'What's more he got a right ticking off from your mam while you were out making your snowmen. He's been sulking in his room ever since, an' as far as I'm concerned he can stay there, 'cause I don't want him fetching his sour face down here, an' that's a fact!' She didn't say it in so many words, but she had never cared for the boy.

Cathy was surprised. As a rule, Jack was in favour with her mother. 'Why was he told off?'

'Too much to say for himself as usual,' Ruby retorted. 'I don't know it all, but for some reason known only to herself, your mam seems to have taken against him ... wants him to go away to school after all, an' she's told your father the same.' Nodding her head in the direction of the door, she added softly, 'Yer mam and dad are in the study talking it over.'

'She really *likes* Jack.' Cathy was puzzled. 'Why would she want him to go away?'

'If you ask me, he's been getting above himself, that's why.' Ruby reminded herself to guard her tongue. Jack wasn't the only one Rita had been getting at lately. Only the other day she herself had got the length of Rita's tongue for nothing at all. 'If you ask me, I don't think yer mam's well.' She had seen the changes in Rita Blackthorn these past weeks. She had also been the one to clear up the morning sickness, and now she would stake her life on her mistress's being with child.

'What's wrong with her?' Cathy hadn't noticed anything. But then she was never allowed to stay in her mother's presence long enough to know whether she was ill or in the pink.

Ruby shrugged her shoulders. It was time to clam up, she thought. 'Don't ask me, lass,' she said innocently, 'I keep meself to meself, then I'm not likely to get in no bother.' Giving Cathy a sideways glance, she suggested, 'Happen it'd be best if you asked her yerself, eh? Now off you go, lass. Leave old Ruby to get on with her chores.'

On her way to the sitting room, Cathy paused outside her father's study. She could hear her parents, still arguing. On tiptoe she moved away.

Margaret bent to her work. 'Give me an hour,' she told Cathy. 'If I don't mark this work before dinner, I'll regret it later.' On seeing Cathy's thoughtful expression she put down her pen. 'What is it, sweetheart?'

'They're rowing ... about Jack.'

Margaret nodded. 'I know,' she said. 'But it's nothing for you to worry about. It's just a question of whether he is sent away to school or not.'

'But he doesn't want to go.'

'Your father doesn't want him to go either. Your mother does, and they can't agree on it.' Putting an arm round Cathy's shoulders, she advised, 'Whatever you or I say, they'll make

491

their own minds up on the matter.'

Cathy was angry. She had suffered her parents' neglect long enough to know how they could hurt others. 'They don't care about people's feelings,' she declared. Casting her gaze to the table she saw the pile of correspondence there. Having taken up enough of Margaret's time, she was mortally sorry to have put her way behind on her work. 'I'll go and talk to Jack,' she said. 'He must be feeling miserable.' Before Margaret could object, she was out of the room and going up the stairs two at a time.

Jack was hopping mad. All his best laid plans were going out of the window. Having been fairly confident that he'd secured a worthy inheritance, he now sensed something going wrong. Lately there had been a definite lessening of Rita's affections. There was something about her that worried him, and he couldn't quite put his finger on the reason. 'Who is it?' The knock on the door startled him.

'It's Cathy.'

'Come to gloat, have you? Glad to see the back of me, are you?' At first he hadn't minded being sent to school. It seemed a laugh. Now, he felt he was losing control of the situation. He didn't want that at all.

'I've come to see if you're all right?'

'I'll be all right when people stop pushing me around. Now clear off and let me think.' He heard her run down the stairs, and for a minute he wondered whether he'd done the right thing in sending her away. After all, wasn't she one of the prizes?

Going to the mirror, he stared into it, admiring his reflection and thinking what a good-looking fellow he was. 'Don't forget she's the daughter of a landowner, and the prettiest thing you've ever seen ... yours for the taking, if you're very cunning.' And he prided himself on being the most cunning fellow there ever was. Sometimes, though, he longed for the streets again, ducking and diving and keeping an eye out for the richest pickings. The more he thought on it, the harder it was to keep up the identity he had adopted. In his mind he was back on the streets, and it felt good. 'Yer a bleedin' fool. 'Course she's a pretty little thing, an' there's no doubt she fancies yer.' He fancied himself too, swaggering a little and winking at the mirror. 'But she ain't what you come 'ere for. Why don't yer stuff yer pockets with all yer can carry an' make off?' The thought amused him. 'Ah! But then you'd lose it all, wouldn't yer, eh? The land, this big house, the cottage where the old lady lives...' He recalled the fight with David and a dark hatred rose in him. 'And think what a pleasure it would be to turf the Leytons out of house and home.'

There was something else too. Something he had kept to himself for too long. 'What about the precious Rita Blackthorn?' he asked himself; several times he had seen her and Owen Leyton, and each time had been an eye-opener. 'What would her old man say if he knew she'd been larking about with one of the peasants, eh? Skin her alive, like as not.' Falling on the bed, he stretched himself full-length. 'That's a card I've not played yet. I mean... it wouldn't be clever to rock the boat that's carrying me to a fortune. Oh, but let her talk him into sending me away and I just might be forced to make things very unpleasant for her.' He softly laughed at the idea.

He was still laughing to himself when suddenly there was pandemonium from downstairs. Panic-stricken, Frank's voice carried to every corner of the house as he ran into the hall. 'Margaret! Come quick. It's Rita!' He sounded frantic. 'Dear God above, I think she's dead!'

Rita wasn't dead, but according to the doctor, who was fetched to the house in no time at all, 'She's totally exhausted... in a state of anxiety.' He made sure she was recovered enough to sit up in bed before telling Frank, who was waiting outside the bedroom, 'You'll have to make certain she doesn't overdo things.'

'Oh, I won't!' Frank had suffered the fright of his life. Rita was everything to him, and he would be only half a man without her. 'Just tell me what I'm to do,' he pleaded. 'It was all my fault. We had an argument... Rita got excited and lost her temper.' He laughed nervously. 'You know how it is with these women.'

Looking sternly at Frank, the doctor chided, 'You should know better. I've already told your wife to take things easy and now it looks as if I'll have to confine her to bed for the duration of her pregnancy.' He saw the colour drain from Frank's face. 'You mean your wife hasn't told you?'

Frank couldn't believe his ears. 'Are you saying, she's... with child?'

'That's exactly what I'm saying. I'm sorry to have spoiled the surprise, but you would have known soon enough. Better now, when you can keep an eye on her.' He found himself talking to thin air as Frank rushed back into the bedroom. Shaking his head, the doctor went downstairs smiling. Margaret, equally astonished to discover that Rita was expecting, was waiting at the bottom with Ruby. 'See Mrs Blackthorn gets these as prescribed.' Handing a prescription to Ruby, he spoke briefly to Margaret before bidding them good day.

Upstairs, Frank caught hold of Rita's hand, his eyes sparkling with tears and his face aglow with love. 'You don't know how happy you've made me,' he said brokenly. 'Carrying my child...' He shook his head in disbelief. 'And you never even told me.' His trusting gaze roved his wife's handsome face, and he was stricken with such ferocious love that it frightened him. 'Oh, Rita! Rita! Why didn't you tell me?'

She wanted to tell him. But not the things he wanted to hear. She longed to say how it wasn't *his* child growing in her belly. She ached to belittle him by describing how she and Owen Leyton had made wild passionate love... the kind of love he could never give her. Love that he could never understand. But it was too early for the truth. She and Owen would be gone from here soon enough. When the plans were made and Owen came for her, she would tell Frank everything, and enjoy every minute of it. For now she had to play the game, however obnoxious. 'I suppose I should have told you, but no matter. You know now.' Pretending to be weak, she languished deeper into the bed. Draping her arm across her face, she whispered, 'I'm tired. Let me sleep.' All she wanted was to be rid of him. The touch of his hands on hers made her shrivel inside.

Bending to kiss her, he didn't realise how she cringed from him. 'Thank you, my darling,' he murmured. 'You've made me a very happy man.' His eyes lit up as he dreamed aloud. 'A son maybe. Who knows?'

Thoughts of Jack prompted her to speak. At first she had

allowed that dirty urchin into the house only to spite Cathy. Later she had come to believe he really could be a son to her. Now she wasn't sure whether he knew about her and Owen. Certainly he must have seen her leaving the barn that day. Then again, maybe he hadn't seen her at all. She might have imagined it, because he had never mentioned the incident. All the same, she could no longer abide being in the same house with him. 'Promise me you'll send the boy away.'

Even now, Frank was loth to do so. 'The doctor says you're not to worry or exert yourself.' He was greatly attached to Jack, which wasn't so surprising when the boy was his own flesh and blood. However, if Rita was to give him a son, he might find himself swayed by her wishes. Until then he must be careful not to upset her. Being evasive, he pleaded cautiously, 'Rest now, and I promise we'll talk about it when you're stronger.'

It would be weeks before Rita felt stronger. Meantime she was confined to her bed, growing more frustrated and bitter by the day. News of her condition quickly spread, the townspeople gossiped, and Owen, who still hadn't planned a way out of the awful situation, thanked his lucky stars that he had been temporarily reprieved. Then the snows came in earnest and many of the roads were cut off.

'When will it end?' Frank insisted on bringing her tray each morning. He brought it on this Friday and his smile was as loving as ever. 'I'll have to get a message to Owen Leyton,' he said. 'The timber yard has had to close, and as far as I know Leyton's the only one with a sizeable stock pile of logs. He'll fetch us a load, I'm sure of it.'

Rita could hardly hide her excitement. The thought of seeing Owen after all these weeks, even from a distance, was something to look forward to. 'You must ask him at once,' she urged. 'Ride over yourself if needs be.'

That was exactly what Frank did. From her bed, Rita craned her neck to look through the window. She watched him go and she watched him return. An hour later, just when she had given up hope and was lying miserably in her bed, she heard the scrunch of wheels in the snow.

Putting on her robe, she went to the window. It was him! Handsome as ever, Owen sat up front, his son directly behind

495

him, and the logs piled so high they were in danger of rolling over the sides of the cart.

Eager to catch his attention she pressed herself close to the pane, waving her hand and softly calling his name. Concentrating on his work, he was oblivious to her. In a moment, though, her chance came. Jumping off the wagon to clear a way through to the outer yard, David left his father to check the horse, which had seemed to be limping. Rita held her breath. Owen was directly beneath her window. Seeing him so close and yet not being able to touch him was more than she could bear. Throwing caution to the winds, she began knocking on the window. At last he looked up, his eyes widening with fear when he saw it was Rita trying desperately to catch his attention. He would have turned away, pretending not to see her, but he knew if he did she would only persist. Suddenly Frank was alongside him, looking up too, waving and smiling, making silent words with his mouth. For the briefest moment she disappeared from their view, hiding behind the curtains until she felt sure that Frank had applied his attentions to other matters. When she peeped out again, he was standing back; never one for too much labour he was happy now to leave it all to others.

In that split second before Owen drove the cart on, he glanced up. When she blew a kiss, he seemed highly nervous, flicking his gaze from Frank to her. For one angry moment she thought he would leave without acknowledging her. An unreasonable rage took hold of her. But then he winked, and was instantly forgiven. In her joy, she couldn't know that he too was playing a game; the same kind of cruel game she was playing with Frank.

Cathy had seen the horse and cart arrive. From the scullery window she watched David help his father offload the logs. 'Do you think I should talk to him?' she asked Ruby.

'No, I don't!' Ruby was adamant. 'A lady would never run after a man.' She had been bending over the oven and her face was raspberry red. 'Let the men come after you,' she declared stoutly.

Disillusioned, Cathy put on her hat, coat and mittens and stood by the back door. She kept watch until all the logs were off and the empty cart pulled away. As it swung round towards her, David's gaze met hers. For one heart-stopping minute it seemed he would say something. Until he remembered how she had told Teresa she never wanted to speak with him again. Hurt and bewildered, he deliberately looked the other way.

'See that?' Ruby also had witnessed it. 'He ain't worth a second thought, lass.' Reluctantly, Cathy had to concede that Ruby might be right.

'What's up with you, son?' Even though Owen was steeped in his own problems, he couldn't help but notice how despondent David was. Easing the wagon along the snowbound lane, he glanced sideways at the young man. 'Something playing on your mind, is it?' Plagued with guilt, he was afraid David might have guessed at his affair with Rita Blackthorn.

'I'm all right.' That was all he said, but what he felt was far from it. He was heart-broken, and nothing would console him. Since losing Cathy, he had thrown his whole self into his work. At the end of the day he would come into the house dripping with sweat and bone tired; he washed and ate and did all the things that made a day pass quickly. In the evening he read the books which Cathy had brought to the house, going over the exercises and mastering the most difficult texts. But it didn't help. Nothing did.

Owen and his son continued the journey in silence, each heavy with his own heartache and each wondering how it had been allowed to come about. At the end of the journey, when the horse was unharnessed and the wagon upended against the barn wall, Owen strode through the snow to the house, while David sat for a while in the barn. Stony-faced and racked with regrets, he let Cathy swamp his thoughts.

The snows fell relentlessly over the next few weeks. It was well into December before the streets of Langho were clear and folk could move about in relative ease. The doctor visited Rita several times, and each time he was more pleased with her progress. 'Keep it up,' he told her, 'and it's possible I could let you sit downstairs of a morning.'

It wasn't enough for Rita. She wanted to go out. She needed to visit Owen, to persuade him that the time was right for them to go. She didn't want to have the baby here, nor did she want to spend one minute longer with Frank. She felt trapped, and all of her scheming wasn't enough to free her. She was even frustrated in her desire to have Jack sent away. On her first morning allowed downstairs, Frank made her comfortable in the drawing room before leaving to collect the tenants' rents. A few moments later, Jack came to see her.

'Thought I should come and see how you are,' he said. When he'd tapped on her door she hadn't realised who it was. If she had, he would never have gained admittance.

'I'm not well enough for visitors.' She was impatient and it showed.

'Just want a word with you, that's all.' He made no move towards her. Instead he closed the door and remained there, leaning against the wall, hands in pockets and looking every inch a cunning scoundrel. When he spoke again, his voice conveyed a threat. 'It's about me being sent to school.'

'What about it?'

'I'm not ready to leave yet.' He grinned. 'Same as you, eh? Biding my time ... enjoying the things that keep me here.'

'What are you trying to say?' Her face grew red with anger. She knew well enough what he was getting at.

'That's just it. I don't want to say anything,' he replied meaningfully. 'Besides, I reckon it would be a real pity if you and me couldn't keep a secret, wouldn't it, eh? You and me ... and Owen Leyton.' His sly grin left nothing to her imagination.

Incensed, she stared at him, her green eyes narrowed to dark glittering slits. 'You'll rue the day you ever threatened me!' she hissed.

He didn't reply but smiled a little then departed, leaving Rita shaking with rage. 'I won't let *anyone* spoil things,' she whispered after him, and there was murder in her heart.

Just as suddenly as the snows had started, they stopped. Two days before Christmas, the roads were clear and it was as if there had been no snow at all. Feeling cooped up, Jack decided to go for a walk across the fields. Cathy went with Margaret into Manchester, where they planned to buy all their Christmas presents. 'I wonder if David will send me a card?' she said when they climbed off the tram at the boulevard. 'I really miss him.'

'I thought you said he ignored you when he and his father brought those logs to the house?'

'He did.' For days she had thought about it, and even now it hurt to remember.

Margaret smiled at her. 'In that case, don't you think you should forget all about him?' She was secretly hurt by the way the Leytons had treated them both . . . David deliberately ignoring Cathy, and Maria passing her in the street without a word of greeting. 'It doesn't do to dwell on what's gone.'

For a while Cathy lapsed into a deep and thoughtful silence. 'What's gone' Margaret had said, and it was true. David didn't want her any more and she must accept that. But it was the hardest thing she had ever been made to do.

The shops were full to bursting with Christmas cheer, presents and toys for even the most discerning buyer and, grateful that they were no longer trapped in their homes by the deluge of snow, people had poured out of their homes. For two hours, Cathy accompanied Margaret round the shops, wide-eyed and excited by the wonder of Christmas: the organ players lining the streets, the hot chestnut barrow and the vendors shouting their wares from the shop fronts.

'Fancy a rest?' Cathy's attention had been caught by the corner café from where the aroma of hot pies and fresh baked barm-cakes filled her nostrils. 'I'm starving,' she said. More than that, her arms ached from carrying all the things she'd bought. The meagre allowance she received from her father had been carefully put away until today. She had no need of money generally, so it was all kept for birthdays and Christmas. Giving brought more pleasure than receiving, she always thought.

'I shan't be sorry to rest my feet.' Margaret had spied the café and was already making for it. 'We'll have a cup of tea and a bite to eat, then we'll catch the next tram home. How's that?' With a grateful sigh she sat herself in the nearest chair and dropped her bags to the floor. Cathy sat opposite, her gaze drawn to the counter and the range of delicious cakes there.

'Yes, ma'am?' The waitress was a thin little thing, with wispy hair and two front teeth missing. 'Can I help you?' Taking the pen from behind her ear and the notepad from her pocket, she waited, impatiently tapping her foot against the floor tiles.

Cathy ordered a cup of tea and a custard slice, while Margaret was gasping for 'Just a big pot of tea, dear.' When the waitress had gone, she remarked, 'A bit surly, wasn't she?'

'I expect her feet ache,' Cathy said. She'd noticed how the waitress hobbled away, as though she had a marble under each shoe. Margaret agreed the poor thing must have been on her feet all day, and gave her a shilling tip. That brought the smile back to her sulky features.

On the homeward journey, Cathy made mention of something else that was on her mind. 'I think Mother's taken against Jack.'

'What makes you say that?' Margaret too had noticed the very same, but had kept the observation to herself.

'Just a feeling, that's all. She snaps at him all the time, and can't seem to bear him near her.' Something else had played on her mind and she had to mention it or burst. 'Margaret?'

'Yes?'

Cathy hesitated, but only for the briefest minute. 'Do you think Jack looks like Father?' Now that the words were out in the open, she felt curiously afraid.

Margaret stared at her, then shook her head and softly laughed. 'My! You do have a vivid imagination. No, I can't say I've noticed a likeness. But then, as the boy is no way blood-related to the family, I wouldn't expect to, would I?' Even so, Cathy had set her thinking. *Was* there a likeness between the boy and Frank? Could it be remotely possible that the boy was his? After all, he often spent time away in London, and Frank was no more resistant to temptation than any other man. Though he adored Rita, she was a cold and forbidding soul. A man like Frank needed warmth and affection. If he couldn't get it from his own wife, then he may well have fallen for the passing charms of some other woman; no doubt bitterly regretting it later. The idea grew in her mind. If he really *was* the boy's father, it would explain so many things ... not least why he had brought a stranger into his home and taken him for adoption. It was certainly a fascinating and awful idea. Also, if it were true, Cathy would never see her father's money. Nor could she ever hope to win his favour because, when all was said and done, a man valued his son above all else; although where Frank was concerned, it was Rita who owned his soul.

The next day was Christmas Eve. Jack was in good spirits after being told he was not going away to school for at least another year. Margaret found herself studying him at every opportunity, searching for a likeness yet not being altogether certain. Rita stayed in her bed all morning. Ruby was 'Run off me feet!' preparing for Christmas Day. Frank bustled about getting ready to collect the weekly rents and, in the hope of seeing David, Cathy had no intention of letting her father go without her.

'Surely you're not collecting rents on Christmas Eve?' Margaret was appalled. 'Especially when they're not due until the end of the month.'

'If I left it till then they'd have spent the lot.' Putting on his warmest overcoat, he then grabbed a flat tweed cap from the hallstand and rammed it over his ears; next came a long brown scarf which he wrapped several times round his neck before peeling on a pair of thick kid gloves. 'Christmas Eve or not, I mean to have what's mine.' Slamming out of the door, he hurried to the barn, where he put the horse to the trap and led the ensemble out into the open.

'You don't mind if I come along, do you?' Cathy had followed him out. Dressed in boots and long coat with a blue beret pulled over her long fair hair, she was not prepared to take no for an answer. Before he'd opened his mouth to reply she had climbed on to the trap. 'I can hold the horse while you go in for your rents,' she offered brightly.

Exasperated, he climbed in alongside her. 'Damn and blast! I hadn't counted on taking a passenger.'

'Please, Father.'

Glancing sideways at her, he was momentarily shaken by her beauty. The girl is grown into a woman, he thought, and I never even noticed.

'You have a look of your mother,' he said, his voice filled with wonder. 'The same wonderful green eyes.' Cathy, however, had something Rita did not . . . a softness, a gentle quality that shone from her face and threw into the shade everything around her. For a time he was dazzled, unable to take his eyes off her. He had neglected her shamefully, but it was of no consequence. All the same, a huge surge of guilt fired his anger. 'You should have been a boy!' he snapped.

Though his words cut deep, Cathy made no comment. Her

silence only compounded his guilt. 'Hold on, dammit! If you fall off, I'll not stop to pick you up.' Grabbing the crop from its cradle, he snatched the reins and flicked them across the horse's rump. With a jolt it lurched forward, taking them at a frenzied pace along the winding lanes. If there had been anything coming in the opposite direction the two would have collided head on.

With her two hands clutching the bars either side of her, Cathy hung on for grim death. Only when they came in sight of the Leyton house did she begin to relax. The trap skidded to a halt. 'Stay where you are,' Frank ordered, jumping to the ground. 'And don't excite the horse.' Without a backward glance he went straight to the front door, where he banged his clenched fist loudly against the wood panel.

Getting down from her seat, Cathy stood by the horse's head. White foam was oozing out of its mouth and its back was sleek with sweat. 'And he told *me* not to excite you!' she remarked, tutting in disgust. Taking off her glove, she first wiped the foam away then ran the clean side along the animal's back. 'There, that must feel better,' she murmured. Her reward was a soft nuzzle and a wet face pressed into her hand. 'You stand still and behave,' she said, 'while I see if I can find you a bite to eat.'

She hoped David might be in the barn, but he wasn't. Disappointed, yet wondering whether he might have snubbed her yet again, she took a handful of hay from the stable and carried it out to the horse. 'Here were are.' Pushing a small handful towards him, she watched him greedily devour it. Soon the hay was gone and her father was striding down the path from the house, muttering to himself all the way.

'Damn tenants!' he snarled, climbing into the seat beside her. 'They never want to pay their way.'

As they passed the far field, David caught a glimpse of them. He mentioned it to Teresa on his return to the house. 'Happen if I'd been here, Cathy and I could have patched up our differences,' he said hopefully.

'I don't think so,' she answered, shaking her head and deliberately dashing his hopes. 'Her father was here demanding the rent early ... got quite upset when he had to wait while Mam fetched her purse. As for the girl, well, I should put her right out of your mind if I were you.' She spoke quietly, hiding the malice that dwelt in her heart. 'She's no better than the rest of them. At least her father lowered himself to set foot in the house. Not her though. Oh, no. *She*'d rather stay out in the cold keeping the horse company.'

'Happen she thought she wouldn't be welcome.' He was clutching at straws.

'Don't you believe it.' Keeping her voice deliberately soft, she went on, 'I even went out to invite her in for a cup of tea. "Warm your bones it will," I said. But she wasn't having it. She simply shook her head and that was that.' She made a noise that sounded like a sigh. 'I'm sorry, David, but I did try my best to make friends, I really did.'

'No need for you to be sorry, sis,' he said bitterly. 'I reckon we'd best forget Miss Cathy Blackthorn.' His dark eyes blazed. 'It's plain to me now ... we're not good enough for her any more.'

'Isn't that what I've been saying all along,' Maria declared, coming into the room. 'Her sort will allus think they have a God-given right to insult the likes of us.' She was thinking more of Rita Blackthorn, her husband's latest plaything. For days now she had toyed with the idea of confronting him, but it would cause uproar and she didn't want the children to know. It was too shameful, and besides they had no idea their father could be capable of such badness. The time was close though when she would have to say something, for she had suffered in silence long enough.

Nan Foster met them at the door. 'Come in, do,' she said, ushering them inside and smiling graciously. 'I expect you've come for the rent?'

Frank was taken aback. 'How did you know that?' he mused aloud. 'It's not due for another week.'

'Oh, I'm not such an old fool as you might think,' she answered through a bright smile. 'You're a businessman. It would make sense to collect your money today ... before folks could spend it on Christmas foolishness.'

Taking off his cap he returned her smile. He and this gentle old lady hardly ever exchanged words, perhaps once a week, during the few minutes it took to sign her rent book and take her money. But the strangest thing happened to him whenever he was near her. He felt humbled somehow, inferior to her yet without knowing why. She had a peculiarly calming effect on him. Just now he had arrived in a sour mood and banged on her door every bit as hard as he had banged on the Leytons'. But the mere sight of the old lady standing there, with her serene face and quiet manner, had sobered him again. 'I do apologise for collecting the rent on Christmas Eve,' he told her. 'But, as you say, if I left it till next week there may well be none to collect.'

'I have it ready,' she declared. Going to the sideboard she opened a drawer and took out her rent book; inside was a small envelope, and inside that were a number of coins. She gave the book and envelope to him, and while he counted the coins into the palm of his hand she asked, 'How is your wife?'

After scribbling his signature into the rent book, he looked up. 'Why, she's much better, thank you.'

'Are you going away for Christmas, Nan?' Cathy had stood patiently by, but now she felt it was right to intervene.

'Away?' She shook her head. 'Where would I go? Who in their right mind would want an old woman like me at their Christmas table?'

'*I* would!' Cathy declared.

'And so would I!' Frank would never know what prompted him to offer such an invitation, but having blurted it out he felt obliged to follow it through. 'In fact, Mrs Foster, my wife and I would be pleased to have you as our Christmas guest.'

Cathy beamed from ear to ear, while Nan could only stare at her landlord with amazement. 'Oh, no. I couldn't impose. I didn't mean . . .'

'Please, Nan, do come.' Now that her father had done such an unpredictable thing, Cathy couldn't let it go. 'Father wouldn't have asked you if he didn't really want you to come.' Turning to Frank, she left him no way out. 'You do want her to come, don't you, Father?'

Wondering what possessed him, he stammered and coughed and finally remarked, 'Of course. Why else would I ask?' Suddenly the prospect didn't seem so daunting. 'Besides, isn't it the custom to share your dinner with those less fortunate than yourself?' His own words embarrassed him and he blushed to the roots of his hair. 'Do forgive me,' he pleaded. 'There are times when my tongue tends to run away with me.'

Nan smiled at that. 'As it did just now, when you asked me to sit at your table?' Before he could respond, she raised her long slim hand. 'I'm sorry, that was very ungracious of me. Of course I would be honoured to accept your kind invitation.' Her smile was telling. 'Though I'm not sure I agree with you . . . about me being less fortunate than yourself.'

As he chivvied the horse and trap along the lanes, Frank still couldn't believe he had done such a foolhardy thing. 'Your mother will not be pleased.' Glancing at Cathy as though by some miracle she might rectify the situation, he wiped his hand over the sweat on his brow. 'What in God's name made me ask a complete stranger to Christmas dinner?'

'She's not a stranger.' In fact Cathy knew the old lady better even than she knew her own mother. 'Nan has impeccable manners and Mother will like her, I know.'

Rita was furious. 'I won't have that old woman at my table!'

'Be reasonable, dear.' Her grim face lowered Frank's spirits. 'All right, all right!' Thinking a compromise would pacify her, he said, 'My invitation had extended to the whole day, but I can restrict it to the evening meal only. Will that do?'

'I don't want her here at all. You must have been out of your mind. How dare you invite one of your tenants to sit at my table?' Frustrated because she had not heard one word from Owen, and suspecting he may have grown cold towards her, she took her temper out on the nearest person: Frank. 'If you insist on bringing that woman into this house, I shall remain in my room for the entire Christmas period.'

'It will be a happier Christmas without her,' Margaret quipped. But he didn't see it that way. Instead, he waited for Christmas Day like a man waiting for the gallows.

That night Cathy sat by her bedroom window counting the stars. Then she was counting the happy times she and David had spent together, and after a while, when the memories grew painful, she began counting the hours to when Nan would arrive.

Morning came and with it a clear bright day that chased away the deeper shadows of winter. 'Can I come with you to fetch Nan?' Cathy bombarded her father at breakfast. 'What time are you going for her? How long will she stay? Have you talked Mother round?'

'For goodness' sake!' Frank passed his hands over his closed eyes and bowed his head to the table. Looking up with hang-dog eyes, he said in slow deliberate tones, 'No, I have not talked your mother round. I have not yet decided the exact hour when I shall have to drag myself out in the cold to bring Mrs Foster here, nor have I an exact hour when I shall drive her home again. And, no! You may not come with me.' He glanced fondly at Jack, who was pretending to keep out of it all. 'As it happens, I've already promised Jack he can come for a ride.'

Jack couldn't resist a sly little smile. 'Sorry about that, Cathy,' he said. 'How was I to know you wanted to go?'

Sighing heavily, Frank addressed Cathy in a harsher voice. 'I hope that answers all your questions. Now kindly eat your breakfast, and don't say another word on the matter. I wish to God I had never invited the wretched woman in the first place.' His nerves were still jangling from Rita's tantrum when he'd taken up her tray just now.

Cathy wasn't finished though. All through breakfast she forced herself to keep quiet. But later, when her father strode across the hall towards the stairs, she waylaid him. 'Why won't Mother let me and Margaret put up a Christmas tree in the hall?'

'Because your mother is poorly, and if she is not in the mood for Christmas, then that's the end of that.' Glaring at her, he insisted, 'There will be no tree in this house, and no further argument on the matter. Is that clear?'

'If you say so.' Yet again he had managed to dampen her spirits.

She stood at the bottom of the stairs watching him climb every step as though it was the side of a mountain. At the top, he squared his shoulders and went at a smarter pace towards Rita's bedroom. From where she stood, Cathy heard him open the door and his voice as he called out, 'Hello, sweetheart. Here I am come to see you.'

The door closed and Rita's voice carried through it. 'Do you still mean to bring that woman here?' Frank must have answered yes, because in the next minute she was screeching like a fishwife, 'Damn you! Get out!'

On hearing the door flung open and her father's footsteps hurrying along the landing, Cathy wisely withdrew to the sitting room, where Margaret was putting out the presents. 'Are you sure you don't want to open yours now?' she asked as Cathy came in.

'No.' Cathy had already explained, 'I want us all to open our presents after dinner, when Nan's here.' The thought gave her a cosy feeling. 'Because Father hasn't allowed a tree, we'll have to set them out in the hearth. But it'll look nice, won't it?' She was more disappointed about the absence of a tree than she was prepared to admit. However, Margaret assured her that it would not take away the spirit of Christmas, and that Cathy was to 'Enjoy every minute of it.' And that was exactly what she decided to do.

The day rushed by; lunch was a brief affair, with only Margaret and Cathy at the table. 'Thank Gawd for that,' Ruby sighed, clearing away afterwards. 'I'm tuckered out. Lord knows I've enough to keep me busy, what with the house to clean and the washing to be done whether it rains or shines. On top of that I've been baking till I'm cross-eyed.' Staring at them both, she shook her head. 'There's enough mince pies, sausage rolls an' biscuits in that larder to feed a blessed army.' Waving her hand over the crockery on the table, she moaned, 'There's this lot to be washed and put away, the turkey to keep on basting, vegetables to be peeled and got ready, and on top of all that I've now got an extra guest to wait on at dinner.' She groaned as though someone had trodden on her bunions. 'What's a poor old soul to do, eh?' she asked, rolling her eyes to heaven and loudly tutting. 'I don't know.'

'I'll help you, Ruby.' Getting out of her chair, Cathy began gathering up the plates. No sooner had she collected two than they were snatched from her grasp.

'The very idea!' Ruby was bristling. 'You'll do no such thing, my girl. What! If I let you clear away the dishes, you'd be washing them up next. After that you'd want to make the beds and hang out the laundry. And what would Ruby do then, eh? She'd be out of a job and twiddling her thumbs, that's what.' Collecting the remaining plates she waddled out of the room, complaining all the way: 'The very idea! Ruby loves her work, that she does.'

At the door she flung them a challenging glance. 'And don't go telling folks I'm in a bad mood, because I ain't. Once the meal's ready and I'm ready to serve dinner, I shall have on me best pinnie, *and* me best smile. So don't forget *that*!'

With Ruby out of the room, Margaret couldn't help but laugh out loud. 'I think we'd better stay on the right side of Ruby,' she suggested. 'She's certainly got a bee in her bonnet today.'

'Do you think she's angry because Nan's coming to dinner?' Cathy couldn't recall Ruby ever being so annoyed.

'No. Of course not.' When she thought about it though, Margaret wasn't so sure. After all, Ruby was a proud little soul and she might take offence at having to wait on someone the mistress clearly didn't want at her table.

At precisely four o'clock, Frank and his son left for Nan Foster's cottage. Cathy watched them go. 'Nan won't be very comfortable squashed between those two,' she remarked.

Margaret came to the sitting-room window in time to see the trap turning the corner. 'I don't know why Jack wanted to go in the first place,' she commented. 'He doesn't even like Nan.'

'I don't think she's too fond of him either.' Frustration rose in Cathy. 'Do you think they'll be long before they're back?'

'Oh, about an hour, I should think. The snow deepened the potholes and with Nan aboard your father will have to drive more carefully than usual.'

Nan Foster was waiting for him. 'I'm not coming,' she said, before inviting the man and the boy inside. She was still wearing the same clothes she had worn the day before, her hair was very slightly dishevelled and there were dark rings beneath her eyes that suggested she had suffered a bad night.

'Are you ill?' Frank could barely hide his relief at her change of heart.

'No, I'm not ill,' she replied. 'Though I must admit I've had a sleepless night.' Taking a deep breath, she invited the man to be seated, but not the boy. Instead, she made a request. 'I would be very grateful if you could perhaps go for a short walk along the lanes? I have something very private to discuss with Mr Blackthorn.' Anxiously she glanced from one to the other. 'I assumed you would be alone,' she told Frank. Addressing Jack, she said, 'I'm sorry, but it shouldn't take too long.'

Frank was intrigued, but irritated. 'And *I'm* sorry if you're about to ask for a rent reduction, because the answer must be a resounding no.'

'It has nothing to do with the rent,' she assured him, beginning to relax. It was good to know that she had him at a disadvantage.

'And it can't wait? This "private" discussion?'

'It's waited too long already.' All night she had listened to her conscience and it told her she must reveal the truth before it was too late. She saw how the situation was developing between the boy and the man, and sensed that it must be now or never.

'Off you go then, Jack.' Reluctantly Frank dismissed his son. 'Don't wander too far though. I'm sure this little matter won't keep me.'

But it did keep him. More than that, he was shocked to the core when Nan Foster told him what was on her mind. First, though, she made him as comfortable as possible, and then she began her story. It was an astonishing one, a tale of adultery and unhappiness, of two people going their separate ways; it was a harrowing account of innocent children and desertion, of regrets and heartbreaking secrets. 'Please hear me out before you say anything,' she begged. 'I want you to know that I'm telling you all of this not for gain or spite, but to right a wrong. After it's done, I'll go away and never come back, if that's what you want.'

While she told her tale, Frank listened in silence, gasping now and then with horror and reeling back in the chair with astonishment. 'I was young and naive when I married Joshua Blackthorn. If you have learned anything at all about your father, you must know he was the laziest man on God's earth, a philanderer who gambled away most of your inheritance, a womaniser who broke my heart time and again. I stood it all, until one evening he arrived home drunk, in a foul and fighting mood after having lost a great deal of money. I knew I couldn't stand it much longer, and so I planned to leave him.'

'Are you telling me . . .' Frank swallowed hard, unable for a minute to mouth the words that pounded his brain. Shaking his head slowly from side to side, he spoke in a low choking voice. 'Are you saying . . . you're my . . . *mother*?' Convinced he was in the throes of a dream, he actually smiled.

She hesitated, lowering her gaze to the floor as it all came flooding back. 'I wanted to take you and Margaret with me, but he wouldn't allow it. He threatened to track me down and punish me if I took you away. And I have no doubt that's exactly what he would have done. If I believed for one minute that he might have hurt you or your sister, I would never have left you there. But, for all his failings, he adored his children . . . especially you, Frank, his only son.' She wrung her hands in despair as the guilt that had haunted her all these years bore down on her. 'I loved you too, but so help me, I could not stay one minute longer with a man who beat me so much that the child I carried was lost.' She saw the growing horror on Frank's face and had to assure him, 'Oh, yes, but for him you might have had another sister, or even a brother. Oh, I'm not saying there weren't times when he could be a good man, but as he grew older the other times became more and more frequent until I didn't even know him any more.'

As he listened to her story, all manner of emotions assailed him. He suspected his father had been everything she said. But he and Margaret had grown up hating the mother who had deserted them. If this was she, if this woman was his mother, he wanted to hurt her as she had hurt him. 'How do I know you're telling me the truth!' Springing out of the chair, he stood over her. 'For all I know you're an imposter, out for what you can get. Do you plan to lay claim to the estate? Is that what this is all about? Because I'm warning you now, I'll fight you all the way.'

'I'm telling you the truth.' Her voice was calm, her manner gracious. Going to the dresser drawer, she took out a sheaf of papers. 'It's all there,' she told him softly. 'The marriage certificate, birth certificates and other proof.' When he snatched them up and pored upon their every word, she went on softly, 'I've never stopped loving you. Wherever I went, you and Margaret were in my heart.'

In a rage he threw the papers at her. 'All right!' He had seen for himself that she was indeed the same woman who had deserted them long ago, and hatred burned in him like a beacon. 'So you're who you say you are . . . Joshua's wife . . . my mother.' His voice broke on a sob. 'What do you expect me to do? Would you like me to fall at your feet and thank the good Lord for bringing you back? Well, I can't! I WON'T!' The tears rolled down his face. 'How can I ever forgive you? And Margaret? What do you expect of us? Tell me, dammit!'

'I don't expect anything at all.' The old lady knew she had hurt him, but it had to be done. 'Not for myself anyway.' She could feel herself trembling all over. The ordeal had been too much, yet she had to go on. For Cathy's sake, she must see it through. 'Your father and I were never divorced. After he died I could have stepped in and claimed his estate, but I didn't. And I won't now.' Soberly regarding him, she went on in a calm deliberate voice, 'I won't make a nuisance of myself. Unless, of course, you mean to cheat Cathy out of her rightful inheritance.'

'Explain yourself.' He was so chilled with loathing he could hardly speak.

'This boy . . . Jack. If you have a mind to place him above Cathy, to make him sole beneficiary of your will, I can't stand by and see that happen.' She smiled then, a smile that told him to be cautious. 'Of course you could assure me that was not the case, but I would never be sure. To that end, I have taken the liberty of making an appointment with my solicitor in Blackburn. No doubt he can produce a watertight and legal document that will safeguard Cathy's rights.'

'You won't get a penny out of me!'

She rose from the chair, her manner every bit that of a hostess seeing off her guest. 'Goodbye, Frank,' she said a little sadly. 'What a pity you've chosen the hard way. You've seen the documents, and you know I have a substantial claim. As I said, I don't want anything for myself, but I will not allow that urchin to rob my grand-daughter.' With that, she went to the door and opened it wide. 'So kind of you to invite me to dinner,' she said in a matter-of-fact voice, 'but you can see now why I really could not accept.'

Storming past her, he paused, glowering down on her through

rage-filled eyes. 'I want you out of here tonight. This is *my* property.'

'Are you sure?' she asked, and her smile infuriated him.

Curious, Jack had hidden himself beneath the window. He had heard every word and was fascinated. When the door was opened, he quickly scurried round the back, emerging only when his name was called. As he sauntered to the trap, he looked back at the old lady and a hardness came into his voice as he murmured, 'So, you reckon you'll undo everything I've done so far, do you?' He chuckled. ''Fraid not, lady. The day ain't 'ere when an old woman can get the better o' me.'

'Look at that! It's a crying shame, that's what it is.' Ruby stood at the head of the table with her hands on her hips and a look of frustration on her face. 'What's going on? Where is everybody? And what's the matter with you two? Lost yer appetite, 'ave yer, eh?' Having slaved all day in the kitchen and set out the most beautiful Christmas table, she was deeply upset to see only Margaret and Cathy attend for dinner, and neither of them in good spirits. 'Is it me food? 'Ave I disappointed yer?' She looked from one to the other, waiting for some kind of explanation.

Cathy had been lost in thought, but at Ruby's hurt tones she looked up with a quick smile. 'Please don't take offence, Ruby,' she pleaded. 'It's nothing to do with you. The food is lovely and I'm sure you've set the best Christmas table in the whole of Lancashire.' She hated seeing that dear soul so upset.

'If that's the case, why ain't yer eating yer dinner?'

'I'm not all that hungry at the moment,' Cathy admitted. 'But I intend to have a little of everything.' Taking up her plate she collected a slice of plump white turkey, two roasted potatoes, half a dozen small round brussels, and a measure of cranberry sauce. 'I'll eat it all,' she promised. 'Afterwards I mean to have a helping of your delicious pudding and a mince pie.' Picking up her knife and fork she ate the first mouthful, and, though it was beautifully cooked, it stuck in her throat like a piece of wood. She'd had visions of everyone enjoying their Christmas dinner together . . . like a real family. Now, it was all spoiled.

Ruby watched her for a minute then, coming to where she

sat, put her hand on Cathy's head, saying fondly, 'Aw, it don't matter, lass. You don't have to force it down just to please old Ruby. I know how disappointed you are that the old lady couldn't come to dinner, and I know yer'd rather ye mam and dad were seated at the table with yer.' She didn't mention Jack because she still saw him as an intruder in this household. She had been here many long years and had learned to ride the storms. But that boy was unnatural. It didn't matter to Ruby that her master was besotted with his 'son'. He didn't belong, that was all, and as far as she was concerned, he never would.

Glancing at Margaret who as yet had said nothing, she apologised softly. 'I'm sorry, Miss. The both of yer 'ave allus been good friends to me, and if there's summat on yer minds that teks away yer appetites, well, what I mean is, I ain't got no right to make yer feel guilty.'

'It's us who should apologise,' Margaret insisted. 'We know how hard you've worked, and honestly, Ruby, it really is a lovely spread.' She looked regretfully at the table. 'But I'm afraid you're right. We *do* seem to have lost our appetites.' Since Frank returned from Nan Foster's there had been a very disturbing atmosphere in this house. It had seemed to affect all of them, with the exception of Ruby, who was no doubt too busy preparing this feast to sense anything unusual.

'Aye, well, happen everyone will feel peckish enough to finish the lot before you go to bed, eh?' Ruby was living in hope.

'Ruby?' Cathy reached up to touch her hand.

'What is it, lass?'

'Has Father said anything to you?'

'What about?'

'About why Nan Foster didn't come to dinner?' She had been waiting at the door when he returned. But when she ran out to ask why Nan wasn't with him, he impatiently brushed past her and went into his study. He hadn't been out since.

Ruby shook her grey head. 'He ain't said a blessed word. 'Course I noticed the Foster woman weren't here, an' I wondered whether I should set a place for her at the table.' Her irritation was betrayed when she looked fiercely towards the door. 'Twice I tapped on the study door to ask what I should do, an' all I got for me trouble was the order to "Go away, damn you!" ' She looked at Cathy, then she looked at Margaret, and her face tightened. 'I ask you, Miss, is that the way to speak to folks as is just trying to help?'

'It's no way to speak at all, Ruby,' Margaret agreed. 'You're quite right to be angry.' Something puzzled her. 'Have you seen Jack since he and Mr Blackthorn returned?'

'Ain't seen hide nor hair of 'im.' She didn't want to neither.

'And Mrs Blackthorn?'

'She won't even let me take a tray up.' Her little round body stiffened. 'What's more, she sent me off with the length of her tongue. Humph! Seems manners are a thing o' the past.' Looking down at Jack's place, she added haughtily, 'And that boy is just as rude. Where is he, eh? Why isn't he at the table, that's what I'd like to know.' Thinking she might overstep the mark, or that the master would suddenly appear and give her what for, she thought it time to excuse herself. 'Eat what you fancy,' she told them. 'The rest will allus keep.'

When she had disappeared into the kitchen, Cathy's curiosity got the better of her. 'Where *is* Jack, do you think?'

Margaret had no idea. 'I saw him only briefly when your father returned.' As she recalled, the boy had been deep in thought, almost colliding with her when she crossed the hall. 'I expect he's gone to his room.' She dabbed the napkin at each corner of her mouth. 'I mean to have words with him at the first opportunity. If he had no intention of joining us for dinner, he might have had the common courtesy to let Ruby know.'

'He's not in his room.'

'Oh? How do you know that?'

'Because when I came past just now, the door was wide open.'

'Well, he can't have gone far.' Margaret glanced at the mantel-piece clock which told her it was five minutes to eight. A glimpse through the window prompted the remark, 'It's dark outside, so I should imagine he must be in the study with your father.' She recalled Frank's red face and obvious rage when he returned from Nan's. The boy, too, had been in a strange mood. 'He may well have incurred your father's displeasure for some reason or another,' she deduced. 'He's probably getting a ticking off right this minute.'

Cathy thought about that and was forced to reply, 'If he is, it's a very quiet ticking off, because I haven't heard a sound since Father went into his study.' All the same it wasn't important enough for her to dwell on it. 'I think I'll go and see if Mother wants a tray.'

'Rather you than me.' Margaret was always humbled by the manner in which Cathy refused to be shut out of her mother's life. 'It's a kind idea,' she encouraged. 'It isn't healthy for her to go without food in her condition. By now I should imagine she must be starving, though I don't expect she'll admit it.'

Cathy tapped gently on the door. 'Mother, would you like me to fetch you a tray? Ruby's cooked a wonderful Christmas dinner. I know she'd be pleased if I brought you a few titbits?'

The answer was a harsh one. 'Get away from my door. I want nothing, do you understand? I want *nothing!*' Taking a paperweight from the dresser, Rita flung it with all her strength against the door. She heard a small cry as Cathy reeled back from the almighty thud, then the sound of footsteps as her daughter reluctantly retreated.

Laughing aloud Rita threw herself on the bed, her laughter turning to tears as the pain pierced her side. Gripping her stomach with both hands she rocked herself back and forth. 'I'm hurt,' she moaned. Her voice rose to a higher pitch as she surveyed the dent in the wood-panelled door, beneath which the paperweight lay. 'Why can't you all leave me alone... knocking on my door, worrying me about this or that? Now see what you've done!' Writhing from side to side in a frenzy, she whispered hoarsely, 'I want none of you. Only Owen. *He's* all that matters to me now.'

Rising from the bed she hobbled to the dressing table, where she studied herself in the mirror. 'Where is he?' she asked in anguish. 'He must know I'm house-bound. Why hasn't he found a way to let me know what he's planned?' Groaning from the depths of her soul, she ran her hands distractedly through her hair, wincing when it caused her pain.

Agitated beyond endurance, she dropped into the chair and bent her head into her hands. 'I can't stand being cooped up in this house any longer!' Looking up with wild eyes, she stared into the mirror, examining her every feature as though she was examining a stranger. 'You're very beautiful, Rita,' she murmured deviously. 'Any man would want you for his own, and Owen is no exception.' She regarded herself carefully; smiling into the cat-green eyes, tenderly touching the wonderful high cheekbones and caressing the long dark hair that hung round her shoulders like the spill of midnight.

'Tomorrow morning, Owen,' she whispered, and the smile slid from her face. The pain was shooting all over her body, but she was determined. 'You've had enough time to get in touch with me. Now I must come and find you. I need you to tell me you have a plan now, a plan to get us away from here, to set us up somewhere together, you and me and our son.' She touched her fingers against the mound beneath her robe. 'It's growing inside me, Owen,' she muttered. 'Your seed is growing inside me.'

Suddenly she was ripping the clothes from her back. In a frantic moment she was stark naked. Turning sideways she regarded the mound of pink skin, a swollen tight mass that was pushing out from her slim form. 'You've made me ugly,' she whispered bitterly. 'I was never made for carrying children. But this is your son, Owen, yours and mine, and you have to take us away from here.' Swinging round to see herself full on, she said softly, 'In the morning, Owen.' The thought gave her a deal of pleasure. 'You've had time enough.'

Downstairs, Frank paced his study like a caged animal. 'I can't tell Margaret,' he moaned to himself. 'How can I tell her the woman we thought was dead so long ago is here, renting our cottage . . . waiting to rob us of everything we own?' His eyes glittered as a thought struck home. 'My God! It wouldn't surprise me if Margaret didn't know already. Of course! That's why she's befriended the old witch. And Margaret has never taken to Jack . . . wanted him out the minute he set foot across the threshold. It all becomes clear now . . . the pair of them are in on it!' He was so astounded by his thoughts that he had to sit down.

His mind was racing ahead, telling him this, telling him that. 'NO!' Common sense prevailed. 'Margaret is too honest. If she'd known who that woman was, she would have told me long ago. The truth is more likely to be that the cunning Foster woman is out to rob Margaret as well.' He began pacing again. 'Should I tell her?' He shook his head. 'No. Think, Frank. Think hard about what happened after she ran out on you. Remember how your sister cried for her mother ... how, when she was old enough she searched long and hard, until Father was forced to say that Mother had died? Remember how Margaret ached for her ... yearned for her? My God! If I was to tell her what was told me this very day, she'd likely throw herself into the arms of that old witch ... rejoicing at the return of her long-lost mother.' The idea was unthinkable.

Going to the desk, he leaned his hands on it and straightened his back, his head bent forward and his eyes closed. 'I can't tell her, and I can't let any of them dictate my life. I *won't!*'

Beating his fist on the desk, he opened his eyes just a little, lost in a trance as he stared at the brass ink-holder. 'If that witch thinks I'm just going to stand back and let her tell me what to do, she couldn't be more wrong. *I'll see her dead first!*'

Margaret was coming across the hall when Frank came bursting out of the study, almost careering into her as he rushed to the front door. He was further irritated when she dared to question him. 'Where on earth are you going at this time of night?'

'Out!' he snapped. 'I have to get some fresh air.'

'Oh, you'll get that all right.' She smiled. 'It's bitter cold out there.' Glancing at his attire, she remarked thankfully, 'At least you're dressed for the night air.' He had on his cap and coat, and was even wearing gloves.

Affording her a withering glance, he advised, 'Don't concern yourself about where I'm going. Or when I'm likely to be back.' With that he stormed out, slamming the door behind him.

When Margaret turned round it was to see Cathy approaching. 'That's funny,' Cathy remarked thoughtfully.

'Oh? What's that?'

'Ruby said Jack was in with Father. Getting a ticking off, she said.' Cathy looked from the study door to the foot of the stairs, and finally brought her gaze to rest on the door through which her father had just departed. 'If he was in the study with Father, where is he now?'

Shrugging her shoulders, Margaret suggested, 'He probably went straight up to his room after your father was finished with him.' A little smile curled the corners of her mouth. 'And from what I've just seen of my dear brother, I can imagine Jack got more than a ticking off. In fact, it wouldn't surprise me if we didn't see him until tomorrow morning.' Draping her arm around Cathy's shoulders, she suggested, 'How about you and me sewing some more squares for Nan's eiderdown?'

'I'd like that,' Cathy replied. It was to be a surprise for Nan's next birthday, a beautiful chequered eiderdown to match her pretty cushions. It was a slow tedious job, and they would need every spare minute to have it finished in time.

As the two of them walked to the drawing room, they chatted about all the things that had recently touched them ... Rita's continuing foul moods, Frank's obsession with her, and Jack. He was the apple of Frank's eye, the apple that had upset the cart. Margaret couldn't really forgive him for that, but she kept that particular thought to herself. And, though Cathy had cause to resent him more than most, she had gone out of her way to accept him. Albeit in different ways, she saw in him a soul as lonely and deprived as herself, though she still hadn't altogether forgiven him for having picked a fight with David and ruining what had been a beautiful friendship.

'If there's time enough, I thought we might perhaps sew two pillow-cases to match the eiderdown.' Going up the stairs to her bedroom where the sewing was kept, Margaret glanced at Cathy. 'What do you think, sweetheart?' Cathy hadn't heard. She seemed a million miles away. 'Cathy? Did you hear what I said?'

Talking about Jack had raised thoughts of David. She thought of him often. She was thinking of him now. And she missed him so much.

'Sorry, yes, I heard what you said,' she apologised. 'I think it's a lovely idea and if we're going to get it all done, we'll have to work extra hard.' In fact it occurred to her that the eiderdown and pillow-cases might be a blessing in disguise, for if the sewing took up her every spare minute it might ease the loneliness of being without David.

Nan Foster felt unusually disquieted. Ever since her confrontation with Frank, she had been swamped with guilt. 'You did right though.' Rocking back and forth in the old wooden chair, she chided herself, 'No one can blame you for what you did all those years ago.'

518

All the same she wished it hadn't come to this, threatening her own son. 'I came here to be close to my children,' she murmured regretfully. 'Margaret is everything I hoped she would be, and Frank is blinded only by his obsession for that wife of his. As for the boy, he's rotten at the core. I feel in my bones he has no real affection for Frank. He's out to get what he can, even at the expense of Cathy.'

Her eyes softened at the mention of Cathy's name. 'What a darling creature she is,' she whispered lovingly. 'No wonder Margaret adores her. And how can I stand by and see her robbed?' Her determination had not wavered.

Tired out by events which had overtaken her, she closed her eyes and rocked a while. The warmth of the fire was soothing, lulling her thoughts and bringing a glow to her face. She slumbered awhile, her dreams uneasy.

She didn't hear the intruder creeping up on her. The log came crashing down against her temple and she fell sideways, her eyes still open, still staring. It took a few frantic minutes to search for valuables, then there was a burst of soft laughter as the intruder fled, leaving the door wide open and the cold dark night rushing in.

'I tell you, I don't want a doctor. He'll only make me stay in bed. I'll go mad if I don't soon get out of this house.' Rita was in a shocking state, clutching her side and crying in agony. 'It was *her* . . . that daughter of yours. *She* did this!'

Frank was a man in torment. 'What do you mean? How could Cathy do this to you?' When he'd returned home late, Rita was waiting for him at the bedroom door. She had replaced the paperweight on the dresser, and as yet he hadn't seen the dent in the door-panel, so when she accused Cathy he was concerned and curious all at the same time.

'By getting me all riled up, that's how!' came the retort. 'All I want is a drink . . . something stronger than tea.' Rolling on to the bed, she gave a little cry of pain.

'You'll have a doctor, that's what you'll have,' he said, easing her into the bed. And no amount of bullying from Rita could change his mind.

When the doctor arrived, Cathy was wide awake. After looking out of the window and seeing whose trap had come to the house, she went into Margaret's room. 'The doctor's here,' she whispered. Together the two of them went out on to the landing. Jack was there. Bleary-eyed and dishevelled, he lazily tied the belt of his robe. 'What's going on?'

When told it was the doctor, come to see Rita, he yawned. 'Oh, that's all right then.' He seemed relieved. A minute later he was back in his bed, with the door closed against the world.

Rita's bedroom door opened and Frank came out. His face was a ghastly shade of grey and there were bags under his eyes. 'I should have been here,' he moaned. Rubbing his hand over his face, he peered at them through his fingers. 'God almighty, I should have been here. If she loses that child . . . if anything happens to my Rita, I'll never forgive myself.'

The three of them waited and waited, and it seemed an age before the doctor emerged. 'She'll be fine,' he promised. Taking Frank by the arm, he walked with him to the foot of the stairs. 'She's twisted a muscle, that's all, though of course she can be forgiven for thinking it might be much worse.' He smiled reassuringly. 'Women easily frighten when they're with child.'

Frank nearly fainted with relief. 'She'll be all right then? Her and the child?'

'She's stronger than when I last saw her, and yes, they'll be all right, Mr Blackthorn. However, just to be on the safe side, I've confined her to bed for at least another week.' He saw the look on Frank's face, and patted him on the shoulder. 'I know she doesn't like it, but doctor knows best, I think.' He went then, leaving Frank to face the bitter end of his wife's tongue.

The strange thing was, Rita had very little to say. After relaying the doctor's diagnosis to Margaret and Cathy, who had been anxiously waiting, Frank returned to his wife's bedroom. 'Please be patient, my dear,' he begged, closing the door. 'I know how you loathe being shut up, but it won't be for long, and it is for your own good after all . . .' He would have gone on, but her stillness silenced him. 'Rita?' Creeping up to the bed, he was fearful of what he might find.

What he found was Rita seemingly fast asleep, so he drew the blankets over her shoulders, kissed her on the forehead and tiptoed out. 'Good night, my dear,' he whispered from the door. 'I'll see you in the morning.'

When the door was closed, her eyes instantly opened, and they were alive with hatred.

In the morning, the whole house was rudely awakened by the sound of Ruby hammering on her master's door. 'Come quickly, Sir,' she cried. 'It's the authorities to see you. Real urgent, they said.'

Cathy was the first one out on the landing. Running across the carpet in bare feet, she asked breathlessly, 'What is it, Ruby? What's the matter?'

Before she could reply, Frank flung open his door. 'Have you all gone mad? What do you mean by hammering on my door at this time of morning? I've had no sleep... no sleep at all, dammit!' All night long he had drifted in and out of sleep, waking with a sweat on him, his every nerve-ending crying out to lie with his wife, to feel the warmth of her body against his. And now to be jolted out of his first few minutes of real sleep was more than he could stand. 'Out with it, woman! What is so important that you have to knock down my door?'

Her manner somewhat subdued by the sight of him with his hair standing on end and his robe flung wide open, Ruby stepped back a pace. 'I know it's only seven o'clock,' she answered. 'I'm really sorry, Sir, but it's the authorities, you see.'

'The authorities? What in God's name do they want with me?'

'They didn't say exactly, only that I was to wake you as it was urgent.'

He pursed his lips and thought hard before briskly ordering, 'Very well. Inform them I'll be right down. Oh, and wake Miss Margaret, would you?'

Margaret was already awake. She and Cathy were washed, dressed and only five minutes behind him. When they arrived in the drawing room, it was to find Frank seated in a chair. There were two constables standing by the door, and seated opposite Frank was a thin balding man in a dark blue suit. On Margaret and Cathy's arrival, he stood up and greeted them. 'Good morning. Forgive me for getting you from your beds at this hour.' Addressing Margaret, he declared, 'I assume you must be Miss Margaret Blackthorn?'

'That's right.' Drawing Cathy closer, she explained, 'And this is my niece, Cathy Blackthorn.'

'I am Inspector Collins, and these are my colleagues.' Pointing to the uniformed men, he told them sharply, 'It might be better if you waited outside in the hall.'

Frank spoke in a low serious voice. 'The girl.' Glancing at Cathy, he flicked a hand to dismiss her. 'There is no need for her to stay.'

Margaret instinctively knew it was the right decision. 'It might be best if you go and talk to Ruby,' she suggested.

Reluctantly, but with little choice, Cathy went without delay. As she closed the door behind her, she heard her father relating the awful news to Margaret, and his words struck horror to her young heart.

'It's that friend of yours and Cathy's . . . Mrs Foster.' There was a slight pause, then, 'Young David Leyton was making a delivery of logs early this morning when he found the door wide open and the old lady still in her rocking chair.' Another pause, while Cathy lingered with her heart in her mouth. '*Murdered!*'

Unable to believe what she was hearing, Cathy fled to the kitchen where she fell sobbing into Ruby's arms, pouring out what she had overheard. 'It's not true, Ruby,' she begged. 'It can't be true.'

Ruby held her close, crying with her. 'Aw, lass, I'm sorry,' she said brokenly. 'I know you thought the world of the old lady. Take heart, lass.' Clutching Cathy tight, she promised, 'Old Ruby's 'ere, and she won't let go of yer no how.'

CHAPTER SEVEN

On 8 January 1901, Annette Rosalind Foster was laid to rest. Never having been divorced from Joshua Blackthorn she could have kept his name, but in order to hide her true identity had adopted the name Foster. Right up to the day she was savagely murdered, she kept her anonymity.

There were few mourners. The only representatives of the Langho community were two traders who'd delivered her supplies over the years; though, as the grocer remarked afterwards, 'None of us really knew her.' Owen and his son David attended, as did Margaret and Cathy. Frank was there in his capacity as landlord to the unfortunate woman. Throughout the service he bowed his head and prayed. Only once did he glance at the coffin. Not for one moment throughout did he regard its contents as being the remains of his own mother. She had been a tenant of his, that was all.

Cathy quietly sobbed. Seated some way behind, David longed to hold and comfort her. At the end, when she walked past him, he lowered his gaze, afraid she would hurt him again. Cathy saw this and took it as yet another sign that he had finished with her. Margaret saw it too, and hurried Cathy out to the trap where Frank was impatiently waiting to be away. 'Thank God that's over,' he muttered as they climbed in. 'The whole business is damned inconvenient though, because now the cottage has to be cleared. After that I've got to find a new tenant.'

Unsure as to what evidence the old lady had left behind, Frank took it on himself to visit the cottage that very afternoon. In the sideboard he found a quantity of old porcelain figures. 'They should fetch a good price at auction,' he remarked, turning the beautiful figurines over in his grasping hands. 'I dare say I'm entitled to have first call on anything of value.' Probing into every corner, he chuckled wickedly. 'Especially if I make it known that she was badly in arrears with her rent.'

There were two framed paintings of modest value, he thought, and a rather old but attractive wicker chair in the bedroom. A more thorough search gave up a small treasure trove, skilfully hidden in a locked compartment at the back of a drawer. It took only a moment to prise the compartment open. Inside was a cash box containing a number of letters and official-looking documents. Beside the cash box was a blue velvet wallet.

'What's this, I wonder?' he whispered, gingerly opening the wallet. When the brooch was laid bare, his eyes almost popped out of his head. 'Good God!' Taking it out, he laid it in the palm of his hand, a feeling of wonder washing over him. 'Good God!' The brooch was delicately crafted of sapphires and platinum. 'It's exactly the same as the necklace at the house.' He stared at it for what seemed an age, turning it over in his hands as though he was handling something too precious to see daylight. 'Of course! It's a set. She must have taken the brooch when she ran off.' If he needed more proof that the old lady really was his mother, it was here in the palm of his hand.

He knew he dared not keep it. 'Can't show it to Rita, or she would accuse me of having kept it from her all these years. Can't sell it either,' he mused aloud, 'or it might be traced back, and how would I explain it?' He sat in the very chair where Nan had been found. 'Oh, but it *is* splendid,' he groaned, continuing to stare at the brooch. 'I haven't the heart to destroy it. What am I to do then?' He thought a while, debating on the best course of action. 'Left her husband and two children behind, but stayed long enough to pack the brooch, eh?' His face darkened. 'Well, it's mine now, and this little trinket is worth a pretty shilling. After all, with the old lady gone and the cottage empty, there's no rent coming in. Because I'm bound to suffer, I have a right to compensation where I can find it.' He chewed on his bottom lip as he had a manner of doing when faced with a dilemma. 'I can't afford not to be careful though,' he reminded himself. 'Don't want folks knowing the old biddy was related.'

He began pacing the floor. 'What to do? What to do?' He

stopped and gazed out of the window, his face growing red with frustration. 'Let me think! I can't think straight here ... with all this round me.' He shifted his eyes round the room, visibly shivering when they came to rest on the chair where Nan had been bludgeoned to death. 'She's still here ... watching me.' His lips moved but no words would come. They moved again, and this time he heard himself saying what he had not said for too many years: 'Mother ... my mother.'

Overcome with emotion, he sank into the nearest chair, bent his head and was silent for a moment. Then he sat up straight, threw back his shoulders and laughed like a man tormented. 'My mother!' His laughter turned to tears. The years fled away and he was a child again, a child deserted, a child whose innocent heart was racked by sobs, just as his guilty heart was racked by sobs now.

He had tasted the word 'Mother' on his lips. It had been a bitter taste and, for the remainder of his life, he would never utter that word again.

When his emotions were drained, he took one more lingering look at the brooch. Then he slipped it into his pocket and turned his attention to the cash box. The letters were written in the most beautiful copperplate by his mother, addressed to his father Joshua, but never posted. For one crippling minute he fought within himself; should he open them, or would he live to regret it? 'I've done many things I regret,' he said wryly, 'one more won't matter either way.' Opening the first letter he started to read:

Dear Joshua,

I know you must hate me for what I have done. Yet, I could not stay with you. There is nothing to be gained by going into the reasons for my leaving. Let it be sufficient for me to say you have changed beyond recognition from the man I married. Or perhaps you never changed, I just didn't see you as you really were.

I can't regret leaving you, but with all my heart I regret leaving my children. I know what you said when I left, that you would never allow me to have them, and that you would move heaven and earth to keep them from me. I know you can do that. I know only too well what cruelty you are capable of.

I beg of you, Joshua, don't be so heartless. Send me word that I may return for them. I shall wait at the address above for the next week only. After that, I leave the area, with no plans to return.

Annette

The letter was nigh on forty years old, almost as old as Frank himself. It had yellowed round the edges and the blue ribbon that bound it to the others was frayed with age.

Frank read it again and again, and each time he wondered why she had never posted it. 'WHY DIDN'T YOU POST IT?' His cry rang from the heart. 'Was it because you were so afraid of him? Or could it be that you never posted it because you changed your mind!' He was beside himself with rage. 'Whatever the reason, you left without us, and I for one will not forgive you.'

He was screaming at the letter, twisting it over and over in his fist. 'Damn you! Damn you!' Long-buried emotions overwhelmed him and it was all too much. Desperate, he thrust the whole batch of letters into the fire-grate, where he set light to them.

When the papers were curled and blackened beyond recognition, he put his mind to the official papers. They amounted to nothing more than domestic bills, circulars, invoices, and a brief acknowledgement from a local solicitor which read:

Dear Mrs Foster,

In answer to your letter, I would be pleased to see you on 2 January at 10 am as requested.

It would have been helpful if you had briefly explained what you require. However, on the last point, the making of your will, I will be able to advise you better on the day. To that end, I look forward to seeing you.

Yours sincerely,

Bartholomew Wright

Frank breathed a sigh of relief. 'Had it all in hand, didn't you, Mrs Foster?' he said through clenched teeth. 'Well now, it's just as well for me and mine that you couldn't keep the appointment with your solicitor.'

Tearing off the address at the top of the letter, he crumpled the remainder in his hand. Throwing it into the grate he watched it follow the same fate as his mother's personal letters to his father. 'Annette and Joshua Blackthorn, I commit your ashes to eternity,' he said savagely. 'And I hope the pair of you burn in hell!' He grew quiet, observing an odd kind of reverence as the evidence crumbled away. 'One way or another you're both to blame,' he murmured. 'If I'm weak and selfish, it's your fault. If I'm only half the man I should be, who else is there to blame but you two? Joshua Blackthorn, whose wild ways drove you away, and *you*, a woman who deserted all her responsibilities. For years after you left, I felt so very lonely, a lost soul, without purpose or sense of belonging.' His eyes filled with tears. 'Until Rita came along.' There was great joy in his voice now. 'She gave me what you took away, and now she's *everything* to me. Why should I mourn your loss, either of you? I don't need you. As long as I have my Rita, I don't need any of you.'

His emotions deeply stirred, he began shouting, oblivious to the fact that he might be overheard. Even here, miles away from anywhere, a voice might carry, a secret might be lost. 'Ssh, Frank!' he whispered. 'Don't lose your mind. Not now. Not when there is so much at stake.'

The following week he arranged a date when a band of men would clean out the cottage and make it ready for the next tenant. On the day before they were due to start work, Cathy asked Margaret, 'Could we have one last look before they go in?' The idea of strangers in hobnail boots treading over Nan's pretty rugs and poking about in that delightful place was distressing to her.

Margaret had much the same idea. 'Why not? It is Sunday after all.' She glanced out of the window at a clear January morning. 'It's a perfect day for a walk.' Getting up from the chair where she had been sewing, she warned Cathy, 'However, it's still very cold out, so mind you put on your boots and beret.'

Well wrapped up against the cold, with Margaret in long coat and fur hat, and Cathy looking exceptionally lovely in her blue beret and matching coat, wearing leather gloves and a pretty white scarf tucked round her throat, the two of them left the house. 'Can we go by way of the streets?' Cathy loved to see the people chatting in the streets, and the children playing hopscotch on the pavements. She liked to see the babies in their prams and, whenever the opportunity presented itself, would stop and chat to the old folk, who smiled back through toothless gums. Old and wise they were, happily minding the children and singing their praises; full of the kind of love she had never known from her own parents.

Margaret agreed, and soon they were walking down the narrow cobbled street. Though it was chilly and the children wore little more than rags, they ran and played and hopped to their games, the dogs ran in and out of their legs and the street was alive with laughter.

From one end of the street to the other, women in turbans were on their knees, white-stoning their steps and mopping the area immediately round their front doors. Men of all ages stood about, leaning on the walls, hands in pockets and voices raised in light-hearted banter as they argued about the state of the world. One mother had braved the cold to sit on a chair in the fresh air and openly breast-feed her baby. Poor they were, and no doubt hungry from time to time, but there was a carefree air about this street, a special bonding of souls, a will to survive as long as they pulled together. These were good people. This was a street filled with love. And Cathy thought it a world away from the sorry house where she lived.

'Mornin', luv. Off fer a walk, are you?' The old woman had passed the time of day with Cathy before.

Recognising her at once, Cathy guided Margaret over to where the old woman was seated. 'We're going to see Nan Foster's cottage before the workmen move in,' she explained sadly.

'I see.' The old woman's red-rimmed eyes looked from Cathy to Margaret, and it was Margaret she addressed. 'Dreadful business that. By! What's the world coming to when an old woman can't sit by her own fireside without having her brains bashed out?' She saw how her words were cutting Cathy and quickly asked, 'Did the old lady leave any next-of-kin?'

A younger woman might have thought twice about questioning a Blackthorn, but age had made her bold. Age, poverty and a sense of survival had chipped away at the niceties of her existence, until now she saw only the *faces* of people. The expensive cut of a dress or the silk ribbon round a bonnet didn't bother her. Not any more. Not since she had suckled her last child and fought with dogs on the pavement for a meaty bone when her husband was out of work.

Margaret had already talked to Frank about the possibility of Nan's having relatives. 'As far as we can tell she had no kin.' Her mind wandered back over the many pleasant conversations she and Nan had shared, and not once could she recall Nan's ever having mentioned family. The old lady's kind gentle face came to mind, and with it a bitter-sweet sensation. 'She was such a loving soul,' she said wistfully, thinking how a woman like Nan was made to have a family. Glancing at Cathy, she said softly, 'We shall miss her.'

'Poor bugger.' The old woman shook her grey head. 'We're all here today and gone tomorrow, an' that's a fact. Still, from what I hear the old lady weren't badly off . . . paid her bills on time by all accounts and never asked for credit. Then, o' course, she had a nice little home, didn't she, eh?' Without waiting for an answer, she rushed on, lost in her own thoughts and not talking to anyone in particular, 'I expect there's another tenant already lined up to fill her shoes, ain't there? I mean . . . the cottage wouldn't be my idea of heaven, but there's plenty who'd love it.'

Seeming mentally to shake herself and realise she was conversing with them from the big house, she screwed herself into a tight little ball, like a hedgehog might do when faced with danger. 'No, I couldn't stand living out there amongst the wind and the trees, with nary a soul in sight.' Squinting up at Cathy, she smiled warmly. 'Me, I like the sound o' childer around me arse, an' the smell of a man's pipe up me nostrils. I like to see the babbies at their mams' titties, an' listen at night through the walls when a fella demands his rights.' She laughed raucously. 'Shame yer, do I?' Grinning sheepishly at Cathy, she apologised. 'I ain't as bad as I sound, me beauty. But I'm a street woman an' there ain't nothing in the world to change me.'

'I understand,' Cathy replied, and she did.

The old woman smiled. ''Course yer do, dearie. A cottage is fine fer them as can stand the loneliness, an' like I say, there's plenty folk who'd be glad of a little place like that.' Cocking her head to look at Margaret, she studied her a moment before asking boldly, 'Got a tenant already, 'ave yer?'

'To tell you the truth, I don't know,' Margaret answered. 'My brother deals with all of that.'

''Course he does, me dear,' came the retort. 'Ain't men allus the same? Like to think they're in charge, ain't that the case, eh? Lost my old fella many year ago ... a drunken ol' bugger he were.'

Margaret bade her good day. 'We have much to do yet,' she explained.

'Yer should be like me then,' replied the harmless old soul. 'If yer ain't got no money nor property, then yer ain't got nothing to worry about.'

'Do you think she's very old?' Cathy asked as they went down the lane towards the cottage.

'Ancient, I'd say.' Margaret laughed softly at the old woman's wise philosophy. 'I certainly believe she could teach us a thing or two.'

With the key that Margaret had brought, Cathy opened the cottage door. The scene that greeted them was utter mayhem. Cathy stood there dumbfounded. 'Someone's ransacked it!' she cried. They had no idea it was Frank who had turned the place upside down. Every room told the same story; cupboard doors flung open, drawers thrown to the floor and their contents strewn over the rugs. There were remnants of burnt paper littering the hearth, and several of Nan's precious ornaments had been swiped from the dresser shelves and left in fragments on the floor.

'Who could have done such a terrible thing?' Like Cathy, Margaret was close to tears.

It took almost an hour for them to clean up the mess, but the things that were broken could never be mended. 'And even if we could repair them, who would they belong to? What would we do with them?' Cathy asked. 'Father said Nan didn't leave a will, and he hasn't been able to trace any relatives.' She

530

lovingly caressed a small plate that had been one of Nan's favourites. Darkest blue with a pattern of flowers round the brim, it had hung over the mantelpiece all these years. 'Isn't it beautiful?' she whispered, looking at Margaret with tearful eyes. 'Like *all* her pretty things. And now someone has been in here and destroyed them.'

'People can be very cruel, sweetheart,' Margaret consoled her. 'Take the plate and keep it safe. I'm sure Nan would like that.' She remembered something else and her eyes went straight to the sideboard. 'The box,' she said. 'The one Nan so wanted you to have.' Going to the dresser she pulled out the small top drawer which only a minute ago Cathy had carefully replaced. The box wasn't there. It wasn't anywhere to be found. 'Whoever came in here must have taken it.'

'It doesn't matter,' Cathy said wistfully. 'It was very lovely, and I know Nan wanted me to have it,' – she pressed the plate close to her heart – 'but I'll be happy just to have this. Nan loved it so, and it will always remind me of her.' She couldn't stand to be in that room where she and Margaret had enjoyed the old lady's company. It wasn't the same any more.

On the way home they talked about Nan. 'What will happen to her furniture?' Cathy wondered. When Margaret explained how she herself would organise either a sale for charity, or even a gift to a poor family in Langho, she was partly comforted. 'Nan would be pleased to know she was helping others,' she replied. One thing she was sure of – never again did she want to enter that cottage. Nan had lived and been brutally killed there. Now she was gone, and with her all of the gentleness that had filled that little place. 'Do you think they'll find the person who killed her?' She daren't even think about what kind of monster he must be.

'Who knows, sweetheart?' Margaret had been thinking the very same. 'He may be long gone from the area by now. My thinking is it must have been a stranger... someone who couldn't have known Nan.'

Glancing back to the cottage, Cathy was filled with rage. 'Someone evil,' she said harshly, 'or totally insane.' It had to be a stranger, she reasoned, because anyone who knew of that delightful soul would never have hurt her. 'I hope they do catch him, but as you say, he's probably long gone.'

Time passed and the police still hadn't caught the murderer. Much to Frank's dismay, people seemed wary of living in a place that had seen such horror. 'I've spent good money on having it cleared out and repainted,' he moaned to Rita. 'I didn't even get the chance to sell the furniture because Margaret snatched it from under my nose and gave it away to one of her wretched families. I've paid out a large sum of money on advertising for tenants, and I've dropped the rent by sixpence. And still I haven't found anyone willing to take it on.'

'I'm not interested.' Still frail but now allowed out of bed and enjoying the run of the house, Rita had more important matters on her mind. She was toying with the idea of paying a visit to Owen's house. Not to see him, but to confront his wife with the truth. Lately there had been a growing suspicion in her mind, and it had caused her many a sleepless night. Only yesterday she had seen Owen pass by at the bottom of the lane. He and David were carting a load of logs to Langho. Filled with excitement at the sight of him, she had waved from the window, expecting him to look towards the house, hoping he was missing her as much as she was missing him. Instead he kept his gaze averted, apparently engaged in deep conversation with his son. Not once did he glance her way.

The incident had unnerved her, and from it the seed of doubt was sown. Had Owen grown cold towards her? Was he preparing to turn his back on her? Would he leave her carrying his child and not lay claim to it? No! Not if she had her way. Before she would let that happen, she would see him ruined.

'Did you hear what I said?' Frank bent to her, a gentler expression on his face. 'Would *you* like to live in the cottage, my dear? We could sell this place and have an extra room or two built on the cottage if you like.'

Already disturbed by her own thoughts, Rita laughed in his face. 'You must be mad!'

'Not mad, my dear,' he said, straightening his back and looking down at her with disappointment. 'Sensible, perhaps? It would help our finances, do you see? As you know we've never been what you might call rich. I'm already paying out a crippling fee for Jack's schooling, and now we've lost the rent from the cottage.' Anticipating an argument, he went on, 'Oh, I know what you're going to say. You're about to remind me that Margaret owns half of this house, *and* the cottage. I've thought of that, and I'm sure she'll agree. After all, I do believe she's had enough of residing under the same roof as the two of us ... especially since we took Jack under our wing. And she wouldn't be going away empty-handed because this house would fetch a fine profit.'

'Are you saying we're desperate for money?' Rita was not altogether astonished. Frank had a way of letting money run through his fingers like water with his frequent trips to London, his weakness for a game of cards and his liking for best whisky and cigars. Then there was the boy ... expensive shopping trips, extravagant gifts, and now the tutor's crippling fees. It wasn't surprising the money went out faster than it came in. No, she wasn't altogether astonished.

But she was glad of something else, and that was her own astuteness where money was concerned, because now she was comfortably off in her own right. Since the day they were married, she had carefully put away every shilling that had come into her own hands. She had jewellery that was worth a small fortune, and a dazzling sapphire necklace left by Joshua Blackthorn. That alone would keep her in luxury if she chose to sell it.

'I have no intention of living in that cottage.' In fact she had no intention of living *anywhere* with him. She too had plans, but they did not include Frank Blackthorn.

'Don't dismiss the idea out of hand, my dear,' he pleaded. 'Think about it while I'm gone to collect my one remaining rent.'

He had her attention now. 'Are you going to the Leytons'?' Her green eyes were shining as she got from the chair and walked with him to the door. 'Would you give Mrs Leyton my regards?'

'Really?' He was surprised and it showed. 'I hope you're not developing Margaret's tiresome trait of compassion for your neighbours.'

'No, but I think you should ask ...' Frowning, she pretended: 'Goodness, I've forgotten his name.' Putting her arm through her husband's, she smiled up at him. 'Well, anyway, I think it

533

might be a good idea if you asked Mr Leyton to deliver a load of his logs to the house.'

Frank was delighted she could not recall the man's name. After all, Owen Leyton was a fine figure of a man, with a certain look that would turn any woman's head. Oh, but not Rita's, he thought. Rita has eyes for no one but me. 'His name is Owen, my dear,' he said, kissing her on the forehead. 'It isn't like you to forget a thing like that. But of course you would have no reason to remember it.'

She shivered, not because she was cold – though it served her purpose for him to think that – but because the wetness of his kiss disgusted her. 'The house is so chilly. I would hate us to run out of logs.'

He was mortified. Looking towards the fire he was pleased to see a pile of logs blazing cheerily away. 'I'll get Ruby to keep the fire piled up, my dear,' he promised. 'We do have a good stock of logs, but seeing as you're still not well and feel the cold more than most, I'll have Owen Leyton deliver another load. Will that suit you?'

'You're a good man,' she purred, thinking what a fool he was. 'Hurry now, or he won't be able to get here before dark.'

Jack was in the kitchen, stuffing his face with what was left of an apple pie. It was the first place Frank looked. 'I need a hand, son,' he said, beckoning him out. 'Get the trap ready while I fetch my rent-ledger from the study.'

'If you're going to the Leytons', can I come with you?' What with one thing and another, Jack had felt neglected lately, and it peeved him.

'Why not? You'll need to know how to conduct a gentleman's business once the estate comes to you.' Frank's smile was all embracing, 'Meantime it behoves me to keep it profitable, wouldn't you say?'

'Too true!' And the sooner it comes to me the better, Jack thought. Even now, with the old lady gone . . . and with her the threat of being ousted, he still didn't feel altogether secure. On top of that he was missing the excitement of the streets. Langho was a quaint mixture of town and countryside and, though he had tried, he felt his face didn't really fit there. But London town? Now *there* was a place! Alive with vendors and reeking with the smell of hot chestnuts, villains round every corner and painted dolls selling their bodies for a few shillings. Carriages taking the gentry to their posh clubs; pockets to pick when their owners had swallowed a few bevvies; fist-fights in the alleys and rozzers on the beat. Alive and throbbing, that's what London was, and he was sore at heart to be parted from it.

Jack had long known the familiar streets were calling him back, and suspected there might be a day when he would return. But not yet. Oh, no, not until he had got what he came here for. He had suffered the starched collars and the discipline; he had sat through hours of being tutored; endured mealtimes when he was a spectacle; and felt the hostility of Margaret Blackthorn. There was a woman with a quick and suspicious mind, a woman he would have to watch if he was to fulfil his plans. There was no doubt he had been tempted many times, occasions when he could quite happily have rammed his pockets full of valuable trinkets and made his way back to London town. But it wasn't enough. When he had properties and land to sell, a fat balance in the bank and money in his pocket, now that would be another matter altogether . . .

He chuckled inwardly at the idea of turning up at his mam's door in a hansom cab, stepping out of it dressed in a toff's clobber and flaunting his newfound wealth to all and sundry. His mam might be reproachful at his having left her to the mercies of that awful fellow who slept alongside her. But, oh, just wait until she saw what he'd made of himself! Wait until he pushed a wad of notes into her grubby hand. She would have a change of heart then, no doubt. But it was still a long way off. And he had a great many cunning plans to undertake before he saw the light of that day.

When the trap was ready, Frank emerged from the house. 'By! It's a cutting breeze,' he exclaimed, climbing on to the seat. Though he was wrapped up warm in a woollen muffler and cap, with his long coat tucked round his legs, he felt the wind go right through his bones. 'Are you warm enough, son?' he asked, noting Jack's short jacket and bare head.

'Warm as a toasted muffin,' came the reply. There was nothing like the promise of an inheritance to make a body feel rosy, he thought.

Teasing the horse off to a careful start on the slippery ground,

Frank chuckled. 'You young blighters don't feel the cold. What it's like to be young, eh?' Shaking his head, he silently congratulated himself for providing a better childhood for his own son Jack than his parents had ever done for him. It never occurred to him that he was sorely guilty of neglecting Cathy, in the same way he himself had been neglected as a child.

As they passed the end of the lane which led to Nan Foster's cottage, Jack remarked, 'Shame about the old biddy.'

'*Lady*,' Frank corrected. 'Mrs Foster was always a *lady*. With her fine features and genteel manner, she could have been an aristocrat.' He felt a pang of guilt at having ransacked her home.

'Give you a shock, did it, when she were killed like that?'

Frank was quiet for a moment before answering in a low voice, 'She didn't deserve to be killed in that way. And, yes, it was a shock.'

The journey continued in silence. When they got to Owen's house there was another shock in store.

'I'm giving a month's notice,' Owen told Frank. 'It's time I moved on to pastures new.'

He didn't reveal that Maria had given him an ultimatum. She knew about him and Rita, and was adamant: 'Either you take me and the children miles away from here, or I'll have words with Frank Blackthorn. I'm sure he'll have something to say about the way you and his wife have been carrying on!'

Now Frank was taken aback. 'You can't leave!' Slamming the rent-ledger down on to the table, he glared at Owen. 'You've got a good thing going on here, Leyton. . . . prime land at a reasonable rent, a solid house for your family, and a landlord who doesn't interfere. What makes you think you can do better elsewhere?'

'It's just time I spread me wings, Mr Blackthorn.' Owen could feel his wife's presence at the back of the room, and his hair stood up on end. Terrified she might blurt out the truth, he gabbled on, 'Me and the wife . . . we've already made the decision, and there's no going back. In a month's time I'll be leaving the area altogether. Don't worry, the rent will be paid up, and I'll take nothing that isn't mine.'

'You're damn right you'll take nothing that isn't yours!' Seeing yet another source of revenue disappear was almost too much for Frank. Thumping his fist on the table, he shouted, 'It's a damned inconvenience, that's what it is. A damned inconvenience.' It was more than that. It was a further squeezing of the purse strings, and Rita wouldn't take kindly to it.

'If I've caused you a problem, then I'm sorry.' Owen was more sorry for himself. He loved this land, and if it wasn't for the mess he'd got himself into, he would be content for his bones to be laid here. He was a weak man where attractive women were concerned. Maria knew that, and so far had turned a blind eye. This time it was different. Oh, there would be temptation again, he was in no doubt about that. But with Rita Blackthorn he'd been too careless, and now she was carrying his child. Because of it, he was having to leave this place, to tramp the roads looking for work and hoping to earn a roof over their heads. What a bloody fool he'd been!

When Frank and the boy were gone, with Frank sending the horse down the lane at a furious pace, Maria told her husband the same. 'You've been a bloody fool, Owen Leyton.'

'I've done what you want.' Irritated, he stared her out. 'Let it go, Maria. We'll be leaving here soon enough. I just hope you don't come to regret it.'

'And if I do . . . if we have to rough it and live in the hedgerows, if I die from lack of warmth and food, whose fault will that be, eh?' Exhausted and weakened by her long illness, she sat in the chair and hung her head. 'I'm sorry.' She had never been a vindictive woman.

Owen came to her then. 'No, Maria, it's *me* who should be sorry,' he murmured. 'We both know it's time to move on, and you're right about its being my fault.'

Looking up with tear-stained face, she spoke to him in a softer voice. 'In many ways you're a strong man,' she told him, 'but you have a weakness for women. I've known it all along, but it hasn't really bothered me. You've always come back to me.' She wiped her eyes and sighed. 'This time it's different.'

'How different, Maria?' He knew she was right, but wanted her to spell it out.

'Rita Blackthorn is a dangerous woman. She won't let you go as easily as the others.' Squaring herself up to him, she studied him for a while, the handsome face with its strong square chin and dark eyes; eyes that held a fear she had never seen before. In a soft voice that held a world of conviction, she declared, 'You meant to leave us, didn't you? You really meant to set up home with that woman?'

The question rocked him on his feet. Yet he couldn't deny it. Instead he lovingly stroked her hair and remained silent for what seemed an age. Then he sighed deeply and turned away. 'How could you know that?'

She reached up to grasp his hand. 'Look at me, Owen Leyton,' she said, and when he turned there was a smile on her face.

'I know because I'm a woman,' she whispered. 'Women have a way of sensing such things. Call it instinct, or mebbe fear. All I know is what I feel here.' She tapped her breast.

'Can you forgive me?'

'Haven't I always?'

'You're a good woman, Maria Leyton, and I don't deserve you.'

There was no answer to this. She smiled and squeezed his hand, and he was satisfied.

Teresa heard the entire conversation. Having returned from the barn where David was sawing logs, she remained in the scullery, hidden from view but able to see her parents through the crack in the door. Still undetected, she crept out again, returning with a bucket in hand and clattering it to make sure she was heard. 'David!' Owen's voice rang out. 'Is that you?'

As he came towards the scullery, Teresa showed herself. 'David's sawing logs in the barn,' she told him. 'Is everything all right?'

'You'd better call him in. There's something he should know, something you should *both* know.'

A few minutes later, the family were gathered in the tiny parlour. Maria and her daughter were seated at the table. David stood behind them, his face clouded with anxiety. Owen stood with his back to the fireplace, desperately thinking of the best way to break the news to them. His first remark was addressed to his son, whose dark eyes were intent on him. 'No doubt you saw the landlord pass the barn on his way here?'

David looked at Teresa and nodded. 'Yes. We saw him ... come to collect the rent, I expect?'

'That's right, son. He collected something else too.'

'Oh?' Sensing trouble, David stiffened, his hand going invol-
untarily to his mother's shoulder.

'I gave him a month's notice.'

'What? You mean to leave here?' David couldn't believe his
ears. 'Why? What's happened?' Foremost in his mind was Cathy,
and the awful knowledge that if they were to leave here he
might never see her again.

'Nothing's happened.' Owen had no intention of revealing the
truth to his own son: that he was to blame for having bedded
Frank Blackthorn's wife. 'We've been here long enough, that's
all you need to know. Your mam and I have decided it's time
to leave.'

'But you can't!' Stepping forward, David confronted his
father. 'You love this place. Your heart's in it . . . and so is mine!
When we came here the land was fit for nothing. Now it's rich
and fertile. Why would you want to leave? WHY?'

'The decision is made.' Owen felt the despair in his son, and
his guilt was tenfold. 'Don't question it.'

During this exchange, Maria and the girl remained silent.
They were still silent when David swung round and strode out
of the house. 'I'll go after him.' Teresa rose from the chair. 'He's
bound to be bitter.'

'What about you?' Maria had been astonished when her
daughter took the news calmly.

Shrugging, Teresa thought for a moment then said, 'I think
you're right, and I for one won't be sorry to see the last of this
place.' Having successfully ruined the relationship between her
brother and Cathy, she was growing restless. Besides, now she
knew what had been going on between her father and Rita
Blackthorn, it was best they should make tracks, and the sooner
the better.

Owen was relieved. 'Happen you can persuade your brother
to think the same way?'

'Don't worry about David. I'll go and talk to him now.'

'No. Leave him be.' Owen knew how shaken David was by
the news. More than that, he had not forgotten how devoted to
Cathy his son was. There were times when a man needed to be
alone, and he sensed this was one of them. 'Just see where
he's gone.'

Teresa was in and out in no time. 'He's making his way to

the top field,' she said. 'He always goes there when he wants to think.'

For the first time, Maria wondered whether they were doing the right thing. 'It's hard on him,' she murmured. 'He's given his heart to this land, and he's known such happiness here.'

Ignoring her mother's remark, Teresa sullenly declared, 'If you ask me, he was getting too pally with that Blackthorn girl.' Eyeing Owen through spiteful eyes she said meaningfully, 'No good can come of things like that.'

Disturbed, yet not really knowing why, Owen snapped at her, 'Seeing as David's made himself scarce and I have the tractor to mend, do you think you're capable of delivering a load of logs?'

''Course I am!'

'Good. Then you'll need a warm coat and a pair of stout boots.'

He waited while she disappeared into the scullery, a moment later showing herself at the door, wearing her boots and carrying a long coat. 'I'm ready.'

Squaring his shoulders, he led the way to the barn. Here the two of them got ready the horse and cart, and in a surprisingly short time it was loaded high with freshly sawn logs. 'Take your time, and watch out for potholes in the road,' he warned.

Climbing into the hard seat, she asked for the umpteenth time, 'Where am I delivering?'

Beads of sweat ran down his temples as he stared up at her. His back ached and his heart even more. He had been all kinds of a fool and now he was paying the worst price. 'Blackthorn House. He brought the order with him this morning.' He gave a strange little laugh. 'In his temper, he forgot to pay for them, but never mind. I'll stop it out of next week's rent.' To tell the truth he was already toying with the idea of leaving before the rent could be collected. Now the hardest decision was made, he had a hankering to put it all behind him.

When the girl was gone, Owen looked round the barn with sad eyes. 'David's right,' he whispered. 'It's going to be a heart-breaking wrench. We've put a lot of years and back-breaking work into this place, and it's part of us now.' Every word was like a stab to his heart.

The familiar sights and smells overwhelmed him: the high pitched roof which he and David had mended so many times he'd lost count; the timber rails that divided the bays; the stable and the hay loft with its long narrow ladder ... all lovingly created by himself and his son. Groaning, he wiped the palms of his hands over his face. Through the gaps between his fingers, he peered out in anguish. 'What will we do? Where will we go?' His voice trembled with emotion. With shoulders drooping, he bent his head and gave vent to his feelings. The sobs shook his body, and the soft sound of his crying echoed from the walls. 'You've gone too far this time, Leyton,' he whispered. 'For the sake of a fling with Rita Blackthorn, you've lost it all, and damned well serve you right!'

Frank was still in a fury. On his return, he found Rita in the drawing room. Desperate to see Owen, she had positioned herself by the window, eagerly awaiting the sound of his horse and wagon. On the chair beside her lay a long dark shawl; she was wearing a burgundy high-necked dress and neat ankle boots. Her face was flushed with excitement as she turned to greet her husband. 'You look angry,' she remarked. 'What's wrong?' Not that she cared. But she wondered whether his sour mood had anything to do with Owen.

Instead of answering he made a remark of his own. 'Good heavens, look at you, my dear.' He saw how she was dressed and was both irritated and curious. 'Anyone would think you were ready to go out.' Rushing across the room he urged, 'Come away from the window, my dear, you know how draughty these old frames are. I don't want you to catch your death of cold.'

'Stop fussing!' Pushing his hand from her shoulder, she rounded on him angrily. 'You suffocate me,' she snapped. 'Why can't you leave me alone?' His stern features and turned-down mouth alerted her. 'What's the matter?' she demanded, keeping her distance. 'Something bad has happened. Tell me at once. Is it Owen Leyton? Has he angered you in some way? Speak up, can't you?'

He grimaced and clenched his fist, his next words making her heart sink. 'Yes, I'm afraid something *has* happened, my dear. And, yes, it *has* to do with the Leyton fellow.' Forcing himself to smile, he assured her, 'However, you're not to worry. I have it all in hand.'

'But I do worry, and I want to know.'

He sighed, a long breathy noise that repelled her. 'I'm afraid we'll have to be careful about the money we spend ... at least until we've secured new tenants.'

'You're not making sense. I already know you're looking for tenants to take the cottage.' She looked curiously at him. 'It isn't the cottage though, is it? Tell me, Frank. I need to know.'

'It's that damned Leyton fellow.' He clenched his fists and punched one hard against his thigh. 'Would you believe he's had the gall to give me a month's notice?' When she was too surprised to answer, he began pacing the room. 'If I didn't want every penny I can squeeze from him, I'd throw him out here and now ... but, of course, apart from the rent, I need the time to find a new tenant, and God knows I'm having no luck at all with the cottage. If I have *both* properties left vacant, it will mean a considerable loss of income.' He paused to look at her anxious face. 'But, like I said, my dear, you're not to worry. I won't have it.'

She was too busy thinking about this new turn of events to worry about his loss of income. 'Why is he leaving? Where does he mean to go? Has he explained?' At first she had been enraged, but now she was beginning to wonder if it wasn't all for her sake.

He laughed aloud. 'Explained? Not a word of it. All I'm told is that he's leaving, and that's as much as I know.'

Hope rose in her, bringing a smile to her face. 'I expect our Mr Owen Leyton has plans.' Certain that these plans included her, she could afford to be pleasant. 'A man like that, well, I suppose he likes to be secretive about what he means to do. No doubt he's been making these plans a long time, so you'll just have to accept it, I'm afraid.'

'You sound almost pleased?' He was staring at her with interest.

'Not at all.' Owen would be here soon, she told herself, and when he asked her, she would go with him to the ends of the earth.

'He should be here shortly with the logs I ordered.' Frank

542

glanced out of the window. 'I'm not in the mood to deal with him. I have other problems to think about.' As he left, he told her kindly, 'Do stay away from that draughty window, my dear, and remember what I said . . . you're not to worry. If you want me, I'll be in my study.' With that he went out of the room and down the hallway; leaving Rita smiling triumphantly to herself as she waited for Owen to arrive.

Her smile widened when she saw the horse and wagon approaching. It faded when she realised it was not Owen who drove it, but his daughter. Throwing the shawl over her shoulders, she met the wagon at the rear of the house. 'I was told your father would deliver the logs.' Though she tried hard not to show her disappointment it was easily evident to the girl.

Clambering down from the lofty seat, Teresa set about unloading the logs. 'As you can see, he's not here,' she answered sourly.

'Where is he then?'

'Working.'

'You're a very surly young woman.'

Teresa made a little bow. 'Sorry, Ma'am,' she said with a sly lilt to her voice. 'And I'm sorry if you're disappointed not to see my father. You'll just have to put up with me.'

Rita was instinctively cautious. 'I beg your pardon?' Sounding suitably offended, she demanded, 'What are you implying?'

This time the girl stopped in her work to look up. 'I know what the pair of you have been up to, and it's no use you denying it. But it's over. We're leaving the area and he'll never see you again.' She took delight in every word.

As the truth sank in, Rita turned a deathly shade of grey. 'What are you saying?' Faltering, she reached out and steadied herself against the wall of the house. 'Who told you these things?'

'It don't matter who told me. The plain truth is we're leaving, and he wants nothing more to do with you.'

'Liar!'

'Oh?' Stepping closer, Teresa pushed her face into the other woman's face. 'If I'm a liar, why is he running away with our mam instead of with you?' She turned her attention to Rita's swollen stomach. 'I wonder what your husband would say if he knew the brat you're carrying ain't his?'

The remark was too much for Rita. With a scream, she lunged forward. 'You liar!' Lashing out, she scored her sharp nails down the girl's face. Teresa struck out in defence and soon the two of them were fighting like wildcats.

When the horrified Ruby pulled them apart, the girl was laughing hysterically. 'You little vixen!' Ruby gasped. 'The master will have your hide for this.'

'I don't think so.' Tearing herself from Ruby's grasp, she stared at Rita with crafty eyes. 'I won't say anything if you don't.'

It was a form of blackmail and Rita was not ready for the truth to come out. Not yet. 'Let her go,' she told Ruby through bruised lips.

Triumphant, the girl clambered on to the half-emptied wagon. As she careered out of the yard at hair-raising speed, the remaining logs spewed from all sides and at one point, when the wheels became entangled in the rolling debris, it seemed as though the whole equipage would topple over. 'Good Lord above! She's mad as a hatter,' Ruby remarked. 'Whatever's got into the creature?'

'Forget it, Ruby,' Rita ordered. 'And you're not to say a word to the master.'

'Whatever you say, Ma'am.' But Ruby was immensely curious, believing there was more here than met the eye.

As she led Rita back to the house, she said nothing more. At times like these it was best to keep your mouth shut and mind your own business. She had her suspicions, though, and they included Owen Leyton.

In the peace of her own room, Rita sat impatiently while Ruby dabbed at the bruises and cuts to her face. Ruby worked silently, her mind going over what had taken place in the yard. She still couldn't believe the mistress had allowed the Leyton girl to get away with attacking her. 'The hoyden,' she remarked angrily. 'She deserves a whipping.'

Pushing Ruby away, Rita reminded her, 'You're to say nothing about this, not to the master, nor to anyone else. Do you understand?'

Ruby shook her head. 'No, Ma'am, I don't,' she said with the boldness of age. 'But you've told me not to say anything and I won't.' Gathering her bowl and towel, she asked, 'Is there anything else I can do for you, Ma'am? Happen a nice hot cup of tea to steady yer nerves?'

Realising Ruby was confused by her decision not to have the girl punished, and not wanting to mystify her any further, Rita decided to humour her. In a kinder voice she replied, 'Thank you, Ruby. A cup of tea would be nice.'

'Don't worry about the bruises, Ma'am,' Ruby assured her. 'A cold-water swab and they're gone in no time.' Her chest swelled with pride. 'I'm a good nurse if I do say so myself.'

Rita was not in the mood for chit-chat. 'Miss Margaret and the girl. Where are they?'

'Gone to Langho. Madge Penny's old man did a runner last week and her eighth bairn is due any minute.' Ruby chuckled. 'You know how Miss Margaret likes to help. She had me sorting out the linen cupboard at the crack of dawn. Her and Miss Cathy left the house some time back, loaded down with all manner of things. Sheets and pillow-cases, towels, nightdresses, and goodness knows what else.'

'And the boy?'

'I ain't seen him since breakfast, Ma'am. I expect he's gone off on one of his little secret missions.' She smiled, but it was without humour. 'The master's still in his study. Do you want me to fetch him?'

'No. I just want to be left alone. In fact, if he shows himself, tell him I'm very tired and don't want to be disturbed.'

'I'll fetch your tea, then I'll see no one comes near.'

When Ruby had gone, Rita sat in the pink wicker chair, her mind on fire from what the girl had told her. 'You lied,' she muttered through clenched teeth. 'Owen wants *me*. I'm carrying his child. I know he would never leave without me.'

Rising from the chair, she went to the window and looked out. Angry tears ran down her face. 'He does love me,' she told a cloudy sky, 'but he *is* leaving. Frank told me he was leaving.' The idea that he might go without her was unbearable. The longer she thought on it, the more confused her mind grew. 'No! He would never leave without me!' A crafty smile transformed her face. 'He's probably waiting for me right now.' A kind of madness took hold of her. Turning on the spot she spun faster and faster until she fell into the chair, dizzy with joy. 'Of course! He daren't come to me, so I have to go to him.' She laughed aloud until Ruby knocked on the door and she was forced to reply in a more serious voice: 'Come in.'

'Here you are, Ma'am.' Ruby had heard her laughing, but thought it best to say nothing. These days she had seen a strangeness in Rita Blackthorn, but to tell the truth she wasn't altogether surprised. Placing the tray on the small table, she quickly withdrew to the quietness of her own kitchen.

Sipping the tea and collecting her thoughts, Rita knew what must be done. 'I'll go to him this very night,' she told herself in the mirror. 'We'll be together for all time.' Softly singing, she lay down on her bed and dreamed of how it would be.

Madge Penny made a loud noise when she made love, and she made a frightening noise when giving birth. Her eighth labour was no exception. The ear-splitting screams could be heard from one end of the street to the other. 'Lord help us!' she cried, squeezing Margaret's hand until it grew numb. 'Where's Widow Carter?'

'She'll be here any minute.' Margaret would never admit it but she was frightened by Madge's awful wailing.

Clutching wildly at her sleeve, Madge writhed on the bed, her plump face contorted with agony. 'For God's sake, get her here . . . tell her I've started and it's bad.' A long crippling pain set her off in a howl that shook the room.

Margaret was beside herself with worry. Never having delivered a child, she was fraught with all manner of doubts as to her own ability. 'Hold on if you can,' she pleaded. 'I've sent for the widow and I'm sure it won't be long before she's here.' She wiped the wet flannel over the woman's face and coaxed her to be quiet. 'Cathy will go with the boy again. Don't worry now.'

'I'm sorry, luv.' Madge Penny was a good soul at heart, but it peeved her to have the gentry woman at her bedside instead of the widow who had given birth to nine of her own and knew what a woman had to endure. 'I've been through it all afore and happen I should know better than to scream and shout,' she said with a little chuckle, 'but it helps, y'see. The louder I shout the easier it is, so don't fear it means I'm dying.'

'I don't fear that.'

'To look at you, anybody would think it were *you* who were giving birth.' Margaret's kindly face was bathed in sweat, and she intermittently paced the room, staring out of the window in search of the widow's homely figure.

'I've never attended a birthing before,' Margaret confessed. 'But you can rely on me. I'll stay until help comes. Meanwhile, just tell me what I have to do.'

The older woman sat up in bed, her long mouse-coloured hair matted with sweat and her face red from exertion. 'The little sod's resting now,' she explained, 'but it won't be long afore it kicks up again with a vengeance.' She rubbed both hands across her stomach and groaned. 'Let's hope the widow's here by then.' Patting at Margaret's hand, she thanked her for all her kindness. 'I reckon we've time for a brew,' she suggested. 'Make it hot and black . . . oh, and put a drop o' booze in it. You'll find it hidden behind the sideboard.' Laughing aloud, she pointed to her stomach. 'That should shift the bugger!'

Margaret was relieved and it showed. 'I could do with a cup of tea myself,' she revealed. 'I'll be as quick as I can. But first, let me make sure you're comfortable.'

Downstairs in the parlour, Cathy waited with Madge's seven children. The room was tiny, no bigger than the shed at the foot of her father's garden. But it was more of a home than Cathy's own. In spite of the poverty that surrounded her, Madge Penny had made the old house into a cosy refuge. The parlour walls were painted green, the black iron fire-range was brightly polished and the long window was covered with respectable lace curtains. The square table was spread with a serviceable green chenille cloth, and in the centre stood a pot plant, green and thriving, making the place surprisingly cheery.

Cathy was seated in the big horse-hair armchair by the fire. Every now and then she would gaze round at the faces of the children. At eleven years of age John was the eldest; small-boned and quiet, he sat in the chair opposite Cathy. The four girls sat round the table, one of the smaller boys sat by Cathy's feet sucking his shirt, and the youngest, a boy not yet two, lay asleep in his makeshift cot under the window. For over an hour they had suffered the howls and wails that issued from upstairs, and now the ensuing silence was unnerving. 'Is she dead?' John stared at Cathy with great big frightened eyes.

Suppressing her own fears, she smiled. 'No, sweetheart. She's having a rest, that's all,' she answered wisely.

'Why's it gone all quiet then?' His voice trembled with emotion.

'She doesn't have to shout *all* the time, silly!' At nine years of age Jessie was the eldest girl. She believed she knew everything, and her brother's questions appeared to amuse and irritate her. 'Honestly, John Penny!' she chided, 'Don't you remember how Mam said she would shout a bit, then be quiet a bit?' She tutted and shook her head like a little old woman. 'Boys are softies,' she told Cathy with a frown. '*You're* not frightened, are you?'

Cathy was honest. 'Just a bit,' she said apologetically.

'Have you heard a baby being born before?'

'No.'

'That's all right then. When our mam had her,' she pointed to the smaller girl beside her, 'I was frightened too.' She cast a glance of derision at her brother John. '*He* shouldn't be frightened though, 'cause he's heard our mam have *all* her babies and she ain't dead yet!'

Cathy smiled. 'Do you want it to be a boy or a girl?' she asked. The idea of a new baby enthralled her.

The girl shrugged her shoulders. 'Don't much care,' she remarked casually. 'They're all the same anyway ... shit theirselves and scream all night they do. Our mam says she wished she'd drowned us all at birth.'

John gave her an angry stare. 'She never meant that and you know it!'

Sensing a row brewing, the smallest child at the table began crying. 'I don't want to be drowned,' she wailed, looking up at her big sister with appealing eyes. When the older girl put an arm round her and promised, 'Not you, Peg. Our mam didn't want to drown *you*,' she spread her little fingers on the table and began proudly entertaining everyone by counting up to four.

At that point Margaret returned to the parlour to tell them, 'Your mother's fine. It won't be long before you have a baby brother or sister.' Her words were greeted with a smile from Jessie, a confused look from John and a bevy of questions from the smaller children. 'In a minute,' Margaret answered patiently. Addressing herself to John, she said, 'Run to Widow Carter's ... tell her your mother needs her right away, that she's close to birthing.' When he jumped from the chair and thankfully headed for the door, she told Cathy, 'Go with him. Make sure the widow knows it's urgent.' That said, and the two of them gone at a run down the street, she turned her attention to Jessie. 'I'd be grateful if you could make a pot of tea while I talk to the young ones.'

'That's our mam,' the girl replied with a grin. 'Always wanting her brew.' While she set about making it, Margaret couldn't help but think how mature she seemed, when in fact she was only a bairn.

As Jessie came back in through the scullery door with a mug of tea for her mam, Widow Carter came rushing in through the other door, with John and Cathy hurrying behind. 'I couldn't come afore,' she explained in a slurred voice. 'Got into a deep sleep and couldn't find me way out of it.' She grinned through numerous gaps between her blackened teeth. 'Truth is I sank a few too many bevvies last night.'

Margaret hurried down the narrow stairs when she heard Widow Carter arrive.

'I'm sure Mrs Penny will be glad you're here now,' Margaret said with relief. She went on to explain that they had arrived earlier to find the poor woman already in the throes of labour.

'Right then!' Rolling up her sleeves, Widow Carter demanded in a sergeant-major voice, 'Plenty of hot water and towels ... and keep that lot out of me way.' Pointing to the children, she wagged a finger. 'You behave yerselves down here. If I know yer mam I'll have enough to do keeping her quiet.'

She laughed as she made for the stairs. Cathy followed with the mug of tea. 'Old Madge ain't the easiest in the world,' the widow called out to her as she went. 'All women is different when it comes to birthing. What! I've heard the buggers scream blue murder, and I've seen 'em cry like babbies ... I've had to hold 'em down and fight with 'em till I'm black and blue. Then there's them as sees it all as something wonderful and can't wait

549

to hold the little 'un in their arms. But Madge!' She chortled, almost losing her footing as she began her way up the stairs. 'What! She'll scream like a banshee from beginning to end.' Poking a gnarled finger in her ear, she complained wryly, 'I've delivered every one o' Madge's, and now I'm nearly deaf for me thanks.'

Once inside the bedroom, the widow took charge. Giving Madge a scolding, she said, 'You might have waited till I felt capable. I've a head on me like three, and me tongue's stuck to the roof o' me mouth. I'm tired and sick, and it ain't fair yer should wake an old 'un from her bed.'

Madge replied that if she felt ill, it served her right for boozing, and if she didn't soon get on with it, the babby would be here and there'd be no need for her services. 'Miss Blackthorn here's done a wonderful job,' she said, taking great gulps from the mug of tea which Cathy handed her.

'I'm sure she has.' The widow smiled at Margaret, who asked if there was anything more she could do. 'Not a thing,' came the reply. 'In fact, if yer want to make yer way home, I'll say goodnight to yer.' It was clearly a dismissal, and Margaret was quick to realise she was no longer required.

She said her goodbyes and assured Madge that if she needed anything she must send one of the children to Blackthorn House. Madge thanked her profusely, and within minutes Cathy and Margaret had left the house and were on their way down the street. As they reached the corner, Madge's dreadful howls brought them to a halt. 'Is it always like that?' asked Cathy.

Margaret shook her head. 'No,' she replied kindly. 'According to Widow Carter, Madge is unique. Never having had a child myself I'm no expert, but it seems every woman deals with childbirth in a different way. I remember when your mother had you, she was in labour for only two hours and never uttered a sound.'

Cathy dwelt on these words for a long time. Deep in her heart she had hoped that she and David would marry and have children. Now that dream was gone, and she was left with an emptiness that nothing could fill. 'I thought it was so lovely in that house ... all the children, I mean.' She glanced back down the street. 'When you have brothers and sisters you're never lonely, are you?' Not like *she* was lonely, she thought. Even though she had her beloved Margaret, there were still times when she felt all alone in the world.

In the lamplight Margaret looked into her face, and it struck her that at sixteen Cathy was already a woman, with a woman's heart. It was evident in those strong green eyes and that lovely heart-shaped face whose expression was now thoughtful. 'I think you were made to be a wife and mother,' she said softly. 'And it will happen, I know. One day it will happen, sweetheart.'

'But it won't be with David will it?' Cathy's voice trembled, betraying her most private fears. And if it couldn't happen with David, she didn't want it to happen at all.

Margaret's answer was to put her arm round Cathy's shoulders and draw her close. As they walked on, the silence was soothing to them both.

Behind them a child was brought into the world. 'What in God's name were yer thinking of?' Widow Carter had kept her opinions to herself until mother and bairn were safe. 'Fancy letting the gentry near yer . . . especially at a time like this!' Apart from a fervent belief that gentry and ordinary folk should be kept miles apart, Widow Carter had a natural suspicion of anyone who lived in a big house.

'She's no different from you nor me,' Madge retaliated. 'Miss Blackthorn and that young niece of hers have been good to me and mine, and I'll not hear a word agin 'em.'

'Oh aye!' Widow Carter hadn't forgotten the shocking fate of someone else who had got too close to Margaret and Cathy Blackthorn. 'An' weren't she good to poor Nan Foster? An' didn't that poor soul have 'er brains bashed in?' She washed Madge, then she washed the bairn, and all the time she grumbled through the wide gaps between her blackened teeth. 'Yer want to be careful o' the company yer keep, Madge Penny,' she warned. 'Or yer might rue the day.'

As they approached the house, Cathy's attention was caught by a flurry of movement against the far hedge. Glancing across, she saw a dark hurrying figure. 'There's someone there,' she whispered, drawing Margaret to a halt. 'Did you see?'

Margaret peered through the darkness. There was nothing. 'A trick of the moonlight,' she suggested. 'Unless of course it's Jack. I wouldn't be at all surprised to see *him* sneaking about at all hours.'

'There *was* someone there, I'm certain of it!' Linking her arm through Margaret's, Cathy quickened her steps towards the house.

Ruby was waiting for them. 'Wherever have yer been till now?' she demanded. When told the whole story, she made them each a mug of cocoa and saw them off to bed. 'Everyone else has been asleep long since,' she declared. 'And now that the two of you are home, I'll not be long afore I'm off to me own bed.'

What with the excitement at Madge Penny's and then the conviction that she had seen someone skulking about as they approached the big house, Cathy couldn't sleep. For a long time she wandered about her bedroom, restless and disturbed but not knowing why. She thought about David and suffered the same painful regrets. She cried a little and chided herself for doing so. She sat by the window and looked over the darkened gardens below, and finally, when a thirst came on her, she put her robe round her shoulders and crept down to the kitchen – almost jumping out of her skin when Jack opened the door just as she had her hand on the door-knob. 'Goodness! You gave me a fright,' she gasped. 'I didn't think anyone would be down here.'

Putting his hands on her arms he drew her inside the kitchen. 'I was on my way to bed,' he said, 'but I'd rather stay and keep you company. I can't sleep anyway.'

Whether Cathy wanted his company or not didn't bother him. 'You were late coming in,' he recalled. 'And you've been gone for most of the day.' He followed her to the pantry. 'You're very quiet. Is anything wrong?'

Pouring the sarsaparilla, she lifted her eyes to stare at him. 'Does it look as though there's something wrong?'

Thrusting his hands into his pockets he warned himself to be careful. If he questioned her, she might feel obliged to question him. That would never do, because his secrets were his own. 'No. I just wondered, that's all.' Pointing to the sarsaparilla he said, 'You can pour me one while you're at it.'

When they were sitting at either end of the table, it was Cathy's turn to ask a question. 'What time did you get in?'

'Ages ago. I've been cooped up and needed a breath of fresh air, so I went for a walk across the fields.' Already he was on his guard. 'Why do you ask?'

Cathy didn't answer straight away. Instead she took her time while recalling the furtive figure she had seen hurrying from the house. 'Did someone visit tonight?'

He shrugged his shoulders. 'Not sure.'

'How long has Father been in bed?'

'He was in the study when I got back. A short time later he went upstairs and there was one hell of a row. He came rushing down again and told Ruby he was feeling ill and going to his bed ... said he didn't want her disturbing him till tomorrow morning.' He leaned back in his chair and studied her. 'As far as I know he's been in his room since, and no, I don't think he's had any visitors.'

'What about Mother?'

'Been in bed for most of the day ... sulking as usual.' He rolled his eyes to the ceiling. 'I heard Ruby knock on the door to tell her she'd brought a tray of refreshments. Next minute she was going down the stairs in a bad mood after being sent packing, tray and all.' He eyed Cathy curiously. 'What's all this about?'

'Nothing. Just that when we came back from Mrs Penny's, I thought I saw someone leaving the house.'

'Mrs Penny, eh?' he sneered. 'Who's that? One of your poor folk?'

Cathy didn't like the way he put the question, so she chose not to answer it. Instead she quickly drank her sarsaparilla and bade him good night.

'You're not leaving me here on my own, are you?' He got to the door before her. 'I don't want you to go,' he murmured, deliberately barring her way.

'I'm tired.'

'You weren't tired a minute ago.'

'Well, I am now.' She had welcomed Jack into this house and been a friend to him, but, since he had deliberately picked a fight with David and spoiled their relationship, her feelings towards him had begun to change. 'Let me pass.' Though she felt threatened, her voice was low and calm. 'I don't feel like talking any more.'

He gazed at her lovely face and a kind of anger surged through him. 'You haven't forgiven me, have you?' he remarked bitterly.

She could have evaded the subject, pretending she didn't understand what he meant. But she *did* understand and now that he had raised the matter she had to reply. 'No, I haven't forgiven you. What you did in goading David into a fight was petty and unnecessary, and because of you, he and I are strangers.'

'All the more reason for you and me to be closer.' Sensing an opportunity he was quick to grasp it. Reaching out he caught her by the back of the neck. 'After all, we're not *really* brother and sister, are we?' Pressing his mouth to hers, he kissed her long and hard.

Taken completely by surprise, Cathy was shocked rigid for a minute, but then rage flowed through her. Lifting her hands, she grabbed his ears and twisted them until he cried out, 'Bitch!' Stumbling in pain he backed away, clutching his ears and staring at her in disbelief. 'What did you do that for?'

'I'm surprised you have to ask.' As she stared at him indignantly her face was set like stone. 'It saddened me that Aunt Margaret could never take to you. I see now she had good reason.'

Enraged and humiliated, he grabbed her by the arm. 'I don't give tuppence for what anybody thinks of me, least of all her. But *you're* different. Your precious Margaret might not have taken to *me*, but I took to you right from the start.' He would have stroked her face but she backed away. Her action further infuriated him. Darting to the door, he slammed it shut.

Up to that point, Cathy had felt all kinds of emotion towards him: anger, indignation, even a touch of loathing. But she had not felt fear until the moment when he slammed shut the door. 'Get out of my way!' she snapped. 'NOW!' Suddenly he was not the brother who had been foisted on her, the waif she had pitied and gone out of her way to befriend. Instead he was a dangerous creature.

He smiled at her words, shaking his head as though it was inconceivable that she should ask him to go. 'You're forgetting, I have as much right in this house as you now.' Taking hold of her by the shoulders, he stared at her long and hard, his smiling eyes boring into hers, making her turn away with disgust. When he tugged her forward she struggled like a wildcat. But he was the stronger. 'Don't want to kiss me, eh?' he murmured. 'Think I'm not good enough for you, is that it?' His voice took on a hard edge. 'Oh, but you'd kiss *him* right enough, wouldn't you, eh? You'd let David Leyton put his hands on you?' Bringing his leg up, he pushed his knee between her legs. 'How many times have you done it with him, eh? You can tell me, Cathy.' When she struggled fiercely, he shook her hard. 'HOW MANY TIMES?'

Unyielding she stared him out, at the same time frantically wondering how she could be rid of him. She could scream and wake the entire household, but deep down she realised there were those who would blame her and not him. Besides, even though he was being cruel and unpleasant, she couldn't believe he meant to harm her, not really. She decided to remain calm and be dignified. Surely he would respond similarly. In a quiet voice she told him, 'David is worth ten of you, and you know it.'

Her words seem to surprise him. Softly laughing, he said incredulously, 'It's plain as a pikestaff you'd want him above me.' Squeezing her shoulders, he enjoyed it when she winced. 'You love him, don't you?'

'That's my business. Now get out of my way.' Burning with shame and anger she pushed her hands against his chest, but she was no match for his brute strength.

Suddenly he released her, sending her off balance. 'Go on then!' he urged, opening the door. 'Get back to your bed and dream of your precious David.' He wanted her more than he had ever wanted anything. The want rose in him like a black tide, swamping every other emotion. Now, as she brushed past him, it was all he could do not to take her.

When she left him there, he remained by the door, watching her as she walked along the hallway, his lascivious eyes following her as she went towards the staircase. She had a special kind of grace and a loveliness of nature that he had never before encountered. 'You're beautiful,' he whispered, and the want was overwhelming, spreading through him unchecked, firing his veins and smothering his reason.

On soft footsteps he followed her like a shadow, only a heart-beat behind. Soon he would be leaving this house. He couldn't go without first tasting of Cathy's loveliness.

Unaware that she was being pursued, but deeply unnerved by the incident, she sped along the upper landing towards her bedroom, her soft bare feet making no sound against the carpet. Like a breath of air, David came into her mind, into her heart, warming her senses, making her happy, making her sad. 'Oh, David,' she murmured, coming quietly into her room, 'I wish you were here now.'

As she half turned to close the door, Jack was on her. Fired by lust and hating her because she would always be good and he would always be bad, he clamped his hand over her mouth and pushed her to the floor. The more she struggled, the more brutal he became. In the half-light he saw the terror in her eyes. 'I won't hurt you,' he said. 'But you shouldn't have said those things to me.' Nuzzling his face against hers, he groaned, 'You've made me wild, y'see. And I've always been a bad lot when I'm wild.'

With her arms pinned down and the weight of him on top, she couldn't move. Her heart was beating as though it would burst and when he tore at her nightgown the fear in her was tenfold. As he ravaged her, the fear became horror, then immense pain, and then it was a strange and shocking numbness.

After he moved away, she lay like a stone at his feet. 'Happen you'd like to tell your precious David about that,' he snarled. When she didn't answer or look at him, he kicked her. 'No doubt he'll come after me. Well, let him. Life on the streets taught me how to look after myself. You'd be surprised how good I am with a knife.'

Still she didn't look up, nor did she move. For one awful minute he thought she might be dead. But then he saw the shocked green eyes blink and the tears roll down her face. He sighed with relief. 'You tell him to come after me if you like,' he bragged. 'But be warned ... I'll be waiting. One dark night when he least expects it, I'll jump on him from some alley.' He grinned, and in the moonlight he looked half crazy. 'I can promise you this, my lovely. If he comes after me, he won't walk away.' Bending his face to hers, he whispered, 'Best if you're sensible, eh? If I were you, I wouldn't tell *anybody*... not David, and certainly not your precious Margaret. Because if you did, I would have to hurt them, and then you'd never forgive yourself, would you, eh?' Prodding her with his foot, he demanded, 'You can hear me, can't you? You do know I mean what I say?'

Cathy heard his every word. Torn and hurting, she waited, silently biding her time. Her first instinct was to kill him. In her pain and confusion, she wondered why the good Lord had not struck him down in front of her. That would be a fitting punishment for what he had done.

'Remember what I said,' he warned grimly. 'Tell whoever you like. But *I* won't be the one to pay... it'll be them. O' course, there's always the chance I might be caught and made to answer for what's happened. But that wouldn't do you no good neither, because I'd only deny it till I'm blue in the face.' He chuckled. 'Though I say it meself, I'm a good liar. It wouldn't take much to convince them that it was your precious David who came here and attacked you. What! I even saw the fella with me own eyes... ran off like the coward he was. Oh, yes, I'll tell a good story, and it'll see him thrown inside for a very long time, I reckon.' He pressed his face against hers. 'You know they'd believe me. After all, anyone could see the way you two felt about each other.'

Grabbing a hank of her long hair, he said with a moan, 'Don't make the mistake of thinking I wouldn't do it. Oh, I've sat across the table from you. I've eaten from your mother's dainty plates and I've studied the ways of a gentleman. But here where it matters' – he dug his thumb into his chest – 'I'm a chancer, a rogue made hard and cruel from living on his wits. You don't really know me. None of you do. Open your mouth, say one word about this to anybody, and I swear you'll rue the day. It won't be me who faces the consequences. It'll be the others... them you think the world of. I'll see they suffer one way or another.' His voice trembled with hatred. 'If I can't promise you anything else, I can promise you that.'

Like the shadow that had followed her in, he left, silent and unseen by her, a creature with badness born in him.

When the door closed behind him, Cathy lay where she was, dazed and bleeding, tears streaming down her face. After a while she struggled up. Going to the washbowl she bathed herself from head to toe time and again, until the water was all gone and the towel stained with her blood. Taking it and the torn nightgown she put them into the pillow-case and pushed them under the bed. She went to the drawer and took out a clean nightgown which she put on, shivering with cold and tainted by the awful memory of what had taken place here in this very room where she had always felt safe. She didn't feel safe now. She might never feel safe again. The thought was nauseating.

For a while she was lost, not knowing what to do. She paced the floor then sat on the edge of the bed, thinking, not thinking, hardly alive inside.

After an hour she sat in the wicker chair and stared out of the window. The night was very beautiful and the moon was high in a clear dark sky; stars twinkled like tiny jewels and she knew the Maker was watching. 'Help me,' she pleaded. 'Forgive me.' In some way she blamed herself, yet couldn't see why. Folding her arms across her breast, she began rocking back and forth. The clock on the mantelpiece ticked and the hours went by. Soon the dawn was rising and his last words echoed over and over in her tortured mind. She whispered them now and every one etched itself in her heart. 'The others ... them you think the world of. I'll see they suffer one way or another. If I can't promise you anything else, I can promise you that.'

Going to the window, she pressed her face close to the pane. It was cold and hard. The tears came again, bitter painful tears that tore her in two. 'I can't tell,' she cried softly. 'He knows I can never tell.'

The burden of what had happened would be her secret, hers and the fiend who had violated her. For all her life she would have to live with it, and never be able to take comfort from confiding in those who loved her. It was a daunting prospect. Yet Cathy knew in her heart that she would be strong enough. To be weak now would put others in danger, and she could never bring herself to do such a thing.

At long last, emotionally scarred and mentally exhausted, she curled up in bed and sank into a fretful sleep.

Out on the landing, another creature of the night emerged. Twice Rita had inched open her door to peer out. The first time she had seen Jack enter her daughter's room; she had seen how he pushed her inside and suspected his intention. But she did not intervene. To intervene might have jeopardised her own plans and she couldn't have that. And anyway, what did she care about Cathy's fate? Or even Jack's for that matter?

The second time she looked out, it was to see Jack creeping away. From his wicked secretive smile she suspected something awful had taken place in Cathy's room. But her concern was only fleeting. She had other more important matters to attend to. Matters that concerned her and Owen, their future, their child, and she was excited beyond endurance. She waited a while longer until she was certain Jack wouldn't see her; though she was curious when, instead of going in the direction of his room, he went down the stairs. But again, she had neither time nor inclination to dwell on it.

She waited again to see if he might return. He didn't. Convinced he must either be in the kitchen or the sitting room, she carefully ventured out.

Fully dressed and with a hooded cloak hiding her, she went quickly down the stairs and out of the house. 'Be ready, Owen,' she muttered lovingly. The thought of being with him made her quicken her steps.

As she hurried away, Rita was unaware of the young man who watched. Fascinated to see the mistress of the house wandering the fields at night, Jack took up pursuit. Two dark hearts, bent on their own gratification, without remorse or conscience, and with not one saving grace between them.

The night was dark outside, but here in the house she had made cozy Maria sat by a cheery fire. In the light from the blazing logs, she studied her husband's face. 'You're still a handsome man, Owen Leyton,' she said proudly. 'Happen that's the trouble ... happen if you'd been an ugly old bugger the women wouldn't fall head over heels for you.' She shook her head. 'But they do. And you, like the fool you are, can't refuse the temptation offered you.' She sighed and smiled a little. But then the smile slipped away and a look of concern replaced it. 'If our David knew the things you'd done, he'd have you out that door afore your feet could touch the ground.'

That was the one thing Owen was afraid of. 'David must never know,' he pleaded. 'Teresa neither. If you were to tell them, I couldn't forgive you.'

She laughed at that. 'Oh, I see! If I were to tell our children how you've bedded one woman after another, made a nonsense of our marriage vows and caused us to move on because of your shameful behaviour... you'd never forgive me? Is that what you're saying?' Her eyes popped out of her head and her mouth hung open with astonishment.

'I know I have no right to ask anything of you.'

'Well, at least you're man enough to admit that.'

'You won't tell them then?'

She studied him before assuring in a warmer voice, 'No, I'll not tell 'em. You can rely on it.' Settling back into her chair she stared into the flames. 'I must be getting soft in the head in me old age.'

'You're far from old, Maria.' He had never seen her as old and never would. 'And you're certainly not soft in the head.'

'Hmph!' She smiled at him. 'I must be, because you've given me a great deal of heartache over the years, and still I've stood by you.' A deep and weary sigh issued from her. 'Any other woman would hate you for what you've done. But so help me, I must be as big a fool as you, because I can't do without you.'

Suddenly he was on his knees before her. 'And I can't do without you, Maria,' he confessed. 'Why do you think I want us away from here? Why haven't I gone off with Rita Blackthorn? I'll tell you why. Because it's *you* I want. Other women tempt me like you said, and yes I'm weak... and stupid, and I don't deserve someone like you. But in spite of everything, I can't see a life without you. I couldn't survive that, and you know it.' Only when it seemed he might lose her, did he realise how much she really meant to him.

But Maria knew. 'You don't have to tell me,' she said, touching her fingers against his face. 'I've always known we belong together. Oh, the women came and they went, you cheated me time and again, but I always knew it wouldn't last with them. You and me, we're a pair. That's the way it is.' A cold hand took hold of her heart. 'There was only ever one woman who frightened me. One woman who I thought would take you from me.' She visibly shivered. 'I don't have to say her name, do I?'

He shook his head. 'I was afraid too,' he revealed. 'Rita Blackthorn is a witch like no other. I found myself being suffocated ... wondering what life with her would be like.' He closed his eyes and groaned. 'I never wanted that.'

'Then the sooner we're gone from here, the better.' She shivered again. 'Is there a window open?' She looked round, searching for the means by which a chill could enter the room; she wasn't aware that the chill was in their thoughts.

'Not unless David's left a window open in his bedroom again.'

'Go and look, will you? The cold's crept right through me bones.'

Going to the fireplace he took two logs from the basket. Wedging them into the grate, he waited for them to catch alight. When they did he turned to her and said softly, 'It's been a while since we made love in front of the fire, Maria.'

'Has it?'

'The other two won't be back till early light. You know what they're like ... especially David. He won't come home without something to show for a night's poaching.'

'You're right. It *has* been a long time, and to tell the truth I don't know if I could ... not tonight.' She had never felt right making love on the floor. It didn't seem proper. The look on his face prompted her to remark cynically, 'All the same, if I refuse I've no doubt you'll find somebody else only too willing, eh?' Not so long ago she wouldn't have minded even that. But now, since Rita Blackthorn, she saw the risk and didn't want to lose him. 'All right, yer bugger,' she whispered, staring round the room as though afraid someone might overhear. 'But we'll have to be quick. I don't want the children surprising us.'

He came to her and cupped her face in his hands. 'I do love you, Maria.'

'So you should!'

'You have the loveliest blue eyes.'

561

'Pity you didn't notice 'em when you were gallivanting about.'

'I *always* noticed them.'

'And did you notice the sallow skin and the bags under me eyes?'

'Never!'

'Liar.'

'Don't talk, Maria. Let's enjoy each other.'

'You mean let *you* enjoy me.'

'Shh. Just hold me.' Reaching down he plucked away her shawl and dropped it on the rug. 'Remember how it used to be, before you were took ill,' he urged softly. Raising her skirt, he fondled her soft thighs, then after undoing his trousers he placed his hands beneath and drew her to the edge of the chair. He was kissing her full on the mouth when he entered her, and he knew from her long contented sigh that she was remembering. 'I need you, Maria,' he whispered against her face. 'I will always need you.'

It seemed like a lifetime since she had felt the warmth of his bare skin against her. The warmth invaded her senses and, like a young woman in love for the first time, she clung to him, her legs wide apart and he between them. In that fevered moment there was no other woman, no regrets; only joy of a kind she had almost forgotten.

Rita Blackthorn emerged from the darkness and made her way towards the house. Her hair was dishevelled and the hem of her dress torn where it had tangled in the brambles; her feet ached and her body was wet with sweat. She had trudged a long way and was weary. The only thought that spurred her on was that soon she and Owen would leave this place for good.

Like the bold creature she was, she went straight to the front door and knocked on it. When there was no answer she knocked again. Still no answer. Resting for a moment against the wall she recovered her breath and tidied the straying strands of her hair. A moment later she was creeping softly around the house, towards the one lighted window she had seen on her approach. She thought it odd that the house was so quiet, especially when a family of four lived within its walls.

Light from the window shafted into the night. The curtains

were not closed and so she peered in. She could see only half the room. It looked warm and cosy, the logs danced and crackled in the fireplace, throwing flickering shadows on the walls and lighting up the pretty pictures that hung there.

In the cold night air, balancing on a mound of dry earth in order to see inside, she felt impatient and uncomfortable. Seeing no one, and assuming the room was empty, she was about to move away when a sound caught her attention; it was a strange noise, a grated sigh, the guttural moan of a wounded animal – or like the sound she knew Owen made when he was in the throes of love.

Shifting position so it was easier to see the entire room, she craned her neck and looked to the right of the fireplace. At first she didn't understand. But then, as her senses took it in, her eyes grew round with horror. She saw it all; Maria, naked from the waist down, half-sitting, half-lying in the chair, her arms stretched wide with fingers gripping the chair-arm. Owen too was half-naked, on his knees, with his trousers round his ankles; his whole body rose and fell as he feverishly thrust forward. Then, in the moment when Rita reeled away, he fell on his wife's body, his face bathed with a look of ecstasy.

Insane with jealousy and fired by it, Rita ran to the front door and slammed her fists against it. 'BASTARD!' Her voice cut viciously through the night air. The door was flung open and there stood Maria, white-faced and angry. '*You!*' Momentarily taken aback, she stared open-mouthed.

Rita used the moment to push her way past. 'It's not you I want,' she snapped. 'You know that!' Made insane by what she had seen through the window, she still intended that nothing would stand in the way of her and Owen being together.

Fearful that everything she had achieved was in danger of being spoiled, Maria followed her. 'You won't have him!' she yelled. 'He doesn't want you, can't you understand that? Get out of here! Who the devil do you think you are ... barging your way into my home?'

Suddenly Owen was there, his face dark with rage. 'She's right,' he said in a firm low voice. 'I *don't* want you. I never really wanted you ... not in the way you thought.'

Something about his calm manner stilled her, though inside

563

she was bubbling with such hatred she could have strangled him with her bare hands. For what seemed an age she didn't speak. Instead she stared at him, stared *through* him, her eyes dark with rage as they raked his handsome face. 'I could kill you,' she whispered harshly, and as she spoke her fists clenched and unclenched, twisting the sides of her dress until it tore.

'I want her out!' Maria stumbled against the sideboard, her breathing hard and shallow, her cold blue gaze going from one to the other. 'Tell her it's finished. Tell her if she doesn't leave, *I'll* be the one to do the killing.'

Owen didn't look at his wife. His eyes were on Rita, and even now he was stunned by her beauty. 'You heard what my wife said,' he told her. 'She wants you to leave.'

Rita had seen the fleeting admiration in his eyes. She sensed his dilemma. Her smile was triumphant as she slyly regarded him. 'You still want me, I can see.'

'You're mad.' The assurance in his voice belied the awful truth, for he did still want her. Even now, after having made love to his wife, his loins burned for this woman.

Rita shook her head. 'I saw you . . .' She glanced at Maria, who appeared to be struggling for breath, her face drawn and pale. 'You and her.' There was disgust in her face. 'How could you?' she asked, her voice darkening. 'How could you couple with her, when I'm here for the asking?'

'Because I love her.' Owen was desperately struggling. In that minute, even with Maria looking on, he could hardly hide his need for Rita. His weakness was shocking, making him wish he had never been born. But it was there and Rita knew it. Worse . . . Maria knew it too.

'You can't love her. It's me you really want . . . me and the child.' She glanced at Maria once more and her mouth twisted in a wicked smile. Then she was addressing Owen again. 'I should hate you for what you've done, but I can't. Nor can I leave here without you.'

Coming forward, Maria stood between them. Her voice trembled as she addressed Owen. 'What does she mean . . . she said her and *the child*. What child, Owen?'

'Please, Maria.' He looked sadly at her before dropping his gaze to the floor. 'Can't you see she means to break up this marriage?'

This time Maria would not be pacified. 'What child, Owen? I want to know the truth.'

Rita was delighted. 'Tell her, Owen.' She pressed the flat of her hand to her stomach. 'Tell her I'm carrying our love child.'

Maria's action took them both by surprise. Launching herself at Rita, she got her by the throat, shaking with a strength that amazed even her. Before Owen could separate them, the two women had fallen to the floor. With a sickening thud, Rita's head hit the corner of the fender. 'Leave her, Maria!' cried Owen, grabbing her by the shoulders and pulling her away. 'For God's sake, do you want to kill her?'

Maria herself was ill, weakened by the struggle and heart-broken by what Rita had told. 'Yes, I want to kill her,' she replied, watching him as he lifted Rita to her feet. 'Just tell me . . . is it true? Is she carrying your child?' All the time she spoke she was aware that his arm was round Rita, that Rita was staring at her, hating her. Maria told herself it wouldn't have mattered if she *had* killed the witch.

Owen turned his face from Rita's. 'It's all right,' he said, easing her into a chair. 'She isn't badly hurt.' Rita was dazed and there was a trickle of blood coming from the back of her head. But she was recovered, and enjoying the friction between husband and wife.

'Answer me, Owen. Is she carrying your child?'

'I was going to tell you.' He was frantic. 'Once we were away from here, I meant to tell you everything.'

'You're a liar. I've forgiven you for your womanising,' she said in a chillingly flat voice, 'I've always forgiven you because I've believed you were weak and couldn't help yourself. I've forgiven you because I love you above all else.' She looked at Rita's smirking face and her anger was tenfold. 'But you kept this from me. You didn't have the courage to tell me you'd got her with child. That much I can't . . . won't . . . forgive.'

'What difference does it make?' He had never seen her like this and he was destroyed. 'I don't want her, and I don't want the child.' He scowled at Rita, not noticing how the colour had drained from her face. 'Besides, how do I know it's mine? It could be anybody's.'

Maria was indignant. 'Oh, it's yours all right,' she said. 'I know when a woman's telling the truth about such a thing.' He went to touch her but she recoiled. 'Get her out of here. Pack your things and go with her. And don't ever come back.'

'No, Maria. You don't know what you're saying!'

'Do as I ask, or when David comes back I'll ask him to throw you out.'

'I thought we'd agreed you would never say anything to him?'

'That was before I knew she was carrying your child.' She had no intention of sharing his shame with David, but it wouldn't hurt to let Owen suffer for his sins.

'But why should her carrying my child make any difference?'

'You wouldn't understand.' There was a great sadness in her voice. 'Only a woman could understand.'

'All right, Maria, I'll go.' He saw no point in arguing now; he was arrogant enough to believe that when Rita was out of the way he would make Maria see sense. 'But only until the morning. Once you've had a chance to think about this, you'll be sorry, I know.'

She laughed softly and he saw a side to her he never knew existed. 'No, Owen. It's *you* who'll be sorry.' Turning away, she sat in the chair where only a short while ago they had made love. Softly she began to rock herself, back and forth, her arms crossed and her sorry gaze directed towards the dying flames in the firegrate.

'There's no talking to you like this,' he protested. 'Think what you're doing to us, Maria. I'll be back in the morning. We'll talk then.'

After collecting his hat and coat from the nail on the door, he dressed for the night air. 'You'd best be on your way,' he told Rita in a sour voice. 'You've caused enough trouble here, damn your eyes.'

Maria heard the front door close, but she didn't move. She was too filled with pain and shame.

'You *are* coming with me, aren't you?' Leaning against the wall of the house, Rita studied his face in the moonlight. She felt exhilarated, yet just a little afraid. 'It's what we wanted, isn't it?' she urged. 'You and me . . . and the child?'

Rounding on her, he snarled, 'It might be what *you* wanted, but it was never my intention to break up with Maria.' Clenching his fist he slammed it against the wall. 'What possessed you to do it? Why did you come here?'

'I came for you.'

Ignoring her remark, he groaned, 'I hope to God I can put right what you've done this night.' Catching hold of her arm, he propelled her away from the house. 'I'm taking you home.'

Struggling, she argued, 'I don't want to go home. I want to go with you.'

'That's out of the question, and you know it!' The very thought of it made him quicken his steps. 'You really are mad.' Convinced he must get her home and confess all to Frank Blackthorn, he dragged her at a smarter pace down the lane.

Rita argued all the way. 'I have money put away ... enough to keep us in a grand style. The child will be a boy, I know it will.' She wanted to seduce him, she longed for it to be like it was before. The very thought of resuming some sort of existence in Frank Blackthorn's house left her cold. 'The child will be a son, Owen ... a son for you and me. We'll have a fine life, and we'll be happy together, you'll see.' The faster he rushed her, the more breathless she became. She was in pain, dazed and confused. The wound on her head was throbbing and the blood was gushing out; she could feel it warm and sticky on her neck.

Incensed by her ceaseless argument, he suddenly stopped and shook her hard, his fingers digging into her shoulders and making her cry out. 'STOP IT!' he yelled. 'FOR GOD'S SAKE, LEAVE IT BE!' Slamming her against the trunk of a tree, he pushed his face close to hers. All need of her was gone. Only a sense of desperation remained. 'Listen to me,' he pleaded. 'As far as I'm concerned, we had nothing special. We had a fling ... slept together. A bit of fun, that's all.' Shaking her again, he demanded, 'Do you hear what I'm saying? You were nothing more than a bit of fun. If I had my way I'd put an end to you and the brat here and now.' Pressing his fist to her stomach, he snarled, 'If it hadn't been for this, Maria would have forgiven me. Now I'm not so sure, damn you!'

Through a haze she saw the hatred in his face. It kindled a kind of love in her, and something else, some strange feeling she could not control. Slowly she slid from his grasp, and as she fell, the moonlight faded, her senses reeled, and she knew she was close to losing consciousness.

'Rita!' He fell to his knees beside her. It was then he realised how ill she was, how pale and racked with pain. The blood from her head wound trickled down her neck; it stuck to his hand and frightened him. 'I'll get you home,' he told her in a kinder voice. 'Don't worry, I'll get you home.'

To his surprise she pushed him away. 'I don't need you to take me home!' she protested. 'Get back to your wife.'

'I'm sorry,' he said penitently, moving away.

'Oh, you will be,' she promised. 'You *will* be sorry for what you've done to me.' Struggling to her feet, she stumbled away. Twice he attempted to help, and each time she threw him off, screaming abuses and lashing out.

'All right. If that's the way you want it.' Dejected, he took another direction.

The journey to Blackthorn House seemed to take forever. Driven on by rage and a burning need for revenge, Rita was only a few steps from the house when a figure lurched from the shadows and struck her, again and again, each time harder than before. In the moonlight she saw the silhouette of her attacker. She saw the face and she knew it well. The next time she was hit, her senses darkened and she slithered to the ground.

It was morning before Rita Blackthorn was found. Ruby wasn't certain whether what she saw was a figure or a poacher's sack. When she realised it was the mistress, badly hurt or even dead, she ran screaming into the house, going straight to the study where Frank was sleeping across his desk.

When some time later Rita was gently carried into the doctor's carriage, he climbed in beside her. Margaret was there, with Cathy and Ruby. They watched in shocked silence as he closed the doors.

Still deeply affected by what had happened earlier between herself and Jack, Cathy could hardly take it in. 'Will she die?' she asked, and Margaret's heart went out to her.

'All we can do is pray,' she said.

Aware that Cathy was in a state of shock, Margaret talked to her all the way back to the house. Behind them, Ruby sniffled loudly into her handkerchief. As for Jack, he seemed unusually preoccupied, kicking at the ground with his boot and planning his next move.

At the Infirmary, Rita was quickly taken to a room where the doctors attended her without delay. But there was little they could do. Frank sat by her side, watching helplessly as she drifted in and out of consciousness, her green eyes silently pleading with him but her mind dwelling on Owen and his wife. 'Who did it, sweetheart?' he pleaded through a blur of tears. 'Who hurt you like this?'

When she became agitated, he called the doctor, who gave her laudanum. 'She'll rest now,' he told Frank. 'But you can stay if you like.'

He was inconsolable. 'Have the police arrived yet?' he demanded. When told they had not, he rolled his eyes and looked at Rita's face once more. 'Who could do such a thing?' he pleaded.

Both men were startled when she answered, '*He* did it.' The doctor would have quietened her, but she was frantic. In a broken voice she confessed, 'The child . . . it's . . . Owen Leyton's. He wanted me . . . dead.'

In that moment she looked radiant. As she raised her eyes to the ceiling her voice was almost inaudible. 'Forgive me, Owen,' she whispered. 'But I can't leave without you.'

When Rita Blackthorn died two days later, she took her lover with her, just as surely as if she had stabbed him through the heart.

On her accusation he was instantly arrested. Spots of blood were found on the Leytons' hearth. Maria Leyton, still smarting from the confrontation, herself gave an account of how her husband was Rita's lover, and that she was carrying his child. She revealed how Owen and Rita had quarrelled on the night of the attack. She told how Owen went with Rita from the house, and of how she had heard them outside, shouting at each other, with Owen threatening to 'put an end to you and the brat'. She said all that in a surge of terrible rage. Then, when it was all too late, she regretted every shocking word.

Owen Leyton was charged with murder. At his trial the jury swiftly returned a verdict of guilty. The judge donned his black cap and pronounced that Owen Leyton would be hanged by the neck until he was dead.

The courtroom was packed. Frank did not attend. Since Rita's death he seemed to have lost his purpose in life. While Owen Leyton was standing trial, Frank was standing at Rita's graveside. Before that he had drunk himself insensible, as he had done every day and night since that awful day.

When the sentence was delivered, Maria's cry echoed from the walls and, gazing at her, Owen desperately pleaded his innocence.

Their two children stood close by: Teresa cold and unmoved; David tall and strong, but inwardly broken. As he left the court, his face was set like granite, his gaze fixed straight ahead. He was aware that Cathy was only an arm's reach away but dared not look up. The precious love they had shared was now lost to him forever. He could never go to her. Not now. Not when his own father had murdered her mother.

Though it was hard to realise her mother was gone, Cathy's heart went out to David in his grief. She followed him with sad lonely eyes, aching to go to him but knowing he must turn her away. 'Now, he will never want to know me, will he?' she said when Margaret came to her side.

'I think it's best if you put him out of your mind,' came the quiet reply. 'Put it *all* out of your mind.'

Jack was arrogant as ever, appearing untouched by all that had happened. Overhearing what Cathy had said, he remarked sourly, 'The Leytons aren't worth *that*!' Raising his hand he clicked his fingers and gave a small laugh, becoming instantly silent when Margaret glared at him.

Cathy's answer was to stare at him hard and long. 'I think I told you once before ... David Leyton is worth *ten* of you!' she said menacingly. The dark anger in his face was all the satisfaction she needed. One day he would pay dearly for what he had done to her. One day, in the future, he would get his just punishment.

CHAPTER EIGHT

The hanging of Owen Leyton sent ripples of reaction through the whole of Lancashire. A month after the event, people still gathered on street corners and whispered of it; boozy men sat in dark corners of ale-houses, grinning and making snide comments about how they wouldn't have minded 'laying bare-arsed' across the beautiful Rita Blackthorn. Every man jack who knew the tale spread it far and wide; Frank Blackthorn became a figure of fun while Maria Leyton drew a mixture of pity and scorn, considering that, in her testimony to the authorities, she had helped her wretched husband on his way just as surely as if she had put the rope round his neck with her own two hands.

One bright spring morning, Cathy rose early from her bed. 'Is Aunt Margaret up yet?' she asked as Ruby came bustling out of the kitchen.

'Not yet, dear.' Ruby had on a new pinafore, a gaudy thing with a pattern of huge red roses and forget-me-nots all over. Her hair was meticulously curled and she had a certain look in her eye; the kind of look that made Cathy suspect she might have a suitor. 'There's neither your aunt nor your father out of their beds yet,' Ruby pronounced sternly. 'As for that surly young fella Jack – well, since your father doesn't keep an eye on him any more, he just seems to get lazier.'

Even the mention of Jack's name turned Cathy's stomach. The memory of a certain night was too alive in her, too bitter. Ignoring Ruby's comment, she said, 'I suppose you know my father was drunk when he came in last night?' It saddened her to see how little life meant to him since losing his beloved wife.

Ruby's face dropped. 'I'm sorry, dearie,' she said quietly. 'I know how hard it must be for you. But I'm sure he'll pull round. People suffer grief in different ways, and he was devoted to her as you know better than I do.' Her face brightened. 'It'll come right, you'll see. Nature has a habit of mending even the sorest wounds.'

Cathy was hopeful too. 'Bless you for that, Ruby,' she said, on impulse leaning down to kiss the dear soul on the cheek. 'I honestly don't know what we'd do without you.'

'Same as we've all got to do without our Queen Victoria,' Ruby said. 'We soldier on, that's what.' The news of Queen Victoria's passing had shocked and saddened the nation. 'For them as are left behind, life has to go on. As for you, Cathy Blackthorn, you've got enough of your own troubles to contend with, but you're made of the right stuff to carry you through.'

She looked at Cathy now and in that instant realised she had matured into a real beauty; her shining fair hair spilled over her shoulders in deep waves, and her stunning green eyes were deep with warmth and compassion. Lovely in looks, lovely in nature, Ruby mused. And made to suffer things not of her making. Since she was a bairn in arms, Cathy had forever captured a little corner of Ruby's heart.

Ruby seemed full of the joys of spring. Winking naughtily at Cathy, she said brightly, 'I was hoping everyone would be up and about early, so I could get the table cleared and everything spick and span before the ten o'clock tram into Blackburn.'

'What? Are you off shopping then, Ruby?'

'No, no, dear,' she replied guardedly. 'I'm just going to see a friend.' She blushed again, and Cathy thought better of pursuing the matter.

'Now then, young lady, I expect you're hungry?' Chattering all the way, Ruby hurried off to the kitchen. 'I'll have your breakfast on the table before you can bat an eyelid. It's all but ready.'

In a matter of minutes the aroma of sizzling bacon had filled the house. 'Will you mind very much if I don't have any breakfast, Ruby?' Cathy's stomach was turning somersaults at the very thought of food. She had lain awake until the early hours, waiting for her father to come home from the ale-house. A few minutes after he went into his study she crept down and opened the door; he was lying on the floor, blind drunk and raving incomprehensibly. The experience of these past weeks had

572

taught her it was no use trying to move him, so she made him as comfortable as possible, put a pillow beneath his head, laid a blanket over him, and left him to sleep it off.

Even then she had hardly slept a wink, going downstairs at regular intervals to check on him. Now, all she wanted was a breath of fresh air. The sun was shining outside and the garden called. 'I need a walk, that's all,' she explained. 'To blow the cobwebs away.'

Too many 'cobwebs' clung to her. Darling Nan and her mother, the way those two had met with their awful end . . . her father's inconsolable grief and the insatiable drinking that would ruin them all . . . the way Jack had defiled her. And David. Oh, David! How she missed his tender affection and the warmth of his smile. Every day she loved and needed him a little more. Every day she wondered how she could mend the terrible rift that had grown between them. But it was not to be. He was lost to her, and she must learn to live with that; just as she must learn to live with all the other misfortunes that had touched her life. Such bad memories, yet in a strange way they were still very much alive, living and breathing, each a burden in its own way. Cobwebs, clinging shadowy cobwebs, which little by little threatened to suffocate her.

After drinking the cup of tea Ruby insisted on brewing for her, Cathy went out into the garden. Though the sun was shining, the air carried a cutting chill, but wrapped up in a long coat and scarf she felt cosy and warm.

The garden was pitifully overgrown. Weeds and brambles had invaded the lawns, the shrubs were tangled and the path that led to the rustic bench was made narrower by the encroachment of creeping foliage. Seating herself on the bench, Cathy took stock of all that surrounded her. 'When the weather breaks, I'll get Aunt Margaret to help me clear this mess away,' she murmured.

Just for a moment she turned her thoughts to Ruby's comments regarding Queen Victoria. It did seem strange though, for that grand lady had been Queen for all of Cathy's life and many long years before. She also realised that, no matter how grand or humble a person was, they all had to face the same God one day.

Margaret appeared at the other end of the garden. 'Mind if

I join you?' she called. When Cathy's answer was to shift along the bench, she came and sat beside her. Shivering, Margaret pulled her scarf tighter round her shoulders. 'Isn't it too cold for you to be sitting out here?'

'I just had to get out of the house.' Cathy had never been really happy there, and lately the walls felt as though they were closing in on her.

'You should have woken me,' Margaret chided.

Cathy chuckled at that. 'Don't think I wasn't tempted,' she teased. However, she knew Margaret was also having sleepless nights. On three occasions this past week when Cathy couldn't sleep and sought refuge in the kitchen, she had found Margaret already there. Each time the two of them had sat until dawn, sipping tea and talking.

Margaret settled back in her seat, the damp wood chilling her bones. 'How long do you mean to stay out here?' Folding her arms, she hugged herself. 'Ruby said you didn't want any breakfast. Why's that?' Lately, she had been concerned about Cathy. She suspected that something very secret was preying on her mind. And it wasn't only the sequence of tragedies that had overtaken this family.

Cathy answered two questions in one. 'I don't seem to have any appetite this morning. I had a bad night and thought a few minutes in the open air would do me good.' Afraid that Margaret meant to quiz her further, she quickly added, 'Give me half an hour, then I'll be ready to come with you to the churchyard.'

'Well now, that's why I came to find you.' Shifting in her seat so she could look into Cathy's curious eyes, she paused, wondering how to impart the news she had heard from the solicitor. 'Yesterday I had a very important letter. I needed to discuss it with your father then, but he was never in the house for more than two minutes at a time.'

Something in Margaret's voice alarmed Cathy. 'Is anything wrong?' she asked anxiously.

'Oh, I'm sure it's something and nothing. But the sooner I speak with your father, the better.' She took a great gulp of fresh air and slowly breathed it out while appearing to think hard, then she patted Cathy's hand and smilingly reassured her.

'There's nothing for you to worry about. And anyway, it should only take half an hour at the very most.'

Cathy was not altogether convinced. 'Can I ask you who the letter was from?' she enquired softly.

Loath to explain how the solicitor's letter had warned her of sales that had been made by Frank without her knowledge, Margaret answered, 'It's to do with our land and property.'

'Does Father know you want to talk with him?'

'Not yet, but I hope he's up to it.' Margaret wore a wry expression. 'He emerged from the study as I came out, and from the look of him, I wonder if he's in a fit state to talk about *anything* at the minute.'

'While he's still drunk. Isn't that what you mean?' There was a deal of sadness in Cathy's voice, but resignation too. She had long stopped fooling herself where her father was concerned.

Cursing herself for being so insensitive, Margaret lowered her gaze. 'I'm sorry,' she murmured. 'But, yes, that is what I meant.'

'It's all right. I'm old enough not to be shocked any more.'

'I know.' Margaret looked into Cathy's troubled eyes and was ashamed. 'That's something else I'm sorry about. I also know it must have been you who covered him over and made him comfortable.' She shook her head angrily. 'Oh, Cathy! Your father goes from bad to worse. Why can't he bear his grief with dignity?'

Cathy's voice was cold. 'Because he's a weakling.'

Margaret was shocked. Usually, Cathy sprang to her father's defence, yet here she was condemning him. 'He misses Rita dreadfully,' she said, summoning a little compassion for Frank. 'I suppose we'll just have to be patient with him.'

'What did the letter say?'

'What letter?' She pretended to have forgotten that important issue.

Cathy stared at her in disbelief. 'The letter you mentioned just now . . . the one about our land and property. Is it very serious?'

Margaret gave a small embarrassed laugh. 'Oh! *That* letter?' She was sorry she had ever mentioned it. 'It's just one of those irritating letters that remind you of your responsibilities, that's all,' she said casually. In fact the letter was very disturbing.

'Oh.' Cathy sensed it was more than that. Margaret was

575

worried and it showed. 'Do you want me to wait for you?'

'It seems a shame for you to hang about.' Worried that Cathy might overhear the imminent argument between herself and Frank, Margaret decided, 'No. You go ahead. I need to stretch my legs. I'll go for a little walk round the house before I disturb your father . . . give myself time to think.'

'Are you sure?' Cathy sensed the letter meant more than Margaret was saying. Just now she had complained about the cold and here she was, talking about going for a walk. 'I can wait for you.'

'No. I'd rather you went on, sweetheart. I'll follow as soon as I've talked with your father.'

It was agreed. Margaret set out for her few quiet minutes in which to prepare for what she assumed would be a confrontation with Frank, while Cathy made her way back to the house.

In the kitchen Ruby was waiting to get ready the flowers. 'I've had them standing in water, so they're still nice and fresh,' she told Cathy. 'It's the wrong time of year for a colourful show, but these daffodils are long-lasting and should keep well.'

Taking the bright yellow flowers out of the jug, she separated them into two bunches and wrapped them in greaseproof paper. 'There you are,' she said, laying them on the draining board. 'And while you're at the church, I'd be grateful if you'd light a penny candle for me old dad. Been gone these past thirty years he has . . . a miserable, spiteful old sod he were, so I reckon he still needs to be shown the way to heaven!'

Taking two copper pennies out of her purse, she laid them on the table. 'Happen you'd better light *two* candles, eh?' she chuckled.

Cathy was intrigued. 'I've never heard you talk about your father before. But I'll light the candles, of course I will.' She reached out to collect the coppers and was surprised when Ruby snatched them back.

'On second thoughts,' she said, dropping the coins into her purse, 'if he ain't got to heaven by now, there ain't much chance of him getting there at all, is there, eh?' That said she took off her pinnie and put on her hat and coat. 'Being Sunday there's only a skeleton tram service, so I'd best get a move on.' Ushering Cathy out of the kitchen, she suggested, 'You can walk me to the end of the lane and see me on the tram if you like.'

'Yes, I will,' Cathy agreed. 'First I'll just go and see if Father's all right.'

'He's gone back into his study,' Ruby told her. 'If you ask me he should be in his bed.' As far as she was concerned, Frank Blackthorn was beyond saving.

First Cathy knocked on the study door. When there was no answer, she knocked again and was told in a gruff voice to 'Enter'.

Going into the study, she was struck by the smell: stale alcohol and sweat. The window was tightly shut and her father was seated at his desk, his body leaning forward and his arms stretched across the polished top. 'What is it? I'm not in the mood for visitors.' Looking up with bleary eyes he peered at her face as if he had never seen it before. 'Is that you, Cathy?'

'Yes, Father.' In spite of his neglect of her all these years, it broke her heart to see him like this.

'What do you want?' As he spoke he slammed his fist on the desk.

'I've just come to see if you're all right.'

'Hmph! Do I *look* all right?' In fact he looked shocking. With swollen bloodshot eyes and a face that hadn't seen a razor for many days, he resembled the worst kind of vagabond. 'Do I look like Rita Blackthorn's husband?' he asked with a leer.

'No. Neither do you look like my father.' There was condemnation in Cathy's expression. 'You've changed, and not for the better.'

He sat up at that, his eyes wider and his whole countenance ready to pounce. 'Oh? And you don't like what you see, is that what you're saying?' he demanded.

'I don't like what you're doing to yourself.' She came to the desk and stood before him, like a criminal before a magistrate. But he was shamed and she was dignified. 'If I don't like what I see, it's only because I love you.'

'Well, I don't . . . love . . . you,' he said cruelly, the words issuing slowly and spitefully.

'I know you don't.' It cost Cathy dearly to say what was in her heart. 'I believe you've *never* loved me.'

'Does it matter?'

'There was a time when it mattered more than anything in the whole world.'

'Your mother loved you even less.'

Cathy gave no answer to that. But she had to know. 'Why does it please you to hurt me, Father?'

'Because you're not her, and you can't take her place.' Suddenly he was crying. 'She's not gone, you know,' he muttered. 'She's still here.'

He gazed round the room. 'She's all around ... everywhere I look. But don't you see? It's worse. It's agony because I can see her but not hold her. She's with me all the time, but when I reach out to touch her she moves away.' He gave a strangled laugh. 'It's always been like that between me and your mother.' He bent his head over the desk and cried, great racking sobs that shook his frame.

Cathy came forward and touched his head with great tenderness. 'Please, Father, don't punish yourself so.' It was awful to see him like this. 'If only you'd let me help, I know things could be better.'

With one mighty swipe he sent her staggering backwards across the room. 'I DON'T WANT YOUR HELP!' Standing now, he glowered at her from behind his desk, clinging to its edge for support. 'Your mother hated you, and so do I,' he hissed. 'Now get out!'

Shocked to the core, she turned away, glancing at him from the door before quietly departing. She wanted to cry but couldn't. Instead a cold, hard feeling came over her. Something changed in that moment; something which had once been very precious was now gone forever. It may have been the last hope clinging on from childhood ... or the desperate need of a young woman to be loved by her parents; it may have been the helpless sense of belonging that had existed even when she was never sure they wanted her. She couldn't tell what it was exactly. All she knew was that her feelings could never be the same again.

'Put you out on your ear, has he?' Jack's harsh voice infiltrated her thoughts. 'Still, I don't care. The more he hates you, the more money he'll leave to me when he goes to hell.'

She looked up to see him smirking at her, lolling against the banister in that lazy manner he had. She recalled Ruby's words:

'Since your father's been neglecting him, he seems to get lazier.' In fact he was hardly ever in the house; his shirt was in need of a wash, his hands were filthy and his thick fair hair was unkempt. Yet when his small hazel eyes smiled on her, he was still as arrogant and self-important as ever.

Cathy knew he was waiting for her to make a comment. But she had no intention of saying anything. With head held high and her expression giving nothing away she walked straight past him, towards the kitchen where Ruby was waiting. 'It won't be long now!' he shouted after her. 'The way the old man's going, he'll soon be rotting in the ground with *her*! If it were me, I'd be glad to be shut of her. When all's said an' done she never wanted him . . . went to the grave with another man's brat inside her, didn't she, eh?'

Enraged, Cathy swung round. But he was gone. Ruby came out to meet her. 'I heard what he said,' she murmured. 'I only hope the master didn't.' Her nervous gaze flickered towards the study. But all was still.

The silence was broken by Margaret's footsteps. Totally unaware of what had just taken place and surprised to see Cathy, she asked, 'Still here? I thought you would have been gone by now.'

Cathy's bright smile and quick answer belied the turmoil inside her. 'I wanted to see Father before I went.'

'Oh? And where did you find him?'

'In the study.'

'Is he in a better mood?'

Cathy hesitated. Ever since she was a little girl she had shared her most secret thoughts with Margaret, but now she found herself suppressing those deeper feelings as she answered, 'You might say he's the same as usual.' Rushing towards the kitchen, she explained, 'I'd best be off. Ruby's kept the flowers fresh and they should make a lovely show in the vases.'

As she hurried away she fought to keep the tears down. Her whole world was falling apart, with only Margaret and Ruby keeping it together. What she felt for them could never be expressed in mere words. They were like candles in the dark, warm and glowing, keeping her sane.

Margaret made her way to Frank's study, while Ruby and Cathy went away from the house. At the bottom of the lane they parted company; Ruby to the tram-stop, and Cathy to take the narrow footpath that led to the church of St Peter. 'Mind how you go now,' Ruby warned. 'Make sure you stay close by the church so your aunt can find you.'

'Stop worrying,' Cathy gently chided. 'You just go and enjoy yourself.'

Ruby saw the glint in Cathy's eye and blushed a fierce shade of pink. 'Whatever do you mean?'

'You've been blushing all morning, you're dressed up in your very best clothes, and you've curled your hair. You look pretty enough to meet a gentleman, that's what I mean.'

Ruby blushed again. 'Cheeky young madam!' she muttered. But she didn't deny it and, when she went at a faster trot down the lane, suddenly burst out singing one of her favourite Irish ditties; all of which only served to convince Cathy that Ruby did have a suitor after all.

As she neared the church, Cathy's heart grew lighter. The walk to St Peter's was a delight in any weather, but on a day like today when the sun was shining, there was a timelessness about the scene that took her breath away.

She came through the spinney and out into the open again. At the top of the rise, she stood and looked out over the landscape. Immediately in front of her the bracken, shrubs and heather were already budding up. The fields stretched beyond as far as the eye could see, a huge magnificent patchwork quilt . . . green and gold, brown and russet, trimmed with hedges and low stone walls. Horses grazed contentedly, with curious hares standing bolt upright at a distance, watching the proceedings before leaping away, with ears pricked high and powerful hind legs driving them along. Heavily pregnant sheep dotted the open fields, heads down as they munched at the grass. In the distance the church bells could be heard calling the community to Sunday Mass, and above it all the birds twittered and sang in the treetops.

On such a day, there was something uniquely peaceful about God's earth. Just being part of it brought a soothing calm to Cathy's turbulent spirit. Lighter of heart, she went on her way, her steps more leisurely now. By the time she got to the church the worshippers would have gone home. Somehow she didn't feel able to mingle with a crowd. Not today.

Having arranged the first bunch of flowers in the stone vase, Cathy said a little prayer over Nan Foster's grave. She told her how much she still missed her, and promised, 'I'll never forget you.' Then, with tears in her eyes, she got up from her knees and walked to the other side of the churchyard, where her mother lay.

It was not hard to talk to Nan; to say all the things that were close to Cathy's heart. But here, with her mother not six feet beneath where she stood, Cathy always found herself afraid. Afraid to let her mother know what she was thinking, afraid she had been too harsh in her judgement, too condemnatory, too selfish and greedy in ever wanting Rita to cherish her. As a small child, rejected and unloved, she'd yearned so much for a 'real' mother, someone who would sit in the firelight with her and share those things that mother and daughter share; someone who would sing her to sleep or tell her a story, filling her world with dreams and wonderful things, someone who would smile and hold her when she was hurt. Most of all, someone who, when childhood was slipping away, could explain all the things that were constantly changing. This was what Cathy had yearned for.

Now, as a young woman, she saw it all in a different light. 'Some things are meant to be, and some are not,' she murmured. 'I can't understand why you couldn't love me, Mother, but I can't hate you for that.' She dropped to her knees and busied herself in arranging the flowers. 'Father is so unhappy,' she whispered. 'He misses you so, I'm afraid he'll kill himself with all the drinking.'

She remained on her knees a little longer, imagining her mother alive, so beautiful, so magnificent, even in the blackest mood. 'If ever I marry and have a child, whether it's a boy or a girl, I must never make the same mistake,' she whispered. 'I will love it with all my heart.'

Stepping back she looked on the grey granite headstone, a splendid thing, the best money could buy, with letters engraved in gold and an angel standing guard at its base.

There was nothing more to say. Without a backward glance,

she went across the lawn, down the gravel footpath and into the church. Here she dropped four pennies into the money box. Taking up four tiny candles, she wedged them into the wrought-iron stands and, striking a match, touched the wicks one after the other, until all four were throwing out a warm bright flame. Kneeling behind a pew, she folded her hands and closed her eyes, softly murmuring, 'One for Mother, one for Nan, one for Ruby's father... though Ruby might not approve,' she whispered with a little smile. 'And another for any poor soul who hasn't yet found its way to heaven.'

Three times she went to the gate to see whether Margaret was in sight. When on the third attempt there was no sign of her, Cathy returned to the churchyard, where she wandered at will, occasionally reading the interesting inscriptions on the headstones; on one ancient granite cross it told how a young woman by the name of Elizabeth Arnam had died in childbirth at the age of nineteen. Close to the church door, in the same spot for a hundred years, stood a tall and beautiful statue of the Sacred Heart; this was the last resting place of an entire family: 'Slain by a madman on this very spot'. But the one that saddened Cathy above all others was that of a small child by the name of Lucy Lane, who had been 'Caught between the wheels of a wagon'. In the same place lay Lucy's mother who, by all accounts, had 'Died of a broken heart'.

Seated on the bench, watching the horizon for Margaret's familiar figure and with her face warmed by the sun, Cathy thought on brighter things, like who was Ruby's suitor, and why she was being so secretive. The idea of Ruby strolling arm in arm with a man, looking up at him with shy, shining eyes, brought a smile to her face. 'I hope you've found a partner, Ruby,' she whispered. 'Nobody deserves one more than you.'

The joy that had flooded her heart at thinking Ruby might have found someone to love was suddenly swamped by thoughts of David. She wondered what he was doing now, right this very minute. Was he tending the horses? Perhaps he was logging in the spinney, or maybe walking the fields... or he might be heading for the spot near the brook where he always found comfort. He had taken Cathy there, and she thought it the most beautiful place on God's earth. 'Where are you, David?' she murmured. Leaning back, she lifted her face to the sun and closed her eyes to think of him.

With a jolt she sat up straight, her heart lurching as she remembered, 'It's tomorrow! Tomorrow you'll be leaving and I'll never see you again.' The thought was too awful to contemplate, so she tried to shut it from her mind. But it wouldn't be denied. Tomorrow, David would be gone from these parts, he and his family; with the exception of his beloved father who was buried somewhere in the prison grounds. Cathy had half expected him to be gone before now, but it was almost as though he could not bear to wrench himself away.

Agitated, Cathy went once more to see whether Margaret was on her way. There was still no sign of her. But Cathy was both astonished and thrilled when she saw two other familiar figures approaching. She recognised them straight away as David and his sister Teresa.

Cathy only had eyes for David. He looked wretched, just as he had looked on leaving the court after his father was sentenced. His face was thinner, almost gaunt; the dark eyes that had so often smiled at her, turning her heart inside out, now stared straight ahead. He seemed older somehow, not a boy but a man. Each footstep brought him closer; his long strides purposeful as ever. But there was a loneliness about him that struck her deep. In him she saw a kindred spirit and, more than ever, she wanted to be with him.

His sister walked alongside, sometimes running to keep up with him. She had a willow stick in her hand and with it she slashed at the trees. Her face was hard but not grief-stricken. Occasionally she would laugh and expect David to laugh with her. When he merely nodded, she kicked at the ground like a sulky child. She seemed impatient, angry, appearing to have come along only to guard him, just as she had always guarded him.

Keeping out of sight, Cathy waited until they had gone by. At one point David was so close she could have reached out and touched him. Somehow he sensed her presence, pausing for a moment and looking round before going on.

When Cathy emerged from her hiding place, it was to see him going through the great oak doors which led into the church. 'Of course . . . you've come to talk with your father,' she said softly. 'I can understand that.' Staring at the doors she somehow believed that David would come out again and things would be the same as before, but of course that couldn't be.

She felt uneasy, deeply disturbed and torn in so many ways. She wanted to go to him but dare not. She wanted to leave but could not. There must be something left between us, she told herself angrily. What happened was not your fault, David, nor was it mine. She paced the grounds and all the time her gaze was focused on the doors of the church. If he was to come out now, what would you do? she asked herself. Could you face him after all that has happened? The thought was paralysing.

Without even realising, she found she had walked along the path to the church, and now here she was standing inside the porch, with only the great oak doors between herself and her love. She was trembling, cold with fear. What would he say? How would he greet her? Her heart told her one thing, her head another. Yet she must know! Before he left forever, she must know whether he really hated her.

With shaking hands, she reached up and closed her fingers over the door-knob. Ever so slowly she eased the door open. When it creaked and groaned she held it still for a second, her heart wildly beating. When, after what seemed an age, she had the door open wide enough for her to peer inside, she saw him there; he was kneeling in the pew closest to the altar, his dark eyes raised and his hands clasped together in prayer. He looked a sad lonely figure, so very different from the carefree laughing youth she had known.

Slowly, as though he was bearing a great weight on his broad shoulders, he stood up and strode towards the wrought-iron stand where Cathy's four candles still brightly burned. Here, he dropped a penny into the tin and collected a candle from the box. Reaching out he actually lit the candle from one of Cathy's before easing it into a nearby space. That done, he looked up at the face of the Virgin Mary; he didn't pray, nor did he move for almost a full minute, just gazed on that peaceful loving face, lost in thought. He was a man in deep pain, a man confused and desperately hurt by the loss of his beloved father.

Summoning every ounce of courage, Cathy took a step forward, hesitating when a harsh voice spoke out behind her. It was Teresa.

'I wouldn't go in there if I were you.' Pushing herself in front of Cathy, she quietly closed the door. 'I think you should know he hasn't forgiven you.'

Cathy looked at her, at the hard face that rarely smiled. 'What happened between your father and my mother was no more my fault than yours,' she replied calmly. 'Hating me won't change anything. I want David to know that.'

'He won't listen.'

'I have to try.'

'And deepen his grief?' Teresa played her part well. 'One way or another your family have ruined us. Oh, I know it was your mother who was murdered and they say my father did it. But, to tell you the truth, I'll never believe that, and neither will David. The real truth is your mother pursued my father. She came to the house and caused a terrible scene. Yes, they'd had an affair, but it was over. She couldn't see it that way though. Whichever way you look at it, a good man lies buried in the prison yard. Your mother's here, beneath the trees and sur-rounded by flowers. *She's* the guilty one, yet the man she used lies in a cold forbidding place. I don't care what sentence was passed on him, Owen Leyton was innocent! But he can't even be buried in consecrated ground. No wonder David wants to get out of this place as quick as he can!'

'If I could make amends, I would. You have to believe that.'

'No! It's too late. Leave him be. Let him leave without further trouble.' The last thing Teresa wanted was for these two to meet up, for she knew that if they did David would take Cathy in his arms and she would be on the outside again. All the time Cathy Blackthorn and David were finding happiness with each other, *she* could only watch and envy. The thought drove her almost crazy. 'Go away and leave us alone!' she hissed. 'Surely you can under-stand why David never wants to set eyes on you again?'

'I think I can. Only I don't want to believe we can't talk about what's happened. David and I have always been able to talk things through.'

Taking a chance, Teresa stepped aside. 'All right! Go in! Destroy him a little more. Cause a terrible scene in the church!

If that's what you want, then go in.'

Fighting all manner of emotions, Cathy hesitated. 'I never wanted him to hate me,' she said. 'If we must part I'd like it to be as friends. Is that so impossible now?'

Teresa was delighted to see she had set the doubts in Cathy's mind. '*I* don't hate you,' she lied, 'but David is a different matter. He hates like only a man can hate. It's been the devil's own job keeping him away from Blackthorn House... from burning it to the ground and all of you inside.' Straightening her back, she took a deep breath. '*That's* how much he hates. Go on. Go inside... let him tell you himself. He misses his father every minute of every day. Who knows? He might just strangle you and then he could be laid to rest in the prison yard, reunited with the father he adored.'

It seemed an age before Cathy answered. Every word uttered by Teresa had been like a stab to the heart. She didn't realise he could hate that much. How could she approach him now? How could she lay him open to such pain? And in God's house? Of course he missed his father. No one ever loved his father as much as David loved Owen; no son ever had such a wonderful relationship with his father as David had enjoyed. Of course he hated the woman who had brought it on them. And the family of that woman, because wasn't it true what Teresa had said, that in one way or another the Blackthorn family had ruined them?

In a quiet voice Cathy answered, 'I *can* understand David's reasons for hating me. I wish it didn't have to be this way, but things have happened, awful painful things, which affect all our lives. I wish I could turn the clock back, but none of us can.'

'Like I say, *I* don't hate you.'

'Thank you for that.' Cathy had no reason to disbelieve her. Glancing at the great oak door which was now firmly closed between her and David, she murmured before leaving, 'I hope your family can find happiness and peace wherever you are.' She doubted whether, without David, she herself would ever find real happiness.

Setting off in the direction of Blackthorn House, Cathy could think of nothing but what Teresa Leyton had said. The words spilled from her lips as she walked. 'He hates like a man... the devil's own job to keep him from Blackthorn House...

from burning it to the ground and all of you inside.' The tears fell then, hot scalding tears that tumbled down her face and made long meandering streaks dried by the sun. 'You'll never know it, David,' she murmured, 'but however much you hate me, it won't stop me from loving you.'

Somehow the thought of that love, the memory of his strong handsome face and the laughter they had shared before events had destroyed their happiness, brought a rush of immense joy. His memory was all she had now. And it would have to last her a long, long time.

While Cathy made her way home, Teresa waited for her brother to emerge from the church. She was impatient to put a distance between them and Cathy Blackthorn, who could still be seen walking along the footpath. 'I thought you were taking up residence in there,' she said when David appeared. 'Can we go now?'

Thrusting his hands in his pockets, he flexed his shoulders and took a deep invigorating breath of air. The church was cold and damp inside, and he felt a chill clinging. 'Aren't you going into the church?' His dark eyes were quizzical. 'I thought that was why you came with me.' Gazing over the fields, he felt a kind of peace settle on him. But it was an uneasy, short-lived peace. 'Go in if you want,' he urged. 'Like I say, I'm in no hurry to leave.'

Teresa was frantic. If *he* wasn't in a hurry to leave, she certainly was. Casting a cursory glance towards the church doors, she replied sullenly, 'I won't go in if it's all the same to you. There's nothing for me in there.'

He saw how distressed she was and misunderstood the real reason; he wasn't to know about the exchange between her and Cathy. Putting a brotherly arm round her shoulders, he said warmly, 'You can find peace, Teresa, if only you'll let yourself believe that.' Yet, except for a fleeting moment when he emerged from God's house, he had not found peace. Without Cathy, he was a lost man.

'I just want to go. There's still a lot to do.' She glanced worriedly at Cathy's retreating figure, grateful that he had not seen it. 'If you must know I can't wait to see the back of this damned place ... the house, the barns, everything!'

'I understand.' Kissing her lightly on the forehead, he acknowledged, 'We'd best get back. Like you say, there's still a lot to do, and Mam will be getting anxious.'

Aware that Cathy was still in full view, Teresa began walking away in the opposite direction, following the route that had brought them here. 'Come on, David,' she pleaded. 'Like you say, Mam will be waiting, eager to start packing. I don't want her to be lifting things ... she's still not strong enough.' The truth was, it didn't matter to her whether her mam hurt herself or not. If Maria Leyton was to die tomorrow, it would be an inconvenience that was all. In fact, Teresa often dreamed of there being only her and David. The idea was very pleasing indeed.

David turned to make sure the church doors were closed. As he swung round, he raised his eyes to the horizon. Recognising Cathy's tall graceful figure, he gasped aloud, 'Has Cathy been *here*?'

Teresa knew there was no use denying it. That footpath led almost directly from Blackthorn House and ended at the church. Feverishly she searched her mind and came up with the same devious lie that had separated her brother and his sweetheart from the very start; the same wicked idea that had *kept* them apart ever since and, if she had her way, would keep them apart for all time. 'I didn't tell you because it was too painful.' She even managed to sound tearful. 'Please don't blame me, David. I didn't tell you because I think you've been hurt enough.'

'What are you saying?' Bent over her, staring at her with dark pained eyes, he could not see the evil in her. 'You should have told me. You know I'd give my right arm for the chance to make amends to Cathy.'

'If she was prepared to give you that chance, or even if she could show the same gentleness you have for her, I *would* have told you.' A superb liar, she wounded him with every cruel, carefully calculated word. 'But Cathy Leyton is not forgiving like you, David. She's changed. I don't think even you could care for her any more.'

'For God's sake, Teresa! Don't tell me how I feel.' Believing he was venting his anger on an innocent, he raised his face to the sky and calmed himself. In a softer voice he told her, 'If only I'd known she was here. You should have told me!'

Wiping away pretend tears, she implored him, 'You know I would have told you. But she said the most awful things.' She bent her head. 'Terrible things that don't bear repeating. And I won't tell you.'

'I want to know!' He had his hands on her shoulders, his fingers bruising her flesh. 'Out with it, Teresa! What awful things did she say?'

She paused, looked up and paused again, seeming afraid to go on. Then, after taking a deep breath, she wiped away another pretend tear, whispering in a shaking voice, 'She said she hated you ... hated me and Mam. She said we should *all* have been hanged.' Gulping hard and rubbing her hands over her face, she went on, 'She swore that, as long as she lived here, she would never forgive the man who had murdered her mother ... or his family, and that we couldn't be gone soon enough for her.'

Having spilled out her poison, she paused to let it sink in; her conscience hardened against the look of pain on his face. 'I'm sorry, David,' she lied, pressing herself close to him. 'Now you know why I didn't want to say anything.'

Bitter and hurt, he stroked her shoulders where only a minute ago he had held her in a vicious grip. 'It's all right,' he assured her. 'I know you didn't want to tell me, but now I know, and it's just as well.' He dropped his hands from her shoulders, looked into her eyes and murmured, 'If Cathy Blackthorn wants us gone from her father's land, then we'd better get back. Like you say, there's still a lot to be done.'

As they made their way back, an uncomfortable silence descended over them. Teresa was hoping David would never discover how she had deceived him. As for David, he realised that the last remaining hope he had had of ever reconciling himself with Cathy was now an impossible dream. He felt her anguish and her anger and, because of it, he loved her all the more.

Drunk and insensible, Frank pushed away his chair and struggled to stand. 'What do you want with me? I didn't ask you to come into my study, so I'd be obliged if you'd get out!'

Margaret stood her ground. 'I'll get out when you've answered my questions and not before.' She came closer, throwing out her arms and pointing to him. 'Look at you, Frank! You're dirty and unkempt. Ever since Rita died, you've let yourself go. There's hardly a day goes by without you're drunk, or gallivanting into Blackburn ... gambling and doing goodness knows what else.'

'I'll do what I please, damn it! I don't want you or anybody else telling me how to run my life.' With a cry he fell heavily into the chair.

'Well, whether you want it or not, *I* mean to tell you a few home truths.' Placing her two hands on the desk she leaned forward, eyes blazing as she went on, 'I appreciate you miss her. I know how much you loved her, and if I could bring her back for you, you know I would.'

'GET OUT!' He hit out with clenched fist, but his co-ordination was dulled by booze and the fist merely flailed in the air before falling to the desk with a thud. 'I'll swing for the bastards, you see if I don't.'

'They'll be gone soon enough.'

'I should have seen it,' he cried out as though in great pain. 'I could have put a stop to it, and now it's too late.' Rising in his chair he pulled at the roots of his hair. 'I should have seen it. They must have known all along. They're laughing at me. I want them out now ... today. I want them off my land.'

'It's not them I'm worried about. They'll be leaving tomorrow, and besides, they have their own grief to cope with.' She looked at him now and it struck her that he was losing his mind. 'Frank, you have to realise it wasn't your fault. You didn't know what was going on between Rita and Owen Leyton. Nobody knew.'

'*They* knew.'

'Listen to me, Frank. It's *you* I'm concerned about now. I've pleaded with you and I've done my best to make you see what you're doing to yourself and to this family, but you wouldn't listen. Now you've come so far down you're almost in the gutter. No decency, no sense of dignity. And what about Cathy? Have you conveniently forgotten you have a daughter? Have you stopped to wonder whether she might need help? That she might just be missing her mother?'

'You take care of her, like you've always done.'

Her manner changed then. Placing the letter on the desk, she told him cynically, 'I'd be happy to do that, Frank, but I'm not sure whether you won't put us all in the workhouse first.'

He stared up at her, then at the letter, his bleary eyes narrowing to concentrate. Gingerly touching it, he asked impatiently, 'What's this? I'm in no mood for reading.'

Relieved to have gained his attention, she told him harshly, 'It's a letter from our solicitor. He claims you've been selling land and property... a great deal of land, Frank... and the cottage too. Tell me it isn't true?' She prayed there might be some sort of explanation. 'Tell me you haven't sold nearly all of our holdings?' Her hopes were dashed by his reply.

'And if I have, what do you intend to do about it?' Suddenly he seemed sober. Fear had a way of sobering a drunken man.

Trembling with anger, she composed herself and pulled up a chair. Sitting down straight-backed, she met his frightened stare with accusing eyes. 'I think you had better explain, don't you?' Folding her hands on the desk, she waited for him to tell her the worst.

It was more damaging than she had thought. When he had finished blurting out the details, she was ashen with shock. 'Are you telling me that all we have left is this house and the Leyton place?'

There was no remorse, no sign of regret for what he had done. 'Don't be ungrateful, my dear,' he said arrogantly. 'I was shrewd enough to keep a small amount of land with each property, and when we find a new tenant for the Leyton place, there will still be a modest income.'

'What have you done with the money you got from the sales?'

He actually smiled. 'Gone, my dear... every last penny.'

'Then you've all but ruined us.' Her voice shook, but she remained seated, stiff and straight, her eyes boring into his.

'Come, that's rather a harsh thing to say. We still have a roof over our heads, and I'm sure it won't be long before we secure a good tenant for the Leyton place.'

'I think you've lost your mind. If all our capital is gone we have nothing to fall back on. It could be months before we find a good tenant, and even when we do, the rent won't bring in enough to feed and clothe five people.'

He outstared her. 'There won't be five, my dear. There'll be you, me and the girl.'

'And what of Jack? And Ruby?'

'Ruby will have to go. I'm sure you and the girl can take up her duties. As for Jack, he must return to the streets where I found him.'

Her mouth fell open with astonishment. 'You really *have* lost your mind!' Taking up Ruby's duties would be no real hardship, but it wasn't as simple as that. There was Ruby herself to consider. Cathy too.

'What I do is no concern of yours.' Growing bold, he sat back, his fingers curled over the arms of the chair and a smug little smile on his face. 'I'm glad we've got it all out in the open,' he said. 'Now, if there is nothing else, I would prefer to be left alone.' Taking the letter, he screwed it up in his fist and dropped it into the wastepaper basket.

'Give me the letter, Frank.'

Something about her manner and voice made him retrieve the letter. After straightening it out he handed it back to her. 'Really, there's nothing you can do. The deals are signed and sealed, and the money has gone forever.' He chuckled. 'Regrets won't help. Not that I have any.'

'Oh, *I* have, Frank,' she informed him bitterly. 'I deeply regret not instructing the solicitor to make certain that all legal papers should bear *both* our signatures, not just yours. But that is now rectified, so thank God your hands are tied. Most of all, I am mortally ashamed that I allowed you to squander Cathy's inheritance.'

'It's done, I tell you.' Crashing out of the chair, he thumped both fists on the desk. 'You'll find a way to take care of the girl. Ruby will be one less mouth to feed, and tomorrow, when that wretched family leave, Jack can be sent on his way too. Oh don't worry, he's lived on his wits before. The young bugger's too cunning to starve, and I'll be sure to find him a few trinkets before he goes.' Dismissing her anxieties with a flick of his hand, he explained, 'I haven't plundered the family silver yet . . . nor the porcelain.' His eyes glazed over. 'Rita did so enjoy that. She always enjoyed nice things.' In a burst of renewed energy he went on, 'Of coure there are her beautiful jewels. But I shall never let them go. Never!' Drawing himself up to his full height he told her sternly, 'You may hate me for what I've done, but I would like you to know that I am penning a letter to cut Jack out of my will so that, in the event of my demise, whatever remains of this estate will come to you.' Swallowing hard, he wiped his hands over his face. 'Now, please get out and leave me to my thoughts.'

Even before she was halfway across the room he had fallen into the chair and thrown himself across the desk in a stupor. 'In spite of what you've done, I can't help but pity you,' she murmured, reflecting on their conversation. 'But it will be a long time before I ever forgive you.'

Outside the door, Jack kept his ear pressed to the panel. He had heard the entire conversation and was shocked to the core. 'After all I've done, you must be out of your mind if you think I'd leave empty handed,' he muttered. 'I would never have done what I've done if I didn't think there'd be a pot o' gold at the end. And now you say I'm to be sent on me way! What's it all been for, eh?'

His face was dark with rage as he planned a suitable vengeance. All the bad things rose in him ... latent murderous instincts at having been denied what he had come to believe was rightfully his.

CHAPTER NINE

'My! You're down early.' Ruby hated being caught unawares. 'It's only six o'clock. I've the firegrates to clean out yet, and umpteen other little jobs to do afore I start the breakfast.'

She was in the throes of cleaning the pantry shelves when Cathy came into the kitchen. 'These days I can't seem to catch me own tail,' she chuckled. Fetching an armful of half-empty jars out of the pantry, she set them down on the table. 'I must be getting old,' she said wistfully. 'Once upon a time I'd have had the whole house sparkling by six of a morning, and be enjoying a leisurely brew afore the family came down for their breakfast.' Sinking into the chair, she looked up at Cathy with mischievous eyes. 'Serve me right for staying out late of a night, don't it, eh?' she said with a little smile.

'I wondered about that,' Cathy admitted, her green eyes shining.

'Oh? And what else did you wonder about?'

'Whether you had got yourself a suitor.' Cathy made herself comfortable in the chair opposite, her arms stretched out and her hands covering Ruby's. 'Oh, Ruby! *Have* you got one?'

'Happen I have, and happen I haven't.'

'You'd rather not talk about it, is that it?' She was angry with herself for having pried. 'I'm sorry, Ruby, only I really would be delighted if you had found someone of your very own ... a good man who could take care of you.'

Ruby put a finger to her mouth to silence her. 'I know you would,' she said. 'And there *is* someone. But I'm afeared to count on it in case it all melts away and I'm on me own again.' She winked. 'I promise, if anything comes of it, you and Miss Margaret will be the first to know, but just now I'd rather keep it to meself. You do understand, don't you?'

Cathy was quick to reassure her. 'Of course I do. I had no right in asking you about it in the first place.' She felt a peace offering was called for. 'Now you sit there while I make you a brew of tea.'

Ruby was horrified. 'You'll do no such thing!' she cried, scrambling out of the chair. But Cathy was already round the table and pressing the little woman back. 'Now then, Ruby!' she gently chided. 'Didn't you just say you missed the days when you were able to enjoy a nice leisurely brew before the family came down?'

'That was *then*, young 'un. Them days are long gone, more's the pity.'

'Then we'll turn the clock back.' Before Ruby could protest again, Cathy had put on the kettle and laid a pretty tray. In less than no time the kettle was puffing out steam and the tea was made. Setting the tray in the centre of the table, she asked in a rather grand manner, 'Would you mind if I joined you?' She didn't sit down until Ruby replied.

'It would be a pleasure, m'lady.' Smiling profusely, Ruby did a servile little bow from the waist. 'Would "modom" like to pour?'

'Why, how kind!' Cathy declared. And the tea was poured.

Twice more the rose china cups were filled, and the two women chatted like old friends. 'It don't seem right though,' Ruby commented thoughtfully.

'What doesn't seem right, Ruby?'

'You and me ... lady and servant ... seated together at the kitchen table and sharing the same teapot.'

Cathy smiled at that. 'Shame on you, Ruby,' she said. 'Since when did we ever worry about things like that?'

Ruby nodded. 'Aye, you're right,' she acknowledged. 'You and Miss Margaret have allus been like family to me, and I love you for it.' Her eyes grew round and fearful as she stared at the door. 'All the same, there are them as would take a very dim view of it. Certainly if the master was to walk in this very minute, he'd have summat to say an' no mistake!'

'As long as he doesn't want to share our teapot.' Cathy had seen Ruby was nervous, and wanted to put her at ease.

Ruby threw back her head and laughed with relief. 'Cathy Blackthorn, you're a scamp!' she said, her whole body shaking with mirth. After another cup of tea, she tidied the crockery on to the tray, telling Cathy with affection, 'You're a ray of sunshine to an old fool, that's what you are.'

'You're not an old fool,' Cathy reprimanded her. 'You're a friend.'

'Well, if I am, I'm glad of it,' Ruby answered softly. 'Lord knows you need all the friends you can get in this cruel world.'

Cathy sipped at her tea, a faraway look in her eyes. 'Friends are very special, aren't they, Ruby?' she asked. 'I've been lucky. You, Nan and Aunt Margaret have always been my friends.' It almost choked her to say it, but it fell from the tip of her tongue. 'David too. He was a very special friend.'

Ruby knew Cathy must have suffered a bad night, because of the dark shadows under her eyes, and because she had risen so early. 'Will it help to talk about it?'

'I don't think so, but thank you, all the same.' The things she felt were not for others to know; not Ruby, not even Margaret. But she was grateful for Ruby's concern. 'I'm fine now,' she lied.

The lie was written on her face. 'I might not be able to help, but I'm a good listener,' Ruby gently insisted. 'What's troubling you? Is it the fact you've lost your mam?'

Cathy put a great deal of thought into her answer. 'I'm sorry she had to die, but I don't miss her as much as I thought I might.' Suddenly ashamed, she leaned forward on the table and asked in a hushed voice, 'Oh, Ruby! Is that such a terrible thing to say?'

'No, it isn't. It would only be terrible if you lied to yourself. Shameful though it is, we both know Rita Blackthorn could have been a better mother to you.'

'I didn't understand, but I won't condemn her for that.'

'That's because you've a good, kind heart.'

Cathy would always regret the way it had been between her and her mother. 'I don't know how to explain it,' she confessed, 'but I don't miss her as much as I miss the love we never shared.' She couldn't explain, and didn't really want to. 'It wasn't my mother I was thinking about. It was someone else.'

Ruby smiled knowingly. 'You're pining for David, aren't you?'

Cathy felt a surge of relief. 'I can't hide anything from you, can I?'

Shaking her head slowly from side to side, Ruby quietly

regarded the younger woman. 'He'll be gone soon. If you're ever again to have peace of mind, you must accept that.'

'I have accepted it.' In a way she had, but it didn't ease the agony of losing him. She glanced up and her eyes were dull with pain. 'I'm sorry. I shouldn't be burdening you.'

'I only wish I could help. It seems such a shame that the two of you couldn't make amends.'

Something occurred to Cathy then, and she dared not tell Ruby. But if she was to act it must be quickly. 'I think I'll go back to bed.' She had no intention of going back but Ruby mustn't know that or she might rouse Margaret.

'I think that's a very good idea, young lady. Come down nearer eight o'clock and I'll have breakfast all ready.' Pushing her chair back Ruby cleared away the tray. From the cupboard beneath the sink she took out a box filled with polishing rags and half-used tins of blacklead. 'Meanwhile, there's umpteen jobs to be done.' Bursting into a tuneful melody, she ambled from the room. 'You get your beauty sleep while you've a chance!' she called over her shoulder. 'When you get to my age you'll be glad of every wink.' Laughing, she went into the drawing room and shut the door.

Cathy moved quickly, up the stairs and into her room where she hurriedly washed and dressed, choosing a brown dress and dark boots, and a long coat. Flicking her long corn-coloured hair outside the coat-collar, she ran down the stairs and out through the front door. She didn't stop running until she reached the footpath, where she slowed to a fast walking pace. The thought of seeing David spurred her on. She didn't want to miss him. Even now, she still hoped David might have a change of heart.

The bitter cold wind howled round her ears. It made her face raw and froze her fingertips, but still she pushed on. She recalled a conversation she'd had with Margaret only the night before. Her aunt had asked, 'Do you know where David might be headed?' And she had answered, 'No, but I wish I was going with him.'

She wished it now, then in the same breath was ashamed. Ashamed because of what had happened between her mother and David's father; ashamed of the outcome; ashamed because it seemed a harsh thing to say when Margaret needed her more than it appeared David did. And yet, she would gladly have walked barefoot behind the cart if it meant she could be with him.

Even while she was thinking these things, a sense of outrage welled up in her, spilling over until she cried out, 'Don't cheapen yourself, Cathy Blackthorn! If he doesn't want you, then to hell with him!' But words themselves were cheap, and it cost her nothing to say that. It cost her more to let him go without making that one last try. She adored Margaret. But it was a different kind of love she felt for David; the kind that grew in your heart, only to break it.

Margaret had said something else too. She had told Cathy, 'In teaching him to read, you've given David something he must cherish forever.'

Cathy thought about that now, and it warmed her heart. All in a moment it came rushing back: the long precious hours she and David had leaned over their books together; the way he laughed whenever he mastered a word; the closeness of his body, the smell of newly mown hay after he'd been out in the fields, and the shining black dampness of his hair when he washed it under the pump.

She remembered it all as though it was only yesterday, and her spirit was both drained and elated. 'David had a quick and clever mind,' she murmured aloud. 'Whatever he chooses to do when he leaves here, I know he'll be a great success.' Silent for the remainder of the journey, she was glad to lose herself in bitter-sweet memories. Even now it was hard to accept that he had turned against her with such loathing.

As he harnessed the horse to the wagon, David's thoughts were very close to Cathy's. 'I thought there'd come a day when she and I would be man and wife,' he told the sad-eyed horse, 'but it wasn't to be.' Pausing for a minute, he stroked the horse's head and nuzzled his face against its nose. 'I'm lost without her,' he whispered. 'What can I do? I love her with all my heart, and she won't have anything to do with me.'

Teresa stepped out of the shadows. 'Talking to yourself is a dangerous thing. Folks will be thinking you've gone out of your mind.'

He laughed at that. 'Happen I have.'

'Not you. You're too strong-minded.'

'Do you think I should go and see Cathy before we leave?'

'Only if you want to hurt her more.'

'The things she said . . . at the church. Do you think she said them in the heat of anger?'

Teresa had to scheme carefully if she was going to stop him from going to Blackthorn House. 'When she said those things to me, she was deadly calm. Believe me, David, going to her now would only make things worse.' Crossing the stable, she linked her arm with his. 'If I thought there was the slightest chance that she'd welcome you, I'd say go on, make one last try to make amends. But I know it would only make matters worse. I saw her face when she said those things, and I promise you . . . she meant every word.'

He glanced down and realised she still seemed upset by what had happened. 'Sorry, sis,' he said bitterly. 'That's what comes of a man like me hankering after someone like Cathy.'

'It's all in the past now,' she said hopefully.

'Best get finished and away,' he said abruptly. 'We're late as it is. I meant to be on the road before the cock crowed.'

'You're sorry to be leaving, aren't you?'

'It's like losing my right arm.' Cathy. Always Cathy. Without her, life was cold and empty.

'I'm not sorry to be going.'

'Well then, take yourself inside and help Mam pack the last few bits and pieces. It'll be a few minutes before I back the cart to the front door. If everything's ready for me to load we can be away in no time.' With that he bent to his task and left Teresa to run back inside and work with a frenzy. 'We're leaving, and the sooner we go the better,' he muttered. But Cathy would go with him wherever he went.

Some fifteen minutes later, the last items were being packed on to the cart. 'Don't damage my sideboard, son,' Maria pleaded. She watched as he wrapped his arms round the oaken bulk and slid it to the edge of the cart. 'Help him, Teresa,' she urged. 'Steady it.' She ran back and forth, nervously biting her handkerchief and issuing instructions.

'Stand back!' David warned as Teresa moved closer. 'If this thing goes it'll slice your toes clean off.'

He inched the heavy article on to the cart, keeping it well balanced and supporting the weight with both arms. The sweat ran down his face and his back ached, but he knew it was safer for him alone to handle it. 'There!' At last it was safely tied to the inside of the cart. 'I don't blame you for being concerned,' he told his mam. 'It's a lovely thing and no mistake.' Taking a moment to admire the oak sideboard, he marvelled at the intricate carving on the doors and panels; the deep fret along the top was edged with sprays of woodland flowers, and each straight sturdy leg culminated in a square foot.

'Your father bought that the day before we were wed,' Maria reminded him. 'And as long as I live, I'll never part with it.'

The box of crockery was last to go on. David wedged it between the eiderdowns, before covering the whole lot over with a canvas to protect it from the weather. 'Ready when you are,' he said. 'I'll just check the barn, while you two take a look inside the house and make sure we've got everything.'

'I'm not setting foot inside that house ever again,' Teresa declared. Climbing on to the back of the cart, she said under her breath, 'As long as I've got all *my* stuff out, that's all I care.'

Maria stood at the door of the house for what seemed an age. Her weary eyes travelled the empty room; where there had been rugs there were now bare floorboards; the walls were stark where once had hung squares of embroidery and small pictures. The huge open hearth was blackened by the many cheery fires that had burned there, but there was no cheery fire now, only dead ashes. 'I should curse you to hell for what you've done to this family, Owen Leyton,' she whispered. 'But, God forgive me, I can't.' On slow tortuous steps, she went into the room, and the memories were overwhelming.

David went to the house to find his mother. She was seated on the hearth, her head bent and her heart breaking. 'How did it all go wrong, son?' she asked, looking up with tear-filled eyes. 'One day we were a family . . . the next we're torn apart. I daren't think what will happen to us now.'

Taking her in his arms, he promised, 'We'll be fine.'

'But we've no money, and nowhere to live. I'm frightened,

son. I can't help but be frightened.'

He felt her shudder in his arms and his determination was tenfold. 'Like I said, Mam, we'll be fine. While I've got a broad back and a pair of strong arms, you'll want for nothing.'

His words soothed her. 'You're a good man,' she said, and when he led her away from the place which had been her home she had great faith that all would come right in the end. Where Teresa was concerned, she had no illusions; besides inheriting some of her father's weak traits, the girl had a tendency towards greed and cruelty. But with her son beside her Maria believed she need not fear the future.

Soon she was seated up on the cart. One last look round, then, 'Let's away from here, son.' Her smile was warm and loving. 'Me and the girl . . . we're in your hands now.' There were no regrets in her voice. Only resignation, and a sense of relief.

Slapping the reins against the horse's rump, David too was impatient to be gone. His dark eyes were turned to the horizon, to the rising sun and the promise of a better day. 'You're wrong, Mam,' he said softly. 'We're in the Good Lord's hands. It's him we'll have to look to before this day ends.' He had an idea where he might find work, and with it a place for them to live. But he wasn't certain. Things changed so quickly, he must be prepared for disappointment.

As the cart rumbled slowly across the uneven ground, Teresa sat on the back, her legs dangling over the side and her brain feverish with mischief. She was elated to be leaving, thrilled at having come between Cathy and David, and now desperate to punish Frank Blackthorn for evicting them from their home. As the idea presented herself, she chuckled with delight.

While David and her mother quietly talked, she slid from the wagon and ran back to the house. Here, she collected a sack of debris which had been swept from the house and left outside. She took it into the parlour and emptied it in the centre of the floor. Next, she went to the kitchen and collected some of the papers left over from her mother's packing. Rolling them into a long thick stick, she dug in her pocket and drew out a box of matches. After striking one against the wall, she put it to the end of the paper torch and waited for it to take hold.

When it was blazing, she dropped it into the pile of debris and watched while the flames leapt high.

Satisfied, she went from the house, secured the door behind her and ran after the cart which was already turning out of the lane. Panting and excited, she silently slipped back on to it, her spiteful eyes fixed on the house until at last it was gone from sight.

At the top of the rise, Cathy paused for breath. But she couldn't stop long. Time was precious. Pressing on, she went over the rise and down the other side, half running, half stumbling, her heart beating like a wild thing's. In the distance she could see the rooftop of the Leyton house. It seemed a million miles away. Her eyes were drawn to the chimney. The sky was clear above it, and she knew what that meant. If there was no fire in the hearth, the family were not there. David was always about before dawn. The first thing he did was to light a fire. So many times she had asked him to describe his day, and she knew what it meant if there was no smoke rising from the chimney. 'He's gone! Please don't let him be gone!' Spurred on, she was oblivious of the sharp thorny bushes and the way they tore at her clothes and face.

Hastening her steps, she ran and ran until her chest was so tight that she could hardly breathe. As she neared the lane she could hear the rumble of wagon wheels. 'David!' Stumbling out of the hedgerow, she could see nothing. The lane was empty, but the sound of wagon wheels was not far off. Going at speed, she followed the lane up and out of the hollow. At the top she saw it; the wagon was a long way ahead and going at a smart pace.

Desperate now, she chased after it, calling again and again, 'DAVID! David, come back. We have to talk.' But the wind drowned her voice and the wagon was soon lost from sight. Dejected and heartbroken, she fell to the ground, and there she lay for some long time, her body racked with sobs.

She was still softly crying when she came to the top of the rise again. Searching the horizon with weary eyes, she realised he was gone and would never be back. About to turn away, she caught sight of a bright flickering light low in the sky. Curious, she shielded her eyes with the palms of her hands and peered closer. The light was a fire, and the flames licked at the air like giant tongues. In an instant it dawned on her. 'It's the Leytons' house!' She couldn't believe what her eyes were telling her. 'It's burning! The house is burning!'

Frantic, she took to her heels. Making straight for Blackthorn House, she ignored the lane and went straight across the fields, her eyes skimming the way ahead, searching for someone, anyone who might help. But there was no one. In that vast and empty place, she was all alone.

Ten minutes later, as she covered the short distance between the house and the rise, Margaret saw her approaching. Filled with relief, she ran to meet her. 'Where on earth have you been?' she cried angrily. 'I've been searching everywhere for you.' And then she saw Cathy's appearance; the torn clothes and deep scratches across her face. 'Good God! Look at you!' Clutching Cathy in her arms, she suddenly recalled how Jack had also left the house earlier, and feared the worst. 'What's happened to you?' she demanded gently, cradling Cathy close to her breast. 'Was it Jack? I need to know. Was it Jack who did this to you?' All her latent suspicions regarding that young man came to the fore.

Cathy caught her breath as the words came out in a rush. 'There's a fire! I saw it as I made my way back ... it's the Leyton house, I'm sure of it.' Drawing away from Margaret she pleaded, 'Leave me ... get help. You must get help!'

'It's you I'm concerned about. If the house was ablaze as you say, there's little to be done to save it now.'

'*Try!* Please try!' Pushing her away, Cathy promised, 'I'm not hurt. Please ... get help.'

Margaret saw the distress in her eyes and realised that the house was all she had left of David. 'I'll be back for you,' she promised. Then she went at a run down the bank and across the field, calling reassurances as she went.

Sinking to the grass, Cathy took great gulps of air. Her lungs felt close to bursting as she followed Margaret's progress. Soon the familiar figure had gone over the horizon and was lost to sight. 'God speed,' Cathy murmured. Getting to her feet, she began following at a steadier pace. In her heart, she knew

Margaret was probably right. There was small hope now of saving the house.

When some short time later the fire wagon clattered through the street of Langho, its bells loudly ringing, the children followed. Raggy-arsed and barefooted, they shouted and laughed, some clinging to the wheels, others hanging from the tail-gate and a few running behind, occasionally cutting across the fields to keep up. This was a treat they couldn't miss, for a real fire in Langho was a rare event.

The house was beyond saving. By the time the firemen arrived, the flames had taken hold and were licking the sky. 'We might have stood a chance if we'd got here earlier,' said one weary man to another, his face streaked with soot and his red eyes weeping from the effects of acrid smoke. The other man shook his head and replied solemnly, 'It was a losing battle. The old place was laden with too much rotten timber.'

It was almost dark when the last man left. The fire was checked and the building gutted. There was nothing else to do but leave the blackened shell to the elements.

Frank was beside himself with rage. 'We're ruined!' Jutting out his chin, he paced up and down the drawing room, hands clenched behind his back. 'I'll have him for it though!' His shifty eyes flicked from Margaret to Cathy. 'Owen Leyton's son did this, and by God I'll make him pay!'

Cathy had heard enough. After being summoned here with Margaret, she had expected to hear some kind of constructive plans for the future. Instead of which her father had strutted about, blaming everyone else for his own misfortune and now threatening to set the law on David. It was the last straw. Springing out of her chair, she faced him with a look as furious as his own. 'I didn't want to attend this meeting in the first place,' she confessed, 'but I came here with my aunt because I thought you might have something useful to say. I was foolish enough to believe you might have found a way of salvaging something out of what we have left. But I was wrong. As I've always been wrong about you. You care for no one but yourself, isn't that the truth?' Now the anger was high in her she couldn't easily suppress it. 'As for David starting that fire, how can you be so sure? How do you know it wasn't just a dreadful accident?'

Momentarily astonished by her outburst, he stared at her with pink bulbous eyes. When he spoke, it was in a low guttural voice that betrayed his dislike of her. 'I know because he's made of the same rotten stuff Owen Leyton was made of. I know, because it's his way of getting back at me for having his father hanged.'

Defiantly, she told him, 'You're wrong about David. I can't defend what his father did, but I can tell you that David Leyton is a fine young man. I know him, and he would never stoop to such a level.'

He laughed at that. 'Oh, I'm quite sure you know him . . . just as your dear mother knew his father. In fact I shouldn't be at all surprised if he hasn't already bedded you, made you with child, like his father made your mother with child.' As the awful words left his lips, his eyes misted over and the tears rolled down his podgy face. 'It's plain enough how he forced himself on her. My Rita would never have betrayed me of her own accord. But *you!* Your poor mother was right about you after all, wasn't she? There's a badness in you . . . just as there's a badness in Owen Leyton's son. He set fire to that house right enough. No doubt the pair of you have been rolling about in the hay, laughing at me. Isn't that the truth, eh?' Taking her by the shoulders, he shook her hard. 'I SAID, ISN'T THAT THE TRUTH?'

Struck silent by the viciousness of his words, Cathy could only stare at him. When Margaret took hold of her, urging, 'He didn't mean it. Can't you see he's crazed with grief?' Cathy shook her off. In a move that took everyone by surprise, she darted forward. Pressing her hands over her father's arms she pinned them to his sides. 'It isn't me and David that's bad,' she told him. 'It's *you!*'

'Take your filthy hands off.' Amazed by her strength, he tried to shake her off but couldn't.

Cathy was relentless. 'There was a time when I loved and respected you. Not any more though. How can I respect a man who doesn't even respect himself? How can a daughter look up to her father when he's lower than the worms in the ground? You spend your life shut away in the study . . . drunk most of the time . . . not caring what goes on around you. You talk about

606

David and his father. But what about you, eh? What about the shocking things *you've* done?'

'What do you mean?' Now he was on the defensive, looking at her with a glint of fear in his eyes.

'I know what you did! The land ... the cottage ... how you sold it all without Aunt Margaret's knowledge.' She had listened with shame and disbelief when, after the Leyton house had burned to the ground, Margaret felt the time was right for her to know the state of things. 'I'm afraid it must affect us badly,' she had said, and Cathy realised that the dear woman was beside herself with worry.

Frank was unrepentant. 'That is none of your concern!'

'Of course it's my concern. You expected to get a handsome rent from the house, didn't you? Enough to keep the wolf from the door, you told Aunt Margaret. What do you intend to do now? The house is a shell. There will be no rent. You've spent every penny got from the sale of other assets, and all that's left is this house. You have cheated your own sister, and still you feel no shame.'

'I'm not her keeper!'

'And I'm sure she wouldn't want you to be. But I can promise you she will come to no harm. Not while I am young enough to find a way of earning a living. Aunt Margaret has been everything to me all these years. She was there for me when you and Mother were not. And I shall always be there for her.' A tide of emotion washed through her, a mighty wave of relief that seemed to release a dam inside. 'You can't hurt me any more. Remember that, Father, when you're filling yourself with drink and shutting out those who might have cherished you ... you can't hurt *either* of us any more.' Shaking and close to tears but keeping them in check, she snatched herself away. With a dignity that made her tower above him, she walked across the room and out of the door.

Once outside she leaned against the wall, strengthened by the depth of her own feelings and astonished that she had found the courage to say what had needed saying for too long.

'Well, now!' Jack's cunning face appeared before her. 'I heard what you said in there, and I reckon it took real guts to turn on him like that.'

Her first instinct was to move away. The very nearness of him turned her stomach. But she was still fired up. 'Be careful, Jack,' she warned in a quiet voice. 'Or I might turn on *you* next.' With that, she went to her bedroom, secure in the knowledge that Margaret would come and talk with her before the night was over.

Jack waited outside the drawing room. The door was open as Cathy had left it, and Margaret was urging Frank, 'Please, you must take stock of yourself. It still isn't too late to win Cathy's affection. The three of us could move away, make a fresh start. Perhaps that would be best for all of us, Frank. Won't you at least think on it?' The scene between father and daughter had upset her, yet she knew it had been a long time in coming, and wasn't all that surprised when it erupted.

'I want nothing from her, and even less from you.' Frank could see no further than his hatred for the Leyton family. 'As for that young dog, David Leyton, I mean to see him punished for what he's done.'

'As Cathy said, how can you be so sure it was David who set fire to the house?'

'I'm sure enough, damn it.' He began pacing the floor again. 'I had it all worked out. The rent from that house would have saved us, and now . . .'

'And now?' Margaret prompted.

For the first time he appeared to be concerned. Coming to the chair he eased himself into it like an old, old man. He didn't look at her, but his voice was broken when he muttered, 'Some of the things she said . . . awful to hear.' When, by her silence, she condoned what Cathy had said, he glanced up, his eyes ugly to look on. 'In answer to your question, Margaret . . . about what might happen now . . . I'm afraid things are out of my hands.'

'What do you mean?'

'I mean, with that wretched house burned down, and with it the prospect of a handsome rent, I can't see which way to turn. As you know, the money is all spent.'

'You still have Rita's jewellery. You said yourself it's very valuable.'

'It's sold!' he lied. 'Every last piece . . . sold!' He eyed her like a cat might a mouse.

'Sold?' She'd never believed he could do that. 'So you've sunk even lower than the few principles you had left? No matter. We still have this house. By all accounts you raised a considerable sum of money from the sale of the cottage and land with it. This place is much grander and should fetch enough to keep us all comfortable. We can find a smaller property, I'm sure. As long as you give up the drink and make yourself useful, and are determined to live more modestly, we'll manage well enough.'

His silence was somehow encouraging, making her feel there might be hope for them after all. It was only when he looked up and she saw his expression that the fear was rekindled. 'There's something you're not telling me,' she said anxiously. 'What is it, Frank? This is no time to be keeping secrets.'

Like the coward he was, he couldn't bear to look at her. Dropping his gaze to the floor, he mumbled, 'It's worse than you think.'

'For God's sake, how can it be worse?'

'I took out a loan against the security of this house, and they're threatening to evict us.'

Margaret's senses swam. For a moment she was unable to answer. She sat in the chair and pressed her hands to her face. She thought of Cathy and of how they would manage.

'It's no use crying over spilt milk,' he said callously.

Her face was stern as she replied, 'I wonder if I can ever forgive you. What you have done would be beyond any decent man.'

'I am my own man, and I will do as I please.'

'Not any more you won't! You have me and Cathy to consider now,' she reminded him. 'And you mustn't forget Jack. After all, you brought the boy here, and now he's your responsibility.'

'He's going back where he came from. I've an idea he might be better off with his own kind.' It was on the tip of his tongue to admit that Jack was his own flesh and blood, but it would serve no purpose. 'Anyway, I've already told you I won't send him away empty-handed.'

'Has he been told of your plans?'

'Not yet.'

'You mean you haven't the courage to tell him.'

'All in good time, my dear.'

'I mean it, Frank. From now on, *I* make the decisions. This house must be put on the market at once. With luck there might be money left after the debt is settled . . . enough for us to make a fresh start.'

'There won't be.'

'For all our sakes, I hope you're wrong.' Regarding him with disdain, she remarked angrily, 'It's a great pity you sold Rita's jewellery, because that might have salvaged at least some future for all of us.'

'Are you after my blood, is that it? Do you think to put me through the grinder for my sins?' Having got the worst off his chest, his arrogance was returning. 'I've confessed everything to you. I've been insulted by my own daughter. The boy is being sent packing, just as you've always wanted, and the changing of my will is in hand. Surely that is enough to satisfy you?'

Margaret was cynical. 'The changing of your will is in hand, you say? I suppose that means instead of leaving your debts to Jack, you'll be leaving them to me? Am I supposed to be grateful for that?' She shook her head forlornly. 'Really, Frank. You never cease to amaze me.'

'It isn't all bad news,' he reminded her. 'Before the day comes when I lie in my grave, you may find a way to restore our fortunes.'

'I believe you really have lost your senses!' Exasperated, she pointed out, 'There is no way I can possibly restore our fortunes, as you put it. As far as I can tell, we have no money and precious little to fall back on. What we have left is this house with one acre of land – both of which are mortgaged.' Looking him straight in the eye, she demanded in a frosty voice, 'I know the house was valued last year for the sum of one hundred guineas. How much is owed on it? And don't fob me off with lies. I want the truth, Frank, however damning.'

'I'm telling you nothing more. You will find out soon enough, I expect.' With each word his chest seemed to expand and his chin jutted out a little further. 'It might be wise for you to bear in mind that I am still head of this household. Now, if you please, I want to go to my study.'

'As you say, Frank, I will find out soon enough what depths you have lowered us all to.' With that she departed the room, leaving him to return to his study and his bottle.

As Margaret made her way up to Cathy, Jack crept out of hiding. Going into the study, he put on a smile and sat himself in the chair before the desk. 'By! What a tartar that one is,' he chuckled. It was an effort not to spring at Frank's throat and throttle the life out of him. Flicking his thumb towards the door, he said admiringly, 'I reckon you handled her very well.'

Surprised and irritated at his intrusion, Frank rounded the desk and took hold of him by the lapels. 'You were not asked to come in here,' he snarled. 'What's more, I don't want your useless opinions.'

Jack's smile grew crafty. 'That's no way to treat me, now is it?' he said, shrugging Frank off. 'I've come in here to talk about my future.'

'Explain.'

'Oh, I thought it might be *you* who'd explain. I heard you meant to send me back where I come from. Is that right? Do you mean to throw me out on me ear?'

Frank's face fell. 'If you heard that, you will also have heard that I don't mean to send you away empty-handed.'

'So you *are* throwing me out on me ear?'

'You never belonged here anyway.'

Jack stared at him for a moment, hatred alive in his face. Then, without another word, he turned away and left.

Frank's next visitor was Ruby. 'Miss Margaret has asked for a supper tray to be served in the drawing room,' she explained. 'I wondered if you might join them?'

'Leave me.'

'Can I bring you a bite to eat? A pot of tea, maybe?'

'I want nothing.' Looking up, he watched as she opened the door to leave. 'Ruby!'

'Yes, sir?'

'Did you post my letter?'

'Yes, sir.'

He gave a deep sigh. 'Very well. Now leave me.'

It was gone midnight when Frank finally climbed the stairs. But he didn't go to his bed. Instead he went to Rita's dressing table where he pulled out the top drawer. Setting it on the floor, he then reached into a hidden cavity. From here he withdrew a small mother-of-pearl cabinet. Placing it on top of the dressing table, he took a key from his waistcoat pocket and unlocked the cabinet. For a long moment he gazed inside, reluctant to let the gems see daylight. 'See here, Rita,' he muttered, looking round the room and pointing to the cabinet, 'I've kept them safe. They think I've sold them, but I could never do that.'

One by one he took out the gems, caressing each one as though it was flesh and blood. Soon they were laid out on the dressing-table top, fourteen pieces in all, glittering and shimmering, and all bought by an adoring husband for a wily ungrateful woman.

He stared at them and touched them, he smiled and he cried, recalling each occasion he had given a piece to Rita, and how she had rewarded him with nights of lovemaking he would never forget.

After a while he fell asleep beside them, his arms folded protectively over them, and his head laid between them; when he lapsed into a deeper slumber, the tears were still damp on his face.

The footsteps came silently into the room. Swamped with alcohol and unconscious with grief, Frank heard not a sound. The footsteps paused by the dressing table, quick practised fingers reached out to stroke the gems. Avaricious eyes devoured their beauty before they were dropped into a small dark bag and thrust into a deeper pocket. The same grubby fingers shook out a rag and pressed it ever so gently over Frank's nose. Asleep with his beloved Rita, he knew nothing. He felt nothing. All too soon it was over, the cabinet was removed and the drawer returned, and all was as before. One more look, making sure there was no trace of what had taken place here, and the footsteps hurried away.

It was Ruby who found him. The night had long gone and a new day had begun, but not for Frank. The news spread far and wide: Frank Blackthorn had died of his terrible grief. There was no mention of murder or robbery. Frank's lies about having sold Rita's jewellery had unwittingly protected his own executioner.

At precisely nine o'clock one morning in February 1901 the solicitor arrived at Blackthorn House. A short balding man with the air of a giant and the voice of a sergeant-major, Mr Reginald Dalton inspired both awe and respect in his many clients.

Cathy let him in. 'Good morning, Mr Dalton,' she said, inviting him through to the dining room where Margaret was already waiting. 'You'll join me and my aunt in a cup of tea, won't you?' As they walked, the grandfather clock in the hall chimed out the hours. The days had been long since David had left, and still she ached for him. But time stands still for no one, she thought.

At Cathy's invitation to accept a cup of tea, Mr Dalton merely nodded but made no verbal reply. She took the nod as being an acceptance. 'I've already asked Ruby to fetch a tray,' she explained politely. 'Your reputation for liking a good cup of tea goes before you.' Her smile was friendly and encouraging, but when he continued to remain silent she began to feel just the slightest bit uncomfortable. 'Aunt Margaret thought we might be more comfortable round the table in the dining room.' Opening the door, she ushered him inside.

Margaret was on her feet. 'Mr Dalton, punctual as usual,' she remarked, offering him her hand.

'I would be no kind of solicitor if I arrived late for the reading of a client's will,' he reprimanded.

Seeing Margaret embarrassed, Cathy chipped in, 'And it's all to your credit, Mr Dalton!' She showed him to the head of the table where he lost no time in laying down his briefcase. Once the women were seated, he settled himself comfortably. 'It's a sorry day,' he said sombrely, glancing first at Margaret and then at Cathy. He saw Jack seated on a chair beneath the window, but took little notice of him. 'Shall we begin?' His question was directed at the two women.

Both nodded, so he opened the briefcase and took out a sheaf of papers. At that moment, there came a knock on the door. It was Ruby. 'I've brought the tray you ordered,' she told Cathy.

'Thank you, Ruby.' She gestured to the end of the table. 'Just set it down there. I'll see to it.' As Ruby put the tray to the table, Cathy noticed that the older woman's hands were trembling, causing the cups and saucers to rattle. 'Are you all right, Ruby?' she asked with concern.

'I'm sorry,' Ruby whispered, casting an anxious glance at Margaret and the solicitor, who were taking this opportunity to discuss other matters. 'Only I'm all at sixes and sevens this morning.'

'You're obviously ailing for something.' Cathy was concerned about her. For days now, Ruby had not been her usual self. She was pale and nervous, seeming to have a great weight on her mind. 'Let the work wait ... go and sit down awhile,' Cathy said gently. 'You don't look at all well.'

'Oh, you mustn't fret about me,' Ruby chided, putting on a little smile. 'You have enough to worry about without me adding to your troubles.'

'It will be a sad day when I don't worry about you,' Cathy told her with a grin. 'Please, Ruby ... do as I ask. Put your feet up and pamper yourself for once.' Taking hold of the work-worn fingers, she gave them an encouraging little squeeze. 'I'll be along to see you when we've finished here.'

'All right, but you will send for me if I'm needed?'

'You won't be needed. Now, do as you're told.'

When the door closed behind Ruby, the short preliminary conversation between Margaret and the solicitor ended. 'If you're all ready now,' he announced, looking from one to the other and saving his most ferocious glare for Jack, 'I'll make a start.'

It was as Margaret and Cathy feared. All their assets had gone, with the exception of the charred remains of the Leyton house and the land on which it stood, and Blackthorn House and contents, all of which were at risk because of money loaned against them. 'The sum owing is quite considerable, I'm afraid,' the solicitor said and mentioned an amount that had his audience gasping.

'Almost its entire worth,' Margaret murmured, and from the look on her face Cathy realised how serious the situation had become.

In conclusion, Mr Dalton announced, 'The new will was received by me on the very day of Frank Blackthorn's death. In it he leaves everything to his sister Margaret. Unfortunately, with the main assets already stripped from the estate, there is much to be done if any monies are to be salvaged. If the debt against the estate is not repaid in full by one month from today, the house and its contents will be seized by the creditors.' Looking over his spectacles, he addressed himself to Cathy. 'It will rest with you and your good aunt to decide on a suitable course of action.'

Her gaze was equally stern. 'I understand,' she assured him. Then, sliding her hand over Margaret's, added in a softer voice, 'We *both* understand.'

Margaret was heartened by Cathy's response. 'We have been prepared for the worst,' she revealed. 'Whatever happens now, we're ready to face it head on.'

'Good! Good!' Beaming from ear to ear, he actually smiled. 'And I'm quite sure you won't mind my making a suggestion?' He took a deep breath and went on, 'Blackthorn House is a very desirable residence. I have a client who would pay a handsome sum of money for such a property... the entire estate, I mean... this house and land, together with the remains of the burned-out property and surrounding land.' Pleased with himself and sensing a favourable response, he added, 'Of course, he would want the contents and furniture included in the price. But you have my word... I will negotiate a handsome sum on your behalf. One that would allow you to leave here with some dignity, together with the ability to set up home elsewhere.' It was to Margaret he now addressed himself. 'In the circumstances, I will of course waive my own professional fee. So can I take it you are you in favour of such an agreement?'

Margaret did seem to be in favour. 'I must admit I haven't relished the thought of seeking a buyer. Certainly your idea has merit.'

'Ah! Then I can make a start?'

Cathy had listened, and not without an inkling of suspicion. Before Margaret could answer, she asked, 'This client of yours... may I ask who he is?'

Mr Dalton was obviously embarrassed. He hummed and hawed and blew his nose into his handkerchief, before saying with an air of indignation, 'At this point in time there is nothing to be served by revealing his identity.'

Cathy was not satisfied. 'Is it *you*, Mr Dalton?' she demanded. 'Are *you* the one who wants to get his hands on Blackthorn House?'

Again he hummed and hawed and glanced at Margaret, who was intent on the conversation. 'Does it matter who the buyer is?' he asked her nervously.

Here Margaret intervened. First she asked Jack to leave the room. When he left in a sulk, she turned on Mr Dalton. 'I believe it is our right to know who the potential buyer is. Also what sum of money we might be talking about. As yet you haven't divulged that very important fact, and I am made to wonder, like Cathy, why all the secrecy?'

'What do you imply by that?' The room was cool, but the sweat was running down his face. Fishing out a clean white handkerchief from his waistcoat pocket, he feverishly dabbed at himself. 'Are you suggesting I intend to acquire the property by devious means?'

It was Cathy who replied. 'What my aunt means, Mr Dalton, is this . . . first of all, why couldn't you say it was you who was hoping to buy the property? And secondly, if you are not prepared to name a figure here and now, we can only be made suspicious. Now, if you would please explain exactly what you mean when you say a "handsome sum"?'

'As I have already explained, after settlement of all debts, the remaining monies will allow you and your aunt to retire in some degree of comfort.'

'But what *sum*, Mr Dalton?' Like a dog with a bone, Cathy would not let go. Looking on, Margaret realised that all the recent trials and disappointments had somehow given her niece a deeper determination.

'I thought . . . one hundred and seventy guineas.' By now his face was shiny and bright pink. 'The sum owed is one hundred and forty . . . leaving you and your aunt with thirty guineas. You can buy a modest house and arrange for a small income with such a sum.'

Cathy's face was set like stone. Pushing away her chair she told him in a hard voice, 'I do believe my aunt would like you to leave now.' She gave a sideways look at Margaret. who was clearly shocked by what amounted to deception by their own trusted solicitor.

Margaret came to stand by Cathy. When she spoke, it was to reiterate what Cathy had already said. 'Yes, I would like you to leave.'

'But what about Blackthorn House, and the remainder?' He saw his mistake and was eager to rectify it. 'I must apologise for not naming myself as the possible buyer ... it's just that I didn't want you to get the wrong idea. And now you have, and I'm embarrassed.'

Cathy gave no quarter. 'So you should be,' she snapped. 'A man in your profession should know better than to deceive the clients who place their trust in you.'

'I am sorry you feel this way, but I have to advise that the figure I offer is a good one, and you'll not get better elsewhere.'

Margaret considered this while Cathy saw him to the door. 'You are wrong about our not being able to get a better price elsewhere,' she informed him. 'Rather than let it go under market value, my aunt and I will consider putting it all to auction.'

He was appalled. 'Do that and you'll be throwing yourselves to the wolves.'

'Maybe. But you have already seen that Blackthorn House is a desirable property. There must be many more who think the same way. Wolves they may be. But if these same wolves are prepared to fight each other for what they want, that can only drive the price up.' Smiling as she closed the door on him, she added softly, 'You obviously thought to be handed everything on a plate. Well, now you can fight for what you want too ... just as my aunt and I must do.'

Margaret was intrigued by Cathy's idea. 'But how will we go about it? I don't know the first thing about auctions ... apart from the fact that Longdon Place went to auction last year and raised more than was expected.'

'There you are then! We have to do it. What we don't know we can find out. Besides, once we put it all in the hands of a reputable auctioneer, we just need to follow the proceedings.'

Excited by the prospect, she urged, 'What do you think? Shall we make some enquiries?'

It was agreed. Margaret, however, placed the burden on Cathy's shoulders, with the plea, 'Forgive me, sweetheart, but I feel drained by it all. Would you mind very much if I returned to my bed?'

Cathy was understanding. 'It's not surprising you feel drained,' she said, going with Margaret to the foot of the stairs. 'First Mother, and all the shocking things that came out about her and Owen Leyton. Nan ... the Leyton house being burned down ... and now Father. And on top of it all, this awful business of having to sell up and pay off enormous debts. It's too much for anyone to bear.'

Margaret smiled at that. 'It isn't too much for you though. And in losing David, you have lost the most precious thing of all.' She shook her head and wondered at Cathy's determination in all of this. 'You're a Godsend to me,' she whispered. 'Where you get your strength from, I will never know.'

'From you,' Cathy assured her. 'I get my strength from you. Whatever I can do to help now will never be enough to thank you for all the years of love you have shown me.'

'Are you sure you'll be all right going to see the auctioneer on your own? Won't you wait until the morning, when I'm sure I'll be able to face it in a better frame of mind?'

'Let me do this. Please.'

'All right. But I don't like you wandering about these auction yards by yourself.'

'We may have to face much harder ordeals before all this is over. There is no one else to do it for us.'

'You're right. Do what you can. I know I can leave it safely in your hands.'

Delighted to be trusted with something so important, Cathy got herself ready. When she came into Ruby's kitchen she looked every inch a businesswoman. Dressed in a straight brown skirt, high-necked blouse and small-heeled boots, with her long grey coat over the top and an official-looking folder tucked under her arm, she took Ruby by surprise. 'Goodness me! You look like you're all set to do battle,' Ruby declared, dropping her paring knife on to the vegetables. 'It's to do with the official gentleman who was just here, is it?'

'That was Mr Dalton, the solicitor,' Cathy explained. 'And yes, in a roundabout way it is to do with him.'

'I didn't take to him at all . . . he had shifty eyes.'

Cathy laughed. 'You always were a good judge of character.'

They chatted for a minute, during which time Cathy asked after Ruby's health, and she said she was feeling much better. Cathy was not altogether convinced and said she would come and sit awhile with Ruby on her return. 'Meantime, would you keep an eye on Aunt Margaret? I think the strain's beginning to tell on her.'

Ruby assured her she most certainly would, and Cathy went on her way with an easier mind.

Margaret came down to the kitchen and told Ruby how she had begged off going to the auctioneers because, 'I feel Cathy would deal with it much better than I ever could. She's making a fine young woman, and appears to have a splendid head for business.'

'Then she takes after you.'

Margaret shook her head in disagreement. 'You're wrong, Ruby,' she murmured. 'If I had been more aware of what was going on . . . if I had kept a closer eye on the business of this estate, we would never have come to this awful predicament. I'm afraid I have a great deal to learn, whereas Cathy has a natural talent for it.' She chuckled. 'It was Cathy who saw right through Mr Dalton's ploy to acquire Blackthorn House at a price advantageous to himself. It was she who virtually threw him out, and it was she who then suggested going to an auctioneer.'

'Oh, she has her head screwed on and no mistake.'

'That she has, Ruby. And I'm afraid from now on it may be a case of me leaning on her.'

'The lass's shoulders are broad enough,' Ruby said gently. 'She's young and strong, and has the heart of a lion.' She laughed aloud. 'In fact, just now she went out of here like a young warrior.'

They both laughed as Margaret said, 'I know what you mean. And in her present mood, I defy anyone to take advantage of her.'

James Armitage was the man everyone turned to when they

had need of an auction. He sold anything and everything, from sticks of furniture to industrial machines, and no one was more astute than he at driving a hard bargain. Small and 'wick', with big white teeth and a mass of ginger hair, he employed twelve good men and had never yet been the subject of complaint.

As was his way when dealing with women, he was charming and efficient. After paying the closest attention to what Cathy had to say, he told her, 'I'm confident we can find any number of well-heeled citizens who would be more than interested in owning such a place as Blackthorn House.'

'How do you mean to present it?' She had thought long and hard about how it should best be done.

'Why, I shall visit the site and value it,' he announced. 'Then, I shall have a catalogue drawn up and distribute it far and wide, together with the usual advertising.'

'I want everyone to know for miles round ... even as far as London.'

He was deeply offended. 'Be assured I will leave no stone unturned to get you the very best price possible. After all, I have my good name and reputation to think of.'

'And a fine commission, I'll be bound! But we can discuss that in a moment. Also, I wasn't questioning your ability. My aunt and I have a great deal to lose if it goes wrong, so with all due respect to your good self, I do have a few thoughts of my own on how it might be handled.'

'I'm listening.'

'First of all, I wouldn't want the entire estate to be sold as one lot.'

'Really?'

'I believe we could raise a better price if we did it another way.'

'Go on.' He had never met such a forthright young lady, and was fascinated that she had put so much thought into what would be for most women a fearsome matter.

'I believe we should sell Blackthorn House with half an acre as one lot, the other half an acre on its own ... which will attract not only those who want Blackthorn House, but also the adjoining farmers and any small landowner who wants to increase his holdings. Another parcel would be the burned-out shell and the land on which it stands. Then the furniture as a separate item.'

'Bearing in mind, of course, that you may wish to keep some of the furniture yourself?'

The very thought made Cathy cringe. 'We want nothing from the house.' She and Margaret had already agreed on this. 'That way we can increase the competition and raise the stakes. Are you in agreement?'

Inspired by her enthusiasm and sharp mind, he commented quietly, 'You are a very unusual young woman.'

'I'm sorry if you think I'm trying to tell you how to do your job, but I must look out for my aunt. You are probably too polite to say so, but I feel you must already know the whole story surrounding Blackthorn House and the family. My aunt has taken it all with great courage and now she needs peace of mind. The monies got from this sale will be all we shall have, so you do understand why I am so concerned to do the best I can? I owe it to my aunt, and to myself.'

He gazed at her before saying warmly, 'Yes, I do know the whole story surrounding Blackthorn House, and I fully understand your need to secure the best price you can for the estate.'

'You think my ideas are workable then? About splitting the estate into four different lots?'

He laughed. 'Do I think your ideas are workable?' He gazed at her again, and the laughter in his eyes became a look of compassion. 'I'll tell you what I think. I think your aunt is in good hands with you to look out for her. I think I should be ashamed I didn't think to split the estate in such a way, and yes, it may well fetch a better price under these circumstances. Rest assured you'll not get a better service from any other auctioneer.'

'Then I'm ready to talk terms.'

The commission he wanted was not acceptable to Cathy, so he reduced it a little. Still it was not acceptable, so he reduced it a little more. And eventually the terms were agreed. 'You will put it all in writing to my aunt,' Cathy instructed as she prepared to leave.

'Of course.' Rarely had he met such a forceful personality, and he was filled with admiration. He saw her out of the office door and led the way to the outer yard. 'Goodbye, Miss Blackthorn,' he said, shaking her by the hand. He had expected her hand to be light and delicate, like a feather in his own. But Cathy gripped his fingers and squeezed with remarkable determination.

'Miss Blackthorn?'

She turned to look at him. 'Yes?'

'I admire your courage.'

'When needs must, we all have to find a certain amount of courage.'

'But you ... so young, losing both parents in such a short time ... and in such circumstances. Now, taking on the responsibility for all this ... for your aunt.' Momentarily choked for words, he smiled encouragingly. 'You really are an exceptional young lady.'

'Thank you.' Cathy didn't know what else to say, although she might have told him how she owed her courage to another 'exceptional' lady. Margaret had taught her to be strong when she had most needed strength. That teaching would serve Cathy all her life.

He bade her good day but before she departed told her solemnly, 'I have two sons, but neither of them has your gumption. If the day should ever come when you need a profession, I would be proud to have you work alongside me.' He chuckled then. 'You might even be able to teach an old dog new tricks.'

Cathy returned his smile. 'I'm flattered by your kind offer. Who knows when our paths may cross again? For now, though, I want the best price for the estate. And be warned, I shall be watching every move you make.'

'I don't doubt that for a minute.'

'You will write to my aunt this very day?'

'The minute you're gone, I promise.'

Inclining her head, she said politely, 'Good day then, Mr Armitage.'

'Good day, Miss Blackthorn.' He watched her go, and wondered why it was that he had begot two layabouts, while a weakling like Frank Blackthorn had spawned such a proud and capable creature.

Margaret listened with interest. 'I'm proud of you,' she declared.

'I knew I was right to leave it all in your hands.'

On the way home, Cathy had entertained her first doubts. 'I hope I've done the right thing in persuading you to go to auction,' she said. 'Perhaps I've been too hasty.'

'While you've been gone, I've been thinking, and I believe you're right. An auction is a splendid idea, and as for suggesting to Mr Armitage that he should split the whole into four lots, well, that was ingenious.'

'I don't know about ingenious, but it seemed to me that some people might want the smaller parcel of land, while others would want only the big house. Then you might have other people who would want neither house nor land, but be glad to buy the furniture.' To give the auctioneer his due, she added, 'I'm certain it would have occurred to Mr Armitage at some point. He is very experienced after all.'

'Perhaps. But it was you who thought of it, and I'm glad you did.' Margaret was feeling a little stronger after her short rest, ready now to face Ruby with the full facts. 'Could you ask Ruby to come in now?' she requested. 'Jack, too . . . if you can find him. It's time they were both put in the picture.'

Jack was in the kitchen stuffing his face with apple pie while Ruby gave him a piece of her mind for not wiping his boots at the back door. 'You're an ungrateful scoundrel!' she told him. 'Not once have you shown any compassion for Miss Margaret or Miss Cathy, and you know how hard it has been for them.' She looked up as Cathy came through the door. 'Oh! I'm sorry,' she said. 'I didn't hear you coming.'

Cathy felt Jack's eyes on her but didn't look at him. Instead she addressed Ruby. 'You're wanted in the drawing room . . . you and . . .' She still couldn't bring herself to look at him, nor could she say his name. 'If you could both make your way there now, my aunt is waiting.'

With Cathy back beside her, Margaret was ready to begin. 'Jack, I would prefer you to sit over here,' she said, shifting her gaze to the window-seat where he sat slouched and surly. 'What I have to say affects us all.'

'I can hear well enough from here.' He glared at her. 'Besides, I've heard enough to know I've been thrown on the slag heap.'

'Very well. Stay where you are if that's the way you want it.' She had no patience with him. 'But I have considered how harshly you've been treated, and I hope I might be able to make some amends for my brother's thoughtlessness.' At once he was across the room and settling himself on a nearby chair. 'That's better.' Margaret gave him a half-hearted smile. 'Now please sit still and pay attention to what I have to say.'

She then went on to explain that the estate was deep in debt. 'There is nothing to be done but to sell it lock, stock and barrel. At the end of it all, I can only hope we raise enough to pay off the debts and have a little left over with which to start again. In a more modest way, of course.'

Jack was the first to respond. 'What's coming to me then? You said you might be able to make amends for the way I've been treated.'

'I can make no promises,' Margaret replied sternly. 'To be honest, I never wanted you in this house, and I shall be glad to see the back of you. But, however misguided and for whatever reason, my brother took it upon himself to bring you here, and now I am taking it on myself to send you on your way with a token gesture . . . hoping, of course, that it might keep you off the streets, at least until you find work and a permanent roof over your head.'

He sat up straight, his eyes gleaming. 'A token gesture, eh? I thought you said you were penniless?'

'No, I did not say that. However, things are very difficult at this moment in time. The house and what remains of the estate will be sold by auction. Until then we have no way of knowing what the outcome will be. That said, I intend to see the bank manager and request a favour . . . a small favour that will compensate you for your time in this house, and allow you to leave it at the first opportunity.'

'Suits me.' He stretched his legs and stood up. 'But I hope the "favour" ain't too small. Don't forget I was led to believe I'd be well off . . . then the old bastard goes and sells it all and changes his will so I can't even lay claim to what's left.'

Cathy stood up at his outburst. In a calm and dignified voice, she told him, 'Your colourful language cuts no ice here. If it was up to me, you'd be sent down the road without shoes or belongings. We none of us want you, so you'd do well to get out now.'

'My! My! Ain't you the bold one, eh?' Shaken by her remarks, he couldn't help but admire her. It was on the tip of his tongue to say how she of all people should know he got what he wanted, because hadn't he already taken her against her will? Oh, yes! She of all people should know he wasn't to be got rid of that easily.

He might have said all this, and more. But something in Cathy's lovely face, in the cold hard stare from her proud green eyes, made him shrink inside. His admiration turned to anger. 'I'll go when I've had my pay-off and not before.' With a sneer, he strode out, but his presence was felt for a long time afterwards.

Though she could see Margaret's motive, Cathy had to voice her disapproval. 'I don't think you should pay him a penny piece.'

'It might make some amends for my brother's foolhardiness in bringing him here in the first place,' Margaret explained. 'It can't be much, I know, and I have never liked that young man. But I will start my new life with a better conscience if it's done. You do understand what I'm trying to say, don't you, Cathy?'

'I understand, but I would rather he was dragged out of here tied to a carriage and four.' Try as she might, she couldn't keep the bitterness out of her voice. He had viciously ravaged her, and she could not forgive him.

Margaret regarded her with curiosity. 'I didn't know your feelings against him ran so deep.'

'I'm sorry.' Realising she had betrayed too much, Cathy was quick to put things right. 'Of course I understand what you're trying to do, and I admire you for it, because I know you don't care for him either. But how can you promise him anything when we don't even know whether we'll have enough to live on when the debts are paid?'

'It will be a small gesture, but a gesture nevertheless.' She turned to Ruby. 'We have just one month before we must leave Blackthorn House forever. As Cathy said, when it's all done we may not even have enough to live on. Do you have any plans, Ruby?'

Ruby was torn two ways. Having been told the full facts, she sat quite still, her face downcast, wringing her hands. As Cathy and Margaret waited for her response, she fought to keep the emotion out of her voice. 'I saw it all coming,' she confessed. 'When that official-looking gentleman came this morning, I knew then . . . I knew you might not be able to stay here. I knew I might have to say goodbye to you . . . to everything.' Her eyes glittered with unshed tears.

Cathy came to sit beside her, to reiterate Margaret's query. 'But . . . do you have any plans, Ruby?'

She surprised them by chuckling. 'I had a man friend,' she revealed. 'A sweetheart, would you believe? I honestly thought he wanted me to wed him. But I were wrong.'

'How do you mean, Ruby?' Cathy recalled how secretive Ruby had been of late, and she could see it all now. Ruby had a sweetheart, and she didn't want the world to know.

'I'm just an old fool, sneaking about, meeting him whenever I had a minute to spare. At my age I should have known better than to think any man would fancy me. He's gone, d'you see? Upped and gone, like he were never here.'

Cathy took hold of the older woman's hand. 'Then he wasn't worthy of you,' she said softly.

'Aye, well, it's done now, and I'm left behind, and don't know what the future holds.'

Cathy turned to look at Margaret. 'If all goes well, we can keep Ruby with us, can't we?' she pleaded.

Margaret nodded her head. Smiling, she said to Ruby, 'If there is any way we can keep you with us, you know we will, don't you?'

Ruby's whole countenance brightened. 'I know that, and I'm very grateful,' she answered. 'But you and Miss Cathy here . . . you've yourselves to think about now. You can't be burdened with an old mare like me.'

Cathy laughed at that. 'It's us that's been a burden to you these many years. But if you're trying to say you don't want to be with us, then say it, Ruby.' She knew that tack might work, and it did.

Ruby was bristling. 'Fancy you saying a thing like that, Cathy Blackthorn!' she chided. 'Don't want to be with you indeed! Where else would I want to be, tell me that?'

Laughing, Cathy hugged her, and soon the three of them were

enjoying the little deceit. 'You're a scoundrel, that's what you are,' Ruby told Cathy. 'You always were a cheeky madam.' Addressing Margaret, she said firmly, 'If there's a way you can keep me, I'm yours for the rest of me days.' Something else occurred to her. 'What's more, I've no need of fancy wages. I've saved a little nest egg, and now it ain't needed to feather me own nest, it's yours if you want it.'

'Take your hard-earned wages?' Margaret's features hardened to disbelief. 'Never!' But she assured Ruby, 'Cathy and I have no idea where we might end up, but wherever it is, and if it can be done, we do want you with us.'

'Bless you for that. It's all I can hope for. Till then, I'd best get on with me chores.' Ruby gave her thanks and excused herself.

'She's upset,' Cathy said. 'We have to find a way to keep her with us.'

'And we will.' Margaret also excused herself. 'First, I want rid of Jack. That means a talk with the bank manager. After that, you and I will just have to bide our time and pray things go well at the auction.'

'Do you want me to come with you?'

'Heaven forbid! He's a great pudding of a man, with a history of bronchitis. If I let you loose on him, he's likely to suffer a heart attack.'

Cathy's eyes twinkled. '*Then* where would we get a loan?'

'Shame on you.' Margaret was still smiling when she hurried from the room to get herself ready. 'I'll not be long,' she called, going out of the door. 'Pray he's in a benevolent mood, for if he turns us down, I don't know where next to turn.'

Two hours later, Margaret was back with the news. 'It seems the whole of Lancashire knows the predicament we're in. According to the bank manager, we are now a financial risk. Unlike you and me, Cathy, he does not envisage any profit from the auction.'

'Then he's a fool.' Cathy was up in arms. 'If there was that much of a risk, why is it the lenders have sanctioned the auction? If they were of the same mind as your bank manager, they would have moved heaven and earth to take control. Oh,

627

I know they are closely monitoring it, but they know full well they'll get their pound of flesh.'

'That's because they have us legally bound to repay the debt within a month.'

'And we will . . . and we'll get more besides, I know it.'

'Meanwhile, what do we do? How do we live?'

'We sell one of the silver ornaments. Leave it to me, eh?' Cathy was already on her feet and heading for the door. 'I know the very one . . . that large statuette in Father's study.'

Margaret agreed, and the very next morning Cathy took the statuette into town. Jake Montague, at the jeweller's, examined it through his eye-piece. 'Very nice,' he muttered, scratching the stubble on his long chin. 'Worth half a guinea.'

Cathy gave him one of her most disapproving stares. '*Three* guineas,' she said coldly. 'I know the value of that statuette as well as you.' She didn't, but it was worth a try.

He placed the statuette on the counter and touched it reverently with the tip of his fingers. Apart from its considerable monetary value, he had taken a liking to it and had no real intention of letting it go. '*One* guinea. That's my final offer.'

'Two guineas, or I take it away and sell it to someone who appreciates beautiful things.' Collecting it up, she began wrapping it in the brown paper.

His hand darted out to grab it back. 'All right,' he groaned. '*Two* guineas.'

Cathy's smile displayed her relief. 'Very wise,' she said. 'Even at that, you know you've got a bargain.'

'Hmph! Been robbed more like.' He paid over the money and grunted, 'I should have waited for the auction. Happen I'd have got it for half the price.'

'And you might have had to pay twice as much.' Cathy was satisfied though. 'Anyway, what makes you think my aunt planned to put it in the auction?'

A look of embarrassment crossed his face. Shrugging, he told her, 'It's common knowledge how you and your aunt have been left penniless. Moreover, I know the auctioneer well, and he reckons every stick and ornament will be included in the sale.' Fearing he had offended her, he apologised. 'I suppose he ought not to be discussing such things with me.'

Cathy was not offended. 'On the contrary. Mr Armitage promised to advertise far and wide, and I'm pleased he appears to be doing his job.'

'He'll do his best by you, there's no two ways about that.'

Her parting words made him bless his own good fortune. 'Think about this, Mr Montague,' she urged. 'If you had waited for the sale to acquire that statue, you might well have been bidding against several other would-be buyers. Like as not, you would have been made to pay four times as much as you've got it for today. You've taken advantage of two ladies in dire straits,' she added indignantly. 'Aren't you ashamed?'

He was so ashamed he gave her the three guineas she had at first requested, and she went on her way with a spring in her step.

Ruby came back into the kitchen. When she saw Jack seated at the table stuffing his face with the remains of the muffins, she grabbed the large wooden spoon and smacked him round the ear with it. 'You ungrateful bugger!' she screeched. 'You know very well I were saving them muffins for supper. It's getting harder and harder to make ends meet since the master went. There ain't no money coming in, and them good ladies is living hand to mouth.' She swiped at him again, but he dodged her and ran behind the table. 'You don't belong here, in a fine house with fine ladies. You're scum, that's what you are! Scum!'

Revelling in her distress, he teased, 'Scum I might be, you old ratbag. But I ain't moving till I get what's coming to me.'

'Well now, you might be interested to know that the bank turned Miss Margaret down. There ain't nothing coming from that direction, so you'd best be off and leave us alone.' Hurrying to the dresser, she dropped the wooden spoon and took down the largest meat cleaver she could lay hands on. 'If you ain't out of this house afore I've counted to ten, I'll have the head off your shoulders,' she threatened. And from the look on her face, she meant every word. 'ONE . . .' As she counted, she came towards him, the cleaver raised high in the air. 'TWO . . .'

'What? Yer mean she can't get no money to be rid of me? Yer lying buggers, the lot of yer!'

'THREE . . .' She was so close now he could see the whites of her eyes. 'FOUR . . .'

'You're bleedin' mad!'

629

'FIVE . . .'

'If yer think I'm going empty-handed, yer can think again.'

'SIX . . .'

Fear erupted in a giggle. 'You don't scare me, yer old trollop.'

'SEVEN . . .'

'If yer throw me out, I'll only come back and set fire to the place, then yer fine ladies will be in the same boat as me.'

Ruby was stopped in her tracks. 'You little bastard! It were *you* who set fire to the Leyton house, weren't it? WEREN'T IT?'

'NO! I swear to God it weren't me.'

Advancing, she began counting again, this time quicker. 'EIGHT . . . NINE.' She was only a hand's reach from him.

'I'M TELLING YER, I DIDN'T SET FIRE TO NOTHING!' He was yelling now, terrified like the coward he was. 'GIVE ME ENOUGH MONEY TO GET TO LONDON TOWN AN' I SWEAR YER'LL NEVER SET EYES ON ME AGAIN!' When there came no reply, he crouched, waiting for the blow that would sever the head from his miserable body.

'How much?' Ruby had the cleaver raised, her beady eyes boring into him as he stared up at her. 'How much to get you back to London?'

'To get me there and see I've a roof over me head for long enough to feel me feet . . . I'll need at least two guineas.'

'How much?'

'Less than that ain't enough to keep body and soul together!'

'How much?'

'Yer don't want me starving in the street, do yer?'

'I don't reckon I'd lose any sleep over that.'

'Give me what you've got, yer old bugger! If it's enough, you'll not see hide nor hair of me ever again.'

Taking the cleaver with her and keeping her eyes on him, Ruby went to the dresser. From here she took out her bag, and from the bag she took out a purse, and from the purse she withdrew a handful of silver coins and threw them one at a time on to the table. 'That's every penny I've got. Now piss off and be damned to you!' Stepping back, she waited until he had collected the coins, then she chased him out of the kitchen, through the door and away from the house. 'If that ain't enough, you'll have to sell the clothes on your back, won't you?' she called after him. 'I dare say you've done that an' all afore today.'

She was laughing out loud as she went back into the kitchen. 'Oh, Ruby Adams! Fancy using language that would make the vicar blush!' she chastised herself. 'Still, the rascal's gone, and it did me heart good to see him haring down the lane as though the very devil was at his heels.'

When the tale was related to Margaret and Cathy, the three of them laughed until they cried. 'That should teach him to mess with you,' Cathy said. And, against Ruby's protests, Margaret promised to replace that good woman's savings as soon as ever the opportunity arrived. 'We've sold one statuette and thanks to Cathy got a good price for it. If needs be, we'll sell another piece of silver before the auction.' Ruby would not hear of it, and the matter was left unresolved.

That night, Cathy lay in her bed, dreaming of David one minute and in the next wondering what the future might hold. 'It won't be much of a future without him near,' she thought aloud. Musing on him, seeing his face in her mind and reliving the special times they had together, she settled down to sleep.

As she lay there in the dark with her brooding thoughts, she eventually allowed herself to think of Jack. Glad beyond words to know he was gone, she dared not speculate any further. These past few weeks, she had felt strange within herself, poorly one day and disgustingly healthy the next. Something was different and she wasn't altogether certain what. Yet now the hideous prospect had crept up on her and she was made to face a shocking possibility. The impulse was so strong that she had to get out of her bed and put on the light.

Standing before the mirror, she pressed her hands over her nightgown, drawing the material tight across her stomach. As always it was flat and hard, with no outward sign to confirm her haunting suspicions. But inside she was alive with the memory of that night when he had brutally assaulted her. 'Jack may be gone, but I'm so afraid.' The fear lit her eyes. The whisper seemed to echo from every wall. 'Dear God, don't let me be with child!' Even now, when it seemed more plausible with every passing day, Cathy dared not, *would not*, allow herself to contemplate such a terrible thing.

Unable to sleep now, she went to the window and watched the night sky for a time. The night was beautiful, the stars high in the heavens and the gentle breeze created a melody in the overhanging branches close to her window. Soon the need for sleep came over her. Climbing back into bed, she closed her eyes and thought of David once more. Her thoughts became dreams and her dreams were sweet.

In the thickness of night, Jack approached the house from the rear. Pausing to look up at the window behind which Ruby was slumbering, he softly chuckled. 'Yer might have thought I were miles away by now, but y'see how wrong yer can be?' Coming forward on tiptoe, he made his entry through the pantry window. Ruby had made a rabbit pie for tomorrow's dinner, and the delicious aroma teased his nostrils. In the half light that trickled through the window he spied the pie and his stomach rumbled. 'I didn't come back for no pie,' he muttered, still smiling, 'but there ain't no reason why I shouldn't help meself.' Scooping it from the plate, he held it in both hands, ramming it into his mouth and licking the spilt gravy as it ran through his fingers. 'I'll say this for yer, Ruby yer old sod,' he muttered through a huge mouthful, 'there ain't nobody can bake a better pie than you.'

With his stomach filled to bursting, he replaced the half-eaten pie. Seeing a hessian sack filled with potatoes, he tipped it upside down, emptying them on to the pantry floor. That done, he tucked the sack under his arm and made his way out of the pantry. On tiptoe and keeping alert to every sound, he went along the dimly lit hall until he came to the drawing room. Here, he softly entered. Closing the door, he struck a match on the sole of his boot, losing no time before going round the room collecting all the silver and porcelain pieces. The smaller ornaments went into his pockets, the larger ones into the hessian sack.

Satisfied, he went back the way he had come, and was soon out of the house, lost in the night, congratulating himself on having had the last laugh. 'This little lot should fetch a pretty penny,' he told himself. 'Happen it'll be them in the streets and me with a better roof over me head. Still, it's no more than I deserve. I ain't never been one to carp, so I'm happy enough to cut me losses.' Pausing long enough to look back at the house, his eyes were drawn to one particular upstairs window. 'I ain't sorry about what I did, Cathy,' he said. 'I'm only sorry I couldn't get you to feel the same way about me.' He stood there for more than a full minute, the bulk of his thieving weighing him down. 'I've only got what's mine,' he grumbled. 'But I ain't such a bastard I can't wish yer well with the auction.'

Swinging the sack carefully on to his shoulder, he turned away, a crafty smile on his face. 'I'd like to see the old bugger Ruby's face in the morning, when she finds her precious pie half gone. Still, I did leave 'em a bite or two, didn't I, eh? I could 'ave took the lot, but I didn't. Generous to a fault, that's what I am!' He was still laughing when he ran through the spinney and across the open fields.

The pie was of no importance, but when it was discovered that a thief had removed almost all of the porcelain and silver, Margaret took it badly. 'I've no one but myself to blame,' she declared. 'I should have taken it all to the bank and put it on deposit . . . or given it into the keeping of the auctioneer. Now it's gone, and with it the prospect of making enough to set up elsewhere.'

'You're not to blame yourself.' Cathy had been aware her aunt was coming to the end of her tether and was anxious to protect her. 'I could have suggested putting it in safe keeping but, like you, I believed there was no real need. Now it's gone, as you say, but we mustn't let it drag us down. We *will* have enough to start again, you must believe that.' Her own hopes had been shattered when Ruby ran up to tell them a burglar had struck in the night. Now, though, she was determined they would come through somehow.

At her words, Ruby stopped crying, and Margaret looked up with admiration. 'You make me feel ashamed,' she told Cathy. 'I ought to be looking after you. Yet at every turn it's you, not me, who refuses to be beaten. You don't seem to know the meaning of fear . . . you tend to see the future in a way I cannot.'

'No, you're wrong,' Cathy corrected her. 'I *am* afraid. But no, I will not be beaten by some cowardly thief in the night.' A great rage took hold of her. 'I only wish I'd been downstairs. He might have wished he'd never set foot in this house!'

'Or wished he'd never been born?' Margaret said with the

glimmering of a smile. She was thankful that Cathy had not set eyes on the person who had violated their home. 'We'll have to let the police know. Maybe they can catch him before he sells everything.'

Ruby hurried away to inform the authorities. When some time later two constables arrived, they went over the house with a fine-tooth comb and took statements from them all. Finally they concluded, 'The thief is probably long gone by now. However . . . the list you've given of the stolen items will be circulated, and we shall certainly do our best, but we can't promise we will ever recover them. In cases like this we find the stolen goods are taken right out of the area . . . the silver could be melted down, and then there's no way of tracing it.'

Cathy was shocked. 'You seem to be giving up before you've even started.'

'I'm sorry, Miss, but we've had the bigger houses round here burgled before, and it's never easy to track down the stolen items.' He wisely changed tack. 'Have you any idea who it might have been? Did someone bear a grudge against you?' His questions were directed at Margaret.

'I can't think of anyone who would do such a thing,' she answered. Jack's name had been on the tip of her tongue but she bit it back.

Cathy was not so reluctant. 'I can think of someone,' she offered. She then told them about Jack, and how he had been sent on his way without the inheritance he had come to expect. 'If you find him, I'm certain you will find everything that's gone missing.'

'He's a bad 'un!' Ruby couldn't resist giving her opinion.

'I see.' The constable asked a few more questions concerning Jack, and wrote all the details in his little book. 'It's something to go on,' he said, and left soon after.

Half an hour later the auctioneer arrived with his foreman. They strolled round the house, through every room, with Mr Armitage also making notes in his little book. 'It's like a circus!' Ruby complained, fetching a tray of tea and toast.

Margaret preferred to sip her tea and await the auctioneer's return while, much to his dismay, Cathy dogged his footsteps. 'Have you had much interest?' she wanted to know.

634

'I'm delighted to say we've had more than a little.'

'Wealthy people, are they?'

'They need to be.' He cast an appreciative glance round the study. 'You do have some very valuable pieces here.' He was staring at the grand walnut desk. 'That alone should fetch a pretty penny.' His gaze went to the shelves. They were stuffed with leather-bound volumes, some of them quite rare. On the dresser stood a silver tray, displaying two handsome silver and crystal decanters with four tumblers to match. 'I have to say, your father had expensive tastes. He certainly liked to surround himself with the best of everything.' He was reluctantly growing to admire a man who'd lived life as he saw fit, and to hell with everyone else.

Cathy was not impressed. 'Not all of these things were my father's,' she said bitterly. In fact the tray and decanters had only recently been brought out from the dark recesses of a cupboard. 'So! I can look forward to a very successful auction, isn't that so?'

'I have high hopes.' He glanced at her and saw the determination in her face. He knew if he didn't promise his best she was quite capable even now of taking her business elsewhere. In that moment he saw his fat commission disappearing and was prompted to assure her, 'As you say, Miss Blackthorn . . . by rights, we should have a very successful auction.'

On the day of the auction they came from far and wide. Hopefuls who saw the opportunity of picking up an expensive piece at half the price; old women who had taken a fancy to Ruby's pine dresser and table; young men who fancied themselves in Frank Blackthorn's leather and oak swivel chair; and hard-faced dealers who thought to buy everything in for a song and sell it out again for a fortune. They crammed into the auction room, catalogues in hand, sparing a smile for one another while secretly lining up for battle. Much to Cathy's delight.

As requested, the auctioneer had arranged for three chairs to be set in the centre of the front row, and here sat the three women from Blackthorn House – three women who had much to lose if the amount raised fell below their expectations. Throughout the auction, Mr Armitage was made nervous by the fact that Cathy's eyes never once left him; vigilantly she watched his every move.

The bidding began with the house itself. After that came the articles of furniture, which were offered with all the atmosphere of a carnival. Item number one was the desk. 'A taster for what's to come,' Mr Armitage told Margaret. 'It'll whet their appetites and persuade them to open their wallets.' And he was right. At first the crowd played a cat and mouse game, waiting for someone else to start the bidding and carry the price towards what they were prepared to pay. When the price climbed and excitement grew to fever pitch, it was everyone for himself.

The lots went quickly, with every piece greedily sought after. 'Oh, Cathy!' Margaret's eyes shone. 'I really think we'll be all right.'

Cathy took hold of her aunt's hand. 'I told you there was nothing to worry about.' She had been mentally calculating, and by her reckoning they would have enough to repay the debts and still have a reasonable sum left over for their own needs.

She proved to be right. 'It was the best attended auction I've ever had,' Mr Armitage proudly declared.

Cathy wandered about then, watching as successful bidders took away their prizes. She didn't feel sad to see the familiar things being removed. She felt oddly regretful that a whole chapter of her life was over forever, but she didn't feel sad.

'Penny for them.' Ruby had come up behind her.

'It's strange, isn't it?' Cathy's attention was drawn to a rather large and well-dressed gentleman who was pawing Frank Blackthorn's desk. He reverently opened every drawer and stroked his hands over the top as though it was a desirable woman. 'I look at my father's desk and I see him seated behind it, just as he always was.' She smiled wryly. 'Whenever I was called to his study, it was to be reprimanded for something or other. Even before I was tall enough to see over the top of it, that desk was like a huge barrier between us, he on one side and I the other.' Memories flooded back. 'When mother was murdered, he took solace in hiding behind it ... drinking and sleeping ... always hiding behind that desk.'

'Aw, lass!' Deeply moved and awash with her own memories of those early days, Ruby put a chubby arm round Cathy's waist and hugged her close. 'It's only a piece of wood, carved and polished to make it look something grand . . . but for all that it's still no more than a piece of wood. If your father chose to derive comfort from that instead of turning to you and your aunt, then we have to feel sorry for him.'

Sensing some other emotion in Ruby's voice, Cathy asked gently, 'You loved my father, didn't you?'

Overcome by all that had happened, Ruby felt the need to sit herself in an armchair close by. Taking out a small white handkerchief, she surreptitiously dabbed at her eyes while pretending to blow her nose. 'Aye, lass. I did have a soft spot for your faither, I'll not deny it. He were a weak man and happen I shouldn't be talking like this, but even though he idolised the very ground she walked on, your mother brought him little happiness.'

'Do you think they're together now, Ruby?' She had often thought about that.

'Who knows, lass?' Ruby had to chuckle at the idea. 'One thing's for sure . . . if they *are* together, there'll be sparks flying and no mistake!'

Intent on each other, Ruby and Cathy didn't see the two men rushing towards them. 'Excuse me, Missus,' the thin, moustached fellow addressed Ruby, 'but I've just bought that chair and unless you want a ride to Wigan I should get yer arse out of it!'

Cheeky as ever, she retaliated, 'Well now, young man, I reckon my arse might enjoy a ride to Wigan. But it would take a better man than you or your mate here to entertain a fine lady such as meself. Besides, I'm particular about the company I keep.' With that she struggled out of the chair and, linking her arm with Cathy's, drew her away.

'You bad old thing,' Cathy laughed. 'Did you see the look on his face?'

'Not a very handsome bloke, was he? If I had a mind to go to Wigan, or anywhere else come to that, it wouldn't be with a fella who had a face like the back of a tram.'

Stifling her laughter, Cathy discreetly turned to glance at the man in question. Tall and thin with a straggly moustache and a face deeply scored with wrinkles, she saw what Ruby meant. In that instant the man glared at her and she had to look away.

'Whatever am I going to do with you, Ruby Adams?' she said, laughing aloud.

It did Ruby's heart good to see Cathy laughing. 'There y'are lass. Memories might hurt, but there'll allus be summat to make you chuckle.'

'Ruby?'

'Yes, lass?'

'Oh, it's nothing.' Cathy had been about to ask her whether she had got over the man who had deserted her. But now she could have bitten out her own tongue.

'It's all right. I know what's on your mind, and no . . . I'm not pining for the bugger who left me. I'll not deny I spent a few miserable nights, and if I'd have got me hands on him there's no telling what I might have done. But now I've had time to think straight, I reckon it's good riddance to him.'

'Sorry, Ruby. You should tell me to mind my own business.'

'What! Then you might tell me the same when I'm being nosy about what *you're* up to.'

'I'm not up to anything.' Terrified that wily old Ruby might have guessed Jack had probably left her with child, Cathy trembled inside.

Pausing to look up at her, Ruby sought for the right words. 'If ever there's anything on your mind, you know I'm a good listener.'

'I know, and thank you, Ruby.' Maybe in the not-so-distant future she might have need of someone to confide in, but for now Cathy knew she must keep her worries to herself. There could just be an outside chance that she was worrying for nothing.

Margaret had good news for them. 'Because he sympathises with our predicament, Mr Armitage says he can settle with me by noon tomorrow, instead of our having to wait the usual week. Apparently most bidders paid cash, and those who paid by other means are known to him.'

Cathy was pleased but surprised. 'I would never have thought he was the kind of businessman to let his heart rule his head.' She regarded Margaret with a mischievous twinkle in her eye. 'He could have his sights set on you, though? *That* would explain it.'

'Mind yer backs!' A great mountain of a woman barged past. 'Make way!' she called out, thrusting herself forward and forging a path for her dutiful husband. The poor little fellow was bow-legged beneath a pile of ladder-back chairs.

As he passed Cathy and the others he winked and sighed. 'She thinks I'm a bloody donkey!' he said wistfully. In fact, with his large head and long ears, he did bear an uncanny resemblance to one.

'Makes you wonder, don't it?' Ruby said with wide eyes as he passed.

Not quite sure what she meant, Cathy concentrated on more mundane matters. 'If Mr Armitage is settling up tomorrow, that means we can settle Father's debts and start looking for a house.'

For the first time in days Margaret appeared relaxed. 'That's something I'm looking forward to,' she said. 'The house and furniture are gone. We'll stay at the hotel in Blackburn as arranged, and then, when things are clearer, we can start looking for a house.'

Cathy agreed, pointing out, 'The rooms at the hotel are costing money we can ill afford, so the sooner we find a new home the better.'

That evening, the three women booked into the hotel. Margaret and Cathy carried a small portmanteau each, while Ruby arrived with two bulging tapestry bags. 'I'm not going nowhere without me precious knick-knacks,' she declared. The day before, when she and Cathy were deciding what to take and what to leave, Cathy vowed she would, 'Leave behind all but the clothes I stand up in, one outfit to change into, and all my underwear.' Margaret felt the same. It was as though each needed to cleanse herself of memories that might cling.

The rooms were clean and pleasantly furnished. In order to save money, Cathy was prepared to share, but Margaret would not hear of it. 'We've all been through a lot,' she explained. 'I think we all deserve some quiet time to ourselves.' Cathy would have preferred to have Margaret with her, but said nothing, thinking it her duty to respect her aunt's views.

The three rooms were on the same floor, though Ruby had

argued, 'I've no right being in a room alongside me employers, and I insist you do not repay the money I gave to that scoundrel Jack and use it instead to pay for me accommodation.' Seated in the small front room, they took a few moments to drink the tea which had been brought up for them by the housemaid. Ruby was adamant. 'I know it's a sorry situation that's brought us all together like this but it ain't right, and I don't feel comfortable, and you might as well know it.'

Margaret told her she would do no such thing as use Ruby's money to pay for the room. 'That money you gave to Jack was your hard-earned savings, and you shall have it back as soon as our debts are paid,' she insisted. Cathy upheld that decision and Ruby was made to concede gratefully.

'All the same,' she persisted, 'once you've found a house, I want me proper place . . . a room alongside the kitchen, or one at the back of the house where servants belong. If yer refuse, I'll find work elsewhere, 'cause I want *my* privacy an' all!' Put that way, neither Margaret nor Cathy could find an argument against it. Satisfied, Ruby went to her bed.

Too tired to talk, Margaret soon retired, and a short time later Cathy went to her own room.

After undressing and strip-washing at the basin, she put on her nightgown, brushed her hair and lay on the bed. Her thoughts wandered gently. 'The house is gone . . . everything's gone,' she murmured with some astonishment. It had all happened with such frightening speed that it seemed unreal. She thought of her mother, and father, and ached with regrets. She thought of David and her heart was like a lead weight inside her. 'Oh, David! David!' Just the taste of his name on her lips brought a sad kind of joy.

The joy was soon swamped by anguish when her thoughts turned to Jack. 'Please God, don't let me be with child,' she prayed, and with that awful thought shadowing her mind, fell into a slumber plagued with nightmares.

The next day was filled with sunshine, and life didn't seem so bad. 'After breakfast, I shall meet Mr Armitage,' Margaret announced. 'Then it's on to the bank where I intend to arrange payments of all our debts. Once that's achieved, it's round to the agent's to find out what houses are available.' Smiling at Cathy, she said, 'We'll find something to suit us, I know.'

Cathy was delighted to see her aunt seeming much brighter after her night's sleep. It was as though a great weight had fallen from her shoulders. 'If you like, Ruby and I could make a start on the house-hunting while you tie up the legal end. What do you say?'

'I need you with me . . . if that's all right?'

'Yes, if that's what you want.'

'And what about me?' Ruby needed to feel useful. 'What can I do?'

Cathy answered, 'You put your feet up and be waited on for a change, Ruby. We shouldn't be too long.'

It was arranged that Cathy and Margaret would meet Mr Armitage before going to the bank and organising payment of the debts. When that was all done, they would return to the hotel and collect Ruby. Cathy would search for a house in one direction, and Ruby would search with Margaret in another. 'Between the three of us, I'm certain we'll find what we're looking for,' Cathy said hopefully.

Unfortunately it wasn't that easy. Over the next few days, they trudged the streets of Blackburn and visited the few agents available. They went in and out of all manner of buildings . . . three-floored tenements and rundown terraced houses, shops with rooms over and smarter dwellings along the embankment. But there was nothing to match their needs, or their purse.

'It's no good.' Margaret was weary, and her spirits flagging. 'We've walked miles and seen nothing that could even begin to look like it might make a decent home.' The three of them were gathered in her room, where she sat huddled in a chair with a blanket across her knees suffering from a streaming cold that had taken all of her strength. 'I'm beginning to think we'll never find anything.'

Cathy recalled one particular house which she had visited along Preston New Road. 'It's the only one that has any potential,' she said. 'Is there no way we can afford it?'

Margaret had gone over the finances time and again, and each time the answer was the same. 'Not unless we lived on dry bread and went in rags for a year.'

'Then we'll just have to keep trying. In fact, we might have to lower our sights.'

'I've been thinking the very same,' Margaret admitted. 'Every penny we pay out at this hotel could be going into a home of our own.'

'Right then!' Cathy saw nothing else for it. 'I'll just have to redouble my efforts.'

'What do you mean... *you* will have to redouble your efforts?'

'I mean you look worn out and you're full of cold. I think you should take things easy for a while.'

'I'll not deny I'm bone tired.'

'That's settled then!' Collecting her bag, she asked Ruby to stay and look after her mistress, 'While I have a scout round the streets nearer to the market square. We've been in every direction but that one.'

'I think you should take Ruby with you,' Margaret suggested. But Cathy ruled that out. 'Right now you need her with you,' she answered, and went out of the door before either of them could change her mind for her.

Boarding the tram, Cathy swept right to the front. From here she could see both sides of the road more clearly, and if there were any empty properties along the route she couldn't possibly miss them. 'Return ticket, please,' she told the conductor. 'To the market square.'

He rang up the ticket on his machine, and gave her a penny change. 'Lovely day,' he said, and Cathy made it all the more lovely by her wide easy smile.

Ten minutes later she climbed off the tram and took a moment to look around. In the warm late-spring sunshine she looked a picture. The straight dark skirt and waist-fitting jacket showed her trim curves to advantage. Her fair hair was brushed to a deep shine and her green eyes sparkled with vitality. Something about her caused many a passerby to glance admiringly in her direction. But, unaware of their attention, she concentrated her mind on the task she had set herself for that day. It was a daunting one: to find a place that could be made into a home; a place they could easily afford; one that wasn't too far from the everyday hustle and bustle, yet far enough to afford them a little quiet when the mood demanded.

'Right, Cathy!' she muttered, straightening her coat and stiffening her shoulders. 'It's do or die. Today is the day when you'll find what you're looking for ... and you're not to stop searching until you've found it ... even if it means walking the streets until midnight.'

Her heart swelling with determination, she started across the cobbled market; there were a few stalls erected, and a bevy of vendors shouting the merits of their goods. Dogs chased each other in and out, and the chatter of passersby created a low hum that gave her a sense of belonging. Blackburn was a grand place, filled with warmhearted folk and teeming with life. 'This is where I want to be,' she murmured. 'Here, where people live out their ordinary lives without fuss or bother.'

Pausing to watch a young couple strolling hand in hand, her heart turned somersaults. Into her mind came a picture of her and David. But she pushed it away. It was still too painful.

As she made her way across the market square and down towards the main street where there was an estate agent's office, Cathy couldn't help but reflect on how she had come to be here, homeless and lonely; for, even with Margaret and Ruby waiting back at the hotel, she felt strangely isolated, almost as though, without even realising it, she had become another person. And, in a way, that was exactly what had happened, because like any one of us Cathy had been shaped by circumstances over which she had no control. When her mother was murdered, she had been just a girl; then later, when her father also was taken, that girl was lost. Something inside her matured and blossomed.

After all the chaos following the will and the ultimate sale of everything familiar to her, Cathy had emerged a woman, a beautiful and accomplished one with ambitions and dreams, some of which might never be fulfilled. She was alive, she could feel the blood coursing through her veins; the sun was warm on her face and the breeze gently ruffled her hair. All of these things told her she was lucky in so many ways. But beneath it all was David, the young man who had awakened something wonderful in her, the young man she had lost, her first and only love.

Now, when memories threatened to overwhelm her, she thrust them from her mind, to concentrate on the task in hand. A few more steps and she was outside the estate agent's. A quick glance in the window showed nothing different from the day before, or the day before that. The announcements were the same; the same expensive houses and the same tatty rundown places that were fit only to be demolished. But she was still hopeful. 'Have you taken on anything new in the past twenty-four hours?' she asked the girl behind the counter ... the same girl who had been there on the four previous visits Cathy had made: a smart creature with rolled-up dark hair and tiny spectacles that perched on the end of her nose.

Looking over her spectacles at Cathy, the girl shook her head. 'Nothing you would be interested in, I'm sorry.'

'But you have taken something new on?'

The girl gestured towards the back office. 'Mr Clegg is dealing with it now ... but, like I say, it's nothing you would be interested in.'

'Might I be the judge of that?' Through the inner office window, Cathy could see Mr Clegg, the manager, and with him was a younger man, aged about thirty, tall and slightly stooped, wearing a suit that looked as if it might have cost a pretty penny. He appeared to be giving instructions while Mr Clegg was hastily writing in his ledger. 'What exactly is it you're taking on?' Cathy could not afford to leave any stone unturned.

The girl came to stand beside her, and together they peered through the window. 'That's Tony Manners,' she said. 'He owns any number of properties across Blackburn ... houses, shops, anything he can make money on. He buys rundown properties ... charges rents that have already put many a family in the workhouse, then he tarts the houses up and sells them on at a profit.' Grimacing, she muttered, 'Tony Manners is a slimy character. I don't know anybody who likes him.' She obviously didn't.

'And what is he selling that I would not be interested in?' Against her better judgement, Cathy was intrigued.

'He's just bought a derelict club in Higher Audley ... means to turn it into some kind of hostel, I shouldn't wonder. Though he might have got a licence to reopen it as a night-club of sorts.' Glancing at Cathy, she went on in a low voice, 'To find the money he needs, he's instructing Mr Clegg to sell three of his houses.'

'Oh? And what makes you think I might not be interested in one of them?'

The girl's eyes grew wide with shock. 'You could *never* want one of Tony Manners' places!' she hissed. 'He's had riff-raff in them ... folks who can work but don't want to ... women who *entertain*, if you know what I mean? The houses are filthy. It wouldn't surprise me if they weren't ridden with rats and swarming with cockroaches!'

She might have gone on, but the office door opened and out came the two men. 'Goodbye, Mr Manners.' The older man shook the other by the hand. 'You can rely on me to find a buyer.'

Tony Manners gave no reply. He had caught sight of Cathy and couldn't take his eyes off her. 'You're not looking for a house by any chance, are you?' he asked boldly. Taking off his trilby he swung it back and forth in his hand. 'I've just instructed Mr Clegg here to sell three of my properties.'

Before Cathy could reply, the girl spoke for her. 'Miss Blackthorn requires a different type of property.' If looks could kill, he would have dropped stone dead to the floor.

Her hostility made no impact on him. Instead he continued to stare at Cathy. 'Miss Blackthorn, eh?' he murmured. Looking her up and down, he came to the conclusion that she was a lady born and bred. It only intrigued him further. 'Yes, I can see you might be looking for something more ... respectable, shall we say?'

Cathy's smile was cold. Like the girl, she had taken a deep dislike to this arrogant man. 'You may say what you like,' she replied politely, 'but it will not make my business any of yours.' With that she turned away and made conversation with the girl, who pretended to be showing her details of other properties; ones which Cathy had already seen and rejected because of the price.

While she listened to the girl, Cathy could feel Tony Manners' eyes on her. But she totally ignored him, and soon he was on his way out. 'Good day, Miss Blackthorn,' he called. 'I hope you find what you're looking for.'

Hearing the door close, Cathy straightened up and glanced round. Mr Clegg was still standing there, so she addressed her remarks to him. 'These houses you've been instructed to sell, might I have the details?'

The girl was horrified. 'You're never going to look at *them*?'

She lapsed into a sulky silence when Mr Clegg reminded her she was here to sell properties – 'Not to make disparaging remarks about the properties we sell, nor to offer personal opinions on our clients ... who I might add ... indirectly pay your wages!'

Cathy stepped forward. 'Mr Clegg, my aunt and I are also your clients, and as you know have searched far and wide for a suitable house. You have houses to sell, and we have cash waiting. Now ... as to Mr Manners' properties, have you any objection to my having the details?'

'None whatsoever. Unlike my assistant here, I make no judgements ... about persons or properties. However, as yet there are no written details. All I can tell you is that the houses are adjacent to one other, situated on William Henry Street, and being offered at sixty pounds each.' He gave a little snigger. 'If I remember rightly, your good aunt mentioned a sum of forty pounds? A shortfall, I think.'

Cathy was quick to reply, 'I'm sure Mr Manners would be prepared to negotiate.'

'I doubt that. But in any case, you haven't even seen the properties.'

'That's what I'm here for, Mr Clegg. You *are* in the business of selling houses, aren't you?' she asked cheekily.

'I haven't even seen them myself.'

'Then perhaps we can see them together?'

'When?' He had eaten and drunk too much the night before and was suffering from a burning pain in his chest. He was in no mood for playing the gentleman.

'Now if you please.'

'As a rule I like to visit the site before allowing clients in.'

Cathy smiled at that. 'Rules were made to be broken, Mr

Clegg.' She walked slowly towards the door. 'Is William Henry Street within walking distance?'

'Five minutes beyond the market square.' Flustered by Cathy's insistence, and feeling quite ill, he snapped at the girl, 'I shall be gone about half an hour. Mind you treat the customers with respect in my absence.'

'Yes, Mr Clegg.'

'Now fetch my hat, girl, and get a move on!'

'Yes, Mr Clegg.' Rushing through to the inner office, she collected his trilby from the hat stand and brought it to him.

Ramming the hat on his head, he muttered out of Cathy's hearing, 'Damned nuisance this! She'll waste my precious time, and run a mile when she sees William Henry Street.'

'Yes, Mr Clegg.'

Sighing at the girl's dumb insolence, he waved her away. 'Come along then, Miss Blackthorn,' he urged, opening wide the door and waiting for her to pass through it. 'As you so rightly pointed out, I am in the business of selling houses after all.' It was just as well he didn't see the grimace the girl made behind his back, or she might have gone out the door and not been allowed back in. But Cathy saw it, and it gave her cause to smile.

They went at a smart pace, along Ainsworth Street, down the entire length of Penny Street and over the bridge to William Henry Street. 'There you are.' Mr Clegg paused for breath at the top of the street. 'Not quite the area you're used to, I'll be bound,' he said smugly.

Cathy chose to ignore his bad temper. Stepping towards the edge of the pavement, she looked down the street and was both shocked and surprised. The cobbled street was teeming with children: little girls in mucky frocks playing with hoops, toddlers climbing in and out of the gutters, and young lads sitting cross-legged on the pavement, throwing five-stones; rolling about on the cobbles a pair of scruffy urchins were knocking hell out of each other, and only two doors from where Cathy stood two women sat breast-feeding, shouting and cackling as each told the other a saucy tale.

The sights and sounds did Cathy's heart good. 'You're wrong, Mr Clegg,' she said softly. 'My aunt and I used to visit families in a street very much like this one.' Warm recollections came to mind of how she and Margaret had struggled that day, arms laden with towels and linen; she recalled the homely woman who had an army of children, and all at once she felt at home. 'Show me the houses you have for sale,' she said, smiling at his astonishment as he led her down the street.

'If you're sure,' he answered, seeming shocked when she stopped to chat with one of the bare-breasted women. His smile never wavered though, because suddenly he had a glimpse of a sale. His step became much brisker. 'These houses were built for the gentry,' he bragged. 'Solid from the foundations up ... made to last, they were.' Filled with hope, he sang their praises. 'I shouldn't think they'll be on my books for long. They're a snip at sixty pounds.'

'Changed your tune, haven't you?' she remarked. In fact it amused her to see he was now desperate to convince her she would be missing out on a real bargain if she didn't buy one of Tony Manners' houses.

Striding down the street, he came to rest outside the last three houses. 'Like I said ... built for the gentry.' He stood, hands on hips, his trilby tipped back at a jaunty angle while he stared admiringly at the properties.

Cathy took stock of the houses. In all three, every window was broken. The door of the middle one was flung wide open to display a narrow dark passage littered with debris. The staircase had been robbed of several steps, probably for firewood to keep body and soul warm, and, even from where she stood, Cathy could see the dark stains where condensation had run down the walls.

The middle house, like the one to its left, had three floors, while the one on the very end of the row had only two. Obviously ravaged by the elements, the cornerstones were black with damp, and part of the chimney was collapsing to one side.

'If you want my opinion, you'll avoid the one on the end,' Mr Clegg advised, 'because it catches a northerly breeze and might be prone to damp.' The thought of sixty pounds going through his hands put a smile on his face. 'The other two, though ... now you could make a decent place of either of them.'

Cathy gave him a look that silenced him. 'As far as I can see, all three houses are unfit for human habitation. I'm surprised Mr Manners has not been reported for renting out such dilapidated dwellings.'

'Dilapidated?' Though he might have agreed, he merely stared at her with feigned amazement. 'You obviously don't know how difficult it is to get good accommodation in the heart of Blackburn town. These houses are large enough for a sizeable family, and I have never known anyone to complain.'

'Well, of course not! Mr Manners is not likely to broadcast his tenants' grudges. In fact he probably throws them out on their ear if they dare to speak out.' Out of the corner of her eye she could see the neighbours peeking at her. 'These people need a champion, I think.'

The implication appalled him. 'Good heavens! You're surely not considering taking on such a task?' Lowering his voice, he turned away from the inquisitive inhabitants. 'Mr Manners is a powerful force in this town, and by all accounts he makes a very formidable enemy.'

Cathy was not impressed. 'I'm sure he does.' Going towards the end house, she took a moment or two to survey the outside. Something about it drew her attention; it had a grandness, a certain style that bore out what Mr Clegg had said about the houses being originally built for the gentry. The stone mullions that framed the windows were intact, and above the thick panelled door was the prettiest lead-lighted window. Three deep wide steps led up to the door. To the right of the house, a narrow flight of steps went from the pavement to the cellar. These were surrounded by black-painted railings of wrought iron, and enclosed at the top with a little gate. 'How many rooms did you say the house has?' Before he could answer, Cathy was already on her way up the steps to the front door.

'Be careful!' Rushing after her, Mr Clegg put the big iron key in the lock and swung open the door. 'Don't hold me responsible if you harm yourself in there.'

Turning, Cathy flashed him a mischievous smile. 'I thought you had your eyes on a fat commission?' she teased. 'Or are you afraid if the roof caved in on me I might sue you for everything you have?'

Red-faced and anxious, he pushed his way in front of her. 'Follow me,' he urged, 'I'll test the floors.' Going gingerly forward, he stretched out his toes, feeling his way along the floor, terrified he might disappear into the cellar at any minute.

As Mr Clegg tiptoed into the parlour, Cathy went straight on, up the stairs and across the landing. It was a full minute before he realised she was missing, then his frantic voice sailed up the stairs. 'Miss Blackthorn? Are you up there? Oh, dear ... I should never have taken these properties on ... they'll be the end of me, they will!' At that moment Cathy stepped on a loose floorboard; it gave out a slow tortuous creak and Mr Clegg below was convinced she had fallen into some terrible black abyss. He started up the stairs, then climbed back down. Staring up from the bottom, he cried at the top of his voice, 'MISS BLACKTHORN, ARE YOU ALL RIGHT?'

'My word, you do panic.' Peeking over the banister, Cathy shook her head in reproof. 'What a coward you are, Mr Clegg,' she teased.

Shamed yet relieved, he went up the stairs at a careful pace. 'This house isn't for you. Come back to the office. I'm certain we'll find another more suitable.' Afraid for his life, it was all he could do not to run down the stairs and out into the street. 'Please ... it's best if we leave now,' he pleaded. All thoughts of his commission had fled. All he could think about was her innocent teasing with regard to suing him for compensation.

Leaving him at the top of the stairs, Cathy went through each bedroom; there were four in all, two at the front and two at the back, the largest being at the end of the corridor with its own little staircase and far enough away from the others almost to be self-contained. 'A place for Ruby to call her own!' Cathy was delighted.

The rooms were all of good size, and each with a large enough window to let the daylight flood in. The big back room had a washbasin installed, and halfway along the corridor Cathy found a small bathroom and in it a rusty old tub. 'That must have been a real luxury when it was installed,' she called out. Mr Clegg was skulking by the stairs, holding on to the handrail as if it was a lifeline. 'Not many houses have a room with a bath.'

'I told you,' he called back, 'these houses were built for the gentry . . . solicitors and the like. As they prospered, they moved to fancier houses on Preston New Road and sold these properties to money-grabbing landlords.' He gave a funny little scream when a bird came tumbling down the chimney and flew past him out of the door. 'PLEASE! I think we should go now.'

'You go if you like,' Cathy told him as she swept by, 'I haven't seen the downstairs yet.'

Downstairs, she went from room to room. She thought the front parlour was the nicest room she had ever seen, although the walls were blackened by soot from the fireplace, and the wallpaper was peeling off at every corner. It had the prettiest cast-iron fireplace, with flowered tiles running down either side of the surround, and a pretty carved mantelpiece with a mirror over. On the wall hung a lovely amber-coloured gas mantle that simply begged to be cleaned and polished. The window-sill was deep enough to make a seat where a body could sit and enjoy seeing the children at play outside the window, and at that hour of the day the sun shone right in through the window to light the whole room.

The back parlour was the heart of the house. 'Whoever left here must have gone in a hurry,' Cathy declared. 'Look.' Pointing above the big old range, she drew his attention to the mantelpiece and the green chenille cloth that covered it from end to end. 'I can't imagine anyone leaving behind such a pretty cloth unless they were made to depart in a rush.' Going to the mantelpiece she fingered the long silk tassels that dangled from the cloth. As she touched them they released a shower of dust, and fell apart in her fingers. 'Fit for nothing now,' she murmured sadly.

The kitchen was large and airy, with a flight of steps running down to the yard. At the foot of the steps were two doors; one leading into the lavatory, and the other into a vast cellar. A ten-foot-high wall surrounded the yard; even so, the sun found a way in, and from a treetop close by the sound of bird-song filled the air. 'Surprisingly pleasant, don't you think?' Mr Clegg remarked; though he would have considered it beneath himself to reside in such an area.

Cathy was secretly excited, but kept her voice cool and disinterested. 'I don't know about that,' she answered, giving a little grimace that dashed his hopes. 'As you so rightly pointed out, William Henry Street is very noisy, and the houses in a terrible state of dilapidation.' She shook her head and looked around her with feigned disgust. 'You say you're pleasantly surprised? Well, I can only say *I'm* surprised this house and others like it have not been put under a demolition order.' With that she departed, smiling to herself when he followed at a run, muttering something about how it might be possible to negotiate a more favourable price with Mr Manners: 'Though he is a hard man to deal with, and I can't promise anything.'

Outside, Cathy waited while he locked the door behind them. 'A more favourable price, you say?' She smiled. 'I'm afraid Mr Manners would have to more than *halve* his price, and even then I doubt whether I could persuade my aunt to step foot inside.' She pointed to a roof tile which was hanging dangerously over the guttering. 'A body could be killed!' she said. 'Besides ... even *you* were afraid the whole place could come falling about your ears.'

He grinned. 'Perhaps I was a little hasty,' he suggested. 'Yes! I'm sure I was a little hasty.'

At the top of the street they parted company, he returning to his office and Cathy making for the tram-stop. 'Should I tell Mr Manners you might be interested?' Taking a huge white handkerchief from his waistcoat pocket, Mr Clegg mopped his brow. It had been an unnerving experience, and this young lady was a trial all by herself.

Deliberately taking her time in answering, Cathy appeared to be deep in thought. Presently she said, 'It isn't what we're looking for, and it does need a great deal of work doing. My aunt and I aren't wealthy. We hadn't counted on buying a place that needed money spent on it.' Sighing, she said wearily, 'But I have to admit we're not having much luck, and this house isn't suitable either ... far from it!' She couldn't let him believe he had a keen buyer, or he wouldn't bring the price down one shilling, let alone by half.

'Not even if I could persuade Mr Manners to drop his price?'

Feigning impatience she said, 'No, Mr Clegg. Not even then.' Bidding him goodbye, she made to cross the road.

'We have your address, so if anything else should come up, we'll be in touch.'

'I doubt if my aunt will want to be bothered,' she replied. 'Not if the best you can offer is a house that needs more spent on it than it's worth!'

All the way back to the hotel, Cathy could hardly contain herself. That house was the one they had been searching for, and oh, she had so much to tell Margaret! Today of all days, though, the short tram journey seemed to take an age.

Margaret was not convinced. 'From what you say, the house needs a lot of improvement, and we simply don't have the money.'

'We will have ... if I can get Mr Manners to halve the price.'

Ruby chuckled. 'He's not likely to do that now, is he?'

Cathy was hopeful. 'He might.' Taking hold of Margaret's hands, she gently shook them. 'At least come and have a look at it. If you don't like the house, I'll forget about it and keep on searching.' When Margaret agreed to view it from the outside, Cathy gave a little whoop. 'You'll love it,' she cried. 'I know you will!'

The following morning, all three went along to William Henry Street.

'Well, I never!' The woman was white-stoning her front doorstep when she noticed Cathy. 'I never thought we'd clap eyes on you again!' she declared. 'It ain't often we get ladies strolling down this 'ere street.' She chuckled and passed a few minutes with them, watching with curiosity when they went down the street to the end house where all three stood looking up, talking about it and wondering whether this was the home they had been looking for. 'What do you think?' Cathy asked. 'Don't you think it has potential?'

Ruby stepped back a pace and regarded the house through narrowed eyes. She hummed and hawed and scratched the end of her nose; she coughed a little and glanced up and down the street, then she looked at Cathy, then she looked at Margaret, and scratched her nose again. 'Could be,' she muttered. 'Aye. Could be.'

Cathy waited patiently while Margaret went down the cellar steps and up again; she went up the front steps to the door and peered through the letter-box, and balanced on the edge of the step, but still couldn't see into the front parlour. 'It might have helped if you'd got the keys so we could go inside,' she said, exasperated.

'I didn't want Mr Clegg to know I'd persuaded you to come here.'

'If we can't get inside, how am I to say whether I like it or not?'

'Do you like the *outside*?' She had expected Margaret to take one look and turn tail and run. When she didn't, Cathy dared to hope. 'Apparently this street once housed the gentry.'

Ruby glared at her. 'Well, aren't *you* the gentry?' she demanded indignantly.

There was a world of pride in Cathy's voice when she answered softly, 'No, Ruby. I don't think so.'

Margaret's remark made them both turn round. 'Yes! I *do* like the outside. I only wish I could see the inside as well.'

Another voice intervened. 'If yer want, *I* can get yer inside, missus.' It was the woman who had been breast-feeding her bairn the day before, and white-stoning her step just now. Without another word she went up the steps and, hooking the tips of her fingers through the letter-box, gave one almighty tug. The door clicked open. 'It's a knack,' she explained dryly.

Cathy led the way up the stairs then down again, and in every room Margaret spent a few minutes describing how she might arrange the furniture. Ruby commented how she would be: 'Well suited to that room upstairs . . . me own stairway to the kitchen, and out of everybody's way.'

As she listened to them, observing their faces as they discussed such things as curtains and carpets, Cathy knew they were home. She even shouted it to the four walls, and soon the three of them were laughing and hugging each other. 'We're home!' Cathy kept saying. 'We're home!'

Just for the briefest moment her excitement was overshadowed by thoughts of David. If only he would walk through that door and smile at her, her happiness would be complete.

Margaret was convinced. 'Well, you found the place, Cathy,' she said. 'Do you really believe you can get the price reduced?'

'*Halved!*' Cathy laughed. 'I'll get it halved.'

The next morning, just as she had predicted, Mr Clegg arrived at the hotel. 'I've come to tell you that I've argued your case with Mr Manners, and he has agreed to reduce the selling price.' He didn't look too pleased, because the lower the price, the lower his own commission. 'But the transaction must be completed swiftly or the house goes back on the market.'

He addressed his remarks to Margaret, but she requested that he direct them to Cathy, who wanted to know, 'Did you tell him we would only consider the house if the price was reduced by half?'

'I did. I also told him that in my opinion it needed far more repairs than he had led me to believe.'

'And has he agreed the price?'

'He has. The property is yours, at half the original asking price.'

Cathy had never really hoped he would agree, but he had, and it was all she could do not to yell for joy. Instead, with a calmness that belied her churning stomach, she glanced at Margaret who was seated bolt upright in the chair, unable to believe that everything had been agreed. 'The decision is my aunt's,' Cathy said coolly. Turning to Margaret, she enquired, 'What do you say? Are you interested?'

Nervously clearing her throat, Margaret answered, 'I think we have a deal, Mr Clegg.'

'Good!' He rubbed his hands and feverishly nodded his head. 'Then I would be obliged if you could instruct your solicitor and get things under way.' Handing her an envelope, he explained, 'Inside you will find all the details you require. Now, if you will please excuse me, I have matters to attend to.'

'And so have we!' After he'd gone, Cathy did a little jig on the spot.

Ruby hugged her, then Margaret. 'There's only one thing that worries me,' said her aunt.

'Oh?' Cathy wasn't worried at all. 'What's that?'

'This Tony Manners ... from what you told me, he seems an undesirable character. I only hope he hasn't taken a fancy to you.'

'He can take a fancy to whoever he likes,' Cathy answered. 'It won't get him anything.'

'I should think not!' Ruby declared. But, like Margaret, she couldn't help wondering whether Tony Manners would be more trouble than he was worth.

CHAPTER TEN

Within weeks, the house on William Henry Street was transformed. Cathy was given the task of choosing curtains and carpets, while Margaret took Ruby with her to browse round the furniture shops. The first priority had been to save the money being spent on rooms at the hotel. 'If we all roll up our sleeves and get stuck in, we'll soon have it ship-shape,' Cathy said, though it was obvious they would have to pay for someone to mend the front door and change the locks, then a plumber to free the blockage in the water pipes, and a handyman to tack back the plasterboard that was hanging from the upstairs ceiling.

Margaret decided to leave the recruiting to Cathy. 'By the time you've finished, they'll likely be pleased to do the work for nothing,' she laughed. Ruby scowled and warned her to be careful who she trusted, and the name of Tony Manners rose to mind.

Cathy enquired among the neighbours and found two workmen who could do all they wanted at a very reasonable price. They were in and out in less than a week, and were every bit as good as Cathy had been told; the ceilings were as new, the plumbing was working smoothly, and all that remained was the scrubbing and cleaning, then the decorating, before the carpets were laid and the furniture delivered. 'Another week and we should be able to move in,' Margaret said with relief, and Ruby began counting the minutes.

The house was a hive of activity. 'Leave the back and front doors wide open to let the fresh air blow through,' Margaret advised, taking up her broom and sweeping every corner in every room.

In her element at having a kitchen at last, Ruby rushed in

657

and out, making tea to keep their spirits up, in between finding all manner of things to do. 'I've never seen so much muck under a sink before,' she declared, loudly tutting and slapping a wet cloth over the shelves.

Cathy spent the best part of a week on her knees. One Monday morning she was on them again, sleeves rolled up and a hessian sack tied round her waist as she scrubbed the living-room floor. 'Get up from there afore yer knees flatten like saucers!' Ruby argued. 'There's a pot o' tea made, an' some fresh Eccles cakes from the corner shop.' She tugged at Cathy's makeshift pinnie. 'I've called Miss Margaret an' she's on her way downstairs, so come on. Let's have yer!'

'Ruby Adams, you're a bully.' In fact, Cathy was ready to stop awhile.

'Mebbe. But you've been on yer knees for over an hour, an' it's time for a break.'

A few minutes later, with their hands washed and pinnies thrown aside, they all sat on upturned boxes, round the big tea chest that served as a table. 'Are you all right?' Margaret had been looking closely at Cathy and, not for the first time of late, wondered whether there was something very wrong.

'I'm quite well,' Cathy lied.

'You look tired.'

'I didn't sleep well last night . . . nothing to worry about.'

The truth was, she knew now without doubt that she was with child. It tortured her to think she must tell Margaret soon.

'You're working too hard.'

'We're *all* working too hard,' Cathy gently reminded her. 'But we've broken the back of it now. If all goes well, we should be in by the end of the week.'

'Thank God for that!' Just as Cathy intended, Margaret's attention was diverted. 'Won't it be wonderful to sit in big soft armchairs, round our very own fireplace?'

In a softer voice filled with conviction, Cathy told her, 'It's no more than you deserve.'

Ruby had been quietly regarding the pair of them, and now she had her little say. 'It's no more than the *both* of you deserve,' she declared. 'Me an' all, because I've missed having me own kitchen, an' it's been far too long since I cooked a proper dinner.'

Cathy stood up. 'Thank you for the tea, Ruby. Now it's back to work, or it'll be a month of Sundays before you have your own kitchen again.'

Margaret resumed her window-cleaning upstairs, and Ruby went into the kitchen to wash the pots. After a while she returned to the living room where Cathy was hard at work. 'Have you got a minute, lass?' she asked, standing over her.

Cathy looked up and the dark circles beneath her eyes were more prominent. 'What is it, Ruby? Is something troubling you?' Wiping her hands on her pinnie, she rose to her feet.

'No, lass, there ain't nothing wrong with me,' Ruby answered softly. 'It's you I'm concerned about.'

'There's no need.' Every instinct in her aching body urged Cathy to confess her troubles. But she couldn't. She wanted to, but God help her, she couldn't bring herself to say the words: 'Jack violated me, and I'm having his baby.' It was too horrible. But sooner or later it would have to be said, and when the news broke it would shatter all their lives; Ruby's because she would be filled with such a rage that she might want to search Jack out and do away with him, and Margaret's because she had borne so much anguish already and, though she tried hard not to let it show, was still haunted by the awful events that had brought them here to William Henry Street.

Ruby suspected there was something Cathy wasn't telling her. She also knew that Cathy was strong-willed and independent, and that the best thing was to leave her be and let her decide when to share her troubles. 'All right, lass,' she said reluctantly. 'But I've told you afore an' I'll tell you again ... I'm here if you want to talk. You an' Miss Margaret are like family to me, an' I'd be offended if summat were deeply troubling you an' you couldn't find the heart to trust old Ruby.'

For a long minute, Cathy was racked with guilt. 'I *do* trust you,' she whispered, 'but I'm well, really I am.' Her eyes swam with tears. It wasn't easy to lie to this dear old soul, but for now she had little choice. 'There's no need for you to worry about me.'

'Hmm.' Biting her tongue, Ruby returned to her kitchen, where she was soon clattering about; though every now and then she peeped out of the doorway to see whether Cathy was all right.

Two days later, the house was finished. The windows were sparkling, the long tapestry curtains were hung, and the floorboards were scrubbed until every line of grain could be seen. At half-past eleven on a Wednesday morning, the carpets and furniture arrived. All morning excitement had been mounting and, now that the moment had finally arrived, Margaret was running round in circles. 'Put the sideboard there,' she instructed the two delivery men. 'Oh, no, that doesn't look right . . . sorry . . . could you please set it against that wall instead?' Four times they shifted the sideboard, and each time Ruby and Cathy hid behind the kitchen door, stifling their giggles. 'If she don't make up her mind soon they'll take the damned thing away and drop it in the cut!' Ruby chuckled. They doubled up with laughter when one of the long-suffering delivery men threatened the very same.

It took a full hour for the furniture to be carted in, and another hour for them to put it all where it was wanted. 'Jesus, Mary and Joseph!' The sweat was teeming down the younger man's face. 'If I'd known the job was like this, I'd 'a gone into farming like me da afore me.'

His face lit up when Margaret gave him and his mate a shilling each. But it was to Cathy he addressed himself. 'I hope everything's to your liking?' he asked shyly, blushing to the roots of his hair when she smiled warmly and thanked the pair of them for their understanding.

'We've worked hard to get this place how we want it,' she explained. 'It's important to have the furniture exactly where it should be.'

As they went out the door, the elder man muttered, 'Hmph! A shilling each won't buy a fat lot over the pub counter.' He had a loud voice and his mutterings were heard by everyone there.

'Go on, yer ungrateful buggers!' Ruby called out. 'Anyway, yer shouldn't be spending yer hard-earned money over the pub counter!'

Shocked that he'd been overheard, the older man turned

round and fell arse over tip down the steps, while the young lad screeched with laughter and got a clip round the ear for his troubles.

'Oh, it's wonderful!' Cathy led the way from room to room. Margaret's bedroom was furnished much like the one she'd had at Blackthorn House in warm dark colours, with brown scatter rugs, a serviceable walnut dressing table and an eiderdown with flowers at each corner. 'I really couldn't wish for anything better,' she told Cathy.

Cathy's room was mainly pink, with cream-coloured rugs and lace eiderdown, and a landscape painting hanging on the wall. It showed a summer scene; in the distance a young couple sat on the grass, deep in conversation and obviously in love. 'It reminds me of David,' she said simply, and there was a world of regret in her voice.

Ruby had given strict instructions as to how she wanted her room furnished. 'Good solid stuff that'll last as long as I do!' She had a narrow bed with a chequered eiderdown, and a tall clothes press with deep drawers and round wooden knobs. The curtains were plain but pretty and at the side of her bed was a soft blue rug which she claimed would 'Tickle me toes'. Her face beamed from ear to ear when she surveyed it all. 'By! We'll be comfortable here an' no mistake,' she said grandly.

The front parlour held a piano, a horsehair settee and two matching chairs, and a small table for taking tea on. 'This can be kept for visitors,' Margaret announced.

'As long as it ain't that sly Mr Manners,' Ruby declared. When she got a stern look from Margaret she announced her intention of making a fresh pot of tea 'To christen our new home', then hurried into the kitchen, muttering all the way.

The following morning, they moved into the house. Neighbours came from everywhere. 'By! You've made it look grand!' Ada Snettleton observed. Fred Arlinton saw they hadn't got a coal-scuttle. 'You've got to have a coal-scuttle,' he instructed, 'else you'll be forever up and down to the cellar with yer shovel.' The woman from the corner shop fetched two big meat and tater pies; somebody else brought the plates. Ruby got a knife from the kitchen and sliced the pies into tiny segments; everybody said how good it was, wished health to their neighbours and washed the victuals down with a drop of Michael Bone's home-made ginger-ale.

Right in the middle of it, Tony Manners turned up and invited Cathy outside to see his new carriage. 'All it needs is a fine lady to grace it,' he said enticingly.

'Then you'd best find yourself one, hadn't you?' she replied.

'I think I've found one in you,' he murmured. Reaching inside the carriage he brought out a huge bunch of flowers.

'I hope you realise I'm proposing,' he said.

Before she could tell him where to go, he kissed her full on the mouth, hopped into the carriage and was gone from the street.

'Good grief!' Cathy gasped. 'And to think we've only just met!'

It was evening before they had the house to themselves again. 'I feel we'll be happy here,' Margaret said.

'Some more than others,' Ruby remarked, stealing a glance at Cathy. She had followed her and Tony Manners outside earlier, and what she saw only fuelled her worst fears.

Cathy didn't know *what* to say, so she remained quiet until Margaret asked her whether she was happy. 'As I'll ever be,' came the answer. Then, 'Yes, of course I am. We've got a home of our own, a full pantry, and good neighbours to drink our health. All in all, it's a perfect end to a perfect day.'

That night she stripped and stood before the mirror. The gentle curve of her stomach was more pronounced and her breasts slightly swollen, but if she breathed in and held herself taut she looked slim and flat as ever. 'Tony Manners would marry you and never know,' she whispered. The idea was both attractive and repugnant. 'What harm would it do?' she argued. 'The child would have a name. There would be no shame, no repercussions.' Torn between love and hate for the child she was carrying, and the bitterness she felt towards its father, she desperately searched for a way out. 'Is marrying Tony Manners the only thing to do?' she asked herself. 'Give yourself to him, and as long as you live you will never be free again.'

She bathed and thought of what it would mean to be tied to

a man like Tony. She put on her nightgown and mused over the prospect. She brushed her hair and thought about the future, and it loomed before her like a long dark tunnel. 'How could you ever marry another man when you still love David ... when you will *always* love David?' It would be hard, perhaps impossible, to pretend. She would have to submit to her husband's demands, lie in bed with him, be a wife in every sense of the word. It was a daunting prospect. 'If you can't have David, what does it matter? Whether you want it or not, this child will be born. It must have a name, so why not the name of Manners? Margaret and Ruby need never know your shame and, by moving out, you will lessen the burden on Margaret.' It was not the ideal solution, but unfortunately it was the only one.

The next morning Cathy's mind was made up. She had spent another restless night, the shadows beneath her eyes had deepened, and when she touched her stomach she imagined she could feel movement inside. 'Don't be silly,' she argued with her image in the mirror. 'It hasn't been long enough.' But time was passing quickly and soon her condition would be apparent to everyone. 'Should I tell Tony the truth?' she asked herself. 'How could I hide the truth from him, even if I wanted to?' It was another dilemma, but: 'If Tony asks me outright to marry him, I'll say yes, and let the consequences take care of themselves.'

As it was, he didn't come anywhere near for several days. 'Good shuts to him,' Ruby said, and was reprimanded by Margaret. 'Like you I don't care much for the charming Mr Manners,' she said, 'but he's polite and friendly, and appears to be genuinely fond of Cathy, and God knows she needs someone to take her out of herself.'

'Ah!' Ruby had said nothing about her concern for Cathy, because she didn't want to worry Margaret unnecessarily, but now that Margaret had mentioned it, she would have her say. 'So you've noticed how unhappy Cathy seems to be of late?'

'Yes, I have noticed.'

'Have you asked her what's wrong?'

'Not yet. I was hoping she would confide in me of her own free will.'

'She won't. I've asked her time and again what's troubling her, but she won't say.' Plucking the clothes out of the dolly tub, she dropped them into the enamel bowl; the hot water made her wince when a trickle of it ran down her arm. Taking another bowl, she placed it under the tap at the bottom, and ran the water off. That done, she tipped the water down the big pot sink, filled it with clean water and rinsed out the newly-washed clothes. 'By! I reckon it would be just as quick to wash the whole blessed lot in the sink,' she complained. Turning to glance at Margaret, who was leaning on the door jamb to stare out of the back window, she enquired softly, 'Where's Cathy now?'

'Next door.'

Ruby wondered if she'd heard right. 'Next door!' Wringing the clothes out one by one, she placed them on the draining board. 'Whatever is she doing next door? The place is empty, ain't it? Dangerous, too, I shouldn't wonder.'

'*He's* with her.'

'Who?' Red-faced from the steam, Ruby wiped her eyes with the back of her hand. 'Surely you don't mean that Manners bloke?'

'Apparently he thinks it unwise to leave the house now we're living here, so he's looking to furnish the place and rent it out. He thinks Cathy has good taste and wants her advice, that's all.'

'Don't you believe it,' Ruby retorted. 'It's the lass herself he wants.' Leaning forward with her arms against the sink she regarded Margaret through red-rimmed eyes. 'Don't that worry you, Miss?'

'Yes, it worries me,' Margaret admitted. 'But I don't think it's right for me to interfere. I've already done her enough harm ... what with persuading her not to go and see David before he left. I was wrong, Ruby. Those two were made for each other and I should have encouraged her to go and talk things through with him. Now he's God knows where, and Cathy will probably never see him again.'

'She'll never stop missing him neither.' Ruby had thought long and hard about it and now she was convinced. 'I reckon that's what's troubling her. Without that young man she's like a summer's day without sunshine.'

Cathy's interest had been aroused. 'I think you should have sensible furnishings ... good solid furniture and curtains with a smooth surface so they won't hold the dust.' Reluctant at first, she was now caught up in the idea of transforming the derelict house next to their own. 'You're right,' she agreed with Tony Manners, 'it has possibilities.'

'I knew you would be the one to ask.' Regarding her from head to foot, he licked his lips like a dog about to be given a chop. 'Let's hear your ideas then, as long as it doesn't cost me a small fortune.'

'If you're going to renovate the house, you might as well do it properly.' Regarding him with a frown, Cathy roved the large empty room. Gingerly tapping at the loose floorboards with the tip of her toe, she remarked, 'Most of the floors are unsafe, so they'll need replacing.' She peeked at him. 'It just might cost you a small fortune after all.'

'The way you're smiling, anyone would think you liked the idea of me parting with my money!'

'I'm sure you don't want some poor unsuspecting soul to plunge through the floor and break his neck?'

He shrugged. 'All right. What's next?'

'The walls. I think they should be painted in soft light colours . . . to reflect sunshine into the room.' She half-smiled at a mental picture of how it might look once Tony Manners had dipped deep into his pocket.

Leaning against the fire-range he watched her moving about. He saw the light in her lovely green eyes and wanted her all to himself. 'Like you?' he murmured, coming forward.

'What did you say?' He was at one end of the room and she at the other, and he had spoken so low she could hardly hear him.

'Paint the walls soft and light, you said . . . so they can reflect sunshine into the room.' He was standing before her now, putting her on her guard. 'That's what *you* do, Cathy . . . reflect the sunshine into the room.'

Something in his manner made her nervous. 'I'd better be going now,' she replied, dashing his hopes. 'You asked for my ideas and I've given them. Whether you choose to use or ignore them is up to you.'

'Oh, I shall use them, of course.' She began to turn away but he caught hold of her hand. 'Have you been thinking about what I asked you the other day?'

'I can't recall your asking me anything.' She knew what he was referring to, but wanted him to spell it out.

He seemed astonished. 'You really can't remember?' Giving a small chuckle, he tugged her towards him. 'And here I was ... thinking you'd been dreaming of me ever since.'

'Hardly!'

'It isn't every day I propose to a beautiful young woman.'

'I should hope not.'

'Well?'

'Well ... what?'

'Was my proposal wasted?'

'Untimely, perhaps. I hardly know you.'

'We can rectify that here and now.' His voice was purring, his hands reaching out to undo the buttons of her dress. 'I've never wanted a woman like I want you.' Looking down on her, his eyes were like a cat's, yellow one minute, dark and seething the next. 'You're very beautiful.'

With her blouse undone and her breasts exposed, she felt like a hussy. When he bent his head to cover her nipple with his open mouth, her every instinct told her to throw him off and run from that place. But she was held by chains that could not be seen ... human chains. The unborn child; Jack; a need to be needed, to belong for the first time in her life. She was angry, fused with a strange longing, yet burning with hate. So much confusion, so many emotions she couldn't explain. Her future was uncertain, yet here he was, offering her a lifeline she could ill afford to refuse. The truth was she desperately needed a father for her child.

She felt his hands move to her waist; a few deft movements, a determined tug, and the skirt fell to her ankles. He didn't stop there, and soon she was standing before him stark naked. The cold air struck like a damp cloth against her shivering skin. But it wasn't the cold air that made her tremble. It was shame. The same deep crippling shame that had stayed with her since Jack took her to himself. RUN CATHY, RUN! It was her own voice, persisting in her head. NOW. GO NOW, CATHY! Sorely tempted to grab up her clothes and cover her nakedness, she smothered the voice, thinking only of a greater shame that lay ahead if she didn't use Tony Manners the way Jack had used her. She was here, and he was touching her, and all she could think of was the price she must pay. Against all her better instincts, she made no move to stop him.

Discarding the last of his garments, Tony Manners fell to his knees before her. 'I knew you felt the same.' Pushing open her legs, he flicked his tongue, shocking her when the moist tip found its mark. 'You want me, don't you?' he moaned. 'Say it . . . say you want me!'

'NO!' Her voice rang out, startling him, startling her. Frantically she pulled away, desperate to be rid of him. 'I can't do this,' she whispered.

He looked up, eyes wide and his face contorted with passion. 'Yes, you can . . . it's what you want. It's what we *both* want.'

Disgust rippled through her. 'I must have been mad to let it go this far!'

She would have wrenched herself away but he held her fast. 'Don't play games with me,' he warned.

When she brought her gaze to him, he saw the revulsion in her eyes. 'If you try and force yourself on me,' she whispered hoarsely, 'I'll kill you.' Every word struck home.

Suddenly he was dressing, his voice laced with fury as he claimed, 'Women don't usually refuse me, and you . . . you led me to believe . . .'

'No!' Quickly pulling on her clothes, she couldn't look at him. 'You led *yourself* to believe.'

'I could give you everything money can buy.'

'There are some things money *can't* buy.'

'Do you know how much I want you?'

'I think so.' They were fully dressed now; he was flushed with passion, while she was pale with the agony she felt inside. 'I should have stopped you earlier. I'm sorry.' It was partly her fault, she knew that.

'I'm sorry too.' Secretly he hated her, but his craving to have her was stronger. He became arrogant, sure of himself, determined not to lose her.

Quickly, before he could detain her, she hurried down the passage to the front door.

Stealthily he followed, vain enough to believe she could not bring herself to walk out on him. When he called her name she paused to look back. He was standing only an arm's reach away. 'You don't have to go,' he pleaded softly. 'I don't want you to go.'

She turned away. 'I'm sorry. I can't stay here ... with you.' Reaching out, she clicked the key in the lock and swung open the door. 'Goodbye,' she whispered. 'Forgive me.'

Realising she meant to leave, that she really didn't want him, was too humiliating. 'Don't fool yourself,' he hissed. 'You're not going anywhere!' Darting forward, he grabbed her by the wrist.

Taken by surprise, Cathy felt herself being dragged away from the door and down the passage-way. Summoning every ounce of her strength she dug her heels into the frayed carpet and set herself against him. 'I don't think you heard me right,' she yelled angrily. 'I don't want you. I *never* wanted you!'

The two of them were struggling harder now, he intent on dragging her into the privacy of the back room, and Cathy equally determined he would not get the better of her. Another scene ran through her mind, of her and Jack. But this time she was stronger. This time she was ready. With one final surge of energy, she jabbed the heel of her shoe into his ankle.

'You bad bugger!' Gritting his teeth he bent to rub the flat of his hand over the broken skin. Taking the chance, Cathy ran. But he was quick. They both reached the door together. As she lunged forward he grabbed at her, causing the hem of her skirt to catch on the iron railings. As she tripped forward, he made another dash to grab her but it was too late. With a cry, she plunged down the steps, knocking her head as she fell. It all happened so quickly. One minute she was fighting him off, and the next she was lying crumpled at the foot of the steps, her face like marble and her body so still he believed she was dead. 'God above!' he muttered, over and over. He made no move to help her but leaned against the door, biting his nails and glancing up and down the street with a kind of animal terror. When he realised there had been no witnesses, he slunk off, keeping close to the wall as he went and glancing back just once to make sure he had not been seen.

It was a few minutes before Cathy was found. One of the neighbours had come out to sit in her chair on the pavement and smoke her pipe. At first she thought it was a bundle of rags lying at the foot of the steps. She came closer, gasping out loud when she saw Cathy's white face. In a minute she had run back to fetch Margaret. Ruby ran off to call for help, and in no time at all Cathy was being whisked to the Infirmary, with Margaret and Ruby beside her. They were both thinking of Tony Manners, and of his probable part in Cathy's 'accident', but neither voiced their suspicions. There'd be time enough for answers when Cathy was awake and well, please God.

She was still unconscious when they rushed her inside. Margaret and Ruby waited in the corridor. The nurse brought them a cup of tea, but it was left to grow cold. 'It's that Tony Manners!' Ruby could hold her tongue no longer. 'It were him who hurt her, an' nobody will tell me otherwise!'

'We don't know, Ruby.' Margaret looked ill. The two of them had waited for half an hour, and still there was no news. 'Until we find out what happened, we mustn't blame anyone.'

Glancing at Margaret, seeing how drawn and worried she looked, Ruby was angry with herself for speaking out of turn. 'You're right,' she said comfortingly. 'The only important thing is for Cathy to be well again.' After that, she kept her opinions to herself.

Another half an hour passed and still no one came to see them. 'What in God's name are they doing in there?' Getting out of her seat, Margaret waylaid a passing nurse. 'Cathy Blackthorn . . . what's happening to her? Is she all right? Why doesn't someone tell us?' She gripped the nurse's arm and wouldn't let her go. 'Please. Is she going to be all right?'

Before the nurse could answer, a plump grey-haired doctor intervened. 'Cathy will be fine,' he said, gesturing for the nurse to leave.

Passing her hand over her face, Margaret almost fell into his arms. 'Thank God!' she whispered. Ruby came to her side and Margaret leaned into her. 'She'll be fine, Ruby . . . Cathy will be fine.' She actually gave a little laugh, and Ruby did the same.

'There! What did I tell yer, eh?' Ruby was full of herself now. 'Didn't I tell yer Cathy were made of strong stuff?'

The doctor spoke softly. 'Your niece suffered a bad fall,' he explained. 'She's still concussed . . . and has two broken ribs.' He saw their expressions change and hesitated. 'But, as I've already told you, she's young and strong, and I'm confident she'll make a full recovery . . .' He took a deep breath. What he had to tell them next was not going to be easy.

Margaret stared at him, her voice quivering as she prompted, 'There's something else, isn't there? Cathy will make a full recovery . . . *but* . . .?' She could tell from his face that there was bad news to come.

The only way to tell it was straight out, without too much emotion but not without a degree of compassion. 'I'm afraid we couldn't save the unborn child.'

His words hung heavy in the ensuing silence. Both women looked at him in disbelief. It was a moment before Margaret spoke, and the word was a whisper. '*Child*?' She was slowly shaking her head from side to side, her confused gaze going from the doctor to Ruby and back again. Ruby too had been stunned by the news. Yet, in their hearts, both women knew there had been something troubling Cathy, something so deep she had not been able to tell them.

Ruby's voice came out in a croak. 'Come and sit down,' she said, leading Margaret to the chair.

The doctor followed. 'I'm sorry.' In cases like this he would rather be anything but a doctor. 'We did all we could, but it wasn't enough.'

Recovered now, Margaret asked, 'Does she know . . . that she's lost the child?'

He pursed his lips, thought for a while and smiled sadly. 'I think she knew even before we did.'

'Can we see her?'

'That would do her good. She hasn't spoken to any of us, and she needs to talk about her loss.' Indicating the double green doors, he led the way. 'However, she's still very weak. I can't let you stay too long.' He saw them to the sister's office, before going about his many duties.

'Just a short time,' the sister said. 'She's very tired.'

Cathy was lying on her side. 'By! She looks like a small child,' Ruby whispered as they came close. 'And she's no colour at all.' Cathy was sleeping, her face stark white and her long slim fingers clutched as though in spasm across her breast.

Leaning forward, Margaret gently touched the folded fingers.

'Once she's home again we'll soon put the colour back in her cheeks,' she said, thinking Ruby was right; Cathy did look like a child.

Hearing the voices of those she loved, she opened her eyes. One look at their faces told her. 'You know about the baby?'

Margaret wrapped her fingers around Cathy's. 'Yes, sweetheart, we know.' Her voice was soft and caressing, relaying all the love she felt. 'We can talk about it later . . . if you want to.'

Against the white skin, Cathy's green eyes looked like large emerald pools; incredibly beautiful, alive with pain. Tears trembled on the long dark lashes. 'I'm so sorry. I should have told you.'

'It doesn't matter,' Margaret said encouragingly. 'What matters now is *you* . . . getting you better so we can take you home.'

'I love you both.' Reaching up awkwardly, Cathy took hold of Ruby's hand. 'I should have told you.' Memories became almost too much to bear. 'I've been bad,' she whispered. 'I can't talk about it.'

'Whenever you're ready, sweetheart.'

'I don't *ever* want to talk about it.'

Sensing that they were getting into deep waters, Margaret assured her, 'It's for you to decide, but when you're better you might feel different.'

Cathy closed her eyes. She felt strange, incredibly tired. The doctor's words echoed in her mind. 'I have to tell you . . . you've lost the child.' In spite of the way it was conceived, she had never consciously wished it harm. It was an innocent, a victim like herself. How could she want it harmed? Yet in her deepest heart had she wanted rid of it? She could never be certain. And now she was beginning to wonder whether all of it was her fault. Had she been too friendly with Jack? Did he take her friendship to mean she felt something stronger for him? And what of Tony Manners? There was no doubt she had seen him as her salvation. She had smiled at him in such a way that he was made arrogantly sure of her. Was it any wonder he saw her as being easy, someone to satisfy his needs and pander to his every whim? A man was only a man after all, and could see no further than his animal desires. But, no! That wasn't true. One man was different from another, just as a woman was different from another. Jack and Tony Manners were two of a kind. David Leyton was another matter altogether. David was kind and good, and had never asked more of her than she was willing to give. If he was here now, she would give him everything she had. But he wasn't here. HE WASN'T HERE!

In all of her life she had never felt so devastated; with the child gone her body felt drained. With David gone there was little to live for. Oh, there was Margaret, and Ruby, and she would always love and need them. But her life was empty, finished. And all she could think of was the child, and David. David! David!

Suddenly she was crying, sobbing as though her heart would break. Margaret was holding her. 'That's right, sweetheart,' she was saying. 'That's right.' But it wasn't right. Cathy feared that nothing could ever be right again.

'Don't worry,' the nurse told Margaret. 'It's only natural she should be weepy after such a shock. On top of losing the child, she's still slightly concussed and the broken ribs will cause her a deal of pain. It's bound to take time, but she will be well again.' While she was talking, Cathy drifted in and out of consciousness, not caring whether she lived or died.

'We'll be there soon as ever they open the doors in the morning.' Intent on keeping Margaret's spirits up, Ruby chattered all the way home. 'It'll not be long afore she's home, then we'll soon get the colour back into her cheeks.'

A week later Cathy came home. Still very weak and in great pain from her broken ribs, she talked and smiled and ate the good broth that Ruby made. She slept well, and sat in the yard, letting the sun warm her face. She read, and she sewed, and just as Ruby had predicted, the roses came back to her cheeks. 'By! She's doing fine,' Ruby declared. Returning to the sitting room after taking Cathy a cup of tea in the yard, she grinned from ear to ear. 'The lass will soon be up to her old tricks . . . rushing about, bossing the pair of us and wanting to put the world to rights.'

'Do you really think she's mending, Ruby?'

'Aye, lass. Mending fast, I reckon.'

Margaret was not of the same mind. Going to the window

she gazed out. 'I'm worried about her,' she said softly. In the wicker chair that Margaret had bought at the market, Cathy was seated against the west wall. It was covered in trellis and pricked with the first blossom of an early-cropping apple-tree. Soon after they first moved into the house, Cathy had knocked the trellis to the wall, and helped Ruby to tie in the tree. 'I shall make some delicious apple pies from that,' Ruby had promised. But that was some time away yet. The blossom had not even begun to shoot.

'I don't know why you're worried about her,' Ruby remarked. 'The lass is eating well, and the pain in her ribs is lessening. The colour's back in her cheeks and her smile is bright as it ever was.'

'I know all that,' Margaret murmured. 'Somehow, though, I have the feeling she's only half alive.'

'By! That's a sorry thing to say.' Ruby had been smiling but now she was looking at Cathy in a different way.

'It's nothing physical, Ruby. Nothing you can put your finger on. It's a feeling, an instinct if you like.' She shivered. 'I don't know what it is, but . . . I'm afraid.'

'Happen we're being too impatient. The lass has been through so much, and losing the child was a terrible thing. You heard what the doctor said . . . it will take time to get over summat like that.'

'Has she spoken to *you* about that, Ruby?'

'Not a word.' Ruby's voice fell to a whisper. 'Lord knows I've given her ample opportunity . . . without pressing her, you understand? But she's said not a word. Not about the bairn, nor about how she came to fall down them steps.'

'Nor to me. And since Tony Manners has made himself scarce, we can't ask him either.'

'That scoundrel has a lot to answer for, I'll be bound.'

'We still can't be sure of that.'

Ruby hesitated to raise the subject again. She and Margaret had discussed it briefly, but neither of them felt it was right to talk about it without Cathy's being present. Yet the burning question hung in the air like a cloud over their heads. 'Do you still think it were David Leyton as made her with child?'

Margaret never took her eyes off Cathy. 'Who else could it

be? David was the only young man she was ever close to. I always believed that Cathy and David would marry one day.' She recalled all those times when she had found them together, two young sweethearts shutting out the world. 'I don't honestly know *what* to believe.'

'If you're concerned about the lass, don't you think you ought to talk with the doctor?'

'No. It isn't a doctor Cathy needs.'

'Who then?' Ruby's eyes lit up. 'It's David, isn't it? You think she's pining for him?'

Still, Margaret kept her gaze on Cathy. 'Maybe. Maybe not. All I know is this... we're losing Cathy, and I can't seem to get through to her. She won't talk to you either, so the only other person I can think of is David.'

'Are you sure about all this?'

'I know her so well, Ruby. Think about it... she's eating, yes, and her health seems to be improving... but do you really believe that forlorn creature down there is the Cathy we know?'

Ruby had to concede, 'Happen you're right. Happen I'm seeing only the good signs and not seeing the truth. I've noticed her spirits are low, and it bothers me that she won't talk about the matters close to her heart.' Margaret's anxiety had conveyed itself to her. 'If you're right though, an' our Cathy *is* fretting inside, what's to be done? Tell me that, lass... what's to be done?'

'I wish I knew.' As she spoke, Cathy glanced up to see them there. Margaret thought she looked cold. 'She's been out there too long, Ruby. I'll fetch her in. You fill a nice hot bath.' With that she went smartly down the steps, leaving Ruby to go on her own way.

'You're an old fusspot.' Cathy would have stayed outside for a time, but Margaret was right. The sun had gone behind a cloud and the breeze had grown chilly. 'I bet you've got Ruby filling a hot bath for me, haven't you?' There was a smile on her face, but it didn't seem to touch her lovely green eyes.

'Don't be cheeky, young lady!' Margaret gently chided. 'Or I might leave you out here until you beg to be brought in.'

'I'm capable of bringing myself in.' In fact she was going up the steps on her own, when previously she'd had to lean heavily on Margaret. 'You see, I'm growing stronger by the day.' Her bright voice belied the trauma inside her. It was true she was growing stronger. But that was on the outside. Inside, where only she could see, something was slowly dying.

That evening, when Ruby was busying herself in the kitchen, Cathy and Margaret sat on the settee. Cathy was watching the sky through the window. 'Do you want to talk?' Margaret asked softly.

Cathy brought her gaze to the older woman. Her voice was soft and surprised. 'What about?'

'Oh, I don't know.' She kept her eyes on Cathy's troubled face. 'Tony Manners perhaps? Or the child? Or we could talk about . . . David.'

The mention of his name brought a glimmer to Cathy's eyes, but it only lasted for a second. 'David's gone,' she said, and the sadness was tenfold.

'You miss him terribly, don't you?' Now that she had got Cathy talking, Margaret didn't want to let the moment go.

Cathy's answer was a curt nod, but it spoke volumes.

'I imagine he's missing you too, sweetheart.'

'No.' How could he be missing her, when she had given him every chance to make amends and he had turned his back on her?

'Cathy, I have to ask . . . was David the father of your child?'

Cathy was shocked. Yet she reasoned it was only natural for Margaret to make such an assumption. 'No,' she answered softly, 'David and I . . . we never actually made love.'

Margaret was at a loss for words. For a long awkward minute she said nothing at all, and then she murmured, 'I didn't mean to pry, you know that.'

'I know.'

'But if David wasn't the father of your child . . .?'

Cathy had said too much already. David was gone. The father of her child was gone, and now so was the poor innocent child itself. There was nothing to be gained from raising the past. 'I'm tired now.' Getting up from the chair she bent to kiss Margaret on the forehead. 'Perhaps we can talk tomorrow?' Margaret made as if to stand up, but stayed put when Cathy told her gratefully, 'I can manage. The stairs are easier for me now.'

It was like climbing a mountain, but Cathy was determined. Racked with pain she went doggedly up the stairs one at a time, pausing for breath after every step. At the top, she turned and smiled at Margaret. 'Good night, God bless.'

'Good night, God bless.' Though she was disappointed that Cathy had curtailed their little talk, Margaret believed she had made a breakthrough. At least now she could put away the idea that David had made Cathy with child. She told Ruby as much.

Ruby was astonished, 'If it ain't David, who the divil is it then?'

'I have my suspicions,' Margaret murmured.

'She might be trying to protect David.'

'It isn't like Cathy to lie.' In fact Margaret's thoughts had been along the same line as Ruby's. 'Mind you, she always had a very protective instinct towards David.'

'There you are then!'

'She misses him dreadfully.'

'Did she say that?'

'Not in so many words, but it was painfully obvious.'

'What about that Tony Manners? Did she say what happened between 'em?'

'She was tired, Ruby. Tomorrow, when she's had a good night's sleep, I'm sure she'll confide in me.'

Cathy didn't have a good night's sleep. At dawn she was still awake, seated by the window and looking at the sky outside, thinking about Margaret's question. Softly she gave the answer again, 'David and I never made love, and now we never will.' In the half-light her eyes glittered with tears. 'She's right though, David . . . I do miss you so.' A solitary tear spilled down her cheek. Wiping it away, she opened the window and braced herself against the rush of cold air.

Dawn peeped over the horizon, and Cathy thought she had never seen a sky more beautiful. Round its edges the golden hue spread like a creeping flame, splintering the silver and black at its heart. She couldn't take her eyes from it, and just for a while its breathtaking beauty brought her a deep sense of peace and contentment.

In the morning, Cathy slept like a child. She slept beyond breakfast time, and into the late morning hours. 'I don't want to wake her,' Margaret said. 'She looked so tired last night.'

At midday, she was still sleeping and Ruby asked, 'Is she unwell, do you think? It ain't like her to sleep such long hours.'

At two o'clock, Margaret woke her. 'You must have something to eat, sweetheart.' Ruby had prepared a tray and the aroma of freshly made tea and muffins filled the room.

Astonished that she had slept for so long, Cathy got out of bed. While Margaret waited she washed and dressed. 'I'm not really hungry,' she said, though on Margaret's insistence she did manage half a muffin and a cup of tea.

While Cathy brushed her hair, Margaret quietly regarded her. She was always shaken nowadays by Cathy's physical appearance; her arms were twig-like, and there was no vitality about her at all. 'How do you feel, sweetheart?' Coming to her side, she put one arm round Cathy's shoulder. 'Is the pain in your ribs lessening?'

'They're getting better. Stop worrying.' It wasn't so much the pain in her ribs that was debilitating. It was the pain in her heart; pain for everything she had lost; pain of a kind she could not explain. Right now, she felt incredibly low, physically drained. But she would overcome it, just as she had always done.

'Ruby wonders whether we should let the doctor see you?'

'I'm mending. There's no need for a doctor.' And to prove her point, she brushed a little rouge on to her cheekbones. 'There! I'm ready for anything now.'

Margaret tutted. 'Shameless hussy,' she said and, hugging each other, they laughed together like they used to.

It was to be a long time before Cathy would laugh like that again. With the assurance that she would follow in a minute, Margaret took the tray downstairs. 'By! Is that all she could manage?' Ruby asked, her manner brightening when she was told how much better Cathy seemed and that she was on her way down. 'Washed, dressed and painted in rouge, would you believe?'

They were still talking when they heard the bump from Cathy's bedroom. Margaret reached her first. 'Get the doctor, Ruby,' she cried. 'Quickly!' Ruby was already halfway down the stairs when Margaret tenderly lifted Cathy from the floor and laid her gently on the bed, shocked at how feather light the girl was in her arms.

The doctor was swift to arrive. He examined Cathy while Margaret and Ruby waited anxiously outside. When he emerged, Ruby went in with Cathy while Margaret accompanied the doctor to the sitting room. 'She's weak and anaemic. I'm not happy about the rate of her recovery.' Snapping his bag shut, he looked at her with an air of frustration. 'Unfortunately, I can't force her to be admitted to the Infirmary.'

Margaret stared at him in disbelief. 'You mean she's refusing?'

'Perhaps you can persuade her?'

Margaret tried but couldn't, and Ruby didn't even make the effort. 'I've come to think you're right,' she said. 'It ain't a doctor Cathy wants. It's someone to share her secrets with. Someone her own age ... someone she thinks to have lost for good.'

'You mean David?'

'Aye, that's who I mean.'

Over the following week, the doctor visited every day, and every day he said the same thing. 'See she takes her tablets, and try to get her eating more.' Cathy took her tablets, and Ruby stood over while she ate the good broth they'd made her. But Cathy grew weaker, and it was heartbreaking to see. 'Please, lass ... will you go to the Infirmary and let them get you well again?' Ruby pleaded. Margaret too sat by her bed and did her utmost to persuade Cathy that she should do as the doctor said.

'I won't get better in the Infirmary.' She was adamant. 'I want to be here, with you. I'll soon be up and about, you'll see.' She made them promise not to send her away, and they prayed they would not live to regret such a promise.

The days flew by, and still Cathy's recovery was painfully slow. 'She's not getting well, is she, Doctor?' Margaret was at her wit's end.

The doctor was truthful. 'She doesn't seem to *want* to get well. When that happens, I'm afraid there's very little we can do.'

'Well, there's something we can do!' Ruby declared when he'd gone. 'We can find David. Fetch him here and then you'll see that bonny lass grow stronger.'

'I've been wondering about that, Ruby.' Margaret was ready to try anything. 'It might work. Cathy has so much unhappiness inside her... pain and heartache that goes back a long long way... to when she was small.' Bowing her head, she covered her face with her hands, recalling how she alone had been both mother and father to that lonely little girl.

Suddenly she was pacing the room. 'We mustn't lose her.' Excited and hopeful, she began to make plans. 'There isn't much money left, but we'll manage. We'll get a private detective and find David at whatever cost. It may not be the answer; he may not want to know... after all, he did turn his back on her, didn't he?' She sat down on the sofa, jerking her head back and forth, desperately making herself believe. 'It's our only hope, Ruby. I'll hire a detective today... tell him all we know about David Leyton and his family. Oh, Ruby... Pray God we're making the right decision!'

Ruby had no doubts. 'If anybody can help her, you mark my words, it's that young man.' She took the liberty of seating herself right next to Margaret. 'But I don't think you should spend your remaining nest egg on a private detective. He'll take your last penny and might not find him anyway.'

Margaret was aware of that. 'But what else can we do?'

'You can send *me*!' Before Margaret could argue, she went on, 'I know what David Leyton looks like. I know what he and the lass meant to each other. When I find him, I can get to the bottom of why he turned his back on her. I've allus wondered about that.' She grinned mischievously. 'Besides, what would you want a private detective for? If anybody can find a needle in a haystack, it's ol' Ruby! What's more, it won't cost yer a farthing... except o' course, there'll be the cooking and such like to do.'

'That's no hardship. And it's a labour of love to look after Cathy.'

'I can go then?'

'With my heartfelt thanks, Ruby.'

A look passed between them that showed their love for Cathy, and for each other. 'I'll find him,' Ruby promised. 'What happens after that. I can't say.'

An hour later, she was ready to leave. Before she said her goodbyes to Margaret, she went up the stairs to Cathy's room.

Gazing down on the sleeping girl, she made a mental note of how thin and drawn that darling face had become; she touched the long fair hair and murmured a promise. 'David never stopped loving yer, lass . . . I know that. In your heart you must know it too. But he hurt yer, didn't he, eh? He hurt yer and he should stand afore yer to say why.' She bent to kiss the sleeping face. 'I'm off to fetch him, lass. If I have to search all the four corners of the earth, I promise you, I'll find him.' As she spoke, the tears ran down her face. 'I'll fetch the bugger back, you see if I don't!'

Margaret gave her enough money to see her all right for at least a week. 'It should be me going, not you,' she argued.

'And why's that?' Ruby asked indignantly. 'Reckon I'm too old, is that it?' Collecting her big tapestry bag, she put the wallet inside. 'I may be long in the tooth, but I can take care of meself, don't you worry about me.'

Margaret waved her off, and she knew she would worry every minute of every day until Ruby returned.

Upstairs, Cathy stirred. 'Ruby?' Hoisting herself on to one elbow, she looked round the room. 'Ruby, is that you?' When there was no answer, she fell back into the pillow and closed her eyes, but she could still hear Ruby's promise.

'Ruby's bringing David home,' Cathy whispered. And, for the first time in many long months, the burden began to lift from her heart.

PART TWO

1901

. . . Come True

CHAPTER ELEVEN

The heat was unbearable. From the first day of June, the sun had beaten down, parching the earth and singeing the crops. Since then, there had been no let up; no breeze, no flicker of clouds in the sky; all was still. Even the branches drooped.

Two men laboured in the field; one a man of about sixty, the other a strapping young fellow with thick dark hair and smiling black eyes. Stripped to the waist, his tanned shoulders glistened with sweat in the merciless sun. Since the early hours they had laboured in the field, layering the hedges and clearing the land beneath. It was hard back-breaking work, but when he stepped back to survey the end result, David was proud. 'That's a good job done, Ted,' he remarked, and the older man was quick to agree.

Taking off his cap to wipe the sweat from his eyes, David peered at the approaching figure. 'Looks like Barney,' he said.

The older man joined him. 'Aye, it's him right enough.'

David was puzzled. 'What's he doing right out here?' Barney was the gentleman farmer's runabout.

'Summat's up, I reckon.' A deep frown etched itself into his old weathered features. 'That bugger don't stir from the comfort of his office unless there's a good enough reason.'

Together they waited, anxious now, expecting the worst.

Barney Lent was a little man in every sense of the word; no more than five foot tall, with close-set eyes and thin brown hair, he puffed and panted, out of sorts and out of temper. 'I've been sent to fetch you,' he panted. 'The boss wants you back at the farm, and he wants you now!'

David grinned, his straight white teeth lighting up a face darkened with sweat and earth. 'You needn't have bothered coming all the way out here,' he said. 'We're just about to pack up and make our way back.'

Barney's temper wasn't improved. 'Get on then!' he snapped. 'The boss is waiting, and you know what an impatient bugger he can be!' With that he swung away and began to retrace his steps through the rows of prime cabbages. 'Get on! Get on!' he called behind him. 'I've done what he asked and I can't do no more!'

David couldn't see rhyme nor reason in Barney's trudging all the way back when he could have a ride on the wagon. 'Get on the cart,' he yelled. 'We'll take you back with us in half the time.'

Barney was disgusted. 'What! Climb on that filthy contraption, and me in my decent clothes. Be buggered!'

His reply had the two men in fits of laughter. 'Oh, la de da!' spluttered the older man, his eyes round and mocking. 'Mustn't get our pretty clothes dirty ... and we certainly mustn't sit aside two men covered with muck and sweat. Whatever next?'

David didn't care much for Barney, but he felt bad about mocking him. All the same, he couldn't help but laugh. 'Honest to God,' he remarked, watching the irate figure step daintily in and out of the market crop, 'it beats me how a fussy bloke like Barney ever came to work on a farm.'

''Course ... being here only three months, you wouldn't know, would you?' queried the older man. 'When Mr Reed Barton bought the farm and moved into the big house, Barney came with him. Apparently he was butler to Reed Barton when they resided in the heart of London town.' He winked. 'Mind you, I reckon there were more to it than master and butler ... have you seen the way them two look at each other?'

David was intrigued. 'Can't say I have.'

'Aye, well, that's because you live at the cottage some two mile away, and I live at the back of the big house.' He chuckled. 'There ain't much I miss, I can tell you.'

'Better not.'

'What you don't know you can't tell, eh?'

'Something like that.' David had wondered about the relationship between the boss and Barney Lent. But that was their business, not his. 'We'd best get back,' he said, slipping on his shirt.

'Aye,' the other man agreed sombrely. 'We wouldn't want Barney to get in trouble with his sweetheart.' He laughed out loud, and David couldn't help but smile. But beneath the smile was an aching heart as he thought of a sweetheart he once had. Time and again he had wondered about Cathy, about why she had turned against him the way she did. Surely to God she must have known he would have moved heaven and earth for things to have been different. What happened between their parents was no more his fault than it was Cathy's. One day, when he could trust himself not to grab her in his arms, he would seek her out and tell her that. Until then, he had to live without her, and never expect to hold her in his arms again.

As always when his heart was pained with memories of Cathy, he distracted himself with other things. Soon the wagon was loaded with the pitchforks and axes, and the two of them were seated up top. David slapped the reins and got the horses gently moving, and the older fellow quietly smoked his pipe. 'I wonder why the boss wants to see us?' David mused aloud. 'It must be important for Barney to be sent.'

'Summat and nothing, I expect.'

'No, I think it's more than that.' Coming towards the back of the house, David glanced at the other man. 'When have you ever known him to send Barney after us?'

'Never.' They were lost in thought, each with their own explanation, each with their own worries. 'You've got me wondering proper now.' Tapping out his pipe on the side of the wagon, Ted went on, 'Summat's always puzzled me about Reed Barton.'

'You've already said.'

'No. I don't mean about whether them two lie in the hay together.' The very idea was unnatural to him. 'If they want to tickle each other's fancy, that's up to them . . . so long as they don't want to tickle *mine*!' His face hardened to a serious expression. 'What I'm saying is this . . . why would a businessman . . . a gent from the city . . . why would he move to the outskirts of Ilford and buy a market gardening business? You have to admit, he doesn't know the first thing about farming. I mean, he relies on you for everything. I'm old and knackered, but he's latched on to you as his saviour. It's you as says what crops need planting, you as buys and sells, and he leans on you for every little thing. In the short time you've been here you've worked miracles. You've been to auction and bought his stallions, sorted the mares and found the finest hunters round here for miles. You plan his working diary . . . and all you get for your trouble is a labourer's wage and a three-bedroomed cottage.'

'It'll do me for now, Ted.' He had his ambitions though. One day he meant to have his own farm, and his own big house. One day . . .

'Can you explain why a gent like that should move out of the city and live in the country? It ain't natural. He's like a fish outta water. The man don't belong here. Any fool can see he's not happy.'

'Happen he's had enough of city life.'

'If that's the case, why is he there more than he is here?' Ted tapped David on the arm. 'Answer me that! If he's so fed up with city life, why is he allus popping back and leaving you in charge?'

'I don't know, and I'm not sure I want to.'

The old fellow leaned back in his seat and sighed. 'And I'm not sure I want to know why he's sent for us. I've been expecting him to pay me off. He knows I'm past my best. He wants rid, that's what'll it be . . . got some strapping young fella such as yourself to take my place.' His voice broke. 'I don't know what I'd do if he asked me to leave. I've lived in that cottage for over thirty years . . . me and the missus, till she passed on five year since.'

'So you weren't much older than me when you first came here?' It wasn't hard to imagine him as a young man. Ted was still broad of back and walked as upright as a man half his age. He had a strong craggy face, with twinkling blue eyes and a smile that revealed a kind happy nature.

'I were coming up twenty-nine, newly wed, and excited to be moving into our first real home.' His eyes misted over. 'We loved that cottage from first sight. The owners were a fair-minded couple, and they paid good wages. Oh, aye, apart from never having children, we had a good life, me and the missus. When the owners retired, Reed Barton bought this place with me as part of the fixtures and fittings.' He sighed deeply. 'I were a fitter man then. These days I'm a bloody old crock!'

'Don't belittle yourself, Ted.' David had grown fond of him. 'You might be a few years older and a bit slower, but you give a good day's work for a good day's pay. Besides, you know farming inside out, and he's well aware of that.' Playfully thumping him on the shoulder, David smiled encouragingly. 'Reed Barton won't get rid of you,' he told him confidently. 'Don't concern yourself about that.'

'You'd speak up for me, would you?'

There was a smile on David's lips as he glanced at him. 'I don't know about that . . .' he teased.

The old fella chuckled. 'You're a grand 'un!' he said. 'Salt of the earth.'

When they drew into the yard there was no sign of Barney. 'The bugger ain't fell down a rat'ole has he?' chuckled Ted. And the two of them were still chuckling as they reported to the office.

Barney Lent's office was a converted outbuilding at the back of the house. It was only a stone's throw from Ted's humble abode, though the two buildings were separated by a high laurel hedge that afforded Ted all the privacy he needed.

Mr Reed Barton was seated behind the desk. A huge man with staring eyes and an abundance of dark hair round his face and chin, he presented a formidable sight. 'Where's that fool Barney?' he demanded in a rasping voice. 'I want him here.'

It was David who answered. 'He's on his way.'

'Why the hell didn't he ride back on the wagon with the two of you?'

'You'll have to ask *him* that.' It was all David could do not to chuckle.

'Oh! I see.' The slightest hint of a smile lifted the corners of the big man's mouth. 'Too particular to ride with the peasants, eh?' He coughed and cleared his throat, and got out of the chair. 'We'll wait for the daft bugger!' he said.

Clutching his hands together behind his back, he walked to the window and looked out across the fields. Struggling towards the house was Barney. 'Here he is now,' he observed. He watched the door for Barney's entrance.

It was only a few minutes before he tumbled in, gasping and moaning, and swearing beneath his breath. 'Look at my boots!'

he grumbled, pointing to his mud-caked feet. The pungent smell of damp manure filled the air.

'Bugger your boots! You stink to high heaven!' The big man gestured for him to sit behind the desk. 'But take your boots off first and leave them far enough away so we won't be choked.' As Barney struggled to untie his laces, he added impatiently, 'It's beyond me how you managed to make such a mess of yourself when there hasn't been a drop of rain in over a week!'

It was hard for David to keep a straight face as he surmised, 'I expect he came by way of the onion beds. That ground is prone to dryness, so I fill in the trenches with horse manure ... helps keep the moisture in.' He bit his lip to stem the rising laughter, and beside him Ted choked as he too kept a straight face. 'Before the dry spell we had a deluge of rain as you know,' David explained. 'As the field slopes to the onion bed, I expect Barney sank in to his ankles.' He glanced at Barney, who was taking off the other boot. 'He might as well throw them away because they'll never be the same again.'

The big man followed David's glance, and when he saw Barney, barefoot and red in the face, he laughed out loud. 'Serves you right!' he cried. 'Next time you might be glad of a ride on the wagon.'

As suddenly as he had laughed, he became hard-faced. 'Get out of my sight. Come back when you smell a bit sweeter, damn you!' He waited until Barney had scuttled away then seated himself behind the desk once more, his staring eyes fixed on the two men. 'You're no doubt wondering why I've sent for you?' His question was addressed to David, who was also looking grim-faced.

'That's right.' Sensing there was bad news to come, he had no desire to prolong the inevitable.

'Right. Well ... I won't keep you in suspense,' he said. 'The truth is, I was never a farmer. Buying this place suited me at the time, but now I'm selling up.' Leaning back in the chair, he tucked the tips of his thumbs behind his broad leather braces. 'You shouldn't be too surprised,' he remarked harshly. 'You must have known I was out of my element.'

Ted grew bold. 'Will you be selling everything, sir?'

'Lock, stock and barrel.' Anticipating the next question, he looked from one to the other. 'I'm sorry, Ted ... the cottages are included. *Both* of them.' He looked at David. 'You won't find it hard to get another job. I have nothing but praise for you.'

'Not much consolation though.' David had half expected this, but it was a bitter blow, especially coming when his mother was bedridden and with Teresa going off the rails.

The big man spoke to Ted. 'I can't promise anything,' he commented, 'and I won't make it a condition of sale, but I will have a word on your behalf with whoever buys this place.'

'If they chuck me off, sir, that'll be the end of me.' There were tears in his eyes. 'But I'd be grateful for anything you could do to let me keep my cottage.'

'Remember, I'm making no promises.'

'No, sir.'

'Now get off home.'

'There's the wagon and horses to see to first.' He sounded heart-weary.

David touched him on the shoulder. 'It's all right, Ted,' he said quietly. 'I'll see to the horses. You go and put your feet up.'

'Will you call in on your way home?'

'If you want me to.'

Ted nodded, excused himself to the boss, and shuffled out. David turned his attention to the man behind the desk. 'Losing his home means losing everything. He's no family, and all his memories are in that cottage.'

'Not my problem.'

'Then what you said to him ... about having a word on his behalf? Just talk was it?'

'Nobody's going to keep Ted on.'

David's blood was boiling. 'You've no right to get his hopes up like that.'

'They'd keep *you* on though.'

'I dare say they would.'

'Do you want me to keep that in mind?'

'Maybe. Maybe not.'

David's quiet smile made him curious. 'You always were a deep bugger.' He got out of his chair and came round the desk. 'Got plans have you?'

'A man always has plans.' David had been careful with his

money, but for something like this farm it was nowhere near enough. 'Would you rent the farm to me?'

The big man shook his head, took out a cigar and chewed on it. 'Sorry. I need the money.'

'Would you rent the field . . . the one we keep for market-gardening?'

'Not even a handkerchief square.'

'Then there's no more to be said.' He could see he was wasting his time, and he had to get home. Teresa had stayed away again last night. She was causing their mother a deal of heartache, and it was time for a showdown. 'How long will it be before we're paid up?'

'You've got until I sell the property . . . could be a week, a month . . . a bit longer. It can't be soon enough for me.' Having got the worst over, he could afford to be arrogant. 'Ted will manage, so will you . . . especially you. You're young and strong, and you've a good head on your shoulders, and I dare say there'll come a day when it'll be *you* paying the wages. You're a man to be reckoned with, young Leyton!'

'You're right about that.' David's ambitions were strengthened by this setback.

Going to the door, the big man opened it wide. 'I expect you think I'm insane . . . giving up this place. But you see, I'm a city man bred and born. Once this lot's auctioned off, I'll pocket the money and be away, and you'll never set eyes on me again.'

Ted wasn't surprised to hear Reed Barton couldn't wait to get away. 'The city's where he belongs,' he said. 'Leave the country-side to them as loves it.'

'I'm sorry I said he wouldn't get rid of you. I had an idea he wouldn't stay too long round these parts, but I honestly didn't think he'd sell up so soon.'

'His sort come and go.' Ted had been rocking himself back-wards and forwards in the big wooden rocker that he had made with his own hands, but now he brought it to a halt. 'I've been so busy thinking about myself I never gave you and yours a thought. What with your mam and your sister, you've *three* to worry about. What will you do, son? Back on the road, is it?'

'Mebbe.' His answer was given in a soft thoughtful tone.

The older man was intrigued. 'You've summat up your sleeve, I can tell.'

'A dream, Ted.' David had never lost sight of his ambition of one day being his own master. 'I've always wanted my own land, and I shan't rest till I have it.'

Ted shook his head and sighed. 'By! There's no justice in the world. Reed Barton has no love for the land, yet he owns a farm that you'd give your right arm for.'

David smiled. 'I don't know about my right arm. What use would I be without that, eh?'

'I wish to God the farm were yours. I'd have a better chance of keeping this 'ere cottage then, wouldn't I, eh?'

'A man who works like you do? Goes without saying.'

'I don't suppose there's a way?' He was shaking his head even as he asked. 'No . . . that would be asking too much.'

David had been racking his brain. 'Nobody wishes more than I do that I could get hold of the farm,' he admitted. 'Or even the five-acre field we were working in today. That would be enough to get me started.' He took a deep invigorating breath, letting it out noisily through his nose. 'I can't see it happening though . . . not without a miracle, and that's not about to happen.' He was used to wanting things and not having them. Look how often he'd prayed that a miracle might fetch Cathy back to him. And he was still waiting.

'Happen he'll not find a buyer.' Ted brightened at the thought.

'Oh, he'll find a buyer right enough!' Striding to the door, David prepared to leave. 'I'll see you the morrow then?'

'Unless the good Lord decides otherwise.'

'He'd better not!' Going out of the door, David cheered him up. 'You tell him there's half a field of spuds to be bagged yet.'

'Get away home with you!'

As a rule David whistled as he walked home. But not tonight. Tonight he was too deep in thought. 'If there was a way to buy that field and the cottages, I'd walk through burning coals in my bare feet,' he muttered. But it took more than courage to buy land. It took money, and as yet he had none to speak of.

Maria had spent the last half hour watching through the bed-room window for her son to come home. When she saw him striding towards the house, she rattled the window with her stick, frantically waving at him when his attention was caught.

He came into the cottage at a run. 'Are you all right, Mam?' Rushing into the bedroom, he was relieved when she nodded her head and struggled to sit up. 'Here, lean on me.' Stretching out his arms, he pressed his shoulder to hers. 'I'm sorry to be late,' he apologised, thinking that was why she had panicked. 'I called in on Ted as I made my way home.' She seemed more settled now, so he sat in the rocking chair and regarded her more closely. Always a little woman, she seemed lately to have shrunk and, with her large pale eyes, looked like a little doll.

While she settled herself comfortably, he glanced curiously round the room. Something occurred to him. Just now, when he came through the cottage, there had been no sign of his sister. 'Where's Teresa?' Searching Maria's face he knew there was something wrong. 'She should have been home from work long since,' he said, looking at the bedside clock; it was ten minutes past five. 'She's always home soon after midday. The draper knows she has to be back for you ... he never keeps her late.' He was on his feet now, angry that Maria had been left on her own for so long.

'It doesn't matter now, son.' She wanted no trouble. '*You're* home now. That's all as matters.'

'Where is she, Mam?' His dark eyes glittered angrily.

'She'll be back when she's ready, I dare say.'

'You knocked the window when you saw me coming ... you've been waiting for me ... wanting to tell me something. What, Mam? What is it you're worried about?'

'She won't listen.' Maria began crying. 'I've argued with her till I'm blue in the face, and she'll not listen to a word I say.'

'She'll listen to *me*, the bugger!' Taking a handkerchief from the bedside drawer, he tenderly wiped her eyes, afterwards putting the handkerchief into her hand. 'What the devil's she been up to now? Will she never give you any peace?'

Maria was loth to tell him, but she had to. Teresa was getting in over her head, and unless she came to her senses was bound to come to a bad end. If anybody could talk sense into her, it was David. 'You know she's been restless for weeks now?'

'Aye. Ever since she met that slimy bloke from the City.'

David was listening intently. 'Go on, Mam . . . what's happened?'

'She didn't go to work this morning. When I asked her why, she flew into a temper . . . said she'd packed the work in . . . said she was sick to death of living hand to mouth, and wanted something more glamorous than being a draper's assistant.' She rolled her eyes. 'That Manners fella told her she had a good singing voice . . . said he could make her rich.'

'She's gone to London, is that it?' He was angry with himself, 'I should have seen it coming.'

Maria shook her head. 'Teresa has a mind of her own, and she's always been devious. I honestly thought she'd seen the badness in that fella, but I was wrong, because that's where she's gone right enough. Packed her bag and left early this morning.' Turning on her side she winced, her blue eyes closing in agony. 'Right bloody man about town that Manners bloke – apparently he has his fingers in all kinds of deals, North *and* South.'

'God Almighty! You've been on your own all day!'

Maria forced a smile. 'I've come to no harm,' she assured him. 'But I'm glad you're home now, son.' She hesitated to ask, especially when she knew he'd been working on the land since early light. She looked at his face, such a strong handsome face. He never talked about Cathy, but Maria knew he would never forget her. She thought it sad that the girl had blamed David for all that happened. 'I'm sorry,' she murmured. 'Your sister and I are a great burden to you.'

'You're never that, Mam. As for Teresa, she's headstrong and easily led. She has to grow up, and the sooner the better.'

He lapsed into deep thought, deciding what to do. 'Look at me, son,' Maria said softly, and he raised his dark eyes to hers. 'Will you fetch her?' she asked. 'Will you go to the city and fetch our Teresa home?'

The dark eyes smiled, a deep-down smile that put her heart at ease. 'Oh, I'll fetch her, don't you worry about that,' he promised. The tension was over. 'There's time enough. I expect she'll be in that club where I found her once before . . . it's less than a half hour away, so I've time to get us both something to eat. After I'm washed and changed, I'll backtrack and fetch Ted . . . he'll be glad to keep you company while I'm gone.' His jaw worked angrily. 'I'm not leaving you on your own again.'

It was settled. In no time at all, David had sliced the ham, boiled four eggs, made the tea, and set it all out on two trays, with a large chunk of bread for himself and a smaller one for Maria. 'It's too much for me,' she complained, but she ate both eggs and half the bread. After that she swallowed two cups of tea and asked for another.

Washed and changed into a clean blue shirt and dark trousers, David was gone less than ten minutes before he returned with Ted. 'The two of you can keep each other company,' he told Maria, and she urged him to make tracks and find his sister. She also reminded him, 'You don't know how long it'll take for you to find her. Late evening can get chilly, so you'd best take your jacket.'

Kissing her fleetingly, he took his leave. 'Hopefully I'll be back before dark,' he told them. Whether or not he would have Teresa with him was another matter altogether. She had a way of losing herself when it suited her.

Tony Manners sat in the darkest corner, tapping his feet to the music and wondering whether he had done the right thing in getting tangled up with the Leyton woman. He said as much to his colleague, a red-headed fellow with stubble on his chin and a down-turned mouth that betrayed his surly nature. 'Women is nothing but trouble!' the fellow drawled. 'Take my woman ... you've seen her in here, ain't yer?'

'Maggie, isn't it?' He'd seen her time and again; a slim-built creature with big sad eyes, and no wonder when she was kept little more than a beggar, and stayed beholden to a man who beat her till she was black and blue. But then, women did that to a man; they had a habit of bringing the worst out in even the mildest of chaps. Look how Cathy Blackthorn had led him on and then caused him to run. And now, because of her, he had to keep his distance from Blackburn ... William Henry Street in particular. Still, though he might be a rogue and a coward, and only just managed to stay on the right side of the law, he didn't see himself as being as rotten as this fellow beside him. If it wasn't for the fact that he did a lot of underhand deals with the foul-smelling scoundrel, he'd tell him to piss off.

The last thing he wanted was to sit here and pass precious time with him. They had already done their business for the night, and now he had an urge to take Teresa upstairs.

The other fellow eyed him suspiciously. 'I'm surprised you remembered her name. But you're right, it is Maggie.' He tested Tony further. 'Hey! You've not got a hankering for her, 'ave yer?'

Tony Manners pointed to Teresa, who was preparing to sing. 'I've got my own entertainment,' he chuckled. 'Why would I hanker after anyone else's?'

The surly fellow turned his attention on Teresa. 'You know how to pick 'em, I'll say that for yer. She's a good looker an' no mistake.' Eyeing her up and down, he fancied her himself; a big girl in every respect, she had the most striking blue eyes, long brown hair that shone like silk in the hazy half-light, and a personality that drew every man's eyes to her. He sniggered. 'Good between the sheets, is she?'

'Wouldn't entertain her if she weren't.'

'Sings like a bird too. By all accounts, she'd do it for nothing more than the attention it gets her.' He tapped the side of his nose and winked. 'Clever of you to wheedle a paypacket out of the proprietor here. As a rule, he wouldn't part with the drippings of his nose.'

'She sings ... he pays. You don't get nothing for nothing.'

'He pays and you pocket it, eh?'

'None of your business.'

'All right, matey! Just being friendly.' Settling back in his seat, he made the snide comment, 'All the same, fancy you remembering Maggie's name.' He didn't want her, but he would cut the heart out of any man who thought he could take her from him.

'Don't make such a thing out of it,' Tony Manners warned. 'I've a good head for names, that's all. You can ask me the name of every man jack in this room, and I dare say I could tell you.' In the shady business of 'buying and selling', he had to know whose company he was keeping.

The other fellow seemed satisfied, but secretly he vowed to question Maggie about it later. 'There was a time when she was a raving beauty, but not now. Gone to seed she has.' He guffawed so loud everyone turned to glare at him, but they quickly averted their attention when he glared back. 'Fit for nothing now she is,' he continued. 'Can't seem to keep me satisfied no more. Yer can't blame a man for wandering, can yer, eh?' Drawing deeply on his cigar he exhaled the smoke over the man on his other side, but the man didn't complain. He didn't fancy being left for dead in the alley one dark night.

'Wander a lot, do you?'

'Every chance I get, matey.' Leaning sideways, he whispered, 'Being a man of the world yerself, you must have had yer fair share?'

'I'm not complaining.'

'Like me, I expect you've suffered for the sake of making a profit?'

'I don't follow.'

'What I mean is . . . sometimes you have to butter a woman up, however much you'd rather put a bag over her head.' He sighed impatiently and took another drag on his cigar. 'There were this woman, d'yer see? Ruby I think 'er name were.' He coughed and spluttered and laughed through his words. 'Some bloody Ruby! You'd think with a name like that she'd be hot to the touch and raring to go. Not this one! This partic'lar Ruby were sixty if she were a day, and well past 'er prime.'

'So why would you want to butter her up?' In spite of himself he was intrigued.

'Use your brains, man! I found meself out in the country, stalking a young bugger who thought he could get one over on me. The housekeeper were a means to an end, weren't she? She worked in this big house . . . had access to silver and the like. Through her, I got inside information, didn't I, eh? The silly old cow thought we'd be wed. She couldn't see I were using 'er.' He smiled from ear to ear. 'Trusting she were . . . lonely and trusting. When they're like that, they tell yer things they don't even know they're telling yer.'

'I thought *I* were bad enough.'

'You've a long way to go afore you catch up wi' me.' His dirty face shone with pride.

The music softened and the order was given, 'Quiet now, men! Let the young lady sing.' The compère stepped back and

Teresa came into the spotlight. Her voice rang out loud and clear, vibrant and filled with emotion. All eyes were on her, and for a time you could have heard a pin drop.

Tony Manners congratulated himself on having acquired such a prize. On top of that, she doted on him. It couldn't be easier. With her voice and his shrewd business acumen, he believed he would be a richer man in no time. His temper shortened when the burly fellow interrupted. 'Never met Maggie's son, 'ave yer?'

'Can't say I have.' Picking up his glass, he took a long gulp of whisky. 'He's not *your* son, then?'

'She says he is, but there's times when I wonder.' A murderous look came into his face. 'Them two's as thick as thieves. Some time back he cleared off.' A dark satisfaction came into his face. 'He thought I couldn't find out where he were... hadn't reckoned on somebody being as artful as himself, the cocky bastard! But I never once let him know I were on to him. Oh no! I let him go on thinking he were getting one over on me, when all the time I were closer than his bleedin' shadow.'

'Watching him, were you?'

'Oh, I were doing much more than that.' He licked his lips. 'Anyway, after a while... back he comes, large as life, and his pockets bulging.' He groaned as though in pain. 'He never shared it with me though, the crafty bugger! Took off, he did, an' I ain't seen hide nor hair of him since.' Ramming the cigar into his mouth, he narrowed his eyes and spoke around it. 'If he knows what's good for him, he'll stay outta my way altogether.' There was menace in his voice, and madness in his eyes. 'I've an idea his mam knows where her precious Jack is. But if the pair of 'em think to cheat me out of my share, they'd best think again.'

'And you reckon this Jack might not be yours, eh?' Sniggering, Tony observed cunningly, 'Sounds to me like he's a chip off the old block.'

'Happen he's mine, and happen he ain't, but there's no two ways about it... Jack is a bad bugger all right.' He got a deal of satisfaction out of adding spitefully, 'Maggie thinks the sun shines out of his arse, but I keep telling her, one o' these fine days he'll swing from the end of a rope.'

'That's what people say about you.' Tony was taking his life into his hands, but thought himself a match for this clumsy bag of wind.

The burly fellow roared with laughter. 'Oh, an' they'd be right an' all!' he cried, much to the irritation of a nearby group who were intent on listening to Teresa sing. 'What the bloody hell are yer staring at, eh?' he yelled. 'Keep yer eyes frontard where they belong . . . less yer want 'em gouged outta yer head!' He laughed again when they turned away. But the music had stopped and Teresa was coming towards them. From the look on her face it was plain she did not like being upstaged.

'You might have the bloody decency to listen when I put myself out for you!' With her hands on her hips she stood in front of them, staring from one to the other and saving her most withering look for Tony Manners.

In a minute he was at her side, charming as ever, mentally calculating whether he should still demand payment from the proprietor. 'What makes you think I wasn't listening?' he coaxed. 'There might be some who don't appreciate you, my love, but not me.' He glanced scathingly at the burly fellow. 'I *know* a true songbird when I hear one.'

'Let's get out of here.' Sidling closer to him, she murmured in his ear, 'You and me on our own, eh? We could go back to your flat. You've been promising for ages to show me your place, but you never have.' It was a bone of contention with her. Before Tony came along, the only man in her life was her brother David. 'You know I worship the ground you walk on, but don't make a fool of me,' she muttered. 'I can be all the things you want, but one thing I *won't* be is a plaything you can use and throw away.'

He didn't like the tone of her voice, and he didn't care much for being threatened by any woman, yet he had to tread carefully, because though she talked like a navvy, she had the voice of an angel and *that* was what attracted him, nothing else. Still, he could play her game if that's what she wanted. 'I told you I'd take you to my place, and I will,' he told her. 'First things first, my beauty.'

Propelling her back-stage, he urged, 'Finish your song or we won't get paid, and if we don't get paid, how am I expected to provide a little love nest, eh?' He was a master of charm and deception.

'Put like that, how can I refuse?' Kissing him brazenly, she followed like a dog.

A few minutes later, she was on stage again; this time the house was quiet and her mentor had moved to a table far away from interruptions. He had made an investment in Teresa Leyton, and he was counting on a high return for his time and effort.

When she finished singing, the house erupted into applause. She bowed and smiled, and kept her beady eyes on the man who had brought her. 'I've done what you wanted,' she reminded him later. 'Now it's time you did what I want.' She put on her coat and wouldn't take no for an answer. As they passed him on their way out, the burly fellow winked obscenely. 'If you don't want her, I'll take her off your hands,' he offered in a slurred voice. When Teresa replied she would rather sleep with a hairy monkey, he fell back in his seat and howled with laughter.

He was still laughing a short time later when David came through the door. Convinced he had seen David before, he engaged him in conversation. 'Ain't you the brother of the one who sings here?' Recalling how she had snapped at him, he went on to describe her as 'the songbird with a sharp beak.' David ignored him, so he persisted, 'If I remember rightly, you and 'er boyfriend almost came to blows.' He thought it was an opportunity missed because he loved a good punch-up, but the cowardly Tony Manners took off rather than have his face put out of shape.

Not recognising the fellow, David didn't pay him much mind until he heard him sneer, 'You've missed the buggers this time, matey. They were 'ere one minute and gone the next.'

Peering through the rising clouds of tobacco smoke, David made certain Teresa was nowhere to be seen. Reluctantly, he asked the burly fellow, 'Was she with Tony Manners?'

'All over him.' He grinned meaningfully.

'Mind your mouth!' David stood over him, his dark eyes smouldering and fists clenched. 'I'm in no mood for your filthy jokes.'

The burly fellow sat up straight, his boozy features drooping to a scowl. He didn't take kindly to being spoken to like that. However, he took careful stock of this young man; the strong broad shoulders and the upright stance . . . the look of determination in the dark eyes. He knew he'd met his match. 'Get a move on, and you might catch 'em,' he grumbled. 'They ain't been gone above five minutes.'

David gave no answer. He left then, searching the dim-lit streets outside, looking for the familiar figure of his sister.

Seeing a likely chance, Maggie stepped forward from the alley where she'd been talking with her son, Jack. 'Got a spare coin for a poor lady?' Stretching out her hand she stared solemnly at David, smiling her gratitude when he thrust his hand into his trouser pocket and dropped a shilling into her palm. 'Thank you, sir,' she murmured, and would have slipped away if he hadn't called her back.

'Have you seen a couple come out of there in the last few minutes?' he asked anxiously. 'The man looks a slimy devil ... you couldn't mistake him.' Pointing to the club, he explained, 'The young woman sings here occasionally ... long brown hair ... taller than you.'

Maggie laughed. 'Every woman in London must be taller than me!' she said. She saw how he was frantically searching up and down the street, and was sorry she couldn't help. 'I've only just come along meself,' she explained. 'Me and my son 'ere.' Turning, she called out, 'You ain't seen no couple come out o' the club, 'ave yer?' Only silence greeted her. 'Musta gone.' She smiled. 'I'll say good night, young fella, though I hope you find who you're looking for.'

'Thank you.' He didn't hear her reply. He was already making his way to the driver of a cab waiting nearby.

Maggie searched the alley. 'Jack!' All was quiet. Only the plaintive mewing of a cat disturbed the silence. 'Jack, you ignorant sod! Where are you?' She nearly jumped out of her skin when he stepped out of a doorway. 'Good God above! What the devil d'you think you're playing at?'

His crafty face leered at her under the lamplight. 'I might ask you the same thing, mother dear,' he mocked.

'What d'you mean?'

'Well! Darting out like that ... begging for a copper. I've already told you we can set our sights higher now.'

'Bad habits die hard, our Jack.'

'We can take time to think what to do now.' He jutted out

his chin and smiled knowingly. 'Now that we've got summat tucked away ... where *he'll* never find it.' He jerked a thumb in the direction of the club. When he looked at Maggie again she had a guilty expression on her face. 'Hey!' He took her by the shoulders and shook her. 'You've not told him, have you? Because if you have, I'm off, and this time I won't be back!'

'No.' Pushing him away she answered truthfully, 'I promised you I wouldn't tell, and I won't.' She lowered her head and stared at the ground. 'It's just that I'm frightened he'll find out somehow.' She raised her sad eyes. 'He knows you've come home flush ... he don't know about the silver and such but he knows summat.'

'Let him think what he likes. He'll not find out. There's only you and me know what's stashed away.' Bunching his fists together, he hissed, 'It's all this bloody waiting! I want to get rid of the stuff *now* ... any of the fences would turn it over for me. Tony Manners would give me a good price for it. But I daren't put the word out. Not yet. Not until the rozzers have given up on it.'

'Do you think they're on to you?'

'Naw, I don't think that. But they must be searching far and wide.' He glanced to the end of the alley. 'That bloke ... the one you spoke to just now ...'

'What about him?'

'He could be looking for me.'

'Why should he be looking for you? Anyway, you're wrong. He was asking after a couple.'

'Tricks! They're up to all manner o' tricks.' Lowering his voice he confided, 'That bloke knows the family I stole from. I fancied my chances with a young beauty called Cathy, but that bugger there scotched any hope o' that!' The memory of the night he took her against her will brought a flush of delight to his face. 'But I got to taste her afore I took off.'

Maggie grabbed him by the coat collar, her voice gruff as she told him, 'I hope you don't mean what I think you mean! If you're going the same way as him in there, I'll disown you, so help me I will!' She too had been taken against her will many times, and loathed the idea that her own son could cause another woman the pain and humiliation she herself had to suffer.

Pointing to her neck, she bared a long jagged scar. 'That great bully nearly did for me,' she grumbled. 'I don't want you ending up like him, d'you hear?'

'Get your paws off me!' Shaking her loose, he stepped back a pace. 'I don't know what I'm saying, that's all,' he lied. 'Seeing that bloke has put me right off me stride. His name's David Leyton.' Instinctively he stroked his face, momentarily feeling the crunch of David's fist. 'Him and me ... we had a bad run-in. One sniff that I'm here, an' he'll keep after me like a dog with a bone.'

'So that's why you hid just now?'

'Huh! Don't go away with the wrong idea. I didn't hide because I'm scared of the bugger. It's just that there's no sense looking for trouble, is there, eh?'

'You're right, son.' Glancing furtively about, she suggested, 'You'd best make tracks, but keep outta sight.' Glancing anxiously behind her, she hissed, 'I'd best be off. If I don't go inside now, he'll be out looking for me.'

Together they walked to the end of the alley. Long after Maggie had gone inside, Jack remained, his eyes turned towards the top of the street where David stood talking to the cab-driver.

'Want a fare, matey?' The driver was seated up top, warmly wrapped against the evening and enjoying his clay pipe.

'Not yet,' David answered. He explained he was looking for a couple; the young woman was his sister and he had to find her. When the cab-driver shook his head and said he'd been taking a nap while he waited, David thanked him. 'I'll walk the length of the street and ask in a few of the cafés,' he decided. 'But I've a feeling I'll not find her tonight.'

'The city's a big place. If you want the advice of them as knows, you'd do better to get off home and start again in the daylight.'

'I reckon you're right. But I can't give up so easily.' He glanced back at the club. 'Wait here,' he said. 'I'll only be a minute'

'I'll wait half the night as long as you pay me,' came the chirpy retort.

Inside the club, David sought out the proprietor. 'Sorry, but I can't help you.' Beads of sweat ran down the podgy face as he blatantly lied to the young man who had caused trouble here

702

once before. 'I've no idea where Tony Manners might have gone with your sister.'

'Do you know where he lives?'

'Not a clue!'

'Are they likely to come back tonight?'

'Naw. She's done her singing for the evening. Mr Manners didn't book her in again.' He smiled cunningly. 'Happen he's got her booked in at the Palladium,' he jeered. 'Manners has his sights set higher than a flea-pit like this. He's got the push and she's got the voice. It wouldn't surprise me if he didn't get her right to the top.' He lowered his voice. 'From what I'm told, he owns properties in the North. Happen he's taken her there?'

'And happen you're trying to send me on a wild-goose chase!' David had taken an instant dislike to this greasy fellow. 'Another Manners in the making,' he muttered as he returned to the cab. 'You're right,' he admitted to the cab-driver, 'I'll not find her tonight. The rat's returned to his hole and he's taken her with him, but he's bound to show his face again, and when he does, I'll be waiting.' With that he gave directions and settled back in his seat. 'Property in the North, eh?' he mused aloud. 'I wonder?' It could be a ruse as he suspected. He didn't doubt that Manners owned properties everywhere. Scavengers like that made good by climbing on the backs of others. Manners was a bad lot and, one way or another, David had to make Teresa see that.

Maria took the news well. 'You've done your best,' she said. 'You can't do no more.'

'I'll make another search tomorrow night,' he promised.

Maria wouldn't hear of it. 'No! I've been giving it some thought, and I've decided she's caused us both enough heart-ache. Now she can get on with it. She'll come home of her own accord, you'll see. When she realises what a bad 'un she's got mixed up with, she'll run home with her tail between her legs. Till then, we'll leave her to her own devices. She'll not listen to anything we say; so let her learn the hard way.' She was ada-mant, and nothing David could say would convince her otherwise.

The runner fell against the wall, gasping for breath, his feet aching, and his heart pounding. 'Must want my head tested!' he groaned. 'Who the hell would want to run round Whitechapel at this time of night – and all for a bleedin' shilling!' Looking up at the big old building, he was just thankful he had the right place. The derelict warehouse had been turned into a tenement, with each room rented out to make the owner a fortune. 'Shouldn't be surprised if Manners don't own *this* place an' all,' he grumbled, going inside.

At the top of the stairs, he took out the note which the proprietor had given him. After reading it, he glanced along the doors and smiled when his eyes alighted on the right one. 'Number four,' he muttered, quickening his steps towards it. 'That's the one!'

He knocked on the door for a third time, and still there was no answer. Gingerly, he pushed open the door and poked his head inside. 'Mr Tony Manners?' He knew this fellow's reputation and didn't want to get on the wrong side of him. 'Anybody there?' he called. From the adjoining room came a series of grunts and strange noises. 'Hello?' He came into the room, shouted again, then went carefully towards the second door. It was slightly open, so he bent his head to peep inside. What he saw brought a smile to his face and held him mesmerised.

Teresa was lying on top of the bed with her legs wide open, and in between them lay Tony Manners, feverishly working up and down, his hands clutching her breasts. 'GO ON!' she was crying. 'NOW! NOW!' The two of them were rocking the bed until the floorboards bounced.

'Bleedin' hell! They'll be through the floor next!' The more they worked themselves into a frenzy, the wider grew the runner's eyes, until they were all but popping from his head.

Excited to fever pitch himself, he made a noise that caused Tony Manners to jerk round. 'We've got a Peeping Tom.' Teresa just giggled.

Manners jumped off the bed and ran across the room. The onlooker was slow to move, his attention held by Manners' erect penis as he rushed towards him. The next thing he felt was a fist in his face.

When he awoke again Manners was standing over him, fully

dressed and bursting with rage. 'You'd best explain yourself!' he snapped. 'Well? I'm waiting!'

Teresa was waiting too; lounging on the bed and smiling at him with wicked eyes. He had the feeling she was ready for more, and she didn't care who mounted her.

Struggling to his feet, the runner gasped, 'I've come from the club . . . the boss sent me.' Quickly, before he could get another smack in the mouth, he grabbed the crumpled letter from his pocket and thrust it at Manners.

After reading the letter, he ordered the runner out, kicking his arse as he went. 'Tell your boss he's lucky I didn't have your head from your shoulders!' he yelled. But the runner was long gone, down the stairs, away up the street, and looking for a woman, *any* woman. What he'd seen was enough to send a man crazy!

'What does it say?' Teresa watched as Manners read the letter again.

'He's persistent, I'll say that for him.' He flung the letter at her. 'I might have to go to drastic lengths to keep your brother off my back.'

She scanned the letter and dropped it to the floor. 'You'll not lay a finger on him,' she warned. Getting up from the bed she came and stood before him. Opening her robe to show her nakedness, she invited brazenly, 'Ready to finish, are you?'

His hands shot out and grabbed her by the throat. 'Don't *ever* tell me who I can and can't lay a finger on.' His fingers tightened. When she began to choke, he took one hand away and fetched it so hard across her mouth that she was thrown to the bed. Then he stripped off, got on top of her, and the two of them were soon once again finding delight in each other.

Afterwards he fell asleep. She went to the mirror and examined herself; her throat was still red-raw, a trickle of blood had dried on her mouth, and her face was badly bruised. 'This is *your* fault, Mam!' she muttered. 'Yours and David's . . . To hell with the pair of you!' With that she splashed her face with cold water from the bowl, then climbed back into bed and snuggled up to her man. 'It wasn't your fault,' she murmured. 'I don't blame you, sweetheart.' She hugged him closer when he stirred. He slyly smiled, and planned how he might use her.

Maria was right. The week after David haunted the nightspots of London looking for her, Teresa turned up. Late on Saturday afternoon, in a blistering heatwave, she got out of a cab in the village and started across the fields. It was quite a walk and, still weak from yet another fierce beating at the hands of Tony Manners, she stopped several times for a rest. 'Bloody place!' she grumbled. 'Only rabbits and vermin live this far away from civilisation.' Three times she tripped over molehills, and once she stepped on an ants' nest. She rested, and swore, rested again and strode out; until at last, though it was still a good way off, she had the cottage in sight.

Hot and tired, with her best shoes covered in a film of dust and the hem of her skirt knitted with bracken, she was itching for a fight . . . with her mam . . . with David . . . it didn't matter. She blamed them both for her dilemma and she was here to let them know it.

David arrived home at twenty minutes to five; he had been at work since quarter to six that morning, and was glad to be back under his own roof. 'Your mam's asleep,' said Nancy Proctor, a dear old soul who lived on a nearby farm. Taken on by David to look after his mam while he was out at work, she was strong as an ox, trustworthy, and used to ruling the roost. 'I've a nice rabbit stew cooking,' she announced, giving him a wrinkly smile. 'It'll be on the table in half an hour. Time enough for you to wash and change.'

'Smells wonderful!' David replied enthusiastically. He hadn't the heart to say he would have preferred a cold pie or a hank of bacon and some fresh baked bread.

A peek into Maria's room showed she was still asleep, so he quietly closed the door and went upstairs to his room. Here he sat on the bed edge, his head in his hands and his mind far away. Since leaving Cathy behind there had been days when he questioned the purpose of what he was doing; days when he thought he couldn't go on without her. Today had been such a day. 'Oh, Cathy! Cathy! Without you, nothing seems worthwhile any more.' He let the wonderful memories flow through him, before shaking her from his thoughts.

Washed and changed, he went back downstairs. He was making his way to Maria's room when Nancy Proctor's voice gently called out, 'Don't disturb her. She's still fast and hard asleep. Time enough to wake her when the dinner's ready.'

Feeling a little lost, he wandered outside. The sun was still hot, and there was no breeze whatsoever. Rolling up the sleeves of his shirt, he went to the pump and filled the two buckets there. Taking them to the kitchen, he was told, 'Your mam's awake now. Fetch her to the table if you like. So long as she's well supported, it'll do her good.'

Maria was thrilled. 'I like it when the two of us sit down together,' she said, smiling up at him as he tucked her safely into the carver. 'It'll be like old times.'

They talked, and laughed, and for a while Teresa was forgotten. Mrs Proctor washed and dried the dishes and quietly left when her husband came to fetch her on the cart. David and his mam remained at the table, talking about this and that; mainly about when David would likely lose his job, and what they might do when the time came. 'Don't you worry your head about it,' he insisted. 'Happen it'll be a blessing in disguise.'

'You're up to summat,' she answered. 'Come on, out with it.'

'When the auction comes up, I mean to be there,' he confessed. 'I mean to buy the field for market gardening, and the two cottages with it.'

Maria was astounded, but she didn't dash his hopes altogether. 'It's all very well wanting to be a property owner, son,' she said kindly, 'and I don't doubt that one day you'll get what you're after. But, well ... where would you ever get that kind of money?'

'I've been working every hour God sends, and though it probably isn't enough, I've saved a fair bit.' His smile was that of a confident man. 'I may never get another chance like this, Mam,' he said softly. The smile dropped away and his face was set with determination. 'Trust me. I'll have the money on the day because, by one means or another, I intend to have that field, this cottage, and Ted's as well. He's a good man, and he'll be invaluable when I start up my own market-gardening business.'

Teresa's voice cut through the air, startling them. 'Why don't you ask Tony Manners to lend you the money? He'll deal with *anyone*, even you.' There was malice in her face. But it wasn't the malice David saw. It was the dark bruises on her cheekbone, and the angry wound to the top of her neck.

Springing to his feet, he took hold of her by the shoulders, his dark eyes examining the marks. 'He did this to you, didn't he?' he demanded angrily. 'The cowardly bastard! Well, now he'll get a taste of his own medicine. Where is he? Where's he hiding?' If he had Tony Manners here he wouldn't be able to control himself. 'You might as well tell me where he's hiding, because however long it takes, I'll find him anyway.'

Twisting from his grasp, Teresa faced him with hostility. 'Search from one end of London to the other, you won't find him.'

'Oh, I'll find him all right, and when I do, it'll be a long time before he beats a woman again.'

'He's gone away . . . on business.'

Maria had remained silent until now. When she spoke it was to Teresa, and in a voice that her daughter didn't easily recognise. 'Answer me one thing,' she asked harshly. 'Do you mean to go back to the fella as did this to you?'

Teresa laughed out loud. 'If he'll have me, yes.'

'Then you should be ashamed of yourself.'

'Well, I'm not!'

David couldn't believe his ears. 'Then it's *us* who should be ashamed of you.' His dark gaze raked her. 'Do you really mean to take up with him again?'

'Just as soon as I'm able.' She narrowed her eyes. 'If you come between us, I'll hate you for as long as I live.'

Something in her manner touched him deep down. 'Don't worry,' he answered stiffly. 'I won't stain my hands with him. If you still want the coward after he's done that to you . . .' – he raised his hand and gestured angrily to her face— 'then I reckon the two of you deserve each other.' That said, he lifted Maria from the seat and carried her back to her bed as though she weighed no more than a child.

'She's her own worst enemy,' Maria murmured sadly. 'She'll break our hearts, and I'd still have to love her.'

On 8 June Cathy took a turn for the better. For days she had

708

been delirious with a fever that even the doctor didn't understand, and had at last been taken to the Infirmary. At one stage he warned Margaret to: 'Prepare yourself for the worst.' Margaret stayed by her bedside and prayed through the night. 'Don't leave me, sweetheart,' she whispered, and slowly but surely Cathy fought her way back. They told Margaret a deep infection had invaded Cathy's body. Margaret listened but was convinced it was not Cathy's body that had been invaded but her heart and soul.

'You want me to see a *priest*?' Cathy was sitting up now, allowed out of her bed for two hours at a time when she would sit for a while in the chair or take a gentle walk down the ward on Margaret's arm. 'Why would I want to see a priest?' She smiled and her face was lit with a special kind of beauty. 'Unless you think I should confess my sins?' she said. It struck her then, that she did have sins to confess. Sins that had weighed her down until she was crippled. Yet she wasn't ready to talk about the things that remained hidden deep down inside her. Maybe she never would be.

'I'm not suggesting you have sins to confess,' Margaret explained. 'And I thank God that you are getting stronger by the day. But I won't rest until you shed the pain inside. There are things you've never talked about, Cathy... things that almost took you from me. Awful things that you keep so deep inside that they grow and fester.' Taking Cathy's hands in hers, she pleaded, 'Please, sweetheart. If you can't talk to me about it, then talk to a man of God... let *him* help you come to terms with what troubles you.'

Cathy raised her eyes, soft green pools that shone with love for this woman who had given her everything. She didn't speak. Instead she met Margaret's gaze until the tears spilled over her lashes and trickled down her nightgown. There was so much pain that it tore at her like a claw. All the years of her young life she had lived every minute, every hour, every day, always yearning for what she could never have. She had weathered the storms and dismissed her mother's hatred, making herself believe it didn't really matter; after all, she had Margaret, and that was enough. She told herself these things, not fully realising that the yearning to be loved and wanted by her own mother would never really go away. And later so many awful things, all adding to that hard knot that grew daily inside her ... the child she had lost, the love she would never have. The grieving, the disappointments and the broken dreams, all suppressed. Maybe it was time to let them out, to destroy them before they destroyed her.

'You don't need to say anything,' Margaret assured her. 'Not now. Wait until you're feeling a little stronger, then maybe we'll talk again ... if you want to?'

Cathy clung to her. 'I want to,' she promised, and just admitting her need seemed to lighten the burden a little.

Hopeful now, and knowing that Cathy would think about what she had said, Margaret told her, 'I had a letter from Ruby this morning.' Anticipating Cathy's next question, she went on, 'Apparently she's traced David as far as Cambridge, where he worked on a farm for a while. But he's moved on ... gone nearer to London.'

'I'm not sure she should be tramping the roads like that.' Since Margaret had confirmed that Ruby had indeed promised to bring David back, Cathy had fretted over her. 'I think you should ask her to come home. Even if she finds David, he won't want to see me. When he left he was filled with loathing. Nothing has happened to change that.'

Margaret was coy. 'Are you saying you never want to see him again?'

'Not if he still hates me.'

'You don't know that. After he left, he may have realised how much he misses you.'

Cathy smiled a sad smile. 'I don't think so, otherwise he would have come back. And don't say he wouldn't know where to start looking, because if he wanted to find me badly enough, he would leave no stone unturned.' Like I would, she thought. If I believed for one minute that he loved me, I would spend my life searching the four corners of the earth. 'Bring Ruby home,' she pleaded. 'I miss her.'

'If that's what you really want?'

'It is.'

'All right.' In a strange way, Margaret was relieved. 'I'll put pen to paper and post a letter this very evening.'

'You mustn't worry about me now,' Cathy told her. 'I'm

stronger in myself, and the doctor says it won't be too long before I'm home.' Kissing her goodbye, she said quietly, 'About . . . the priest. I promise I'll keep in mind what you said.'

'That's all I ask, sweetheart.' Margaret left then, and Cathy thought about their conversation. One thing was certain. 'Ruby's coming home. And David really has gone for good.' She must come to terms with it, in the same way she must learn to come to terms with everything else that had shaped her life. Since losing the child, and then suffering the illness that had sapped her will to live, she had seen nowhere to turn. She would talk to the priest, and ask God's forgiveness for letting the badness grow inside her.

True to her word, Margaret wrote to Ruby at the address she had been given in the last correspondence:

Dear Ruby,

It's time you came home. Like Cathy, I feel you have done more than was expected of you.

Cathy believes David can't love her, and now I believe she may be right. She wants you home, and so do I. We miss you.

Love from us both.

Margaret

CHAPTER TWELVE

Ruby thanked the blacksmith. 'Morton Farm, you say? You're certain it's a Mr David Leyton who works there?'

'The very same.' Taking a rag from his apron pocket, he blew his nose; a surprisingly small nose for a giant of a man. 'Him and Ted fetch the shires in regular . . . loves his animals, does David.' He blew his nose again. 'It's a pity the farm's being sold off next month. By rights a man like that should have his own land.'

After all her searching, Ruby had to be sure. 'What does he look like?'

The blacksmith chuckled. 'It's your man all right,' he declared. 'David Leyton by name . . . tall and built like a young bull, brown-eyed with a mop of dark hair.' He thought for a minute before saying cautiously, 'He always has a smile and a cheery word, but I get the feeling he has troubles he keeps to himself.'

'What kind of troubles?'

'Who knows what troubles a man has? Money troubles . . . woman troubles. All I know is he's got troubles of a family kind, what with his mam being old and frail, and that sister of his coming and going all the time. But if you ask me it has nothing at all to do with any of that. Oh, no. It's summat he doesn't talk about, and who can blame him? Sometimes a man has secrets he doesn't want spread about.'

'If you'll kindly point me in the right direction, I'll be on my way.' Ruby was relieved and delighted to have found him at last, though she was faintly apprehensive about the reception she might receive. According to Cathy, David had left with feelings of animosity towards her. Maybe he still felt the same. But, for Cathy's sake, she had to find out once and for all.

713

'I'll take you there if you like?' he offered. 'I've a quiet morning for a change ... first cob not arriving till mid-morning, and only two fillies to shoe after that.'

The cart was surprisingly comfortable. The bench was padded, and the springs had been treated so they easily rode the bumps. 'Built this myself,' the blacksmith told her. 'Took me nigh on a year.' He stroked it like a baby. Ruby broadened his smile by saying she thought it was the grandest cart she had ever ridden on.

Inside the cottage, Maria was demanding the answers to a few questions. 'What makes you want to stay with a man who could treat you like that?'

Teresa's temper had not improved in the few days she had spent here. 'I don't pry into your personal life!' she snapped.

'That's because I don't have one,' came the swift reply.

'Just leave me alone.' She had been brushing her hair but threw the brush across the room. 'I'll not trouble you any longer than I have to,' she snarled. 'Matter of fact, I'll be glad to see the back of you ... nag nag nag! That's all you've done since I got here.'

Maria reached out of bed to collect the brush from the floor where it had landed. 'If you can't behave in a civilised manner, I'll be glad to see the back of *you* an' all,' she declared.

Walking across the room, Teresa remained defiant but a little subdued. 'I hate it here,' she moaned. 'I've got used to the bright lights. That's where I want to be. In the heart of London's night-life.'

In spite of everything, Maria loved her daughter, and it showed in her voice as she said softly, 'With *him*? After what he did to you?'

'I'd rather be with him than with anyone ... even you.'

Maria's eyes clouded over. 'You know how to hurt your mam,' she said. 'But I won't always be here, so you must do what you feel right for yourself.'

'Oh, I will.' Collecting the brush from Maria's hand she moved away, standing before the mirror, attending to her hair and examining the fading bruises on her neck and face. 'I think I've been here long enough to teach the bugger a lesson. Come tomorrow, I'll be on my way.'

'Will we see you again?'

'Not if I can help it.'

'Don't be cruel, our Teresa,' Maria pleaded. 'I'll always love you, you know that.' She hated the rift her daughter had caused. 'It would do my heart good if you could make it up with David. He loves you too . . . in spite of everything.' When Teresa gave no answer, she went on, 'While we have a roof over our heads, you'll always be welcome, you know that.'

Smiling slyly, Teresa taunted, 'Seems to me it's a good job I can take care of myself, because as far as I can see, once the farm's sold, *I* might be the only one with a roof over my head.'

'You're a wicked little bugger!'

'But you love me, eh?' She counted on it.

'God help me for it.' Maria was angry with herself. 'But I'm still your mam when all's said and done.'

Leaning on the cupboard, Teresa regarded her mother with a thoughtful expression. 'I seem to remember you always saved for a rainy day,' she said coaxingly. 'Have you got anything hidden away?'

'I might have.' Maria could read her mind, but she feigned ignorance. 'Why?'

'I need to borrow a few shillings . . . enough to get me back to London. Come to think of it, a guinea would suit me fine.'

Maria laughed. 'I expect it would,' she replied. 'But you'll not get a guinea from me, my girl!'

'A few shillings then?'

'We'll see.'

'I could find your money and take it. You couldn't stop me.'

'You'd better think again!' Reaching down under the bedclothes, Maria drew out the long sturdy stick which David had made for her. Pointing it at Teresa she said coldly, 'Try taking what ain't yours, and you might be sorry.'

Knowing she would have to change her approach if she was to get what she needed, Teresa laughed out loud. 'I was only fooling,' she lied, 'I would never take what wasn't mine.'

Not altogether satisfied, Maria nodded. Putting the stick away, she was surprised to hear a knock on the front door. 'Whoever's that?' she queried, craning her neck to see through the window. 'We don't usually get visitors out here.'

'Happen it's Tony . . . full of remorse and come to find me!'

Rushing out of the room, she ran to the front door. As she opened it, her mouth fell open when she saw who it was. For a split second she hadn't been certain, but then it all came flooding back ... her father's affair with the wife of his landlord ... Rita Blackthorn's murder ... the hanging ... and more than that, she recalled David's fondness for Cathy Blackthorn, a fondness that had deepened to love.

Her first instinct urged her to strike out, to send Ruby flying into the mud, but she hadn't forgotten her own part in it all ... the deception that split her brother from his sweetheart ... the deliberate firing of the cottage. Her mind raced ahead. She must play it clever, like before. Fear cautioned her, sweetening her tongue. 'It's Ruby Adams, isn't it?'

In spite of Teresa's smile, Ruby had the feeling she wasn't welcome. 'For a minute there, I thought you might have forgotten me.'

Ignoring her comment, Teresa remarked, 'You're a long way from home. What's brought you here ... to *this* house?' All kinds of possibilities flew through her guilty mind. 'What is it you want with us?'

'I've come to see your brother.'

'He's not home.' She was more than curious. 'Can I help?'

'I don't think so. I've come on a delicate matter.' Ruby spoke softly. 'It's to do with Cathy. She had an unfortunate accident.' It was on the tip of her tongue to explain that Cathy had lost the child because of her fall, but something stopped her. That kind of information was not for everyone's ears. 'She's very ill. Her aunt and I feel it would help her if David could spare the time to come and see her. They parted on such bad terms, you see.' Before Teresa could take it all in, she went on, 'The big house was sold soon after you left the area. We're living in Blackburn town now ... William Henry Street.'

Teresa's fears heightened. If David should ever find out how she'd come between him and Cathy, he might seek his revenge by doing the same with her and Tony. She had to think fast. 'I'm sorry to hear about Cathy Blackthorn,' she lied convincingly. 'But I have to tell you, your journey has been wasted.'

'Oh?' Ruby had feared as much. 'Why is that?'

Convinced she would get away with her lies, Teresa actually

invited Ruby in, but was glad when the invitation was gratefully declined. 'David's feelings haven't changed,' she went on. 'He has never forgiven Cathy or her family for what happened to our dad. We've made a good life out here. David has a new love now. She's carrying his child, and they're due to be wed soon.' She looked dejected. 'I'm so sorry,' she sighed. 'David can be stubborn when he puts his mind to it. He was closer to our dad than anyone, and now he'll never forget or forgive. He's trying to put it all behind him. If you have any thought for him at all, you'll leave us be.' Inwardly panic-stricken, she reached out to touch Ruby's hand. 'Please,' she begged. 'You must see it's all for the best?'

Ruby was devastated. Her journey was all for nothing. She was hurt to think that David could not find it in his heart to forgive, and she might have said as much, but there was no point. It would not mend things between Cathy and David, though it might easily deepen his bitterness. 'A bairn on the way, and soon to be wed, eh?' she murmured, and her heart went out to Cathy.

Secretly gloating, Teresa dared to insist that she come in for a cup of tea. 'You look like you could do with one.'

Ruby shook her head. 'No. You're very kind, but I must be on my way home now.' Half-turning, she said, 'Happen it'll be best if you don't mention it to David that I've been here. As you say, if he still harbours bad feeling, there'll be nothing gained by him knowing of my visit.' As an afterthought she said kindly, 'I hope he'll be happy with his new love. Good day to you now.'

When the cart had rumbled away, taking Ruby with it, Maria called out to Teresa. She sat bolt upright in her bed and demanded to know, 'Why did you tell her such a pack of lies?'

'You heard then?' She was unrepentant, concerned only that Maria might tell David what had taken place here.

'I should have called out . . . told the poor woman what a liar you are!'

'Then what? Think what you're saying, you old fool!' Threateningly, she came towards the bed. 'David has no thought for any other woman but Cathy Blackthorn. If he knew how I'd deceived him before – well, like as not he'd strangle me with his bare hands. And if he were to find out she's ill and asking

717

for him, he would move heaven and earth to be with her. Don't imagine for one minute that he'd give *you* a second thought. Especially when I tell him how *you* are as much to blame for letting him believe Cathy wanted no truck with him!'

The awful words tumbled from her mouth to frighten her mother half out of her wits. 'What! He'd be gone, and you'd be left here on your own, because *I* don't intend to stay around a minute longer than I have to.' She bent her head to stare Maria in the face. 'Is that what you want, Mam? To have him flay me alive, and then to be left on your own?' Maria huddled into herself, more afraid than she had ever been in her life. 'Answer me! Is that what you want?'

The whisper was barely audible. 'I won't tell him.'

'Of course you won't, Mam.' Teresa was smiling again, pleased with herself. 'Now, about that guinea?' Holding out her palm, she waited.

Maria had no intention of letting her see where she kept her cash. 'Later,' she said, 'I'll find you a guinea later.' Then she fell back into the bed and lay with her eyes wide open and her breathing irregular. 'You'll be the death of me yet,' she muttered.

'Not till I've got my guinea.' Teresa left the room giggling. This time tomorrow she would be back with Tony. The thought of it made her burst into song.

Having eavesdropped on the conversation between Ruby and the young woman, the blacksmith turned it all over in his mind as they travelled back to Ilford. After a long silence, he decided to speak his mind. 'You can say it's none of my business,' he began, 'but I told you I had an idea there was something troubling that young fella . . .'

Ruby wasn't paying much attention. Instead she was thinking of Margaret and Cathy. 'Sorry, what were you saying?'

Drawing into the kerb, he climbed down and proceeded to help Ruby off the cart. 'I was just saying how I had an idea there was something troubling him.' He cocked his head and grinned at having learned a secret. 'All the same, I would never have guessed he was about to become husband and father all at the same time.'

'What do I owe you?' Now that it was over, she couldn't wait to get home to those she loved.

'Nothing at all.' Before she could offer him a fare he quickly drove the equipage away, geeing up the old horse as he went.

That very evening, Ruby was given a letter that had been forwarded from her previous boarding house. 'I hope it isn't bad news, my dear,' the kindly landlady said.

It wasn't bad news. Margaret was calling her home. 'It's me who'll be carrying bad news to you,' Ruby murmured as she packed her bag. Cathy had been right. David may have adored her once, but that was a lifetime ago.

CHAPTER THIRTEEN

Cathy was adamant. Seated in the chair at her hospital bedside, she looked first at Ruby, then Margaret. 'I expect you've found David,' she said calmly. 'He isn't here, so I can only think he wants nothing to do with me.'

Margaret quietly regarded her niece, and for the first time in her life came close to deception. Cathy was still very poorly. It was true she had recovered from the infection that nearly took her from them, and it was true that with every day she grew a little stronger. But she was painfully thin, and her face was white as chalk. Her lovely green eyes still held a deep secret agony, and Margaret was afraid for her. 'Ruby's home with us now,' she said evasively. 'Soon you'll be home as well, and the three of us can start rebuilding our lives. Isn't that enough for now?'

Cathy remained calm, her hands gripping the chair-arms, the need to know overriding everything else. 'Please. I have to know what he said.'

Uncomfortable beneath Cathy's intent gaze and knowing how she was bound to be hurt, Margaret hesitated. Lowering her gaze to the floor, she wondered how she might soften the blow.

Cathy sensed her dilemma. 'I know he's never coming back to me,' she said, and just for a second her voice broke on a sob. When she spoke again, it was with great dignity. There was no trace of anguish in her face. Looking at Ruby, she said softly, 'When I realised you had gone to search for David, I was angry and hurt. But I know you did it because you love me, and I'm deeply grateful for that.'

More than once since her return, Ruby had regretted ever having gone; she regretted it now. 'It was wrong of me,' she

721

answered. 'But I thought I were doing it for the best.'

Putting out her hand to hold Ruby's, Cathy told her honestly, 'I know that, Ruby, and I love you for it.' Returning her attention to Margaret, she said, 'I know you were both thinking of me. Now, though, if you want me to rebuild my life, I have to know everything. How was David? Where is he working? What did he say?' Hardening her heart against him was difficult, but she had to do it if she was ever to grow away from him. 'Please . . . I need to know.'

Margaret pondered. There was no way to soften the truth, and so she came right out with it. 'David is about to be wed.' She took a deep breath, waiting for Cathy's reaction, waiting to comfort her. She had deliberately kept back the fact that David was also about to become a father. Margaret had not forgotten it was losing the child that had almost pushed Cathy over the edge. For reassurance, she glanced at Ruby, visibly relaxing when Ruby gave her a nod.

Reeling inside from the news that David had found himself a new love, a woman he was about to make his wife, Cathy fought with the turmoil of emotions that threatened to overwhelm her. She remembered every word he had ever said to her, every gesture, every promise. He had told her lovingly that one day he would make *her* his wife. It had been the dream that carried her into womanhood, and now it was gone. The dream was over, and he was making a life with someone else.

'I'm sorry, sweetheart.' Margaret knew the news must have shaken Cathy to her soul. She was angry too. 'If he could hate you for what someone else did, then he isn't worth a second thought. Put him out of your mind.'

Cathy had seen the look that passed between her aunt and Ruby. She knew them of old. 'There's something you're not telling me,' she persisted. 'I need to know *everything*.'

This time it was Ruby who answered, and it was in the softest of voices. 'What your aunt says is right, child,' she remarked. 'A man who could turn his back on you like that . . . well, he ain't worth spit.' She wrinkled her face in disgust.

'You *are* keeping something from me, Ruby? What is it?'

She hesitated. It was obvious Cathy would not be satisfied until she knew it all. 'You allus did know what were going on in ol' Ruby's mind,' she admitted with a helpless smile. 'You're right. There *is* summat else.' Taking a deep breath she went on, 'David is getting wed right enough. He's also on his way to being a father.' Like Margaret she feared what the news might do to Cathy. After all she'd been through, it was one more blow.

'Thank you for telling me.' Cathy sat back in her seat, her hands fiercely gripping the chair-arms and her eyes closed. It had all come as a shock, yet in one way she was not surprised. 'It's only natural that David should make a new life,' she said presently. 'He's a handsome hard-working man, with a good kind heart.' Before they could question such a statement, she went on, 'I don't blame him for feeling the way he did . . . and for wanting to make a fresh start.'

Margaret was not so forgiving. 'All the same, he had no call to blame you.'

Sitting up straight, she looked at Margaret, her smile warm and reassuring. 'I know,' she admitted simply. 'I could never harbour any hatred for him, but we all have to deal with loss in our own way. He was always close to his father, so his loss was greater than mine.' In her heart she had always understood David's bitterness about his father's hanging. 'I wish him well,' she went on. 'I'm glad he's found a new love. In fact, I'm grateful for it, because now I can put him behind me and look forward to a new life of my own.'

'By! You never fail to amaze me, child.' Shaking her head slowly from side to side, Ruby admired her determination. She had seen this lovely young woman suffer one crisis after another, and each time Cathy had found the strength to overcome it.

Margaret said nothing but got out of her chair and came to where her niece sat. Putting an arm round her shoulders, she hugged her close and for a precious moment the two of them remembered how it all used to be. Ruby's eyes swam with tears; she murmured her goodbyes, and tactfully left them alone.

Some moments later, when Margaret joined her outside, she asked worriedly, 'Do you reckon the lass'll be all right?'

'I think so, Ruby. It won't be easy for her, but now she knows David is out of her reach, she has little choice but to forget he ever existed.'

'What about the child she lost? That's summat else that's preyed on her mind.'

'Like I said, Ruby, it won't be easy.' Margaret had one hope above all else. 'Just now, she promised to see the priest when she comes home. I feel he can help.'

'D'you think she'll tell him who fathered the child?'

'I don't know. For her own sake, I pray she'll tell him everything.'

Waiting on the side of the road for the wagons and carriages to pass, Ruby had a dreadful thought. 'If she's to start afresh, I hope it isn't with that awful Tony Manners!'

Margaret had no time to reply because suddenly there was a gap in the traffic and the two of them ran across the road. All the way home, she considered Ruby's comment, and it raised all manner of anxieties in her mind.

'I see your visitors have gone?' The nurse, with her big blue eyes and masses of fair hair spilling from beneath her cap, had a waist that was no bigger than a child's. She tidied the bed and smiled like nurses do, then hurried away.

Cathy sat in the chair for what seemed an age. Supper came and went. She was ushered into bed and soon afterwards the lights were put out for the night. From her bed she watched the nurses change shift, and smiled when the auxiliary dropped the contents of a bedpan all over the floor.

After a while all was quiet. She thought about Margaret and Ruby, and vowed never again to do anything that would make them worry about her. She thought about David and his new love and her heart was like a lead weight inside her. 'Be happy, David,' she murmured. She smiled at the memories, and her eyes clouded when she thought about the way it had all gone wrong.

Suddenly her love for him was like a great rushing tide inside her; regrets, emotions and lost dreams, all mingled together, washing everything else before them. Steeling herself against the feelings that threatened to destroy her, she buried her head in the pillow. Then the sobs came, long aching sobs that racked her body and carried her to a restless nightmare-haunted slumber. She would be strong. She would be all that Margaret and Ruby wanted. But she could not be happy. Never again could she be truly happy without him.

On 1 July, Cathy went into Blackburn market for the first time in months. Margaret insisted on accompanying her. 'You may be well, thank God,' she argued, 'but you're still not strong enough to be out on your own.'

'All right,' Cathy conceded. 'But only if we can walk all the way.'

At the kitchen doorway, Ruby stood beaming with delight. She and Margaret had worried about Cathy, but the lass was good as her word; she got up in the morning with a smile on her face, and she spent the day keeping herself busy. She had even taken on the task of teaching one of the street children to read. She laughed and chatted, and it was good to see how happy she was becoming.

'Let the lass walk,' Ruby called out. 'It's a grand day and the market ain't too far.' As they went out of the door, she ran after them. 'Fetch me some darning thread,' she instructed. 'I caught me stockings on the mangle and now there's a hole as big as a midden.' Taking a sixpence from her pinnie pocket, she put it into Cathy's hand. 'I'm that proud of you, lass,' she muttered, and with that she went at a run back into her kitchen. 'Me muffins!' she cried. 'The buggers'll be burnt to a crisp!'

As they went down the street, womenfolk stopped them to chat. 'Good to see you home again, young lady,' commented Ada Snettleton. One neighbour pointed out it was time the landlord found a buyer for the empty house. 'There'll be rats running round us feet next!' said Fred Arlinton. Lottie Barnett wanted to know why Tony Manners hadn't been to collect the rent himself. 'He sends a snotty-nosed lad round,' she complained. 'A nasty piece o' work in the making that one.' Her ma-in-law had taken a particular dislike to the young fellow in question. 'He wants dipping in the canal,' she grumbled through her toothless pink gums. 'Looks to me like he ain't had a wash in a month o' Sundays!'

Cathy was still chuckling as they came into the market square. 'I'm glad we moved to William Henry Street,' she said, and Margaret agreed.

They bought the darning thread and a basket load of fresh fruit. Afterwards, they wandered among the many colourful stalls, examining this and that but buying nothing else. Presently they made their way to the little café on the corner.

Here they sat and passed the time of day, and Margaret said warily, 'Have you given up the idea of talking with the priest?'

'I will go and see him,' promised Cathy. 'But not yet.' Somehow she still couldn't bring herself to talk about the things closest to her heart.

'Don't leave it too long, sweetheart,' Margaret advised gently. 'I know how hard you're trying to forget. But it's still there, isn't it? Still hurting as much as ever.'

For a moment it seemed as though Cathy might answer. But the moment passed and she was asking, 'See over there?' Pointing to the draper's stall, she suggested light-heartedly, 'Wouldn't Ruby be pleased if we took her a brand new pair of stockings?'

Margaret understood and chided herself for thinking she knew best. 'All right, sweetheart,' she apologised. 'In your own good time.'

CHAPTER FOURTEEN

It was Thursday, the night when revellers came from all over London to hear the band. By nine o'clock there wasn't a sober man in the place, come ten o'clock there wasn't even standing room, and by the time the musicians played their last melody of the first set, deals of all kinds were being done in every corner of the club.

'I'm no bloody fool!' The burly fellow kept the dainty jewel-box in the palm of his grubby hand. 'You'll have to give me a better price than that, or I'll take me business elsewhere.'

He would have put the box in his jacket pocket, but Tony Manners held out his hand. 'Let me see it again.'

Opening it up, the burly fellow took out a small picture of two infants. Showing it to the other man first, he then tore it into pieces and threw the pieces into the ash-tray. 'Pictures of kids is worth nothing,' he grumbled. Handing the box over, he said, 'If you want this, though, you're gonna have to pay for it.'

Tony Manners turned the box over and over in his palm. It was a beautiful thing; small and heart-shaped, made of platinum and gold, and encrusted with rubies. It was obvious that some-one had cherished it, someone from a grand house. 'A thing like this might be fitting for a lady,' he observed softly, and straightaway Cathy came to mind. 'I don't normally ask where you get your stuff,' he remarked, 'but this is different . . . better class than you usually fetch me.' Instinctively he stared round, looking for strange faces, anyone who might look suspicious. 'Look here, I don't want the rozzers on my back,' he said harshly.

The burly fellow laughed. 'Relax! Like I said, I'm no bloody fool. That box was taken months back. I've kept it hidden all this time, and you can take my word there'll be no rozzers on your back.'

'Straightforward burglary, was it?' Something about that box made his blood turn cold.

'That's my business.' He wasn't about to admit that he'd brutally murdered an old woman for it. Agitated by the sight of it, he snarled, 'Do you want it or don't you?'

'I want it.'

'Name your best offer?'

'Half a guinea?'

'To hell with that!' Snatching the box, he put it back in his pocket.

At that moment, Teresa returned from the dressing-room. 'He wants me to sing another number,' she explained. 'I told him I'd check with you first.'

'Tell him you'll do it, and that I'll expect to talk terms with him after closing.' Tony watched as she made her way back. When he turned he saw how the burly fellow was watching her too. 'Fancy her, do you?' he asked.

'Bursting out me pants, I am.'

'I should break your legs for that.'

'You could try.'

'How badly do you want her?'

The burly fellow stared at him in disbelief. 'Are you saying what I think you're saying?'

'The price I've offered ... and *her*.'

'Jesus!' He started trembling. 'She won't do it ...'

'She'll do as she's told.'

'It's a deal. But I'll hang on to the box for now.'

'I've another deal waiting.' Standing up, Tony said softly, 'I'll be back before she's finished singing.'

'I'll be waiting, matey.' Just then Teresa came on stage and went straight into a rendering of 'I'll take you home again, Kathleen'. The burly fellow watched, his eyes raking her body. 'Sing your heart out, my lovely,' he croaked hoarsely. 'Afterwards, I'll show you what a *real* man can do.'

Jack was getting nervous. 'Where the hell have you been?' he hissed as Tony Manners approached, and slunk back into the shadows. 'You know I don't want my old man to clap eyes on me.'

'Better get a move on then.' He was amused by the constant game of cat and mouse between the burly fellow and Jack. 'He's in there now, impatient for me to go back inside.'

Taking a small sack from beneath his coat, Jack opened it and took out a silver statuette. 'That's the last of the big ones,' he whispered, thrusting it into the older man's hands. 'Gimme the same as before and let me get out of here.'

While Tony Manners counted out the coins, a row erupted inside the club. 'Get a move on!' urged Jack. 'For God's sake, get a bloody move on!'

No sooner were the words out of his mouth than the club doors were flung open and out came a very irate Teresa, with the burly fellow hard on her heels. 'Tony, you bastard!' Rushing up the alley, she flung herself at him. 'Is it right what he says?' In the lamplight tears glittered in her eyes. 'Did you really tell him I'd sleep with him?' Her voice fell to a sob. 'You didn't say that, did you? Tell me you didn't say that.' She was plucking at his coat, desperate for him to deny it.

Angry that she had interrupted his deal, he glared at her. 'One night, that's all, you stupid cow! It's important to me, or I wouldn't ask.'

Suddenly all hell was let loose. Jack and the burly fellow caught sight of each other, and it was only seconds before they were rolling about on the ground, punching and gouging at each other. Somebody got excited and yelled, 'Garn! Teach the big bugger a lesson, Jack!' Another drunk shouted for the big fellow and soon the whole crowd was in turmoil, fists flying and blood spattering everywhere. The proprietor called for help, and the sound of a police whistle sent Tony Manners fleeing away down the alley, with Teresa in tow.

As he looked back, he saw a swarm of blue uniforms gathering round the crowd. 'Mindless fools!' he groaned. 'My money's scattered all over the alley and I've got bugger all to show for it. I've dropped the statuette, and thanks to you, I don't expect to clap eyes on that box again.' Raising his fist, he brought it down heavy over Teresa's face. 'Next time I make you part of a deal, you'd do well not to question it.'

As she fell to the ground he gave her a kick in the groin for good measure.

CHAPTER FIFTEEN

Maria sat up in bed and supped at the tea David had brought her. 'I do miss her, son,' she said. 'Bad as she is, she's still my lass.'

'I know that, Mam,' he acknowledged. 'And nobody prays harder than me that she'll come to her senses before too long.'

'I only wish she were more like you in nature.' After draining her cup she gave it to him and watched while he replaced it on the tray. 'You're a good man,' she told him softly. 'You don't deserve a sister like that . . . nor a silly old woman like me for a mother. There must be times when you wish you were miles away from the pair of us.'

Regarding her with dark smiling eyes, he asked softly, 'Do you really believe that?'

She shook her head and chuckled. 'Naw,' she confessed. 'But if I were you, I'd 'a dropped the pair of us long ago.'

'No, you wouldn't,' he chided. 'I may be stubborn, but I'll never see the day when I can match you.' With a wry smile he added in a regretful voice, 'Or Teresa, come to that.'

'Being stubborn isn't a good thing, son. It's being strong that counts, and we'll neither of us ever have the strength that was born in you.' She had been riddled with guilt since the day when Teresa turned Ruby away from the door with a pack of lies. Night and day it had rested uneasy on her conscience. Looking at him now, knowing how hard it had been for him to leave his Cathy behind, she was tempted to tell him and to hell with Teresa's threats. 'Son . . .?'

He was at the door now, ready to take the cob into Ilford. At the sound of her voice, he came back, 'What is it, Mam?'

Her courage deserted her. 'Nothing. Go on, be off with you.'

'Is there anything else you want before I go?'

'Is Ted coming to stay with me?'

'He's on his way.'

'Then I want for nothing.'

'I'll not be long. I should be back from Ilford by half-past seven . . . an hour to see the cob settled in his stable, and ten minutes across the field to home.' Grinning, he called behind him as he went from the cottage, 'Ask Nancy to have the kettle on for quarter to nine. I'll have a thirst on me like a fire.'

Outside the cob was restless. 'We'll soon have you a new set of shoes, you old devil.' Tickling it under the chin, he lifted himself on to its back. Gently squeezing his knees into its belly, he urged it on, away from the cottage and across the fields in the direction of Ilford town. He went slowly at first, then the cob broke into a trot, and the summer breeze strengthened. It was an exhilarating experience, riding on the strong broad back, across the hills and valleys with no hedge or fence to mar your path. 'Go on, boy! Go on!' As they crossed the stream the breeze played around them, spurring them on. David bent low over the cob's back, his eyes raw where the breeze whipped into them, and his dark hair spilling back from his forehead.

As they came nearer to town, he brought his mount back to a slower pace. Smacking it fondly on the neck, he confided, 'It'll be a sorry day when the farm's sold. There's no telling where either of us will end up.' He'd had time to mull over the changes ahead. 'If I can find my way to keep the field, I'll find a way to keep you an' all,' he promised. 'But it's a sad day all the same, when things have to change. Though change they must, and sometimes we have to part from them we've come to love.'

Cathy was always on his mind, always in his heart, but sometimes, as now when he was out in the fields with only nature around him, she crept right into his soul. 'I had a sweetheart once,' he told the cob. 'Her name was Cathy . . . and she was the loveliest creature on God's earth.' A great ache grew in his heart and, as he relived those precious times he'd spent with her, he felt as though his life was ended. 'She's gone now,' he whispered. 'Strange how easily her love died when mine never could.'

For the remainder of the journey, he thought about other

things: the old cob; the farm and when it might be auctioned; his mother and how he would do anything to avoid her having to move house and home again; Teresa and the way of life she was caught up in. All these thoughts washed through his mind, leaving him more determined than ever that he wouldn't take it all without a good fight.

He didn't have to think about Cathy. She was just there, not a thought or a memory but the very essence of his being. She was with him every minute of every day, and would be for the rest of his life.

The blacksmith was expecting him. 'You're the last of the day,' he said with a grateful sigh. 'The old back's playing me up again, sod it.'

Jumping down from the cob's back, David led it by the reins into the yard. 'You'll have to think about retiring soon,' he told the older man. 'I recall you telling me when I first came here that you were looking for someone to take over.'

'Aye, an' I were. But I've stopped looking now, because men who could do this job are few and far between.' Suddenly his eyes brightened and he stepped back to look at David's fine figure. '*You* could do it though,' he suggested hopefully. 'When the farm's closed you'll be looking for work.'

'True enough. But I'm hoping to be my own boss.'

'That takes money.'

'You don't have to tell me that.' Rubbing his hand reassuringly up and down the horse's shoulder he smiled knowingly, winking as he revealed confidently, 'I'll do it though. I don't know how yet, but I will do it.'

The blacksmith was impressed. David's determination only made him more persistent. 'I can see you've had enough of working for others, so how about if I offered you a share? How about if, instead of earning your wages, you worked for a share in the business with me?'

It was an offer out of the blue, and David didn't want to sound ungrateful, but blacksmithing wasn't for him. Holding out his hands, he said in a serious voice, 'See these?'

'Aye, and I can see they're strong and capable . . . you'd make a fine blacksmith.'

'What I'm trying to say is these hands are used to working

733

with God's good earth. Though I thank you kindly for your offer, I have to say no.'

'More's the pity.' Sighing, the blacksmith prepared to shoe the horse. 'It's a lonely job and no mistake,' he chattered on while David watched him turn the hot iron in the heat of the fire. 'Happen I should do as you say ... retire and find myself a woman.' He chuckled. 'A nice homely sort like the one as came to see you the other day.' His chuckling erupted into a full-bellied laugh. 'I don't mind telling you, I took a shine to that lady. Mind you, I tend to fancy every woman I clap eyes on. Trouble is, they don't fancy me.'

David thought the other fellow must be confused. 'You've got me mixed up with somebody else,' he said. 'I've had no lady visit me ... homely or otherwise.'

The blacksmith was affronted. 'I might have a bad back,' he said in an injured voice, 'but I ain't senile ... not yet I ain't!' Taking the hot iron to the cob, he raised its hoof and seared the shoe into place. 'I took her out to your place on the cart. She spoke to that sister o' yourn, and then I fetched her back again. I didn't charge her a penny. If I can't give a lift to a lady when it's needed, what kind of a gentleman am I, eh?'

David was paying more attention now. 'I wasn't told about this.' Suspicions of Teresa came into his mind. 'The visitor ... did she give her name?'

'Nope.'

'What did she look like?' His heart was racing. Somehow he dared to hope it might have to do with Cathy. But then, how could it?

The blacksmith looked up. 'I'd say she were in her late fifties, maybe a little older, but presentable if you know what I mean.' He frowned. 'I'll tell you what, though. She looked troubled ... didn't have much to say for herself. Deep in thought most of the time.'

David's mind was racing ahead. Why would a woman like that want to see *him*? 'So she never mentioned what her business was?'

'Oh, aye! Her business were *you*. She came here especially to see you ... asking after you she was. Knew your name, knew your family. On the way out to your place, she had a smile on her face. On the way back it was wiped off. Whatever your sister told her, it dampened the poor creature's spirits, that's for sure.' He thought it best not to mention how he'd overheard the conversation between Teresa and the visitor.

The blacksmith finished his work and tried his luck once more before David left. 'Are you sure you won't change your mind about coming into business with me?'

Now astride the cob's back, David was eager to get away, to ask his mam about this mysterious visitor. 'I'm not made for blacksmithing,' he declared. 'When a man's heart is in the soil, that's where his ambitions lie.'

'Good luck to you then.'

Hot and sweating from the race across the fields, David tethered the cob and ran into the cottage. Maria was awake. When she realised he knew about Ruby Adams calling, she lied with conviction. 'If she came here I must have been asleep, son, because I know nothing about a visitor.' Feigning tiredness, she yawned and slid beneath the sheets. 'Ted's just gone,' she said, desperately trying to turn his attention from the delicate issue. 'He's a grand neighbour . . . nothing's too much trouble for him.' Observing David out of the corner of her eye, she hated herself for deceiving him.

'Did Teresa say if she'd be coming home again?'

'You know what she's like, son. Here one minute an' gone the next. She can be gone weeks, or turn up when you least expect it.'

'Who do you reckon the visitor was, Mam?' Happen he was clutching at straws thinking it might be something to do with Cathy. There was no reason to think such a thing, yet he couldn't shake the feeling off.

'Some old gypsy woman, I expect. They're allus at the door, after one thing or another.'

'By all accounts it was no gypsy woman.' He recalled the blacksmith's very words. 'She asked for me by name. What do you make of that?'

'Somebody heard the farm were up for sale . . . sent her maid-servant to offer you work.'

'Teresa had no right not letting me know.'

'If it had been important, I'm sure she would have.'

'Happen I should make it my business to find out.'

A thought struck her then, making her sit up in her bed. 'You're never going to the city to find her? Good God! Look at you ... you've worked yourself to a standstill. You've the cob to take back yet, and when you've trekked your way across the fields, I dare say it'll be gone midnight.' She tutted with frustration. 'You're never telling me you mean to go to the city at this time of a night? And what for, eh? To ask your sister about some poor old bugger who, for all we know, might have been looking for work herself?' She tutted again. 'And do you intend waking Ted from his bed, eh? Or are you gonna leave your old mam on her own at the mercy of every rambler?' Fear of his finding out the truth was evident in her voice.

Misinterpreting her fear, he was quick to assure her. 'Don't worry. You'll not be left alone, Mam, and I wouldn't be so callous as to wake Ted. You forget, I know how hard he works, so I know how much he needs his sleep.' Her arguments began to make sense. 'You're right. If it had been important Teresa would have let me know. When all's said and done, it might well have been somebody asking after work. It's no secret that I mean to raise the money for that field. It follows that folk might believe there'll be work going.' All the same, he couldn't help but be curious.

Settling his mam down, he told her, 'I'll stable the cob here in the shed for tonight. It won't hurt.'

All night long, Maria tossed and turned. Visions of Teresa haunted her dreams. Once, when the dreams became nightmares, she woke up screaming. In a minute David was by her side. 'Hush now,' he murmured. 'It's all right ... I'm here. You're safe.'

The night hours lengthened into the dawn, and during the long vigil he patted her forehead with cold water, soothed her with a quiet voice, and wondered what had triggered such terrible nightmares. Even when she was awake, they seemed real. Twice she startled him by calling out Cathy's name. When she called out his father's, he thought she had been dreaming of the hanging. 'No, no, it's all over,' he coaxed. 'Everything's all right.' Yet he knew that for him it would never be all right again.

CHAPTER SIXTEEN

On Saturday mornings, Ruby had got into the habit of baking a dozen loaves. Cathy would put them in the oven when they were risen, and take them out again when they were baked and crusty. 'You'll soon be doing me out of a job,' Ruby complained, but secretly she was delighted to see Cathy coming back to full health.

When the bread was wrapped in muslin and placed in the deep wicker baskets, Cathy would take these and place them on the front doorstep; just as she did on this warm and pleasant Saturday afternoon. Half an hour later, she opened the door and took the empty baskets inside again. 'You were right about not taking the bread to their doors,' Margaret acknowledged as Cathy replaced the baskets in the cupboard. 'I would never have thought about doing that.'

'These folk are very proud,' Cathy acknowledged. 'They would much rather help themselves than have us take the bread to their doorsteps. It can't be easy for them to accept charity.'

'It's never easy,' Ruby answered from the kitchen doorway. 'Most of the menfolk down this street were in work when we first came here. Now every other household is finding it hard to scrape by.' She chuckled mischievously. 'It's funny though how the bread just vanishes like that, as though the fairies come out of their hidey-holes and whisper it away.' Winking, she declared, 'One o' these days I'm gonna peek out from behind the parlour curtain.'

Margaret clicked her tongue. 'You'll do no such thing, Ruby Adams,' she said. 'Besides, Cathy can tell you who has the bread, and who doesn't.'

'Oh?'

'It goes to those who need it most,' Cathy explained. 'When I asked Molly Turnbull to let it be known that the bread was there for anyone who needed it, she put the word round. She says it's going to the right folk ... the poorer families, where the men have lost their work.' It was good to help, even if it wasn't enough. She was humbled by such God-fearing folk. 'Sometimes it's the children who come for the bread.' Pausing, she wondered about something Molly Turnbull had revealed. 'She told me how no one else would ever take the bread that was meant for these families. The ones who had enough for their own would never take from the mouths of others.'

'Good job we're among honest folk,' Ruby declared, wiping her hands on her pinnie. 'Else the baskets would be spirited away along with the bread. Then I'd be after strangling somebody, 'cause them baskets is me pride and joy!' That said, she ambled back into the kitchen and busied herself with the making of a plum duff.

Following Ruby into the kitchen, Cathy took the bucket to the tap and half filled it. 'What the divil d'you think *you're* doing?' Ruby swung round, showering Cathy with flour from her hands. 'I'm not having you cleaning them windows, my girl! You've not been out of the Infirmary five minutes, and you think you can do what you like.' She rubbed her nose and sneezed when it was covered in flour. 'Leave it to me, lass. I'll clean the windows when I've put the pudding on to steam.'

'You do too much already,' Cathy argued. 'Besides, I've got nothing else to do.'

Ruby glanced at the clock. It was gone two. 'Ah! So young Tommy Turnbull ain't turned up, is that it?'

Cathy tried to hide her disappointment. 'I'd best make a start on the window.'

'What you want is a nice quiet little pastime. Your aunt's embroidering. I'm sure you'd rather do that than clean the front window?' she asked hopefully. One look at Cathy's face told her otherwise, so she shook her head and smiled. 'Not for you, eh? Go on then, you young divil! Clean the blessed window. And don't dare leave a smear else I just might make you do it all over again.'

Cathy had cleaned only one corner of the window when she

was interrupted by Molly Turnbull's son, a big lad with a crippled foot and a smile that would light the blackest day. 'Hello, Mrs Cathy.' However much she told him she was not a 'Mrs', he insisted on addressing her in the same way. Holding up a small exercise book, he told her proudly, 'I've brought my book. And I learned that word just like you told me.'

Cathy clambered down the steps. 'Hello, Tommy.' She was delighted to see him. 'You had me worried. I thought you weren't coming to see me.' Taking the book, she opened it to the first page. Written down in big bold lettering was the word 'Blackburn'. 'Good boy,' she enthused, giving him a big hug. 'Come and sit beside me.' She patted the step and he sat alongside her. 'Do you remember how to say the word?'

Opening his mouth he formed the letters. It was a painfully slow procedure. 'Bl... ack... b... urn.' When he'd finished he clapped himself and Cathy clapped too. His smile broadened and he broke out in a fit of giggles.

'What does the word mean, Tommy?'

'It's where I live.'

'Is it the name of the street?'

He shook his head.

'What then?'

'It's...' He had to think for a minute, recalling what Cathy had told him. Suddenly he was grinning from ear to ear. 'It's the *town* where I live.'

'Right. Now then, get your pencil out and let me see you write your name again, and remember to say the letters as you write them down.'

'Aren't we going inside?'

'Do you want to?'

'Naw. I want to stay on the doorstep.'

'So do I,' she agreed. 'The sun's shining out here.' It was so good to feel the sun on her face, to feel the strength running back into her body.

Wondering why Cathy was so long, Ruby came to the door and peeped out. When she saw Cathy and the boy earnestly studying, she crept away and went to tell Margaret. 'It does my old heart good to see her teaching that lad,' she said brokenly. 'I don't mind telling you there was a time when I thought we'd lose that lass. God was good when he brought her back to us.'

Margaret put away her sewing and went to the front parlour. From the window there she had a clear view of Cathy and the boy. She gazed at her niece for a long time, thinking how well she had begun to look; her long fair hair shone in the sunlight, and her green eyes were dazzling as she laughed and giggled with the boy. But there was still a faraway look in those lovely eyes, a lost and lonely look that betrayed the truth beneath. 'You'll get over him, sweetheart,' she whispered, closing the curtains. As she wandered back to the sitting room, she sent up a little prayer that Cathy's extraordinary strength would carry her through.

Later that night, when Ruby had gone to her bed, Cathy made two mugs of hot cocoa; one for her and one for Margaret. 'Tommy's coming on a treat,' she said. While she spoke she stood by the window, absent-mindedly watching the trailing stars in a beautiful sky. 'He has a real thirst to learn.'

Margaret hoped she wasn't trespassing in matters best left alone when she asked softly. 'Teaching that lad ... it reminds you of David, doesn't it?'

At first Cathy didn't answer; it was as though she was searching for the right response, when of course there was only one answer. 'Yes.' Turning round, she came to the chair opposite Margaret. Sitting down, she placed her mug of cocoa in the hearth. '*Everything* reminds me of David,' she answered simply. 'Teaching Tommy to read and write ... the sunshine ... the night sky.' Her smile was wonderful. 'He's everywhere I turn.'

'I'm sorry.' Margaret had been afraid to open old wounds, and now she had. 'I should not have asked you such a question.'

'I'm glad you did.' With each passing day, Cathy knew she had to come to terms with all that happened. 'I think I'm learning to put it behind me.'

'You will. Oh, I'm not saying you will ever forget David because I know you won't. But, with God's help, there will come a day when you'll be able to remember without pain. You do believe that, don't you?'

'I have to.' Taking up her mug of cocoa she sipped at it, her mind wandering back to the past, and her heart warming. 'I did love him,' she murmured. 'I *do*.'

'Do you want to talk about the child?' She knew that until Cathy let go of the pain, she would never fully recover. 'Or the child's father? You know what they say ... a trouble shared is a trouble halved.'

'Soon maybe. Not yet.' Visions of Jack tearing at her clothes assailed her. She visibly shivered. Since coming out of the Infirmary she had agonised over a certain promise she had made to Margaret. In that moment she made up her mind. 'Tomorrow morning, I mean to go and see the priest.'

'Oh, Cathy, if only you can open your heart to someone, I know it will all come right.'

The following morning, Cathy put on her best cream skirt and blue linen jacket. Her hair hung to her shoulders in a thick straight line, and for the first time in many a month she walked down the street with a spring in her step. Now that she had made the decision, she was actually looking forward to talking to the priest.

Two children swinging on a lamp-post stopped to stare at her as she went by. 'Cor, ain't she pretty?' cried the chubby girl with the egg-splattered smock. 'She ain't as pretty as my Auntie Pat!' yelled the buster of a boy. In a minute they were going at each other like a pair of dogs, with the girl astride the boy and the boy screaming for mercy.

After Cathy successfully intervened, she scolded the pair of them, explaining to the little girl, 'That wasn't a very ladylike way to behave.'

'That's 'cause she's a scruffpot!' snorted the lad, and if Cathy hadn't taken the girl home there might well have been blood spilled. When peace was restored, she went down the road, chuckling. Before she turned the corner at the bottom of William Henry Street, she could hear them going hammer and tongs at each other again.

The frantic knocking on the door sent Ruby up the passage at a run. 'Wait a minute, for heaven's sake!' As she flung open the door, she was shaken to see David standing there, taller, broader of shoulder, and more handsome than she remembered. 'You!' She stared open-mouthed. 'What the divil do *you* want?'

Margaret was equally shocked to see him. Having followed

Ruby to the door she was even more astonished when David pleaded, 'I have to see Cathy. Please ... tell her I'm here.'

Ruby snapped at him. Believing he was here to cause Cathy more pain, she couldn't hide the hostility in her voice. 'She doesn't want you here. None of us do.'

He turned to Margaret. 'You have to let me see her!'

'Why should I?' Like Ruby, Margaret thought he would only cause Cathy a deal more heartache. 'From what I understand, you're due to be married. I believe double congratulations are in order ... you're also about to become a father, isn't that right?'

David shook his head. 'No, it is not right.' Relieved that he had found the place where Cathy was, and sensing somehow that she must be in better health, his dark eyes melted into a smile. 'Look, I have to talk to her,' he told Margaret in a calmer voice. 'Teresa gave out a pack of lies. I'm not about to be wed, and there's no woman carrying my child.' He laughed wryly. 'The only woman I've ever wanted is Cathy.' Looking beyond the two women, he glanced down the passage. 'Please ... tell her I'm here.'

Ruby and Margaret glanced at each other; the news he had brought was the best they could have heard. Ruby laughed out loud. 'You're not even courting?' Her laughter turned to tears, and she couldn't say another word. Instead she wiped her eyes on her pinnie and trembled all over.

Margaret felt the same, but managed to hide her emotions. After all, she had to be certain. 'You'd better come in,' she said, stepping aside for David to pass. 'Ruby, I'm sure a cup of tea and a slice of your fruit cake would be most welcome.' On her mistress's instructions, Ruby scuttled away.

David followed Margaret into the sitting room. 'I have to see Cathy,' he groaned. Realising he was being scrutinised, he grew agitated. 'I don't blame you for being suspicious, especially when Teresa also led you all to believe that I blamed Cathy for what her mother did.' Standing in the doorway, he ran his hands through his hair and bowed his head in despair. 'Don't you understand what I'm telling you?' he pleaded. 'I believed it was Cathy who loathed me! For some wicked reason that gave her pleasure, Teresa played us off against each other. She wanted to separate me and Cathy, and by God she did!' Turning his head he called up the stairs, 'CATHY!' His voice echoed in the silence. He couldn't see her, couldn't hear her. It was more than he could bear.

Margaret's calm voice broke in. 'It's no good your calling her, Cathy isn't here.'

His dark eyes widened with fear. 'Not here? Where then? For pity's sake! Where is she?'

If she'd had any doubts about his love for Cathy, they fell away in the face of his anguish. 'She isn't too far away,' she answered. 'She's well again, but ... she's missed you, David ... missed you like nothing on this earth.' Shaking her head, she invited, 'Sit down with me. Tell me everything, so I can understand.' Gesturing to the two armchairs by the fire-grate, she waited for him to accept. When he hesitated, she went and sat down, her eyes never leaving him for one moment.

'You won't tell me where she is until I do, will you?' He was quiet yet inwardly in turmoil, he knew how Margaret had always protected Cathy, and he admired her for that.

'I have to know Cathy won't be hurt again,' she explained. 'When we've talked, and I can be sure, *then* I'll tell you where to find her.'

Realising he had no choice, he walked across the room and sat in the chair opposite, his dark eyes filled with pain as he told her how he had found out about Ruby's visit from the blacksmith, and how, deep down, he'd sensed it might be something to do with Cathy. He couldn't let it go and so he found Teresa and she told him everything.

'The man she was with had a habit of beating her. But when he tried to force her into prostitution, she turned on him. I brought her home and she was filled with remorse at what she had done. She told me what Ruby had said ... how Cathy was ill and needed me.' When the tears welled up in his eyes, he paused to choke them back. 'You can't know what that did to me.' He paused again before going on, 'Teresa confessed how she had deliberately put poison between me and Cathy ... leading us to believe each loathed the other for what happened between our parents.' Taking a deep breath, he bowed his head and spoke in a quieter voice. 'I've been distraught,' he murmured. 'Now I just want to hold Cathy in my arms, to tell her how much I love and need her.'

When he lifted his gaze, Margaret was shocked by the depth of emotion in his face. 'I believe you,' she said.

Relief flowing through him, he closed his eyes and leaned back in the chair. In a moment he was standing beside her. 'I must go to Cathy now.' His voice was low and firm. The need for her was like a clenched fist inside him.

Realising the significance of the moment, Margaret stood up. 'I'll take you to her.'

As she went to fetch her jacket, she took a moment to think of Cathy. 'He's home, sweetheart,' she murmured. 'David has come home for you.'

Father Goldstone looked at Cathy with compassion. 'From what you've told me, life hasn't treated you too well. First your parents and their inability to love you as they should ... the young man you loved and lost ... the other young man, a wicked and cruel creature ... then the agony of losing that little innocent child.' His soft gaze enveloped her. 'I know how hard it can be, but you have to forgive. If you don't, you'll only succeed in destroying yourself.' He looked at her, at her lovely face and clear green eyes, and he saw the spirit beneath. 'It's only when we learn to forgive that we become strong enough to go on.'

'I understand that, Father.' Coming here had been the right thing to do. 'I am beginning to put it all behind me. The cruel things, the precious things I never had ... I can accept that now.' Her love for David was overwhelming. 'But I did have something very precious with David.' Her voice trembled. 'However hard I try, I can't seem to put that behind me.'

'When you experience a love such as you feel for your young man, you may *never* be able to put it behind you,' he answered honestly. 'But you still have to go on. There will be another love, I dare say.'

Cathy smiled wistfully. 'No, Father,' she whispered. 'There will never be another love for me.'

Outside, Margaret and David approached the church. 'I'll wait here,' she suggested. 'You go ahead.' She meant to stay just long enough to see them reunited, and then she would sneak away. The tower clock chimed ten. 'Cathy would have got here at about nine-thirty; I expect she'll be coming out at any minute now.'

Cathy opened the door and let herself out. In the fresh air she took a long deep breath. As she raised her eyes to the sunshine, a strange feeling came over her: that of being watched. Slowly, with beating heart, she turned her head. There was a young man making his way down the path towards her, a tall dark-haired young man. His long quick stride was oddly familiar. Suddenly he was running. Their eyes met and her breath caught in a gasp. '*David*?' The name came out in a whisper. She was shaking her head in disbelief, the tears streaming down her face as he called her name.

'CATHY! OH, CATHY!'

Before she could get her breath they were in each other's arms, crying and laughing, lost to everything but the joy of each other. An old couple smiled as they passed. 'Young lovers,' said the man to his wife, and as they looked on, they too were young again.

From a distance, Margaret watched the emotional reunion. She saw the radiance in Cathy's face. She heard the laughter as David swung her round again and again. She even cried a little. Then she went quietly away to tell Ruby the wonderful news.

All day Sunday, Cathy's head was in the clouds. In the afternoon she and David walked in the park, content in each other, she with her arm linked through his, and he walking tall and proud beside her. 'I don't think I'll ever forgive Teresa for what she did,' he said, leaning over the rail beside the lake. 'If it hadn't been for the blacksmith, I might never have known Ruby had come to find me.'

'I've thought hard about Teresa,' Cathy admitted. 'And about what the priest said.' Smiling up at him, she took pleasure in the warmth of his dark eyes, saying softly, 'If we don't forgive, we'll only destroy ourselves ... it's only when we forgive that we find the strength to go on. That's what the priest said. And that's why we have to forgive Teresa.'

He gazed down on her, thinking what a lucky man he was to have found such a gem. 'I love you,' he said.

'No more than I love you,' she answered simply. When he bent to kiss her, a great warmth spread through her. She'd never thought to see this day and now it was here and she was in David's arms. Glimpsing the blue sky above she sent up a silent prayer of thanks.

CHAPTER SEVENTEEN

On 14 September 1901 Cathy and David were married, joined together in wedlock by the same priest to whom Cathy had turned in her greatest need. Margaret attended her. Dressed in a pale blue outfit and holding a small posy, she looked ten years younger.

Throughout the service, whenever Cathy glanced up at David, he was glancing down at her. Though she could feel his hand in hers and hear the priest giving his blessing, she still found it hard to believe that she was actually here in God's house, being married to the man she'd feared had gone from her life forever.

When the service was almost over and the words 'I pronounce you man and wife' were spoken, she looked up into David's dark eyes and saw her own deep emotion mirrored there. 'You look lovely, Mrs Leyton,' he murmured. They kissed for the first time as man and wife, and when they walked down the aisle – he looking smart and debonair in a dark suit, and she looking radiant in a white silk gown made by Margaret's own hands – there was never a couple better suited to each other.

As they passed the pews, all eyes turned towards them. Ted and Maria were there, Maria seated at the end of the pew in an old bathchair that Ted bought in a house sale. As Cathy brushed by, she reached out her hand to wrap her fingers round Maria's; in that briefest touch a lifelong friendship was forged. Teresa had promised to be here but was not. Ruby sniffled into her hankie until her nose looked like a ripe tomato, and in the back pews a number of neighbours and regular churchgoers broadly smiled and wished the couple well as they went by.

Afterwards they gathered in the house on William Henry

Street where Ruby and a few of the neighbours had laid out a spread fit for a king. They ate and chatted and danced to the tune of Mr Entwhistle's accordion. By two o'clock the party spilled on to the streets where the neighbours were having their own knees-up, and soon it was time for David and Cathy to leave.

'Enjoy yourselves!' shouted Ada Snettleton, wiping a snuffy dewdrop from her nose. 'God go with yer!' shouted the old drunk from the top house. As the carriage pulled away, Cathy fell into David's arms and the two of them laughed until they were out of sight of William Henry Street.

Once they were on the train going south, they spent the hours talking about their future. 'Are you sure you don't mind us living with my mam for a while?' David asked. He had other plans under way, but there was time enough for him to tell Cathy all about those later.

'As long as I'm with you, I don't really care where we are,' she assured him. 'As long as your mam doesn't mind.' All the same she had been giving it a great deal of thought. 'When the farm's sold, I expect we'll all have to move on ... where will we go?'

'Don't worry your head about that,' he said. 'We're on our honeymoon ... booked into a little country hotel with a whole week to enjoy each other.' He breathed a sigh of relief when she rested her head on his shoulder, closed her eyes and lightly slept.

The hotel was small but friendly. Though it was very late, the proprietor's wife served a delicious cold meal. 'Could you wake us early in the morning?' David asked the proprietor's wife. 'We have an important appointment.'

'What appointment?' In the privacy of their own room, Cathy was curious.

Taking her in his arms, he whispered in her ear, 'I'm going to get you the best wedding present in the whole world.'

She didn't reply because he was peeling off her clothes. 'Are you going to take advantage of me?' she asked coyly.

'I might ... or don't you want me to?' He was teasing and she loved it.

'I want you to.' She spoke the words into his mouth as he pushed her gently on to the bed, kissing her with the tenderness of a lover.

First he gripped her hands and spread her arms out, then he licked her nipples with the tip of his tongue, and now he was stroking his fingers over the outline of her breast. 'You're beautiful,' he whispered hoarsely.

'Love me,' she coaxed, softly kissing him on the curve of his neck. 'Make love to me now.'

He rolled on top of her. Lying against her body, he kissed her all over, every now and then returning to kiss her passionately on the mouth, and all the while he murmured sweet endearments, taking his time in loving her, his heart bursting and the feel of her in his arms almost more than he could bear.

Cathy stroked his thick dark hair, whispering into his ear all the things she had never been able to tell him. She could sense his great love for her. Soon their passion rose and he eased open her legs. She felt the thickness of him hard against her thigh. Slowly at first, he entered her. Sighing with pleasure, she arched towards him, wrapping her arms around his back. Their bodies entangled and as he pushed in and out of her, caressing and wooing her, their passion was roused to fever pitch.

Filled with wonder, she gave herself to him, revelling in the touch of his bare flesh, clinging to him, needing him like she had never needed anything in the whole of her life. Too soon it was over. They held on to each other, breathless and fulfilled. 'I adore you, Mrs Leyton,' he murmured softly against her face. And she could only hold him as though she would never let him go.

The following morning they awoke early and made love again. Later, they enjoyed their breakfast before boarding a carriage. 'Where are you taking me?' Cathy wanted to know.

'Wait and see,' came the answer. 'If I tell you now it won't be a surprise, will it?'

When the carriage pulled into the farmyard, Cathy thought the driver had made a wrong turn. 'There's a sale going on,' she exclaimed, craning her neck to see the crowd of people surging round the auctioneer's rostrum.

Jumping out of the carriage, David offered a helping hand. 'Well, are you coming or not?'

There was a mischievous smile on his face that made her suspicious. 'Why would I want to watch a sale?' she asked cautiously.

'All right. Stay where you are.' He began striding away.

'No, wait!' Scrambling from her seat, Cathy ran after him. 'What are you up to, David Leyton?' she demanded.

Turning round, he put his hands on her shoulders and pushed her gently towards a hay bale. First he kissed her full on the mouth. 'I want you to trust me, Mrs Leyton,' he declared, kissing her again when she began to protest. 'I promised you the best wedding present ever, didn't I?'

'You did,' she retorted playfully. 'So where is it?'

Stretching his arms wide, he swung round, embracing all the land as far as the eye could see. 'This is it,' he said, and there was wonder in his voice.

Amazed, she followed his gaze; looking from the land to the outbuildings and then to the big farmhouse. 'This *farm*!' Her voice came out in a strange little croak. 'Are you saying this *farm* is my wedding present?'

Grabbing her by the hand, he ran her across the gravel yard to where the auctioneer was offering the farmhouse. 'Together with thirty acres of prime agricultural land.'

As the bidding began, David stood back, letting them take the price as far as they could; until one by one the bidders dropped out, each having reached his own financial limit. It was then that he put in his bid. Twice he had to raise it, and each time the other man stood against him. Anxious now, David put forward a bid of seven hundred guineas; that was as far as he could go. Feeling the sweat trickle down the back of his neck he nodded at the other man. The other man nodded back. It was a calculated game of bluff. David smiled confidently; the auctioneer asked the other man if he wanted to raise his bid. The man looked at David once more, took a moment to think it through, then shook his head and, disappointed, slunk quietly away. The hammer went down.

'SOLD TO MR DAVID LEYTON!'

A cheer went up and Cathy felt herself being lifted through

the air as David swung her high in his arms. 'We're landowners!' he cried, hugging her until she thought her bones would break. 'I have my Cathy, and now I have the land I've always dreamed of.' His dark eyes glowing, he murmured, 'What more could any man want?'

'A child,' she answered. David's child to complete her joy.

CHAPTER EIGHTEEN

Though David had saved a tidy sum of his own, it was the blacksmith who had made it possible for him to buy the farm. Because of his recurring back trouble and an urge to try another line of work, he had entered into a partnership with David. For five years David would pay the blacksmith a small income from the farm, together with regular payments to reduce the loan. It was a fair and satisfactory arrangement, releasing the blacksmith from the work that was crippling him, and giving David the opportunity to farm the land that would one day be his own.

Over the next five years, tended by David's strong hand and shrewd business mind, the farm prospered. Two days before the agreement ran out, he had repaid every penny to the blacksmith who then decided to become a trader and buy two shops in the heart of London town.

Teresa was never seen again in Ilford. She stayed with Tony Manners and went on to be a famous singer.

Jack was jailed for ten years after admitting a string of offences, including the theft of a quantity of silver and other valuables from the big house in Langho. His father, who claimed he was only looking after his son's interests, confessed to murdering two people ... Nan Foster and Frank Blackthorn. He was duly sentenced to hang, but cheated the hangman when he died of gangrene before the day of execution.

Both men vehemently denied killing Rita Blackthorn. There were those who whispered that it was her own husband who had ended her life, rather than let her share it with another man. Over the years the rumours grew, for no one else was ever brought to answer for her murder.

The police were able to return most of the valuables stolen

from Blackthorn House. Margaret and Ruby remained in the house on William Henry Street, living modestly and contentedly; they lived to be very old.

Margaret never learned the truth about Nan; in the circumstances perhaps it was just as well. Sometimes more pain is caused by knowing than not knowing. Some things are best left to merge quietly with the past.

On 4 April 1902 Maria and Ted were married in a registrar's office. David made them a present of Ted's cottage, and they lived there happily for many years.

Two years after their marriage vows, Cathy and David were blessed with a son. Cathy was thrilled. 'He has your dark looks,' she observed, holding him close to his father's face.

The following July, she gave birth to a daughter, with fair hair and lovely green eyes. Cradling the tiny infant in her arms, she whispered a heartfelt promise: 'You and your brother will never want for love,' she said. 'Whenever you need me, I'll be here.' The tears rolled down her face as she remembered her own lonely childhood. But it was over. With her husband and their two lovely children, she had a wonderful future to look forward to. A future she had thought would never be hers.

'Come out here, sweetheart.' David's voice carried into the house. With their son cuddled against her shoulder, and the tiny girl tucked in her other arm, Cathy went to him. 'Look at that,' he said, his dark eyes encompassing the sun-kissed landscape. 'Did you ever dare to think that one day such a beautiful place would be ours?'

Cathy wasn't looking at the landscape. Her gaze was intent on his face; on that rich dark hair and those dark glowing eyes that could turn her heart over with one glance. 'I never dared to believe *you* would be mine,' she murmured softly. 'Can you ever know how much I love you?'

Slowly he turned his head and looked at her, and his heart was full. 'There will never be a single day in the whole of our lives when I don't know that,' he answered. 'How could I not know it, when I feel your every heartbeat?' Embracing his small

son with one arm, he stretched out the other, drawing Cathy and their daughter close to his heart. 'What we have, my lovely,' he whispered in her ear, 'will last a lifetime.'

And it did.